THE VIKI⬛⬛⬛⬛⬛⬛⬛⬛⬛⬛ARY

AMERI⬛⬛⬛

James Nagel, J. O. Eids⬛⬛⬛⬛⬛⬛⬛⬛⬛⬛⬛⬛can Literature at the University of Geor⬛⬛⬛⬛⬛⬛⬛⬛⬛⬛udies in American Fiction and was its eui̇tor ior twenty years. He is the General Editor of the *Critical Essays on American Literature* series, published by Macmillan, that now contains over 130 volumes. He was one of the founders of the American Literature Association and serves that organization as its Executive Coordinator. Among his seventeen books are *Stephen Crane and Literary Impressionism*, *Ernest Hemingway: The Oak Park Legacy*, and *Hemingway in Love and War*, which was selected by *The New York Times* as one of the outstanding books of 1989. This book was made into a major motion picture, *In Love and War*, released by New Line Productions in January of 1997. He has published over seventy articles in scholarly journals and books, and he has lectured on American literature in fifteen countries.

Tom Quirk is Professor of English at the University of Missouri–Columbia. He is the author of *Melville's Confidence Man*, *Bergson and American Culture*, *Coming to Grips with Huckleberry Finn*, and *Mark Twain: A Study of the Short Fiction*. He is the editor or co-editor of several books, including *Writing the American Classics*, *American Realism and the Canon*, *Mark Twain: Tales Speeches, Essays, and Sketches*, and *Biographies of Books*.

Each volume in The Viking Portable Library either presents a representative selection from the works of a single outstanding writer or offers a comprehensive anthology on a special subject. Averaging 700 pages in length and designed for compactness and readability, these books fill a need not met by other compilations. All are edited by distinguished authorities, who have written introductory essays and included much other helpful material.

The Portable

AMERICAN REALISM READER

Edited and with Introductions by
JAMES NAGEL
AND TOM QUIRK

PENGUIN BOOKS

PENGUIN BOOKS
Published by the Penguin Group
Penguin Putnam Inc., 375 Hudson Street,
New York, New York 10014, U.S.A.
Penguin Books Ltd, 27 Wrights Lane,
London W8 5TZ, England
Penguin Books Australia Ltd, Ringwood,
Victoria, Australia
Penguin Books Canada Ltd, 10 Alcorn Avenue,
Toronto, Ontario, Canada M4V 3B2
Penguin Books (N.Z.) Ltd, 182–190 Wairau Road,
Auckland 10, New Zealand

Penguin Books Ltd, Registered Offices:
Harmondsworth, Middlesex, England

First published in Penguin Books 1997

1 3 5 7 9 10 8 6 4 2

LIBRARY OF CONGRESS CATALOGING IN PUBLICATION DATA
The portable American realism reader/edited and with
introductions by James Nagel and Thomas Quirk.
p. cm.—(The Viking portable library)
ISBN 0 14 02.6830 8 (pbk.)
1. American fiction—19th century. 2. American fiction—20th
century. 3. Short stories, American. 4. Naturalism—Fiction.
5. Realism—Fiction. I. Nagel, James. II. Quirk, Tom, 1946– .
III. Series.
PS658.P67 1997
813'.408012—dc21 97–12448

Printed in the United States of America
Set in Sabon

CONTENTS

PART III
NATURALISM

INTRODUCTION

The Historical Context

On April 9, 1865, at the McClean farmhouse in the village of Appo-mattox, Virginia, General Robert E. Lee signed the terms of peace written in General Ulysses S. Grant's own hand. America's Civil War was at an end. The "rebels" were permitted to retain their side arms and, if they could establish a claim to them, their horses and mules, in order that they might return home to work their small farms. This event, in these humble surroundings, marked a moment of quiet and tragic dignity that has entered our national folklore. Grant admonished his excited troops, eager to gloat over their victory, with a simple remark: "The war is over; the rebels are our countrymen again." On June 28, 1919, the Treaty of Versailles ending World War I was signed in a rather different environment—high ceilings and heavy drapery, pomp and circumstance, idealistic public rhetoric and private realpolitik. Woodrow Wilson had worked hard to make the establishment of a League of Nations an important part of the treaty, but his hopes for American participation in it were quickly dashed; the Senate refused to ratify the treaty, and, officially, the United States was at war with Germany until the Treaty of Berlin was ratified in 1921. By 1919, the United States had once and for all joined the community of nations, nevertheless.

These two events may serve to bracket the historical era to which this volume of short fiction is devoted. The differences epitomized by the McClean farmhouse and the Palace of Versailles suggest the distance (cultural, political, and other) that America had traveled in so brief a time. That era and the qualities that defined it have been characterized in various ways. Mark Twain and Charles Dudley Warner named their times the Gilded Age, though the literary historian Vernon Parrington thought they might more aptly be called the Great Barbecue. Other literary historians would apply other phrases to characterize the age. It was a time in "ferment" or a time when Americans were reaping "the harvests of change" or experiencing the moral and social consequences of a "universe of force." It was an "age of energy," an "age of excess," and an "age of reform." American culture, for George Santayana, was dominated by a tradition that was hopelessly "genteel." For Thomas Beer the 1890s was a "mauve decade"; and for Larzer Ziff it was the time of a "lost generation." The opening years of the twentieth century have been deemed "the confident years," the "progressive era," the "era of good feelings." For Walter Lord they were simply the "good years"; for Henry May, the same period marked the "end of American innocence."

One could multiply adjectives. The fifty years between a local war to preserve the Union, a war that had something to do with a "peculiar institution" and that left more than a half a million dead, and the "Great War," a war to end all wars, may be regarded from various angles. In 1865, Walt Whitman sought comfort in the word *reconciliation*— "Word over all, beautiful as the sky"—and wished to believe that "the hands of the sisters Death and Night incessantly softly wash again, and ever again, this soil'd world." In 1901, Mark Twain, disgusted with the crass materialism of the day, rewrote the "Battle Hymn of the Republic":

> *Mine eyes have seen the orgy of the launching of the Sword;*
> *He is searching out the hoardings where the stranger's wealth is*
> *   stored;*
> *He hath loosed his fateful lightnings, and with woe and death has*
> *   scored;*
> *His lust is marching on.*

Warren Harding, in the aftermath of World War I, was cheerier and more blunt; he called for "a return to normalcy."

The era that we shall designate as the age of realism and naturalism (knowing full well that realists and naturalists made at best short and temporary inroads into the American cultural sensibility) was anything but normal. To a significant degree, American realism was a call for men and women to attend to the actualities of life as it is lived, not as it is dreamed or feared. As a literary rebellion, realism was conducting its battles on two fronts, however. Pious sentimentalities, whether they were found in the parlor, in the street, or on the battlefield, were the particular enemies of the realist literary agenda. In *The Rise of Silas Lapham* (1885), William Dean Howells has his Reverend Sewell characterize novels of noble self-sacrifice as "psychical suicide." Novelists might do a real service to the moral life, he continues, "if they painted life as it is, and human feelings in their true proportion and relation." For Howells, sentimentalists were devoted to spiritual absolutes and eternal certainties and, in their basically antiempirical and antiscientific attitude, were willing to sacrifice the experience of life to familiar platitudes.

On the other hand, the scientific mindset was equally eager for abstract generalizations, the enunciation of natural laws that hovered above and apart from lives as they are lived but somehow explained those lives nonetheless. The universe, it was supposed, was composed of Energy and Matter, and the relation between them could be understood in exclusively mechanistic terms. Science and technology, however, often proved desiccating and diminishing to actual experience and to familiar acquaintance. Though generally empirical in their attitude, realists, unlike naturalists, were not willing to allow scientists the final word on matters of value and human freedom. Women writers, in particular, often portrayed the scientific mindset in unsympathetic ways. Sarah Orne Jewett, in "A White Heron," could depict her ornithologist who invades the Maine woods with quiet disdain and amusement. Kate Chopin, in *The Awakening* (1899), had Dr. Mandelet define Edna Pontellier's emotional moral predicament as merely another piece of evidence that proves Nature "takes no account of moral consequences" and supplies feelings of desire as a "decoy to secure mothers for the race." Charlotte Perkins Gilman was more severe: in her feminist utopian novel she sent three unsympathetic male scientists to "Herland"; and, in "The Yellow Wallpaper," she dramatized with special violence the effects of Dr. S. Weir Mitchell's "rest cure." These fictive counterstatements notwithstanding, science and technology enjoyed an unprecedented authority in our national life.

This was an era that witnessed mind-boggling technological "improvements": interchangeable parts, huge and powerful dynamos (such as the one that powered the Philadelphia Centennial Exposition or the one at the World's Fair in Paris that so disturbed Henry Adams); mail-order clothes and even mail-order houses; the Gatling gun and smokeless gunpowder (a technical improvement that Howells wryly observed allows one "to see the man drop that you kill"); the Pullman car, the electric trolley, and the bicycle (a device the young Willa Cather vigorously pedaled around Pittsburgh); barbed wire, the telephone, the phonograph, and the incandescent light. In 1885 the internal combustion engine was patented; 1903 marked the founding of the Ford Motor Company and the flight at Kitty Hawk. Mark Twain, in *A Connecticut Yankee in King Arthur's Court* (1889), gave imaginative and comic embodiment to his "gospel of progress" by introducing many of these improvements into sixth-century England and by having his hero, Hank Morgan, blast his way across Camelot and challenge rank superstition, aristocratic privilege, and Church mandate.

No reasonable person could dispute the blessings of technological progress, of course. Each advance seemed to corroborate a mechanistic view of the cosmos, and yet it also seemed to impose a concomitant sense of the interchangeability of experience and a diminishment of the individual. William Dean Howells would say that realism was "nothing more and nothing less than the truthful treatment of material," and Theodore Dreiser could be even more succinct—the whole substance of literary and social morality was comprehended in three words: "Tell the truth." But the truth of experience was not so easy to come by. In his *Pragmatism* (1907), William James observed that individual "impressions" and independent thought were elusive at best; our thoughts and perceptions seemed to have been "peptonized and cooked for our consumption," and reality, one might say, has been already *"faked."*

Insofar as the view of literary realists had a philosophic foundation, James's pragmatism may serve as the belated statement of it. Another sort of realist writer, one that in the twentieth century has become known as a "literary naturalist," discerned more sinister and remote influences shaping human destiny. Biological and economic forces determined the character of society and the fate of the individual, not moral choice. Naturalists were apt to take their cues from Marx, Darwin, or Spencer. Both realists and naturalists, at any rate, shared a contempt for sentimental pieties and spiritual absolutes, and they might equally subscribe to James's prophetic plea: "The earth of things, long thrown into shadow by the glories of the upper ether, must resume its rights."

This was an age of rich and, from a literary point of view at least, sometimes fruitful tensions and confusions combined with disturbingly lucid certainties. In the nineteenth century, scientific philosophers such as Herbert Spencer or Ernst Haeckel believed, and spoke with the authority of that belief, that the riddles of nature had been solved once and for all. The laws of matter were the highest laws, and chief among them for Spencer was the law of evolution—the passage of matter from an "indefinite, incoherent homogeneity to a definite, coherent, heterogeneity," as he defined it. For many Americans, Spencer's optimistic vision of evolutionary progress was vaguely reassuring because it seemed to make comprehensible an otherwise baffling array of discrete facts, technological innovations, and momentous events. The world after the Civil War had become vastly more complicated, more "heterogeneous," to be sure, but one might be reconciled to complexities in the name of progress and providence. Indeed, John Fiske (in *Outlines of Cosmic Philosophy* [1874]) and Henry Ward Beecher (in *Evolution and Religion* [1885]) had undertaken to show that the evolutionary point of view was compatible with religious faith.

However, it was was no easy task for the average American to hold in solution these two ultimately antagonistic points of view, and the stress fractures in the American sensibility made for discomfiting compromises in everyday life. William James in his *Pragmatism* had discerned in the welter of American experience two prevailing mental

types: the "tender minded" and the "tough minded." The first was idealistic, optimistic, religious, and dogmatic; the second materialistic, pessimistic, pluralistic, and sceptical. Most people are a mixture of these
two positions, he observed, the philosophical layman "never being a
radical, never straightening out his system, but living vaguely in one
plausible compartment of it or another to suit the temptations of successive hours." Only a few years later, in "America's Coming of Age"
(1915), Van Wyck Brooks applied different but analogous terms to iden-
tify the dichotomies of the American cultural scene. "Highbrows," he
said, were principled and virtuous, but inept and condescending; "Low-
brows" are likeable but coarse and vulgar. Both camps, Brooks wrote,
"are equally undesirable, and they are incompatible; but they divide
American life between them."

American culture, Brooks insisted, had no solid foundation or established point of reference, and American literature was distinguished by
its utter lack of personality. Brooks scanned the horizon of America's
literary past and, save in Walt Whitman, saw no vital expression of
American life, no middle plane between "vaporous idealism" and "self-
interested practicality." This bifocal vision could have other construc-
tions, and even more hurtful consequences. The theory of the
naturalness of "separate spheres" is another example of nineteenth-
century doubleness, and it was the ready answer to women suffragists.
Charlotte Perkins Gilman supplied her rebuttal to this view in her essay
"Are Women Human Beings?" (1912). W. E. B. Du Bois, in *The Souls
of Black Folk* (1903), wrote of the "double consciousness" of the African American, a "sense of always looking at one's self through the
eyes of others, of measuring one's soul by the tape of a world that looks
on in amused contempt and pity. One ever feels his two-ness,—an
American, a Negro: two souls, two thoughts, two unreconciled strivings;
two warring ideals in one dark body, whose dogged strength alone keeps
it from being torn asunder." The felt "two-ness" of identity, though by
no means so degrading or debilitating as it was for the African American, was general nevertheless.

Brooks lamented the absence of personality in American literature,
but the existence and nature of the "self" was itself a vexed question,
and it is a remarkable fact that there was an abundance of autobiographies published during this period. They are notable for the sheer
variety of narrative approaches to the writing of a life. Zitkala-Sä's
autobiographical essays about her youth, published in *The Atlantic
Monthly*, are at once the record of the theft of her Dakota Sioux identity
and a representation of tribal life swiftly passing from existence. Jane
Addams also begins *Twenty Years at Hull House* with impressions of
her childhood, but soon chronology is abandoned and her own history

is blended with the history of the settlement house itself, so that the story of one is the story of the other. In his autobiography, Mark Twain also deliberately abandoned chronology in favor of whatever might occur to him at the given moment of his dictation, and the intended result was a voice that spoke from beyond the grave in a book that would not, in fact could not, ever be completed. Abraham Cahan wrote a five-volume autobiography that detailed his experience as a Jewish immigrant and, if only by example, attempted to shatter stereotypical views of the Jew in America. More privileged by far than these others, Henry Adams privately published *The Education of Henry Adams*. In it, Adams would tell his life in the third person and thus suggest that whatever "self" he possessed seemed to float upon the surfaces of forces quite beyond his control. Henry James, in an initial effort to commemorate his recently deceased brother, William, wrote three autobiographical volumes that were a series of vivid memories and impressions of his own youth but were sustained by the subtleties and maturities of his late style. Hamlin Garland, too, wrote of his life as the "son of the middle border," but the recovery of past events in the imaginative act of memory called forth an ever shifting point of view that blurs even as it enhances the reader's understanding of frontier identity.

The principal motive for autobiography, surely, is to explain oneself to others, to displace comfortable prejudices, correct racial or gender stereotypes, or to question idealized prepossessions with a full and truthful accounting of the actualities of a life as it has been lived. In that, these autobiographies share with the realist and naturalist fiction of the period a common motive: to cleanse the vision of prepared or culturally conditioned understanding; to correct roseate conviction with hard fact. For a variety of reasons, postbellum America was plagued by troubling uncertainties, and, ironically, for that same reason formulaic or platitudinous conceptions were often that much more attractive to the dominant culture.

Many writers of the period took special pleasure in unmasking the falsehood of conventionally understood and rather fixed ideas about the separate roles of the sexes, the nature of heroism, the sanctioned privileges of class, and so forth. Harriet Beecher Stowe, in "The Minister's Housekeeper," reveals in comic terms how incompetent and ignorant the parson is about the supposed masculine business of farm life and how efficient and knowing is his housekeeper. In Mary Wilkins Freeman's "The Revolt of 'Mother,' " it is the willful and domineering husband, not the wife, who at last breaks down and cries. At the conclusion of Charlotte Perkins Gilman's "The Yellow Wallpaper," it is not the "hysterical" wife but the "rational" husband John who has apparently fainted from shock. In Stephen Crane's parodic Western tale "The Bride

Comes to Yellow Sky," the renegade Scratchy Wilson is bested in a
"show-down," not with his customary adversary Sheriff Potter, however, but with an unarmed and innocent bride. Henry James's Miss
Churm and Oronte, it appears, are more adept at representing aristocratic manners than the Monarchs, who are "the real thing." William
Dean Howells's character George Gearson goes to fight in a war he
personally condemns and as a consequence becomes a military "hero,"
but only because he lacks the courage to oppose the wishes of his fian-
cée, Editha. Realist writers were fond of such ironic inversions, and in
a hundred different ways they sought to disarm the authority of the
ideal by dramatizing actualities of life as it is really lived.

Realist and naturalist writings may be defined according to their literary manner or their subject matter, but the same qualities and impulses may also be discovered in the motives of the writers themselves.
For that reason, realists did not feel exclusively tied to mimetic representation as the only creative avenue to render the truths of experience
or to disclose to the reader the falseness of certain piously held notions.
Fables, parables, burlesques, parodies, ghost stories, satires, utopian
novels, fantasy, science fiction, and other fictive forms might participate
in the realist cultural agenda by awakening readers to the truths of life
as they knew it. Madelene Yale Wynne's fantastic tale, "The Little
Room," artfully and rather mildly suggests that women enjoy a delicious
freedom only when they are free from attachments to men. In several
comic tales of good little boys and bad little boys Mark Twain gleefully
challenged the prevailing notion that Providence rewarded virtue and
punished vice; similarly, Edith Wharton, in *The House of Mirth* (1905),
and without a whiff of comedy, showed Lily Bart's virtue to be her
tragic flaw. Kate Chopin, in *The Awakening*, called into deep question
the transcendent satisfactions of being a "mother woman"; Harold
Frederic scrutinized the tranquil confidence of untested faith of a Methodist minister in *The Damnation of Theron Ware* (1896).

Darwinian notions of the "survival of the fittest" might be enlisted
to show that millionaire industrialists were not robber barons but providentially authorized heroes, but in *The Rise of Silas Lapham* (1885)
Howells dramatized the incommensurable relation between material
prosperity and moral conduct. Instead of celebrating the myth of the
yeoman farmer, Willa Cather and Hamlin Garland exposed the harshness and deprivation of frontier life. John Oskison and Zitkala-Sä wrote
of the doubtful blessings of American missionary work among the Indians. Constance Fenimore Woolson, in "Rodman, the Keeper," surveyed the consequences of the war in personal rather than political
terms. In a rather different way, so did Charles W. Chesnutt, in "The
Wife of His Youth." Ambrose Bierce's bitterly ironic tales of soldiers

and civilians leave little room for uncompromised notions of military heroism and virtue. Edgar Watson Howe's *The Story of a Country Town* (1883), Mark Twain's "The Man That Corrupted Hadleyburg" (1899), Sherwood Anderson's *Winesburg, Ohio* (1919), and many other works dramatized the meanness and narrowness of America's "idyllic" villages. Crane, in *Maggie: A Girl of the Streets* (1893) and "An Experiment in Misery" (1894), Dreiser, in "The Curious Shifts of the Poor" (1899) and *Sister Carrie* (1900), and Paul Laurence Dunbar, in *The Sport of the Gods* (1902), depicted in very different ways the dehumanizing brutality of the cities.

The gulf between rich and poor seemed to widen with each successive year, and particularly in the cities the close proximity of splendor and squalor made the contrasts more visible. The era witnessed astonishing industrial growth; between 1860 and 1920 the numbers of industrial workers increased sixfold. But startling economic progress was punctuated with financial crises. The financial panic of 1893, for example, prompted social protest and encouraged Populist sentiments. Armies of the poor demonstrated their discontent. Jack London was a soldier in one such gathering, but only Jacob Coxey's "army" of five hundred men reached the nation's capital. Before Coxey could address the crowd who gathered there, however, he was arrested for walking on the grass. The morally outraged assertions of fiction writers were documented and verified by books such as Jacob Riis's *How the Other Half Lives* (1890) or Lincoln Steffens's *The Shame of the Cities* (1904). Howells's novel *A Hazard of New Fortunes* (1890) was largely motivated by his anger over the massacre of protesters in the Haymarket Riot of 1886 and the unjust trial of its supposed agitators. Rebecca Harding Davis, in "Life in the Iron Mills" (1861), and Frank Norris, in "A Deal in Wheat" (1902), traced the bland decisions of capitalist powerbrokers to their ultimate consequences in human suffering. Gaudy millionaires feasted on ten-course dinners at Delmonico's, and Thorstein Veblen wrote *The Theory of the Leisure Class* (1899). John D. Rockefeller distributed dimes to the needy, and Ida Tarbell wrote the *History of the Standard Oil Company* (1904). Henry George argued the advantages of his single-tax theory in *Progress and Poverty* (1877–79), and Hamlin Garland published "Under the Lion's Paw" in 1889.

The end of Reconstruction in 1877 and the installment of Jim Crow throughout the South permitted violent crimes against blacks to occur with alarming frequency and virtual impunity. The massacre of innocent black citizens by white supremacists in Wilmington, North Carolina, in 1898 was the subject of Charles W. Chesnutt's *The Marrow of Tradition* (1901). Paul Laurence Dunbar and Theodore Dreiser wrote short stories about lynching; James Weldon Johnson described the burning of a man in *Autobiography of an Ex-Colored Man* (1912). Mark Twain sardonically named his country "The United States of Lyncherdom." W. E. B. Du Bois, as editor of *The Crisis*, founded in 1910 as the official publication of the NAACP, resolved to keep the national crime of lynching in public view.

This inventory of historical events and fictional representations is but a shorthand way of saying that realists and naturalists were committed to fusing imaginative literature with the urgency of social problems and public policy as well as to rendering and recording the quieter and more intimate phases of American life. In part, the social commitment of realists participated in the broad effort to repair the wounds of the Civil War, to restore the union through a more comprehensive and sympathetic awareness of the common human condition. To be sure, that condition was modified and expressed by differences in race, class, gender, and section, but only gradually did it become apparent that America was too complex a subject for a single book or a single writer.

In 1868, John De Forest published in *The Nation* "The Great American Novel." In that essay he called for a novel that would contain and faithfully describe the diversity of America at the same time that it identified the commonalities, the "Americaness," of the national life. De Forest nominated *Uncle Tom's Cabin* (1850–51) as the only novel that had thus far approached the richness and broadness of this subject, but De Forest himself had attempted the novel he described in *Miss Ravenal's Conversion from Secession to Loyalty* (1867). Though Henry James would try to get at the national character in *The American* (1877), and Howells would follow De Forest's attempt to bring in vivid contact the varieties of American class and condition in *A Hazard of New Fortunes* (1890), it soon became apparent that the subject was too vast for a single, unified work. Harriet Beecher Stowe herself had turned from the large national narrative that was *Uncle Tom's Cabin* to writing stories and novels about her native New England. In his preface to the 1892 edition of *The Hoosier Schoolmaster* (1871), Edward Eggleston noted that a general yearning for the great American novel had swiftly passed in favor of the novels of sections. William Dean Howells observed that the attempt to capture American life in a single work was much like trying to put "a bushel measure in a pint cup." In 1895, Twain remarked that American writers are content to lay "plainly before you the ways and speech and life of a few people grouped in a certain place." Together, many such writers give us "a hundred patches of life and groups of people in a dozen widely separated cities," and, together, they may give us the whole of American life.

As early as the 1830s, local colorist and regionalist writers were intent on capturing the distinctive quality of life as it was expressed in the dialect, folklore, customs, and landscape of a particular place at a particular time. After the Civil War, the general appetite for such fiction increased for several reasons. The war had exposed many men, who otherwise might never have traveled outside of their county in upstate New York or their local parish in middle Tennessee, to unfamiliar varieties of weather, landscape, customs, and dialect. And at the home front, men, women, and children anxiously read the war news with increased personal interest in places, such as Gettysburg or Chickamauga, that were clearly beyond the orbit of the family farm or their house in the city. What is more, after the war there was a restless movement of large segments of the population in search of finer opportunities. Successive waves of immigrants came to the United States to secure some portion of its bright democratic promise. Most of them would stay in the cities, some would secure farms in the Middle West; in either case they typically found their eager and hopeful ambitions thwarted or delayed. Natives frequently left the village or the farm to work in industry in the North. Some might try to improve their circumstance on free lands in the West, but by 1891 the frontier was officially closed. The more adventurous or the more desperate went in pursuit of instant wealth in one of the successive silver or gold strikes in Nevada, California, or Alaska.

In any and virtually all cases, large segments of the population were for the first time being exposed to, and often competing with, people of richly diverse cultural backgrounds, and the fact was making a lot of people nervous. Particularly at the end of the century, xenophobic cries for an "Anglo-Saxon" culture and an "Anglo-Saxon" literature, whether they came from Teddy Roosevelt, William Randolph Hearst, or elsewhere, were maliciously influential in shaping popular sentiment. Charles W. Chesnutt had one of his characters refer to white supremacists as the "Angry Saxon" race; Finley Peter Dunne used his persona, Mr. Dooley, to express in comic terms his anger over these vaunted claims of racial superiority. However, the public at large may have been especially susceptible to the mythic appeal of an Anglo-Saxon culture because they were deeply distressed by the radical changes in their everyday lives. In the realm of conduct and manners, these changes made for large confusions. The times bred what David R. Shi has called a "spectatorial vision"; under new and alien conditions, people were watching people, anxious for any clue about how to act and what to say.

From a literary point of view, this condition might result in comedies of misunderstanding (as in Twain's "Buck Fanshaw's Funeral") or a tragedies of misapprehension (as in Crane's "The Blue Hotel"). For the immigrant writer, such as Sui Sin Far or Abraham Cahan, it provided the occasion to measure what had certainly been lost from the old world against what might possibly be gained in the new. But the intricacies of modern life also cultivated a yearning for a simpler time, real or imagined, when such troubling uncertainties seemed far away. Some, like Charlotte Perkins Gilman in *Herland* (1915), Howells in *A Traveler from Altruria* (1894), and Edward Bellamy in *Looking Backward* (1888), imagined utopian societies in some distant place or time, where rational social arrangements encouraged human happiness. Some, Mark Twain among them, sought tonic relief in the simple recall of youth and innocence. Others described the actualities of local life but frequently colored their accounts with romantic sentiment.

Regionalist and local-color writing prospered and proliferated under this double and somewhat contradictory inheritance. On the one hand, there was a widespread and ready curiosity about other places and other people, even in one's own land, and a host of talented writers were willing to gratify it. At the same time, there was a sense that the peculiarities of custom, place, and speech were rapidly passing away, being chewed up by a voracious appetite for progress and made quaint and ineffectual by a general homogenizing of American culture. Mary Wilkins (Freeman) wrote Hamlin Garland that, while she believed that she was writing of the New England of her present, she had "a fancy that my characters belong to a present that is rapidly becoming *past* and that a few generations will cause them to disappear." In this sense, regionalist and local-color writing, motivated by sympathetic and familiar acquaintance, was often drawn toward nostalgia and sentimentality and tempted to fuse romantic conventions with realist subject matter. Many talented regionalists such as Wilkins avoided these temptations, however, and brought deliberate artistic restraint and immense literary sophistication to their project.

What is perhaps most important, these writers could gain a national audience and reputation in the ever-multiplying number of magazines. Between the wars, the population of the nation's cities increased seven times and the literacy rate rose sharply. There was also what Frank Luther Mott has called a "mania" for creating new magazines; the number of popular magazines increased from around two hundred in 1860 to eighteen hundred by the end of the century. As a consequence, writers found a relatively easy and profitable outlet for their wares, and with the passage of an international copyright law in 1891 American writers could compete with European writers for a national readership on an equal economic footing. The law of supply and demand governed the enormous production of short stories during this period, but it did not likewise produce an exponential rise in the number of gifted writers. The best of them, however, produced enduring and memorable fiction and took their stand on a piece of native soil that, in creative terms, was both their subject matter and their muse. Zona Gale claimed Wisconsin as her special precinct; for Sarah Orne Jewett it was Maine. Hamlin Garland depicted the heroic fight of the farmer in the Dakotas; Willa Cather said she hit the "home pasture" when she began to write of her native Nebraska. Kate Chopin and Alice Dunbar-Nelson frequently wrote of Creole culture and customs. The Pacific Slope of gold-rich California was widely known as Bret Harte Country. Mary Noailles Murfrees told affectionate tales of Tennessee mountain folk; Constance Fenimore Woolson wrote local-color stories set in Ohio and, later, in the South during Reconstruction. George Washington Cable attempted to render the complex culture of Lousiana; Joel Chandler Harris had his Uncle Remus speak an authentic dialect at the same time that he conveyed something of the character and feeling of postbellum Georgia. Mary Austin produced pictures of life in the desert Southwest.

Regionalist writing was not the only beneficiary of the explosion in the number of popular magazines. The appeal of the short story soon surpassed in popularity the serialized novel. Understood as a distinct genre, the short story was a relatively new phenomenon. In 1884, Brander Matthews published "The Philosophy of the Short-story," the first attempt, he said, to articulate the rules and distinctive features of the form. Matthews admitted that much of what he had to say had been derived from Edgar Allan Poe's review of *Twice-Told Tales*, but his description of the story's aesthetic features was sometimes taken to be a formula for success. The "art" of the short story, it was thought in some quarters, could be learned easily enough. This art was taught in the schools and the subject of several "how to" handbooks. The wide popularity of Frank Stockton's "The Lady or the Tiger," or the example of O. Henry's lucrative career, built as it was on his popular and rather predictable narrative twists at the end, created the impression that the imaginative story was but one more commodity that could be fashioned according to recipe. More serious artists did not take their cues from handbooks, however. Kate Chopin sought to emulate Mauppassant, not O. Henry. Henry James took the compression required of a short story as an exhilarating challenge; he recorded in his notebook his ambitions for a story that would become "The Real Thing"—it should be "a little gem of bright, quick, vivid form." Sarah Orne Jewett offered her advice to a young Willa Cather: "One must know the world *so well* before one can know the parish." For her part, when she wrote a preface to a collection of Jewett's fiction in 1925, Cather insisted that Jewett's stories had outlasted other New England stories because she was never tempted to dramatize "arresting situations" nor given to mere "clever story-making."

Howells, who in his editorial capacity at *The Atlantic*, and later at *Harper's*, was apt to read and pass judgment on more stories than most, believed the American short story was nearer perfection than any other country's, except perhaps those being published in Russia. He thought the short story ideally suited to bring about a "literary decentralization" of our culture. Women writers in particular, he said, excelled in the form, and their stories seemed "faithfuler and more realistic than than those of the men, in proportion to their number." Their dialect freshened our language, and their pictures of life expanded the bounds of our understanding and sympathy. "The arts must become democratic," Howells proclaimed; and he took pleasure in the fact that the whole range of American life, as it was then being rendered by men and women from every section of the country and from every class and condition, was "getting represented with unexampled fulness."

To retrieve something of that fulness is the ambition of this collection of short fiction. Novels of the era better convey the social and political ethos of the country or explore the psychological depth of characters, perhaps. But, together, the following stories disclose a representative spectrum of concerns and commitments and display a remarkable array of styles and techniques in ways that we believe suggest something important and fundamental about these years. Literary naturalists undoubtedly suffer under such an arrangement, however. Those writers who took Émile Zola's slender monograph "The Experimental Novel" (1880) as doctrine and his thick novels as exempla required a larger canvas than the short story provides. Zola had complained that today "an exaggerated emphasis is given to form" and that literature is "rotten with lyricism." Dreiser, London, Norris, and others wished to diagnose the influences of large, and largely impersonal, forces, whether they originated from without, as disturbing social realities, or from within, as animalistic biological impulses. The discursive imagination is by nature ill-adapted to dramatize compact moments of being. Still, naturalists did not avoid short fiction altogether and at times delivered original and powerful tales in brief compass. The icy tundra or an indifferent sea provided settings in which a Jack London or a Stephen Crane might explore elemental passions in spare, clean prose. Norris's "A Deal in Wheat" and to a lesser extent Dreiser's "Curious Shifts of the Poor" achieve a montage effect that predicts modernist narrative strategies.

In any event, what this gathering of short fiction may lose in depth and complexity, it proposes to gain in extent and variety. Many important American writers of the time had abandoned the once popular idea that there might be some overarching expression of the American character; in 1891 Howells believed that he had detected a "universal rule against universalizing" in our literature. In the short story, at least, gifted writers were content to contribute what they could to the hundred "patches" that might make up in quiltlike fashion a representative American literature. Together, diverse in their purposes and variable in their approach to their material, they nevertheless did broad justice to their historical and cultural moment. This may have been what Howells had in mind, after all, when he spoke of the "democratic" mission of the American writer.

Tom Quirk

INTRODUCTION

The Literary Context

The writers of Realism and Naturalism humanized American fiction, using common characters, colloquial language, and normative situations for the creation of literary art. This era, 1865 to 1918, saw the development of the short story as a major genre and the maturation of the realistic "novel." During these decades women became a major force in American letters, as did minority writers of a broad spectrum of ethnic and religious backgrounds. The subject of literature also changed in this period, addressing the regional differences of the expanding United States, the moral dilemmas of everyday life, the role of the emerging New Woman, the burgeoning industrial revolution, the influence of scientific methodology, the implications of evolution and agnosticism for traditional religious beliefs, the rapidly growing immigrant population drawn by the American dream for themselves and their children, and the problems of assimilation into a mainstream American culture that was itself a blend of many traditions and systems of values. It was the most dramatic period of transformation the country had ever seen, and it changed forever the language, the literature, and the fundamental values of American society.

Nowhere were these changes more evident than in American fiction. Prior to the Civil War, the most important American narratives were essentially Romances based on a set of philosophic assumptions that regarded reality as fundamentally spiritual in nature. The concept of Transcendentalism, as elucidated in the essays of Ralph Waldo Emerson and Henry David Thoreau, rested on the notion that physical facts were merely an indication of the more important spiritual facts behind them. Specific items in nature were "symbolic" of their spiritual essence in the ubiquitous "oversoul" that invests the universe, setting the physical world in "correspondence" with the ethereal, uniting people with nature into a spiritual whole. The fiction of the Romantic period in America addressed similarly grand conceptions, reaching for universals, surpassing mundane concerns to explore the generic state of human existence. In Herman Melville's *Moby-Dick*, for example, the whale takes on a significance far beyond its role as an aquatic mammal, becoming a physical manifestation of the mysterious (either good or evil depending upon interpretation), the object of Ahab's obsessive quest. Nathaniel Hawthorne's *The Scarlet Letter* is more than a study in morality and punishment, for it seems to enlist cosmic forces (as when lightning scribes a scarlet *A* in the heavens) in its psychologically insightful portrayal of the destructiveness of hidden sin and the conflict between the individual and society.

The basic congruence between Romantic ideas and aesthetics becomes even more evident in the study of the short fiction of the period, for the Romantics wrote primarily either "tales" (accounts of mysterious events involving symbolic or personified characters) or "sketches" (a portrait of a character type with little plot development). An example of the first is Hawthorne's "Young Goodman Brown," which features as protagonist the righteous "Good Man" leaving his wife, Faith, to encounter the evil in the human heart in a midnight ceremony in the dark woods. The obvious personification of these characters, and of the deceptive "Devil" they encounter, infuses the events of the story with universal significance, suggesting that the acceptance of evil in the human heart is a necessary awareness for a mature existence. Since the pure Goodman is never able to accept evil in his wife or in himself, his happiness is destroyed, and he lives in bitterness and defeat until his death. Perhaps the most famous *sketch* of the period is Washington Irving's "Rip Van Winkle," a highly sophisticated narrative that drew on centuries of lore of legendary sleepers (among them King Arthur, Odin, and Sleeping Beauty) who returned to active life in a later era. Drawing on the ancient German tale of Peter Klaus, with its mysterious events and life-enhancing return, Irving Americanized the material by setting it in upstate New York at the time of the Revolutionary War, by introducing a locally legendary figure (Henry Hudson, Captain of the *Halfmoon*), and by supplying enough details of a Dutch village in the Catskills to create an aura of plausibility. In its portrayal of an impossibly lengthy sleep, its mythic explanation of the origin of thunder, and its utilization of the mysterious, nonhuman crew of the ship, the tale well exemplifies the fiction of the period, norms that the Realists were to reject in the aftermath of the war.

But the transformation from a spiritual Romanticism, with its elevated language and sophisticated concerns, to a secularized Realism, told in common language about ordinary events, did not occur as a single event. It was, rather, an evolution of a spectrum of tendencies that coalesced in the trauma of the war, after which the optimism of Emersonian idealism seemed tragically absurd. But even during the Romantic period there were literary elements that tended toward the depiction of unadorned reality, one of which was the need to establish a physical foundation for transcendent allegories, with the result that nearly all Romantic fiction contains passages of detailed description and plain conversation. Another stream of influence tending toward realism derived from the humor traditions in America, all of which had localized, "earthy" characters speaking in the vernacular, capturing the personality and mannerisms of a section of the country. The Yankee peddler, the Southern trickster, the garrulous cracker-barrel philosopher of the West, the country bumpkin of the "middle-boarder" were all character types used for humorous effects, but they spoke the language of earthy people, they struggled against ordinary obstacles, and they inhabited the "real" world of physical existence. The humor traditions also offered a mockery of the social superiority of the sophisticated characters and language of the Romantic tradition, puncturing the inflated concerns of transcendental philosophy.

By roughly the time of the Civil War, these literary influences combined with a spectrum of social transformations to pave the way for the local-color tradition of regional stories, an important movement of the day. The Civil War brought about a renewed concern for the social character of the restored Union, and there followed a period of national self-definition, an accounting of the peoples, dialects, folkways, and diverse traditions of the geographic sections of the United States, with much of the emphasis on the South. Indeed, late in 1865, *The Nation* magazine initiated a series of articles on "The South As It Is," and within a decade both *Scribner's Monthly* and *Harper's Monthly* had commissioned similar series. Soon, magazines were flooded with stories depicting virtually all of the regions of the country in much the same manner, with an emphasis on a highly localized setting and provincial, rustic characters who spoke a regional dialect. The local-color story subordinated plot to the revelation of personality; it avoided sophisticated language to capture the speech patterns of unlettered Americans; it most distinctly rejected any sense of capturing universal Truth. But that fact does not mean that the movement was not vital in American culture, nor was the term essentially pejorative in implication. The local-color story represented a distinct focus on uniquely American characters, settings, and language patterns, a rejection of European models, and the formation of an indigenous literary tradition. In *Crumbling Idols* in 1894, Hamlin Garland made clear that he regarded this tradition as central to the establishment of a national literature, and it was widely accepted in these terms by writers in all sections of the country.

The tales in the humor traditions of the prewar years appeared primarily in newspapers, the principal outlet for short fiction. In contrast, the local-color story was more the product of the burgeoning magazines that blanketed the country after the war, joining the ever-growing list of successful newspapers as outlets for fiction. The list of new magazines is impressive: *Galaxy* was founded in 1866, *Overland Monthly* and *Lippincott's Magazine* in 1868, *Appleton's Journal* in 1869, *Scribner's Monthly* in 1870 (evolving into *Century Magazine* 1881, which made room for *Scribner's Magazine* in 1887), to name only a few of the 3,300 magazines in America by 1885. The new outlets joined the more established magazines, such as *The Atlantic Monthly, The Nation, The Ladies' Home Journal,* and *Harper's Monthly.* Additional newspapers were also founded in this period, among them some of the very best, including the *Kansas City Star,* the *New York Evening Post,* and the *New York Morning Journal.* The number of new magazines reflected a growing reading public, a phenomenon that allowed the increase of the *New York World* readership from 20,000 in 1883 to more than 250,000 in 1886. The inception of the newspaper syndicate, made possible by the telegraph, also allowed for a wide distribution, and the country was crying for regional materials, particularly for local-color stories.

Although narratives with localized descriptions occur as early as Irving's tales of the 1820s, Augustus Baldwin Longstreet's *Georgia Scenes* in 1835, and Harriet Beecher Stowe's *The Pearl of Orr's Island* in 1862, the local-color movement is generally regarded to have begun with the publication of Mark Twain's "The Celebrated Jumping Frog of Calaveras County" in 1865 and Bret Harte's "The Luck of Roaring Camp" in 1868, stories that utilize a distinctly Western setting, provincial character types, and definable regional dialect for humorous effect. Since the genre of the movement was distinctly the short story, with relatively few novels in the mode, there were thousands of such stories published between the end of the war and the turn of the century, so many that more than 150 volumes of local-color stories were collected in the 1890s. Among the notable contributions were stories of New England by Harriet Beecher Stowe, Rose Terry Cooke, Sarah Orne Jewett, and Mary E. Wilkins Freeman. In the South the style was represented by George Washington Cable, Alice Dunbar-Nelson (an important African-

American local colorist), and Grace Elizabeth King, all from New Orleans, as well as Mary Noailles Murfree of Tennessee and Joel Chandler
Harris of Georgia. These stories expanded the thematic boundaries of
regionalism by introducing other issues beyond the capturing of local
folkways, so that in "A Church Mouse" Freeman shows the conservative thinking of a New England village but also explores the restrictions
on the lives of women. Stowe's "The Minister's Housekeeper" is representative of the use of regional dialect and folkways in the New England humor tradition that evolved into Local Colorism. More focused
on personality and language than moral conflict, the story comes to a
predictable and amusing conclusion with the marriage of Parson Carryl
and Huldy, his attractive and capable young housekeeper.

Although the local-color story emphasized character over plot, setting over theme, dialogue over event, both Kate Chopin's "Athénaïse"
and Sarah Orne Jewett's "A White Heron" involve dramatic plot developments that require an important decision by the protagonist, a
device more common to the stories of realism. However, in that the
decisions to be made are distinctly tied to regional values in circumstances unlikely to be duplicated in another area of the country, the
local-color designation seems appropriate. The local colorists explored
a broad range of subjects and themes, but their unifying emphasis is on
the qualities of regional identity, the mores and backgrounds unique to
the geographic section of the country.

By the time of the Civil War, the short narratives of the humorous
traditions and local colorism evolved into the realistic short story, which
offered a strong narrative line, a plot involving a central conflict, believable characters and dialogue, and a normative portrait of American
life. Part of the impetus for this transformation came from foreign influences, literary imports that greatly altered the character of fiction in
America. For example, the earliest use of the term "Realism" to describe
literature seems to have been a review of Balzac published in the *West-
minster Review* in England in 1853, although the concept was being
used in Paris to describe the new wave in painting. Edmond Duranty
established a review entitled *Réalisme* in 1856, and by the end of the
decade the term seemed well established in Europe, with the appearance
of Turgenev's *A Sportsman's Sketches* in 1852, Tolstoy's *Sevastopol* in
1856, and Flaubert's *Madame Bovary* the same year. European immigrants into the United States brought their literary traditions with them,
of course, and important Realistic subjects and techniques came along
with Scandinavian settlers (already exposed to the harsh dramas of
Henry Ibsen) as well as those from France, Spain, Germany, Italy, and
elsewhere on the continent. Their ideas and techniques were quickly

absorbed into American fiction, and their descendants were to become the most important writers of the next generation.

The fundamental assumptions of Realism were quite distinct from Romanticism: In his *Devil's Dictionary*, Ambrose Bierce defined Realism as "the art of depicting nature as it is seen by toads." For the Realists, the emphasis was on physical existence, not Transcendental spirituality, and compared with the prewar writers, they were unabashedly anthropocentric. Their literature was fundamentally democratic, dealing with average characters in mundane situations, struggling with the social, racial, economic, and moral issues of terrestrial life. Ethics were regarded as intrinsic to human interaction, rather than a set of regulations imposed by a supernatural deity. Fundamentally, the underlying assumption of the Realists was not that their fiction constituted "reality" itself but rather that reality could be understood and made the basis of art by capturing the "common vision." The physical world was sufficiently stable and available to empirical scrutiny to depict in literature, the concept of "mimetic representation." This thinking led to a variety of approaches, one of them being slice-of-life fiction, a mode close to journalism, in which the story rendered a moment of experience for a character. More often, however, the central character was placed in a position of ethical crisis. Since reality was physical, stable, and comprehensible, the conflicts focused on the responsibility of characters for choices they were free to make, giving protagonists "agency" to act in accord with their own moral values. This idea also perpetuated the assumptions of American individualism that give primacy to personal experience and judgment. In *The Rise of Silas Lapham*, for example, William Dean Howells placed the central character in a position to choose between his wealth and his sense of ethical integrity, a key conflict in a capitalist society based on free enterprise. In Mark Twain's *Adventures of Huckleberry Finn*, the climactic moment comes when Huck must choose between his regard for the humanity and decency of a runaway slave and the social and legal ethic that demands that he surrender him to the authorities. It is perhaps the most dramatic decision in American literature, one illustrative of the kinds of issues that served as conflicts in realistic fiction.

The other elements of the fiction within the realistic mode were congruent with these subjects and themes. Stories about the struggles of common people needed to be told by the ordinary people themselves, in first person, or by a third-person narrative intelligence identified with the mind of a single character, usually the protagonist. Characters interacting in a physical world do not lend themselves to personification, so the fictional personalities in Realism tended to be described in terms of their appearance or earthly function, revealing themselves dramatically in action or dialogue. Supernatural omniscience was no longer in vogue, hence there was no access to the life stories of all the characters, unless they spoke about themselves to another character. This limited method of narration did not provide access to a frame of reference that would allow for symbolization; instead, the Realists presented images derived from experience or metaphors arising from the events in a story; there are few formal symbols in American Realism.

Nature, a benevolent, Pantheistic entity in Romanticism, is portrayed as indifferent to the human condition in Realism, although the underlying notion that there is a "moral" presence in Nature lingered in fiction for more than a century. Formal religion, and direct allusions to a deity, are rare in Realism; when organized religious institutions are described, as they are in *Huck Finn* and Harold Frederic's *The Damnation of Theron Ware*, they are usually the subject of satire, a tradition that culminates in the twentieth century with Sinclair Lewis's *Elmer Gantry*. All of these matters should be taken as tendencies in the fiction of the period, not absolutes, but they were sufficiently widespread to constitute a movement in the short story, one that had an effect on American literature for more than a century, producing many of its finest works. Of course no short story fits the mold of Realism perfectly, but many of the best stories in American literature are essentially Realistic.

Within these parameters, writers explored the important issues of the late nineteenth century. The national and personal destructiveness of war was an unavoidable subject for the time, and stories based on the Civil War, the most devastating event in national history, as well as on the Spanish-American War and World War I, expressed the central ideas of Realism. William Dean Howells's "Editha," set during the Spanish-American War, focuses on the moral consequences of a young woman's need to have her betrothed enlist to become worthy of her, a sacrifice with unforeseen but devastating consequences. Ambrose Bierce's "An Occurrence at Owl Creek Bridge" is one of the great stories in English, capturing, in the workings of the mind of a condemned man, the meaning of a military execution. Garland's "The Return of a Private" shows the aftermath of war, the human cost of political idealism, the grim impoverishment that awaits the antiheroic arrival of a humble farmer coming home to his family. No story presents a more devastating account of a battle than does Bierce's "Chickamauga," a powerful story not only for its subject, an engagement as seen by a small child, but also for its method, as the narrative perspective identifies with the child's mind, revealing the truth of the scene as he comes to a startling, haunting, realization.

Other writers used Realistic techniques to explore the dynamics of gender, a concern that resulted in the New Woman theme in the 1890s and went on, in the suffragist movement, to the political enfranchisement of women. Perhaps the best novel on the New Woman theme is Kate Chopin's *The Awakening*. The most well known feminist story of the period is Charlotte Perkins Gilman's "The Yellow Wallpaper," a brilliant evocation of emotional pathology and misguided, destructive attempts to treat it. Mary Wilkins Freeman's "The Revolt of 'Mother' " captures a moment of female assertion with both humor and sensitivity. Edith Wharton's "The Other Two" concerns a distinctly "modern" subject, the divorced and remarried woman. Jewett's "Miss Tempy's Watchers" deals with the more gentle issue of "communities of women," using psychological transformation, rather than physical event, for the climax. Willa Cather's "A Wagner Matinée" similarly focuses on another sensitive matter that emerges in this era, the essence of the aesthetic sensibility, the importance of art in human existence.

Ethnic and racial topics were also an important part of Realism, for few subjects seemed so central to the melting pot of America as the definition of the values of various groups as a precursor to the assimilation of them into one symbiotic society. With vast numbers of immigrants from a broad range of backgrounds, with differing languages, religions, and customs, the expanding nation presented an unlimited number of possibilities for stories in this vein. Charles W. Chesnutt's "The Wife of His Youth" utilizes African-American issues in a typically Realistic manner, presenting the protagonist at an intense moment of ethical crisis, when a decision will forever change the course of his life. Zitkala-Sä's "The Trial Path" uses a Native American legend to illustrate the process of justice among the Lakota people. Alice Dunbar-Nelson, an African-American writer from New Orleans, unites racial and regional concerns in "Sister Josepha," and Abraham Cahan, the first important Jewish writer in American fiction, gives expression to his background in "A Providential Match." These are only a sample of the varied subjects that Realistic writers addressed in their stories, but their work brought the fruition of the short story in American literary history.

By the 1890s the central concept of Realism was well established in American literature, and its basic principles were to dominate fiction for the next century, but there also evolved two related movements with somewhat different fundamental assumptions: Naturalism and Impressionism. Naturalism was not, as is often assumed, simply a more pessimistic form of Realism. Indeed, the underlying ideas of the nature of human life, the extent to which people are responsible for their actions, the method of presenting narratives, the kinds of characters used, the handling of plot, the presentation of images, the tone, the genre, and even the style of Naturalism differed from Realism in important ways.

If Realism had its origins in painting, Naturalism can be thought to have evolved from science, specifically from a book by a French physician, Claude Bernard, entitled *An Introduction to the Study of Experimental Medicine*, which presented the startling idea that medical treatment should involve an assessment of the cause of a condition as a basis for curing the patient. Illness was not, in Bernard's view, a matter of divine will, and heavenly intervention was not a preferred therapy, an attitude that proved controversial. The duty of a physician was to establish the physiological etiology of a pathological phenomenon, alter the causative agent, and cure the patient. Émile Zola, impressed by this thinking, applied the same logic to the role of a novelist in *The Experimental Novel* (1880). The obligation of a novel was to portray social pathology, analyzing its causative forces, and, by suggesting ways of altering these factors, improve society. Naturalism was, unabashedly, a reformist movement.

Beginning in the 1890s in America, Naturalistic fiction was very effective in achieving these ends, and, through alliance with the Populist movement, with governmental agencies seeking to improve conditions in the cities and on the farms, and later with Socialism, the Naturalists were able to influence the direction of American society. They were also informed by developments in psychology, political philosophy, and science, particularly by Charles Darwin's *The Origin of Species by Means of Natural Selection* in 1859, which contributed to Naturalistic thinking not only the idea that homo sapiens are related to the lower forms of animals but that people are capable of an atavistic regression to a savage state, that modern behavior can be the product of biologically determined forces, that there is nothing transcendent in human life. Life is a struggle for survival in which not the fittest but the most ruthless prevail.

Out of these ideas developed the dominant theme in Naturalism of pessimistic Determinism, the notion that characters are the victims of the Promethean forces of heredity, society, and a hostile nature, powers outside the control of the protagonists and for which they are thus not to be held responsible. In this sense individuality, crucial in Realism, is deemphasized in Naturalism, since personal attributes make little difference in a character driven by overwhelming external forces or internal biological necessities. The plots of Naturalism thus tend to exhibit the expression of Deterministic power; there is little ethical struggle within a character since personal choice makes no difference. Naturalistic fiction is normally set in a hostile environment, in urban slums, in rural poverty, in the jungle, or the arctic. The characters tend to be uneducated, representative, lower-class "types" of some oppressed group, most often uncomprehending of the forces that impel them toward tragedy, unable to grasp the situation or articulate a protest. Such characters could not narrate their own stories, of course, since they have no knowledge of the powers that drive them to ruin; Naturalistic narrators are nearly always omniscient voices, in possession of the long causative history of the situation, able to have access to the minds of all of the characters, able to see into the future as well as the past. Such narrators tend to be intrusive, commenting directly on the meaning of the events presented, analyzing the responsibility for the destructive circumstances. As a reform movement, Naturalism was not noted for artistic effects or stylistic grace; but animal and jungle images, figures drawn from war, metaphors from prehistoric savagery, and dominant symbols of obsessive characters traits (lust, greed, hatred, revenge) emphasize the underlying themes.

These ideas produced some great novels, among them Theodore Dreiser's *Sister Carrie*, Frank Norris's *McTeague*, Jack London's *The Sea-Wolf*, John Steinbeck's *The Grapes of Wrath*, and, in 1940, Richard Wright's *Native Son*, perhaps the last great novel in this tradition. Because an analysis of causative forces tends to be ponderous, the short story was not the normal genre for Naturalism, although there were powerful stories produced in the mode. One of the most frequently cited is Norris's "A Deal in Wheat," which well illustrates the theme of economic determinism, as greed in the grain market ruins the life of a farmer and his family. Hamlin Garland's "Under the Lion's Paw" develops a related theme, the exploitation of tenant farmers in the uncontrolled economy of the late nineteenth century. Social injustice is also the theme of Stephen Crane's "An Experiment in Misery" and "The Men in the Storm," both Bowery tales of urban poverty and despair. London's "To Build a Fire" illustrates the hostility of nature, life as a struggle for survival, and "The Law of Life" reveals the tragic acceptance of death. In "The Lynching of Jube Benson," Paul Lawrence Dunbar, an important early African-American writer, and John M. Oskison, who wrote from a Native American perspective, both present Naturalistic ideas functioning in minority cultures, and Dreiser's "The Second Choice" explores the restricted options available to lower-class women of the time.

Literary Impressionism, as did Realism, had it origins in painting, although it quickly found expression in music and literature. The term was first used to describe a Parisian art exhibit in 1874, one displaying paintings by Cézanne, Degas, Pissaro, and Renoir, and which featured Claude Monet's *Impression, Sunrise*, which gave a name to the new movement. Within three years a new art journal was founded, *The Impressionist*, which signaled public acceptance of the still controversial new methodology. Although there was no ideological or artistic homogeneity among the thirty painters originally identified with the term, there were at least some central ideas that gave cohesion to a set of artistic tendencies. For the Impressionists, actuality was not stable and understood, as the Realists assumed, but constantly in flux, yielding only momentary sensory "impressions," primarily visual, from which only a tentative and fragmentary understanding of the situation could be inferred. Cézanne declared that "art should not imitate nature but should express the sensations aroused by nature." From this point of view, reality is a matter of perception; it is objective in the sense that the impressions originate in physical nature, and subjective to the extent that individual human minds receive and interpret the sensations.

These ideas were quickly exported to America. In 1874 the Foreign Exhibition in Boston displayed Impressionistic works by Monet, Manet, Pissaro, Renoir, and Sisley, and by 1886 there were major shows in New York: that year James F. Sutton of the American Art Association arranged an exhibition of more than 300 Impressionist paintings. By this time there were young American artists who were attracted to the mode, among them Theodore Robinson, James Whistler, Mary Cassatt, John Twatchman, Childe Hassam, J. Alden Weir, and Willard Metcalf, and they formed the Academy of American Impressionism. The central ideas of Impressionism quickly influenced American writers as well, since the ideas were being discussed in hundreds of articles in intellectual magazines, among them Cecilia Waern's "Some Notes on French Impressionism" in the *Atlantic Monthly* in 1892. But there were other avenues of exposure: Stephen Crane moved into the Art Students' League in 1892, living with young painters all studying, and discussing, impressionistic painting. The next year Hamlin Garland spoke at the opening of the Impressionist exhibit at the Columbia Exhibition in Chicago, and he later devoted a chapter to Impressionism in his *Crumbling Idols*. Other writers attended lectures on the movement or viewed the traveling displays of Impressionistic paintings that brought the new art to the small towns and villages across America.

The strategy of the Impressionist writer was to present the sensory details that the central character could receive in an instant of experience, what the painters called a *vistazo*. The central structural principle of Impressionistic fiction is thus the episode, brief scenes strung together in sequence, each separate but each contributing to the growing aggregate of information. The characters in such fiction are in a constant state of having to interpret the world around them. Impressionistic narrators do not possess omniscience, nor do they have an understanding of a stable "reality" that allows for ethical struggle; they must limit their information to the flow of sensations of a character. They do not intrude with interpretive comment; they do not know the past or the future; they are focused on the sensations of the moment. They know nothing of supernatural spirituality, nor is there any "symbolism" in Impressionism, only sensory images and the dramatic metaphors inspired by the flow of events. The significance of Impressionistic images thus grows out of the immediate context; in contrast, the meaning of Naturalistic *symbols* derives from a long history of cultural associations. In Impressionism the issue is a struggle to comprehend the truth of a situation. The conflicts of Impressionism thus do not involve determinism or moral crisis but the incremental acquisition of knowledge, leading to a climatic epiphany, a dramatic moment when a character, usually a young person still learning about life, suddenly sees the truth of a situation. The central themes of such fiction involve truth and illusion, delusion, epistemological growth, and sudden realizations, a set of ideas at once psychologically realistic and yet startlingly modern in literature.

The central ideas and artistic methods of Impressionism, however, did not develop sufficient acceptance or momentum to constitute an entirely separate movement; they are better understood as a set of tendencies within Realism, with which it shared characters and language, ordinary situations, and a concern for the details of literary "art." Unlike Naturalism, they both avoided authorial comment, dominant symbols, deterministic themes, and political didacticism. In the American novel, the most notable authors employing Impressionistic techniques and ideas were Stephen Crane, whose *The Red Badge of Courage* is a classic work of Impressionism, Henry James, Kate Chopin, Ambrose Bierce, and Harold Frederic. In the short story, these tendencies have a role in some of the best stories of the period: The first section of Bierce's "An Occurrence at Owl Creek Bridge," which presents the objective sensations of the protagonist, is a prime example of Impressionistic restriction; the third section, which presents fantasy as actual experience, is a good example of the subjective pole of Impressionistic narration. The center section, an omniscient presentation of the prehistory of the situation, is not an Impressionistic device. In "Chickamauga," by restricting the center of intelligence and presenting the sensations of a deaf-mute child, Bierce also utilized Impressionism, as he did for the climax of that story, a dramatic epiphany. An epiphany also serves as the climax of Chopin's "Désirée's Baby," in which a new realization changes the meaning of everything, very close to the role of "recognition" in classical tragedy, the very issue that concludes James's "The Beast in the Jungle." Impressionism was not the major movement of its day (that role was left to Realism), but it had an influence on the direction of American literature for several decades beginning in the 1890s. The Imagist movement in poetry, for example, has it roots in Impressionism, as did certain aspects of the Modernism that developed in the 1920s.

Many stories of the period, particularly around the turn of the century, display multiple tendencies, lending them to a variety of interpretations in these terms. In Crane's "The Open Boat," for example, Nature is initially portrayed as hostile (with the snarling of the waves and the threat of the shark), but the correspondent grows to see it as indifferent. The fight for survival is replaced as a central issue by the new realization of the central character, his development of compassion, and the sense of community, a "brotherhood" that unites the men in the boat. "The Blue Hotel" provides the basis for a reading in all three modes, although the results are very different. As Naturalism, the theme involves the hostility of the storm about the hotel, the compulsions of "character" within the Swede, the fight for survival of the gambler. The Swede is the victim of deterministic forces, and no one is personally responsible. As Realism, the story is about the assessment of culpability for the death of the Swede, the issue the Easterner and the Cowboy discuss at the end, and many characters can be seen as contributory actors, for which they cannot escape blame. The role of Impressionism is related to narrative method, as "the Easterner's mind, like a film, took lasting impressions of the three men," putting the emphasis on the sensory experiences of the central character and his realizations in the conclusion. Each of these approaches have interpretive validity, and yet no one of them accounts for all of the artistry and ideas that enrich this remarkable story.

Many stories defy easy categorization, even when certain aspects of them fit a movement perfectly. Jewett's "A White Heron," for example, is Regional in tone, dialect, and setting, but the conflict involves precisely the kind of ethical dilemma that typifies Realism. But even though no story fits one category in all respects, and the definitions of the movements do not account for all of the devices and themes that the stories contain, still a working definition of the local-color movement, Realism, Naturalism, and Impressionism help to elucidate the variety of themes that were current in this period and to serve as a reminder of the spectrum of considerations that go into a full interpretation of a story. This was a period, 1865 to 1918, that saw the short story come into maturity in America, and the short fiction that emerged in this era confronted the most pressing issues of a dynamic age. It is a rich literary legacy, one that finds partial expression in the stories in this volume.

James Nagel

SUGGESTIONS FOR FURTHER READING

Ahnebrink, Lars. *The Beginnings of Naturalism in American Fiction: A Study of the Works of Hamlin Garland, Stephen Crane, and Frank Norris with Special Reference to Some European Influences, 1891–1903*. Cambridge: Harvard University Press, 1950.

Auerbach, Erich. *Memesis: The Representation of Reality in Western Literature*. Princeton: Princeton University Press, 1953.

Baguley, David. *Naturalist Fiction: The Entropic Vision*. Cambridge: Cambridge University Press, 1990.

Becker, George L., ed. *Documents of Modern Literary Realism*. Princeton: Princeton University Press, 1963.

Bell, Michael Davitt. *The Problem of American Realism: Studies in the Cultural History of a Literary Idea*. Chicago: University of Chicago Press, 1993.

Bernardette, Jane, ed. *American Realism: A Shape for Fiction*. New York: Putnam, 1972.

Berthoff, Warner. *The Ferment of Realism: American Literature, 1884–1919*. New York: Free Press, 1965.

Block, Haskell M. *Naturalistic Triptych: The Fictive and the Real in Zola, Mann, and Dreiser*. New York: Random House, 1970.

Boller, Paul F., Jr. *American Thought in Transition: The Impact of Evolutionary Naturalism, 1865–1900*. Chicago: Rand McNally, 1969.

Borus, Daniel H. *Writing Realism: Howells, James, and Norris in the Mass Market*. Chapel Hill: University of North Carolina Press, 1989.

Brooks, Van Wyck. *New England: Indian Summer: 1865–1915*. New York: Dutton, 1940.

Cady, Edwin H. *The Light of Common Day: Realism in American Fiction*. Bloomington: Indiana University Press, 1971.

Cargill, Oscar. *Intellectual America: Ideas on the March*. New York: Macmillan, 1941.

Carter, Everett. *Howells and the Age of Realism*. Philadelphia: Lippincott, 1954.

Chase, Richard. *The American Novel and Its Tradition*. Garden City: Doubleday Anchor, 1957.

Conder, John J. *Naturalism in American Fiction: The Classic Phase.* Lexington: University Press of Kentucky, 1984.

Conn, Peter. *The Divided Mind: Ideology and Imagination in America, 1898–1917.* Cambridge: Cambridge University Press, 1983.

Donovan, Josephine. *New England Local Color Literature: A Women's Tradition.* New York: Ungar, 1983.

Fetterley, Judith, and Marjorie Pryse. *American Women Regionalists 1850–1910.* New York: Norton, 1992.

Fiedler, Leslie A. *Love and Death in the American Novel.* New York: Criterion, 1960.

Furst, Lilian R., and Peter N. Skrine. *Naturalism.* London: Methuen, 1971.

Fussell, Edwin. *Frontier: American Literature and the American West.* Princeton: Princeton University Press, 1965.

Geismar, Maxwell. *Rebels and Ancestors: The American Novel, 1890–1915.* Boston: Houghton Mifflin, 1953.

Habegger, Alfred. *Gender, Fantasy, and Realism in American Literature.* New York: Columbia University Press, 1982.

Hakutani, Yoshinobu, and Lewis Fried, eds. *American Literary Naturalism: A Reassessment.* Heidelberg: Carl Winter, 1975.

Hicks, Granville. *The Great Tradition: An Interpretation of American Literature Since the Civil War.* New York: Macmillan, 1993.

Hook, Andrew. *American Literature in Context III, 1865–1900.* London: Methuen, 1983.

Howard, June. *Form and History in American Literary Naturalism.* Chapel Hill: University of North Carolina Press, 1985.

Hubbell, Jay B. *The South in American Literature, 1607–1900.* Durham: Duke University Press, 1954.

Kaplan, Amy. *The Social Construction of American Realism.* Chicago: University of Chicago Press, 1988.

Kaplan, Harold. *Power and Order: Henry Adams and the Naturalist Tradition in American Fiction.* Chicago: University of Chicago Press, 1981.

Karolides, Nicholas J. *The Pioneer in the American Novel, 1900–1950.* Norman: University of Oklahoma Press, 1967.

Kazin, Alfred. *On Native Grounds: An Interpretation of Modern American Prose Literature.* New York: Reynal and Hitchcock, 1942.

Kolb, Harold H., Jr. *The Illusion of Life: American Realism as a Literary Form.* Charlottesville: University Press of Virginia, 1969.

Krause, Sydney J., ed. *Essays on Determinism in American Literature.* Kent: Kent State University Press, 1964.

Lamprecht, Sterling P. *The Metaphysics of Naturalism.* New York: Appleton-Century-Crofts, 1967.

Levin, Harry. *The Gates of Horn: A Study of Five French Realists.* New York: Oxford University Press, 1963.

McElderry, Bruce R., Jr., ed. *The Realistic Movement in American Writing.* New York: Odyssey, 1965.

McKay, Janet H. *Narration and Discourse in American Realistic Fiction.* Philadelphia: University of Pennsylvania Press, 1982.

Martin, Jay. *Harvests of Change: American Literature, 1865–1914.* Englewood Cliffs: Prentice-Hall, 1967.

Martin, Ronald E. *American Literature and the Universe of Force.* Durham: Duke University Press, 1981.

Michaels, Walter Benn. *The Gold Standard and the Logic of Naturalism: American Literature at the Turn of the Century.* Berkeley: University of California Press, 1987.

Mitchell, Lee Clark. *Determined Fictions: American Literary Naturalism.* New York: Columbia University Press, 1989.

Nagel, James, ed. *American Fiction: Historical and Critical Essays.* Boston: Northeastern University Press, 1977.

Nagel, James, and Richard Astro, eds. *American Literature: The New England Heritage.* New York: Garland, 1981.

Nagel, James. *Stephen Crane and Literary Impressionism.* University Park: Pennsylvania State University Press, 1980.

Parrington, Vernon Louis. *The Beginnings of Critical Realism in America, 1860–1920.* Vol. 3 of *Main Currents in American Thought.* New York: Harcourt, Brace, 1930.

Pattee, Fred Lewis. *The Development of the American Short Story: An Historical Survey.* New York: Harper, 1923.

———. *A History of American Literature Since 1870.* New York: Century, 1915.

Pizer, Donald. *The Cambridge Companion to American Realism and Naturalism: Howells to London.* New York: Cambridge University Press, 1995.

———. *Realism and Naturalism in Nineteenth-Century American Literature.* Carbondale: Southern Illinois University Press, 1966.

———. *The Theory and Practice of American Literary Naturalism: Selected Essays and Reviews.* Carbondale: Southern Illinois University Press, 1993.

———. *Twentieth-Century American Literary Naturalism: An Interpretation.* Carbondale: Southern Illinois University Press, 1982.

Pizer, Donald, and Earl Harbert, eds. *American Realists and Naturalists.* Vol. 12 of the *Dictionary of Literary Biography.* Detroit: Gale Research, 1982.

Schneider, Robert W. *Five Novelists of the Progressive Era.* New York: Columbia University Press, 1965.

Seltzer, Mark. *Bodies and Machines.* New York: Routledge, 1992.

Shi, David E. *Facing Facts: Realism in American Thought and Culture, 1850–1920.* New York: Oxford University Press, 1995.

Simpson, Claude M. *The Local Colorists: American Short Stories, 1857–1900.* New York: Harper and Brothers, 1960.

Smith, Henry Nash. *Virgin Land: The American West as Symbol and Myth.* Cambridge: Harvard University Press, 1950.

Stegner, Wallace. *Selected American Prose 1841–1900: The Realistic Movement*. New York: Holt, Rinehart and Winston, 1958.

Stein, Allen. *After the Vows Were Spoken: Marriage in American Literary Realism*. Columbus: Ohio University Press, 1984.

Stromberg, Roland N., ed. *Realism, Naturalism, and Symbolism: Modes of Thought and Expression in Europe*. New York: Walker, 1968.

Sundquist, Eric J., ed. *American Realism: New Essays*. Baltimore: Johns Hopkins University Press, 1982.

Taylor, Gordon O. *The Passages of Thought: Psychological Representation in the American Novel, 1870–1900*. New York: Oxford University Press, 1969.

Thorp, Willard. *American Writing in the Twentieth Century*. Cambridge: Harvard University Press, 1960.

Thorp, Willard, ed. *Great Short Works of American Realism*. New York: Harper & Row, 1968.

Trachtenberg, Alan. *The Incorporation of America: Culture and Society in the Gilded Age*. New York: Hill and Wang, 1982.

Trilling, Lionel. *The Liberal Imagination*. New York: Viking, 1950.

Walcutt, Charles C. *American Literary Naturalism: A Divided Stream*. Minneapolis: University of Minnesota Press, 1956.

Warfel, Harry R. and G. Harrison Orians. *American Local Color Stories*. New York: Cooper Square, 1970.

Westbrook, Perry D. *Free Will and Determinism in American Literature*. Rutherford: Fairleigh Dickinson University Press, 1979.

Wilson, Christopher P. *The Labor of Words: Literary Professionalism in the Progressive Era*. Athens: University of Georgia Press, 1985.

Ziff, Larzer. *The American 1890s: Life and Times of a Lost Generation*. New York: Viking, 1966.

CHRONOLOGY

Political and Social History

1865—
Thirteenth Amendment abolishes
   slavery
Lee surrenders at Appomattox
Lincoln assassinated
Andrew Johnson president 1865–9

1866—
Atlantic cable completed

1867—
Reconstruction Act
Howard University founded
Purchase of Alaska
Alfred Nobel perfects dynamite

1868—
Effort to impeach President Johnson
   narrowly fails
Fourteenth Amendment guaranteeing
   civil rights

1869—
Ulysses S. Grant, president 1869–77
Suez Canal opens
Union Pacific–Central Pacific trans-
   continental railroad completed
Knights of Labor
Prohibition Party
Wyoming passes first woman's suf-
   frage act

1870—
Franco-Prussian War
John D. Rockefeller founds the Stan-
   dard Oil Company

Literature

1865—
Mark Twain, "The Celebrated Jumping Frog of Calaveras County"

1867—
Bret Harte, *Condensed Novels*
John W. De Forest, *Miss Ravenel's
   Conversion from Secession to
   Loyalty*
George Washington Harris, *Sut Lov-
   ingood Yarns*

1868—
Louisa Alcott, *Little Women*

1869—
Harriet Beecher Stowe, *Oldtown
   Folks*

1870—
Bret Harte, *The Luck of Roaring
   Camp and Other Sketches*

1871—
Chicago destroyed by fire
Charles Darwin, *The Descent of Man*
Smith College founded

1872—
Crédit Mobilier scandal

1873—
Financial Panic of 1873
Herbert Spencer, *The Study of
    Sociology*

1874—
Woman's Christian Temperance
    Union founded
First impressionist exhibition in Paris
John Fiske, *The Outlines of Cosmic
    Philosophy*

1876—
Disputed election of 1876 between
    Samuel J. Tilden and Rutherford B.
    Hayes
Alexander Graham Bell invents the
    telephone
Centennial Exposition in Philadelphia
Custer defeated at the Battle of Little
    Big Horn

1877—
End of Reconstruction
Railroad strikes
Edison patents phonograph

1879—
Edison patents the incandescent lamp
Henry George, *Progress and Poverty*

1871—
Edward Eggleston, *The Hoosier
    Schoolmaster*

1872—
Mark Twain, *Roughing It*

1873—
William Dean Howells, *A Chance
    Acquaintance*
Mark Twain and Charles Dudley
    Warner, *The Gilded Age*

1875—
Bret Harte, *Tales of the Argonauts*

1876—
Mark Twain, *The Adventures of
    Tom Sawyer*

1877—
Henry James, *The American*
Sarah Orne Jewett, *Deephaven*

1878—
Henry James, *Daisy Miller*

1879—
George Washington Cable, *Old Cre-
    ole Days*

1880—
Henry Adams, *Democracy*
George Washington Cable, *The
    Grandissimes*
Lew Wallace, *Ben-Hur*

1881—
President James A. Garfield is
assassinated
Chester A. Arthur, president 1881–5
Booker T. Washington establishes
Tuskegee Institute
American Federation of Labor
founded

1881—
Joel Chandler Harris, *Uncle Remus*
Henry James, *The Portrait of a Lady*

1882—
Chinese exclusion act

1882—
William Dean Howells, *A Modern
Instance*
Deaths of Ralph Waldo Emerson and
Henry Wadsworth Longfellow

1883—
Pendleton Act, establishing Civil
Service
Northern Pacific transcontinental rail-
road completed
Brooklyn Bridge opens
First Chicago skyscraper

1883—
E. W. Howe, *The Story of a Country
Town*
Mark Twain, *Life on the Mississippi*

1884—
Mugwump liberal wing of Republi-
can party contributes to defeat of
James G. Blaine by Grover Cleve-
land, president 1885–9, 1893–7
National Bureau of Labor

1884—
Mary Noailles Murfree, *In The Tennessee Mountains*
Mark Twain, *Adventures of Huckleberry Finn*

1885—
Internal combustion engine patented
Ulysses S. Grant, *Personal Memoirs*

1885—
William Dean Howells, *The Rise of
Silas Lapham*

1886—
Haymarket Riot in Chicago, anar-
chists blamed
Karl Marx, *Capital* published in
English
Andrew Carnegie, *Triumphant
Democracy*

1887—
Interstate Commerce Act
First electric streetcars

1887—
William Dean Howells begins the
"Editor's Study" for *Harper's
Monthly*
Sarah Orne Jewett, *A White Heron
and Other Stories*
Constance Fenimore Woolson, *East
Angels*

Mary Wilkins Freeman, *A Humble Romance and Other Stories*
Joseph Kirkland, *Zury: The Meanest Man in Spring County*

1888—
Nicholas Tesla invents the first electric motor
George Eastman perfects the box camera

1888—
Edward Bellamy, *Looking Backward*
Henry James, *The Aspern Papers*

1889—
Benjamin Harrison, president 1889–93
Oklahoma "Land Rush"
Hull House opens in Chicago

1889—
Lafcadio Hearn, *Chita*
Mark Twain, *A Connecticut Yankee in King Arthur's Court*

1890—
Sherman Anti-Trust Act
William James, *The Principles of Psychology*
Jacob Riis, *How the Other Half Lives*

1890—
Emily Dickinson, *Poems*
William Dean Howells, *A Hazard of New Fortunes*

1891—
First International Copyright Law

1891—
Deaths of Herman Melville and James Russell Lowell
Ambrose Bierce, *Tales of Soldiers and Civilians*
Mary Wilkins Freeman, *A New England Nun and Other Stories*
Hamlin Garland, *Main-Travelled Roads*
William Dean Howells, *Criticism and Fiction*

1892—
Strike riots at Carnegie Steel Company, Homestead, Penn.
Formation of the People's Party (Populists)
Ellis Island opens as immigration center

1892—
Death of Walt Whitman
Charlotte Perkins Gilman, "The Yellow Wallpaper"

1893—
Grover Cleveland, president 1893–7
Wall Street Panic of 1893 begins depression (to 1897)
Anti-Saloon League formed
World's Columbian Exposition in Chicago
Frederick Jackson Turner, "The Sig-

1893—
Stephen Crane, *Maggie: A Girl of the Streets*
Henry B. Fuller, *The Cliff-Dwellers*

nificance of the Frontier in American
History"

1894—
Pullman Company strike in Chicago
followed by nationwide rail strike
Coxey's Army marches on
Washington
First kinetoscope (motion picture)
opens in New York

1895—
Marconi invents radio telegraphy
Röntgen discovers X-rays

1896—
William Jennings Bryan's "Cross of
Gold" speech at Democratic
Convention
Beginning of Klondike Gold Rush
Nobel Prizes established

1897—
William McKinley, president 1897–
1901
William James, *The Will to Believe*

1898—
Spanish-American War
The *Maine* incident (Battle of Manila
Bay)
Annexation of Hawaii
United States ceded the Philippines
and Puerto Rico
Charlotte Perkins Gilman, *Women
and Economics*

1899—
Beginning of Philippine insurrection
(to 1902)
Boer War in South Africa (to 1902)
John Dewey, *The School and Society*
Thorstein Veblen, *The Theory of the
Leisure Class*

1894—
Kate Chopin, *Bayou Folk*
Hamlin Garland, *Crumbling Idols*
William Dean Howells, *A Traveller
from Altruria*
Mark Twain, *The Tragedy of
Pudd'nhead Wilson*

1895—
Stephen Crane, *The Red Badge of
Courage*
Hamlin Garland, *Rose of Dutcher's
Coolly*

1896—
Death of Harriet Beecher Stowe
Abraham Cahan, *Yekl: A Tale of the
New York Ghetto*
Paul Laurence Dunbar, *Lyrics of a
Lowly Life*
Harold Frederic, *The Damnation of
Theron Ware*
Sarah Orne Jewett, *The Country of
the Pointed Firs*

1897—
Richard Harding Davis, *Soldiers of
Fortune*
Henry James, *The Spoils of Poynton*
Edwin Arlington Robinson, *The Chil-
dren of the Night*

1898—
Death of Harold Frederic
Stephen Crane, *The Open Boat and
Other Tales of Adventure*
Finley Peter Dunne, *Mr. Dooley in
Peace and War*

1899—
Charles W. Chesnutt, *The Conjure
Woman*
Kate Chopin, *The Awakening.*
Stephen Crane, *The Monster and
Other Stories*

1899— (*cont'd.*)
Edwin Markham, *The Man with the Hoe and Other Poems*
Frank Norris, *McTeague*
Alice Dunbar-Nelson, *The Goodness of St. Rocque and Other Stories*

1900—
Paris International Exhibition
Eugene Debs, Socialist Party candidate for president
Sigmund Freud, *The Interpretation of Dreams*
Theodore Roosevelt, *The Strenuous Life*

1900—
Death of Stephen Crane
Charles W. Chesnutt, *The House Behind the Cedars*
Theodore Dreiser, *Sister Carrie*
Robert Herrick, *The Web of Life*
Mark Twain, *The Man That Corrupted Hadleyburg*

1901—
William McKinley reelected (1900) and assassinated; succeeded by Theodore Roosevelt, president 1901–9
Death of Queen Victoria
J. P. Morgan organizes United States Steel Corporation
Booker T. Washington, *Up From Slavery*

1901—
Frank Norris, *The Octopus*

1902—
William James, *The Varieties of Religious Experience*

1902—
Death of Frank Norris
Ellen Glasgow, *The Battle-Ground*
Owen Wister, *The Virginian*

1903—
Wright Brothers' first flight
Founding of the Ford Motor Company
W. E. B. Du Bois, *The Souls of Black Folk*

1903—
Henry James, *The Ambassadors*
Jack London, *The Call of the Wild*
Frank Norris, *The Pit* and *The Responsibilities of the Novelist*

1904—
Russo-Japanese War (to 1905)
Saint Louis Exposition
American Academy of Arts and Letters founded
Lincoln Steffens, *The Shame of the Cities*
Ida Tarbell, *The History of the Standard Oil Company*

1904—
Death of Kate Chopin
Henry James, *The Golden Bowl*
Jack London, *The Sea-Wolf*

1905—
Revolutionary violence in Russia
International Workers of the World
(IWW) founded
Einstein formulates special theory of
relativity

1906—
San Francisco earthquake
Pure Food and Drug Act

1907—
Financial Panic of 1907
William James, *Pragmatism*

1909—
William Howard Taft, president
1909–13
Henry Ford begins mass production
of Model T
Robert E. Peary reaches the North
Pole
W. E. B. Du Bois helps found the
National Association for the Ad-
vancement of Colored People
(NAACP)
Sigmund Freud lectures in the United
States

1910—
Jane Addams, *Twenty Years at Hull
House*

1911—
Supreme Court orders dissolution of
the Standard Oil Company and the
American Tobacco Company
Roald Amundsen reaches the South
Pole

1912—
Three-way presidential election, with
Woodrow Wilson defeating Wil-
liam Howard Taft and Theodore
Roosevelt

1905—
Robert Herrick, *The Memoirs of an
American Citizen*
Edith Wharton, *The House of Mirth*

1906—
Death of Paul Laurence Dunbar
Jack London, *White Fang*
Upton Sinclair, *The Jungle.*
Mark Twain, *What Is Man?*

1907—
Henry Adams, *The Education of
Henry Adams*
Henry James, *The American Scene*

1908—
Jack London, *The Iron Heel*

1909—
Ezra Pound, *Personae*
Gertrude Stein, *Three Lives*

1910—
Death of Mark Twain

1911—
Theodore Dreiser, *Jennie Gerhardt*
Edith Wharton, *Ethan Frome*

1912—
Theodore Dreiser, *The Financier*
James Weldon Johnson, *The Autobi-
ography of an Ex-Colored Man*
Poetry magazine founded in Chicago

1912— (cont'd.)
American marines occupy Nicaragua
Titanic sinks on maiden voyage
Mary Antin, *The Promised Land*

1913—
Sixteenth Amendment authorizes federal income tax
Armory Show on modern art in New York

1913—
Willa Cather, *O Pioneers!*
Robert Frost, *A Boy's Will*
Ellen Glasgow, *Virginia*
Edith Wharton, *The Custom of the Country*

1914—
World War I begins following the assassination of Archduke Ferdinand
Panama Canal opens
United States marines land at Vera Cruz, Mexico.

1914—
Theodore Dreiser, *The Titan*
Robert Frost, *North of Boston*
Vachel Lindsay, *The Congo*

1915—
Lusitania sunk

1915—
Edgar Lee Masters, *Spoon River Anthology*
Van Wyck Brooks, *America's Coming of Age*

1916—
San Francisco Preparedness Day bombing

1916—
Deaths of Henry James and Jack London
E. A. Robinson, *The Man Against the Sky*
Carl Sandburg, *Chicago Poems*

1917—
U.S. enters World War I
Bolsheviks seize power in Russia

1917—
T. S. Eliot, *Prufrock and Other Observations*
Garland, *Son of the Middle Border*
H. L. Mencken, *A Book of Prefaces*
Edna St. Vincent Millay, *Renascence*

1918—
Armistice declared in World War I
Wilson submits his "Fourteen Points" for peace

1918—
Willa Cather, *My Ántonia*
Ezra Pound, *Pavannes and Divisions*

Part I

REGIONALISM AND
LOCAL COLOR

MARK TWAIN

Jim Smiley and His Jumping Frog

This memorable piece of vernacular humor launched Mark Twain's national literary reputation and, in a way, remained his signature piece for many years to come. Twain had heard a man named Ben Coon tell the story in a mining camp on California's Western Slope, and, seeing something literary in it, he recorded in bare-boned fashion the incidents of the tale. What most struck Twain was Ben Coon's deadpanned way of telling the yarn—for Coon was evidently unaware that there was anything funny about what he was saying. When Artemus Ward requested a contribution from Twain for a collection he was putting together, Twain wrote up the story. The completed tale arrived too late to be included in Ward's collection, however, and instead was first published in the New York *Saturday Review* for November 18, 1865. It was subsequently reprinted in newspapers throughout the country, and Mark Twain became an instant celebrity.

The author had chosen to cast this story in the familiar form of the frame tale, in which a genteel and refined character begins the story, a vernacular character spins his yarn, and the genteel narrator returns in the final paragraph. Twain adopted the form to his own purposes, however, and, unlike other humorists, refused to condescend to his created character or to make fun of him. Wheeler's genuine admiration of the exploits of Jim Smiley and the mysterious stranger, combined with his vivid and often fantastic vernacular metaphors, makes for an affecting as well as a hilarious specimen of Twain's humor.

* * *

Mr. A. Ward,
    Dear Sir:—Well, I called on good-natured, garrulous old Simon Wheeler, and I inquired after your friend Leonidas W. Smiley, as you requested me to do, and I hereunto append the result. If you can get any information out of it you are cordially welcome to it. I have a lurking suspicion that your Leonidas W. Smiley is a myth—that you never knew such a personage, and that you only conjectured that if I asked old Wheeler about him it would remind him of his infamous *Jim* Smiley, and he would go to work and bore me nearly to death with some infernal reminiscence of him

as long and tedious as it should be useless to me. If that was your design, Mr. Ward, it will gratify you to know that it succeeded.

I found Simon Wheeler dozing comfortably by the barroom stove of the little old dilapidated tavern in the ancient mining camp of Boomerang, and I noticed that he was fat and bald-headed, and had an expression of winning gentleness and simplicity upon his tranquil countenance. He roused up and gave me good-day. I told him a friend of mine had commissioned me to make some inquiries about a cherished companion of his boyhood named Leonidas W. Smiley—Rev. Leonidas W. Smiley—a young minister of the gospel, who he had heard was at one time a resident of this village of Boomerang. I added that if Mr. Wheeler could tell me anything about this Rev. Leonidas W. Smiley, I would feel under many obligations to him.

Simon Wheeler backed me into a corner and blockaded me there with his chair—and then sat down and reeled off the monotonous narrative which follows this paragraph. He never smiled, he never frowned, he never changed his voice from the quiet, gently-flowing key to which he turned the initial sentence, he never betrayed the slightest suspicion of enthusiasm—but all through the interminable narrative there ran a vein of impressive earnestness and sincerity, which showed me plainly that so far from his imagining that there was anything ridiculous or funny about his story, he regarded it as a really important matter, and admired its two heroes as men of transcendent genius in finesse. To me, the spectacle of a man drifting serenely along through such a queer yarn without ever smiling was exquisitely absurd. As I said before, I asked him to tell me what he knew of Rev. Leonidas W. Smiley, and he replied as follows. I let him go on in his own way, and never interrupted him once:

There was a feller here once by the name of *Jim* Smiley, in the winter of '49—or maybe it was the spring of '50—I don't recollect exactly, some how, though what makes me think it was one or the other is because I remember the big flume wasn't finished when he first come to the camp; but anyway, he was the curiosest man about always betting on anything that turned up you ever see, if he could get anybody to bet on the other side, and if he couldn't he'd change sides—any way that suited the other man would suit *him*—any way just so's he got a bet, *he* was satisfied. But still, he was lucky—uncommon lucky; he most always come out winner. He was always ready and laying for a chance; there couldn't be no solitry thing mentioned but what that feller'd offer to bet on it—and take any side you please, as I was just telling you: if there was a horse race, you'd find him flush or you find him busted at the end of it; if there was a dog-fight, he'd bet on it; if there was a cat-fight, he'd bet on it; if there was a chicken-fight, he'd bet on it; why if there was two birds setting on a fence, he would bet you which one would fly first—or if there was a camp-meeting he would be there reglar to bet on parson Walker, which he judged to be the best exhorter about here, and so he was, too, and a good man; if he even see a straddle-bug start to go any wheres, he would bet you how long it would take him to get wherever he was going to, and if you took him up he would foller that straddle-bug to Mexico but what he would find out where he was bound for and how long he was on the road. Lots of the boys here has seen that Smiley and can tell you about him. Why, it never made no difference to *him*—he would bet on *anything*—the dangdest feller. Parson Walker's wife laid very sick, once, for a good while, and it seemed as if they warn't going to save her; but one morning he come in and Smiley asked him how she was, and he said she was considerable better—thank the Lord for his inf'nit mercy—and coming on so smart that with the blessing of Providence she'd get well yet—and Smiley, before he thought, says, "Well, I'll resk two-and-a-half that she don't, anyway."

Thish-yer Smiley had a mare—the boys called her the fifteen-minute nag, but that was only in fun, you know, because, of course, she was faster than that—and he used to win money on that horse, for all she was so slow and always had the asthma, or the distemper, or the consumption, or something of that kind. They used to give her two or three hundred yards' start, and then pass her under way; but always at the fag-end of the race she'd get excited and desperate-like, and come cavorting and spraddling up, and scattering her legs around limber, sometimes in the air, and sometimes out to one side amongst the fences, and kicking up m-o-r-e dust, and raising m-o-r-e racket with her coughing and sneezing and blowing her nose—and always fetch up at the stand just about a neck ahead, as near as you could cipher it down.

And he had a little small bull-pup, that to look at him you'd think he warn't worth a cent, but to set around and look ornery, and lay for a chance to steal something. But as soon as money was up on him he was a different dog—his underjaw'd begin to stick out like the for'castle of a steamboat, and his teeth would uncover, and shine savage like the furnaces. And a dog might tackle him, and bully-rag him, and bite him, and throw him over his shoulder two or three times, and Andrew Jackson—which was the name of the pup—Andrew Jackson would never let on but what he was satisfied, and hadn't expected nothing else—and the bets being doubled and doubled on the other side all the time, till the money was all up—and then all of a sudden he would grab that other dog just by the joint of his hind legs and freeze to it—not chaw, you understand, but only just grip and hang on till they throwed up the sponge, if it was a year. Smiley always came out winner on that pup till he harnessed a dog once that didn't have no hind legs, because they'd been sawed off in a circular saw, and when the thing had gone along far enough, and the money was all up, and he came to make a snatch for his pet holt, he saw in a minute how he'd been imposed on, and how the other dog had him in the door, so to speak, and he 'peared surprised, and then he looked sorter discouraged like, and didn't try no more to win the fight, and so he got shucked out bad. He gave Smiley a look as much as to say his heart was broke, and it was *his* fault, for putting up a dog that hadn't no hind legs for him to take holt of, which was his main dependence in a fight, and then he limped off a piece, and laid down and died. It was a good pup, was that Andrew Jackson, and would have made a name for hisself if he'd lived, for the stuff was in him, and he had genius—I know it, because he hadn't had no opportunities to speak of, and it don't stand to reason that a dog could make such a fight as he could under them circumstances, if he hadn't no talent. It always makes me feel sorry when I think of that last fight of his'on, and the way it turned out.

Well, thish-yer Smiley had rat-terriers and chicken cocks, and tom-cats, and all them kind of things, till you couldn't rest, and you couldn't fetch nothing for him to bet on but he'd match you. He ketched a frog one day and took him home and said he cal'lated to educate him; and so he never done nothing for three months but set in his back yard and learn that frog to jump. And you bet you he *did* learn him, too. He'd give him a little hunch behind, and the next minute you'd see that frog whirling in the air like a doughnut—see him turn one summerset, or maybe a couple, if he got a good start, and come down flat-footed and all right, like a cat. He got him up so in the matter of ketching flies, and kept him in practice so constant, that he'd nail a fly every time as far as he could see him. Smiley said all a frog wanted was education, and he could do most anything—and I believe him. Why, I've seen him set Dan'l Webster down here on this floor—Dan'l Webster was the name of the frog—and sing out, "Flies! Dan'l, flies," and quicker'n you could wink, he'd spring straight up, and snake a fly off'n the counter there, and flop down on the floor again as solid as a gob of mud, and fall to scratching the side of his head with his hind foot as indifferent as if he hadn't no idea he'd done any more'n any frog might do. You never see a frog so modest and straightfor'ard as he was, for all he was so gifted. And when it come to fair-and-square jumping on a dead level, he could get over more ground at one straddle than any animal of his breed you ever see. Jumping on a dead level was his strong suit, you understand, and when it come to that, Smiley would ante up money on him as long as he had a red. Smiley was monstrous proud of his frog, and well he might be, for fellers that had travelled and ben everywheres all said he laid over any frog that ever *they* see.

Well, Smiley kept the beast in a little lattice box, and he used to fetch him down town sometimes and lay for a bet. One day a feller—a stranger in the camp, he was—come across him with his box, and says:

"What might it be that you've got in the box?"

And Smiley says, sorter indifferent like, "It might be a parrot, or it might be a canary, maybe, but it ain't—it's only just a frog."

And the feller took it, and looked at it careful, and turned it round this way and that, and says, "H'm—so 'tis. Well, what's *he* good for?"

"Well," Smiley says, easy and careless, "He's good enough for *one* thing I should judge—he can out-jump ary frog in Calaveras county."

The feller took the box again, and took another long, particular look, and give it back to Smiley and says, very deliberate, "Well—I don't see no points about that frog that's any better'n any other frog."

"Maybe you don't," Smiley says. "Maybe you understand frogs, and maybe you don't understand 'em; maybe you've had experience, and maybe you ain't only a amature, as it were. Anyways, I've got *my* opinion, and I'll resk forty dollars that he can outjump ary frog in Calaveras county."

And the feller studied a minute, and then says, kinder sad, like, "Well—I'm only a stranger here, and I ain't got no frog—but if I had a frog I'd bet you."

And then Smiley says, "That's all right—that's all right—if you'll hold my box a minute I'll go and get you a frog;" and so the feller took the box, and put up his forty dollars along with Smiley's, and set down to wait.

So he set there a good while thinking and thinking to hisself, and then he got the frog out and prized his mouth open and took a teaspoon and filled him full of quail-shot—filled him pretty near up to his chin —and set him on the floor. Smiley he went out to the swamp and slopped around in the mud for a long time, and finally he ketched a frog and fetched him in and give him to this feller and says:

"Now if you're ready, set him alongside of Dan'l, with his forepaws just even with Dan'l's, and I'll give the word." Then he says, "one— two—three—jump!" and him and the feller touched up the frogs from behind, and the new frog hopped off lively, but Dan'l give a heave, and hysted up his shoulders—so—like a Frenchman, but it wasn't no use— he couldn't budge; he was planted as solid as a anvil, and he couldn't no more stir than if he was anchored out. Smiley was a good deal surprised, and he was disgusted too, but he didn't have no idea what the matter was, of course.

The feller took the money and started away, and when he was going out at the door he sorter jerked his thumb over his shoulder—this way—at Dan'l, and says again, very deliberate, "Well—*I* don't see no points about that frog that's any better'n any other frog."

Smiley he stood scratching his head and looking down at Dan'l a long time, and at last he says, "I do wonder what in the nation that frog throwed off for—I wonder if there ain't something the matter with him—he 'pears to look mighty baggy, somehow"—and he ketched Dan'l by the nap of the neck, and lifted him up and says, "Why blame my cats if he don't weigh five pound"—and turned him upside down, and he belched out about a double-handful of shot. And then he see how it was, and he was the maddest man—he set the frog down and took out after that feller, but he never ketched him. And——

[Here Simon Wheeler heard his name called from the front-yard, and got up to go and see what was wanted.] And turning to me as he moved away, he said: "Just sit where you are, stranger, and rest easy—I ain't going to be gone a second."

But by your leave, I did not think that a continuation of the history of the enterprising vagabond Jim Smiley would be likely to afford me much information concerning the Rev. Leonidas W. Smiley, and so I started away.

At the door I met the sociable Wheeler returning, and he buttonholed me and recommenced:

"Well, thish-yer Smiley had a yaller one-eyed cow that didn't have no tail only just a short stump like a bannanner, and——"

"O, curse Smiley and his afflicted cow!" I muttered, good-naturedly, and bidding the old gentleman good-day, I departed.

BRET HARTE

The Luck of Roaring Camp

This story was published in 1868 in the second issue of the California journal *The Overland Monthly*, of which Harte was the founding editor and frequent contributor. The piece appeared unsigned, and though many local readers objected to its coarseness, when it was reprinted in the East the tale was welcomed with unreserved enthusiasm. When the author's name was disclosed, Harte became an overnight sensation and the most celebrated exponent of local-color writing. The manner of this and other stories is distinctly literary, however, and owes more to Dickens and Hawthorne than to the vernacular energy of California mining communities. Nevertheless, the charm of the tale resides in the author's seemingly effortless fusion of diverse, even paradoxical, elements. The illegimate offspring of a prostitute, "Cherokee Sal," works a redemptive change on the maimed and violent citizens of Roaring Camp, their awkward and unaccustomed attempts to care for the child serving as better burlesque of genteel customs than deliberate satire. On the other hand, the child they christen "Thomas Luck" may or may not be their savior; the transformations of the local roughs may be little more than the ill-fitting garments of sentimentality. The child, at all events, is, as Kentuck admiringly describes him, a "d——d little cuss" in more ways than one. If his birth recalls a homespun version of the Nativity, the manner of his death is reminiscent of the deluge God sent to rid the world of wickedness. The net effect of this ambiguous story is at once amusingly parodic (of both Western manners and strained religiosity) and genuinely affecting.

*   *   *

There was commotion in Roaring Camp. It could not have been a fight, for in 1850 that was not novel enough to have called together the entire settlement. The ditches and claims were not only deserted, but "Tuttle's grocery" had contributed its gamblers, who, it will be remembered, calmly continued their game the day that French Pete and Kanaka Joe shot each other to death over the bar in the front room. The whole camp was collected before a rude cabin on the outer edge of the clearing. Conversation was carried on in a low tone, but the name of a woman was frequently repeated. It was a name familiar enough in the camp,—"Cherokee Sal."

Perhaps the less said of her the better. She was a coarse, and, it is to be feared, a very sinful woman. But at that time she was the only woman in Roaring Camp, and was just then lying in sore extremity, when she most needed the ministration of her own sex. Dissolute, abandoned, and irreclaimable, she was yet suffering a martyrdom hard enough to bear even when veiled by sympathizing womanhood, but now terrible in her loneliness. The primal curse had come to her in that original isolation which must have made the punishment of the first transgression so dreadful. It was, perhaps, part of the expiation of her sin, that, at a moment when she most lacked her sex's intuitive tenderness and care, she met only the half-contemptuous faces of her masculine associates. Yet a few of the spectators were, I think, touched by her sufferings. Sandy Tipton thought it was "rough on Sal," and, in the contemplation of her condition, for a moment rose superior to the fact that he had an ace and two bowers in his sleeve.

It will be seen, also, that the situation was novel. Deaths were by no means uncommon in Roaring Camp, but a birth was a new thing. People had been dismissed the camp effectively, finally, and with no possibility of return; but this was the first time that anybody had been introduced *ab initio*. Hence the excitement.

"You go in there, Stumpy," said a prominent citizen known as "Kentuck," addressing one of the loungers. "Go in there, and see what you kin do. You've had experience in them things."

Perhaps there was a fitness in the selection. Stumpy, in other climes, had been the putative head of two families; in fact, it was owing to some legal informality in these proceedings that Roaring Camp—a city of refuge—was indebted to his company. The crowd approved the choice, and Stumpy was wise enough to bow to the majority. The door closed on the extempore surgeon and midwife, and Roaring Camp sat down outside, smoked its pipe, and awaited the issue.

The assemblage numbered about a hundred men. One or two of these were actual fugitives from justice, some were criminal, and all were reckless. Physically, they exhibited no indication of their past lives and character. The greatest scamp had a Raphael face, with a profusion of blond hair; Oakhurst, a gambler, had the melancholy air and intellectual abstraction of a Hamlet; the coolest and most courageous man was scarcely over five feet in height, with a soft voice and an embarrassed, timid manner. The term "roughs" applied to them was a distinction rather than a definition. Perhaps in the minor details of fingers, toes, ears, etc., the camp may have been deficient, but these slight omissions did not detract from their aggregate force. The strongest man had but three fingers on his right hand; the best shot had but one eye.

Such was the physical aspect of the men that were dispersed around the cabin. The camp lay in a triangular valley, between two hills and a river. The only outlet was a steep trail over the summit of a hill that faced the cabin, now illuminated by the rising moon. The suffering woman might have seen it from the rude bunk whereon she lay,—seen it winding like a silver thread until it was lost in the stars above.

A fire of withered pine-boughs added sociability to the gathering. By degrees the natural levity of Roaring Camp returned. Bets were freely offered and taken regarding the result. Three to five that "Sal would get through with it"; even, that the child would survive; side bets as to the sex and complexion of the coming stranger. In the midst of an excited discussion an exclamation came from those nearest the door, and the camp stopped to listen. Above the swaying and moaning of the pines, the swift rush of the river, and the crackling of the fire, rose a sharp, querulous cry,—a cry unlike anything heard before in the camp. The pines stopped moaning, the river ceased to rush, and the fire to crackle. It seemed as if Nature had stopped to listen too.

The camp rose to its feet as one man! It was proposed to explode a barrel of gunpowder, but, in consideration of the situation of the mother, better counsels prevailed, and only a few revolvers were discharged; for, whether owing to the rude surgery of the camp, or some other reason, Cherokee Sal was sinking fast. Within an hour she had climbed, as it were, that rugged road that led to the stars, and so passed out of Roaring Camp, its sin and shame forever. I do not think that the announcement disturbed them much, except in speculation as to the fate of the child. "Can he live now?" was asked of Stumpy. The answer was doubtful. The only other being of Cherokee Sal's sex and maternal condition in the settlement was an ass. There was some conjecture as to fitness, but the experiment was tried. It was less problematical than the ancient treatment of Romulus and Remus, and apparently as successful.

When these details were completed, which exhausted another hour, the door was opened, and the anxious crowd of men who had already formed themselves into a queue, entered in single file. Beside the low bunk or shelf, on which the figure of the mother was starkly outlined below the blankets stood a pine table. On this a candle-box was placed, and within it, swathed in staring red flannel, lay the last arrival at Roaring Camp. Beside the candle-box was placed a hat. Its use was soon indicated. "Gentlemen," said Stumpy, with a singular mixture of authority and *ex officio* complacency,—"Gentlemen will please pass in at the front door, round the table, and out at the back door. Them as wishes to contribute anything toward the orphan will find a hat handy." The first man entered with his hat on; he uncovered, however, as he looked about him, and so, unconsciously, set an example to the next. In such communities good and bad actions are catching. As the procession filed in, comments were audible,—criticisms addressed, perhaps, rather to Stumpy, in the character of showman,—"Is that him?" "mighty small specimen"; "hasn't mor'n got the color"; "ain't bigger nor a derringer." The contributions were as characteristic: A silver tobacco-box; a doubloon; a navy revolver, silver mounted; a gold specimen; a very beautifully embroidered lady's handkerchief (from Oakhurst the gambler); a diamond breastpin; a diamond ring (suggested by the pin, with the remark from the giver that he "saw that pin and went two diamonds better"); a slung shot; a Bible (contributor not detected); a golden spur; a silver teaspoon (the initials, I regret to say, were not the giver's); a pair of surgeon's shears; a lancet; a Bank of England note for £5; and about $200 in loose gold and silver coin. During these proceedings Stumpy maintained a silence as impassive as the dead on his left, a gravity as inscrutable as that of the newly born on his right. Only one incident occurred to break the monotony of the curious procession. As Kentuck bent over the candle-box half curiously, the child turned, and, in a spasm of pain, caught at his groping finger, and held it fast for a moment. Kentuck looked foolish and embarrassed. Something like a blush tried to assert itself in his weather-beaten cheek. "The d—d little cuss!" he said, as he extricated his finger, with, perhaps, more tenderness and care than he might have been deemed capable of showing. He held that finger a little apart from its fellows as he went out, and examined it curiously. The examination provoked the same original remark in regard to the child. In fact, he seemed to enjoy repeating it. "He rastled with my finger," he remarked to Tipton, holding up the member, "the d—d little cuss!"

It was four o'clock before the camp sought repose. A light burnt in the cabin where the watchers sat, for Stumpy did not go to bed that night. Nor did Kentuck. He drank quite freely, and related with great gusto his experience, invariably ending with his characteristic condemnation of the new-comer. It seemed to relieve him of any unjust implication of sentiment, and Kentuck had the weaknesses of the nobler sex. When everybody else had gone to bed, he walked down to the river, and whistled reflectingly. Then he walked up the gulch, past the cabin, still whistling with demonstrative unconcern. At a large redwood tree he paused and retraced his steps, and again passed the cabin. Half-way down to the river's bank he again paused, and then returned and knocked at the door. It was opened by Stumpy. "How goes it?" said Kentuck, looking past Stumpy toward the candle-box. "All serene," replied Stumpy. "Anything up?" "Nothing." There was a pause—an embarrassing one—Stumpy still holding the door. Then Kentuck had recourse to his finger, which he held up to Stumpy. "Rastled with it,— the d—d little cuss," he said, and retired.

The next day Cherokee Sal had such rude sepulture as Roaring Camp afforded. After her body had been committed to the hillside, there was a formal meeting of the camp to discuss what should be done with her infant. A resolution to adopt it was unanimous and enthusiastic. But an animated discussion in regard to the manner and feasibility of providing for its wants at once sprung up. It was remarkable that the argument partook of none of those fierce personalities with which discussions were usually conducted at Roaring Camp. Tipton proposed that they should send the child to Red Dog,—a distance of forty miles,—where female attention could be procured. But the unlucky suggestion met with fierce and unanimous opposition. It was evident that no plan which entailed parting from their new acquisition would for a moment be entertained. "Besides," said Tom Ryder, "them fellows at Red Dog would swap it, and ring in somebody else on us." A disbelief in the honesty of other camps prevailed at Roaring Camp as in other places.

The introduction of a female nurse in the camp also met with objection. It was argued that no decent woman could be prevailed to accept Roaring Camp as her home, and the speaker urged that "they didn't want any more of the other kind." This unkind allusion to the defunct mother, harsh as it may seem, was the first spasm of propriety,—the first symptom of the camp's regeneration. Stumpy advanced nothing. Perhaps he felt a certain delicacy in interfering with the selection of a possible successor in office. But when questioned, he averred stoutly that he and "Jinny"—the mammal before alluded to—could manage to rear the child. There was something original, independent, and heroic about the plan that pleased the camp. Stumpy was retained. Certain articles were sent for to Sacramento. "Mind," said the treasurer, as he pressed a bag of gold-dust into the expressman's hand, "the best that can be got,—lace, you know, and filigree-work and frills,—d—m the cost!"

Strange to say, the child thrived. Perhaps the invigorating climate of the mountain camp was compensation for material deficiencies. Nature took the foundling to her broader breast. In that rare atmosphere of the Sierra foot-hills,—that air pungent with balsamic odor, that ethereal cordial at once bracing and exhilarating,—he may have found food and nourishment, or a subtle chemistry that transmuted asses' milk to lime and phosphorus. Stumpy inclined to the belief that it was the latter and good nursing. "Me and that ass," he would say, "has been father and mother to him! Don't you," he would add, apostrophizing the helpless bundle before him, "never go back on us."

By the time he was a month old, the necessity of giving him a name became apparent. He had generally been known as "the Kid," "Stumpy's boy," "the Cayote" (an allusion to his vocal powers), and even by Kentuck's endearing diminutive of "the d—d little cuss." But these were felt to be vague and unsatisfactory, and were at last dismissed under another influence. Gamblers and adventurers are generally superstitious, and Oakhurst one day declared that the baby had brought "the luck" to Roaring Camp. It was certain that of late they had been successful. "Luck" was the name agreed upon, with the prefix of Tommy for greater convenience. No allusion was made to the mother, and the father was unknown. "It's better," said the philosophical Oakhurst, "to take a fresh deal all round. Call him Luck, and start him fair." A day was accordingly set apart for the christening. What was meant by this ceremony the reader may imagine, who has already gathered some idea of the reckless irreverence of Roaring Camp. The master of ceremonies was one "Boston," a noted wag, and the occasion seemed to promise the greatest facetiousness. This ingenious satirist had spent two days in preparing a burlesque of the church service, with pointed local allusions. The choir was properly trained, and Sandy Tipton was to stand god-father. But after the procession had marched to the grove with music and banners, and the child had been deposited before a mock altar, Stumpy stepped before the expectant crowd. "It ain't my style to spoil fun, boys," said the little man, stoutly, eying the faces around him, "but it strikes me that this thing ain't exactly on the squar. It's playing it pretty low down on this yer baby to ring in fun on him that he ain't going to understand. And ef there's going to be any godfathers round, I'd like to see who's got any better rights than me." A silence followed Stumpy's speech. To the credit of all humorists be it said, that the first man to acknowledge its justice was the satirist, thus stopped of his fun. "But," said Stumpy, quickly, following up his advantage, "we're here for a christening, and we'll have it. I proclaim you Thomas Luck, ac-cording to the laws of the United States and the State of California, so help me God." It was the first time that the name of the Deity had been uttered otherwise than profanely in the camp. The form of christening was perhaps even more ludicrous than the satirist had conceived; but, strangely enough, nobody saw it and nobody laughed. "Tommy" was christened as seriously as he would have been under a Christian roof, and cried and was comforted in as orthodox fashion.

And so the work of regeneration began in Roaring Camp. Almost imperceptibly a change came over the settlement. The cabin assigned to "Tommy Luck"—or "The Luck," as he was more frequently called—first showed signs of improvement. It was kept scrupulously clean and whitewashed. Then it was boarded, clothed, and papered. The rosewood cradle—packed eighty miles by mule—had, in Stumpy's way of putting it, "sorter killed the rest of the furniture." So the rehabilitation of the cabin became a necessity. The men who were in the habit of lounging in at Stumpy's to see "how The Luck got on" seemed to appreciate the change, and, in self-defence, the rival establishment of "Tuttle's grocery" bestirred itself, and imported a carpet and mirrors. The reflec-tions of the latter on the appearance of Roaring Camp tended to pro-duce stricter habits of personal cleanliness. Again, Stumpy imposed a kind of quarantine upon those who aspired to the honor and privilege of holding "The Luck." It was a cruel mortification to Kentuck—who, in the carelessness of a large nature and the habits of frontier life, had begun to regard all garments as a second cuticle, which, like a snake's, only sloughed off through decay—to be debarred this privilege from certain prudential reasons. Yet such was the subtle influence of inno-vation that he thereafter appeared regularly every afternoon in a clean shirt, and face still shining from his ablutions. Nor were moral and social sanitary laws neglected. "Tommy," who was supposed to spend his whole existence in a persistent attempt to repose, must not be disturbed by noise. The shouting and yelling which had gained the camp its infelicitous title were not permitted within hearing distance of Stumpy's. The men conversed in whispers, or smoked with Indian gravity. Profanity was tacitly given up in these sacred precincts, and throughout the camp a popular form of expletive, known as "D—n the luck!" and "Curse the luck!" was abandoned, as having a new personal bearing. Vocal music was not interdicted, being supposed to have a soothing, tranquillizing quality, and one song, sung by "Man-o'-War Jack," an English sailor, from her Majesty's Australian colonies, was quite popular as a lullaby. It was a lugubrious recital of the exploits of "the Arethusa, Seventy-four," in a muffled minor, ending with a prolonged dying fall at the burden of each verse, "On b-o-o-o-ard of the Arethusa." It was a fine sight to see Jack holding The Luck, rocking from side to side as if with the motion of a ship, and crooning forth this naval ditty. Either through the peculiar rocking of Jack or the length of his song,—it contained ninety stanzas, and was continued with conscientious deliberation to the bitter end,—the lullaby generally had the desired effect. At such times the men would lie at full length under the trees, in the soft summer twilight, smoking their pipes and drinking in the melodious utterances. An indistinct idea that this was pastoral happiness pervaded the camp. "This 'ere kind o' think," said the Cockney Simmons, meditatively reclining on his elbow, "is 'evingly." It reminded him of Greenwich.

On the long summer days The Luck was usually carried to the gulch, from whence the golden store of Roaring Camp was taken. There, on a blanket spread over pine-boughs, he would lie while the men were working in the ditches below. Latterly, there was a rude attempt to decorate this bower with flowers and sweet-smelling shrubs, and generally some one would bring him a cluster of wild honeysuckles, azaleas, or the painted blossoms of Las Mariposas. The men had suddenly awakened to the fact that there were beauty and significance in these trifles, which they had so long trodden carelessly beneath their feet. A flake of glittering mica, a fragment of variegated quartz, a bright pebble from the bed of the creek, became beautiful to eyes thus cleared and strengthened, and were invariably put aside for "The Luck." It was wonderful how many treasures the woods and hillsides yielded that "would do for Tommy." Surrounded by playthings such as never child out of fairyland had before, it is to be hoped that Tommy was content. He appeared to be securely happy albeit there was an infantine gravity about him— a contemplative light in his round gray eyes that sometimes worried Stumpy. He was always tractable and quiet, and it is recorded that once having crept beyond his "corral,"—a hedge of tessellated pine-boughs,

which surrounded his bed,—he dropped over the bank on his head in
the soft earth, and remained with his mottled legs in the air in that
position for at least five minutes with unflinching gravity. He was ex-
tricated without a murmur. I hesitate to record the many other instances
of his sagacity, which rest, unfortunately, upon the statements of prejudiced friends. Some of them were not without a tinge of superstition.
"I crep' up the bank just now," said Kentuck one day, in a breathless
state of excitement, "and dern my skin if he wasn't a talking to a jaybird
as was a sittin' on his lap. There they was, just as free and sociable
as anything you please, a jawin' at each other just like two cherry-
bums." Howbeit, whether creeping over the pine-boughs or lying lazily
on his back blinking at the leaves above him, to him the birds sang, the
squirrels chattered, and the flowers bloomed. Nature was his nurse and
playfellow. For him she would let slip between the leaves golden shafts
of sunlight that fell just within his grasp; she would send wandering
breezes to visit him with the balm of bay and resinous gums; to him
the tall red-woods nodded familiarly and sleepily, the bumble-bees
buzzed, and the rooks cawed a slumbrous accompaniment.

Such was the golden summer of Roaring Camp. They were "flush
times,"—and the Luck was with them. The claims had yielded enor-
mously. The camp was jealous of its privileges and looked suspiciously
on strangers. No encouragement was given to immigration, and, to
make their seclusion more perfect, the land on either side of the mountain wall that surrounded the camp they duly preempted. This, and a
reputation for singular proficiency with the revolver, kept the reserve of
Roaring Camp inviolate. The expressman—their only connecting link
with the surrounding world—sometimes told wonderful stories of the
camp. He would say, "They 've a street up there in 'Roaring,' that would
lay over any street in Red Dog. They've got vines and flowers round
their houses, and they wash themselves twice a day. But they're mighty
rough on strangers, and they worship an Ingin baby."

With the prosperity of the camp came a desire for further improvement. It was proposed to build a hotel in the following spring, and to
invite one or two decent families to reside there for the sake of "The
Luck,"—who might perhaps profit by female companionship. The sacrifice that this concession to the sex cost these men, who were fiercely
sceptical in regard to its general virtue and usefulness, can only be accounted for by their affection for Tommy. A few still held out. But the
resolve could not be carried into effect for three months, and the minority meekly yielded in the hope that something might turn up to prevent it. And it did.

The winter of 1851 will long be remembered in the foot-hills. The
snow lay deep on the Sierras, and every mountain creek became a river,

and every river a lake. Each gorge and gulch was transformed into a tumultuous watercourse that descended the hillsides, tearing down giant trees and scattering its drift and débris along the plain. Red Dog had been twice under water, and Roaring Camp had been forewarned. "Water put the gold into them gulches," said Stumpy. "It's been here once and will be here again!" And that night the North Fork suddenly leaped over its banks, and swept up the triangular valley of Roaring Camp.

In the confusion of rushing water, crushing trees, and crackling timber, and the darkness which seemed to flow with the water and blot out the fair valley, but little could be done to collect the scattered camp. When the morning broke, the cabin of Stumpy nearest the river-bank was gone. Higher up the gulch they found the body of its unlucky owner; but the pride, the hope, the joy, the Luck, of Roaring Camp had disappeared. They were returning with sad hearts, when a shout from the bank recalled them.

It was a relief-boat from down the river. They had picked up, they said, a man and an infant, nearly exhausted, about two miles below. Did anybody know them, and did they belong here?

It needed but a glance to show them Kentuck lying there, cruelly crushed and bruised, but still holding the Luck of Roaring Camp in his arms. As they bent over the strangely assorted pair, they saw that the child was cold and pulseless. "He is dead," said one. Kentuck opened his eyes. "Dead?" he repeated feebly. "Yes, my man, and you are dying too." A smile lit the eyes of the expiring Kentuck. "Dying," he repeated, "he's a taking me with him,—tell the boys I've got the Luck with me now"; and the strong man, clinging to the frail babe as a drowning man is said to cling to a straw, drifted away into the shadowy river that flows forever to the unknown sea.

MARK TWAIN

The Story of the Old Ram

This humorous sketch was interpolated into *Roughing It* (1872), where it first appeared. It perfectly illustrates the rules for telling a humorous tale, which Twain formulated in his essay "How to Tell a Story" (1895): it wanders about and strings together incongruities and absurdities at its leisure; the narrator, Jim Blaine, is perfectly unaware that there is anything funny in what he is saying; and, largely through masterful punctuation, it conveys the sense of an absentminded immediateness of presentation. Of course, telling a story and writing a story that gives the reader the imaginary feeling of hearing a tale told are two different matters. For that reason, Twain, functioning as the genteel narrator who introduces a vernacular character, provides something of a user's manual in the opening paragraph. He sets the scene, gives us the dramatic occasion for the tale, and carefully describes the almost reverential quality of Jim Blaine's voice and the inebriated abstraction of his mood. Once Blaine commences, however, he is never interrupted, and his tale bubbles along in a single meandering paragraph. Twain may claim that he has been hoodwinked or "sold" at the end, but readers are more apt to feel that they have been treated to an awfully good time.

* * *

Every now and then, in these days, the boys used to tell me I ought to get one Jim Blaine to tell me the stirring story of his grandfather's old ram—but they always added that I must not mention the matter unless Jim was drunk at the time—just comfortably and sociably drunk. They kept this up until my curiosity was on the rack to hear the story. I got to haunting Blaine; but it was of no use, the boys always found fault with his condition; he was often moderately but never satisfactorily drunk. I never watched a man's condition with such absorbing interest, such anxious solicitude; I never so pined to see a man uncompromisingly drunk before. At last, one evening I hurried to his cabin, for I learned that this time his situation was such that even the most fastidious could find no fault with it—he was tranquilly, serenely, symmetrically drunk —not a hiccup to mar his voice, not a cloud upon his brain thick enough to obscure his memory. As I entered, he was sitting upon an empty powder-keg, with a clay pipe in one hand and the other raised to command silence. His face was round, red, and very serious; his throat was bare and his hair tumbled; in general appearance and costume he was a stalwart miner of the period. On the pine table stood a candle, and its dim light revealed "the boys" sitting here and there on bunks, candle-boxes, powder-kegs, etc. They said:

"Sh—! Don't speak—he's going to commence."

THE STORY OF THE OLD RAM

I found a seat at once, and Blaine said:

"I don't reckon them times will ever come again. There never was a more bullier old ram than what he was. Grandfather fetched him from Illinois—got him of a man by the name of Yates—Bill Yates—maybe you might have heard of him; his father was a deacon—Baptist—and he was a rustler, too; a man had to get up ruther early to get the start of old Thankful Yates; it was him that put the Greens up to jining teams with my grandfather when he moved West. Seth Green was prob'ly the pick of the flock; he married a Wilkerson—Sarah Wilkerson—good creatur, she was—one of the likeliest heifers that was ever raised in old Stoddard, everybody said that knowed her. She could heft a bar'l of flour as easy as I can flirt a flapjack. And spin? Don't mention it! Independent? Humph! When Sile Hawkins come a-browsing around her, she let him know that for all his tin he couldn't trot in harness alongside of *her*. You see, Sile Hawkins was—no, it warn't Sile Hawkins, after all—it was a galoot by the name of Filkins—I disremember his first name; but he *was* a stump—come into pra'r meeting drunk, one night, hooraying for Nixon, becuz he thought it was a primary; and old deacon Ferguson up and scooted him through the window and he lit on old Miss Jefferson's head, poor old filly. She was a good soul—had a glass eye and used to lend it to old Miss Wagner, that hadn't any, to receive company in; it warn't big enough, and when Miss Wagner warn't noticing, it would get twisted around in the socket, and look up, maybe, or out to one side, and every which way, while t'other one was looking as straight ahead as a spy-glass. Grown people didn't mind it, but it most always made the children cry, it was so sort of scary. She tried packing it in raw cotton, but it wouldn't work, somehow—the cotton would get loose and stick out and look so kind of awful that the children couldn't stand it no way. She was always dropping it out, and turning up her old dead-light on the company empty, and making them oncomfortable, becuz *she* never could tell when it hopped out, being blind on that side, you see. So somebody would have to hunch her and say, 'Your game eye has fetched loose, Miss Wagner dear'—and then all of them would have to sit and wait till she jammed it in again—wrong side before, as a general thing, and green as a bird's egg, being a bashful cretur and easy sot back before company. But being wrong side before warn't much difference, anyway, becuz her own eye was sky-blue and the glass one was yaller on the front side, so whichever way she turned it it didn't match nohow. Old Miss Wagner was considerable on the borrow, she was. When she had a quilting, or Dorcas S'iety at her house she gen'ally borrowed Miss Higgins's wooden leg to stump around on; it was considerable shorter than her other pin, but much *she* minded that. She said she couldn't abide crutches when she had company, becuz they were so slow; said when she had company and things had to be done, she wanted to get up and hump herself. She was as bald as a jug, and so she used to borrow Miss Jacops's wig—Miss Jacops was the coffin-peddler's wife—a ratty old buzzard, he was, that used to go roost-

ing around where people was sick, waiting for 'em; and there that old
rip would sit all day, in the shade, on a coffin that he judged would fit
the can'idate; and if it was a slow customer and kind of uncertain, he'd
fetch his rations and a blanket along and sleep in the coffin nights. He
was anchored out that way, in frosty weather, for about three weeks,
once, before old Robbins's place, waiting for him; and after that, for as
much as two years, Jacops was not on speaking terms with the old man,
on account of his disapp'inting him. He got one of his feet froze, and
lost money, too, becuz old Robbins took a favorable turn and got well.
The next time Robbins got sick, Jacops tried to make up with him, and
varnished up the same old coffin and fetched it along; but old Robbins
was too many for him; he had him in, and 'peared to be powerful weak;
he bought the coffin for ten dollars and Jacops was to pay it back and
twenty-five more besides if Robbins didn't like the coffin after he'd tried
it. And then Robbins died, and at the funeral he bursted off the lid and
riz up in his shroud and told the parson to let up on the performances,
becuz he could *not* stand such a coffin as that. You see he had been in
a trance once before, when he was young, and he took the chances on
another, cal'lating that if he made the trip it was money in his pocket,
and if he missed fire he couldn't lose a cent. And by George he sued
Jacops for the rhino and got jedgment; and he set up the coffin in his
back parlor and said he 'lowed to take his time, now. It was always an
aggravation to Jacops, the way that miserable old thing acted. He
moved back to Indiany pretty soon—went to Wellsville—Wellsville was
the place the Hogadorns was from. Mighty fine family. Old Maryland
stock. Old Squire Hogadorn could carry around more mixed licker, and
cuss better than most any man I ever see. His second wife was the
widder Billings—she that was Becky Martin; her dam was deacon Dunlap's first wife. Her oldest child, Maria, married a missionary and died
in grace—et up by the savages. They et *him*, too, poor feller—biled
him. It warn't the custom, so they say, but they explained to friends of
his'n that went down there to bring away his things, that they'd tried
missionaries every other way and never could get any good out of
'em—and so it annoyed all his relations to find out that that man's life
was fooled away just out of a dern'd experiment, so to speak. But mind
you, there ain't anything ever reely lost; everything that people can't
understand and don't see the reason of does good if you only hold on
and give it a fair shake; Prov'dence don't fire no blank ca'tridges, boys.
That there missionary's substance, unbeknowns to himself, actu'ly converted every last one of them heathens that took a chance at the barbecue. Nothing ever fetched them but that. Don't tell *me* it was an
accident that he was biled. There ain't no such a thing as an accident.
When my uncle Lem was leaning up agin a scaffolding once, sick, or

drunk, or suthin, an Irishman with a hod full of bricks fell on him out
of the third story and broke the old man's back in two places. People
said it was an accident. Much accident there was about that. He didn't
know what he was there for, but he was there for a good object. If he
hadn't been there the Irishman would have been killed. Nobody can
ever make me believe anything different from that. Uncle Lem's dog
was there. Why didn't the Irishman fall on the dog? Becuz the dog
would a seen him a-coming and stood from under. That's the reason
the dog warn't appinted. A dog can't be depended on to carry out a
special providence. Mark my words it was a put-up thing. Accidents
don't happen, boys. Uncle Lem's dog—I wish you could a seen that
dog. He was a reglar shepherd—or ruther he was part bull and part
shepherd—splendid animal; belonged to parson Hagar before Uncle
Lem got him. Parson Hagar belonged to the Western Reserve Hagars;
prime family; his mother was a Watson; one of his sisters married a
Wheeler; they settled in Morgan County, and he got nipped by the
machinery in a carpet factory and went through in less than a quarter
of a minute; his widder bought the piece of carpet that had his remains
wove in, and people come a hundred mile to 'tend the funeral. There
was fourteen yards in the piece. She wouldn't let them roll him up, but
planted him just so—full length. The church was middling small where
they preached the funeral, and they had to let one end of the coffin
stick out of the window. They didn't bury him—they planted one end,
and let him stand up, same as a monument. And they nailed a sign
on it and put—put on—put on it—sacred to—the m-e-m-o-r-y—of
fourteen y-a-r-d-s—of three-ply—car-pet—containing all that was—
m-o-r-t-a-l—of—of—W-i-l-l-i-a-m—W-h-e—"

Jim Blaine had been growing gradually drowsy and drowsier—his
head nodded, once, twice, three times—dropped peacefully upon his
breast, and he fell tranquilly asleep. The tears were running down the
boys' cheeks—they were suffocating with suppressed laughter—and
had been from the start, though I had never noticed it. I perceived that
I was "sold." I learned then that Jim Blaine's peculiarity was that whenever he reached a certain stage of intoxication, no human power could
keep him from setting out, with impressive unction, to tell about a wonderful adventure which he had once had with his grandfather's old
ram—and the mention of the ram in the first sentence was as far as any
man had ever heard him get, concerning it. He always maundered off,
interminably, from one thing to another, till his whisky got the best of
him and he fell asleep. What the thing was that happened to him and
his grandfather's old ram is a dark mystery to this day, for nobody has
ever yet found out.

HARRIET BEECHER STOWE

The Minister's Housekeeper

"The Minister's Housekeeper," which draws heavily on Stowe's experiences as the daughter of one minister and the wife of another, was
included in *Oldtown Fireside Stories* in 1872. Representative of both
the New England humor tradition and the increasing popularity of
local-color stories, this story is one of a series told by the fictional Sam
Lawson, a village miscreant who avoids work but glories in the telling
of garrulous tales. Much of the charm of his narration comes from his
use of regional dialect and the revelation of the personalities and folkways of the mythical Oldtown, based on South Natick, Massachusetts.
This story contains Lawson's amusing depiction of the ethereal Parson
Carryl, who, when he had a point to prove in a sermon, could "drive
all the texts ahead o' him like a flock o' sheep," but who lacks the
capacity to deal with "temporal" matters. At issue is his relationship
with his housekeeper, an attractive young woman who keeps house for
him after the death of his wife. The gossip about their relationship drives
the minister to a futile attempt to take care of his own household and
to the predictable conclusion that resolves the issue. Although the Sam
Lawson stories lack the moral fervor of Stowe's abolitionist writing,
they contributed to the growing literature of regional character that
dominated American magazines in the years after the Civil War, and
they further established her as an important voice in the movement
toward American realism.

*   *   *

SCENE.—The shady side of a blueberry-pasture.—Sam Lawson with the boys, picking blueberries.—Sam, *loq.*

Wal, you see, boys, 'twas just here,—Parson Carryl's wife, she died
along in the forepart o' March: my cousin Huldy, she undertook to
keep house for him. The way on't was, that Huldy, she went to take
care o' Mis' Carryl in the fust on't, when she fust took sick. Huldy was
a tailoress by trade; but then she was one o' these 'ere facultised persons
that has a gift for most any thing, and that was how Mis Carryl come
to set sech store by her, that, when she was sick, nothin' would do for
her but she must have Huldy round all the time: and the minister, he
said he'd make it good to her all the same, and she shouldn't lose nothin'
by it. And so Huldy, she staid with Mis' Carryl full three months afore

she died, and got to seein' to every thing pretty much round the place.

"Wal, arter Mis' Carryl died, Parson Carryl, he'd got so kind o' used to hevin' on her 'round, takin' care o' things, that he wanted her to stay along a spell; and so Huldy, she staid along a spell, and poured out his tea, and mended his close, and made pies and cakes, and cooked and washed and ironed, and kep' every thing as neat as a pin. Huldy was a drefful chipper sort o' gal; and work sort o' rolled off from her like water off a duck's back. There warn't no gal in Sherburne that could put sich a sight o' work through as Huldy; and yet, Sunday mornin', she always come out in the singers' seat like one o' these 'ere June roses, lookin' so fresh and smilin', and her voice was jest as clear and sweet as a meadow lark's—Lordy massy! I 'member how she used to sing some o' them 'are places where the treble and counter used to go together: her voice kind o' trembled a little, and it sort o' went thro' and thro' a feller! tuck him right where he lived!"

Here Sam leaned contemplatively back with his head in a clump of sweet fern, and refreshed himself with a chew of young wintergreen. "This 'ere young wintergreen, boys, is jest like a feller's thoughts o' things that happened when he was young: it comes up jest so fresh and tender every year, the longest time you hev to live; and you can't help chawin' on't tho' 'tis sort o' stingin'. I don't never get over likin' young wintergreen."

"But about Huldah, Sam?"

"Oh, yes! about Huldy. Lordy massy! when a feller is Indianin' round, these 'ere pleasant summer days, a feller's thoughts gits like a flock o' young partridges: they's up and down and everywhere; 'cause one place is jest about as good as another, when they's all so kind o' comfortable and nice. Wal, about Huldy,—as I was a sayin'. She was jest as handsome a gal to look at as a feller could have; and I think a nice, well-behaved young gal in the singers' seat of a Sunday is a means o' grace: it's sort o' drawin' to the unregenerate, you know. Why, boys, in them days, I've walked ten miles over to Sherburne of a Sunday mornin', jest to play the bass-viol in the same singers' seat with Huldy. She was very much respected, Huldy was; and, when she went out to tailorin', she was allers bespoke six months ahead, and sent for in waggins up and down for ten miles round; for the young fellers was allers 'mazin' anxious to be sent after Huldy, and was quite free to offer to go for her. Wal, after Mis' Carryl died, Huldy got to be sort o' housekeeper at the minister's, and saw to every thing, and did every thing: so that there warn't a pin out o' the way.

"But you know how 'tis in parishes: there allers is women that thinks the minister's affairs belongs to them, and they ought to have the rulin' and guidin' of 'em; and, if a minister's wife dies, there's folks that allers has their eyes open on providences,—lookin' out who's to be the next one.

"Now, there was Mis' Amaziah Pipperidge, a widder with snappin' black eyes, and a hook nose,—kind o' like a hawk; and she was one o' them up-and-down commandin' sort o' women, that feel that they have a call to be seein' to every thing that goes on in the parish, and 'specially to the minister.

"Folks did say that Mis' Pipperidge sort o' sot her eye on the parson for herself: wal, now that 'are might a been, or it might not. Some folks thought it was a very suitable connection. You see she hed a good property of her own, right nigh to the minister's lot, and was allers kind o' active and busy; so, takin' one thing with another, I shouldn't wonder if Mis' Pipperidge should a thought that Providence p'inted that way. At any rate, she went up to Deakin Blodgett's wife, and they two sort o' put their heads together a mournin' and condolin' about the way things was likely to go on at the minister's now Mis' Carryl was dead. Ye see, the parson's wife, she was one of them women who hed their eyes everywhere and on every thing. She was a little thin woman, but tough as Inger rubber, and smart as a steel trap; and there warn't a hen laid an egg, or cackled, but Mis' Carryl was right there to see about it; and she hed the garden made in the spring, and the medders mowed in summer, and the cider made, and the corn husked, and the apples got in the fall; and the doctor, he hedn't nothin' to do but jest sit stock still a meditatin' on Jerusalem and Jericho and them things that ministers think about. But Lordy massy! he didn't know nothin' about where any thing he eat or drunk or wore come from or went to: his wife jest led him 'round in temporal things and took care on him like a baby.

"Wal, to be sure, Mis' Carryl looked up to him in spirituals, and thought all the world on him; for there warn't a smarter minister no where 'round. Why, when he preached on decrees and election, they used to come clear over from South Parish, and West Sherburne, and Old Town to hear him; and there was sich a row o' waggins tied along by the meetin'-house that the stables was all full, and all the hitchin'-posts was full clean up to the tavern, so that folks said the doctor made the town look like a gineral trainin'-day a Sunday.

"He was gret on texts, the doctor was. When he hed a p'int to prove, he'd jest go thro' the Bible, and drive all the texts ahead o' him like a flock o' sheep; and then, if there was a text that seemed gin him, why, he'd come out with his Greek and Hebrew, and kind o' chase it 'round a spell, jest as ye see a fellar chase a contrary bell-wether, and make him jump the fence arter the rest. I tell you, there wa'n't no text in the Bible that could stand agin the doctor when his blood was up. The year arter the doctor was app'inted to preach the 'lection sermon in Boston, he made such a figger that the Brattlestreet Church sent a committee right down to see if they couldn't get him to Boston; and then the Sherburne folks, they up and raised his salary; ye see, there ain't nothin' wakes folks up like somebody else's wantin' what you've got. Wal, that fall they made him a Doctor o' Divinity at Cambridge College, and so they sot more by him than ever. Wal, you see, the doctor, of course he felt kind o' lonesome and afflicted when Mis' Carryl was gone; but railly and truly, Huldy was so up to every thing about house, that the doctor didn't miss nothin' in a temporal way. His shirt-bosoms was pleated finer than they ever was, and them ruffles 'round his wrists was kep' like the driven snow; and there warn't a brack in his silk stockin's, and his shoe buckles was kep' polished up, and his coats brushed; and then there warn't no bread and biscuit like Huldy's; and her butter was like solid lumps o' gold; and there wern't no pies to equal hers; and so the doctor never felt the loss o' Miss Carryl at table. Then there was Huldy allers oppisite to him, with her blue eyes and her cheeks like two fresh peaches. She was kind o' pleasant to look at; and the more the doctor looked at her the better he liked her; and so things seemed to be goin' on quite quiet and comfortable ef it hadn't been that Mis' Pipperidge and Mis' Deakin Blodgett and Mis' Sawin got their heads together a talkin' about things.

" 'Poor man,' says Mis' Pipperidge, 'what can that child that he's got there do towards takin' the care of all that place? It takes a mature woman,' she says, 'to tread in Mis' Carryl's shoes.'

" 'That it does,' said Mis' Blodgett; 'and, when things once get to runnin' down hill, there ain't no stoppin' on 'em,' says she.

"Then Mis' Sawin she took it up. (Ye see, Mis' Sawin used to go out to dress-makin', and was sort o' jealous, 'cause folks sot more by Huldy than they did by her). 'Well,' says she, 'Huldy Peters is well enough at her trade. I never denied that, though I do say I never did believe in her way o' makin' button-holes; and I must say, if 'twas the dearest friend I hed, that I thought Huldy tryin' to fit Mis' Kittridge's plumb-colored silk was a clear piece o' presumption; the silk was jist spiled, so 'twarn't fit to come into the meetin'-house. I must say, Huldy's a gal that's always too ventersome about takin' 'sponsibilities she don't know nothin' about.'

" 'Of course she don't,' said Mis' Deakin Blodgett. 'What does she know about all the lookin' and seein' to that there ought to be in guidin' the minister's house. Huldy's well meanin', and she's good at her work, and good in the singers' seat; but Lordy massy! she hain't got no experience. Parson Carryl ought to have an experienced woman to keep house for him. There's the spring house-cleanin' and the fall house-cleanin' to be seen to, and the things to be put away from the moths;

and then the gettin' ready for the association and all the ministers' meetin's; and the makin' the soap and the candles, and settin' the hens and turkeys, watchin' the calves, and seein' after the hired men and the garden; and there that 'are blessed man jist sets there at home as serene, and has nobody 'round but that 'are gal, and don't even know how things must be a runnin' to waste!'

"Wal, the upshot on't was, they fussed and fuzzled and wuzzled till they'd drinked up all the tea in the teapot; and then they went down and called on the parson, and wuzzled him all up talkin' about this, that, and t'other that wanted lookin' to, and that it was no way to leave every thing to a young chit like Huldy, and that he ought to be lookin' about for an experienced woman. The parson he thanked 'em kindly, and said he believed their motives was good, but he didn't go no further. He didn't ask Mis' Pipperidge to come and stay there and help him, nor nothin' o' that kind; but he said he'd attend to matters himself. The fact was, the parson had got such a likin' for havin' Huldy 'round, that he couldn't think o' such a thing as swappin' her off for the Widder Pipperidge.

"But he thought to himself, 'Huldy is a good girl; but I oughtn't to be a leavin' every thing to her,—it's too hard on her. I ought to be instructin' and guidin' and helpin' of her; 'cause 'tain't everybody could be expected to know and do what Mis' Carryl did;' and so at it he went; and Lordy massy! didn't Huldy hev a time on't when the minister began to come out of his study, and want to tew 'round and see to things? Huldy, you see, thought all the world of the minister, and she was 'most afraid to laugh; but she told me she couldn't, for the life of her, help it when his back was turned, for he wuzzled things up in the most singular way. But Huldy she'd jest say 'Yes, sir,' and get him off into his study, and go on her own way.

" 'Huldy,' says the minister one day, 'you ain't experienced out doors; and, when you want to know any thing, you must come to me.'

" 'Yes, sir,' says Huldy.

" 'Now, Huldy,' says the parson, 'you must be sure to save the turkey-eggs, so that we can have a lot of turkeys for Thanksgiving.'

" 'Yes, sir,' says Huldy; and she opened the pantry-door, and showed him a nice dishful she'd been a savin' up. Wal, the very next day the parson's hen-turkey was found killed up to old Jim Scroggs's barn. Folks said Scroggs killed it; though Scroggs, he stood to it he didn't: at any rate, the Scroggses, they made a meal on't; and Huldy, she felt bad about it 'cause she'd set her heart on raisin' the turkeys; and says she, 'Oh, dear! I don't know what I shall do. I was just ready to set her.'

" 'Do, Huldy?' says the parson: 'why, there's the other turkey, out there by the door; and a fine bird, too, he is.'

Sure enough, there was the old tom-turkey a struttin' and a sidlin'
and a quitterin,' and a floutin' his tail-feathers in the sun, like a lively
young widower, all ready to begin life over agin.

" 'But,' says Huldy, 'you know *he* can't set on eggs.'

" 'He can't? I'd like to know why,' says the parson. 'He *shall* set on
eggs, and hatch 'em too.'

" 'O doctor!' says Huldy, all in a tremble; 'cause, you know, she
didn't want to contradict the minister, and she was afraid she should
laugh,—'I never heard that a tom-turkey would set on eggs.'

" 'Why, they ought to,' said the parson, getting quite 'arnest: 'what
else be they good for? you just bring out the eggs, now, and put 'em in
the nest, and I'll make him set on 'em.'

"So Huldy she thought there wern't no way to convince him but to
let him try: so she took the eggs out, and fixed 'em all nice in the nest;
and then she come back and found old Tom a skirmishin' with the
parson pretty lively, I tell ye. Ye see, old Tom he didn't take the idee at
all; and he flopped and gobbled, and fit the parson; and the parson's
wig got 'round so that his cue stuck straight out over his ear, but he'd
got his blood up. Ye see, the old doctor was used to carryin' his p'ints
o' doctrine; and he hadn't fit the Arminians and Socinians to be beat
by a tom-turkey; so finally he made a dive, and ketched him by the neck
in spite o' his floppin', and stroked him down, and put Huldy's apron
'round him.

" 'There, Huldy,' he says, quite red in the face, 'we've got him now;'
and he travelled off to the barn with him as lively as a cricket.

"Huldy came behind jist chokin' with laugh, and afraid the minister
would look 'round and see her.

" 'Now, Huldy, we'll crook his legs, and set him down,' says the
parson, when they got him to the nest: 'you see he is getting quiet, and
he'll set there all right.'

"And the parson, he sot him down; and old Tom he sot there solemn
enough, and held his head down all droopin', lookin' like a rail pious
old cock, as long as the parson sot by him.

" 'There: you see how still he sets,' says the parson to Huldy.

"Huldy was 'most dyin' for fear she should laugh. 'I'm afraid he'll
get up,' says she, 'when you do.'

" 'Oh, no, he won't!' says the parson, quite confident. 'There, there,'
says he, layin' his hands on him, as if pronouncin' a blessin'. But when
the parson riz up, old Tom he riz up too, and began to march over the
eggs.

" 'Stop, now!' says the parson. 'I'll make him get down agin: hand
me that corn-basket; we'll put that over him.'

"So he crooked old Tom's legs, and got him down agin; and they

put the corn-basket over him, and then they both stood and waited.
" 'That'll do the thing, Huldy,' said the parson.
" 'I don't know about it,' says Huldy.
" 'Oh, yes, it will, child! I understand,' says he.
"Just as he spoke, the basket riz right up and stood, and they could
see old Tom's long legs.

" 'I'll make him stay down, confound him,' says the parson; for, ye
see, parsons is men, like the rest on us, and the doctor had got his
spunk up.

" 'You jist hold him a minute, and I'll get something that'll make
him stay, I guess;' and out he went to the fence, and brought in a long,
thin, flat stone, and laid it on old Tom's back.

"Old Tom he wilted down considerable under this, and looked railly
as if he was goin' to give in. He staid still there a good long spell, and
the minister and Huldy left him there and come up to the house; but
they hadn't more than got in the door before they see old Tom a hippin'
along, as high-steppin' as ever, sayin' 'Talk! talk! and quitter! quitter!'
and struttin' and gobblin' as if he'd come through the Red Sea, and got
the victory.

" 'Oh, my eggs!' says Huldy. 'I'm afraid he's smashed 'em!'
"And sure enough, there they was, smashed flat enough under the
stone.

" 'I'll have him killed,' said the parson: 'we won't have such a critter
'round.'

"But the parson, he slep' on't, and then didn't do it: he only come
out next Sunday with a tip-top sermon on the "Riginal Cuss' that was
pronounced on things in gineral, when Adam fell, and showed how
every thing was allowed to go contrary ever since. There was pig-
weed, and pusley, and Canady thistles, cut-worms, and bag-worms, and
canker-worms, to say nothin' of rattlesnakes. The doctor made it very
impressive and sort o' improvin'; but Huldy, she told me, goin' home,
that she hardly could keep from laughin' two or three times in the
sermon when she thought of old Tom a standin' up with the corn-basket
on his back.

"Wal, next week Huldy she jist borrowed the minister's horse and
side-saddle, and rode over to South Parish to her Aunt Bascome's,—
Widder Bascome's, you know, that lives there by the trout-brook,—and
got a lot o' turkey-eggs o' her, and come back and set a hen on 'em,
and said nothin'; and in good time there was as nice a lot o' turkey-
chicks as ever ye see.

"Huldy never said a word to the minister about his experiment, and
he never said a word to her; but he sort o' kep' more to his books, and
didn't take it on him to advise so much.

"But not long arter he took it into his head that Huldy ought to have a pig to be a fattin' with the buttermilk. Mis' Pipperidge set him up to it; and jist then old Tim Bigelow, out to Juniper Hill, told him if he'd call over he'd give him a little pig.

"So he sent for a man, and told him to build a pig-pen right out by the well, and have it all ready when he came home with his pig.

"Huldy she said she wished he might put a curb round the well out there, because in the dark, sometimes, a body might stumble into it; and the parson, he told him he might do that.

"Wal, old Aikin, the carpenter, he didn't come till most the middle of the arternoon; and then he sort o' idled, so that he didn't get up the well-curb till sun down; and then he went off and said he'd come and do the pig-pen next day.

"Wal, arter dark, Parson Carryl he driv into the yard, full chizel, with his pig. He'd tied up his mouth to keep him from squeelin'; and he see what he thought was the pig-pen,—he was rather near-sighted, —and so he ran and threw piggy over; and down he dropped into the water, and the minister put out his horse and pranced off into the house quite delighted.

" 'There, Huldy, I've got you a nice little pig.'

" 'Dear me!' says Huldy: 'where have you put him?'

" 'Why, out there in the pig-pen, to be sure.'

" 'Oh, dear me!' says Huldy: 'that's the well-curb; there ain't no pig-pen built,' says she.

" 'Lordy massy!' says the parson: 'then I've thrown the pig in the well!'

"Wal, Huldy she worked and worked, and finally she fished piggy out in the bucket, but he was dead as a door-nail; and she got him out o' the way quietly, and didn't say much; and the parson, he took to a great Hebrew book in his study; and says he, 'Huldy, I ain't much in temporals,' says he. Huldy says she kind o' felt her heart go out to him, he was so sort o' meek and helpless and larned; and says she, 'Wal, Parson Carryl, don't trouble your head no more about it; I'll see to things;' and sure enough, a week arter there was a nice pen, all ship-shape, and two little white pigs that Huldy bought with the money for the butter she sold at the store.

" 'Wal, Huldy,' said the parson, 'you are a most amazin' child: you don't say nothin', but you do more than most folks.'

"Arter that the parson set sich store by Huldy that he come to her and asked her about every thing, and it was amazin' how every thing she put her hand to prospered. Huldy planted marigolds and larkspurs, pinks and carnations, all up and down the path to the front door, and trained up mornin' glories and scar-let-runners round the windows. And she was always a gettin' a root here, and a sprig there, and a seed from somebody else: for Huldy was one o' them that has the gift, so that ef you jist give 'em the leastest sprig of any thing they make a great bush out of it right away; so that in six months Huldy had roses and geraniums and lilies, sich as it would a took a gardener to raise. The parson, he took no notice at fust; but when the yard was all ablaze with flowers he used to come and stand in a kind o' maze at the front door, and say, 'Beautiful, beautiful: why, Huldy, I never see any thing like it.' And then when her work was done arternoons, Huldy would sit with her sewin' in the porch, and sing and trill away till she'd draw the meadow-larks and the bobolinks, and the orioles to answer her, and the great big elm-tree overhead would get perfectly rackety with the birds; and the parson, settin' there in his study, would git to kind o' dreamin' about the angels, and golden harps, and the New Jerusalem; but he wouldn't speak a word, 'cause Huldy she was jist like them wood-thrushes, she never could sing so well when she thought folks was hearin'. Folks noticed, about this time, that the parson's sermons got to be like Aaron's rod, that budded and blossomed: there was things in 'em about flowers and birds, and more 'special about the music o' heaven. And Huldy she noticed, that ef there was a hymn run in her head while she was 'round a workin' the minister was sure to give it out next Sunday. You see, Huldy was jist like a bee: she always sung when she was workin', and you could hear her trillin', now down in the corn-patch, while she was pickin' the corn; and now in the buttery, while she was workin' the butter; and now she'd go singin' down cellar, and then she'd be singin' up over head, so that she seemed to fill a house chock full o' music.

"Huldy was so sort o' chipper and fair spoken, that she got the hired men all under her thumb: they come to her and took her orders jist as meek as so many calves; and she traded at the store, and kep' the accounts, and she hed her eyes everywhere, and tied up all the ends so tight that there want no gettin' 'round her. She wouldn't let nobody put nothin' off on Parson Carryl, 'cause he was a minister. Huldy was allers up to anybody that wanted to make a hard bargain; and, afore he knew jist what he was about, she'd got the best end of it, and everybody said that Huldy was the most capable gal that they'd ever traded with.

"Wal, come to the meetin' of the Association, Mis' Deakin Blodgett and Mis' Pipperidge come callin' up to the parson's, all in a stew, and offerin' their services to get the house ready; but the doctor, he jist thanked 'em quite quiet, and turned 'em over to Huldy; and Huldy she told 'em that she'd got every thing ready, and showed 'em her pantries, and her cakes and her pies and her puddin's, and took 'em all over the house; and they went peekin' and pokin', openin' cupboard-doors, and lookin' into drawers; and they couldn't find so much as a thread out o' the way, from garret to cellar, and so they went off quite discontented. Arter that the women set a new trouble a brewin'. Then they begun to talk that it was a year now since Mis' Carryl died; and it r'ally wasn't proper such a young gal to be stayin' there, who everybody could see was a settin' her cap for the minister.

"Mis' Pipperidge said, that, so long as she looked on Huldy as the hired gal, she hadn't thought much about it; but Huldy was railly takin' on airs as an equal, and appearin' as mistress o' the house in a way that would make talk if it went on. And Mis' Pipperidge she driv 'round up to Deakin Abner Snow's, and down to Mis' 'Lijah Perry's, and asked them if they wasn't afraid that the way the parson and Huldy was a goin' on might make talk. And they said they hadn't thought on't before, but now, come to think on't, they was sure it would; and they all went and talked with somebody else, and asked them if they didn't think it would make talk. So come Sunday, between meetin's there warn't nothin' else talked about; and Huldy saw folks a noddin' and a winkin', and a lookin' arter her, and she begun to feel drefful sort o' disagreeable. Finally Mis' Sawin she says to her, 'My dear, didn't you, never think folk would talk about you and the minister?'

" 'No: why should they?' says Huldy, quite innocent.

"Wal, dear,' says she, 'I think it's a shame; but they say you're tryin' to catch him, and that it's so bold and improper for you to be courtin' of him right in his own house,—you know folks will talk,—I thought I'd tell you 'cause I think so much of you,' says she.

"Huldy was a gal of spirit, and she despised the talk, but it made her drefful uncomfortable; and when she got home at night she sat down in the mornin'-glory porch, quite quiet, and didn't sing a word.

"The minister he had heard the same thing from one of his deakins that day; and, when he saw Huldy so kind o' silent, he says to her, 'Why don't you sing, my child?'

"He hed a pleasant sort o' way with him, the minister had, and Huldy had got to likin' to be with him, and it all come over her that perhaps she ought to go away; and her throat kind o' filled up so she couldn't hardly speak; and, says she, 'I can't sing to-night.'

"Says he, 'You don't know how much good you're singin' has done me, nor how much good *you* have done me in all ways, Huldy. I wish I knew how to show my gratitude.'

" 'O sir!' says Huldy, '*is* it improper for me to be here?'

" 'No, dear,' says the minister, 'but ill-natured folks will talk; but there is one way we can stop it, Huldy—if you will marry me. You'll make me very happy, and I'll do all I can to make you happy. Will you?'

"Wal, Huldy never told me jist what she said to the minister,—gals never does give you the particulars of them 'are things jist as you'd like 'em,—only I know the upshot and the hull on't was, that Huldy she did a consid'able lot o' clear starchin' and ironin' the next two days; and the Friday o' next week the minister and she rode over together to Dr. Lothrop's in Old Town; and the doctor, he jist made 'em man and wife, 'spite of envy of the Jews,' as the hymn says. Wal, you'd better believe there was a starin' and a wonderin' next Sunday mornin' when the second bell was a tollin', and the minister walked up the broad aisle with Huldy, all in white, arm in arm with him, and he opened the minister's pew, and handed her in as if she was a princess; for, you see, Parson Carryl come of a good family, and was a born gentleman, and had a sort o' grand way o' bein' polite to women-folks. Wal, I guess there was a rus'lin' among the bunnets. Mis' Pipperidge gin a great bounce, like corn poppin' on a shovel, and her eyes glared through her glasses at Huldy as if they'd a sot her afire; and everybody in the meetin' house was a starin', I tell *yew*. But they couldn't none of 'em say nothin' agin Huldy's looks; for there wa'n't a crimp nor a frill about her that wa'n't jis' *so;* and her frock was white as the driven snow, and she had her bunnet all trimmed up with white ribbins; and all the fellows said the old doctor had stole a march, and got the handsomest gal in the parish.

"Wal, arter meetin' they all come 'round the parson and Huldy at the door, shakin' hands and laughin'; for by that time they was about agreed that they'd got to let putty well alone.

" 'Why, Parson Carryl,' says Mis' Deakin Blodgett, 'how you've come it over us.'

" 'Yes,' says the parson, with a kind o' twinkle in his eye. 'I thought,' says he, 'as folks wanted to talk about Huldy and me, I'd give 'em somethin' wuth talkin' about.' "

GEORGE WASHINGTON CABLE

Belles Demoiselles Plantation

"Belles Demoiselles Plantation" was originally published in *Scribner's Monthly* in 1874, the second of Cable's important stories to appear, and anthologized in *Old Creole Days* in 1879. Set in New Orleans in the early nineteenth century, it combines the mythic elements of Gothic Romanticism with local-color detail and the ethical conflicts of the emerging realism. At the heart of the story is the historical curse of abandonment and betrayal within the De Charleu family and the complex relationship between the aristocratic Creole Colonel and his Choctaw relative, Injin Charlie, a situation deeply suggestive of the divided heritage that plagued the South. That the two men speak English to each other, rather than their first languages, underscores their problems of true communication and intimacy. When the lazy and sybaritic aristocrat, driven by his beautiful but self-indulgent daughters, attempts to cheat his relative out of his property, the central issues of guilt, responsibility, and ethical stature dramatically emerge. As the tragic events of the story unfold, and the family mansion collapses, the two men discover the depth of their loyalty and sympathy for each other and the moral superiority of the "inferior" man. The stories in *Old Creole Days* and the masterful novel *The Grandissimes* helped make Cable the foremost local colorist of his region.

*   *   *

The original grantee was Count——; assume the name to be De Charlen; the old Creoles never forgive a public mention. He was the French king's commissary. One day, called to France to explain the lucky accident of the commissariat having burned down with his account books inside, he left his wife, a Choctaw *comtesse*, behind.

Arrived at court, his excuses were accepted, and that tract granted him where afterward stood Belles Demoiselles Plantation. A man cannot remember everything! In a fit of forgetfulness he married a French gentlewoman, rich and beautiful, and "brought her out." However, "all's well that ends well"; a famine had been in the colony, and the Choctaw *comtesse* had starved, leaving nought but a half-caste orphan family lurking on the edge of the settlement, bearing our French gentlewoman's own new name, and being mentioned in Monsieur's will.

And the new *comtesse*—she tarried but a twelvemonth, left Monsieur a lovely son, and departed, led out of this vain world by the swamp fever.

From this son sprang the proud Creole family of De Charleu. It rose straight up, up, up, generation after generation, tall, branchless, slender, palmlike; and finally, in the time of which I am to tell, flowered with all the rare beauty of a century plant, in Artemise, Innocente, Felicité, the twins Marie and Martha, Leontine and little Septima; the seven beautiful daughters for whom their home had been fitly named Belles Demoiselles.

The count's grant had once been a long *pointe*, round which the Mississippi used to whirl, and seethe, and foam, that it was horrid to behold. Big whirlpools would open and wheel about in the savage eddies under the low bank, and close up again, and others open, and spin, and disappear. Great circles of muddy surface would boil up from hundreds of feet below, and gloss over, and seem to float away—sink, come back again under water, and with only a soft hiss surge up again, and again drift off, and vanish. Every few minutes the loamy bank would tip down a great load of earth upon its besieger, and fall back a foot—sometimes a yard—and the writhing river would press after, until at last the *pointe* was quite swallowed up, and the great river glided by in a majestic curve, and asked no more; the bank stood fast, the "caving" became a forgotten misfortune, and the diminished grant was a long, sweeping, willowy bend, rustling with miles of sugar cane.

. Coming up the Mississippi in the sailing craft of those early days, about the time one first could descry the white spires of the old St. Louis Cathedral, you would be pretty sure to spy, just over to your right under the levee, Belles Demoiselles Mansion, with its broad veranda and red painted cypress roof, peering over the embankment, like a bird in the nest, half-hid by the avenue of willows which one of the departed De Charleus—he that married a Marot—had planted on the levee's crown.

The house stood unusually near the river, facing eastward, and standing four square, with an immense veranda about its sides, and a flight of steps in front spreading broadly downward, as we open arms to a child. From the veranda nine miles of river were seen; and in their compass, near at hand, the shady garden full of rare and beautiful flowers; farther away broad fields of cane and rice, and the distant quarters of the slaves, and on the horizon everywhere a dark belt of cypress forest.

The master was old Colonel De Charleu—Jean Albert Henri Joseph De Charleu-Marot, and "Colonel" by the grace of the first American governor. Monsieur—he would not speak to anyone who called him "Colonel"—was a hoary-headed patriarch. His step was firm, his form erect, his intellect strong and clear, his countenance classic, serene, dignified, commanding, his manners courtly, his voice musical—fascinating. He had had his vices—all his life; but had borne them, as his race do, with a serenity of conscience and a cleanness of mouth that left no outward blemish on the surface of the gentleman. He had gambled in Royal Street, drunk hard in Orleans Street, run his adversary through in the dueling ground at Slaughterhouse Point, and danced and quarreled at the St. Philippe Street Theatre quadroon balls. Even now, with all his courtesy and bounty, and a hospitality which seemed to be entertaining angels, he was bitter proud and penurious, and deep down in his hard-finished heart loved nothing but himself, his name, and his motherless children. But these!—their ravishing beauty was all but excuse enough for the unbounded idolatry of their father. Against these seven goddesses he never rebelled. Had they even required him to de-fraud old De Carlos—

I can hardly say.

Old De Carlos was his extremely distant relative on the Choctaw side. With this single exception, the narrow threadlike line of descent from the Indian wife, diminished to a mere strand by injudicious alli-ances, and deaths in the gutters of old New Orleans, was extinct. The name, by Spanish contact, had become De Carlos; but this one surviving bearer of it was known to all, and known only, as Injin Charlie.

One thing I never knew a Creole to do. He will not utterly go back on the ties of blood, no matter what sort of knots those ties may be. For one reason, he is never ashamed of his or his father's sins; and for another—he will tell you—he is "all heart!"

So the different heirs of the De Charleu estate had always strictly regarded the rights and interests of the De Carloses, especially their ownership of a block of dilapidated buildings in a part of the city, which had once been very poor property, but was beginning to be valuable. This block had much more than maintained the last De Carlos through a long and lazy lifetime, and, as his household consisted only of himself and an aged and crippled Negress, the inference was irresistible that he "had money." Old Charlie, though by *alias* an "Injin," was plainly a dark white man, about as old as Colonel De Charleu, sunk in the bliss of deep ignorance, shrewd, deaf, and, by repute at least, unmerciful.

The colonel and he always conversed in English. This rare accom-plishment, which the former had learned from his Scotch wife—the latter from upriver traders—they found an admirable medium of com-munication, answering, better than French could, a similar purpose to that of the stick which we fasten to the bit of one horse and breast gear of another, whereby each keeps his distance. Once in a while, too, by way of jest, English found its way among the ladies of Belles Demoi-selles, always signifying that their sire was about to have business with old Charlie.

Now a long-standing wish to buy out Charlie troubled the colonel. He had no desire to oust him unfairly; he was proud of being always fair; yet he did long to engross the whole estate under one title. Out of his luxurious idleness he had conceived this desire, and thought little of so slight an obstacle as being already somewhat in debt to old Charlie for money borrowed, and for which Belles Demoiselles was, of course, good, ten times over. Lots, buildings, rents, all, might as well be his, he thought, to give, keep, or destroy. "Had he but the old man's heritage. Ah! He might bring that into existence which his *belles demoiselles* had been begging for, 'since many years'; a home—and such a home—in

the gay city. Here he should tear down this row of cottages and make
his garden wall; there that long rope walk should give place to vine-
covered arbors; the bakery yonder should make way for a costly conservatory; that wine warehouse should come down, and the mansion go
up. It should be the finest in the state. Men should never pass it, but
they should say—'the palace of the De Charleus; a family of grand
descent, a people of elegance and bounty, a line as old as France, a fine
old man, and seven daughters as beautiful as happy; whoever dare attempt to marry there must leave his own name behind him!'

"The house should be of stones fitly set, brought down in ships from
the land of '*les Yankees*,' and it should have an airy belvedere, with a
gilded image tiptoeing and shining on its peak, and from it you should
see, far across the gleaming folds of the river, the red roof of Belles
Demoiselles, the country seat. At the big stone gate there should be a
porter's lodge, and it should be a privilege even to see the ground."

Truly they were a family fine enough, and fancy-free enough to have
fine wishes, yet happy enough where they were, to have had no wish
but to live there always.

To those, who, by whatever fortune, wandered into the garden of
Belles Demoiselles some summer afternoon as the sky was reddening
toward evening, it was lovely to see the family gathered out upon the
tiled pavement at the foot of the broad front steps, gaily chatting and
jesting, with that ripple of laughter that comes so pleasingly from a bevy
of girls. The father would be found seated in their midst, the center of
attention and compliment, witness, arbiter, umpire, critic, by his beautiful children's unanimous appointment, but the single vassal, too, of
seven absolute sovereigns.

Now they would draw their chairs near together in eager discussion
of some new step in the dance, or the adjustment of some rich
adornment. Now they would start about him with excited comments to
see the eldest fix a bunch of violets in his buttonhole. Now the twins
would move down a walk after some unusual flower and be greeted
on their return with the high pitched notes of delighted feminine
surprise.

As evening came on they would draw more quietly about their
paternal center. Often their chairs were forsaken, and they grouped
themselves on the lower steps, one above another, and surrendered
themselves to the tender influences of the approaching night. At such
an hour the passer on the river, already attracted by the dark figures of
the broad-roofed mansion, and its woody garden standing against the
glowing sunset, would hear the voices of the hidden group rise from the
spot in the soft harmonies of an evening song; swelling clearer and
clearer as the thrill of music warmed them into feeling, and presently

joined by the deeper tones of the father's voice; then, as the daylight passed quite away, all would be still, and he would know that the beautiful home had gathered its nestlings under its wings.

And yet, for mere vagary, it pleased them not to be pleased.

"Arti!" called one sister to another in the broad hall, one morning —mock amazement in her distended eyes—"something is goin' to took place!"

"*Comm-e-n-t?*"—long-drawn perplexity.

"Papa is goin' to town!"

The news passed up stairs.

"Inno!"—one to another meeting in a doorway—"something is goin' to took place!"

"*Qu'est-ce-que c'est!*"—vain attempt at gruffness.

"Papa is goin' to town!"

The unusual tidings were true. It was afternoon of the same day that the colonel tossed his horse's bridle to his groom, and stepped up to old Charlie, who was sitting on his bench under a China-tree, his head, as was his fashion, bound in a Madras handkerchief. The "old man" was plainly under the effect of spirits, and smiled a deferential salutation without trusting himself to his feet.

"Eh, well Charlie!"—the colonel raised his voice to suit his kinsman's deafness—"how is those times with my friend Charlie?"

"Eh?" said Charlie, distractedly.

"Is that goin' well with my friend Charlie?"

"In de house—call her"—making a pretense of rising.

"*Non, non!* I don't want"—the speaker paused to breathe—"ow is collection?"

"Oh!" said Charlie, "every day he make me more poorer!"

"What do you hask for it?" asked the planter indifferently, designating the house by a wave of his whip.

"Ask for w'at?" said Injin Charlie.

"De *house!* What you ask for it?"

"I don't believe," said Charlie.

"What you would *take* for it!" cried the planter.

"Wait for w'at?"

"What you would *take* for the whole block?"

"I don't want to sell him!"

"I'll give you *ten thousand dollah* for it."

"Ten t'ousand dollah for dis house? Oh, no, dat is no price. He is blame good old house—dat old house." (Old Charlie and the colonel never swore in presence of each other.) "Forty years dat old house didn't had to be paint! I easy can get fifty t'ousand dollah for dat old house."

"Fifty thousand picayunes; yes," said the colonel.

"She's a good house. Can make plenty money," pursued the deaf man.

"That's what make you so rich, eh, Charlie?"

"*Non,* I don't make nothing. Too blame clever, me, dat's de troub'. She's a good house, make money fast like a steamboat, make a barrelful in a week! Me, I lose money all de days. Too blame clever."

"Charlie!"

"Eh?"

"Tell me what you'll take."

"Make? I don't make *nothing.* Too blame clever."

"What will you *take?*"

"Oh! I got enough already—half-drunk now."

"What will you take for the 'ouse?"

"You want to buy her?"

"I don't know"—(shrug)—"may*be,* if you sell it cheap."

"She's a bully old house."

There was a long silence. By and by old Charlie commenced—

"Old Injin Charlie is a low-down dog."

"*C'est vrai, oui!*" retorted the colonel in an undertone.

"He's got Injin blood in him."

The colonel nodded assent.

"But he's got some blame good blood, too, ain't it?"

The colonel nodded impatiently.

"*Bien!* Old Charlie's Injin blood says, 'sell de house, Charlie, you blame old fool!' *Mais,* old Charlie's good blood says, 'Charlie! If you sell dat old house, Charlie, you low-down old dog, Charlie, what de Comte De Charleu make for you grace-gran'muzzer, de dev' can eat you, Charlie, I don't care.' "

"But you'll sell it anyhow, won't you, old man?"

"No!" And the *no* rumbled off in muttered oaths like thunder out on the Gulf. The incensed old colonel wheeled and started off.

"Curl!" (Colonel) said Charlie, standing up unsteadily.

The planter turned with an inquiring frown.

"I'll trade with you!" said Charlie.

The colonel was tempted. " 'Ow'l you trade?" he asked.

"My house for yours!"

The old colonel turned pale with anger. He walked very quickly back, and came close up to his kinsman.

"Charlie!" he said.

"Injin Charlie,"—with a tipsy nod.

But by this time self-control was returning. "Sell Belles Demoiselles

to you?" he said in a high key, and then laughed "Ho, ho, ho!" and
rode away.

A cloud, but not a dark one, overshadowed the spirits of Belles Demoiselles' plantation. The old master, whose beaming presence had always
made him a shining Saturn, spinning and sparkling within the bright
circle of his daughters, fell into musing fits, started out of frowning
reveries, walked often by himself, and heard business from his overseer
fretfully.

No wonder. The daughters knew his closeness in trade, and attributed to it his failure to negotiate for the Old Charlie buildings—so to
call them. They began to deprecate Belles Demoiselles. If a north wind
blew, it was too cold to ride. If a shower had fallen, it was too muddy
to drive. In the morning the garden was wet. In the evening the grass-
hopper was a burden. *Ennui* was turned into capital; every headache
was interpreted a premonition of ague; and when the native exuberance
of a flock of ladies without a want or a care burst out in laughter in
the father's face, they spread their French eyes, rolled up their little
hands, and with rigid wrists and mock vehemence vowed and vowed
again that they only laughed at their misery, and should pine to death
unless they could move to the sweet city. "Oh, the theater! Oh, Orleans
Street! Oh, the masquerade! The Place d'Armes! The ball!" and they
would call upon Heaven with French irreverence, and fall into each
other's arms, and whirl down the hall singing a waltz, end with a grand
collision and fall, and, their eyes streaming merriment, lay the blame on
the slippery floor, that would some day be the death of the whole seven.

Three times more the fond father, thus goaded, managed, by
accident—business accident—to see old Charlie and increase his offer;
but in vain. He finally went to him formally.

"Eh?" said the deaf and distant relative. "For what you want him,
eh? Why you don't stay where you halways be 'appy? Dis is a blame
old rathole—good for old Injin Charlie—da's all. Why you don't stay
where you be halways 'appy? Why you don't buy somewheres else?"

"That's none of your business," snapped the planter. Truth was, his
reasons were unsatisfactory even to himself.

A sullen silence followed. Then Charlie spoke:

"Well, now, look here; I sell you old Charlie's house."

"*Bien!* And the whole block," said the colonel.

"Hold on," said Charlie. "I sell you de 'ouse and de block. Den I go
and git drunk, and go to sleep, de dev' comes along and says, 'Charlie!
old Charlie, you blame low-down old dog, wake up! What you doin'
here? Where's de 'ouse what Monsieur le Comte give your grace-
gran'muzzer? Don't you see dat fine gentyman, De Charleu, done gone

and tore him down and make him over new, you blame old fool, Charlie, you low-down old Injin dog!' "

"I'll give you forty thousand dollars," said the colonel.

"For de 'ouse?"

"For all."

The deaf man shook his head.

"Forty-five!" said the colonel.

"What a lie? For what you tell me 'What a lie?' I don't tell you no lie."

"*Non, non!* I give you *forty-five!*" shouted the colonel.

Charlie shook his head again.

"Fifty!"

He shook it again.

The figures rose and rose to—

"Seventy-five!"

The answer was an invitation to go away and let the owner alone, as he was, in certain specified respects, the vilest of living creatures and no company for a fine gentyman.

The "fine gentyman" longed to blaspheme—but before old Charlie! —in the name of pride, how could he? He mounted and started away.

"Tell you what I'll make wid you," said Charlie.

The other, guessing aright, turned back without dismounting, smiling.

"How much Belles Demoiselles hoes me now?" asked the deaf one.

"One hundred and eighty thousand dollars," said the colonel, firmly.

"Yass," said Charlie. "I don't want Belles Demoiselles."

The old colonel's quiet laugh intimated it made no difference either way.

"But me," continued Charlie, "me—I'm got le Comte De Charleu's blood in me, any'ow—a litt' bit, any'ow, ain't it?"

The colonel nodded that it was.

"*Bien!* If I got out of dis place and don't go to Belles Demoiselles, de peoples will say—dey will say, 'Old Charlie he been all doze time tell a blame *lie!* He ain't no kin to his old grace-gran'muzzer, not a blame bit! He don't got nary drop of De Charleu blood to save his blame low-down old Injin soul! No, sare! What I want wid money, den? No, sare! My place for yours!"

He turned to go into the house, just too soon to see the colonel make an ugly whisk at him with his riding whip. Then the colonel, too, moved off.

Two or three times over, as he ambled homeward, laughter broke through his annoyance, as he recalled old Charlie's family pride and the presumption of his offer. Yet each time he could but think better of—

not the offer to swap, but the preposterous ancestral loyalty. It was so much better than he could have expected from his "low-down" relative, and not unlike his own whim withal—the proposition which went with it was forgiven.

This last defeat bore so harshly on the master of Belles Demoiselles that the daughters, reading chagrin in his face, began to repent. They loved their father as daughters can, and when they saw their pretended dejection harassing him seriously they restrained their complaints, displayed more than ordinary tenderness, and heroically and ostentatiously concluded there was no place like Belles Demoiselles. But the new mood touched him more than the old, and only refined his discontent. Here was a man, rich without the care of riches, free from any real trouble, happiness as native to his house as perfume to his garden, deliberately, as it were with premeditated malice, taking joy by the shoulder and bidding her be gone to town, whither he might easily have followed, only that the very same ancestral nonsense that kept Injin Charlie from selling the old place for twice its value prevented him from choosing any other spot for a city home.

But by and by the charm of nature and the merry hearts around him prevailed; the fit of exalted sulks passed off, and after a while the year flared up at Christmas, flickered, and went out.

New Year came and passed; the beautiful garden of Belles Demoiselles put on its spring attire; the seven fair sisters moved from rose to rose; the cloud of discontent had warmed into invisible vapor in the rich sunlight of family affection, and on the common memory the only scar of last year's wound was old Charlie's sheer impertinence in crossing the caprice of the De Charleus. The cup of gladness seemed to fill with the filling of the river.

How high that river was! Its tremendous current rolled and tumbled and spun along, hustling the long funeral flotillas of drift—and how near shore it came! Men were out day and night, watching the levee. On windy nights even the old colonel took part, and grew lighthearted with occupation and excitement, as every minute the river threw a white arm over the levee's top, as though it would vault over. But all held fast, and, as the summer drifted in, the water sunk down into its banks and looked quite incapable of harm.

On a summer afternoon of uncommon mildness, old Colonel Jean Albert Henri Joseph De Charleu-Marot, being in a mood for reverie, slipped the custody of his feminine rulers and sought the crown of the levee, where it was his wont to promenade. Presently he sat upon a stone bench, a favorite seat. Before him lay his broad-spread fields; near by, his lordly mansion; and being still—perhaps by female contact—somewhat sentimental, he fell to musing on his past. It was hardly wor-

thy to be proud of. All its morning was reddened with mad frolic, and
far toward the meridian it was marred with elegant rioting. Pride had
kept him well-nigh useless, and despised the honors won by valor; gam-
ing had dimmed prosperity; death had taken his heavenly wife; volup-
tuous ease had mortgaged his lands; and yet his house still stood, his
sweet-smelling fields were still fruitful, his name was fame enough; and
yonder and yonder, among the trees and flowers, like angels walking in
Eden, were the seven goddesses of his only worship.

Just then a slight sound behind him brought him to his feet. He cast
his eyes anxiously to the outer edge of the little strip of bank between
the levee's base and the river. There was nothing visible. He paused,
with his ear toward the water, his face full of frightened expectation.
Ha! There came a single plashing sound, like some great beast slipping
into the river, and little waves in a wide semicircle came out from under
the bank and spread over the water!

"My God!"

He plunged down the levee and bounded through the low weeds to
the edge of the bank. It was sheer, and the water about four feet below.
He did not stand quite on the edge, but fell upon his knees a couple of
yards away, wringing his hands, moaning and weeping, and staring
through his watery eyes at a fine, long crevice just discernible under the
matted grass, and curving outward on either hand toward the river.

"My God!" he sobbed aloud; "my God!" and even while he called,
his God answered: the tough Bermuda grass stretched and snapped, the
crevice slowly became a gape, and softly, gradually, with no sound but
the closing of the water at last, a ton or more of earth settled into the
boiling eddy and disappeared.

At the same instant a pulse of the breeze brought from the garden
behind, the joyous, thoughtless laughter of the fair mistresses of Belles
Demoiselles.

The old colonel sprang up and clambered over the levee. Then forcing
himself to a more composed movement, he hastened into the house and
ordered his horse.

"Tell my children to make merry while I am gone," he left word. "I
shall be back tonight," and the horse's hoofs clattered down a byroad
leading to the city.

"Charlie," said the planter, riding up to a window, from which the
old man's nightcap was thrust out, "what you say, Charlie—my house
for yours, eh, Charlie—what you say?"

"Ello!" said Charlie; "from where you come from dis time of
tonight?"

"I come from the Exchange in St. Louis Street." (A small fraction of
the truth.)

"What you want?" said matter-of-fact Charlie.

"I come to trade."

The low-down relative drew the worsted off his ears. "Oh, yass," he said with an uncertain air.

"Well, old man Charlie, what you say: my house for yours—like you said—eh, Charlie?"

"I dunno," said Charlie; "it's nearly mine now. Why you don't stay dare youse'f?"

"*Because I don't want!*" said the colonel savagely. "Is dat reason enough for you? You better take me in de notion, old man, I tell you—yes!"

Charlie never winced; but how his answer delighted the colonel! Quoth Charlie:

"I don't care—I take him!—*mais,* possession give right off."

"Not the whole plantation, Charlie; only—"

"I don't care," said Charlie; "we easy can fix dat. *Mais,* what for you don't want to keep him? I don't want him. You better keep him."

"Don't you try to make no fool of me, old man," cried the planter.

"Oh, no!" said the other. "Oh, no! But you make a fool of yourself, ain't it?"

The dumbfounded colonel stared; Charlie went on:

"Yass! Belles Demoiselles is more wort' dan tree block like dis one. I pass by dare since two weeks. Oh, pritty Belles Demoiselles! De cane was wave in de wind, de garden smell like a bouquet, de white cap was jump up and down on de river; seven *belles demoiselles* was ridin' on horses. 'Pritty, pritty, pritty!' says old Charlie. Ah! *Monsieur le père,* 'ow 'appy, 'appy, 'appy!'"

"Yass!" he continued—the colonel still staring—"le Comte De Charleu have two familie. One was low-down Choctaw, one was high up *noblesse.* He gave the low-down Choctaw dis old rat hole; he give Belles Demoiselles to you gran' fozzer; and now you don't be *satisfait.* What I'll do wid Belles Demoiselles? She'll break me in two years, yass. And what you'll do wid old Charlie's house, eh? You'll tear her down and make you' se'f a blame old fool. I rather wouldn't trade!"

The planter caught a big breathful of anger, but Charlie went straight on:

"I rather wouldn't, *mais* I will do it for you; just the same, like Monsieur le Comte would say, 'Charlie, you old fool, I want to shange houses wid you.' "

So long as the colonel suspected irony he was angry, but as Charlie seemed, after all, to be certainly in earnest, he began to feel conscience-stricken. He was by no means a tender man, but his lately discovered misfortune had unhinged him, and this strange, undeserved, disinter-

ested family fealty on the part of Charlie touched his heart. And should
he still try to lead him into the pitfall he had dug? He hesitated; no, he
would show him the place by broad daylight, and if he chose to overlook the "caving bank," it would be his own fault;—a trade's a trade.

"Come," said the planter, "come at my house tonight; tomorrow we
look at the place before breakfast, and finish the trade."

"For what?" said Charlie.

"Oh, because I got to come in town in the morning."

"I don't want," said Charlie. "How I'm goin' to come dere?"

"I git you a horse at the liberty stable."

"Well—anyhow—I don't care—I'll go." And they went.

When they had ridden a long time, and were on the road darkened
by hedges of Cherokee rose, the colonel called behind him to the "low-
down" scion:

"Keep the road, old man."

"Eh?"

"Keep the road."

"Oh, yes; all right; I keep my word; we don't goin' to play no
tricks, eh?"

But the colonel seemed not to hear. His ungenerous design was beginning to be hateful to him. Not only old Charlie's unprovoked goodness was prevailing; the eulogy on Belles Demoiselles had stirred the
depths of an intense love for his beautiful home. True, if he held to it,
the caving of the bank, at its present fearful speed, would let the house
into the river within three months; but were it not better to lose it so,
than sell his birthright? Again—coming back to the first thought—to
betray his own blood! It was only Injin Charlie; but had not the De
Charleu blood just spoken out in him? Unconsciously he groaned.

After a time they struck a path approaching the plantation in the
rear, and a little after, passing from behind a clump of live oaks, they
came in sight of the villa. It looked so like a gem, shining through the
dark grove, so like a great glow worm in the dense foliage, so significant
of luxury and gaiety, that the poor master, from an over-flowing heart,
groaned again.

"What?" asked Charlie.

The colonel only drew his rein, and, dismounting mechanically, contemplated the sight before him. The high, arched doors and windows
were thrown wide to the summer air; from every opening the bright
light of numerous candelabra darted out upon the sparkling foliage of
magnolia and bay, and here and there in the spacious verandas a colored
lantern swayed in the gentle breeze. A sound of revel fell on the ear, the
music of harps; and across one window, brighter than the rest, flitted,

once or twice, the shadows of dancers. But oh, the shadows flitting across the heart of the fair mansion's master!

"Old Charlie," said he, gazing fondly at his house, "you and me is both old, eh?"

"Yaas," said the stolid Charlie.

"And we has both been bad enough in our time, eh, Charlie?"

Charlie, surprised at the tender tone, repeated, "Yaas."

"And you and me is mighty close?"

"Blame close, yaas."

"But you never know me to cheat, old man!"

"No"—impassively.

"And do you think I would cheat you now?"

"I dunno," said Charlie. "I don't believe."

"Well, old man, old man"—his voice began to quiver—"I shan't cheat you now. My God! Old man, I tell you—you better not make the trade!"

"Because for what?" asked Charlie in plain anger; but both looked quickly toward the house! The colonel tossed his hands wildly in the air, rushed forward a step or two, and giving one fearful scream of agony and fright, fell forward on his face in the path. Old Charlie stood transfixed with horror. Belles Demoiselles, the realm of maiden beauty, the home of merriment, the house of dancing, all in the tremor and glow of pleasure, suddenly sank, with one short, wild wail of terror— sank, sank, down, down, down, into the merciless, unfathomable flood of the Mississippi.

Twelve long months were midnight to the mind of the childless father; when they were only half-gone, he took his bed; and every day, and every night, old Charlie, the "low-down," the "fool," watched him tenderly, tended him lovingly, for the sake of his name, his misfortunes, and his broken heart. No woman's step crossed the floor of the sick chamber, whose western dormer windows over-peered the dingy architecture of old Charlie's block; Charlie and a skilled physician, the one all interest, the other all gentleness, hope, and patience—these only entered by the door; but by the window came in a sweet-scented evergreen vine, transplanted from the caving bank of Belles Demoiselles. It caught the rays of sunset in its flowery net, and let them softly in upon the sick man's bed; gathered the glancing beams of the moon at midnight, and often wakened the sleeper to look, with his mindless eyes, upon their pretty silver fragments strewn upon the floor.

By and by there seemed—there was—a twinkling dawn of returning reason. Slowly, peacefully, with an increase unseen from day to day, the light of reason came into the eyes, and speech became coherent; but withal there came a failing of the wrecked body, and the doctor said that monsieur was both better and worse.

One evening, as Charlie sat by the vineclad window with his fireless pipe in his hand, the old colonel's eyes fell full upon his own, and rested there.

"Charl—" he said with an effort, and his delighted nurse hastened to the bedside and bowed his best ear. There was an unsuccessful effort or two, and then he whispered, smiling with sweet sadness—

"We didn't trade."

The truth, in this case, was a secondary matter to Charlie; the main point was to give a pleasing answer. So he nodded his head decidedly, as who should say—"Oh, yes, we did, it was a bonafide swap!" but when he saw the smile vanish, he tried the other expedient and shook his head with still more vigor, to signify that they had not so much as approached a bargain; and the smile returned.

Charlie wanted to see the vine recognized. He stepped backward to the window with a broad smile, shook the foliage, nodded and looked smart.

"I know," said the colonel, with beaming eyes, "—many weeks."

The next day—

"Charl—"

The best ear went down.

"Send for a priest."

The priest came, and was alone with him a whole afternoon. When he left, the patient was very haggard and exhausted, but smiled and would not suffer the crucifix to be removed from his breast.

One more morning came. Just before dawn Charlie, lying on a pallet in the room, thought he was called, and came to the bedside.

"Old man," whispered the failing invalid, "is it caving yet?"

Charlie nodded.

"It won't pay you out."

"Oh, dat makes not'ing," said Charlie. Two big tears rolled down his brown face. "Dat makes not'in'."

The colonel whispered once more:

"*Mes belles demoiselles!* In paradise; in the garden; I shall be with them at sunrise"; and so it was.

CONSTANCE FENIMORE WOOLSON

Rodman the Keeper

"Rodman the Keeper," a dramatic story that depicts John Rodman, a Union officer in charge of a military cemetery, caring for a dying Southern soldier, was originally published in the *Atlantic Monthly* in 1877. In the magazine version, the story concluded with a fierce exchange between Rodman and Bettina Ward on the welfare of African Americans in the South. Rodman maintains that the lack of educational opportunity for people of all races, not simply Northern exploitation, has led to the desolation of the region. Aware of the sensitivity of these issues, Woolson deleted this passage when the story was published in *Rodman the Keeper: Southern Sketches* in 1880. Even without this inflammatory issue, the story reveals the depth of regional feeling in the years after the war, a period in which reconciliation and cooperation seemed highly problematic. Even though she wrote within the local-color tradition, stressing character over plot, description over action, Woolson constructed deeply serious themes with compelling psychological insight, avoiding sentimental resolutions to the conflicts presented in her stories. In "Rodman the Keeper" she offers no mitigation to the deep bitterness the Southern lady feels for the Union officer, concluding instead with an ironic revelation of the mercantile values of New England.

*   *   *

The long years come and go,
    And the Past,
The sorrowful, splendid Past,
With its glory and its woe,
    Seems never to have been.
—Seems never to have been?
    O somber days and grand,
    How ye crowd back once more,
Seeing our heroes' graves are green
By the Potomac and the Cumberland,
And in the valley of the Shenandoah!

When we remember how they died,—
In dark ravine and on the mountain-side,
In leaguered fort and fire-encircled town,
And where the iron ships went down,—
How their dear lives were spent

In the weary hospital-tent,
In the cockpit's crowded hive,
                    —it seems
Ignoble to be alive!

                    THOMAS BAILEY ALDRICH.

"Keeper of what? Keeper of the dead. Well, it is easier to keep the dead than the living; and as for the gloom of the thing, the living among whom I have been lately were not a hilarious set."

John Rodman sat in the doorway and looked out over his domain. The little cottage behind him was empty of life save himself alone. In one room the slender appointments provided by government for the keeper, who being still alive must sleep and eat, made the bareness doubly bare; in the other the desk and the great ledgers, the ink and pens, the register, the loud-ticking clock on the wall, and the flag folded on a shelf, were all for the kept, whose names, in hastily written, blotted rolls of manuscript, were waiting to be transcribed in the new red-bound ledgers in the keeper's best handwriting day by day, while the clock was to tell him the hour when the flag must rise over the mounds where reposed the bodies of fourteen thousand United States soldiers—who had languished where once stood the prison pens, on the opposite slopes, now fair and peaceful in the sunset; who had fallen by the way in long marches to and fro under the burning sun; who had fought and died on the many battlefields that reddened the beautiful state, stretching from the peaks of the marble mountains in the smoky west down to the sea islands of the ocean border. The last rim of the sun's red ball had sunk below the horizon line, and the western sky glowed with deep rose-color, which faded away above into pink, into the salmon tint, into shades of that far-away heavenly emerald which the brush of the earthly artist can never reproduce, but which is found sometimes in the iridescent heart of the opal. The small town, a mile distant, stood turning its back on the cemetery; but the keeper could see the pleasant, rambling old mansions, each with its rose garden and neglected outlying fields, the empty Negro quarters falling into ruin, and everything just as it stood when on that April morning the first gun was fired on Sumter; apparently not a nail added, not a brushful of paint applied, not a fallen brick replaced, or latch or lock repaired. The keeper had noted these things as he strolled through the town, but not with surprise; for he had seen the South in its first estate, when, fresh, strong, and fired with enthusiasm, he, too, had marched away from his village home with the colors flying above and the girls waving their handkerchiefs behind, as the regiment, a thousand strong, filed down the dusty road. That regiment, a weak, scarred two hundred, came back a year later with lagging step and colors tattered and scorched, and the girls could not wave their handkerchiefs, wet and sodden with tears. But the keeper, his wound healed, had gone again; and he had seen with his New England eyes the magnificence and the carelessness of the South, her splendor and negligence, her wealth and thriftlessness, as through Virginia and the fair Carolinas, across Georgia and into sunny Florida, he had marched month by month, first a lieutenant, then captain, and finally major and colonel, as death mowed down those above him, and he and his good conduct were left. Everywhere magnificence went hand in hand with neglect, and he had said so as chance now and then threw a conversation in his path.

"We have no such shiftless ways," he would remark, after he had furtively supplied a prisoner with hardtack and coffee.

"And no such grand ones either," Johnny Reb would reply, if he was a man of spirit; and generally he was.

The Yankee, forced to acknowledge the truth of this statement, qualified it by observing that he would rather have more thrift with a little less grandeur; whereupon the other answered that *he* would not; and there the conversation rested. So now ex-Colonel Rodman, keeper of the national cemetery, viewed the little town in its second estate with philosophic eyes. "It is part of a great problem now working itself out; I am not here to tend the living, but the dead," he said.

Whereupon, as he walked among the long mounds, a voice seemed to rise from the still ranks below: "While ye have time, do good to men," it said. "Behold, we are beyond your care." But the keeper did not heed.

This still evening in early February he looked out over the level waste. The little town stood in the lowlands; there were no hills from whence cometh help—calm heights that lift the soul above earth and its cares; no river to lead the aspirations of the children outward toward the great sea. Everything was monotonous, and the only spirit that rose above the waste was a bitterness for the gained and sorrow for the lost cause. The keeper was the only man whose presence personated the former in their sight, and upon him therefore, as representative, the bitterness fell, not in words, but in averted looks, in sudden silences when he approached, in withdrawals and avoidance, until he lived and moved in a vacuum; wherever he went there was presently no one save himself; the very shopkeeper who sold him sugar seemed turned into a man of wood, and took his money reluctantly, although the shilling gained stood perhaps for that day's dinner. So Rodman withdrew himself, and came and went among them no more; the broad acres of his domain gave him as much exercise as his shattered ankle could bear; he ordered his few supplies by the quantity, and began the life of a solitary, his island marked out by the massive granite wall with which the United States Government has carefully surrounded those sad Southern cemeteries of hers; sad, not so much from the number of the mounds representing youth and strength cut off in their bloom, for that is but the fortune of war, as for the complete isolation which marks them. "Strangers in a strange land" is the thought of all who, coming and going to and from Florida, turn aside here and there to stand for a moment among the closely ranged graves which seem already a part of the past, that near past which in our hurrying American life is even now so far away. The government work was completed before the keeper came; the lines of the trenches were defined by low granite copings, and the comparatively few single mounds were headed by trim little white boards bearing generally the word "Unknown," but here and there a name and an age, in most cases a boy from some far-away Northern state; "twenty-one," "twenty-two," said the inscriptions; the dates were those dark years among the sixties, measured now more than by anything else in the number of maidens widowed in heart, and women widowed indeed, who sit still and remember, while the world rushes by. At sunrise the keeper ran up the stars and stripes; and so precise were his ideas of the accessories belonging to the place, that from his own small store of money he had taken enough, by stinting himself, to buy a second flag for stormy weather, so that, rain or not, the colors should float over the dead. This was not patriotism so-called, or rather miscalled, it was not sentimental fancy, it was not zeal or triumph; it was simply a sense of the fitness of things, a conscientiousness which had in it nothing of religion, unless indeed a man's endeavor to live up to his own ideal of his duty be a religion. The same feeling led the keeper to spend hours in copying the rolls. "John Andrew Warren, Company G, Eighth New Hampshire Infantry," he repeated, as he slowly wrote the name, giving "John Andrew" clear, bold capitals and a lettering impossible to mistake; "died August 15, 1863, aged twenty-two years. He came from the prison pen yonder, and lies somewhere in those trenches, I suppose. Now then, John Andrew, don't fancy I am sorrowing for you; no doubt you are better off than I am at this very moment. But nonetheless, John Andrew, shall pen, ink, and hand do their duty to you. For that I am here."

Infinite pains and labor went into these records of the dead; one hair's-breadth error, and the whole page was replaced by a new one. The same spirit kept the grass carefully away from the low coping of the trenches, kept the graveled paths smooth and the mounds green, and the bare little cottage neat as a man-of-war. When the keeper cooked his dinner, the door toward the east, where the dead lay, was scrupulously closed, nor was it opened until everything was in perfect order again. At sunset the flag was lowered, and then it was the keeper's habit to walk slowly up and down the path until the shadows veiled the mounds on each side, and there was nothing save the peaceful green of earth. "So time will efface our little lives and sorrows," he mused, "and we shall be as nothing in the indistinguishable past." Yet nonetheless did he fulfill the duties of every day and hour with exactness. "At least they shall not say that I was lacking," he murmured to himself as he thought vaguely of the future beyond these graves. Who "they" were, it would have troubled him to formulate, since he was one of the many sons whom New England in this generation sends forth with a belief composed entirely of negatives. As the season advanced, he worked all day in the sunshine. "My garden looks well," he said. "I like this cemetery because it is the original resting place of the dead who lie beneath. They were not brought here from distant places, gathered up by contract, numbered, and described like so much merchandise; their first repose has not been broken, their peace has been undisturbed. Hasty burials the prison authorities gave them; the thin bodies were tumbled into the trenches by men almost as thin, for the whole state went hungry in those dark days. There were not many prayers, no tears, as the dead carts went the rounds. But the prayers had been said, and the tears had fallen, while the poor fellows were still alive in the pens yonder; and when at last death came, it was like a release. They suffered long; and I for one believe that therefore shall their rest be long—long and sweet."

After a time began the rain, the soft, persistent, gray rain of the Southern lowlands, and he stayed within and copied another thousand names into the ledger. He would not allow himself the companionship of a dog lest the creature should bark at night and disturb the quiet. There was no one to hear save himself, and it would have been a friendly sound as he lay awake on his narrow iron bed, but it seemed to him against the spirit of the place. He would not smoke, although he had the soldier's fondness for a pipe. Many a dreary evening, beneath a hastily built shelter of boughs, when the rain poured down and everything was comfortless, he had found solace in the curling smoke; but now it seemed to him that it would be incongruous, and at times he almost felt as if it would be selfish too. "*They* cannot smoke, you know, down there under the wet grass," he thought, as standing at the window he looked toward the ranks of the mounds stretching across the eastern end from side to side—"my parade ground," he called it. And then he would smile at his own fancies, draw the curtain, shut out the rain and the night, light his lamp, and go to work on the ledgers again. Some of the names lingered in his memory; he felt as if he had known the men who bore them, as if they had been boys together, and were friends even now although separated for a time. "James Marvin, Company B, Fifth Maine. The Fifth Maine was in the seven days' battle. I say, do you remember that retreat down the Quaker church road, and the way Phil Kearney held the rearguard firm?" And over the whole seven days he wandered with his mute friend, who remembered everything and everybody in the most satisfactory way. One of the little headboards in the parade ground attracted him peculiarly because the name inscribed was his own: "——Rodman, Company A, One Hundred and Sixth New York."

"I remember that regiment; it came from the extreme northern part of the state. Blank Rodman must have melted down here, coming as he did from the half-arctic region along the St. Lawrence. I wonder what he thought of the first hot day, say in South Carolina, along those simmering rice fields?" He grew into the habit of pausing for a moment by the side of this grave every morning and evening. "Blank Rodman. It might easily have been John. And then, where should *I* be?"

But Blank Rodman remained silent, and the keeper, after pulling up a weed or two and trimming the grass over his relative, went off to his duties again. "I am convinced that Blank is a relative," he said to himself; "distant, perhaps, but still a kinsman."

One April day the heat was almost insupportable; but the sun's rays were not those brazen beams that sometimes in Northern cities burn the air and scorch the pavements to a white heat; rather were they soft and still; the moist earth exhaled her richness, not a leaf stirred, and the whole level country seemed sitting in a hot vapor bath. In the early dawn the keeper had performed his outdoor tasks, but all day he remained almost without stirring in his chair between two windows, striving to exist. At high noon out came a little black bringing his supplies from the town, whistling and shuffling along, gay as a lark. The keeper watched him coming slowly down the white road, loitering by the way in the hot blaze, stopping to turn a somersault or two, to dangle over a bridge rail, to execute various impromptu capers all by himself. He reached the gate at last, entered, and, having come all the way up the path in a hornpipe step, he set down his basket at the door to indulge in one long and final double-shuffle before knocking. "Stop that!" said the keeper through the closed blinds. The little darkey darted back; but as nothing further came out of the window—a boot, for instance, or some other stray missile—he took courage, showed his ivories, and drew near again. "Do you suppose I am going to have you stirring up the heat in that way?" demanded the keeper.

The little black grinned, but made no reply, unless smoothing the hot white sand with his black toes could be construed as such; he now removed his rimless hat and made a bow.

"Is it, or is it not warm?" asked the keeper, as a naturalist might inquire of a salamander, not referring to his own so much as to the salamander's ideas on the subject.

"Dunno, mars'," replied the little black.

"How do *you* feel?"

" 'Spects I feel all right, mars'."

The keeper gave up the investigation, and presented to the salamander a nickel cent. "I suppose there is no such thing as a cool spring in all this melting country," he said.

But the salamander indicated with his thumb a clump of trees on the green plain north of the cemetery. "Ole Mars' Ward's place—cole spring dah." He then departed, breaking into a run after he had passed the gate, his ample mouth watering at the thought of a certain chunk of taffy at the mercantile establishment kept by Aunt Dinah in a corner of her one-roomed cabin. At sunset the keeper went thirstily out with a tin pail on his arm, in search of the cold spring. "If it could only be like the spring down under the rocks where I used to drink when I was a boy!" he thought. He had never walked in that direction before. Indeed, now that he had abandoned the town, he seldom went beyond the walls of the cemetery. An old road led across to the clump of trees, through fields run to waste, and following it he came to the place, a deserted house with tumble-down fences and overgrown garden, the outbuildings indicating that once upon a time there were many servants and a prosperous master. The house was of wood, large on the ground, with encircling piazzas; across the front door rough bars had been nailed, and the closed blinds were protected in the same manner; from long want of paint the clapboards were gray and mossy, and the floor of the piazza had fallen in here and there from decay. The keeper decided that his cemetery was a much more cheerful place than this, and then he looked around for the spring. Behind the house the ground sloped down; it must be there. He went around and came suddenly upon a man lying on an old rug outside of a back door. "Excuse me. I thought nobody lived here," he said.

"Nobody does," replied the man; "I am not much of a body, am I?"

His left arm was gone, and his face was thin and worn with long illness; he closed his eyes after speaking, as though the few words had exhausted him.

"I came for water from a cold spring you have here, somewhere," pursued the keeper, contemplating the wreck before him with the interest of one who has himself been severely wounded and knows the long, weary pain. The man waved his hand toward the slope without unclosing his eyes, and Rodman went off with his pail and found a little

shady hollow, once curbed and paved with white pebbles, but now neglected, like all the place. The water was cold, however, deliciously cold.
He filled his pail and thought that perhaps after all he would exert
himself to make coffee, now that the sun was down; it would taste better
made of this cold water. When he came up the slope, the man's eyes
were open.

"Have some water?" asked Rodman.

"Yes; there's a gourd inside."

The keeper entered, and found himself in a large, bare room; in one
corner was some straw covered with an old counterpane, in another a
table and chair; a kettle hung in the deep fireplace, and a few dishes
stood on a shelf; by the door on a nail hung a gourd; he filled it and
gave it to the host of this desolate abode. The man drank with eagerness.

"Pomp has gone to town," he said, "and I could not get down to the
spring today, I have had so much pain."

"And when will Pomp return?"

"He should be here now; he is very late tonight."

"Can I get you anything?"

"No, thank you; he will soon be here."

The keeper looked out over the waste; there was no one in sight. He
was not a man of any especial kindliness—he had himself been too
hardly treated in life for that—but he could not find it in his heart to
leave this helpless creature all alone with night so near. So he sat down
on the doorstep. "I will rest awhile," he said, not asking but announcing
it. The man had turned away and closed his eyes again, and they both
remained silent, busy with their own thoughts; for each had recognized
the ex-soldier, Northern and Southern, in portions of the old uniforms,
and in the accent. The war and its memories were still very near to the
maimed, poverty-stricken Confederate; and the other knew that they
were, and did not obtrude himself.

Twilight fell, and no one came.

"Let me get you something," said Rodman; for the face looked
ghastly as the fever abated. The other refused. Darkness came; still,
no one.

"Look here," said Rodman, rising, "I have been wounded myself,
was in hospital for months; I know how you feel. You must have
food—a cup of tea, now, and a slice of toast, brown and thin."

"I have not tasted tea or wheaten bread for weeks," answered the
man; his voice died off into a wail, as though feebleness and pain had
drawn the cry from him in spite of himself. Rodman lighted a match;
there was no candle, only a piece of pitch pine stuck in an iron socket
on the wall; he set fire to this primitive torch and looked around.

"There is nothing there," said the man outside, making an effort to speak carelessly; "my servant went to town for supplies. Do not trouble yourself to wait; he will come presently, and—and I want nothing."

But Rodman saw through proud poverty's lie; he knew that irregular quavering of the voice, and that trembling of the hand; the poor fellow had but one to tremble. He continued his search; but the bare room gave back nothing, not a crumb.

"Well, if you are not hungry," he said briskly, "I am, hungry as a bear; and I'll tell you what I am going to do. I live not far from here, and I live all alone too; I haven't a servant as you have. Let me take supper here with you, just for a change; and, if your servant comes, so much the better, he can wait upon us. I'll run over and bring back the things."

He was gone without waiting for reply; the shattered ankle made good time over the waste, and soon returned, limping a little, but bravely hasting, while on a tray came the keeper's best supplies, Irish potatoes, corned beef, wheaten bread, butter, and coffee; for he would not eat the hot biscuits, the corncake, the bacon and hominy of the country, and constantly made little New England meals for himself in his prejudiced little kitchen. The pine torch flared in the doorway; a breeze had come down from the far mountains and cooled the air. Rodman kindled a fire on the cavernous hearth, filled the kettle, found a saucepan, and commenced operations, while the other lay outside and watched every movement in the lighted room.

"All ready; let me help you in. Here we are now; fried potatoes, cold beef, mustard, toast, butter, and tea. Eat, man; and the next time I am laid up you shall come over and cook for me."

Hunger conquered, and the other ate, ate as he had not eaten for months. As he was finishing a second cup of tea, a slow step came around the house; it was the missing Pomp, an old Negro, bent and shriveled, who carried a bag of meal and some bacon in his basket. "That is what they live on," thought the keeper.

He took leave without more words. "I suppose now I can be allowed to go home in peace," he grumbled to conscience. The Negro followed him across what was once the lawn. "Fin' Mars' Ward mighty low," he said apologetically, as he swung open the gate which still hung between its posts, although the fence was down, "but I hurred and hurred as fas' as I could; it's mighty fur to de town. Proud to see you, sah; hope you'll come again. Fine fambly, de Wards, sah, befo' de war."

"How long has he been in this state?" asked the keeper.

"Ever sence one ob de las' battles, sah; but he's worse sence we come yer, 'bout a mont' back."

"Who owns the house? Is there no one to see to him? has he no friends?"

"House b'long to Mars' Ward's uncle; fine place once, befo' de war; he's dead now, and dah's nobuddy but Miss Bettina, an' she's gone off somewhuz. Propah place, sah, fur Mars' Ward—own uncle's house," said the old slave, loyally striving to maintain the family dignity even then.

"Are there no better rooms—no furniture?"

"Sartin; but—but Miss Bettina, she took de keys; she didn't know we was comin'—"

"You had better send for Miss Bettina, I think," said the keeper, starting homeward with his tray, washing his hands, as it were, of any future responsibility in the affair.

The next day he worked in his garden, for clouds veiled the sun and exercise was possible; but, nevertheless, he could not forget the white face on the old rug. "Pshaw!" he said to himself, "haven't I seen tumble-down old houses and battered human beings before this?"

At evening came a violent thunderstorm, and the splendor of the heavens was terrible. "We have chained you, mighty spirit," thought the keeper as he watched the lightning, "and some time we shall learn the laws of the winds and foretell the storms; then, prayers will no more be offered in churches to alter the weather than they would be offered now to alter an eclipse. Yet back of the lightning and the wind lies the power of the great Creator, just the same."

But still into his musings crept, with shadowy persistence, the white face on the rug.

"Nonsense!" he exclaimed; "if white faces are going around as ghosts, how about the fourteen thousand white faces that went under the sod down yonder? If they could arise and walk, the whole state would be filled and no more carpetbaggers needed." So, having balanced the one with the fourteen thousand, he went to bed.

Daylight brought rain—still, soft, gray rain; the next morning showed the same, and the third likewise, the nights keeping up their part with low-down clouds and steady pattering on the roof. "If there was a river here, we should have a flood," thought the keeper, drumming idly on his windowpane. Memory brought back the steep New England hillsides shedding their rain into the brooks, which grew in a night to torrents and filled the rivers so that they overflowed their banks; then, suddenly, an old house in a sunken corner of a waste rose before his eyes, and he seemed to see the rain dropping from a moldy ceiling on the straw where a white face lay.

"Really, I have nothing else to do today, you know," he remarked in an apologetic way to himself, as he and his umbrella went along the old road; and he repeated the remark as he entered the room where the man lay, just as he had fancied, on the damp straw.

"The weather *is* unpleasant," said the man. "Pomp, bring a chair."

Pomp brought one, the only one, and the visitor sat down. A fire smoldered on the hearth and puffed out acrid smoke now and then, as if the rain had clogged the soot in the long-neglected chimney; from the streaked ceiling oozing drops fell with a dull splash into little pools on the decayed floor; the door would not close; the broken panes were stopped with rags, as if the old servant had tried to keep out the damp; in the ashes a corncake was baking.

"I am afraid you have not been so well during these long rainy days," said the keeper, scanning the face on the straw.

"My old enemy, rheumatism," answered the man; "the first sunshine will drive it away."

They talked awhile, or rather the keeper talked, for the other seemed hardly able to speak, as the waves of pain swept over him; then the visitor went outside and called Pomp out. "*Is* there anyone to help him, or not?" he asked impatiently.

"Fine fambly, befo' de war," began Pomp.

"Never mind all that; is there anyone to help him now—yes or no?"

"No," said the old black with a burst of despairing truthfulness. "Miss Bettina, she's as poor as Mars' Ward, an' dere's no one else. He's had noth'n but hard corncake for three days, an' he can't swaller it no more."

The next morning saw Ward De Rosset lying on the white pallet in the keeper's cottage, and old Pomp, marveling at the cleanliness all around him, installed as nurse. A strange asylum for a Confederate soldier, was it not? But he knew nothing of the change, which he would have fought with his last breath if consciousness had remained; returning fever, however, had absorbed his senses, and then it was that the keeper and the slave had borne him slowly across the waste, resting many times, but accomplishing the journey at last.

That evening John Rodman, strolling to and fro in the dusky twilight, paused alongside of the other Rodman. "I do not want him here, and that is the plain truth," he said, pursuing the current of his thoughts. "He fills the house; he and Pomp together disturb all my ways. He'll be ready to fling a brick at me too, when his senses come back; small thanks shall I have for lying on the floor, giving up all my comforts, and, what is more, riding over the spirit of the place with a vengeance!" He threw himself down on the grass beside the mound and lay looking up toward the stars, which were coming out, one by one, in the deep blue of the Southern night. "With a vengeance, did I say? That is it exactly—the vengeance of kindness. The poor fellow has suffered horribly in body and in estate, and now ironical Fortune throws him in my way, as if saying, 'Let us see how far your selfishness will yield.' This is not a question of magnanimity; there is no magnanimity about it, for the war is over, and you Northerners have gained every point for which you fought. This is merely a question between man and man; it would be the same if the sufferer was a poor Federal, one of the carpetbaggers, whom you despise so, for instance, or a pagan Chinaman. And Fortune is right; don't you think so, Blank Rodman? I put it to you, now, to one who has suffered the extreme rigor of the other side—those prison pens yonder."

Whereupon Blank Rodman answered that he had fought for a great cause, and that he knew it, although a plain man and not given to speechmaking; he was not one of those who had sat safely at home all through the war, and now belittled it and made light of its issues. (Here a murmur came up from the long line of the trenches, as though all the dead had cried out.) But now the points for which he had fought being gained, and strife ended, it was the plain duty of every man to encourage peace. For his part he bore no malice; he was glad the poor Confederate was up in the cottage, and he did not think any the less of the keeper for bringing him there. He would like to add that he thought more of him; but he was sorry to say that he was well aware what an effort it was, and how almost grudgingly the charity began.

If Blank Rodman did not say this, at least the keeper imagined that he did. "That is what he would have said," he thought. "I am glad you do not object," he added, pretending to himself that he had not noticed the rest of the remark.

"We do not object to the brave soldier who honestly fought for his cause, even though he fought on the other side," answered Blank Rodman for the whole fourteen thousand. "But never let a coward, a double-face, or a flippant-tongued idler walk over our heads. It would make us rise in our graves!"

And the keeper seemed to see a shadowy pageant sweep by—gaunt soldiers with white faces, arming anew against the subtle product of peace: men who said, "It was nothing! Behold, we saw it with our eyes!"—stay-at-home eyes.

The third day the fever abated, and Ward De Rosset noticed his surroundings. Old Pomp acknowledged that he had been moved, but veiled the locality: "To a frien's house, Mars' Ward."

"But I have no friends now, Pomp," said the weak voice.

Pomp was very much amused at the absurdity of this. "No frien's! Mars' Ward, no frien's!" He was obliged to go out of the room to hide his laughter. The sick man lay feebly thinking that the bed was cool and fresh, and the closed green blinds pleasant; his thin fingers stroked the linen sheet, and his eyes wandered from object to object. The only thing that broke the rule of bare utility in the simple room was a square of white drawing paper on the wall, upon which was inscribed in ornamental text the following verse:

> *"Toujours femme varie,*
> *Bien fou qui s'y fie;*
> *Une femme souvent*
> *N'est qu'une plume au vent."*

With the persistency of illness the eyes and mind of Ward De Rosset went over and over this distich; he knew something of French, but was unequal to the effort of translating; the rhymes alone caught his vagrant fancy. "Toujours femme varie," he said to himself over and over again; and when the keeper entered, he said it to him.

"Certainly," answered the keeper; "bien fou qui s'y fie. How do you find yourself this morning?"

"I have not found myself at all, so far. Is this your house?"

"Yes."

"Pomp told me I was in a friend's house," observed the sick man, vaguely.

"Well, it isn't an enemy's. Had any breakfast? No? Better not talk, then."

He went to the detached shed which served for a kitchen, upset all Pomp's clumsy arrangements, and ordered him outside; then he set to work and prepared a delicate breakfast with his best skill. The sick man eagerly eyed the tray as he entered. "Better have your hands and face sponged off, I think," said Rodman; and then he propped him up skillfully, and left him to his repast. The grass needed mowing on the parade ground; he shouldered his scythe and started down the path, viciously kicking the gravel aside as he walked. "Wasn't solitude your principal idea, John Rodman, when you applied for this place?" he demanded of himself. "How much of it are you likely to have with sick men, and sick men's servants, and so forth?"

The "and so forth," thrown in as a rhetorical climax, turned into reality and arrived bodily upon the scene—a climax indeed. One afternoon, returning late to the cottage, he found a girl sitting by the pallet—a girl young and dimpled and dewy; one of the creamy roses of the South that, even in the bud, are richer in color and luxuriance than any Northern flower. He saw her through the door, and paused; distressed old Pomp met him and beckoned him cautiously outside. "Miss Bettina," he whispered gutturally; "she's come back from somewhuz, an' she's awful mad 'cause Mars' Ward's here. I tole her all 'bout 'em—de leaks an' de rheumatiz an' de hard corncake, but she done gone scole me; and Mars' Ward, he know now whar he is, an' he mad too."

"Is the girl a fool?" said Rodman. He was just beginning to rally a little. He stalked into the room and confronted her. "I have the honor of addressing—"

"Miss Ward."

"And I am John Rodman, keeper of the national cemetery."

This she ignored entirely; it was as though he had said, "I am John Jones, the coachman." Coachmen were useful in their way; but their names were unimportant.

The keeper sat down and looked at his new visitor. The little creature fairly radiated scorn; her pretty head was thrown back, her eyes, dark brown fringed with long dark lashes, hardly deigned a glance; she spoke to him as though he was something to be paid and dismissed like any other mechanic.

"We are indebted to you for some day's board, I believe, keeper— medicines, I presume, and general attendance. My cousin will be removed today to our own residence; I wish to pay now what he owes."

The keeper saw that her dress was old and faded; the small black shawl had evidently been washed and many times mended; the old-fashioned knitted purse she held in her hand was lank with long famine.

"Very well," he said; "if you choose to treat a kindness in that way, I consider five dollars a day none too much for the annoyance, expense, and trouble I have suffered. Let me see: five days—or is it six? Yes. Thirty dollars, Miss Ward."

He looked at her steadily; she flushed. "The money will be sent to you," she began haughtily; then, hesitatingly, "I must ask a little time—"

"O Betty, Betty, you know you cannot pay it. Why try to disguise— But that does not excuse *you* for bringing me here," said the sick man, turning toward his host with an attempt to speak fiercely, which ended in a faltering quaver.

All this time the old slave stood anxiously outside of the door; in the pauses they could hear his feet shuffling as he waited for the decision of his superiors. The keeper rose and threw open the blinds of the window that looked out on the distant parade ground. "Bringing you here," he repeated—"*here;* that is my offense, is it? There they lie, four-teen thousand brave men and true. Could they come back to earth they would be the first to pity and aid you, now that you are down. So would it be with you if the case were reversed; for a soldier is generous to a soldier. It was not your own heart that spoke then; it was the small venom of a woman, that here, as everywhere through the South, is playing its rancorous part."

The sick man gazed out through the window, seeing for the first time the far-spreading ranks of the dead. He was very weak, and the keeper's words had touched him; his eyes were suffused with tears. But Miss Ward rose with a flashing glance. She turned her back full upon the keeper and ignored his very existence. "I will take you home immediately, Ward—this very evening," she said.

"A nice, comfortable place for a sick man," commented the keeper, scornfully, "I am going out now, De Rosset, to prepare your supper; you had better have one good meal before you go."

He disappeared, but as he went he heard the sick man say, deprecatingly: "It isn't very comfortable over at the old house now, indeed it isn't, Betty; I suffered"—and the girl's passionate outburst in reply. Then he closed his door and set to work.

When he returned, half an hour later, Ward was lying back exhausted on the pillows, and his cousin sat leaning her head upon her hand; she had been weeping, and she looked very desolate, he noticed, sitting there in what was to her an enemy's country. Hunger is a strong master, however, especially when allied to weakness; and the sick man ate with eagerness.

"I must go back," said the girl, rising. "A wagon will be sent out for you, Ward; Pomp will help you."

But Ward had gained a little strength as well as obstinacy with the nourishing food. "Not tonight," he said.

"Yes, tonight."

"But I cannot go tonight; you are unreasonable, Bettina. Tomorrow will do as well, if go I must."

"If go you must! You do not want to go, then—to go to our own home—and with me"—Her voice broke; she turned toward the door.

The keeper stepped forward. "This is all nonsense, Miss Ward," he said, "and you know it. Your cousin is in no state to be moved. Wait a week or two, and he can go in safety. But do not dare to offer me your money again; my kindness was to the soldier, not to the man, and as such he can accept it. Come out and see him as often as you please. I shall not intrude upon you. Pomp, take the lady home."

And the lady went.

Then began a remarkable existence for the four: a Confederate soldier lying ill in the keeper's cottage of a national cemetery; a rampant little rebel coming out daily to a place which was to her anathemamaranatha; a cynical, misanthropic keeper sleeping on the floor and enduring every variety of discomfort for a man he never saw before— a man belonging to an idle, arrogant class he detested; and an old black freedman allowing himself to be taught the alphabet in order to gain permission to wait on his master—master no longer in law—with all

the devotion of his loving old heart. For the keeper had announced to
Pomp that he must learn his alphabet or go; after all these years of
theory, he, as a New Englander, could not stand by and see precious
knowledge shut from the black man. So he opened it, and mighty dull
work he found it.

Ward De Rosset did not rally as rapidly as they expected. The white-
haired doctor from the town rode out on horseback, pacing slowly up
the graveled roadway with a scowl on his brow, casting, as he dismounted, a furtive glance down toward the parade ground. His horse
and his coat were alike old and worn, and his broad shoulders were
bent with long service in the miserably provided Confederate hospitals,
where he had striven to do his duty through every day and every night
of those shadowed years. Cursing the incompetency in high places, cursing the mismanagement of the entire medical department of the Confederate army, cursing the recklessness and indifference which left the
men suffering for want of proper hospitals and hospital stores, he yet
went on resolutely doing his best with the poor means in his control
until the last. Then he came home, he and his old horse, and went the
rounds again, he prescribing for whooping cough or measles, and Dob-
bin waiting outside; the only difference was that fees were small and
good meals scarce for both, not only for the man but for the beast. The
doctor sat down and chatted awhile kindly with De Rosset, whose father
and uncle had been dear friends of his in the bright, prosperous days;
then he left a few harmless medicines and rose to go, his gaze resting a
moment on Miss Ward, then on Pomp, as if he were hesitating. But he
said nothing until on the walk outside he met the keeper, and recognized
a person to whom he could tell the truth. "There is nothing to be done;
he may recover, he may not; it is a question of strength merely. He
needs no medicines, only nourishing food, rest, and careful tendance."

"He shall have them," answered the keeper briefly. And then the old
gentleman mounted his horse and rode away, his first and last visit to
a national cemetery.

"National!" he said to himself—"national!"

All talk of moving De Rosset ceased, but Miss Ward moved into the
old house. There was not much to move: herself, her one trunk, and
Marí, a black attendant, whose name probably began life as Maria,
since the accent still dwelt on the curtailed last syllable. The keeper went
there once, and once only, and then it was an errand for the sick man,
whose fancies came sometimes at inconvenient hours—when Pomp had
gone to town, for instance. On this occasion the keeper entered the
mockery of a gate and knocked at the front door, from which the bars
had been removed; the piazza still showed its decaying planks, but

quick-growing summer vines had been planted, and were now encircling the old pillars and veiling all defects with their greenery. It was a woman's pathetic effort to cover up what cannot be covered—poverty. The blinds on one side were open, and white curtains waved to and fro in the breeze; into this room he was ushered by Marí. Matting lay on the floor, streaked here and there ominously by the dampness from the near ground. The furniture was of dark mahogany, handsome in its day: chairs, a heavy pier table with low-down glass, into which no one by any possibility could look unless he had eyes in his ankles, a sofa with a stiff round pillow of hair cloth under each curved end, and a mirror with a compartment framed off at the top, containing a picture of shepherds and shepherdesses, and lambs with blue ribbons around their necks, all enjoying themselves in the most natural and lifelike manner. Flowers stood on the high mantelpiece, but their fragrance could not overcome the faint odor of the damp straw-matting. On a table were books—a life of General Lee, and three or four shabby little volumes printed at the South during the war, waifs of prose and poetry of that highly wrought, richly colored style which seems indigenous to Southern soil.

"Some way, the whole thing reminds me of a funeral," thought the keeper.

Miss Ward entered, and the room bloomed at once; at least that is what a lover would have said. Rodman, however, merely noticed that she bloomed, and not the room, and he said to himself that she would not bloom long if she continued to live in such a moldy place. Their conversation in these days was excessively polite, shortened to the extreme minimum possible, and conducted without the aid of the eyes, at least on one side. Rodman had discovered that Miss Ward never looked at him, and so he did not look at her—that is, not often; he was human, however, and she was delightfully pretty. On this occasion they exchanged exactly five sentences, and then he departed, but not before his quick eyes had discovered that the rest of the house was in even worse condition than this parlor, which, by the way, Miss Ward considered quite a grand apartment; she had been down near the coast, trying to teach school, and there the desolation was far greater than here, both armies having passed back and forward over the ground, foragers out, and the torch at work more than once.

"Will there ever come a change for the better?" thought the keeper, as he walked homeward. "What an enormous stone has got to be rolled up hill! But at least, John Rodman, *you* need not go to work at it; *you* are not called upon to lend your shoulder."

Nonetheless, however, did he call out Pomp that very afternoon and sternly teach him "E" and "F," using the smooth white sand for a black-board, and a stick for chalk. Pomp's primer was a government placard hanging on the wall of the office. It read as follows:

IN THIS CEMETERY REPOSE THE REMAINS OF
FOURTEEN THOUSAND THREE HUNDRED AND TWENTY-ONE
UNITED STATES SOLDIERS.

"Tell me not in mournful numbers
Life is but an empty dream;
For the soul is dead that slumbers,
And things are not what they seem.

"Life is real! Life is earnest!
And the grave is not its goal;
Dust thou art, to dust returnest,
Was not written of the soul!"

"The only known instance of the government's condescending to poetry," the keeper had thought, when he first read this placard. It was placed there for the instruction and edification of visitors; but, no visitors coming, he took the liberty of using it as a primer for Pomp. The large letters served the purpose admirably, and Pomp learned the entire quotation; what he thought of it has not transpired. Miss Ward came over daily to see her cousin. At first she brought him soups and various concoctions from her own kitchen—the leaky cavern, once the dining room, where the soldier had taken refuge after his last dismissal from hospital; but the keeper's soups were richer, and free from the taint of smoke; his martial laws of neatness even disorderly old Pomp dared not disobey, and the sick man soon learned the difference. He thanked the girl, who came bringing the dishes over carefully in her own dimpled hands, and then, when she was gone, he sent them untasted away. By chance Miss Ward learned this, and wept bitter tears over it; she continued to come, but her poor little soups and jellies she brought no more.

One morning in May the keeper was working near the flag staff, when his eyes fell upon a procession coming down the road which led from the town and turning toward the cemetery. No one ever came that way: what could it mean? It drew near, entered the gate, and showed itself to be Negroes walking two and two—old uncles and aunties, young men and girls, and even little children, all dressed in their best; a very poor best, sometimes gravely ludicrous imitations of "ole mars' " or "ole miss'," sometimes mere rags bravely patched together and adorned with a strip of black calico or rosette of black ribbon; not one was without a badge of mourning. All carried flowers, common blossoms from the little gardens behind the cabins that stretched around the town on the outskirts—the new forlorn cabins with their chimneys of piled stones and ragged patches of corn; each little darkey had his bouquet and marched solemnly along, rolling his eyes around, but without even the beginning of a smile, while the elders moved forward with gravity, the bubbling, irrepressible gayety of the Negro subdued by the newborn dignity of the freedman.

"Memorial Day," thought the keeper; "I had forgotten it."

"Will you do us de hono', sah, to take de head ob de processio', sah?" said the leader, with a ceremonious bow. Now, the keeper had not much sympathy with the strewing of flowers, North or South; he had seen the beautiful ceremony more than once turned into a political demonstration. Here, however, in this small, isolated, interior town, there was nothing of that kind; the whole population of white faces laid their roses and wept true tears on the graves of their lost ones in the village churchyard when the Southern Memorial Day came round, and just as naturally the whole population of black faces went out to the national cemetery with their flowers on the day when, throughout the North, spring blossoms were laid on the graves of the soldiers, from the little Maine village to the stretching ranks of Arlington, from Greenwood to the far Western burial places of San Francisco. The keeper joined the procession and led the way to the parade ground. As they approached the trenches, the leader began singing and all joined. "Swing low, sweet chariot," sang the freedmen, and their hymn rose and fell with strange, sweet harmony—one of those wild, unwritten melodies which the North heard with surprise and marveling when, after the war, bands of singers came to their cities and sang the songs of slavery, in order to gain for their children the coveted education. "Swing low, sweet chariot," sang the freedmen, and two by two they passed along, strewing the graves with flowers till all the green was dotted with color. It was a pathetic sight to see some of the old men and women, ignorant field hands, bent, dull eyed, and past the possibility of education even in its simplest forms, carefully placing their poor flowers to the best advantage. They knew dimly that the men who lay beneath those mounds had done something wonderful for them and for their children; and so they came bringing their blossoms, with little intelligence but with much love.

The ceremony over, they retired. As he turned, the keeper caught a glimpse of Miss Ward's face at the window.

"Hope we's not makin' too free, sah," said the leader, as the procession, with many a bow and scrape, took leave, "but we's kep' de day now two years, sah, befo' you came, sah, an we's teachin' de chil'en to keep it, sah."

The keeper returned to the cottage. "Not a white face," he said.

"Certainly not," replied Miss Ward, crisply.

"I know some graves at the North, Miss Ward, graves of Southern soldiers, and I know some Northern women who do not scorn to lay a few flowers on the lonely mounds as they pass by with their blossoms on our Memorial Day."

"You are fortunate. They must be angels. We have no angels here."

"I am inclined to believe you are right," said the keeper.

That night old Pomp, who had remained invisible in the kitchen during the ceremony, stole away in the twilight and came back with a few flowers. Rodman saw him going down toward the parade ground, and watched. The old man had but a few blossoms; he arranged them hastily on the mounds with many a furtive glance toward the house, and then stole back, satisfied; he had performed his part.

Ward De Rosset lay on his pallet, apparently unchanged; he seemed neither stronger nor weaker. He had grown childishly dependent upon his host, and wearied for him, as the Scotch say; but Rodman withstood his fancies, and gave him only the evenings, when Miss Bettina was not there. One afternoon, however, it rained so violently that he was forced to seek shelter; he set himself to work on the ledgers; he was on the ninth thousand now. But the sick man heard his step in the outer room, and called in his weak voice, "Rodman, Rodman." After a time he went in, and it ended in his staying; for the patient was nervous and irritable, and he pitied the nurse, who seemed able to please him in nothing. De Rosset turned with a sigh of relief toward the strong hands that lifted him readily, toward the composed manner, toward the man's voice that seemed to bring a breeze from outside into the close room; animated, cheered, he talked volubly. The keeper listened, answered once in a while, and quietly took the rest of the afternoon into his own hands. Miss Ward yielded to the silent change, leaned back, and closed her eyes. She looked exhausted and for the first time pallid; the loosened dark hair curled in little rings about her temples, and her lips were parted as though she was too tired to close them; for hers were not the thin, straight lips that shut tight naturally, like the straight line of a closed box. The sick man talked on. "Come, Rodman," he said, after a while, "I have read that lying verse of yours over at least ten thousand and fifty-nine times; please tell me its history; I want to have something definite to think of when I read it for the ten thousand and sixtieth."

> *"Toujours femme varie,*
> *Bien fou qui s'y fie;*

> *Une femme souvent*
> *N'est qu'une plume au vent,"*

read the keeper slowly, with his execrable English accent. "Well, I don't know that I have any objection to telling the story. I am not sure but that it will do me good to hear it all over myself in plain language again."

"Then it concerns yourself," said De Rosset; "so much the better. I hope it will be, as the children say, the truth, and long."

"It will be the truth, but not long. When the war broke out I was twenty-eight years old, living with my mother on our farm in New England. My father and two brothers had died and left me the homestead; otherwise I should have broken away and sought fortune farther westward, where the lands are better and life is more free. But mother loved the house, the fields, and every crooked tree. She was alone, and so I stayed with her. In the center of the village green stood the square, white meeting-house, and near by the small cottage where the pastor lived; the minister's daughter, Mary, was my promised wife. Mary was a slender little creature with a profusion of pale flaxen hair, large, serious blue eyes, and small, delicate features; she was timid almost to a fault; her voice was low and gentle. She was not eighteen, and we were to wait a year. The war came, and I volunteered, of course, and marched away; we wrote to each other often; my letters were full of the camp and skirmishes; hers told of the village, how the widow Brown had fallen ill, and how it was feared that Squire Stafford's boys were lapsing into evil ways. Then came the day when my regiment marched to the field of its slaughter, and soon after our shattered remnant went home. Mary cried over me, and came out every day to the farmhouse with her bunches of violets; she read aloud to me from her good little books, and I used to lie and watch her profile bending over the page, with the light falling on her flaxen hair low down against the small, white throat. Then my wound healed, and I went again, this time for three years; and Mary's father blessed me, and said that when peace came he would call me son, but not before, for these were no times for marrying or giving in marriage. He was a good man, a red-hot abolitionist, and a roaring lion as regards temperance; but nature had made him so small in body that no one was much frightened when he roared. I said that I went for three years; but eight years have passed and I have never been back to the village. First, mother died. Then Mary turned false. I sold the farm by letter and lost the money three months afterward in an unfortunate investment; my health failed. Like many another Northern soldier, I remembered the healing climate of the South; its soft airs came back to me when the snow lay deep on the fields and the sharp wind whistled around the poor tavern where the moneyless, half-crippled volunteer sat coughing by the fire. I applied for this place and obtained it. That is all."

"But it is not all," said the sick man, raising himself on his elbow; "you have not told half yet, nor anything at all about the French verse."

"Oh—that? There was a little Frenchman staying at the hotel; he had formerly been a dancing master, and was full of dry, withered conceits, although he looked like a thin and bilious old ape dressed as a man. He taught me, or tried to teach me, various wise saying, among them this one, which pleased my fancy so much that I gave him twenty-five cents to write it out in large text for me."

"Toujours femme varie," repeated De Rosset; "but you don't really think so, do you, Rodman?"

"I do. But they cannot help it; it is their nature. I beg your pardon, Miss Ward. I was speaking as though you were not here."

Miss Ward's eyelids barely acknowledged his existence; that was all. But some time after she remarked to her cousin that it was only in New England that one found that pale flaxen hair.

June was waning, when suddenly the summons came. Ward De Rosset died. He was unconscious toward the last, and death, in the guise of sleep, bore away his soul. They carried him home to the old house, and from there the funeral started, a few family carriages, dingy and battered, following the hearse, for death revived the old neighborhood feeling; that honor at least they could pay—the sonless mothers and the widows who lived shut up in the old houses with everything falling into ruin around them, brooding over the past. The keeper watched the small procession as it passed his gate on its way to the churchyard in the village. "There he goes, poor fellow, his sufferings over at last," he said; and then he set the cottage in order and began the old solitary life again.

He saw Miss Ward but once.

It was a breathless evening in August, when the moonlight flooded the level country. He had started out to stroll across the waste; but the mood changed, and climbing over the eastern wall he had walked back to the flag staff, and now lay at its foot gazing up into the infinite sky. A step sounded on the gravel walk; he turned his face that way, and recognized Miss Ward. With confident step she passed the dark cottage, and brushed his arm with her robe as he lay unseen in the shadow. She went down toward the parade ground, and his eyes followed her. Softly outlined in the moonlight, she moved to and fro among the mounds, pausing often, and once he thought she knelt. Then slowly she returned, and he raised himself and waited; she saw him, started, then paused.

"I thought you were away," she said; "Pomp told me so."

"You set him to watch me?"

"Yes. I wished to come here once, and I did not wish to meet you."

"Why did you wish to come?"

"Because Ward was here—and because—because—never mind. It is enough that I wished to walk once among those mounds."

"And pray there?"

"Well—and if I did!" said the girl defiantly.

Rodman stood facing her, with his arms folded; his eyes rested on her face; he said nothing.

"I am going away tomorrow," began Miss Ward again assuming with an effort her old, pulseless manner. "I have sold the place, and I shall never return, I think; I am going far away."

"Where?"

"To Tennessee."

"That is not so very far," said the keeper, smiling.

"There I shall begin a new existence," pursued the voice, ignoring the comment.

"You have scarcely begun the old; you are hardly more than a child, now. What are you going to do in Tennessee?"

"Teach."

"Have you relatives there?"

"No."

"A miserable life—a hard, lonely, loveless life," said Rodman. "God help the woman who must be that dreary thing, a teacher from necessity!"

Miss Ward turned swiftly, but the keeper kept by her side. He saw the tears glittering on her eyelashes, and his voice softened. "Do not leave me in anger," he said; "I should not have spoken so, although indeed it was the truth. Walk back with me to the cottage, and take your last look at the room where poor Ward died, and then I will go with you to your home."

"No; Pomp is waiting at the gate," said the girl, almost inarticulately.

"Very well; to the gate, then."

They went toward the cottage in silence; the keeper threw open the door. "Go in," he said. "I will wait outside."

The girl entered and went into the inner room, throwing herself down upon her knees at the bedside. "O Ward, Ward!" she sobbed; "I am all alone in the world now, Ward—all alone!" She buried her face in her hands and gave way to a passion of tears; and the keeper could not help but hear as he waited outside. Then the desolate little creature rose and came forth, putting on, as she did so, her poor armor of pride. The keeper had not moved from the doorstep. Now he turned his face. "Before you go—go away for ever from this place—will you write your name in my register," he said—"the visitors' register? The government had it prepared for the throngs who would visit these graves; but with the exception of the blacks, who cannot write, no one has come, and the register is empty. Will you write your name? Yet do not write it unless you can think gently of the men who lie there under the grass. I believe you do think gently of them, else why have you come of your own accord to stand by the side of their graves?" As he said this, he looked fixedly at her.

Miss Ward did not answer; but neither did she write.

"Very well," said the keeper; "come away. You will not, I see."

"I cannot! Shall I, Bettina Ward, set my name down in black and white as a visitor to this cemetery, where lie fourteen thousand of the soldiers who killed my father, my three brothers, my cousins; who brought desolation upon all our house, and ruin upon all our neighborhood, all our state, and all our country?—for the South *is* our country, and not your North. Shall I forget these things? Never! Sooner let my right hand wither by my side! I was but a child; yet I remember the tears of my mother, and the grief of all around us. There was not a house where there was not one dead."

"It is true," answered the keeper; "at the South, all went."

They walked down to the gate together in silence.

"Good-by," said John, holding out his hand; "you will give me yours or not as you choose, but I will not have it as a favor."

She gave it.

"I hope that life will grow brighter to you as the years pass. May God bless you!"

He dropped her hand; she turned, and passed through the gateway; then he sprang after her.

"Nothing can change you," he said; "I know it, I have known it all along; you are part of your country, part of the time, part of the bitter hour through which she is passing. Nothing can change you; if it could, you would not be what you are, and I should not—But you cannot change. Good-by, Bettina, poor little child—good-by. Follow your path out into the world. Yet do not think, dear, that I have not seen—have not understood."

He bent and kissed her hand; then he was gone, and she went on alone.

A week later the keeper strolled over toward the old house. It was twilight, but the new owner was still at work. He was one of those sandy-haired, energetic Maine men, who, probably on the principle of extremes, were often found through the South, making new homes for themselves in the pleasant land.

"Pulling down the old house, are you?" said the keeper, leaning idly on the gate, which was already flanked by a new fence.

"Yes," replied the Maine man, pausing; "it was only an old shell, just ready to tumble on our heads. You're the keeper over yonder, an't you?" (He already knew everybody within a circle of five miles.)

"Yes. I think I should like those vines if you have no use for them," said Rodman, pointing to the uprooted greenery that once screened the old piazza.

"Wuth about twenty-five cents, I guess," said the Maine man, handing them over.

SARAH ORNE JEWETT

A White Heron

In 1886, Sarah Orne Jewett joined the board of directors of the Massachusetts Audubon Society, a group devoted to saving the white heron, which had declined in population because fashionable ladies were wearing feathers in their hats. Related to this experience is one of her most notable short stories, "A White Heron," which portrays a young girl, Sylvia, caught between her desire to ingratiate herself to a handsome young man and her allegiance to the nature she loves. In her final decision, she confirms the deeper loyalty and in the process achieves a more mature knowledge of herself and nature than she had previously known. The story also reveals the historical conflicts between burgeoning industrialization and simple agrarian values and between male and female approaches to nature. Although the story has been faulted for its shifts in point of view, it has found a place in American literary history for the significance of its theme and for its demonstration of Jewett's skill in depicting the people and landscape of her beloved New England.

*   *   *

I.

The woods were already filled with shadows one June evening, just before eight o'clock, though a bright sunset still glimmered faintly among the trunks of the trees. A little girl was driving home her cow, a plodding, dilatory, provoking creature in her behavior, but a valued companion for all that. They were going away from whatever light there was, and striking deep into the woods, but their feet were familiar with the path, and it was no matter whether their eyes could see it or not.

There was hardly a night the summer through when the old cow could be found waiting at the pasture bars; on the contrary, it was her greatest pleasure to hide herself away among the huckleberry bushes, and though she wore a loud bell she had made the discovery that if one stood perfectly still it would not ring. So Sylvia had to hunt for her until she found her, and call Co'! Co'! with never an answering Moo, until her childish patience was quite spent. If the creature had not given good milk and plenty of it, the case would have seemed very different to her owners. Besides, Sylvia had all the time there was, and very little use to make of it. Sometimes in pleasant weather it was a consolation to look upon the cow's pranks as an intelligent attempt to play hide and seek, and as the child had no playmates she lent herself to this amusement with a good deal of zest. Though this chase had been so long that the wary animal herself had given an unusual signal of her whereabouts, Sylvia had only laughed when she came upon Mistress Moolly at the swamp-side, and urged her affectionately homeward with a twig of birch leaves. The old cow was not inclined to wander farther, she even turned in the right direction for once as they left the pasture, and stepped along the road at a good pace. She was quite ready to be milked now, and seldom stopped to browse. Sylvia wondered what her grandmother would say because they were so late. It was a great while since she had left home at half-past five o'clock, but everybody knew the difficulty of making this errand a short one. Mrs. Tilley had chased the hornéd torment too many summer evenings herself to blame any one else for lingering, and was only thankful as she waited that she had Sylvia, nowadays, to give such valuable assistance. The good woman suspected that Sylvia loitered occasionally on her own account; there never was such a child for straying about out-of-doors since the world was made! Everybody said that it was a good change for a little maid who had tried to grow for eight years in a crowded manufacturing town, but, as for Sylvia herself, it seemed as if she never had been alive at all before she came to live at the farm. She thought often with wistful compassion of a wretched geranium that belonged to a town neighbor.

" 'Afraid of folks,' " old Mrs. Tilley said to herself, with a smile, after she had made the unlikely choice of Sylvia from her daughter's houseful of children, and was returning to the farm. " 'Afraid of folks,' they said! I guess she won't be troubled no great with 'em up to the old place!" When they reached the door of the lonely house and stopped to unlock it, and the cat came to purr loudly, and rub against them, a deserted pussy, indeed, but fat with young robins, Sylvia whispered that this was a beautiful place to live in, and she never should wish to go home.

The companions followed the shady wood-road, the cow taking slow steps and the child very fast ones. The cow stopped long at the brook to drink, as if the pasture were not half a swamp, and Sylvia stood still and waited, letting her bare feet cool themselves in the shoal water, while the great twilight moths struck softly against her. She waded on through the brook as the cow moved away, and listened to the thrushes with a heart that beat fast with pleasure. There was a stirring in the great boughs overhead. They were full of little birds and beasts that seemed to be wide awake, and going about their world, or else saying good-night to each other in sleepy twitters. Sylvia herself felt sleepy as she walked along. However, it was not much farther to the house, and the air was soft and sweet. She was not often in the woods so late as this, and it made her feel as if she were a part of the gray shadows and the moving leaves. She was just thinking how long it seemed since she first came to the farm a year ago, and wondering if everything went on in the noisy town just the same as when she was there; the thought of the great red-faced boy who used to chase and frighten her made her hurry along the path to escape from the shadow of the trees.

Suddenly this little woods-girl is horror-stricken to hear a clear whistle not very far away. Not a bird's-whistle, which would have a sort of friendliness, but a boy's whistle, determined, and somewhat aggressive. Sylvia left the cow to whatever sad fate might await her, and stepped discreetly aside into the brushes, but she was just too late. The enemy had discovered her, and called out in a very cheerful and persuasive tone, "Halloa, little girl, how far is it to the road?" and trembling Sylvia answered almost inaudibly, "A good ways."

She did not dare to look boldly at the tall young man, who carried a gun over his shoulder, but she came out of her bush and again followed the cow, while he walked alongside.

"I have been hunting for some birds," the stranger said kindly, "and I have lost my way, and need a friend very much. Don't be afraid," he added gallantly. "Speak up and tell me what your name is, and whether you think I can spend the night at your house, and go out gunning early in the morning."

Sylvia was more alarmed than before. Would not her grandmother consider her much to blame? But who could have foreseen such an accident as this? It did not seem to be her fault, and she hung her head as if the stem of it were broken, but managed to answer "Sylvy," with much effort when her companion again asked her name.

Mrs. Tilley was standing in the doorway when the trio came into view. The cow gave a loud moo by way of explanation.

"Yes, you'd better speak up for yourself, you old trial! Where'd she tucked herself away this time, Sylvy?" But Sylvia kept an awed silence; she knew by instinct that her grandmother did not comprehend the gravity of the situation. She must be mistaking the stranger for one of the farmer-lads of the region.

The young man stood his gun beside the door, and dropped a lumpy game-bag beside it; then he bade Mrs. Tilley good-evening, and repeated his wayfarer's story, and asked if he could have a night's lodging.

"Put me anywhere you like," he said. "I must be off early in the morning, before day; but I am very hungry, indeed. You can give me some milk at any rate, that's plain."

"Dear sakes, yes," responded the hostess, whose long slumbering hospitality seemed to be easily awakened. "You might fare better if you went out to the main road a mile or so, but you're welcome to what we've got. I'll milk right off, and you make yourself at home. You can sleep on husks or feathers," she proffered graciously. "I raised them all myself. There's good pasturing for geese just below here towards the ma'sh. Now step round and set a plate for the gentleman, Sylvy!" And Sylvia promptly stepped. She was glad to have something to do, and she was hungry herself.

It was a surprise to find so clean and comfortable a little dwelling in this New England wilderness. The young man had known the horrors of its most primitive housekeeping, and the dreary squalor of that level of society which does not rebel at the companionship of hens. This was the best thrift of an old-fashioned farmstead, though on such a small scale that it seemed like a hermitage. He listened eagerly to the old woman's quaint talk, he watched Sylvia's pale face and shining gray eyes with ever growing enthusiasm, and insisted that this was the best supper he had eaten for a month, and afterward the new-made friends sat down in the door-way together while the moon came up.

Soon it would be berry-time, and Sylvia was a great help at picking. The cow was a good milker, though a plaguy thing to keep track of, the hostess gossiped frankly, adding presently that she had buried four children, so Sylvia's mother, and a son (who might be dead) in California were all the children she had left. "Dan, my boy, was a great hand to go gunning," she explained sadly. "I never wanted for pa'tridges or gray squer'ls while he was to home. He's been a great wand'rer, I expect, and he's no hand to write letters. There, I don't blame him, I'd ha' seen the world myself if it had been so I could."

"Sylvy takes after him," the grandmother continued affectionately, after a minute's pause. "There ain't a foot o' ground she don't know her way over, and the wild creatures counts her one o' themselves. Squer'ls she'll tame to come an' feed right out o' her hands, and all sorts o' birds. Last winter she got the jay-birds to bangeing here, and I believe she'd 'a' scanted herself of her own meals to have plenty to throw out amongst 'em, if I had n't kep' watch. Anything but crows, I tell her, I'm willin' to help support—though Dan he had a tamed one o' them that did seem to have reason same as folks. It was round here a good spell after he went away. Dan an' his father they did n't hitch,—but he never held up his head ag'in after Dan had dared him an' gone off."

The guest did not notice this hint of family sorrows in his eager interest in something else.

"So Sylvy knows all about birds, does she?" he exclaimed, as he looked round at the little girl who sat, very demure but increasingly sleepy, in the moonlight. "I am making a collection of birds myself. I have been at it ever since I was a boy." (Mrs. Tilley smiled.) "There are two or three very rare ones I have been hunting for these five years. I mean to get them on my own ground if they can be found."

"Do you cage 'em up?" asked Mrs. Tilley doubtfully, in response to this enthusiastic announcement.

"Oh no, they're stuffed and preserved, dozens and dozens of them," said the ornithologist, "and I have shot or snared every one myself. I caught a glimpse of a white heron a few miles from here on Saturday, and I have followed it in this direction. They have never been found in this district at all. The little white heron, it is," and he turned again to look at Sylvia with the hope of discovering that the rare bird was one of her acquaintances.

But Sylvia was watching a hop-toad in the narrow footpath.

"You would know the heron if you saw it," the stranger continued eagerly. "A queer tall white bird with soft feathers and long thin legs. And it would have a nest perhaps in the top of a high tree, made of sticks, something like a hawk's nest."

Sylvia's heart gave a wild beat; she knew that strange white bird, and had once stolen softly near where it stood in some bright green swamp grass, away over at the other side of the woods. There was an open place where the sunshine always seemed strangely yellow and hot, where tall, nodding rushes grew, and her grandmother had warned her that she might sink in the soft black mud underneath and never be heard of more. Not far beyond were the salt marshes just this side the sea itself, which Sylvia wondered and dreamed much about, but never had seen, whose great voice could sometimes be heard above the noise of the woods on stormy nights.

"I can't think of anything I should like so much as to find that heron's nest," the handsome stranger was saying. "I would give ten dollars to anybody who could show it to me," he added desperately, "and I mean to spend my whole vacation hunting for it if need be. Perhaps it was only migrating, or had been chased out of its own region by some bird of prey."

Mrs. Tilley gave amazed attention to all this, but Sylvia still watched the toad, not divining, as she might have done at some calmer time, that the creature wished to get to its hole under the door-step, and was much hindered by the unusual spectators at that hour of the evening. No amount of thought, that night, could decide how many wished-for treasures the ten dollars, so lightly spoken of, would buy.

The next day the young sportsman hovered about the woods, and Sylvia kept him company, having lost her first fear of the friendly lad, who proved to be most kind and sympathetic. He told her many things about the birds and what they knew and where they lived and what they did with themselves. And he gave her a jack-knife, which she thought as great a treasure as if she were a desert-islander. All day long he did not once make her troubled or afraid except when he brought down some unsuspecting singing creature from its bough. Sylvia would have liked him vastly better without his gun; she could not understand why he killed the very birds he seemed to like so much. But as the day waned, Sylvia still watched the young man with loving admiration. She had never seen anybody so charming and delightful; the woman's heart, asleep in the child, was vaguely thrilled by a dream of love. Some premonition of that great power stirred and swayed these young creatures who traversed the solemn woodlands with soft-footed silent care. They stopped to listen to a bird's song; they pressed forward again eagerly, parting the branches—speaking to each other rarely and in whispers; the young man going first and Sylvia following, fascinated, a few steps behind, with her gray eyes dark with excitement.

She grieved because the longed-for white heron was elusive, but she did not lead the guest, she only followed, and there was no such thing as speaking first. The sound of her own unquestioned voice would have terrified her—it was hard enough to answer yes or no when there was need of that. At last evening began to fall, and they drove the cow home together, and Sylvia smiled with pleasure when they came to the place where she heard the whistle and was afraid only the night before.

II.

Half a mile from home, at the farther edge of the woods, where the land was highest, a great pine-tree stood, the last of its generation.

Whether it was left for a boundary mark, or for what reason, no one
could say; the wood-choppers who had felled its mates were dead and
gone long ago, and a whole forest of sturdy trees, pines and oaks and
maples, had grown again. But the stately head of this old pine towered
above them all and made a landmark for sea and shore miles and miles
away. Sylvia knew it well. She had always believed that whoever
climbed to the top of it could see the ocean; and the little girl had often
laid her hand on the great rough trunk and looked up wistfully at those
dark boughs that the wind always stirred, no matter how hot and still
the air might be below. Now she thought of the tree with a new excitement, for why, if one climbed it at break of day could not one see
all the world, and easily discover from whence the white heron flew,
and mark the place, and find the hidden nest?

What a spirit of adventure, what wild ambition! What fancied triumph and delight and glory for the later morning when she could make
known the secret! It was almost too real and too great for the childish
heart to bear.

All night the door of the little house stood open and the whippoor-
wills came and sang upon the very step. The young sportsman and his
old hostess were sound asleep, but Sylvia's great design kept her broad
awake and watching. She forgot to think of sleep. The short summer
night seemed as long as the winter darkness, and at last when the whip-
poorwills ceased, and she was afraid the morning would after all come
too soon, she stole out of the house and followed the pasture path
through the woods, hastening toward the open ground beyond, listening
with a sense of comfort and companionship to the drowsy twitter of a
half-awakened bird, whose perch she had jarred in passing. Alas, if the
great wave of human interest which flooded for the first time this dull
little life should sweep away the satisfactions of an existence heart to
heart with nature and the dumb life of the forest!

There was the huge tree asleep yet in the paling moonlight, and small
and silly Sylvia began with utmost bravery to mount to the top of it,
with tingling, eager blood coursing the channels of her whole frame,
with her bare feet and fingers, that pinched and held like bird's claws
to the monstrous ladder reaching up, up, almost to the sky itself. First
she must mount the white oak tree that grew alongside, where she was
almost lost among the dark branches and the green leaves heavy and
wet with dew; a bird fluttered off its nest, and a red squirrel ran to and
fro and scolded pettishly at the harmless housebreaker. Sylvia felt her
way easily. She had often climbed there, and knew that higher still one
of the oak's upper branches chafed against the pine trunk, just where
its lower boughs were set close together. There, when she made the

dangerous pass from one tree to the other, the great enterprise would really begin.

She crept out along the swaying oak limb at last, and took the daring step across into the old pine-tree. The way was harder than she thought; she must reach far and hold fast, the sharp dry twigs caught and held her and scratched her like angry talons, the pitch made her thin little fingers clumsy and stiff as she went round and round the tree's great stem, higher and higher upward. The sparrows and robins in the woods below were beginning to wake and twitter to the dawn, yet it seemed much lighter there aloft in the pine-tree, and the child knew she must hurry if her project were to be of any use.

The tree seemed to lengthen itself out as she went up, and to reach farther and farther upward. It was like a great main-mast to the voyaging earth; it must truly have been amazed that morning through all its ponderous frame as it felt this determined spark of human spirit wending its way from higher branch to branch. Who knows how steadily the least twigs held themselves to advantage this light, weak creature on her way! The old pine must have loved his new dependent. More than all the hawks, and bats, and moths, and even the sweet voiced thrushes, was the brave, beating heart of the solitary gray-eyed child. And the tree stood still and frowned away the winds that June morning while the dawn grew bright in the east.

Sylvia's face was like a pale star, if one had seen it from the ground, when the last thorny bough was past, and she stood trembling and tired but wholly triumphant, high in the treetop. Yes, there was the sea with the dawning sun making a golden dazzle over it, and toward that glorious east flew two hawks with slow-moving pinions. How low they looked in the air from that height when one had only seen them before far up, and dark against the blue sky. Their gray feathers were as soft as moths; they seemed only a little way from the tree, and Sylvia felt as if she too could go flying away among the clouds. Westward, the woodlands and farms reached miles and miles into the distance; here and there were church steeples, and white villages, truly it was a vast and awesome world!

The birds sang louder and louder. At last the sun came up bewilderingly bright. Sylvia could see the white sails of ships out at sea, and the clouds that were purple and rose-colored and yellow at first began to fade away. Where was the white heron's nest in the sea of green branches, and was this wonderful sight and pageant of the world the only reward for having climbed to such a giddy height? Now look down again, Sylvia, where the green marsh is set among the shining birches and dark hemlocks; there where you saw the white heron once you will see him again; look, look! a white spot of him like a single floating feather comes up from the dead hemlock and grows larger, and rises, and comes close at last, and goes by the landmark pine with steady sweep of wing and outstretched slender neck and crested head. And wait! wait! do not move a foot or a finger, little girl, do not send an arrow of light and consciousness from your two eager eyes, for the heron has perched on a pine bough not far beyond yours, and cries back to his mate on the nest and plumes his feathers for the new day!

The child gives a long sigh a minute later when a company of shouting cat-birds comes also to the tree, and vexed by their fluttering and lawlessness the solemn heron goes away. She knows his secret now, the wild, light, slender bird that floats and wavers, and goes back like an arrow presently to his home in the green world beneath. Then Sylvia, well satisfied, makes her perilous way down again, not daring to look far below the branch she stands on, ready to cry sometimes because her fingers ache and her lamed feet slip. Wondering over and over again what the stranger would say to her, and what he would think when she told him how to find his way straight to the heron's nest.

"Sylvy, Sylvy!" called the busy old grandmother again and again, but nobody answered, and the small husk bed was empty and Sylvia had disappeared.

The guest waked from a dream, and remembering his day's pleasure hurried to dress himself that might it sooner begin. He was sure from the way the shy little girl looked once or twice yesterday that she had at least seen the white heron, and now she must really be made to tell. Here she comes now, paler than ever, and her worn old frock is torn and tattered, and smeared with pine pitch. The grandmother and the sportsman stand in the door together and question her, and the splendid moment has come to speak of the dead hemlock-tree by the green marsh.

But Sylvia does not speak after all, though the old grandmother fretfully rebukes her, and the young man's kind, appealing eyes are looking straight in her own. He can make them rich with money; he has promised it, and they are poor now. He is so well worth making happy, and he waits to hear the story she can tell.

No, she must keep silence! What is it that suddenly forbids her and makes her dumb? Has she been nine years growing and now, when the great world for the first time puts out a hand to her, must she thrust it aside for a bird's sake? The murmur of the pine's green branches is in her ears, she remembers how the white heron came flying through the golden air and how they watched the sea and the morning together, and

Sylvia cannot speak; she cannot tell the heron's secret and give its life away.

Dear loyalty, that suffered a sharp pang as the guest went away disappointed later in the day, that could have served and followed him and loved him as a dog loves! Many a night Sylvia heard the echo of his whistle haunting the pasture path as she came home with the loitering cow. She forgot even her sorrow at the sharp report of his gun and the sight of thrushes and sparrows dropping silent to the ground, their songs hushed and their pretty feathers stained and wet with blood. Were the birds better friends than their hunter might have been,—who can tell? Whatever treasures were lost to her, woodlands and summertime, remember! Bring your gifts and graces and tell your secrets to this lonely country child!

MARY WILKINS FREEMAN

A Church Mouse

"A Church Mouse," one of Freeman's most frequently discussed stories from *A New England Nun and Other Stories* (1891), is typical of her fiction in portraying a woman in conflict with the restrictive traditions of her time, finding within herself, and within a community of other women, the strength to persevere and bring change to society. Freeman's stories usually focus on a strong central plot and feature strong female characters who assert their personal integrity at a moment of crisis. Writing within the local-color tradition, Freeman also emphasized regional dialects and traditions, deftly etched settings, and the poverty of rural New England. In "A Church Mouse" Hetty Fifield upsets historic gender roles by insisting on becoming the church sexton, a startling innovation in this conservative rural community, and she complicates matters by moving into the church itself, lacking anywhere else to live. Overcoming doubts that she can perform the duties of the position, she finally enlists the support of women of the community through a poignant speech to the congregation. There is pathos and humor in this tale of the resourcefulness and humanity of a simple village woman whose determination transforms her life and that of the entire community.

*   *   *

"I never heard of a woman's bein' saxton."

"I dun' know what difference that makes; I don't see why they shouldn't have women saxtons as well as men saxtons, for my part, nor nobody else neither. They'd keep dusted 'nough sight cleaner. I've seen the dust layin' on my pew thick enough to write my name in a good many times, an' ain't said nothin' about it. An' I ain't goin' to say nothin' now again Joe Sowen, now he's dead an' gone. He did jest as well as most men do. Men git in a good many places where they don't belong, an' where they set as awkward as a cow on a hen-roost, jest because they push in ahead of women. I ain't blamin' 'em; I s'pose if I could push in I should, jest the same way. But there ain't no reason that I can see, nor nobody else neither, why a woman shouldn't be saxton."

Hetty Fifield stood in the rowen hay-field before Caleb Gale. He was a deacon, the chairman of the selectmen, and the rich and influential man of the village. One looking at him would not have guessed it. There was nothing imposing about his lumbering figure in his calico shirt and baggy trousers. However, his large face, red and moist with perspiration, scanned the distant horizon with a stiff and reserved air; he did not look at Hetty.

"How'd you go to work to ring the bell?" said he. "It would have to be tolled, too, if anybody died."

"I'd jest as lief ring that little meetin'-house bell as to stan' out here an' jingle a cow-bell," said Hetty; "an' as for tollin', I'd jest as soon toll the bell for Methusaleh, if he was livin' here! I'd laugh if I ain't got strength 'nough for that."

"It takes a kind of knack."

"If I ain't got as much knack as old Joe Sowen ever had, I'll give up the ship."

"You couldn't tend the fires."

"Couldn't tend the fires—when I've cut an' carried in all the wood I've burned for forty year! Couldn't keep the fires a-goin' in them two little wood-stoves!"

"It's consider'ble work to sweep the meetin'-house."

"I guess I've done 'bout as much work as to sweep that little meetin'-house, I ruther guess I have."

"There's one thing you ain't thought of."

"What's that?"

"Where'd you live? All old Sowen got for bein' saxton was twenty dollar a year, an' we couldn't pay a woman so much as that. You wouldn't have enough to pay for your livin' anywheres."

"Where am I goin' to live whether I'm saxton or not?"

Caleb Gale was silent.

There was a wind blowing, the rowen hay drifted round Hetty like a brown-green sea touched with ripples of blue and gold by the asters and golden-rod. She stood in the midst of it like a May-weed that had gathered a slender toughness through the long summer; her brown cotton gown clung about her like a wilting leaf, outlining her harsh little form. She was as sallow as a squaw, and she had pretty black eyes; they were bright, although she was old. She kept them fixed upon Caleb. Suddenly she raised herself upon her toes; the wind caught her dress and made it blow out; her eyes flashed. "I'll tell you where I'm goin' to live," said she. *"I'm goin' to live in the meetin'-house."*

Caleb looked at her. *"Goin' to live in the meetin'-house!"*

"Yes, I be."

"Live in the meetin'-house!"

"I'd like to know why not."

"Why—you couldn't—live in the meetin'-house. You're crazy."

Caleb flung out the rake which he was holding, and drew it in full of rowen. Hetty moved around in front of him, he raked imperturbably; she moved again right in the path of the rake, then he stopped. "There ain't no sense in such talk."

"All I want is jest the east corner of the back gall'ry, where the chimbly goes up. I'll set up my cookin'-stove there, an' my bed, an' I'll curtain it off with my sunflower quilt, to keep off the wind."

"A cookin'-stove an' a bed in the meetin'-house!"

"Mis' Grout she give me that cookin'-stove, an' that bed I've allers slept on, before she died. She give 'em to me before Mary Anne Thomas, an' I moved 'em out. They air settin' out in the yard now, an' if it rains that stove an' that bed will be spoilt. It looks some like rain now. I guess you'd better give me the meetin'-house key right off."

"You don't think you can move that cookin'-stove an' that bed into the meetin'-house—I ain't goin' to stop to hear such talk."

"My worsted-work, all my mottoes I've done, an' my wool flowers, air out there in the yard."

Caleb raked. Hetty kept standing herself about until he was forced to stop, or gather her in with the rowen hay. He looked straight at her, and scowled; the perspiration trickled down his cheeks. "If I go up to the house can Mis' Gale git me the key to the meetin'-house?" said Hetty.

"No, she can't."

"Be you goin' up before long?"

"No, I ain't." Suddenly Caleb's voice changed: it had been full of stubborn vexation, now it was blandly argumentative. "Don't you see it ain't no use talkin' such nonsense, Hetty? You'd better go right along, an' make up your mind it ain't to be thought of."

"Where be I goin' to-night, then?"

"To-night?"

"Yes; where be I a-goin'?"

"Ain't you got any place to go to?"

"Where do you s'pose I've got any place? Them folks air movin' into Mis' Grout's house, an' they as good as told me to clear out. I ain't got no folks to take me in. I dun' know where I'm goin'; mebbe I can go to your house?"

Caleb gave a start. "We've got company to home," said he, hastily. "I'm 'fraid Mis' Gale wouldn't think it was convenient."

Hetty laughed. "Most everybody in the town has got company," said she.

Caleb dug his rake into the ground as if it were a hoe, then he leaned on it, and stared at the horizon. There was a fringe of yellow birches on the edge of the hay-field; beyond them was a low range of misty blue hills. "You ain't got no place to go to, then?"

"I dun' know of any. There ain't no poor-house here, an' I ain't got no folks."

Caleb stood like a statue. Some crows flew cawing over the field. Hetty waited. "I s'pose that key is where Mis' Gale can find it?" she said, finally.

Caleb turned and threw out his rake with a jerk. "She knows where 'tis; it's hangin' up behind the settin'-room door. I s'pose you can stay there to-night, as long as you ain't got no other place. We shall have to see what can be done."

Hetty scuttled off across the field. "You mustn't take no stove nor bed into the meetin'-house," Caleb called after her; "we can't have that, nohow."

Hetty went on as if she did not hear.

The golden-rod at the sides of the road was turning brown; the asters were in their prime, blue and white ones; here and there were rows of thistles with white tops. The dust was thick; Hetty, when she emerged from Caleb's house, trotted along in a cloud of it. She did not look to the right or left, she kept her small eager face fixed straight ahead, and moved forward like some little animal with the purpose to which it was born strong within it.

Presently she came to a large cottage-house on the right of the road; there she stopped. The front yard was full of furniture, tables and chairs standing among the dahlias and clumps of marigolds. Hetty leaned over the fence at one corner of the yard, and inspected a little knot of household goods set aside from the others. There were a small cooking-stove, a hair trunk, a yellow bedstead stacked up against the fence, and a pile of bedding. Some children in the yard stood in a group and eyed Hetty.

A woman appeared in the door—she was small, there was a black smutch on her face, which was haggard with fatigue, and she scowled in the sun as she looked over at Hetty. "Well, got a place to stay in?" said she, in an unexpectedly deep voice.

"Yes, I guess so," replied Hetty.

"I dun' know how in the world I can have you. All the beds will be full—I expect his mother some to-night, an' I'm dreadful stirred up anyhow."

"Everybody's havin' company; I never see anything like it." Hetty's voice was inscrutable. The other woman looked sharply at her.

"You've got a place, ain't you?" she asked, doubtfully.

"Yes, I have."

At the left of this house, quite back from the road, was a little unpainted cottage, hardly more than a hut. There was smoke coming out of the chimney, and a tall youth lounged in the door. Hetty, with the woman and children staring after her, struck out across the field in the little footpath towards the cottage. "I wonder if she's goin' to stay there?" the woman muttered, meditating.

The youth did not see Hetty until she was quite near him, then he aroused suddenly as if from sleep, and tried to slink off around the cottage. But Hetty called after him. "Sammy," she cried, "Sammy, come back here, I want you!"

"What d'ye want?"

"Come back here!"

The youth lounged back sulkily, and a tall woman came to the door. She bent out of it anxiously to hear Hetty.

"I want you to come an' help me move my stove an' things," said Hetty.

"Where to?"

"Into the meetin'-house."

"The meetin'-house?"

"Yes, the meetin'-house."

The woman in the door had sodden hands; behind her arose the steam of a wash-tub. She and the youth stared at Hetty, but surprise was too strong an emotion for them to grasp firmly.

"I want Sammy to come right over an' help me," said Hetty.

"He ain't strong enough to move a stove," said the woman.

"Ain't strong enough!"

"He's apt to git lame."

"Most folks are. Guess I've got lame. Come right along, Sammy!"

"He ain't able to lift much."

"I s'pose he's able to be lifted, ain't he?"

"I dun' know what you mean."

"The stove don't weigh nothin','," said Hetty; "I could carry it myself if I could git hold of it. Come, Sammy!"

Hetty turned down the path, and the youth moved a little way after her, as if perforce. Then he stopped, and cast an appealing glance back at his mother. Her face was distressed. "Oh, Sammy, I'm afraid you'll git sick," said she.

"No, he ain't goin' to git sick," said Hetty. "Come, Sammy." And Sammy followed her down the path.

It was four o'clock then. At dusk Hetty had her gay sunflower quilt curtaining off the chimney-corner of the church gallery; her stove and little bedstead were set up, and she had entered upon a life which endured successfully for three months. All that time a storm brewed; then it broke; but Hetty sailed in her own course for the three months.

It was on a Saturday that she took up her habitation in the meeting-house. The next morning, when the boy who had been supplying the dead sexton's place came and shook the door, Hetty was prompt on the other side. "Deacon Gale said for you to let me in so I could ring the bell," called the boy.

"Go away," responded Hetty. "I'm goin' to ring the bell; I'm saxton."

Hetty rang the bell with vigor, but she made a wild, irregular jangle at first; at the last it was better. The village people said to each other that a new hand was ringing. Only a few knew that Hetty was in the meeting-house. When the congregation had assembled, and saw that gaudy tent pitched in the house of the Lord, and the resolute little pilgrim at the door of it, there was a commotion. The farmers and their wives were stirred out of their Sabbath decorum. After the service was over, Hetty, sitting in a pew corner of the gallery, her little face dark and watchful against the flaming background of her quilt, saw the people below gathering in groups, whispering, and looking at her.

Presently the minister, Caleb Gale, and the other deacon came up the gallery stairs. Hetty sat stiffly erect. Caleb Gale went up to the sunflower quilt, slipped it aside, and looked in. He turned to Hetty with a frown. To-day his dignity was supported by important witnesses. "Did you bring that stove an' bedstead here?"

Hetty nodded.

"What made you do such a thing?"

"What was I goin' to do if I didn't? How's a woman as old as me goin' to sleep in a pew, an' go without a cup of tea?"

The men looked at each other. They withdrew to another corner of the gallery and conferred in low tones; then they went down-stairs and out of the church. Hetty smiled when she heard the door shut. When one is hard pressed, one, however simple, gets wisdom as to vantage-

points. Hetty comprehended hers perfectly. She was the propounder of
a problem; as long as it was unguessed, she was sure of her foothold as
propounder. This little village in which she had lived all her life had
removed the shelter from her head; she being penniless, it was beholden
to provide her another; she asked it what. When the old woman with
whom she had lived died, the town promptly seized the estate for
taxes—none had been paid for years. Hetty had not laid up a cent;
indeed, for the most of the time she had received no wages. There had
been no money in the house; all she had gotten for her labor for a sickly,
impecunious old woman was a frugal board. When the old woman died,
Hetty gathered in the few household articles for which she had stipu-
lated, and made no complaint. She walked out of the house when the
new tenants came in; all she asked was, "What are you going to do
with me?" This little settlement of narrow-minded, prosperous farmers,
however hard a task charity might be to them, could not turn an old
woman out into the fields and highways to seek for food as they would
a Jersey cow. They had their Puritan consciences, and her note of distress would sound louder in their ears than the Jersey's bell echoing
down the valley in the stillest night. But the question as to Hetty Fifield's
disposal was a hard one to answer. There was no almshouse in the
village, and no private family was willing to take her in. Hetty was
strong and capable; although she was old, she could well have paid for
her food and shelter by her labor; but this could not secure her an
entrance even among this hard-working and thrifty people, who would
ordinarily grasp quickly enough at service without wage in dollars and
cents. Hetty had somehow gotten for herself an unfortunate name in
the village. She was held in the light of a long-thorned brier among the
beanpoles, or a fierce little animal with claws and teeth bared. People
were afraid to take her into their families; she had the reputation of
always taking her own way, and never heeding the voice of authority.
"I'd take her in an' have her give me a lift with the work," said one
sickly farmer's wife; "but, near's I can find out, I couldn't never be sure
that I'd get molasses in the beans, nor saleratus in my sour-milk cakes,
if she took a notion not to put it in. I don't dare to risk it."
    Stories were about concerning Hetty's authority over the old woman
with whom she had lived. "Old Mis' Grout never dared to say her soul
was her own," people said. Then Hetty's sharp, sarcastic sayings were
repeated; the justice of them made them sting. People did not want a
tongue like that in their homes.
    Hetty as a church sexton was directly opposed to all their ideas of
church decorum and propriety in general; her pitching her tent in the
Lord's house was almost sacrilege; but what could they do? Hetty jangled the Sabbath bells for the three months; once she tolled the bell for

an old man, and it seemed by the sound of the bell as if his long, calm years had swung by in a weak delirium; but people bore it. She swept and dusted the little meeting-house, and she garnished the walls with her treasures of worsted-work. The neatness and the garniture went far to quiet the dissatisfaction of the people. They had a crude taste. Hetty's skill in fancy-work was quite celebrated. Her wool flowers were much talked of, and young girls tried to copy them. So these wreaths and clusters of red and blue and yellow wool roses and lilies hung as acceptably between the meeting-house windows as pictures of saints in a cathedral.

Hetty hung a worsted motto over the pulpit; on it she set her chiefest treasure of art, a white wax cross with an ivy vine trailing over it, all covered with silver frost-work. Hetty always surveyed this cross with a species of awe; she felt the irresponsibility and amazement of a genius at his own work.

When she set it on the pulpit, no queen casting her rich robes and her jewels upon a shrine could have surpassed her in generous enthusiasm. "I guess when they see that they won't say no more," she said.

But the people, although they shared Hetty's admiration for the cross, were doubtful. They, looking at it, had a double vision of a little wax Virgin upon an altar. They wondered if it savored of popery. But the cross remained, and the minister was mindful not to jostle it in his gestures.

It was three months from the time Hetty took up her abode in the church, and a week before Christmas, when the problem was solved. Hetty herself precipitated the solution. She prepared a boiled dish in the meeting-house, upon a Saturday, and the next day the odors of turnip and cabbage were strong in the senses of the worshippers. They sniffed and looked at one another. This superseding the legitimate savor of the sanctuary, the fragrance of peppermint lozenges and wintergreen, the breath of Sunday clothes, by the homely week-day odors of kitchen vegetables, was too much for the sensibilities of the people. They looked indignantly around at Hetty, sitting before her sunflower hanging, comfortable from her good dinner of the day before, radiant with the consciousness of a great plateful of cold vegetables in her tent for her Sabbath dinner.

Poor Hetty had not many comfortable dinners. The selectmen doled out a small weekly sum to her, which she took with dignity as being her hire; then she had a mild forage in the neighbors' cellars and kitchens, of poor apples and stale bread and pie, paying for it in teaching her art of worsted-work to the daughters. Her Saturday's dinner had been a banquet to her: she had actually bought a piece of pork to boil with the vegetables; somebody had given her a nice little cabbage and some turnips, without a thought of the limitations of her housekeeping.

Hetty herself had not a thought. She made the fires as usual that Sunday
morning; the meeting-house was very clean, there was not a speck of
dust anywhere, the wax cross on the pulpit glistened in a sunbeam slanting through the house. Hetty, sitting in the gallery, thought innocently
how nice it looked.

After the meeting, Caleb Gale approached the other deacon. "Somethin's got to be done," said he. And the other deacon nodded. He had
not smelt the cabbage until his wife nudged him and mentioned it; neither had Caleb Gale.

In the afternoon of the next Thursday, Caleb and the other two
selectmen waited upon Hetty in her tabernacle. They stumped up the
gallery stairs, and Hetty emerged from behind the quilt and stood looking at them scared and defiant. The three men nodded stiffly; there was
a pause; Caleb Gale motioned meaningly to one of the others, who
shook his head; finally he himself had to speak. "I'm 'fraid you find it
pretty cold here, don't you, Hetty?" said he.

"No, thank ye; it's very comfortable," replied Hetty, polite and wary.

"It ain't very convenient for you to do your cookin' here, I guess."

"It's jest as convenient as I want. I don't find no fault."

"I guess it's rayther lonesome here nights, ain't it?"

"I'd 'nough sight ruther be alone than have comp'ny, any day."

"It ain't fit for an old woman like you to be livin' alone here
this way."

"Well, I dun' know of anything that's any fitter; mebbe you do."

Caleb looked appealingly at his companions; they stood stiff and
irresponsive. Hetty's eyes were sharp and watchful upon them all.

"Well, Hetty," said Caleb, "we've found a nice, comfortable place
for you, an' I guess you'd better pack up your things, an' I'll carry you
right over there." Caleb stepped back a little closer to the other men.
Hetty, small and trembling and helpless before them, looked vicious.
She was like a little animal driven from its cover, for whom there is
nothing left but desperate warfare and death.

"Where to?" asked Hetty. Her voice shrilled up into a squeak.

Caleb hesitated. He looked again at the other selectmen. There was
a solemn, far-away expression upon their faces. "Well," said he, "Mis'
Radway wants to git somebody, an'—"

"You ain't goin' to take me to that woman's!"

"You'd be real comfortable—"

"I ain't goin'."

"Now, why not, I'd like to know?"

"I don't like Susan Radway, hain't never liked her, an' I ain't goin'
to live with her."

"Mis' Radway's a good Christian woman. You hadn't ought to speak that way about her."

"You know what Susan Radway is, jest as well's I do; an' everybody else does too. I ain't goin' a step, an' you might jest as well make up your mind to it."

Then Hetty seated herself in the corner of the pew nearest her tent, and folded her hands in her lap. She looked over at the pulpit as if she were listening to preaching. She panted, and her eyes glittered, but she had an immovable air.

"Now, Hetty, you've got sense enough to know you can't stay here," said Caleb. "You'd better put on your bonnet, an' come right along before dark. You'll have a nice ride."

Hetty made no response.

The three men stood looking at her. "Come, Hetty," said Caleb, feebly; and another selectman spoke. "Yes, you'd better come," he said, in a mild voice.

Hetty continued to stare at the pulpit.

The three men withdrew a little and conferred. They did not know how to act. This was a new emergency in their simple, even lives. They were not constables; these three steady, sober old men did not want to drag an old woman by main force out of the meeting-house, and thrust her into Caleb Gale's buggy as if it were a police wagon.

Finally Caleb brightened. "I'll go over an' git mother," said he. He started with a brisk air, and went down the gallery stairs; the others followed. They took up their stand in the meeting-house yard, and Caleb got into his buggy and gathered up the reins. The wind blew cold over the hill. "Hadn't you better go inside and wait out of the wind?" said Caleb.

"I guess we'll wait out here," replied one; and the other nodded.

"Well, I sha'n't be gone long," said Caleb. "Mother'll know how to manage her." He drove carefully down the hill; his buggy wings rattled in the wind. The other men pulled up their coat collars, and met the blast stubbornly.

"Pretty ticklish piece of business to tackle," said one, in a low grunt.

"That's so," assented the other. Then they were silent, and waited for Caleb. Once in a while they stamped their feet and slapped their mittened hands. They did not hear Hetty slip the bolt and turn the key of the meeting-house door, nor see her peeping at them from a gallery window.

Caleb returned in twenty minutes; he had not far to go. His wife, stout and handsome and full of vigor, sat beside him in the buggy. Her face was red with the cold wind; her thick cashmere shawl was pinned tightly over her broad bosom. "Has she come down yet?" she called out, in an imperious way.

The two selectmen shook their heads. Caleb kept the horse quiet while his wife got heavily and briskly out of the buggy. She went up the meeting-house steps, and reached out confidently to open the door. Then she drew back and looked around. "Why," said she, "the door's locked; she's locked the door. I call this pretty work!"

She turned again quite fiercely, and began beating on the door. "Hetty!" she called; "Hetty, Hetty Fifield! Let me in! What have you locked this door for?"

She stopped and turned to her husband.

"Don't you s'pose the barn key would unlock it?" she asked.

"I don't b'lieve 'twould."

"Well, you'd better go home and fetch it."

Caleb again drove down the hill, and the other men searched their pockets for keys. One had the key of his corn-house, and produced it hopefully; but it would not unlock the meeting-house door.

A crowd seldom gathered in the little village for anything short of a fire; but to-day in a short time quite a number of people stood on the meeting-house hill, and more kept coming. When Caleb Gale returned with the barn key his daughter, a tall, pretty young girl, sat beside him, her little face alert and smiling in her red hood. The other selectmen's wives toiled eagerly up the hill, with a young daughter of one of them speeding on ahead. Then the two young girls stood close to each other and watched the proceedings. Key after key was tried; men brought all the large keys they could find, running importantly up the hill, but none would unlock the meeting-house door. After Caleb had tried the last available key, stooping and screwing it anxiously, he turned around. "There ain't no use in it, any way," said he; "most likely the door's bolted."

"You don't mean there's a bolt on that door?" cried his wife.

"Yes, there is."

"Then you might jest as well have tore 'round for hen's feathers as keys. Of course she's bolted it if she's got any wit, an' I guess she's got most as much as some of you men that have been bringin' keys. Try the windows."

But the windows were fast. Hetty had made her sacred castle impregnable except to violence. Either the door would have to be forced or a window broken to gain an entrance.

The people conferred with one another. Some were for retreating, and leaving Hetty in peaceful possession until time drove her to capitulate. "She'll open it to-morrow," they said. Others were for extreme measures, and their impetuosity gave them the lead. The project of forcing the door was urged; one man started for a crow-bar.

"They are a parcel of fools to do such a thing," said Caleb Gale's wife to another woman. "Spoil that good door! They'd better leave the poor thing alone till to-morrow. I dun' know what's goin' to be done with her when they git in. I ain't goin' to have father draggin' her over to Mis' Radway's by the hair of her head."

"That's jest what I say," returned the other woman.

Mrs. Gale went up to Caleb and nudged him. "Don't you let them break that door down, father," said she.

"Well, well, we'll see," Caleb replied. He moved away a little; his wife's voice had been drowned out lately by a masculine clamor, and he took advantage of it.

All the people talked at once; the wind was keen, and all their garments fluttered; the two young girls had their arms around each other under their shawls; the man with the crow-bar came stalking up the hill.

"Don't you let them break down that door, father," said Mrs. Gale.

"Well, well," grunted Caleb.

Regardless of remonstrances, the man set the crow-bar against the door; suddenly there was a cry, "There she is!" Everybody looked up. There was Hetty looking out of a gallery window.

Everybody was still. Hetty began to speak. Her dark old face, peering out of the window, looked ghastly; the wind blew her poor gray locks over it. She extended her little wrinkled hands. "Jest let me say one word," said she; "jest one word." Her voice shook. All her coolness was gone. The magnitude of her last act of defiance had caused it to react upon herself like an overloaded gun.

"Say all you want to, Hetty, an' don't be afraid," Mrs. Gale called out.

"I jest want to say a word," repeated Hetty. "Can't I stay here, nohow? It don't seem as if I could go to Mis' Radway's. I ain't nothin' again' her. I s'pose she's a good woman, but she's used to havin' her own way, and I've been livin' all my life with them that was, an' I've had to fight to keep a footin' on the earth, an' now I'm gittin' too old for't. If I can jest stay here in the meetin'-house, I won't ask for nothin' any better. I sha'n't need much to keep me, I wa'n't never a hefty eater; an' I'll keep the meetin'-house jest as clean as I know how. An' I'll make some more of them wool flowers. I'll make a wreath to go the whole length of the gallery, if I can git wool 'nough. Won't you let me stay? I ain't complainin', but I've always had a dretful hard time; seems as if now I might take a little comfort the last of it, if I could stay here. I can't go to Mis' Radway's nohow." Hetty covered her face with her hands; her words ended in a weak wail.

Mrs. Gale's voice rang out clear and strong and irrepressible. "Of course you can stay in the meetin'-house," said she; "I should laugh if you couldn't. Don't you worry another mite about it. You sha'n't go one step to Mis' Radway's; you couldn't live a day with her. You can stay jest where you are; you've kept the meetin'-house enough sight cleaner than I've ever seen it. Don't you worry another mite, Hetty."

Mrs. Gale stood majestically, and looked defiantly around; tears were in her eyes. Another woman edged up to her. "Why couldn't she have that little room side of the pulpit, where the minister hangs his hat?" she whispered. "He could hang it somewhere else."

"Course she could," responded Mrs. Gale, with alacrity, "jest as well as not. The minister can have a hook in the entry for his hat. She can have her stove an' her bed in there, an' be jest as comfortable as can be. I should laugh if she couldn't. Don't you worry, Hetty."

The crowd gradually dispersed, sending out stragglers down the hill until it was all gone. Mrs. Gale waited until the last, sitting in the buggy in state. When her husband gathered up the reins, she called back to Hetty: "Don't you worry one mite more about it, Hetty. I'm comin' up to see you in the mornin'!"

It was almost dusk when Caleb drove down the hill; he was the last of the besiegers, and the feeble garrison was left triumphant.

The next day but one was Christmas, the next night Christmas Eve. On Christmas Eve Hetty had reached what to her was the flood-tide of peace and prosperity. Established in that small, lofty room, with her bed and her stove, with gifts of a rocking-chair and table, and a goodly store of food, with no one to molest or disturb her, she had nothing to wish for on earth. All her small desires were satisfied. No happy girl could have a merrier Christmas than this old woman with her little measure full of gifts. That Christmas Eve Hetty lay down under her sunflower quilt, and all her old hardships looked dim in the distance, like far-away hills, while her new joys came out like stars.

She was a light sleeper; the next morning she was up early. She opened the meeting-house door and stood looking out. The smoke from the village chimneys had not yet begun to rise blue and rosy in the clear frosty air. There was no snow, but over all the hill there was a silver rime of frost; the bare branches of the trees glistened. Hetty stood looking. "Why, it's Christmas mornin'," she said, suddenly. Christmas had never been a gala-day to this old woman. Christmas had not been kept at all in this New England village when she was young. She was led to think of it now only in connection with the dinner Mrs. Gale had promised to bring her to-day.

Mrs. Gale had told her she should have some of her Christmas dinner, some turkey and plum-pudding. She called it to mind now with a thrill of delight. Her face grew momentarily more radiant. There was a certain beauty in it. A finer morning light than that which lit up the wintry earth seemed to shine over the furrows of her old face. "I'm goin' to have turkey an' plum-puddin' to-day," said she; "it's Christmas." Suddenly she started, and went into the meeting-house, straight up the gallery stairs. There in a clear space hung the bell-rope. Hetty grasped it. Never before had a Christmas bell been rung in this village; Hetty had probably never heard of Christmas bells. She was prompted by pure artless enthusiasm and grateful happiness. Her old arms pulled on the rope with a will, the bell sounded peal on peal. Down in the village, curtains rolled up, letting in the morning light, happy faces looked out of the windows. Hetty had awakened the whole village to Christmas Day.

ROSE TERRY COOKE

How Celia Changed Her Mind

"How Celia Changed Her Mind" is most often read in terms of its biographical resonance, for its parallels to Cooke's own late marriage and her responsibility for raising two children who were not her own. Whether its flagrantly anti-marriage sentiment can be taken as her own is a more complex issue, for her contemporaries considered Cooke's marriage to be a solid one. First published in Cooke's final volume of local-color fiction, *Huckleberries Gathered from New England Hills* (1891), this story explores Celia's feelings about her dissatisfaction with being an "old maid," her contempt for women who have never married, and her change of heart after an unhappy four years as the wife of Deacon Everts, a plot paralleled in the younger generation by the young Rosabel, who dies in childbirth after having left her worthless husband. Representative of the local-color tradition, the story captures the personalities and folkways of rural New England, the regional dialect, and the restricted roles for women in village life. It is also, however, a story of psychological growth toward self-sufficiency and personal resourcefulness that leaves Celia fulfilled at the end in a community of women.

*   *   *

"If there's anything on the face of the earth I *do* hate, it's an old maid!"

Mrs. Stearns looked up from her sewing in astonishment.

"Why, Miss Celia!"

"Oh, yes! I know it. I'm one myself, but all the same, I hate 'em worse than p'ison. They ain't nothing nor nobody; they're cumberers of the ground." And Celia Barnes laid down her scissors with a bang, as if she might be Atropos herself, ready to cut the thread of life for all the despised class of which she was a notable member.

The minister's wife was genuinely surprised at this outburst; she herself had been well along in life before she married, and though she had been fairly happy in the uncertain relationship to which she had attained, she was, on the whole, inclined to agree with St. Paul, that the woman who did not marry "doeth better." "I don't agree with you, Miss Celia," she said gently. "Many, indeed, most of my best friends are maiden ladies, and I respect and love them just as much as if they were married women."

"Well, I don't. A woman that's married is somebody; she's got a place in the world; she ain't everybody's tag; folks don't say, 'Oh, it's nobody but that old maid Celye Barnes;' it's 'Mis' Price,' and 'Mis' Simms,' or 'Thomas Smith's wife,' as though you was somebody. I don't know how 't is elsewheres, but here in Bassett you might as well be a dog as an old maid. I allow it might be better if they all had means or eddication: money's 'a dreadful good thing to have in the house, as I see in a book once, and learning is sort of comp'ny to you if you're lonesome; but then lonesome you be, and you've got to be, if you're an old maid, and it can't be helped noway."

Mrs. Stearns smiled a little sadly, thinking that even married life had its own loneliness when your husband was shut up in his study, or gone off on a long drive to see some sick parishioner or conduct a neighborhood prayer-meeting, or even when he was the other side of the fireplace absorbed in a religious paper or a New York daily, or meditating on his next sermon, while the silent wife sat unnoticed at her mending or knitting. "But married women have more troubles and responsibilities than the unmarried, Miss Celia," she said. "You have no children to bring up and be anxious about, no daily dread of not doing your duty by the family whom you preside over, and no fear of the supplies giving out that are really needed. Nobody but your own self to look out for."

"That's jest it," snapped Celia, laying down the boy's coat she was sewing with a vicious jerk of her thread. "There 't is! Nobody to home to care if you live or die; nobody to peek out of the winder to see if you're comin', or to make a mess of gruel or a cup of tea for you, or to throw ye a feelin' word if you're sick nigh unto death. And old maids is just as li'ble to up and die as them that's married. And as to responsibility, I ain't afraid to tackle that. Never! I don't hold with them that cringe and crawl and are skeert at a shadder, and won't do a living thing that they had ought to do because they're 'afraid to take the responsibility.' Why, there's Mrs. Deacon Trimble, she durstn't so much as set up a prayer-meetin' for missions or the temp'rance cause, because 't was 'sech a reesponsibility to take the lead in them matters.' I suppose it's somethin' of a responsible chore to preach the gospel to the heathen, or grab a drinkin' feller by the scruff of his neck and haul him out of the horrible pit anyway, but if it's dooty it's got to be done, whether or no; and I ain't afraid of pitchin' into anything the Lord sets me to do!"

"Except being an old maid," said Mrs. Stearns.

Celia darted a sharp glance at her over her silver-rimmed spectacles, and pulled her needle through and through the seams of Willy's jacket with fresh vigor, while a thoughtful shadow came across her fine old face. Celia was a candid woman, for all her prejudices, a combination peculiarly characteristic of New England, for she was a typical Yankee. Presently she said abruptly, "I hadn't thought on 't in that light." But then the minister opened the door, and the conversation stopped.

Parson Stearns was tired and hungry and cross, and his wife knew all that as soon as she saw his face. She had learned long ago that ministers, however good they may be, are still men; so to-day she had kept her husband's dinner warm in the under-oven, and had the kettle boiling to make him a cup of tea on the spot to assuage his irritation in the shortest and surest way; but though the odor of a savory stew and the cheerful warmth of the cooking-stove greeted him as he preceded her through the door into the kitchen, he snapped out, sharply enough for Celia to hear him through the half-closed door, "What do you have that old maid here for so often?"

"There!" said Celia to herself,—"there 't is! *He* don't look upon 't as a dispensation, if she doos. Men-folks run the world, and they know it. There ain't one of the hull caboodle but what despises an onmarried woman! Well, 't ain't altogether my fault. I wouldn't marry them that I could; I couldn't—not and be honest; and them that I would hev had didn't ask me. I don't know as I'm to blame, after all, when you look into 't."

And she went on sewing Willy's jacket, contrived with pains and skill out of an old coat of his father's, while Mrs. Stearns poured out her husband's tea in the kitchen, replenished his plate with stew, and cut for him more than one segment of the crisp, fresh apple-pie, and urged upon him the squares of new cheese that legitimately accompany this deleterious viand of the race and country, the sempiternal, insistent, flagrant, and alas! also fragrant pie.

Celia Barnes was the tailoress of the little scattered country town of Bassett. Early left an orphan, without near relatives or money, she had received the scantiest measure of education that our town authorities deal to the pauper children of such organizations. She was ten years old when her mother, a widow for almost all those ten years, left her to the tender mercies of the selectmen of Bassett. The selectmen of our country towns are almost irresponsible governors of their petty spheres, and gratify the instinct of oligarchy peculiar to, and conservative of, the human race. Men must be governed and tyrannized over,—it is an in-born necessity of their nature; and while a republic is a beautiful theory, eminently fitted for a race who are "non Angli, sed Angeli," it has in practice the effect of producing more than Russian tyranny, but on smaller scales and in far and scattered localities. Nowhere are there more despots than among village selectmen in New England. Those who have wrestled with their absolute monarchism in behalf of some charity that might abstract a few of the almighty dollars made out of poverty and distress from their official pockets know how positive and dogmatic is their use of power—*experto crede*. The Bassett "first selectman" promptly bound out little Celia Barnes to a hard, imperious woman, who made a white slave of the child, and only dealt out to her the smallest measure of schooling demanded by law, because the good old minister, Father Perkins, interfered in the child's behalf.

As she was strong and hardy and resolute, Celia lived through her bondage, and at the "free" age of eighteen apprenticed herself to old Miss Polly Mariner, the Bassett tailoress, and being deft with her fingers and quick of brain, soon outran her teacher, and when Polly died, succeeded to her business.

She was a bright girl, not particularly noticeable among others, for she had none of that delicate flower-like New England beauty which is so peculiar, so charming, and so evanescent; her features were tolerably regular, her forehead broad and calm, her gray eyes keen and perceptive, and she had abundant hair of an uncertain brown; but forty other girls in Bassett might have been described in the same way; Celia's face was one to improve with age; its strong sense, capacity for humor, fine out-lines of a rugged sort, were always more the style of fifty than fifteen, and what she said of herself was true.

She had been asked to marry an old farmer with five uproarious boys, a man notorious in East Bassett for his stinginess and bad temper, and she had promptly declined the offer. Once more fate had given her a chance. A young fellow of no character, poor, "shiftless," and given to cider as a beverage, had considered it a good idea to marry some one who would make a home for him and earn his living. Looking about him for a proper person to fill this pleasant situation, he pounced on Celia—and she returned the attention!

"Marry *you?* I wonder you've got the sass to ask any decent girl to marry ye, Alfred Hatch! What be you good for, anyway? I don't know what under the canopy the Lord spares you for,—only He doos let the tares grow amongst the wheat, Scripter says, and I'm free to suppose He knows why, but I don't. No, *sir!* Ef you was the last man in the livin' universe I wouldn't tech ye with the tongs. If you'd got a speck of grit into you, you'd be ashamed to ask a woman to take ye in and support ye, for that's what it comes to. You go 'long! I can make my hands save my head so long as I hev the use of 'em, and I haven't no call to set up a private poor-house!"

So Alfred Hatch sneaked off, much like a cur that has sought to share the kennel of a mastiff, and been shortly and sharply convinced of his presumption.

Here ended Celia's "chances," as she phrased it. Young men were few in Bassett; the West had drawn them away with its subtle attraction of unknown possibilities, just as it does to-day, and Celia grew old in the service of those established matrons who always want clothes cut over for their children, carpet rags sewed, quilts quilted, and comfortables tacked. She was industrious and frugal, and in time laid up some money in the Dartford Savings' Bank; but she did not, like many spinsters, invest her hard-earned dollars in a small house. Often she was urged to do so, but her reasons were good for refusing.

"I should be so independent? Well, I'm as independent now as the law allows. I've got two good rooms to myself, south winders, stairs of my own and outside door, and some privileges. If I had a house there'd be taxes, and insurance, and cleanin' off snow come winter-time, and hoein' paths; and likely enough I should be so fur left to myself that I should set up a garden, and make my succotash cost a dollar a pint a-hirin' of a man to dig it up and hoe it down. Like enough, too, I should be gettin' flower seeds and things; I'm kinder fond of blows in the time of 'em. My old fish-geran'um is a sight of comfort to me as 't is, and there would be a bill of expense again. Then you can't noway build a house with only two rooms in 't, it would be all outside; and you might as well try to heat the universe with a cookin'-stove as such a house. Besides, how lonesome I should be. It's forlorn enough to be an old maid anyway, but to have it sort of ground into you, as you may say, by livin' all alone in a hull house, that ain't necessary nor agreeable. Now, if I'm sick or sorry, I can just step downstairs and have aunt Nabby to help or hearten me. Deacon Everts he did set to work one time to persuade me to buy a house; he said 't was a good thing to be able to give somebody shelter 't was poorer 'n I was. Says I, 'Deacon, I've worked for my livin' ever sence I remember, and I know there's no use in anybody bein' poorer than I be. I haven't no call to take any sech in and do for 'em. I give what I can to missions,—home ones,—and I'm willin', cheerfully willin', to do a day's work now and again for somebody that is strivin' with too heavy burdens; but as for keepin' free lodgin' and board, I sha'n't do it.' 'Well, well, well,' says he, kinder as if I was a fractious young one, and a-sawin' his fat hand up and down in the air till I wanted to slap him, 'just as you'd ruther, Celye,—just as you'd ruther. I don't mean to drive ye a mite, only, as Scripter says, "Provoke one another to love and good works." '

"That did rile me! Says I: 'Well, you've provoked me full enough, though I don't know as you've done it in the Scripter sense; and mabbe I shouldn't have got so fur provoked if I hadn't have known that little red house your grandsir' lived and died in was throwed back on your hands just now, and advertised for sellin'. I see the "Mounting County Herald," Deacon Everts.' He shut up, I tell ye. But I sha'n't never buy no house so long as aunt Nabby lets me have her two south chambers, and use the back stairway and the north door continual."

So Miss Celia had kept on in her way till now she was fifty, and to-day making over old clothes at the minister's. The minister's wife had, as we have seen, little romance or wild happiness in her life; it is not often the portion of country ministers' wives; and, moreover, she had two step-daughters who were girls of sixteen and twelve when she married their father. Katy was married herself now, this ten years, and doing her hard duty by an annual baby and a struggling parish in Dakota; but Rosabel, whose fine name had been the only legacy her dying mother left the day-old child she had scarce had time to kiss and christen before she went to take her own "new name" above, was now a girl of twenty-two, pretty, headstrong, and rebellious. Nature had endowed her with keen dark eyes, crisp dark curls, a long chin, and a very obstinate mouth, which only her red lips and white even teeth redeemed from ugliness; her bright color and her sense of fun made her attractive to young men wherever she encountered one of that rare species. Just now she was engaged in a serious flirtation with the station-master at Bassett Centre,—an impecunious youth of no special interest to other people and quite unable to maintain a wife. But out of the "strong necessity of loving," as it is called, and the want of young society or settled occu-pation, Rosa Stearns chose to fall in love with Amos Barker, and her father considered it a "fall" indeed. So, with the natural clumsiness of a man and a father, Parson Stearns set himself to prevent the matter, and began by forbidding Rosabel to see or speak or write to the youth in question, and thereby inspired in her mind a burning desire to do all three. Up to this time she had rather languidly amused herself by mild and gentle flirtations with him, such as looking at him sidewise in church on Sunday, meeting him accidentally on his way to and from the station, for she spent at least half her time at her aunt's in Bassett Centre, and had even taught the small school there during the last six months. She had also sent him her tintype, and his own was secreted in her bureau drawer. He had invited her to go with him to two sleigh-rides and one sugaring-off, and always came home with her from prayer-meeting and singing-school; but like a wise youth he had never yet proposed to marry her in due form, not so much because he was wise as because he was thoughtless and lazy; and while he enjoyed the society of a bright girl, and liked to dangle after the prettiest one in Bassett, and the minister's daughter too, he did not love work well enough to shoulder the responsibility of providing for another those material but necessary supplies that imply labor of an incessant sort.

Rosabel, in her first inconsiderate anger at her father's command, sat down and wrote a note to Amos, eminently calculated to call out his sympathy with her own wrath, and promptly mailed it as soon as it was written. It ran as follows:—

Dear Friend,—Pa has forbidden me to speak to you any more, or to correspond with you. I suppose I must submit so far; but he did not say I must return your picture [the parson had not an idea that she possessed that precious thing], so I shall keep it to remind me of the pleasant hours we have passed together.

> *"Fare thee well, and if forever,*
> *Still forever fare thee well!"*

Your true friend, ROSABEL STEARNS.
P.S.—I think pa is *horrid!*

So did Amos as he read this heart-rending missive, in which the post-script, according to the established sneer at woman's postscripts, carried the whole force of the epistle.

Now Amos had made a friend of Miss Celia by once telegraphing for her trunk, which she had lost on her way home from the only journey of her life, a trip to Boston, whither she had gone, on the strength of the one share of B. & A. R. R. stock she held, to spend the allotted three days granted to stockholders on their annual excursions, presumably to attend the annual meeting. Amos had put himself to the immense trouble of sending two messages for Miss Celia, and asked her nothing for the civility, so that ever after, in the fashion of solitary women, she held herself deeply in his debt. He knew that she was at work for Mrs. Stearns when he received Rosa's epistle, for he had just been over to Bassett on the train—there was but a mile to traverse—to get her to repair his Sunday coat, and not found her at home, but had no time to look her up at the parson's, as he must walk back to his station. Now he resolved to take his answer to Rosa to Miss Celia in the evening, and so be sure that his abused sweetheart received it, for he had read too many dime novels to doubt that her tyrannic father would intercept their letters, and drive them both to madness and despair. That well-meaning but rather dull divine never would have thought of such a thing; he was a puffy, absent-minded, fat little man, with a weak, squeaky voice, and a sudden temper that blazed up like a bunch of dry weeds at a passing spark, and went out at once in flattest ashes. It had been Mrs. Stearns's step-motherly interference that drove him into his harshness to Rosa. She meant well and he meant well, but we all know what good intentions with no further sequel of act are good for, and nobody did more of that "paving" than these two excellent but futile people.

Miss Celia was ready to do anything for Amos Barker, and she considered it little less than a mortal sin to stand in the way of any marriage that was really desired by two parties. That Amos was poor did not daunt her at all; she had the curious faith that possesses some women, that any man can be prosperous if he has the will so to be; and she had a high opinion of this youth, based on his civility to her. It may be said of men, as of elephants, that it is lucky they do not know their own power; for how many more women would become their worshipers and slaves than are so to-day if they knew the abject gratitude the average woman feels for the least attention, the smallest kindness, the faintest expression of affection or good will. We are all, like the Syrophenician woman, glad and ready to eat of the crumbs which fall from the children's table, so great is our faith—in men.

Miss Celia took the note in her big basket over to the minister's the very next day after that on which we introduced her to our readers. She was perhaps more rejoiced to contravene that reverend gentleman's orders than if she had not heard his querulous and contemptuous remark about her through the crack of the door on the previous afternoon; and it was with a sense of joy that, after all, an old maid could do something, that she slipped the envelope into Rosa's hands, and told her to put it quickly into her pocket, the very first moment she found herself alone with that young woman.

Many a hasty word had Parson Stearns spoken in the suddenness of his petulant temper, but never one that bore direr fruit than that when he called Celia Barnes "that old maid."

For of course Amos and Rosabel found in her an ardent friend. They had the instinct of distressed lovers to cajole her with all their confidences, caresses, and eager gratitude, and for once she felt herself dear and of importance. Amos consulted her on his plans for the future, which of course pointed westward, where he had a brother editing and owning a newspaper. This brother had before offered him a place in his office, but Amos had liked better the easy work of a station-master in a tiny village. Now his ambition was aroused, for the time at least. He wanted to make a home for Rosabel, but, alack! he had not one cent to pay their united expenses to Peoria, and a lion stood in the way. Here again Celia stepped in: she had some money laid up; she would lend it to them.

I do not say that at this stage she had no misgivings, but even these were set at rest by a conversation she had with Mrs. Stearns some six weeks after the day on which Celia had so fully expressed her scorn of spinsters. She was there again to tack a comfortable for Rosabel's bed, and bethought herself that it was a good time to feel her way a little concerning Mrs. Stearns's opinion of things.

"They do say," she remarked, stopping to snip off her thread and twist the end of it through her needle's eye, "that your Rosy don't go with Amos Barker no more. Is that so?"

"Yes," said Mrs. Stearns, with a half sigh. "Husband was rather prompt about it; he don't think Amos Barker ever'll amount to much, and he thinks his people are not just what they should be. You know his father never was very much of a man, and his grandfather is a real old reprobate. Husband says he never knew anything but crows come out of a crow's nest, and so he told Rosa to break acquaintance with him."

"Who does he like to hev come to see her?" asked Celia, with a grim set of her lips, stabbing her needle fiercely through the unoffending calico.

Mrs. Stearns laughed rather feebly. "I don't think he has anybody on his mind, Miss Celia. I don't think there are any young men in Bassett. I dare say Rosa will never marry. I wish she would, for she isn't happy here, and I can't do much to help it, with all my cares."

"And you can't feel for her as though she was your own, if you try ever so," confidently asserted Celia.

"No, I suppose not. I try to do my duty by her, and I am sorry for her; but I know all the time an own mother would understand her better and make it easier for her. Mr. Stearns is peculiar, and men don't know just how to manage girls."

It was a cautious admission, but Miss Celia had sharp eyes, and knew very well that Rosabel neither loved nor respected her father, and that they were now on terms of real if unavowed hostility.

"Well," said she, "I don' know but you will have to have one of them onpleasant creturs, an old maid, in your fam'ly. I declare for't, I'd hold a Thanksgiving Day all to myself ef I'd escaped that marcy."

"You may not always think so, Celia."

"I don't know what'll change me. 'T will be something I don't look forrard to now," answered Celia obstinately.

Mrs. Stearns sighed. "I hope Rosa will do nothing worse than to live unmarried," she said; but she could not help wishing silently that some worthy man would carry the perverse and annoying girl out of the parsonage for good.

After this Celia felt a certain freedom to help Rosabel; she encouraged the lovers to meet at her house, helped plan their elopement, sewed for the girl, and at last went with them as far as Brimfield when they stole away one evening, saw them safely married at the Methodist parsonage there, and bidding them good-speed, returned to Bassett Centre on the midnight train, and walked over to her own dwelling in the full moonshine of the October night, quite fearless and entirely exultant.

But she was not to come off unscathed. There was a scene of wild commotion at the parsonage next day, when Rosa's letter, modeled on that of the last novel heroine she had become acquainted with, was found on her bureau, as per novel aforesaid.

With her natural thoughtlessness she assured her parents that she "fled not uncompanioned," that her "kind and all but maternal friend, Miss Celia Barnes, would accompany her to the altar, and give her support and her countenance to the solemn ceremony that should make Rosabel Stearns the blessed wife of Amos Barker!"

It was all the minister could do not to swear as he read this astounding letter. His flabby face grew purple; his fat, sallow hands shook with rage; he dared not speak, he only sputtered, for he knew that profane and unbecoming words would surely leap from his tongue if he set it free; but he must—he really must—do or say something! So he clapped on his old hat, and with coat tails flying in the breeze, and rage in every step, set out to find Celia Barnes; and find her he did.

It would be unpleasant, and it is needless, to depict this encounter; language both unjust and unsavory smote the air and reverberated along the highway, for he met the spinster on her road to an engagement at Deacon Stiles's. Suffice it to say that both freed their minds with great enlargement of opinion, and the parson wound up with,—

"And I never want to see you again inside of my house, you confounded old maid!"

"There! that's it!" retorted Celia. "Ef I wasn't an old maid, you wouldn't no more have darst to 'a' talked to me this way than nothin'. Ef I'd had a man to stand up to ye you'd have been dumber 'n Balaam's ass a great sight,—afore it seen the angel, I mean. I swow to man, I b'lieve I'd marry a hitchin'-post if 't was big enough to trounce ye. You great lummox, if I could knock ye over you wouldn't peep nor mutter agin, if I be a woman!"

And with a burst of furious tears that asserted her womanhood Miss Celia went her way. Her hands were clinched under her blanket shawl, her eyes red with angry rain, and as she walked on she soliloquized aloud:—

"I declare for 't, I b'lieve I'd marry the Old Boy himself if he'd ask me. I'm sicker 'n ever of bein' an old maid!"

"Be ye?" queried a voice at her elbow. "P'r'aps, then, you might hear to me if I was to speak my mind, Celye."

Celia jumped. As she said afterward, "I vum I thought 't was the Enemy, for certain; and to think 't was only Deacon Everts!"

"Mercy me!" she said now; "is 't you, deacon?"

"Yes, it's me; and I think 't is a real providence I come up behind ye just in the nick of time. I've sold my farm only last week, and I've come to live on the street in that old red house of grand-sir's, that you mistrusted once I wanted you to buy. I'm real lonesome sence I lost my partner" (he meant his wife), "and I've been a-hangin' on by the edges the past two year; hired help is worse than nothing onto a farm, and hard to get at that; so I sold out, and I'm a-movin' yet, but the old house looks forlorn enough, and I was intendin' to look about for a second; so if you'll have me, Celye, here I be."

Celia looked at him sharply; he was an apple-faced little man, with shrewd, twinkling eyes, a hard, dull red still lingering on his round cheeks in spite of the deep wrinkles about his pursed-up lips and around his eyelids; his mouth gave him a consequential and self-important air, to which the short stubbly hair, brushed up "like a blaze" above his forehead, added; and his old blue coat with brass buttons, his homespun trousers, the old-fashioned aspect of his unbleached cotton shirt, all attested his frugality. Indeed, everybody knew that Deacon Everts was "near," and also that he had plenty of money, that is to say, far more than he could spend. He had no children, no near relations; his first wife had died two years since, after long invalidism, and all her relations had moved far west. All this Celia knew and now recalled; her wrath against Parson Stearns was yet fresh and vivid; she remembered that Simeon Everts was senior deacon of the church, and had it in his power to make the minister extremely uncomfortable if he chose. I have never said Celia was a very good woman; her religion was of the dormant type not uncommon nowadays; she kept up its observances properly, and said her prayers every day, bestowed a part of her savings on each church collection, and was rated as a church-member "in good and regular standing;" but the vital transforming power of that Christianity which means to "love the Lord thy God with all thy heart, and mind, and soul, and strength, and thy neighbor as thyself," had no more entered into her soul than it had into Deacon Everts's; and while she would have honestly admitted that revenge was a very wrong sentiment, and entirely improper for any other person to cherish, she felt that she did well to be angry with Parson Stearns, and had a perfect right to "pay him off" in any way she could.

Now here was her opportunity. If she said "Yes" to Deacon Everts, he would no doubt take her part. Her objections to housekeeping were set aside by the fact that the house-owner himself would have to do those heavy labors about the house which she must otherwise have hired a man to do; and the cooking and the indoor work for two people could not be so hard as to sew from house to house for her daily bread. In short, her mind was slowly turning favorably toward this sudden project, but she did not want this wooer to be too sure; so she said: "W-e-ll, 't is a life sentence, as you may say, deacon, and I want to think on 't a spell. Let's see,—to-day's Tuesday; I'll let ye know Thursday night, after prayer-meetin'."

"Well," answered the deacon.

Blessed Yankee monosyllable that means so much and so little; that has such shades of phrase and intention in its myriad inflections; that is "yes," or "no," or "perhaps," just as you accent it; that is at once preface and peroration, evasion and definition! What would all New England speech be without "well"? Even as salt without any savor, or pepper with no pungency.

Now it meant to Miss Celia assent to her proposition; and in accordance the deacon escorted her home from meeting Thursday night, and received for reward a consenting answer. This was no love affair, but a matter of mere business. Deacon Everts needed a housekeeper, and did not want to pay out wages for one; and Miss Celia's position she expressed herself as she put out her tallow candle on that memorable night, and breathed out on the darkness the audible aspiration, "Thank goodness, I sha'n't hev to die an old maid!"

There was no touch of sanctifying love or consoling affection, or even friendly comradeship, in this arrangement; it was as truly a *marriage de convenance* as was ever contracted in Paris itself, and when the wedding day came, a short month afterward, the sourest aspect of November skies threatening a drenching pour, the dead and sodden leaves that strewed the earth, the wailing northeast wind, even the draggled and bony old horse behind which they jogged over to Bassett Centre, seemed fit accompaniments to the degraded ceremony performed by a justice of the peace, who concluded this merely legal compact, for Miss Celia stoutly refused to be married by Parson Stearns; she would not be accessory to putting one dollar in his pocket, even as her own wedding fee. So she went home to the little red house on Bassett Street, and begun her married life by scrubbing the dust and dirt of years from the kitchen table, making biscuit for tea, washing up the dishes, and at last falling asleep during the deacon's long nasal prayer, wherein he wandered to the ends of the earth, and prayed fervently for the heathen, piteously unconscious that he was little better than a heathen himself.

It did not take many weeks to discover to Celia what is meant by "the curse of a granted prayer." She could not at first accept the situation at all; she was accustomed to enough food, if it was plain and simple, when she herself provided it; but now it was hard to get such viands as would satisfy a healthy appetite.

"You've used a sight of pork, Celye," the deacon would remonstrate. "My first never cooked half what you do. We shall come to want certain, if you're so free-handed."

"Well, Mr. Everts, there wasn't a mite left to set by. We eat it all, and I didn't have no more'n I wanted, if you did."

"We must mortify the flesh, Celye. It's hullsome to get up from your victuals hungry. Ye know what Scripter says, 'Jeshurun waxed fat an' kicked.' "

"Well, I ain't Jeshurun, but I expect I shall be more likely to kick if I don't have enough to eat, when it's only pork 'n' potatoes."

"My first used to say them was the best, for steady victuals, of anything, and she never used but two codfish and two quarts of m'lasses the year round; and as for butter, she was real sparin'; she'd fry our bread along with the salt pork, and 't was just as good."

"Look here!" snapped Celia. "I don't want to hear no more about your 'first.' I'm ready to say I wish't she'd ha' been your last too."

"Well, well, well! this is onseemly contention, Celye," sputtered the alarmed deacon. "Le' 's dwell together in unity so fur as we can, Mis' Everts. I haven't no intention to starve ye, none whatever. I only want to be keerful, so as we sha'n't have to fetch up in the poor-us."

"No need to have a poor-house to home," muttered Celia.

But this is only a mild specimen of poor Celia's life as a married woman. She did not find the honor and glory of "Mrs." before her name a compensation for the thousand evils that she "knew not of" when she fled to them as a desirable change from her single blessedness. Deacon Everts entirely refused to enter into any of her devices against Parson Stearns; he did not care a penny about Celia's wrongs, and he knew very well that no other man than dreamy, unpractical Mr. Stearns, who eked out his minute pittance by writing schoolbooks of a primary sort, would put up with four hundred dollars a year from his parish; yet that was all Bassett people would pay. If they must have the gospel, they must have it at the lowest living rates, and everybody would not assent to that.

So Celia found her revenge no more feasible after her marriage than before, and, gradually absorbed in her own wrongs and sufferings, her desire to reward Mr. Stearns in kind for his treatment of her vanished; she thought less of his futile wrath and more of her present distresses every day.

For Celia, like everybody who profanes the sacrament of marriage, was beginning to suffer the consequences of her misstep. As her husband's mean, querulous, loveless character unveiled itself in the terrible intimacy of constant and inevitable companionship, she began to look woefully back to the freedom and peace of her maiden days. She learned that a husband is by no means his wife's defender always, not even against reviling tongues. It did not suit Deacon Everts to quarrel with any one, whatever they said to him, or of him and his; he "didn't want no enemies," and Celia bitterly felt that she must fight her own battles; she had not even an ally in her husband. She became not only defiant, but also depressed; the consciousness of a vital and life-long mistake is not productive of cheer or content; and now, admitted into the free-masonry of married women, she discovered how few among them were more than household drudges, the servants of their families, worked to the verge of exhaustion, and neither thanked nor rewarded for their pains. She saw here a woman whose children were careless of, and ungrateful to her, and her husband coldly indifferent; there was one on whom the man she had married wreaked all his fiendish temper in daily small injuries, little vexatious acts, petty tyrannies, a "street-angel, house-devil" of a man, of all sorts the most hateful. There were many whose lives had no other outlook than hard work until the end should come, who rose up to labor and lay down in sleepless exhaustion, and some whose days were a constant terror to them from the intemperate brutes to whom they had intrusted their happiness, and indeed their whole existence.

It was no worse with Celia than with most of her sex in Bassett; here and there, there were of course exceptions, but so rare as to be shining examples and objects of envy. Then, too, after two years, there came forlorn accounts of poor Rosabel's situation at the west. Amos Barker had done his best at first to make his wife comfortable, but change of place or new motives do not at once, if ever, transform an indolent man into an active and efficient one. He found work in his brother's office, but it was the hard work of collecting bills all about the country; the roads were bad, the weather as fluctuating as weather always is, the climate did not agree with him, and he got woefully tired of driving about from dawn till after dark, to dun unwilling debtors. Rosa had chills and fever and babies with persistent alacrity; she had indeed enough to eat, with no appetite, and a house, with no strength to keep it. She grew untidy, listless, hysterical; and her father, getting worried by her despondent and infrequent letters, actually so far roused himself as to sell his horse, and with this sacrificial money betook himself to Mound Village, where he found Rosabel with two babies in her arms, dust an inch deep on all her possessions, nothing but pork, potatoes, and corn bread in the pantry, and a slatternly negress washing some clothes in a kitchen that made the parson shudder.

The little man's heart was bigger than his soul. He put his arms about Rosa and the dingy babies, and forgave her all; but he had to say, even while he held them closely and fondly to his breast, "Oh, Rosy, I told you what would happen if you married that fellow."

Of course Rosa resented the speech, for, after all, she had loved Amos; perhaps could love him still if the poverty and malaria and babies could have all been eliminated from her daily life.

Fortunately the parson's horse had sold well, for it was strong and young, and the rack of venerable bones with which he replaced it was bought very cheap at a farmer's auction, so he had money enough to carry Rosa and the two children home to Bassett, where two months after she added another feeble, howling cipher to the miserable sum of humanity.

Miss—no, Mrs.—Celia's conscience stung her to the quick when she encountered this ghastly wreck of pretty Rosabel Stearns, now called Mrs. Barker. She remembered with deep regret how she had given aid and comfort to the girl who had defied and disobeyed parental counsel and authority, and so brought on herself all this misery. She fancied that Parson Stearns glared at her with eyes of bitter accusation and reproach, and not improbably he did, for beside his pity and affection for his daughter, it was no slight burden to take into his house a feeble woman with two children helpless as babies, and to look forward to the expense and anxiety of another soon to come. And Mrs. Stearns had never loved Rosa well enough to be complacent at this addition to her family cares. She gave the parson no sympathy. It would have been her way to let Rosabel lie on the bed she had made, and die there if need be. But the poor worn-out creature died at home, after all, and the third baby lay on its mother's breast in her coffin: they had gone together.

Celia felt almost like a murderess when she heard that Rosabel

Barker was dead. She did not reflect that in all human probability the girl would have married Amos if she, Celia, had refused to help or encourage her. It began to be an importunate question in our friend's mind whether she herself had not made a mistake too; whether the phrase "single blessedness" was not an expression of a vital truth rather than a scoff. Celia was changing her mind no doubt, surely if slowly.

Meantime Deacon Everts did not find all the satisfaction with his "second" that he had anticipated. Celia had a will of her own, quite undisciplined, and it was too often asserted to suit her lord and master. Secretly he planned devices to circumvent her purposes, and sometimes succeeded. In prayer-meeting and in Sunday-school the idea haunted him; his malice lay down and rose up with him. Even when he propounded to his Bible class the important question, "How fur be the heathen *ree*-sponsible for what they dun know?" and asked them "to ponder on 't through the comin' week," he chuckled inwardly at the thought that Celia could not evade *her* responsibility; she knew enough, and would be judged accordingly: the deacon was not a merciful man.

At last he hit upon that great legal engine whereby men do inflict the last deadly kick upon their wives: he would remodel his will. Yes, he would leave those gathered thousands to foreign missions; he would leave behind him the indisputable testimony and taunt that he considered the wife of his bosom less than the savages and heathen afar off. He forgot conveniently that the man "who provideth not for his own household hath denied the faith, and is worse than an infidel." And in his delight of revenge he also forgot that the law of the land provides for a man's wife and children in spite of his wicked will. Nor did he remember that his life-insurance policy for five thousand dollars was made out in his wife's name, simply as his wife, her own name not being specified. He had paid the premium always from his "first's" small annual income, and agreed that it should be written for her benefit, but he supposed that at her death it had reverted to him. He forgot that he still had a wife when he mentioned that policy in his assets recorded in the will, and to save money he drew that evil document up himself, and had it signed down at "the store" by three witnesses.

Celia had borne her self-imposed yoke for four years, when it was suddenly broken. A late crop of grass was to be mowed in mid-July on the meadow which appertained to the old house, and the deacon, now some seventy years old, to save hiring help, determined to do it by himself. The grass was heavy and over-ripe, the day extremely hot and breathless, and the grim Mower of Man trod side by side with Simeon Everts, and laid him too, all along by the rough heads of timothy and the purpled feather-tops of the blue-grass. He did not come home at noon or at night, and when Celia went down to the lot to call him he heard no summons of hers; he had answered a call far more imperative and final.

After the funeral Celia found his will pushed back in the deep drawer of an old secretary, where he kept his one quill pen, a bottle of dried ink, a lump of chalk, some rat-poison, and various other odds and ends.

She was indignant enough at its tenor; but it was easily broken, and she not only had her "thirds," but the life policy reverted to her also, as it was made out to Simeon Everts's wife, and surely she had occupied that position for four wretched years. Then, also, she had a right to her support for one year out of the estate, and the use of the house for that time.

Oh, how sweet was her freedom! With her characteristic honesty she refused to put on mourning, and even went to the funeral in her usual gray Sunday gown and bonnet. "I won't lie, anyhow!" she answered to Mrs. Stiles's remonstrance. "I ain't a mite sorry nor mournful. I could ha' wished he'd had time to repent of his sins, but sence the Lord saw fit to cut him short, I don't feel to rebel ag'inst it. I wish't I'd never married him, that's all!"

"But, Celye, you got a good livin'."

"I earned it."

"And he's left ye with means too."

"He done his best not to. I don't owe him nothing for that; and I earned that too,—the hull on't. It's poor pay for what I've lived through; and I'm a'most a mind to call it the wages of sin, for I done wrong, ondeniably wrong, in marryin' of him; but the Lord knows I've repented, and said my lesson, if I did get it by the hardest."

Yet all Bassett opened eyes and mouth both when on the next Thanksgiving Day Celia invited every old maid in town—seven all told—to take dinner with her. Never before had she celebrated this old New England day of solemn revel. A woman living in two small rooms could not "keep the feast," and rarely had she been asked to any family conclave. We Yankees are conservative at Thanksgiving if nowhere else, and like to gather our own people only about the family hearth; so Celia had but once or twice shared the turkeys of her more fortunate neighbors.

Now she called in Nabby Hyde and Sarah Gillett, Ann Smith, Celestia Potter, Delia Hills, Sophronia Ann Jenkins and her sister Adelia Ann, ancient twins, who lived together on next to nothing, and were happy.

Celia bloomed at the head of the board, not with beauty, but with gratification. "Well," she said, as soon as they were seated, "I sent for ye all to come because I wanted to have a good time, for one thing, and because it seems as though I'd ought to take back all the sassy and disagreeable things I used to be forever flingin' at old maids. 'I spoke in my haste,' as Scripter says, and also in my ignorance, I'm free to confess. I feel as though I could keep Thanksgivin' to-day with my hull soul. I'm so thankful to be an old maid ag'in!"

"I thought you was a widder," snapped Sally Gillett.

Celia flung a glance of wrath at her, but scorned to reply.

"And I'm thankful too that I'm spared to help ondo somethin' done in that ignorance. I've got means, and, as I've said before, I earned 'em. I don't feel noway obleeged to him for 'em; he didn't mean it. But now I can I'm goin' to adopt Rosy Barker's two children, and fetch 'em up to be dyed-in-the-wool old maids; and every year, so long as I live, I'm goin' to keep an old maids' Thanksgivin' for a kind of a burnt-offering, sech as the Bible tells about, for I've changed my mind clear down to the bottom, and I go the hull figure with the 'postle Paul when he speaks about the onmarried, 'It is better if she so abide.' Now let's go to work at the victuals."

GRACE ELIZABETH KING

La Grande Demoiselle

"La Grande Demoiselle," one of Grace King's finest works, was first published in *The Century Magazine* before its inclusion in *Balcony Stories* (1893), a series of fourteen stories told by women of an evening sharing tales of family life in the South in the aftermath of the Civil War. The central themes of these stories deal with the fallen aristocracy of New Orleans Creoles, the psychological devastation of their reduced economic and social status, and the resourcefulness of women in coping with their plight. "La Grande Demoiselle" is typical of these stories in its depiction of the extravagance and self-indulgence of young Idalie Sainte Foy Mortemart des Islets and the collapse of her stature after the death of her parents and the Northern occupation of New Orleans during the war. That the events are related as rumor rather than fact, with many unexplained events, and the fact that La Grande Demoiselle never herself speaks during the story, lends a mythic element to this powerful narrative of psychic degradation.

*   *   *

That was what she was called by everybody as soon as she was seen or described. Her name, besides baptismal titles, was Idalie Sainte Foy

Mortemart des Islets. When she came into society, in the brilliant little world of New Orleans, it was the event of the season, and after she came in, whatever she did, became also events. Whether she went, or did not go; what she said, or did not say; what she wore, and did not wear—all these became important matters of discussion, quoted as much or more than what the president said, or the governor thought. And in those days, the days of '59, New Orleans was not, as it is now, a one-heiress place, but it may be said that one could find heiresses then as one finds type-writing girls now.

Mademoiselle Idalie received her birth, and what education she had, on her parents' plantation, the famed old Reine Sainte Foy place, and it is no secret that, like the ancient kings of France, her birth exceeded her education.

It was a plantation, the Reine Sainte Foy, the richness and luxury of which are really well described in those perfervid pictures of tropical life, at one time the passion of philanthropic imaginations, excited and exciting over the horrors of slavery. Although these pictures were then often accused of being purposely exaggerated, they seem now to fall short of, instead of surpassing, the truth. Stately walls, acres of roses, miles of oranges, unmeasured fields of cane, colossal sugar-house—they were all there, and all the rest of it, with the slaves, slaves, slaves everywhere, whole villages of negro cabins. And there were also, most noticeable to the natural, as well as to the visionary, eye—there were the ease, idleness, extravagance, self-indulgence, pomp, pride, arrogance, in short the whole enumeration, the moral *sine qua non,* as some people considered it, of the wealthy slaveholder of aristocratic descent and tastes.

What Mademoiselle Idalie cared to learn she studied, what she did not, she ignored; and she followed the same simple rule untrammeled in her eating, drinking, dressing, and comportment generally; and whatever discipline may have been exercised on the place, either in fact or fiction, most assuredly none of it, even so much as in a threat, ever attainted her sacred person. When she was just turned sixteen, Mademoiselle Idalie made up her mind to go into society. Whether she was beautiful or not, it is hard to say. It is almost impossible to appreciate properly the beauty of the rich, the very rich. The unfettered development, the limitless choice of accessories, the confidence, the self-esteem, the sureness of expression, the simplicity of purpose, the ease of execution—all these produce a certain effect of beauty behind which one really cannot get to measure length of nose, or brilliancy of eye. This much can be said: there was nothing in her that positively contradicted any assumption of beauty on her part, or credit of it on the part of others. She was very tall and very thin with small head, long neck, black eyes, and abundant straight black hair,—for which her hair-dresser deserved more praise than she,—good teeth, of course, and a mouth that, even in prayer, talked nothing but commands; that is about all she had *en fait d'ornements,* as the modistes say. It may be added that she walked as if the Reine Sainte Foy plantation extended over the whole earth, and the soil of it were too vile for her tread. Of course she did not buy her toilets in New Orleans. Everything was ordered from Paris, and came as regularly through the custom-house as the modes and robes to the milliners. She was furnished by a certain house there, just as one of a royal family would be at the present day. As this had lasted from her layette up to her sixteenth year, it may be imagined what took place when she determined to make her début. Then it was literally, not metaphorically, *carte blanche,* at least so it got to the ears of society. She took a sheet of note-paper, wrote the date at the top, added, "I make my début in November," signed her name at the extreme end of the sheet, addressed it to her dressmaker in Paris, and sent it.

It was said that in her dresses the very handsomest silks were used for linings, and that real lace was used where others put imitation,—around the bottoms of the skirts, for instance,—and silk ribbons of the best quality served the purposes of ordinary tapes; and sometimes the buttons were of real gold and silver, sometimes set with precious stones. Not that she ordered these particulars, but the dressmakers, when given *carte blanche* by those who do not condescend to details, so soon exhaust the outside limits of garments that perforce they take to plastering them inside with gold, so to speak, and, when the bill goes in, they depend upon the furnishings to carry out a certain amount of the contract in justifying the price. And it was said that these costly dresses, after being worn once or twice, were cast aside, thrown upon the floor, given to the negroes—anything to get them out of sight. Not an inch of the real lace, not one of the jeweled buttons, not a scrap of ribbon, was ripped off to save. And it was said that if she wanted to romp with her dogs in all her finery, she did it; she was known to have ridden horseback, one moonlight night, all around the plantation in a white silk dinner-dress flounced with Alençon. And at night, when she came from the balls, tired, tired to death as only balls can render one, she would throw herself down upon her bed in her tulle skirts,—on top, or not, of the exquisite flowers, she did not care,—and make her maid undress her in that position; often having her bodices cut off her, because she was too tired to turn over and have them unlaced.

That she was admired, raved about, loved even, goes without saying. After the first month she held the refusal of half the beaux of New Orleans. Men did absurd, undignified, preposterous things for her; and she? Love? Marry? The idea never occurred to her. She treated the most exquisite of her pretenders no better than she treated her Paris gowns, for the matter of that. She could not even bring herself to listen to a proposal patiently; whistling to her dogs, in the middle of the most ardent protestations, or jumping up and walking away with a shrug of the shoulders, and a "Bah!"

Well! Every one knows what happened after '59. There is no need to repeat. The history of one is the history of all. But there was this difference—for there is every shade of difference in misfortune, as there is every shade of resemblance in happiness. Mortemart des Islets went off to fight. That was natural; his family had been doing that, he thought, or said, ever since Charlemagne. Just as naturally, he was killed in the first engagement. They, his family, were always among the first killed; so much so that it began to be considered assassination to fight a duel with any of them. All that was in the ordinary course of events. One difference in their misfortunes lay in that after the city was captured, their plantation, so near, convenient, and rich in all kinds of provisions, was selected to receive a contingent of troops—a colored company. If it had been a colored company raised in Louisiana it might have been different; and these negroes mixed with the negroes in the neighborhood,—and negroes are no better than whites, for the proportion of good and bad among them,—and the officers were always off duty when they should have been on, and on when they should have been off.

One night the dwelling caught fire. There was an immediate rush to save the ladies Oh, there was no hesitation about that! They were seized in their beds, and carried out in the very arms of their enemies; carried away off to the sugar-house, and deposited there. No danger of their doing anything but keep very quiet and still in their *chemises de nuit,* and their one sheet apiece, which was about all that was saved from the conflagration—that is, for them. But it must be remembered that this is all hearsay. When one has not been present, one knows nothing of one's own knowledge; one can only repeat. It has been repeated, however, that although the house was burned to the ground, and everything in it destroyed, wherever, for a year afterward, a man of that company or of that neighborhood was found, there could have been found also, without search-warrant, property that had belonged to the Des Islets. That is the story; and it is believed or not, exactly according to prejudice.

How the ladies ever got out of the sugar-house, history does not relate; nor what they did. It was not a time for sociability, either personal or epistolary. At one offensive word your letter, and you, very likely, examined; and Ship Island for a hotel, with soldiers for hostesses! Madame Des Islets died very soon after the accident—of rage, they say; and that was about all the public knew.

Indeed, at that time the society of New Orleans had other things to think about than the fate of the Des Islets. As for *la grande demoiselle,* she had prepared for her own oblivion in the hearts of her female friends. And the gentlemen,—her *preux chevaliers,*—they were burning with other passions than those which had driven them to her knees, encountering a little more serious response than "bahs" and shrugs. And, after all, a woman seems the quickest thing forgotten when once the important affairs of life come to men for consideration.

It might have been ten years according to some calculations, or ten eternities,—the heart and the almanac never agree about time,—but one morning old Champigny (they used to call him Champignon) was walking along his levee front, calculating how soon the water would come over, and drown him out, as the Louisianians say. It was before a seven-o'clock breakfast, cold, wet, rainy, and discouraging. The road was knee-deep in mud, and so broken up with hauling, that it was like walking upon waves to get over it. A shower poured down. Old Champigny was hurrying in when he saw a figure approaching. He had to stop to look at it, for it was worth while. The head was hidden by a green barege veil, which the showers had plentifully besprinkled with dew; a tall, thin figure. Figure! No; not even could it be called a figure: straight up and down, like a finger or a post; high-shouldered, and a step—a step like a plowman's. No umbrella; no—nothing more, in fact. It does not sound so peculiar as when first related—something must be forgotten. The feet—oh, yes, the feet—they were like waffle-irons, or frying-pans, or anything of that shape.

Old Champigny did not care for women—he never had; they simply did not exist for him in the order of nature. He had been married once, it is true, about a half century before; but that was not reckoned against the existence of his prejudice, because he was *célibataire* to his finger-tips, as any one could see a mile away. But that woman *intrigué'd* him.

He had no servant to inquire from. He performed all of his own domestic work in the wretched little cabin that replaced his old home. For Champigny also belonged to the great majority of the *nouveaux pauvres.* He went out into the rice-field, where were one or two hands that worked on shares with him, and he asked them. They knew immediately; there is nothing connected with the parish that a field-hand does not know at once. She was the teacher of the colored public school some three or four miles away. "Ah," thought Champigny, "some Northern lady on a mission." He watched to see her return in the evening, which she did, of course; in a blinding rain. Imagine the green barege veil then; for it remained always down over her face.

Old Champigny could not get over it that he had never seen her before. But he must have seen her, and, with his abstraction and old age, not have noticed her, for he found out from the negroes that she had been teaching four or five years there. And he found out also—how, is not important—that she was Idalie Sainte Foy Mortemart des Islets. *La grande demoiselle!* He had never known her in the old days, owing to his uncomplimentary attitude toward women, but he knew of her, of course, and of her family. It should have been said that his plantation was about fifty miles higher up the river, and on the opposite bank to Reine Sainte Foy. It seemed terrible. The old gentleman had had reverses of his own, which would bear the telling, but nothing was more shocking to him than this—that Idalie Sainte Foy Mortemart des Islets should be teaching a public colored school for—it makes one blush to name it—seven dollars and a half a month. For seven dollars and a half a month to teach a set of—well! He found out where she lived, a little cabin—not so much worse than his own, for that matter —in the corner of a field; no companion, no servant, nothing but food and shelter. Her clothes have been described.

Only the good God himself knows what passed in Champigny's mind on the subject. We know only the results. He went and married *la grande demoiselle.* How? Only the good God knows that too. Every first of the month, when he goes to the city to buy provisions, he takes her with him—in fact, he takes her everywhere with him.

Passengers on the railroad know them well, and they always have a chance to see her face. When she passes her old plantation *la grande demoiselle* always lifts her veil for one instant—the inevitable green barege veil. What a face! Thin, long, sallow, petrified! And the neck! If she would only tie something around the neck! And her plain, coarse cottonade gown! The negro women about her were better dressed than she.

Poor old Champignon! It was not an act of charity to himself, no doubt cross and disagreeable, besides being ugly. And as for love, gratitude!

KATE CHOPIN

Athénaïse

"Athénaïse," a richly complex story that serves as a thematic counter-point to Chopin's famous novel *The Awakening*, was first published in the *Atlantic Monthly* in 1896, before its inclusion in *A Night in Acadie* in 1897. Indeed, there are many relationships between the story and the novel, including a similar setting, a recurring character, and a good deal of resonance on the issues of marriage and the realization of self, romance and sexual fulfillment, responsibility to children, and the growth of insight that leads to the assumption of agency in one's life. In this story, however, such growth takes place for both the husband and the young wife, she learning to assert herself but coming, through pregnancy, to recognize that she can choose a loving relationship with her husband, and he recognizing that he cannot dominate his wife and that she needs a sense of freedom, volition, and self-respect. It is a richly developed story, subtle in its use of imagistic patterns of nature and the renewal of life, and powerful in its depiction of the issues of the New Woman emerging in the 1890s.

*   *   *

I

Athénaïse went away in the morning to make a visit to her parents, ten miles back on rigolet de Bon Dieu. She did not return in the evening, and Cazeau, her husband, fretted not a little. He did not worry much about Athénaïse, who, he suspected, was resting only too content in the bosom of her family; his chief solicitude was manifestly for the pony she had ridden. He felt sure those "lazy pigs," her brothers, were capable of neglecting it seriously. This misgiving Cazeau communicated to his servant, old Félicité, who waited upon him at supper.

His voice was low pitched, and even softer than Félicité's. He was tall, sinewy, swarthy, and altogether severe looking. His thick black hair waved, and it gleamed like the breast of a crow. The sweep of his mustache, which was not so black, outlined the broad contour of the mouth. Beneath the under lip grew a small tuft which he was much given to twisting, and which he permitted to grow, apparently for no other purpose. Cazeau's eyes were dark blue, narrow and overshadowed. His hands were coarse and stiff from close acquaintance with farming tools and implements, and he handled his fork and knife clumsily. But he was distinguished looking, and succeeded in commanding a good deal of respect, and even fear sometimes.

He ate his supper alone, by the light of a single coal-oil lamp that but faintly illuminated the big room, with its bare floor and huge rafters, and its heavy pieces of furniture that loomed dimly in the gloom of the apartment. Félicité, ministering to his wants, hovered about the table like a little, bent, restless shadow.

She served him with a dish of sunfish fried crisp and brown. There was nothing else set before him beside the bread and butter and the bottle of red wine which she locked carefully in the buffet after he had poured his second glass. She was occupied with her mistress's absence, and kept reverting to it after he had expressed his solicitude about the pony.

"Dat beat me! on'y marry two mont', an' got de head turn' a'ready to go 'broad. C'est pas Chrétien, tenez!"

Cazeau shrugged his shoulders for answer, after he had drained his glass and pushed aside his plate. Félicité's opinion of the unchristianlike behavior of his wife in leaving him thus alone after two months of marriage weighed little with him. He was used to solitude, and did not mind a day or a night or two of it. He had lived alone ten years, since his first wife died, and Félicité might have known better than to suppose that he cared. He told her she was a fool. It sounded like a compliment in his modulated, caressing voice. She grumbled to herself as she set about clearing the table, and Cazeau arose and walked outside on the gallery; his spur, which he had not removed upon entering the house, jangled at every step.

The night was beginning to deepen, and to gather black about the clusters of trees and shrubs that were grouped in the yard. In the beam of light from the open kitchen door a black boy stood feeding a brace of snarling, hungry dogs; further away, on the steps of a cabin, some one was playing the accordion; and in still another direction a little negro baby was crying lustily. Cazeau walked around to the front of the house, which was square, squat and one-story.

A belated wagon was driving in at the gate, and the impatient driver was swearing hoarsely at his jaded oxen. Félicité stepped out on the gallery, glass and polishing towel in hand, to investigate, and to wonder, too, who could be singing out on the river. It was a party of young people paddling around, waiting for the moon to rise, and they were singing Juanita, their voices coming tempered and melodious through the distance and the night.

Cazeau's horse was waiting, saddled, ready to be mounted, for Cazeau had many things to attend to before bed-time; so many things that there was not left to him a moment in which to think of Athénaïse. He felt her absence, though, like a dull, insistent pain.

However, before he slept that night he was visited by the thought of her, and by a vision of her fair young face with its drooping lips and sullen and averted eyes. The marriage had been a blunder; he had only to look into her eyes to feel that, to discover her growing aversion. But it was a thing not by any possibility to be undone. He was quite prepared to make the best of it, and expected no less than a like effort on her part. The less she revisited the rigolet, the better. He would find means to keep her at home hereafter.

These unpleasant reflections kept Cazeau awake far into the night, notwithstanding the craving of his whole body for rest and sleep. The moon was shining, and its pale effulgence reached dimly into the room, and with it a touch of the cool breath of the spring night. There was an unusual stillness abroad; no sound to be heard save the distant, tireless, plaintive notes of the accordion.

II

Athénaïse did not return the following day, even though her husband sent her word to do so by her brother, Montéclin, who passed on his way to the village early in the morning.

On the third day Cazeau saddled his horse and went himself in search of her. She had sent no word, no message, explaining her absence, and he felt that he had good cause to be offended. It was rather awkward to have to leave his work, even though late in the afternoon,—Cazeau had always so much to do; but among the many urgent calls upon him, the task of bringing his wife back to a sense of her duty seemed to him for the moment paramount.

The Michés, Athénaïse's parents, lived on the old Gotrain place. It did not belong to them; they were "running" it for a merchant in Alexandria. The house was far too big for their use. One of the lower rooms served for the storing of wood and tools; the person "occupying" the place before Miché having pulled up the flooring in despair of being able to patch it. Upstairs, the rooms were so large, so bare, that they offered a constant temptation to lovers of the dance, whose importunities Madame Miché was accustomed to meet with amiable indulgence. A dance at Miché's and a plate of Madame Miché's gumbo filé at midnight were pleasures not to be neglected or despised, unless by such serious souls as Cazeau.

Long before Cazeau reached the house his approach had been observed, for there was nothing to obstruct the view of the outer road;

vegetation was not yet abundantly advanced, and there was but a patchy, straggling stand of cotton and corn in Miché's field.

Madame Miché, who had been seated on the gallery in a rocking-chair, stood up to greet him as he drew near. She was short and fat, and wore a black skirt and loose muslin sack fastened at the throat with a hair brooch. Her own hair, brown and glossy, showed but a few threads of silver. Her round pink face was cheery, and her eyes were bright and good humored. But she was plainly perturbed and ill at ease as Cazeau advanced.

Montéclin, who was there too, was not ill at ease, and made no attempt to disguise the dislike with which his brother-in-law inspired him. He was a slim, wiry fellow of twenty-five, short of stature like his mother, and resembling her in feature. He was in shirt-sleeves, half leaning, half sitting, on the insecure railing of the gallery, and fanning himself with his broad-rimmed felt hat.

"Cochon!" he muttered under his breath as Cazeau mounted the stairs,—"sacré cochon!"

"Cochon" had sufficiently characterized the man who had once on a time declined to lend Montéclin money. But when this same man had had the presumption to propose marriage to his well-beloved sister, Athénaïse, and the honor to be accepted by her, Montéclin felt that a qualifying epithet was needed fully to express his estimate of Cazeau.

Miché and his oldest son were absent. They both esteemed Cazeau highly, and talked much of his qualities of head and heart, and thought much of his excellent standing with city merchants.

Athénaïse had shut herself up in her room. Cazeau had seen her rise and enter the house at perceiving him. He was a good deal mystified, but no one could have guessed it when he shook hands with Madame Miché. He had only nodded to Montéclin, with a muttered "Comment ça va?"

"Tiens! something tole me you were coming to-day!" exclaimed Madame Miché, with a little blustering appearance of being cordial and at ease, as she offered Cazeau a chair.

He ventured a short laugh as he seated himself.

"You know, nothing would do," she went on, with much gesture of her small, plump hands, "nothing would do but Athénaïse mus' stay las' night fo' a li'le dance. The boys wouldn' year to their sister leaving."

Cazeau shrugged his shoulders significantly, telling as plainly as words that he knew nothing about it.

"Comment! Montéclin didn' tell you we were going to keep Athénaïse?" Montéclin had evidently told nothing.

"An' how about the night befo'," questioned Cazeau, "an' las' night? It isn't possible you dance every night out yere on the Bon Dieu!"

Madame Miché laughed, with amiable appreciation of the sarcasm; and turning to her son, "Montéclin, my boy, go tell yo' sister that Monsieur Cazeau is yere."

Montéclin did not stir except to shift his position and settle himself more securely on the railing.

"Did you year me, Montéclin?"

"Oh yes, I yeard you plain enough," responded her son, "but you know as well as me it's no use to tell 'Thénaïse anything. You been talkin' to her yo'se'f since Monday; an' pa's preached himse'f hoa'se on the subject; an' you even had uncle Achille down yere yesterday to reason with her. W'en 'Thénaïse said she wasn' goin' to set her foot back in Cazeau's house, she meant it."

This speech, which Montéclin delivered with thorough unconcern, threw his mother into a condition of painful but dumb embarrassment. It brought two fiery red spots to Cazeau's cheeks, and for the space of a moment he looked wicked.

What Montéclin had spoken was quite true, though his taste in the manner and choice of time and place in saying it were not of the best. Athénaïse, upon the first day of her arrival, had announced that she came to stay, having no intention of returning under Cazeau's roof. The announcement had scattered consternation, as she knew it would. She had been implored, scolded, entreated, stormed at, until she felt herself like a dragging sail that all the winds of heaven had beaten upon. Why in the name of God had she married Cazeau? Her father had lashed her with the question a dozen times. Why indeed? It was difficult now for her to understand why, unless because she supposed it was customary for girls to marry when the right opportunity came. Cazeau, she knew, would make life more comfortable for her; and again, she had liked him, and had even been rather flustered when he pressed her hands and kissed them, and kissed her lips and cheeks and eyes, when she accepted him.

Montéclin himself had taken her aside to talk the thing over. The turn of affairs was delighting him.

"Come, now, 'Thénaïse, you mus' explain to me all about it, so we can settle on a good cause, an' secu' a separation fo' you. Has he been mistreating an' abusing you, the sacré cochon?" They were alone together in her room, whither she had taken refuge from the angry domestic elements.

"You please to reserve yo' disgusting expressions, Montéclin. No, he has not abused me in any way that I can think."

"Does he drink? Come 'Thénaïse, think well over it. Does he ever get drunk?"

"Drunk! Oh, mercy, no,—Cazeau never gets drunk."

"I see; it's jus' simply you feel like me; you hate him."

"No, I don't hate him," she returned reflectively; adding with a sudden impulse, "It's jus' being married that I detes' an' despise. I hate being Mrs. Cazeau, an' would want to be Athénaïse Miché again. I can't stan' to live with a man; to have him always there; his coats an' pantaloons hanging in my room; his ugly bare feet—washing them in my tub, befo' my very eyes, ugh!" She shuddered with recollections, and resumed, with a sigh that was almost a sob: "Mon Dieu, mon Dieu! Sister Marie Angélique knew w'at she was saying; she knew me better than myse'f w'en she said God had sent me a vocation an' I was turning deaf ears. W'en I think of a blessed life in the convent, at peace! Oh, w'at was I dreaming of!" and then the tears came.

Montéclin felt disconcerted and greatly disappointed at having obtained evidence that would carry no weight with a court of justice. The day had not come when a young woman might ask the court's permission to return to her mamma on the sweeping ground of a constitutional disinclination for marriage. But if there was no way of untying this Gordian knot of marriage, there was surely a way of cutting it.

"Well, 'Thénaise, I'm mighty durn sorry you got no better groun's 'an w'at you say. But you can count on me to stan' by you w'atever you do. God knows I don' blame you fo' not wantin' to live with Cazeau."

And now there was Cazeau himself, with the red spots flaming in his swarthy cheeks, looking and feeling as if he wanted to thrash Montéclin into some semblance of decency. He arose abruptly, and approaching the room which he had seen his wife enter, thrust open the door after a hasty preliminary knock. Athénaïse, who was standing erect at a far window, turned at his entrance.

She appeared neither angry nor frightened, but thoroughly unhappy, with an appeal in her soft dark eyes and a tremor on her lips that seemed to him expressions of unjust reproach, that wounded and maddened him at once. But whatever he might feel, Cazeau knew only one way to act toward a woman.

"Athénaïse, you are not ready?" he asked in his quiet tones. "It's getting late; we havn' any time to lose."

She knew that Montéclin had spoken out, and she had hoped for a wordy interview, a stormy scene, in which she might have held her own as she had held it for the past three days against her family, with Montéclin's aid. But she had no weapon with which to combat subtlety. Her

husband's looks, his tones, his mere presence, brought to her a sudden
sense of hopelessness, an instinctive realization of the futility of rebellion
against a social and sacred institution.

Cazeau said nothing further, but stood waiting in the doorway. Madame Miché had walked to the far end of the gallery, and pretended to
be occupied with having a chicken driven from her parterre. Montéclin
stood by, exasperated, fuming, ready to burst out.

Athénaïse went and reached for her riding skirt that hung against the
wall. She was rather tall, with a figure which, though not robust, seemed
perfect in its fine proportions. "La fille de son père," she was often
called, which was a great compliment to Miché. Her brown hair was
brushed all fluffily back from her temples and low forehead, and about
her features and expression lurked a softness, a prettiness, a dewiness,
that were perhaps too childlike, that savored of immaturity.

She slipped the riding-skirt, which was of black alpaca, over her
head, and with impatient fingers hooked it at the waist over her pink
linen-lawn. Then she fastened on her white sunbonnet and reached for
her gloves on the mantelpiece.

"If you don' wan' to go, you know w'at you got to do, 'Thénaïse,"
fumed Montéclin. "You don' set yo' feet back on Cane River, by God,
unless you want to,—not w'ile I'm alive."

Cazeau looked at him as if he were a monkey whose antics fell short
of being amusing.

Athénaïse still made no reply, said not a word. She walked rapidly
past her husband, past her brother; bidding good-bye to no one, not
even to her mother. She descended the stairs, and without assistance
from any one mounted the pony, which Cazeau had ordered to be saddled upon his arrival. In this way she obtained a fair start of her husband, whose departure was far more leisurely, and for the greater part
of the way she managed to keep an appreciable gap between them. She
rode almost madly at first, with the wind inflating her skirt balloon-like
about her knees, and her sunbonnet falling back between her shoulders.

At no time did Cazeau make an effort to overtake her until traversing
an old fallow meadow that was level and hard as a table. The sight of
a great solitary oak-tree, with its seemingly immutable outlines, that
had been a landmark for ages—or was it the odor of elderberry stealing
up from the gully to the south? or what was it that brought vividly back
to Cazeau, by some association of ideas, a scene of many years ago?
He had passed that old live-oak hundreds of times, but it was only now
that the memory of one day came back to him. He was a very small
boy that day, seated before his father on horse-back. They were pro-
ceeding slowly, and Black Gabe was moving on before them at a little
dog-trot. Black Gabe had run away, and had been discovered back in

the Gotrain swamp. They had halted beneath this big oak to enable the negro to take breath; for Cazeau's father was a kind and considerate master, and every one had agreed at the time that Black Gabe was a fool, a great idiot indeed, for wanting to run away from him.

The whole impression was for some reason hideous, and to dispel it Cazeau spurred his horse to a swift gallop. Overtaking his wife, he rode the remainder of the way at her side in silence.

It was late when they reached home. Félicité was standing on the grassy edge of the road, in the moonlight, waiting for them.

Cazeau once more ate his supper alone; for Athénaïse went to her room, and there she was crying again.

III

Athénaïse was not one to accept the inevitable with patient resignation, a talent born in the souls of many women; neither was she the one to accept it with philosophical resignation, like her husband. Her sensibilities were alive and keen and responsive. She met the pleasurable things of life with frank, open appreciation, and against distasteful conditions she rebelled. Dissimulation was as foreign to her nature as guile to the breast of a babe, and her rebellious outbreaks, by no means rare, had hitherto been quite open and aboveboard. People often said that Athénaïse would know her own mind some day, which was equivalent to saying that she was at present unacquainted with it. If she ever came to such knowledge, it would be by no intellectual research, by no subtle analyses or tracing the motives of actions to their source. It would come to her as the song to the bird, the perfume and color to the flower.

Her parents had hoped—not without reason and justice—that marriage would bring the poise, the desirable pose, so glaringly lacking in Athénaïse's character. Marriage they knew to be a wonderful and powerful agent in the development and formation of a woman's character; they had seen its effect too often to doubt it.

"And if this marriage does nothing else," exclaimed Miché in an outburst of sudden exasperation, "it will rid us of Athénaïse; for I am at the end of my patience with her! You have never had the firmness to manage her,"—he was speaking to his wife,—"I have not had the time, the leisure, to devote to her training; and what good we might have accomplished, that maudit Montéclin—Well, Cazeau is the one! It takes just such a steady hand to guide a disposition like Athénaïse's, a master hand, a strong will that compels obedience."

And now, when they had hoped for so much, here was Athénaïse, with gathered and fierce vehemence, beside which her former outbursts appeared mild, declaring that she would not, and she would not, and

she would not continue to enact the role of wife to Cazeau. If she had
had a reason! as Madame Miché lamented; but it could not be discovered that she had any sane one. He had never scolded, or called names,
or deprived her of comforts, or been guilty of any of the many repre-
hensible acts commonly attributed to objectionable husbands. He did
not slight nor neglect her. Indeed, Cazeau's chief offense seemed to be
that he loved her, and Athénaïse was not the woman to be loved against
her will. She called marriage a trap set for the feet of unwary and unsuspecting girls, and in round, unmeasured terms reproached her mother
with treachery and deceit.

"I told you Cazeau was the man," chuckled Miché, when his wife
had related the scene that had accompanied and influenced Athénaïse's
departure.

Athénaïse again hoped, in the morning, that Cazeau would scold or
make some sort of a scene, but he apparently did not dream of it. It
was exasperating that he should take her acquiescence so for granted.
It is true he had been up and over the fields and across the river and
back long before she was out of bed, and he may have been thinking
of something else, which was no excuse, which was even in some sense
an aggravation. But he did say to her at breakfast, "That brother of
yo's, that Montéclin, is unbearable."

"Montéclin? Par exemple!"

Athénaïse, seated opposite to her husband, was attired in a white
morning wrapper. She wore a somewhat abused, long face, it is true,—
an expression of countenance familiar to some husbands,—but the expression was not sufficiently pronounced to mar the charm of her
youthful freshness. She had little heart to eat, only playing with the food
before her, and she felt a pang of resentment at her husband's healthy
appetite.

"Yes, Montéclin," he reasserted. "He's developed into a firs'-class
nuisance; an' you better tell him, Athénaïse,—unless you want me to
tell him,—to confine his energies after this to matters that concern him.
I have no use fo' him or fo' his interference in w'at regards you an' me
alone."

This was said with unusual asperity. It was the little breach that
Athénaïse had been watching for, and she charged rapidly: "It's strange,
if you detes' Montéclin so heartily, that you would desire to marry his
sister." She knew it was a silly thing to say, and was not surprised when
he told her so. It gave her a little foothold for further attack, however.
"I don't see, anyhow, w'at reason you had to marry me, w'en there
were so many others," she complained, as if accusing him of persecution
and injury. "There was Marianne running after you fo' the las' five years
till it was disgraceful; an' any one of the Dortrand girls would have

been glad to marry you. But no, nothing would do; you mus' come out on the rigolet fo' me." Her complaint was pathetic, and at the same time so amusing that Cazeau was forced to smile.

"I can't see w'at the Dortrand girls or Marianne have to do with it," he rejoined; adding, with no trace of amusement, "I married you because I loved you; because you were the woman I wanted to marry, an' the only one. I reckon I tole you that befo'. I thought—of co'se I was a fool fo' taking things fo' granted—but I did think that I might make you happy in making things easier an' mo' comfortable fo' you. I expected—I was even that big a fool—I believed that yo' coming yere to me would be like the sun shining out of the clouds, an' that our days would be like w'at the story-books promise after the wedding. I was mistaken. But I can't imagine w'at induced you to marry me. W'atever it was, I reckon you foun' out you made a mistake, too. I don' see anything to do but make the best of a bad bargain, an' shake han's over it." He had arisen from the table, and, approaching, held out his hand to her. What he had said was commonplace enough, but it was significant, coming from Cazeau, who was not often so unreserved in expressing himself.

Athénaïse ignored the hand held out to her. She was resting her chin in her palm, and kept her eyes fixed moodily upon the table. He rested his hand, that she would not touch, upon her head for an instant, and walked away out of the room.

She heard him giving orders to workmen who had been waiting for him out on the gallery, and she heard him mount his horse and ride away. A hundred things would distract him and engage his attention during the day. She felt that he had perhaps put her and her grievance from his thoughts when he crossed the threshold; whilst she—

Old Félicité was standing there holding a shining tin pail, asking for flour and lard and eggs from the storeroom, and meal for the chicks.

Athénaïse seized the bunch of keys which hung from her belt and flung them at Félicité's feet.

"Tiens! tu vas les garder comme tu as jadis fait. Je ne veux plus de ce train là, moi!"

The old woman stooped and picked up the keys from the floor. It was really all one to her that her mistress returned them to her keeping, and refused to take further account of the ménage.

IV

It seemed now to Athénaïse that Montéclin was the only friend left to her in the world. Her father and mother had turned from her in what appeared to be her hour of need. Her friends laughed at her, and refused to take seriously the hints which she threw out,—feeling her way to discover if marriage were as distasteful to other women as to herself. Montéclin alone understood her. He alone had always been ready to act for her and with her, to comfort and solace her with his sympathy and his support. Her only hope for rescue from her hateful surroundings lay in Montéclin. Of herself she felt powerless to plan, to act, even to conceive a way out of this pitfall into which the whole world seemed to have conspired to thrust her.

She had a great desire to see her brother, and wrote asking him to come to her. But it better suited Montéclin's spirit of adventure to appoint a meeting-place at the turn of the lane, where Athénaïse might appear to be walking leisurely for health and recreation, and where he might seem to be riding along, bent on some errand of business or pleasure.

There had been a shower, a sudden downpour, short as it was sudden, that had laid the dust in the road. It had freshened the pointed leaves of the live-oaks, and brightened up the big fields of cotton on either side of the lane till they seemed carpeted with green, glittering gems.

Athénaïse walked along the grassy edge of the road, lifting her crisp skirts with one hand, and with the other twirling a gay sunshade over her bare head. The scent of the fields after the rain was delicious. She inhaled long breaths of their freshness and perfume, that soothed and quieted her for the moment. There were birds splashing and spluttering in the pools, pluming themselves on the fence-rails, and sending out little sharp cries, twitters, and shrill rhapsodies of delight.

She saw Montéclin approaching from a great distance,—almost as far away as the turn of the woods. But she could not feel sure it was he; it appeared too tall for Montéclin, but that was because he was riding a large horse. She waved her parasol to him; she was so glad to see him. She had never been so glad to see Montéclin before; not even the day when he had taken her out of the convent, against her parents' wishes, because she had expressed a desire to remain there no longer. He seemed to her, as he drew near, the embodiment of kindness, of bravery, of chivalry, even of wisdom; for she had never known Montéclin at a loss to extricate himself from a disagreeable situation.

He dismounted, and, leading his horse by the bridle, started to walk beside her, after he had kissed her affectionately and asked her what she was crying about. She protested that she was not crying, for she was laughing, though drying her eyes at the same time on her handkerchief, rolled in a soft mop for the purpose.

She took Montéclin's arm, and they strolled slowly down the lane;

they could not seat themselves for a comfortable chat, as they would have liked, with the grass all sparkling and bristling wet.

Yes, she was quite as wretched as ever, she told him. The week which had gone by since she saw him had in no wise lightened the burden of her discontent. There had even been some additional provocations laid upon her, and she told Montéclin all about them,—about the keys, for instance, which in a fit of temper she had returned to Félicité's keeping; and she told how Cazeau had brought them back to her as if they were something she had accidentally lost, and he had recovered; and how he had said, in that aggravating tone of his, that it was not the custom on Cane river for the negro servants to carry the keys, when there was a mistress at the head of the household.

But Athénaïse could not tell Montéclin anything to increase the disrespect which he already entertained for his brother-in-law; and it was then he unfolded to her a plan which he had conceived and worked out for her deliverance from this galling matrimonial yoke.

It was not a plan which met with instant favor, which she was at once ready to accept, for it involved secrecy and dissimulation, hateful alternatives, both of them. But she was filled with admiration for Montéclin's resources and wonderful talent for contrivance. She accepted the plan; not with the immediate determination to act upon it, rather with the intention to sleep and to dream upon it.

Three days later she wrote to Montéclin that she had abandoned herself to his counsel. Displeasing as it might be to her sense of honesty, it would yet be less trying than to live on with a soul full of bitterness and revolt, as she had done for the past two months.

V

When Cazeau awoke, one morning at his usual very early hour, it was to find the place at his side vacant. This did not surprise him until he discovered that Athénaïse was not in the adjoining room, where he had often found her sleeping in the morning on the lounge. She had perhaps gone out for an early stroll, he reflected, for her jacket and hat were not on the rack where she had hung them the night before. But there were other things absent,—a gown or two from the armoire; and there was a great gap in the piles of lingerie on the shelf; and her traveling-bag was missing, and so were her bits of jewelry from the toilet tray— and Athénaïse was gone!

But the absurdity of going during the night, as if she had been a prisoner, and he the keeper of a dungeon! So much secrecy and mystery, to go sojourning out on the Bon Dieu! Well, the Michés might keep

their daughter after this. For the companionship of no woman on earth
would he again undergo the humiliating sensation of baseness that had
overtaken him in passing the old oak-tree in the fallow meadow.

But a terrible sense of loss overwhelmed Cazeau. It was not new or
sudden; he had felt it for weeks growing upon him, and it seemed to
culminate with Athénaïse's flight from home. He knew that he could
again compel her return as he had done once before,—compel her to
return to the shelter of his roof, compel her cold and unwilling submis-
sion to his love and passionate transports; but the loss of self-respect
seemed to him too dear a price to pay for a wife.

He could not comprehend why she had seemed to prefer him above
others; why she had attracted him with eyes, with voice, with a hundred
womanly ways, and finally distracted him with love which she seemed,
in her timid, maidenly fashion, to return. The great sense of loss came
from the realization of having missed a chance for happiness,—a chance
that would come his way again only through a miracle. He could not
think of himself loving any other woman, and could not think of Athénaïse ever—even at some remote date—caring for him.

He wrote her a letter, in which he disclaimed any further intention
of forcing his commands upon her. He did not desire her presence ever
again in his home unless she came of her free will, uninfluenced by
family or friends; unless she could be the companion he had hoped for
in marrying her, and in some measure return affection and respect for
the love which he continued and would always continue to feel for her.
This letter he sent out to the rigolet by a messenger early in the day.
But she was not out on the rigolet, and had not been there.

The family turned instinctively to Montéclin, and almost literally fell
upon him for an explanation; he had been absent from home all night.
There was much mystification in his answers, and a plain desire to mis-
lead in his assurances of ignorance and innocence.

But with Cazeau there was no doubt or speculation when he accosted
the young fellow. "Montéclin, w'at have you done with Athénaïse?" he
questioned bluntly. They had met in the open road on horseback, just
as Cazeau ascended the river bank before his house.

"W'at have you done to Athénaïse?" returned Montéclin for answer.

"I don't reckon you've considered yo' conduct by any light of decency
an' propriety in encouraging yo' sister to such an action, but let me
tell you"—

"Voyons! you can let me alone with yo' decency an' morality an'
fiddlesticks. I know you mus' 'a' done Athénaïse pretty mean that she
can't live with you; an' fo' my part, I'm mighty durn glad she had the
spirit to quit you."

"I ain't in the humor to take any notice of yo' impertinence, Montéclin; but let me remine you that Athénaïse is nothing but a chile in character; besides that, she's my wife, an' I hole you responsible fo' her safety an' welfare. If any harm of any description happens to her, I'll strangle you, by God, like a rat, and fling you in Cane river, if I have to hang fo' it!" He had not lifted his voice. The only sign of anger was a savage gleam in his eyes.

"I reckon you better keep yo' big talk fo' the women, Cazeau," replied Montéclin, riding away.

But he went doubly armed after that, and intimated that the precaution was not needless, in view of the threats and menaces that were abroad touching his personal safety.

VI

Athénaïse reached her destination sound of skin and limb, but a good deal flustered, a little frightened, and altogether excited and interested by her unusual experiences.

Her destination was the house of Sylvie, on Dauphine Street, in New Orleans,—a three-story gray brick, standing directly on the banquette, with three broad stone steps leading to the deep front entrance. From the second-story balcony swung a small sign, conveying to passers-by the intelligence that within were "*chambres garnies.*"

It was one morning in the last week of April that Athénaïse presented herself at the Dauphine Street house. Sylvie was expecting her, and introduced her at once to her apartment, which was in the second story of the back ell, and accessible by an open, outside gallery. There was a yard below, paved with broad stone flagging; many fragrant flowering shrubs and plants grew in a bed along the side of the opposite wall, and others were distributed about in tubs and green boxes.

It was a plain but large enough room into which Athénaïse was ushered, with matting on the floor, green shades and Nottingham-lace curtains at the windows that looked out on the gallery, and furnished with a cheap walnut suit. But everything looked exquisitely clean, and the whole place smelled of cleanliness.

Athénaïse at once fell into the rocking-chair, with the air of exhaustion and intense relief of one who has come to the end of her troubles. Sylvie, entering behind her, laid the big traveling-bag on the floor and deposited the jacket on the bed.

She was a portly quadroon of fifty or there-about, clad in an ample *volante* of the old-fashioned purple calico so much affected by her class. She wore large golden hoop-earrings, and her hair was combed plainly, with every appearance of effort to smooth out the kinks. She had broad, coarse features, with a nose that turned up, exposing the wide nostrils, and that seemed to emphasize the loftiness and command of her bearing,—a dignity that in the presence of white people assumed a character of respectfulness, but never of obsequiousness. Sylvie believed firmly in maintaining the color line, and would not suffer a white person, even a child, to call her "Madame Sylvie,"—a title which she exacted religiously, however, from those of her own race.

"I hope you be please' wid yo' room, madame," she observed amiably. "Dat's de same room w'at yo' brother, M'sieur Miché, all time like w'en he come to New Orlean'. He well, M'sieur Miché? I receive' his letter las' week, an' dat same day a gent'man want I give 'im dat room. I say, 'No, dat room already ingage'.' Ev-body like dat room on 'count it so quite (quiet). M'sieur Gouvernail, dere in nax' room, you can't pay 'im! He been stay t'ree year' in dat room; but all fix' up fine wid his own furn'ture an' books, 'tel you can't see! I say to 'im plenty time', 'M'sieur Gouvernail, w'y you don't take dat t'ree-story front, now, long it's empty?' He tells me, 'Leave me 'lone, Sylvie; I know a good room w'en I fine it, me.' "

She had been moving slowly and majestically about the apartment, straightening and smoothing down bed and pillows, peering into ewer and basin, evidently casting an eye around to make sure that everything was as it should be.

"I sen' you some fresh water, madame," she offered upon retiring from the room. "An' w'en you want an't'ing, you jus' go out on de gall'ry an' call Pousette: she year you plain,—she right down dere in de kitchen."

Athénaïse was really not so exhausted as she had every reason to be after that interminable and circuitous way by which Montéclin had seen fit to have her conveyed to the city.

Would she ever forget that dark and truly dangerous midnight ride along the "coast" to the mouth of Cane river! There Montéclin had parted with her, after seeing her aboard the St. Louis and Shreveport packet which he knew would pass there before dawn. She had received instructions to disembark at the mouth of Red river, and there transfer to the first south-bound steamer for New Orleans; all of which instructions she had followed implicitly, even to making her way at once to Sylvie's upon her arrival in the city. Montéclin had enjoined secrecy and much caution; the clandestine nature of the affair gave it a savor of adventure which was highly pleasing to him. Eloping with his sister was only a little less engaging than eloping with some one else's sister.

But Montéclin did not do the *grand seigneur* by halves. He had paid Sylvie a whole month in advance for Athénaïse's board and lodging. Part of the sum he had been forced to borrow, it is true, but he was not niggardly.

Athénaïse was to take her meals in the house, which none of the other lodgers did; the one exception being that Mr. Gouvernail was served with breakfast on Sunday mornings.

Sylvie's clientèle came chiefly from the southern parishes; for the most part, people spending but a few days in the city. She prided herself upon the quality and highly respectable character of her patrons, who came and went unobtrusively.

The large parlor opening upon the front balcony was seldom used. Her guests were permitted to entertain in this sanctuary of elegance,— but they never did. She often rented it for the night to parties of respectable and discreet gentlemen desiring to enjoy a quiet game of cards outside the bosom of their families. The second-story hall also led by a long window out on the balcony. And Sylvie advised Athénaïse, when she grew weary of her back room, to go and sit on the front balcony, which was shady in the afternoon, and where she might find diversion in the sounds and sights of the street below.

Athénaïse refreshed herself with a bath, and was soon unpacking her few belongings, which she ranged neatly away in the bureau drawers and the armoire.

She had revolved certain plans in her mind during the past hour or so. Her present intention was to live on indefinitely in this big, cool, clean back room on Dauphine street. She had thought seriously, for moments, of the convent, with all readiness to embrace the vows of poverty and chastity; but what about obedience? Later, she intended, in some roundabout way, to give her parents and her husband the assurance of her safety and welfare; reserving the right to remain unmolested and lost to them. To live on at the expense of Montéclin's generosity was wholly out of the question, and Athénaïse meant to look about for some suitable and agreeable employment.

The imperative thing to be done at present, however, was to go out in search of material for an inexpensive gown or two; for she found herself in the painful predicament of a young woman having almost literally nothing to wear. She decided upon pure white for one, and some sort of a sprigged muslin for the other.

VII

On Sunday morning, two days after Athénaïse's arrival in the city, she went in to breakfast somewhat later than usual, to find two covers laid at table instead of the one to which she was accustomed. She had been to mass, and did not remove her hat, but put her fan, parasol, and prayer-book aside. The dining-room was situated just beneath her own apartment, and, like all rooms of the house, was large and airy; the floor was covered with a glistening oil-cloth.

The small, round table, immaculately set, was drawn near the open window. There were some tall plants in boxes on the gallery outside; and Pousette, a little, old, intensely black woman, was splashing and dashing buckets of water on the flagging, and talking loud in her Creole patois to no one in particular.

A dish piled with delicate river-shrimps and crushed ice was on the table; a caraffe of crystal-clear water, a few *hors d'œuvres,* beside a small golden-brown crusty loaf of French bread at each plate. A half-bottle of wine and the morning paper were set at the place opposite Athénaïse.

She had almost completed her breakfast when Gouvernail came in and seated himself at table. He felt annoyed at finding his cherished privacy invaded. Sylvie was removing the remains of a mutton-chop from before Athénaïse, and serving her with a cup of café au lait.

"M'sieur Gouvernail," offered Sylvie in her most insinuating and impressive manner, "you please leave me make you acquaint' wid Madame Cazeau. Dat's M'sieur Miché's sister; you meet 'im two t'ree time', you rec'lec', an' been one day to de race wid 'im. Madame Cazeau, you please leave me make you acquaint' wid M'sieur Gouvernail."

Gouvernail expressed himself greatly pleased to meet the sister of Monsieur Miché, of whom he had not the slightest recollection. He inquired after Monsieur Miché's health, and politely offered Athénaïse a part of his newspaper,—the part which contained the Woman's Page and the social gossip.

Athénaïse faintly remembered that Sylvie had spoken of a Monsieur Gouvernail occupying the room adjoining hers, living amid luxurious surroundings and a multitude of books. She had not thought of him further than to picture him a stout, middle-aged gentleman, with a bushy beard turning gray, wearing large gold-rimmed spectacles, and stooping somewhat from much bending over books and writing material. She had confused him in her mind with the likeness of some literary celebrity that she had run across in the advertising pages of a magazine.

Gouvernail's appearance was, in truth, in no sense striking. He looked older than thirty and younger than forty, was of medium height and weight, with a quiet, unobtrusive manner which seemed to ask that he be let alone. His hair was light brown, brushed carefully and parted in the middle. His mustache was brown, and so were his eyes, which had a mild, penetrating quality. He was neatly dressed in the fashion of the day; and his hands seemed to Athénaïse remarkably white and soft for a man's.

He had been buried in the contents of his newspaper, when he suddenly realized that some further little attention might be due to Miché's sister. He started to offer her a glass of wine, when he was surprised and relieved to find that she had quietly slipped away while he was absorbed in his own editorial on Corrupt Legislation.

Gouvernail finished his paper and smoked his cigar out on the gallery. He lounged about, gathered a rose for his buttonhole, and had his regular Sunday-morning confab with Pousette, to whom he paid a weekly stipend for brushing his shoes and clothing. He made a great pretense of haggling over the transaction, only to enjoy her uneasiness and garrulous excitement.

He worked or read in his room for a few hours, and when he quitted the house, at three in the afternoon, it was to return no more till late at night. It was his almost invariable custom to spend Sunday evenings out in the American quarter, among a congenial set of men and women,—*des esprits forts,* all of them, whose lives were irreproachable, yet whose opinions would startle even the traditional "sapeur," for whom "nothing is sacred." But for all his "advanced" opinions, Gouvernail was a liberal-minded fellow; a man or woman lost nothing of his respect by being married.

When he left the house in the afternoon, Athénaïse had already ensconced herself on the front balcony. He could see her through the jalousies when he passed on his way to the front entrance. She had not yet grown lonesome or homesick; the newness of her surroundings made them sufficiently entertaining. She found it diverting to sit there on the front balcony watching people pass by, even though there was no one to talk to. And then the comforting, comfortable sense of not being married!

She watched Gouvernail walk down the street, and could find no fault with his bearing. He could hear the sound of her rockers for some little distance. He wondered what the "poor little thing" was doing in the city, and meant to ask Sylvie about her when he should happen to think of it.

VIII

The following morning, towards noon, when Gouvernail quitted his room, he was confronted by Athénaïse, exhibiting some confusion and trepidation at being forced to request a favor of him at so early a stage of their acquaintance. She stood in her doorway, and had evidently been sewing, as the thimble on her finger testified, as well as a long-threaded needle thrust in the bosom of her gown. She held a stamped but unaddressed letter in her hand.

And would Mr. Gouvernail be so kind as to address the letter to her brother, Mr. Montéclin Miché? She would hate to detain him with explanations this morning,—another time, perhaps,—but now she begged that he would give himself the trouble.

He assured her that it made no difference, that it was no trouble whatever; and he drew a fountain pen from his pocket and addressed the letter at her dictation, resting it on the inverted rim of his straw hat. She wondered a little at a man of his supposed erudition stumbling over the spelling of "Montéclin" and "Miché."

She demurred at overwhelming him with the additional trouble of posting it, but he succeeded in convincing her that so simple a task as the posting of a letter would not add an iota to the burden of the day. Moreover, he promised to carry it in his hand, and thus avoid any possible risk of forgetting it in his pocket.

After that, and after a second repetition of the favor, when she had told him that she had had a letter from Montéclin, and looked as if she wanted to tell him more, he felt that he knew her better. He felt that he knew her well enough to join her out on the balcony, one night, when he found her sitting there alone. He was not one who deliberately sought the society of women, but he was not wholly a bear. A little commiseration for Athénaïse's aloneness, perhaps some curiosity to know further what manner of woman she was, and the natural influence of her feminine charm were equal unconfessed factors in turning his steps towards the balcony when he discovered the shimmer of her white gown through the open hall window.

It was already quite late, but the day had been intensely hot, and neighboring balconies and doorways were occupied by chattering groups of humanity, loath to abandon the grateful freshness of the outer air. The voices about her served to reveal to Athénaïse the feeling of loneliness that was gradually coming over her. Notwithstanding certain dormant impulses, she craved human sympathy and companionship.

She shook hands impulsively with Gouvernail, and told him how glad she was to see him. He was not prepared for such an admission, but it pleased him immensely, detecting as he did that the expression was as sincere as it was outspoken. He drew a chair up within comfortable conversational distance of Athénaïse, though he had no intention of talking more than was barely necessary to encourage Madame—He had actually forgotten her name!

He leaned an elbow on the balcony rail, and would have offered an opening remark about the oppressive heat of the day, but Athénaïse did not give him the opportunity. How glad she was to talk to some one, and how she talked!

An hour later she had gone to her room, and Gouvernail stayed smoking on the balcony. He knew her quite well after that hour's talk.

It was not so much what she had said as what her half saying had revealed to his quick intelligence. He knew that she adored Montéclin, and he suspected that she adored Cazeau without being herself aware of it. He had gathered that she was self-willed, impulsive, innocent, ignorant, unsatisfied, dissatisfied; for had she not complained that things seemed all wrongly arranged in this world, and no one was permitted to be happy in his own way? And he told her he was sorry she had discovered that primordial fact of existence so early in life.

He commiserated her loneliness, and scanned his bookshelves next morning for something to lend her to read, rejecting everything that offered itself to his view. Philosophy was out of the question, and so was poetry; that is, such poetry as he possessed. He had not sounded her literary tastes, and strongly suspected she had none; that she would have rejected The Duchess as readily as Mrs. Humphry Ward. He compromised on a magazine.

It had entertained her passably, she admitted, upon returning it. A New England story had puzzled her, it was true, and a Creole tale had offended her, but the pictures had pleased her greatly, especially one which had reminded her so strongly of Montéclin after a hard day's ride that she was loath to give it up. It was one of Remington's Cowboys, and Gouvernail insisted upon her keeping it,—keeping the magazine.

He spoke to her daily after that, and was always eager to render her some service or to do something towards her entertainment.

One afternoon he took her out to the lake end. She had been there once, some years before, but in winter, so the trip was comparatively new and strange to her. The large expanse of water studded with pleasure-boats, the sight of children playing merrily along the grassy palisades, the music, all enchanted her. Gouvernail thought her the most beautiful woman he had ever seen. Even her gown—the sprigged muslin—appeared to him the most charming one imaginable. Nor could anything be more becoming than the arrangement of her brown hair under the white sailor hat, all rolled back in a soft puff from her radiant face. And she carried her parasol and lifted her skirts and used her fan in ways that seemed quite unique and peculiar to herself, and which he considered almost worthy of study and imitation.

They did not dine out there at the water's edge, as they might have done, but returned early to the city to avoid the crowd. Athénaïse wanted to go home, for she said Sylvie would have dinner prepared and would be expecting her. But it was not difficult to persuade her to dine instead in the quiet little restaurant that he knew and liked, with its sanded floor, its secluded atmosphere, its delicious menu, and its obsequious waiter wanting to know what he might have the honor of serving to "monsieur et madame." No wonder he made the mistake, with Gouvernail assuming such an air of proprietorship! But Athénaïse was very tired after it all; the sparkle went out of her face, and she hung draggingly on his arm in walking home.

He was reluctant to part from her when she bade him good-night at her door and thanked him for the agreeable evening. He had hoped she would sit outside until it was time for him to regain the newspaper office. He knew that she would undress and get into her peignoir and lie upon her bed; and what he wanted to do, what he would have given much to do, was to go and sit beside her, read to her something restful, soothe her, do her bidding, whatever it might be. Of course there was no use in thinking of that. But he was surprised at his growing desire to be serving her. She gave him an opportunity sooner than he looked for.

"Mr. Gouvernail," she called from her room, "will you be so kine as to call Pousette an' tell her she fo'got to bring my ice-water?"

He was indignant at Pousette's negligence, and called severely to her over the banisters. He was sitting before his own door, smoking. He knew that Athénaïse had gone to bed, for her room was dark, and she had opened the slats of the door and windows. Her bed was near a window.

Pousette came flopping up with the ice-water, and with a hundred excuses: "Mo pa oua vou à tab c'te lanuite, mo cri vou pé gagni déja là-bas; parole! Vou pas cri conté ça Madame Sylvie?" She had not seen Athénaïse at table, and thought she was gone. She swore to this, and hoped Madame Sylvie would not be informed of her remissness.

A little later Athénaïse lifted her voice again: "Mr. Gouvernail, did you remark that young man sitting on the opposite side from us, coming in, with a gray coat an' a blue ban' aroun' his hat?"

Of course Gouvernail had not noticed any such individual, but he assured Athénaïse that he had observed the young fellow particularly.

"Don't you think he looked something,—not very much, of co'se,—but don't you think he had a little faux-air of Montéclin?"

"I think he looked strikingly like Montéclin," asserted Gouvernail, with the one idea of prolonging the conversation. "I meant to call your attention to the resemblance, and something drove it out of my head."

"The same with me," returned Athénaïse. "Ah, my dear Montéclin! I wonder w'at he is doing now?"

"Did you receive any news, any letter from him to-day?" asked Gouvernail, determined that if the conversation ceased it should not be through lack of effort on his part to sustain it.

"Not to-day, but yesterday. He tells me that maman was so dis-

tracted with uneasiness that finally, to pacify her, he was fo'ced to confess that he knew w'ere I was, but that he was boun' by a vow of secrecy
not to reveal it. But Cazeau has not noticed him or spoken to him since
he threaten' to throw po' Montéclin in Cane river. You know Cazeau
wrote me a letter the morning I lef', thinking I had gone to the rigolet.
An' maman opened it, an' said it was full of the mos' noble sentiments,
an' she wanted Montéclin to sen' it to me; but Montéclin refuse' poin'
blank, so he wrote to me."

Gouvernail preferred to talk of Montéclin. He pictured Cazeau as
unbearable, and did not like to think of him.

A little later Athénaïse called out, "Good-night, Mr. Gouvernail."

"Good-night," he returned reluctantly. And when he thought that
she was sleeping, he got up and went away to the midnight pandemon-
ium of his newspaper office.

IX

Athénaïse could not have held out through the month had it not been
for Gouvernail. With the need of caution and secrecy always uppermost
in her mind, she made no new acquaintances, and she did not seek out
persons already known to her; however, she knew so few, it required
little effort to keep out of their way. As for Sylvie, almost every moment
of her time was occupied in looking after her house; and, moreover, her
deferential attitude towards her lodgers forbade anything like the gos-
sipy chats in which Athénaïse might have condescended sometimes to
indulge with her land-lady. The transient lodgers, who came and went,
she never had occasion to meet. Hence she was entirely dependent upon
Gouvernail for company.

He appreciated the situation fully; and every moment that he could
spare from his work he devoted to her entertainment. She liked to be
out of doors, and they strolled together in the summer twilight through
the mazes of the old French quarter. They went again to the lake end,
and stayed for hours on the water; returning so late that the streets
through which they passed were silent and deserted. On Sunday morning he arose at an unconscionable hour to take her to the French market,
knowing that the sights and sounds there would interest her. And he
did not join the intellectual coterie in the afternoon, as he usually did,
but placed himself all day at the disposition and service of Athénaïse.

Notwithstanding all, his manner toward her was tactful, and evinced
intelligence and a deep knowledge of her character, surprising upon so
brief an acquaintance. For the time he was everything to her that she
would have him; he replaced home and friends. Sometimes she won-

dered if he had ever loved a woman. She could not fancy him loving any one passionately, rudely, offensively, as Cazeau loved her. Once she was so naïve as to ask him outright if he had ever been in love, and he assured her promptly that he had not. She thought it an admirable trait in his character, and esteemed him greatly therefor.

He found her crying one night, not openly or violently. She was leaning over the gallery rail, watching the toads that hopped about in the moonlight, down on the damp flagstones of the courtyard. There was an oppressively sweet odor rising from the cape jessamine. Pousette was down there, mumbling and quarreling with some one, and seeming to be having it all her own way,—as well she might, when her companion was only a black cat that had come in from a neighboring yard to keep her company.

Athénaïse did admit feeling heart-sick, body-sick, when he questioned her; she supposed it was nothing but homesick. A letter from Montéclin had stirred her all up. She longed for her mother, for Montéclin; she was sick for a sight of the cotton-fields, the scent of the ploughed earth, for the dim, mysterious charm of the woods, and the old tumble-down home on the Bon Dieu.

As Gouvernail listened to her, a wave of pity and tenderness swept through him. He took her hands and pressed them against him. He wondered what would happen if he were to put his arms around her.

He was hardly prepared for what happened, but he stood it courageously. She twined her arms around his neck and wept outright on his shoulder; the hot tears scalding his cheek and neck, and her whole body shaken in his arms. The impulse was powerful to strain her to him; the temptation was fierce to seek her lips; but he did neither.

He understood a thousand times better than she herself understood it that he was acting as substitute for Montéclin. Bitter as the conviction was, he accepted it. He was patient; he could wait. He hoped some day to hold her with a lover's arms. That she was married made no particle of difference to Gouvernail. He could not conceive or dream of it making a difference. When the time came that she wanted him,—as he hoped and believed it would come,—he felt he would have a right to her. So long as she did not want him, he had no right to her,—no more than her husband had. It was very hard to feel her warm breath and tears upon his cheek, and her struggling bosom pressed against him and her soft arms clinging to him and his whole body and soul aching for her, and yet to make no sign.

He tried to think what Montéclin would have said and done, and to act accordingly. He stroked her hair, and held her in a gentle embrace, until the tears dried and the sobs ended. Before releasing herself she kissed him against the neck; she had to love somebody in her own way! Even that he endured like a stoic. But it was well he left her, to plunge into the thick of rapid, breathless, exacting work till nearly dawn.

Athénaïse was greatly soothed, and slept well. The touch of friendly hands and caressing arms had been very grateful. Henceforward she would not be lonely and unhappy, with Gouvernail there to comfort her.

X

The fourth week of Athénaïse's stay in the city was drawing to a close. Keeping in view the intention which she had of finding some suitable and agreeable employment, she had made a few tentatives in that direction. But with the exception of two little girls who had promised to take piano lessons at a price that would be embarrassing to mention, these attempts had been fruitless. Moreover, the homesickness kept coming back, and Gouvernail was not always there to drive it away.

She spent much of her time weeding and pottering among the flowers down in the courtyard. She tried to take an interest in the black cat, and a mockingbird that hung in a cage outside the kitchen door, and a disreputable parrot that belonged to the cook next door, and swore hoarsely all day long in bad French.

Beside, she was not well; she was not herself, as she told Sylvie. The climate of New Orleans did not agree with her. Sylvie was distressed to learn this, as she felt in some measure responsible for the health and well-being of Monsieur Miché's sister; and she made it her duty to inquire closely into the nature and character of Athénaïse's malaise.

Sylvie was very wise, and Athénaïse was very ignorant. The extent of her ignorance and the depth of her subsequent enlightenment were bewildering. She stayed a long, long time quite still, quite stunned, after her interview with Sylvie, except for the short, uneven breathing that ruffled her bosom. Her whole being was steeped in a wave of ecstasy. When she finally arose from the chair in which she had been seated, and looked at herself in the mirror, a face met hers which she seemed to see for the first time, so transfigured was it with wonder and rapture.

One mood quickly followed another, in this new turmoil of her senses, and the need of action became uppermost. Her mother must know at once, and her mother must tell Montéclin. And Cazeau must know. As she thought of him, the first purely sensuous tremor of her life swept over her. She half whispered his name, and the sound of it brought red blotches into her cheeks. She spoke it over and over, as if it were some new, sweet sound born out of darkness and confusion, and reaching her for the first time. She was impatient to be with him. Her whole passionate nature was aroused as if by a miracle.

She seated herself to write to her husband. The letter he would get in the morning, and she would be with him at night. What would he say? How would he act? She knew that he would forgive her, for had he not written a letter?—and a pang of resentment toward Montéclin shot through her. What did he mean by withholding that letter? How dared he not have sent it?

Athénaïse attired herself for the street, and went out to post the letter which she had penned with a single thought, a spontaneous impulse. It would have seemed incoherent to most people, but Cazeau would understand.

She walked along the street as if she had fallen heir to some magnificent inheritance. On her face was a look of pride and satisfaction that passers-by noticed and admired. She wanted to talk to some one, to tell some person; and she stopped at the corner and told the oyster-woman, who was Irish, and who God-blessed her, and wished prosperity to the race of Cazeaus for generations to come. She held the oyster-woman's fat, dirty little baby in her arms and scanned it curiously and observingly, as if a baby were a phenomenon that she encountered for the first time in life. She even kissed it!

Then what a relief it was to Athénaïse to walk the streets without dread of being seen and recognized by some chance acquaintance from Red river! No one could have said now that she did not know her own mind.

She went directly from the oyster-woman's to the office of Harding & Offdean, her husband's merchants; and it was with such an air of partnership, almost proprietorship, that she demanded a sum of money on her husband's account, they gave it to her as unhesitatingly as they would have handed it over to Cazeau himself. When Mr. Harding, who knew her, asked politely after her health, she turned so rosy and looked so conscious, he thought it a great pity for so pretty a woman to be such a little goose.

Athénaïse entered a dry-goods store and bought all manner of things,—little presents for nearly everybody she knew. She bought whole bolts of sheerest, softest, downiest white stuff; and when the clerk, in trying to meet her wishes, asked if she intended it for infant's use, she could have sunk through the floor, and wondered how he might have suspected it.

As it was Montéclin who had taken her away from her husband, she wanted it to be Montéclin who should take her back to him. So she wrote him a very curt note,—in fact it was a postal card,—asking that he meet her at the train on the evening following. She felt convinced that after what had gone before, Cazeau would await her at their own home; and she preferred it so.

Then there was the agreeable excitement of getting ready to leave, of packing up her things. Pousette kept coming and going, coming and going; and each time that she quitted the room it was with something that Athénaïse had given her,—a handkerchief, a petticoat, a pair of stockings with two tiny holes at the toes, some broken prayer-beads, and finally a silver dollar.

Next it was Sylvie who came along bearing a gift of what she called "a set of pattern',"—things of complicated design which never could have been obtained in any new-fangled bazaar or pattern-store, that Sylvie had acquired of a foreign lady of distinction whom she had nursed years before at the St. Charles hotel. Athénaïse accepted and handled them with reverence, fully sensible of the great compliment and favor, and laid them religiously away in the trunk which she had lately acquired.

She was greatly fatigued after the day of unusual exertion, and went early to bed and to sleep. All day long she had not once thought of Gouvernail, and only did think of him when aroused for a brief instant by the sound of his foot-falls on the gallery, as he passed in going to his room. He had hoped to find her up, waiting for him.

But the next morning he knew. Some one must have told him. There was no subject known to her which Sylvie hesitated to discuss in detail with any man of suitable years and discretion.

Athénaïse found Gouvernail waiting with a carriage to convey her to the railway station. A momentary pang visited her for having forgotten him so completely, when he said to her, "Sylvie tells me you are going away this morning."

He was kind, attentive, and amiable, as usual, but respected to the utmost the new dignity and reserve that her manner had developed since yesterday. She kept looking from the carriage window, silent, and embarrassed as Eve after losing her ignorance. He talked of the muddy streets and the murky morning, and of Montéclin. He hoped she would find everything comfortable and pleasant in the country, and trusted she would inform him whenever she came to visit the city again. He talked as if afraid or mistrustful of silence and himself.

At the station she handed him her purse, and he bought her ticket, secured for her a comfortable section, checked her trunk, and got all the bundles and things safely aboard the train. She felt very grateful. He pressed her hand warmly, lifted his hat, and left her. He was a man of intelligence, and took defeat gracefully; that was all. But as he made his way back to the carriage, he was thinking, "By heaven, it hurts, it hurts!"

XI

Athénaïse spent a day of supreme happiness and expectancy. The fair sight of the country unfolding itself before her was balm to her vision and to her soul. She was charmed with the rather unfamiliar, broad, clean sweep of the sugar plantations, with their monster sugar-houses, their rows of neat cabins like little villages of a single street, and their impressive homes standing apart amid clusters of trees. There were sudden glimpses of a bayou curling between sunny, grassy banks, or creeping sluggishly out from a tangled growth of wood, and brush, and fern, and poison-vines, and palmettos. And passing through the long stretches of monotonous woodlands, she would close her eyes and taste in anticipation the moment of her meeting with Cazeau. She could think of nothing but him.

It was night when she reached her station. There was Montéclin, as she had expected, waiting for her with a two-seated buggy, to which he had hitched his own swift-footed, spirited pony. It was good, he felt, to have her back on any terms; and he had no fault to find since she came of her own choice. He more than suspected the cause of her coming; her eyes and her voice and her foolish little manner went far in revealing the secret that was brimming over in her heart. But after he had deposited her at her own gate, and as he continued his way toward the rigolet, he could not help feeling that the affair had taken a very disappointing, an ordinary, a most commonplace turn, after all. He left her in Cazeau's keeping.

Her husband lifted her out of the buggy, and neither said a word until they stood together within the shelter of the gallery. Even then they did not speak at first. But Athénaïse turned to him with an appealing gesture. As he clasped her in his arms, he felt the yielding of her whole body against him. He felt her lips for the first time respond to the passion of his own.

The country night was dark and warm and still, save for the distant notes of an accordion which some one was playing in a cabin away off. A little negro baby was crying somewhere. As Athénaïse withdrew from her husband's embrace, the sound arrested her.

"Listen, Cazeau! How Juliette's baby is crying! Pauvre ti chou, I wonder w'at is the matter with it?"

ALICE DUNBAR-NELSON

The Goodness of Saint Rocque

"The Goodness of Saint Rocque" was first published in *The Goodness of Saint Rocque and Other Stories* (1899). Dunbar-Nelson sought to render the exotic and fascinating culture of the Lousiana Creoles. These French-speaking descendants of early Spanish and French settlers had distinctive folkways and a dialect that provided rich material for the regionalist writer. Along with George Washington Cable, Kate Chopin, and Grace Elizabeth King, Alice Dunbar-Nelson wrote many stories and sketches that registered the cadences and depicted the customs and social mores of a Creole culture. Unlike these others, however, Dunbar-Nelson was herself a part of that culture and sometimes lectured on Creole customs. Perhaps for that reason she brought a finer sympathy and greater familiarity to her subject matter. In any event, her rendering of Creole French is masterful, and even in her detached narrator, mostly through innovative syntax, she reproduces Creole cadences. As with much local-color writing, the plot of this story is thin and serves to introduce the reader to the world Manuela inhabits. Manuela seeks to reclaim her authority over Theophilé's affection first, by means of the charm she purchases from the "Wizened One," and second through her prayers at the church. Manuela's wish is gratified. By seating Manuela beside his mother, Theophilé declares his intentions to marry her. The reader is left to decide whether the power of the charm, the goodness of St. Rocque, or Manuela's own beauty and vivacity has worked this local miracle.

* * *

Manuela was tall and slender and graceful, and once you knew her the lithe form could never be mistaken. She walked with the easy spring that comes from a perfectly arched foot. To-day she swept swiftly down Marais Street, casting a quick glance here and there from under her heavy veil as if she feared she was being followed. If you had peered under the veil, you would have seen that Manuela's dark eyes were swollen and discoloured about the lids, as though they had known a sleepless, tearful night.

There had been a picnic the day before, and as merry a crowd of giddy, chattering Creole girls and boys as ever you could see boarded the ramshackle dummy-train that puffed its way wheezily out wide Elysian Fields Street, around the lily-covered bayous, to Milneburg-on-the-

Lake. Now, a picnic at Milneburg is a thing to be remembered for ever. One charters a rickety-looking, weather-beaten dancing-pavilion, built over the water, and after storing the children—for your true Creole never leaves the small folks at home—and the baskets and mothers downstairs, the young folks go upstairs and dance to the tune of the best band you ever heard. For what can equal the music of a violin, a guitar, a cornet, and a bass viol to trip the quadrille to at a picnic?

Then one can fish in the lake and go bathing under the prim bath-houses, so severely separated sexually, and go rowing on the lake in a trim boat, followed by the shrill warnings of anxious mamans. And in the evening one comes home, hat crowned with cool gray Spanish moss, hands burdened with fantastic latanier baskets woven by the brown bayou boys, hand in hand with your dearest one, tired but happy.

At this particular picnic, however, there had been bitterness of spirit. Theophilé was Manuela's own especial property, and Theophilé had proven false. He had not danced a single waltz or quadrille with Man-uela, but had deserted her for Claralie, blonde and petite. It was Claralie whom Theophilé had rowed out on the lake; it was Claralie whom Theophilé had gallantly led to dinner; it was Claralie's hat that he wreathed with Spanish moss, and Claralie whom he escorted home after the jolly singing ride in town on the little dummy-train.

Not that Manuela lacked partners or admirers. Dear no! she was too graceful and beautiful for that. There had been more than enough for her. But Manuela loved Theophilé, you see, and no one could take his place. Still, she had tossed her head and let her silvery laughter ring out in the dance, as though she were the happiest of mortals, and had tripped home with Henri, leaning on his arm, and looking up into his eyes as though she adored him.

This morning she showed the traces of a sleepless night and an aching heart as she walked down Marais Street. Across wide St. Rocque Avenue she hastened. "Two blocks to the river and one below—" she repeated to herself breathlessly. Then she stood on the corner gazing about her, until with a final summoning of a desperate courage she dived through a small wicket gate into a garden of weed-choked flowers.

There was a hoarse, rusty little bell on the gate that gave querulous tongue as she pushed it open. The house that sat back in the yard was little and old and weather-beaten. Its one-story frame had once been painted, but that was a memory remote and traditional. A straggling morning-glory strove to conceal its time-ravaged face. The little walk of broken bits of brick was reddened carefully, and the one little step was scrupulously yellow-washed, which denoted that the occupants were cleanly as well as religious.

Manuela's timid knock was answered by a harsh "Entrez."

It was a small sombre room within, with a bare yellow-washed floor and ragged curtains at the little window. In a corner was a diminutive altar draped with threadbare lace. The red glow of the taper lighted a cheap print of St. Joseph and a brazen crucifix. The human element in the room was furnished by a little, wizened yellow woman, who, black-robed, turbaned, and stern, sat before an uncertain table whereon were greasy cards.

Manuela paused, her eyes blinking at the semi-obscurity within. The Wizened One called in croaking tones:

"An' fo' w'y you come here? Assiezlà, ma'amzelle."

Timidly Manuela sat at the table facing the owner of the voice.

"I want," she began faintly; but the Mistress of the Cards understood: she had had much experience. The cards were shuffled in her long grimy talons and stacked before Manuela.

"Now you cut dem in t'ree part, so—un, deux, trois, bien! You mek' you' weesh wid all you' heart, bien! Yaas, I see, I see!"

Breathlessly did Manuela learn that her lover was true, but "dat light gal, yaas, she mek' nouvena in St. Rocque fo' hees love."

"I give you one lil' charm, yaas," said the Wizened One when the séance was over, and Manuela, all white and nervous, leaned back in the rickety chair. "I give you one lil' charm fo' to ween him back, yaas. You wear h'it 'roun' you' wais', an' he come back. Den you mek prayer at St. Rocque an' burn can'le. Den you come back an' tell me, yaas. Cinquante sous, ma'amzelle. Merci. Good luck go wid you."

Readjusting her veil, Manuela passed out the little wicket gate, treading on air. Again the sun shone, and the breath of the swamps came as healthful sea-breeze unto her nostrils. She fairly flew in the direction of St. Rocque.

There were quite a number of persons entering the white gates of the cemetery, for this was Friday, when all those who wish good luck pray to the saint, and wash their steps promptly at twelve o'clock with a wondrous mixture to guard the house. Manuela bought a candle from the keeper of the little lodge at the entrance, and pausing one instant by the great sun-dial to see if the heavens and the hour were propitious, glided into the tiny chapel, dim and stifling with heavy air from myriad wish-candles blazing on the wide table before the altar-rail. She said her prayer and lighting her candle placed it with the others.

Mon Dieu! how brightly the sun seemed to shine now, she thought, pausing at the door on her way out. Her small finger-tips, still bedewed with holy water, rested caressingly on a gamin's head. The ivy which enfolds the quaint chapel never seemed so green; the shrines which serve as the Way of the Cross never seemed so artistic; the baby graves, even, seemed cheerful.

Theophilé called Sunday. Manuela's heart leaped. He had been spending his Sundays with Claralie. His stay was short and he was plainly bored. But Manuela knelt to thank the good St. Rocque that night, and fondled the charm about her slim waist. There came a box of bonbons during the week, with a decorative card all roses and fringe, from Theophilé; but being a Creole, and therefore superstitiously careful, and having been reared by a wise and experienced maman to mistrust the gifts of a recreant lover, Manuela quietly thrust bonbons, box, and card into the kitchen fire, and the Friday following placed the second candle of her nouvena in St. Rocque.

Those of Manuela's friends who had watched with indignation Theophilé gallantly leading Claralie home from High Mass on Sundays, gasped with astonishment when the next Sunday, with his usual bow, the young man offered Manuela his arm as the worshippers filed out in step to the organ's march. Claralie tossed her head as she crossed herself with holy water, and the pink in her cheeks was brighter than usual.

Manuela smiled a bright good-morning when she met Claralie in St. Rocque the next Friday. The little blonde blushed furiously, and Manuela rushed post-haste to the Wizened One to confer upon this new issue.

"H'it ees good," said the dame, shaking her turbaned head. "She ees 'fraid, she will work, mais you' charm, h'it weel beat her."

And Manuela departed with radiant eyes.

Theophilé was not at Mass Sunday morning, and murderous glances flashed from Claralie to Manuela before the tinkling of the Host-Bell. Nor did Theophilé call at either house. Two hearts beat furiously at the sound of every passing footstep, and two minds wondered if the other were enjoying the beloved one's smiles. Two pair of eyes, however, blue and black, smiled on others, and their owners laughed and seemed none the less happy. For your Creole girls are proud, and would die rather than let the world see their sorrows.

Monday evening Theophilé, the missing, showed his rather sheepish countenance in Manuela's parlour, and explained that he, with some chosen spirits, had gone for a trip—"over the Lake."

"I did not ask you where you were yesterday," replied the girl, saucily.

Theophilé shrugged his shoulders and changed the conversation.

The next week there was a birthday fête in honour of Louise, Theophilé's young sister. Everyone was bidden, and no one thought of refusing, for Louise was young, and this would be her first party. So, though the night was hot, the dancing went on as merrily as light young feet could make it go. Claralie fluffed her dainty white skirts, and cast mischievous sparkles in the direction of Theophilé, who with the maman and Louise was bravely trying not to look self-conscious. Manuela, tall and calm and proud-looking, in a cool, pale yellow gown was apparently enjoying herself without paying the slightest attention to her young host.

"Have I the pleasure of this dance?" he asked her finally, in a lull of the music.

She bowed assent, and as if moved by a common impulse they strolled out of the dancing-room into the cool, quaint garden, where jessamines gave out an overpowering perfume, and a caged mocking-bird complained melodiously to the full moon in the sky.

It must have been an engrossing tête-a-tête, for the call to supper had sounded twice before they heard and hurried into the house. The march had formed with Louise radiantly leading on the arm of papa. Claralie tripped by with Leon. Of course, nothing remained for Theophilé and Manuela to do but to bring up the rear, for which they received much good-natured chaffing.

But when the party reached the dining-room, Theophilé proudly led his partner to the head of the table, at the right hand of maman, and smiled benignly about at the delighted assemblage. Now you know, when a Creole young man places a girl at his mother's right hand at his own table, there is but one conclusion to be deduced therefrom.

If you had asked Manuela, after the wedding was over, how it happened, she would have said nothing, but looked wise.

If you had asked Claralie, she would have laughed and said she always preferred Leon.

If you had asked Theophilé, he would have wondered that you thought he had ever meant more than to tease Manuela.

If you had asked the Wizened One, she would have offered you a charm.

But St. Rocque knows, for he is a good saint, and if you believe in him and are true and good, and make your nouvenas with a clean heart, he will grant your wish.

Part II

REALISM

JOEL CHANDLER HARRIS

Free Joe and the Rest of the World

Harris published this story in the *Century Magazine* in 1886 and collected it in *Free Joe and Other Georgian Sketches* (1887). It was based on a real Free Joe the author had known in his youth in Eatonton, Georgia, and was among Harris's favorite creations. For many readers, this tale of a freed slave who can find no place in the world, either among black slaves or white workers, dramatizes Harris's yearning for the social stability of the antebellum South and his belief that slaves were not worthy of freedom. It is true that Harris was never a totally reconstructed Southerner; however, he knew that a return to a culture of aristocratic planters was neither possible nor desirable. Besides, Free Joe is so thoroughly victimized by events and, more cruelly, by the aptly named "Spite" Calderwood, that his misfortunes approach genuine tragedy. Moreover, there is a basis of identification between the author and his created character. Harris, who was himself called Joe, was extremely self-conscious and shy and may well have felt that like his character he could not "escape the finger of observation." Like Free Joe, too, Harris also felt himself to be something of a social outcast. He was an illegitimate child, whose father had abandoned his mother shortly after his birth, and as a result Harris knew first hand what it felt to be "drifting hither and thither without an owner, to be blown about by all the winds of circumstance."

*   *   *

The name of Free Joe strikes humorously upon the ear of memory. It is impossible to say why, for he was the humblest, the simplest, and the most serious of all God's living creatures, sadly lacking in all those elements that suggest the humorous. It is certain, moreover, that in 1850 the sober-minded citizens of the little Georgian village of Hillsborough were not inclined to take a humorous view of Free Joe, and neither his name nor his presence provoked a smile. He was a black atom, drifting hither and thither without an owner, blown about by all the winds of circumstance, and given over to shiftlessness.

The problems of one generation are the paradoxes of a succeeding one, particularly if war, or some such incident, intervenes to clarify the atmosphere and strengthen the understanding. Thus, in 1850, Free Joe represented not only a problem of large concern, but, in the watchful eyes of Hillsborough, he was the embodiment of that vague and mysterious danger that seemed to be forever lurking on the outskirts of slavery, ready to sound a shrill and ghostly signal in the impenetrable swamps, and steal forth under the midnight stars to murder, rapine, and pillage—a danger always threatening, and yet never assuming shape; intangible, and yet real; impossible, and yet not improbable. Across the serene and smiling front of safety, the pale outlines of the awful shadow of insurrection sometimes fell. With this invisible panorama as a background, it was natural that the figure of Free Joe, simple and humble as it was, should assume undue proportions. Go where he would, do what he might, he could not escape the finger of observation and the kindling eye of suspicion. His lightest words were noted, his slightest actions marked.

Under all the circumstances it was natural that his peculiar condition should reflect itself in his habits and manners. The slaves laughed loudly day by day, but Free Joe rarely laughed. The slaves sang at their work and danced at their frolics, but no one ever heard Free Joe sing or saw him dance. There was something painfully plaintive and appealing in his attitude, something touching in his anxiety to please. He was of the friendliest nature, and seemed to be delighted when he could amuse the little children who had made a playground of the public square. At times he would please them by making his little dog Dan perform all sorts of curious tricks, or he would tell them quaint stories of the beasts of the field and birds of the air; and frequently he was coaxed into relating the story of his own freedom. That story was brief, but tragical.

In the year of our Lord 1840, when a negro speculator of a sportive turn of mind reached the little village of Hillsborough on his way to the Mississippi region, with a caravan of likely negroes of both sexes, he found much to interest him. In that day and at that time there were a number of young men in the village who had not bound themselves over to repentance for the various misdeeds of the flesh. To these young men the negro speculator (Major Frampton was his name) proceeded to address himself. He was a Virginian, he declared; and, to prove the statement, he referred all the festively inclined young men of Hillsborough to a barrel of peach-brandy in one of his covered wagons. In the minds of these young men there was less doubt in regard to the age and quality of the brandy than there was in regard to the negro trader's birthplace. Major Frampton might or might not have been born in the Old Dominion—that was a matter for consideration and inquiry—but there could be no question as to the mellow pungency of the peach-brandy.

In his own estimation, Major Frampton was one of the most accomplished of men. He had summered at the Virginia Springs; he had been to Philadelphia, to Washington, to Richmond, to Lynchburg, and to Charleston, and had accumulated a great deal of experience which he found useful. Hillsborough was hid in the woods of Middle Georgia, and its general aspect of innocence impressed him. He looked on the young men who had shown their readiness to test his peach-brandy as overgrown country boys who needed to be introduced to some of the arts and sciences he had at his command. Thereupon the major pitched his tents, figuratively speaking, and became, for the time being, a part and parcel of the innocence that characterized Hillsborough. A wiser man would doubtless have made the same mistake.

The little village possessed advantages that seemed to be providentially arranged to fit the various enterprises that Major Frampton had in view. There was the auction block in front of the stuccoed courthouse, if he desired to dispose of a few of his negroes; there was a quarter-track, laid out to his hand and in excellent order, if he chose to enjoy the pleasures of horse-racing; there were secluded pine thickets within easy reach, if he desired to indulge in the exciting pastime of cock-fighting; and variously lonely and unoccupied rooms in the second story of the tavern, if he cared to challenge the chances of dice or cards.

Major Frampton tried them all with varying luck, until he began his famous game of poker with Judge Alfred Wellington, a stately gentleman with a flowing white beard and mild blue eyes that gave him the appearance of a benevolent patriarch. The history of the game in which Major Frampton and Judge Alfred Wellington took part is something more than a tradition in Hillsborough, for there are still living three or four men who sat around the table and watched its progress. It is said that at various stages of the game Major Frampton would destroy the cards with which they were playing, and send for a new pack, but the result was always the same. The mild blue eyes of Judge Wellington, with few exceptions, continued to overlook "hands" that were invincible—a habit they had acquired during a long and arduous course of training from Saratoga to New Orleans. Major Frampton lost his money, his horses, his wagons, and all his negroes but one, his body-servant. When his misfortune had reached this limit, the major adjourned the game. The sun was shining brightly, and all nature was cheerful. It is said that the major also seemed to be cheerful. However this may be, he visited the court-house, and executed the papers that gave his body-servant his freedom. This being done, Major Frampton sauntered into a convenient pine thicket, and blew out his brains.

The negro thus freed came to be known as Free Joe. Compelled, under the law, to choose a guardian, he chose Judge Wellington, chiefly because his wife Lucinda was among the negroes won from Major

Frampton. For several years Free Joe had what may be called a jovial time. His wife Lucinda was well provided for, and he found it a comparatively easy matter to provide for himself; so that, taking all the circumstances into consideration, it is not matter for astonishment that he became somewhat shiftless.

When Judge Wellington died, Free Joe's troubles began. The judge's negroes, including Lucinda, went to his half-brother, a man named Calderwood, who was a hard master and a rough customer generally —a man of many eccentricities of mind and character. His neighbors had a habit of alluding to him as "Old Spite"; and the name seemed to fit him so completely that he was known far and near as "Spite" Calderwood. He probably enjoyed the distinction the name gave him, at any rate he never resented it, and it was not often that he missed an opportunity to show that he deserved it. Calderwood's place was two or three miles from the village of Hillsborough, and Free Joe visited his wife twice a week, Wednesday and Saturday nights.

One Sunday he was sitting in front of Lucinda's cabin, when Calderwood happened to pass that way.

"Howdy, marster?" said Free Joe, taking off his hat.

"Who are you?" exclaimed Calderwood abruptly, halting and staring at the negro.

"I'm name' Joe, marster. I'm Lucindy's ole man."

"Who do you belong to?"

"Marse John Evans is my gyardeen, marster."

"Big name—gyardeen. Show your pass."

Free Joe produced that document, and Calderwood read it aloud slowly, as if he found it difficult to get at the meaning:

"To whom it may concern: This is to certify that the boy Joe Frampton has my permission to visit his wife Lucinda."

This was dated at Hillsborough, and signed *"John W. Evans."*

Calderwood read it twice, and then looked at Free Joe, elevating his eyebrows, and showing his discolored teeth.

"Some mighty big words in that there. Evans owns this place, I reckon. When's he comin' down to take hold?"

Free Joe fumbled with his hat. He was badly frightened.

"Lucindy say she speck you wouldn't min' my comin', long ez I behave, marster."

Calderwood tore the pass in pieces and flung it away.

"Don't want no free niggers 'round here," he exclaimed. "There's the big road. It'll carry you to town. Don't let me catch you here no more. Now, mind what I tell you."

Free Joe presented a shabby spectacle as he moved off with his little dog Dan slinking at his heels. It should be said in behalf of Dan, however, that his bristles were up, and that he looked back and growled. It may be that the dog had the advantage of insignificance, but it is difficult to conceive how a dog bold enough to raise his bristles under Calderwood's very eyes could be as insignificant as Free Joe. But both the negro and his little dog seemed to give a new and more dismal aspect to forlornness as they turned into the road and went toward Hillsborough.

After this incident Free Joe appeared to have clearer ideas concerning his peculiar condition. He realized the fact that though he was free he was more helpless than any slave. Having no owner, every man was his master. He knew that he was the object of suspicion, and therefore all his slender resources (ah! how pitifully slender they were!) were devoted to winning, not kindness and appreciation, but toleration; all his efforts were in the direction of mitigating the circumstances that tended to make his condition so much worse than that of the negroes around him—negroes who had friends because they had masters.

So far as his own race was concerned, Free Joe was an exile. If the slaves secretly envied him his freedom (which is to be doubted, considering his miserable condition), they openly despised him, and lost no opportunity to treat him with contumely. Perhaps this was in some measure the result of the attitude which Free Joe chose to maintain toward them. No doubt his instinct taught him that to hold himself aloof from the slaves would be to invite from the whites the toleration which he coveted, and without which even his miserable condition would be rendered more miserable still.

His greatest trouble was the fact that he was not allowed to visit his wife; but he soon found a way out of his difficulty. After he had been ordered away from the Calderwood place, he was in the habit of wandering as far in that direction as prudence would permit. Near the Calderwood place, but not on Calderwood's land, lived an old man named Micajah Staley and his sister Becky Staley. These people were old and very poor. Old Micajah had a palsied arm and hand; but, in spite of this, he managed to earn a precarious living with his turning-lathe.

When he was a slave Free Joe would have scorned these representatives of a class known as poor white trash, but now he found them sympathetic and helpful in various ways. From the back door of their cabin he could hear the Calderwood negroes singing at night, and he sometimes fancied he could distinguish Lucinda's shrill treble rising above the other voices. A large poplar grew in the woods some distance from the Staley cabin, and at the foot of this tree Free Joe would sit for hours with his face turned toward Calderwood's. His little dog Dan would curl up in the leaves near by, and the two seemed to be as comfortable as possible.

One Saturday afternoon Free Joe, sitting at the foot of this friendly poplar, fell asleep. How long he slept, he could not tell; but when he awoke little Dan was licking his face, the moon was shining brightly, and Lucinda his wife stood before him laughing. The dog, seeing that Free Joe was asleep, had grown somewhat impatient, and he concluded to make an excursion to the Calderwood place on his own account. Lucinda was inclined to give the incident a twist in the direction of superstition.

"I 'uz settn' down front er de fireplace," she said, "cookin' me some meat, w'en all of a sudden I year sumpin at de do'—scratch, scratch. I tuck'n tu'n de meat over, en make out I ain't year it. Bimeby it come dar 'gin—scratch, scratch. I up en open de do', I did, en, bless de Lord! dar wuz little Dan, en it look like ter me dat his ribs done grow terge'er. I gin 'im some bread, en den, w'en he start out, I tuck'n foller 'im, kaze, I say ter myse'f, maybe my nigger man mought be some'rs 'roun'. Dat ar little dog got sense, mon."

Free Joe laughed and dropped his hand lightly on Dan's head. For a long time after that he had no difficulty in seeing his wife. He had only to sit by the poplar tree until little Dan could run and fetch her. But after a while the other negroes discovered that Lucinda was meeting Free Joe in the woods, and information of the fact soon reached Calderwood's ears. Calderwood was what is called a man of action. He said nothing; but one day he put Lucinda in his buggy, and carried her to Macon, sixty miles away. He carried her to Macon, and came back without her; and nobody in or around Hillsborough, or in that section, ever saw her again.

For many a night after that Free Joe sat in the woods and waited. Little Dan would run merrily off and be gone a long time, but he always came back without Lucinda. This happened over and over again. The "willis-whistlers" would call and call, like fantom huntsmen wandering on a far-off shore; the screech-owl would shake and shiver in the depths of the woods; the night-hawks, sweeping by on noiseless wings, would snap their beaks as though they enjoyed the huge joke of which Free Joe and little Dan were the victims; and the whippoor-wills would cry to each other through the gloom. Each night seemed to be lonelier than the preceding, but Free Joe's patience was proof against loneliness. There came a time, however, when little Dan refused to go after Lucinda. When Free Joe motioned him in the direction of the Calderwood place, he would simply move about uneasily and whine; then he would curl up in the leaves and make himself comfortable.

One night, instead of going to the poplar tree to wait for Lucinda, Free Joe went to the Staley cabin, and, in order to make his welcome good, as he expressed it, he carried with him an armful of fat-pine splinters. Miss Becky Staley had a great reputation in those parts as a fortune-teller, and the schoolgirls, as well as older people, often tested her powers in this direction, some in jest and some in earnest. Free Joe placed his humble offering of light-wood in the chimney corner, and then seated himself on the steps, dropping his hat on the ground outside.

"Miss Becky," he said presently, "whar in de name er gracious you reckon Lucindy is?"

"Well, the Lord he'p the nigger!" exclaimed Miss Becky, in a tone that seemed to reproduce, by some curious agreement of sight with sound, her general aspect of peakedness. "Well, the Lord he'p the nigger! hain't you been a-seein' her all this blessed time? She's over at old Spite Calderwood's, if she's anywheres, I reckon."

"No'm, dat I ain't, Miss Becky. I ain't seen Lucindy in now gwine on mighty nigh a mont'."

"Well, it hain't a-gwine to hurt you," said Miss Becky, somewhat sharply. "In my day an' time it wuz allers took to be a bad sign when niggers got to honeyin' 'roun' an' gwine on."

"Yessum," said Free Joe, cheerfully assenting to the proposition— "yessum, dat's so, but me an' my ole 'oman, we 'uz raise terge'er, en dey ain't bin many days w'en we 'uz' 'way fum one 'n'er like we is now."

"Maybe she's up an' took up wi' some un else," said Micajah Staley from the corner. "You know what the sayin' is: 'New master, new nigger.'"

"Dat's so, dat's de sayin', but tain't wid my ole 'oman like 'tis wid yuther niggers. Me en her wuz des natally raise up terge'er. Dey's lots likelier niggers dan w'at I is," said Free Joe, viewing his shabbiness with a critical eye, "but I knows Lucindy mos' good ez I does little Dan dar—dat I does."

There was no reply to this, and Free Joe continued:

"Miss Becky, I wish you please, ma'am, take en run yo' kyards en see sump'n n'er 'bout Lucindy; kaze ef she sick, I'm gwine dar. Dey ken take en take me up en gimme a stroppin', but I'm gwine dar."

Miss Becky got her cards, but first she picked up a cup, in the bottom of which were some coffee-grounds. These she whirled slowly round and round, ending finally by turning the cup upside down on the hearth and allowing it to remain in that position.

"I'll turn the cup first," said Miss Becky, "and then I'll run the cards and see what they say."

As she shuffled the cards the fire on the hearth burned low, and in its fitful light the gray-haired, thin-featured woman seemed to deserve the weird reputation which rumor and gossip had given her. She shuffled the cards for some moments, gazing intently in the dying fire; then, throwing a piece of pine on the coals, she made three divisions of the pack, disposing them about in her lap. Then she took the first pile, ran the cards slowly through her fingers, and studied them carefully. To the first she added the second pile. The study of these was evidently not satisfactory. She said nothing, but frowned heavily; and the frown deepened as she added the rest of the cards until the entire fifty-two had passed in review before her. Though she frowned, she seemed to be deeply interested. Without changing the relative position of the cards, she ran them all over again. Then she threw a larger piece of pine on the fire, shuffled the cards afresh, divided them into three piles, and subjected them to the same careful and critical examination.

"I can't tell the day when I've seed the cards run this a-way," she said after a while. "What is an' what ain't, I'll never tell you; but I know what the cards sez."

"W'at does dey say, Miss Becky?" the negro inquired, in a tone the solemnity of which was heightened by its eagerness.

"They er runnin' quare. These here that I'm a-lookin' at," said Miss Becky, "they stan' for the past. Them there, they er the present; and the t'others, they er the future. Here's a bundle"—tapping the ace of clubs with her thumb—"an' here's a journey as plain as the nose on a man's face. Here's Lucinda—"

"Whar she, Miss Becky?"

"Here she is—the queen of spades."

Free Joe grinned. The idea seemed to please him immensely.

"Well, well, well!" he exclaimed. "Ef dat don't beat my time! De queen er spades! W'en Lucindy year dat hit'll tickle 'er, sho'!"

Miss Becky continued to run the cards back and forth through her fingers.

"Here's a bundle an' a journey, and here's Lucinda. An' here's ole Spite Calderwood."

She held the cards toward the negro and touched the king of clubs.

"De Lord he'p my soul!" exclaimed Free Joe with a chuckle. "De faver's dar. Yesser, dat's him! W'at de matter 'long wid all un um, Miss Becky?"

The old woman added the second pile of cards to the first, and then the third, still running them through her fingers slowly and critically. By this time the piece of pine in the fireplace had wrapped itself in a mantle of flame, illuminating the cabin and throwing into strange relief the figure of Miss Becky as she sat studying the cards. She frowned ominously at the cards and mumbled a few words to herself. Then she dropped her hands in her lap and gazed once more into the fire. Her shadow danced and capered on the wall and floor behind her, as if, looking over her shoulder into the future, it could behold a rare spectacle. After a while she picked up the cup that had been turned on the hearth. The coffee-grounds, shaken around, presented what seemed to be a most intricate map.

"Here's the journey," said Miss Becky, presently; "here's the big road, here's rivers to cross, here's the bundle to tote." She paused and sighed. "They hain't no names writ here, an' what it all means I'll never tell you. Cajy, I wish you'd be so good as to han' me my pipe."

"I hain't no hand wi' the kyards," said Cajy, as he handed the pipe, "but I reckon I can patch out your misinformation, Becky, bekaze the other day, whiles I was a-finishin' up Mizzers Perdue's rollin'-pin, I hearn a rattlin' in the road. I looked out, an' Spite Calderwood was a-drivin' by in his buggy, an' thar sot Lucinda by him. It'd in-about drapt out er my min'."

Free Joe sat on the door-sill and fumbled at his hat, flinging it from one hand to the other.

"You ain't see um gwine back, is you, Mars Cajy?" he asked after a while.

"Ef they went back by this road," said Mr. Staley, with the air of one who is accustomed to weigh well his words, "it must 'a' bin endurin' of the time whiles I was asleep, bekaze I hain't bin no furder from my shop than to yon bed."

"Well, sir!" exclaimed Free Joe in an awed tone, which Mr. Staley seemed to regard as a tribute to his extraordinary powers of statement.

"Ef it's my beliefs you want," continued the old man, "I'll pitch 'em at you fair and free. My beliefs is that Spite Calderwood is gone an' took Lucindy outen the county. Bless your heart and soul! when Spite Calderwood meets the Old Boy in the road they'll be a turrible scuffle. You mark what I tell you."

Free Joe, still fumbling with his hat, rose and leaned against the door-facing. He seemed to be embarrassed. Presently he said:

"I speck I better be gittin' 'long. Nex' time I see Lucindy, I'm gwine tell 'er w'at Miss Becky say 'bout de queen er spades—dat I is. Ef dat don't tickle 'er, dey ain't no nigger 'oman never bin tickle'."

He paused a moment, as though waiting for some remark or comment, some confirmation of misfortune, or, at the very least, some endorsement of his suggestion that Lucinda would be greatly pleased to know that she had figured as the queen of spades; but neither Miss Becky nor her brother said anything.

"One minnit ridin' in the buggy 'longside er Mars Spite, en de nex' highfalutin' 'roun' playin' de queen er spades. Mon, deze yer nigger gals gittin' up in de pictur's; dey sholy is."

With a brief "Good night, Miss Becky, Mars Cajy," Free Joe went out into the darkness, followed by little Dan. He made his way to the poplar, where Lucinda had been in the habit of meeting him, and sat down. He sat there a long time; he sat there until little Dan, growing restless, trotted off in the direction of the Calderwood place. Dozing against the poplar, in the gray dawn of the morning, Free Joe heard Spite Calderwood's fox-hounds in full cry a mile away.

"Shoo!" he exclaimed, scratching his head, and laughing to himself, "dem ar dogs is des a-warmin' dat old fox up."

But it was Dan the hounds were after, and the little dog came back no more. Free Joe waited and waited, until he grew tired of waiting. He went back the next night and waited, and for many nights thereafter. His waiting was in vain, and yet he never regarded it as in vain. Careless and shabby as he was, Free Joe was thoughtful enough to have his theory. He was convinced that little Dan had found Lucinda, and that some night when the moon was shining brightly through the trees, the dog would rouse him from his dreams as he sat sleeping at the foot of the poplar tree, and he would open his eyes and behold Lucinda standing over him, laughing merrily as of old; and then he thought what fun they would have about the queen of spades.

How many long nights Free Joe waited at the foot of the poplar tree for Lucinda and little Dan no one can ever know. He kept no account of them, and they were not recorded by Micajah Staley nor by Miss Becky. The season ran into summer and then into fall. One night he went to the Staley cabin, cut the two old people an armful of wood, and seated himself on the doorsteps, where he rested. He was always thankful—and proud, as it seemed—when Miss Becky gave him a cup of coffee, which she was sometimes thoughtful enough to do. He was especially thankful on this particular night.

"You er still layin' off for to strike up wi' Lucindy out thar in the woods, I reckon," said Micajah Staley, smiling grimly. The situation was not without its humorous aspects.

"Oh, dey er comin', Mars Cajy, dey er comin', sho," Free Joe replied. "I boun' you dey'll come; en w'en dey does come, I'll des take en fetch um yer, whar you kin see um wid you own eyes, you en Miss Becky."

"No," said Mr. Staley, with a quick and emphatic gesture of disapproval. "Don't! don't fetch 'em anywheres. Stay right wi' 'em as long as may be."

Free Joe chuckled, and slipped away into the night, while the two old people sat gazing in the fire. Finally Micajah spoke.

"Look at that nigger; look at 'im. He's pine-blank as happy now as a killdee by a mill-race. You can't faze 'em. I'd in-about give up my t'other hand ef I could stan' flat-footed, an' grin at trouble like that there nigger."

"Niggers is niggers," said Miss Becky, smiling grimly, "an' you can't rub it out; yit I lay I've seed a heap of white people lots meaner'n Free

Joe. He grins—an' that's nigger—but I've ketched his under jaw a-tremblin' when Lucindy's name uz brung up. An' I tell you," she went on, bridling up a little, and speaking with almost fierce emphasis, "the Old Boy's done sharpened his claws for Spite Calderwood. You'll see it."

"Me, Rebecca?" said Mr. Staley, hugging his palsied arm; "me? I hope not."

"Well, you'll know it then," said Miss Becky, laughing heartily at her brother's look of alarm.

The next morning Micajah Staley had occasion to go into the woods after a piece of timber. He saw Free Joe sitting at the foot of the poplar, and the sight vexed him somewhat.

"Git up from there," he cried, "an' go an' arn your livin'. A mighty purty pass it's come to, when great big buck niggers can lie a-snorin' in the woods all day, when t'other folks is got to be up an' a-gwine. Git up from there!"

Receiving no response, Mr. Staley went to Free Joe, and shook him by the shoulder; but the negro made no response. He was dead. His hat was off, his head was bent, and a smile was on his face. It was as if he had bowed and smiled when death stood before him, humble to the last. His clothes were ragged; his hands were rough and callous; his shoes were literally tied together with strings; he was shabby in the extreme. A passer-by, glancing at him, could have no idea that such a humble creature had been summoned as a witness before the Lord God of Hosts.

SARAH ORNE JEWETT

Miss Tempy's Watchers

"Miss Tempy's Watchers" was first published in the *Atlantic Monthly* in 1888, before its inclusion in *The King of Folly Island and Other People* later that year and in *Tales of New England* in 1890. Frequently anthologized for its utilization of local-color details, it is also a more subtle story of psychological transformation, social-class interaction, and penuriousness in conflict with altruism. In a sense the most generous act in the story is Miss Tempy's gesture of bringing together her estranged friends, Mrs. Crowe and the unmarried Sarah Ann Binson, to watch over her in death, a situation calculated to bring healing to a community of women. As the two friends grow in understanding and compassion, it is the deceased Miss Tempy who does the watching, as though the dead could trade confidences with the living, guiding Mrs. Crowe to a willingness to share her riches with others and Miss Binson to a new sympathy for her wealthy companion. In the process of their conversation, the two women also elaborate on the character of Miss Tempy, bringing her to life in the story in many acts of financial and psychological charity. The story has the quiet dignity and gentle humor typical of Jewett's remarkable tales of New England.

*   *   *

The time of year was April; the place was a small farming town in New Hampshire, remote from any railroad. One by one the lights had been blown out in the scattered houses near Miss Tempy Dent's; but as her neighbors took a last look out-of-doors, their eyes turned with instinctive curiosity toward the old house, where a lamp burned steadily. They gave a little sigh. "Poor Miss Tempy!" said more than one bereft acquaintance; for the good woman lay dead in her north chamber, and the light was a watcher's light. The funeral was set for the next day, at one o'clock.

The watchers were two of the oldest friends, Mrs. Crowe and Sarah Ann Binson. They were sitting in the kitchen, because it seemed less awesome than the unused best room, and they beguiled the long hours by steady conversation. One would think that neither topics nor opinions would hold out, at that rate, all through the long spring night; but there was a certain degree of excitement just then, and the two women had risen to an unusual level of expressiveness and confidence. Each had already told the other more than one fact that she had determined to keep secret; they were again and again tempted into statements that either would have found impossible by daylight. Mrs. Crowe was knitting a blue yarn stocking for her husband; the foot was already so long that it seemed as if she must have forgotten to narrow it at the proper time. Mrs. Crowe knew exactly what she was about, however; she was of a much cooler disposition than Sister Binson, who made futile attempts at some sewing, only to drop her work into her lap whenever the talk was most engaging.

Their faces were interesting,—of the dry, shrewd, quick-witted New England type, with thin hair twisted neatly back out of the way. Mrs. Crowe could look vague and benignant, and Miss Binson was, to quote her neighbors, a little too sharp-set; but the world knew that she had need to be, with the load she must carry of supporting an inefficient widowed sister and six unpromising and unwilling nieces and nephews. The eldest boy was at last placed with a good man to learn the mason's trade. Sarah Ann Binson, for all her sharp, anxious aspect, never defended herself, when her sister whined and fretted. She was told every week of her life that the poor children never would have had to lift a finger if their father had lived, and yet she had kept her steadfast way with the little farm, and patiently taught the young people many useful things, for which, as everybody said, they would live to thank her. However pleasureless her life appeared to outward view, it was brimful of pleasure to herself.

Mrs. Crowe, on the contrary, was well to do, her husband being a rich farmer and an easy-going man. She was a stingy woman, but for all that she looked kindly; and when she gave away anything, or lifted a finger to help anybody, it was thought a great piece of beneficence, and a compliment, indeed, which the recipient accepted with twice as much gratitude as double the gift that came from a poorer and more generous acquaintance. Everybody liked to be on good terms with Mrs. Crowe. Socially she stood much higher than Sarah Ann Binson. They were both old schoolmates and friends of Temperance Dent, who had asked them, one day, not long before she died, if they would not come together and look after the house, and manage everything, when she was gone. She may have had some hope that they might become closer friends in this period of intimate partnership, and that the richer woman might better understand the burdens of the poorer. They had not kept the house the night before; they were too weary with the care of their old friend, whom they had not left until all was over.

There was a brook which ran down the hillside very near the house, and the sound of it was much louder than usual. When there was silence in the kitchen, the busy stream had a strange insistence in its wild voice, as if it tried to make the watchers understand something that related to the past.

"I declare, I can't begin to sorrow for Tempy yet. I am so glad to have her at rest," whispered Mrs. Crowe. "It is strange to set here without her, but I can't make it clear that she has gone. I feel as if she had got easy and dropped off to sleep, and I'm more scared about waking her up than knowing any other feeling."

"Yes," said Sarah Ann, "it's just like that, ain't it? But I tell you we are goin' to miss her worse than we expect. She's helped me through with many a trial, has Temperance. I ain't the only one who says the same, neither."

These words were spoken as if there were a third person listening; somebody beside Mrs. Crowe. The watchers could not rid their minds of the feeling that they were being watched themselves. The spring wind whistled in the window crack, now and then, and buffeted the little house in a gusty way that had a sort of companionable effect. Yet, on the whole, it was a very still night, and the watchers spoke in a half-whisper.

"She was the freest-handed woman that ever I knew," said Mrs. Crowe, decidedly. "According to her means, she gave away more than anybody. I used to tell her 't wa'n't right. I used really to be afraid that she went without too much, for we have a duty to ourselves."

Sister Binson looked up in a half-amused, unconscious way, and then recollected herself.

Mrs. Crowe met her look with a serious face. "It ain't so easy for me to give as it is for some," she said simply, but with an effort which was made possible only by the occasion. "I should like to say, while Tempy is laying here yet in her own house, that she has been a constant lesson to me. Folks are too kind, and shame me with thanks for what I do. I ain't such a generous woman as poor Tempy was, for all she had nothin' to do with, as one may say."

Sarah Binson was much moved at this confession, and was even pained and touched by the unexpected humility. "You have a good many calls on you"—she began, and then left her kind little compliment half finished.

"Yes, yes, but I've got means enough. My disposition's more of a cross to me as I grow older, and I made up my mind this morning that Tempy's example should be my pattern henceforth." She began to knit faster than ever.

" 'T ain't no use to get morbid: that's what Tempy used to say herself," said Sarah Ann, after a minute's silence. "Ain't it strange to say 'used to say'?" and her own voice choked a little. "She never did like to hear folks git goin' about themselves."

" 'T was only because they're apt to do it so as other folks will say 't wasn't so, an' praise 'em up," humbly replied Mrs. Crowe, "and that ain't my object. There wa'n't a child but what Tempy set herself to work to see what she could do to please it. One time my brother's folks had been stopping here in the summer, from Massachusetts. The children was all little, and they broke up a sight of toys, and left 'em when they were going away. Tempy come right up after they rode by, to see if she couldn't help me set the house to rights, and she caught me just as I was going to fling some of the clutter into the stove. I was kind of tired out, starting 'em off in season. 'Oh, give me them!' says she, real pleading; and she wropped 'em up and took 'em home with her when she went, and she mended 'em up and stuck 'em together, and made some young one or other happy with every blessed one. You'd thought I'd done her the biggest favor. 'No thanks to me. I should ha' burnt 'em, Tempy,' says I."

"Some of 'em came to our house, I know," said Miss Binson. "She'd take a lot o' trouble to please a child, 'stead o' shoving of it out o' the way, like the rest of us when we're drove."

"I can tell you the biggest thing she ever done, and I don't know's there's anybody left but me to tell it. I don't want it forgot," Sarah Binson went on, looking up at the clock to see how the night was going. "It was that pretty-looking Trevor girl, who taught the Corners school, and married so well afterwards, out in New York State. You remember her, I dare say?"

"Certain," said Mrs. Crowe, with an air of interest.

"She was a splendid scholar, folks said, and give the school a great start; but she'd overdone herself getting her education, and working to pay for it, and she all broke down one spring, and Tempy made her come and stop with her a while,—you remember that? Well, she had an uncle, her mother's brother, out in Chicago, who was well off and friendly, and used to write to Lizzie Trevor, and I dare say make her some presents; but he was a lively, driving man, and didn't take time to stop and think about his folks. He hadn't seen her since she was a little girl. Poor Lizzie was so pale and weakly that she just got through the term o' school. She looked as if she was just going straight off in a decline. Tempy, she cosseted her up a while, and then, next thing folks knew, she was tellin' round how Miss Trevor had gone to see her uncle, and meant to visit Niagary Falls on the way, and stop over night. Now I happened to know, in ways I won't dwell on to explain, that the poor girl was in debt for her schoolin' when she come here, and her last quarter's pay had just squared it off at last, and left her without a cent ahead, hardly; but it had fretted her thinking of it, so she paid it all; those might have dunned her that she owed it to. An' I taxed Tempy about the girl's goin' off on such a journey till she owned up, rather 'n have Lizzie blamed, that she'd given her sixty dollars, same 's if she was rolling in riches, and sent her off to have a good rest and vacation."

"Sixty dollars!" exclaimed Mrs. Crowe. "Tempy only had ninety dollars a year that came in to her; rest of her livin' she got by helpin' about, with what she raised off this little piece o' ground, sand one side an' clay the other. An' how often I've heard her tell, years ago, that she'd rather see Niagary than any other sight in the world!"

The women looked at each other in silence; the magnitude of the generous sacrifice was almost too great for their comprehension.

"She was just poor enough to do that!" declared Mrs. Crowe at last, in an abandonment of feeling. "Say what you may, I feel humbled to the dust," and her companion ventured to say nothing. She never had given away sixty dollars at once, but it was simply because she never had it to give. It came to her very lips to say in explanation, "Tempy was so situated;" but she checked herself in time, for she would not betray her own loyal guarding of a dependent household.

"Folks say a great deal of generosity, and this one's being publicsperited, and that one free-handed about giving," said Mrs. Crowe, who was a little nervous in the silence. "I suppose we can't tell the sorrow it would be to some folks not to give, same's 't would be to me not to save. I seem kind of made for that, as if 't was what I'd got to do. I should feel sights better about it if I could make it evident what I was savin' for. If I had a child, now, Sarah Ann," and her voice was a little husky,—"if I had a child, I should think I was heapin' of it up because he was the one trained by the Lord to scatter it again for good. But here's Mr. Crowe and me, we can't do anything with money, and both of us like to keep things same 's they've always been. Now Priscilla Dance was talking away like a mill-clapper, week before last. She'd think I would go right off and get one o' them new-fashioned gilt-and-white papers for the best room, and some new furniture, an' a marble-top table. And I looked at her, all struck up. 'Why,' says I, 'Priscilla, that nice old velvet paper ain't hurt a mite. I shouldn't feel 't was my best room without it. Dan'el says 't is the first thing he can remember rubbin' his little baby fingers on to it, and how splendid he thought them red roses was.' I maintain," continued Mrs. Crowe stoutly, "that folks wastes sights o' good money doin' just such foolish things. Tearin' out the insides o' meetin'-houses, and fixin' the pews different; 't was good enough as 't was with mendin'; then times come, an' they want to put it all back same 's 't was before."

This touched upon an exciting subject to active members of that parish. Miss Binson and Mrs. Crowe belonged to opposite parties, and had at one time come as near hard feelings as they could, and yet escape them. Each hastened to speak of other things and to show her untouched friendliness.

"I do agree with you," said Sister Binson, "that few of us know what use to make of money, beyond every-day necessities. You've seen more o' the world than I have, and know what's expected. When it comes to taste and judgment about such things, I ought to defer to others;" and with this modest avowal the critical moment passed when there might have been an improper discussion.

In the silence that followed, the fact of their presence in a house of death grew more clear than before. There was something disturbing in the noise of a mouse gnawing at the dry boards of a closet wall near by. Both the watchers looked up anxiously at the clock; it was almost the middle of the night, and the whole world seemed to have left them alone with their solemn duty. Only the brook was awake.

"Perhaps we might give a look up-stairs now," whispered Mrs. Crowe, as if she hoped to hear some reason against their going just then to the chamber of death; but Sister Binson rose, with a serious and yet satisfied countenance, and lifted the small lamp from the table. She was much more used to watching than Mrs. Crowe, and much less affected by it. They opened the door into a small entry with a steep stairway; they climbed the creaking stairs, and entered the cold upper room on tiptoe. Mrs. Crowe's heart began to beat very fast as the lamp was put on a high bureau, and made long, fixed shadows about the walls. She went hesitatingly toward the solemn shape under its white drapery, and felt a sense of remonstrance as Sarah Ann gently, but in a business-like way, turned back the thin sheet.

"Seems to me she looks pleasanter and pleasanter," whispered Sarah Ann Binson impulsively, as they gazed at the white face with its wonderful smile. "To-morrow 't will all have faded out. I do believe they kind of wake up a day or two after they die, and it's then they go." She replaced the light covering, and they both turned quickly away; there was a chill in this upper room.

" 'T is a great thing for anybody to have got through, ain't it?" said Mrs. Crowe softly, as she began to go down the stairs on tiptoe. The warm air from the kitchen beneath met them with a sense of welcome and shelter.

"I don' know why it is, but I feel as near again to Tempy down here as I do up there," replied Sister Binson. "I feel as if the air was full of her, kind of. I can sense things, now and then, that she seems to say. Now I never was one to take up with no nonsense of sperits and such, but I declare I felt as if she told me just now to put some more wood into the stove."

Mrs. Crowe preserved a gloomy silence. She had suspected before this that her companion was of a weaker and more credulous disposition than herself. " 'T is a great thing to have got through," she repeated, ignoring definitely all that had last been said. "I suppose you know as well as I that Tempy was one that always feared death. Well, it's all put behind her now; she knows what 't is." Mrs. Crowe gave a little sigh, and Sister Binson's quick sympathies were stirred toward this other old friend, who also dreaded the great change.

"I'd never like to forget almost those last words Tempy spoke plain to me," she said gently, like the comforter she truly was. "She looked up at me once or twice, that last afternoon after I come to set by her, and let Mis' Owen go home; and I says, 'Can I do anything to ease you, Tempy?' and the tears come into my eyes so I couldn't see what kind of a nod she give me. 'No, Sarah Ann, you can't, dear,' says she; and then she got her breath again, and says she, looking at me real meanin', 'I'm only a-gettin' sleepier and sleepier; that's all there is,' says she, and smiled up at me kind of wishful, and shut her eyes. I knew well enough all she meant. She'd been lookin' out for a chance to tell me, and I don' know's she ever said much afterwards."

Mrs. Crowe was not knitting; she had been listening too eagerly. "Yes, 't will be a comfort to think of that sometimes," she said, in acknowledgment.

"I know that old Dr. Prince said once, in evenin' meetin', that he'd watched by many a dyin' bed, as we well knew, and enough o' his sick folks had been scared o' dyin' their whole lives through; but when they come to the last, he'd never seen one but was willin', and most were glad, to go. ' 'T is as natural as bein' born or livin' on,' he said. I don't know what had moved him to speak that night. You know he wa'n't in the habit of it, and 't was the monthly concert of prayer for foreign missions anyways," said Sarah Ann; "but 't was a great stay to the mind to listen to his words of experience."

"There never was a better man," responded Mrs. Crowe, in a really cheerful tone. She had recovered from her feeling of nervous dread, the kitchen was so comfortable with lamplight and firelight; and just then the old clock began to tell the hour of twelve with leisurely whirring strokes.

Sister Binson laid aside her work, and rose quickly and went to the cupboard. "We'd better take a little to eat," she explained. "The night will go fast after this. I want to know if you went and made some o' your nice cupcake, while you was home to-day?" she asked, in a pleased tone; and Mrs. Crowe acknowledged such a gratifying piece of thoughtfulness for this humble friend who denied herself all luxuries. Sarah Ann brewed a generous cup of tea, and the watchers drew their chairs up to the table presently, and quelled their hunger with good country appetites. Sister Binson put a spoon into a small, old-fashioned glass of preserved quince, and passed it to her friend. She was most familiar with the house, and played the part of hostess. "Spread some o' this on your bread and butter," she said to Mrs. Crowe. "Tempy wanted me to use some three or four times, but I never felt to. I know she'd like to have us comfortable now, and would urge us to make a good supper, poor dear."

"What excellent preserves she did make!" mourned Mrs. Crowe. "None of us has got her light hand at doin' things tasty. She made the most o' everything, too. Now, she only had that one old quince-tree down in the far corner of the piece, but she'd go out in the spring and tend to it, and look at it so pleasant, and kind of expect the old thorny thing into bloomin'."

"She was just the same with folks," said Sarah Ann. "And she'd never git more 'n a little apernful o' quinces, but she'd have every mite o' goodness out o' those, and set the glasses up onto her best-room closet shelf, *so* pleased. 'T wa'n't but a week ago to-morrow mornin' I fetched her a little taste o' jelly in a teaspoon; and she says 'Thank ye,' and took it, an' the minute she tasted it she looked up at me as worried as could be. 'Oh, I don't want to eat that,' says she. 'I always keep that in case o' sickness.' 'You're goin' to have the good o' one tumbler yourself,' says I. 'I'd just like to know who's sick now, if you ain't!' An' she couldn't help laughin', I spoke up so smart. Oh, dear me, how I shall miss talkin' over things with her! She always sensed things, and got just the p'int you meant."

"She didn't begin to age until two or three years ago, did she?" asked Mrs. Crowe. "I never saw anybody keep her looks as Tempy did. She looked young long after I begun to feel like an old woman. The doctor used to say 't was her young heart, and I don't know but what he was right. How she did do for other folks! There was one spell she wasn't at home a day to a fortnight. She got most of her livin' so, and that made her own potatoes and things last her through. None o' the young folks could get married without her, and all the old ones was disappointed if she wa'n't round when they was down with sickness and had to go. An' cleanin', or tailorin' for boys, or rug-hookin',—there was nothin' but what she could do as handy as most. 'I do love to work,' —ain't you heard her say that twenty times a week?"

Sarah Ann Binson nodded, and began to clear away the empty plates. "We may want a taste o' somethin' more towards mornin'," she said. "There's plenty in the closet here; and in case some comes from a distance to the funeral, we'll have a little table spread after we get back to the house."

"Yes, I was busy all the mornin'. I've cooked up a sight o' things to bring over," said Mrs. Crowe. "I felt 't was the last I could do for her."

They drew their chairs near the stove again, and took up their work. Sister Binson's rocking-chair creaked as she rocked; the brook sounded louder than ever. It was more lonely when nobody spoke, and presently Mrs. Crowe returned to her thoughts of growing old.

"Yes, Tempy aged all of a sudden. I remember I asked her if she felt as well as common, one day, and she laughed at me good. There, when Mr. Crowe begun to look old, I couldn't help feeling as if somethin' ailed him, and like as not 't was somethin' he was goin' to git right over, and I dosed him for it stiddy, half of one summer."

"How many things we shall be wanting to ask Tempy!" exclaimed Sarah Ann Binson, after a long pause. "I can't make up my mind to doin' without her. I wish folks could come back just once, and tell us how 'tis where they've gone. Seems then we could do without 'em better."

The brook hurried on, the wind blew about the house now and then; the house itself was a silent place, and the supper, the warm fire, and an absence of any new topics for conversation made the watchers drowsy. Sister Binson closed her eyes first, to rest them for a minute; and Mrs. Crowe glanced at her compassionately, with a new sympathy for the hard-worked little woman. She made up her mind to let Sarah Ann have a good rest, while she kept watch alone; but in a few minutes her own knitting was dropped, and she, too, fell asleep. Overhead, the pale shape of Tempy Dent, the outworn body of that generous, loving-hearted, simple soul, slept on also in its white raiment. Perhaps Tempy herself stood near, and saw her own life and its surroundings with new understanding. Perhaps she herself was the only watcher.

Later, by some hours, Sarah Ann Binson woke with a start. There was a pale light of dawn outside the small windows. Inside the kitchen, the lamp burned dim. Mrs. Crowe awoke, too.

"I think Tempy'd be the first to say 't was just as well we both had some rest," she said, not without a guilty feeling.

Her companion went to the outer door, and opened it wide. The fresh air was none too cold, and the brook's voice was not nearly so loud as it had been in the midnight darkness. She could see the shapes of the hills, and the great shadows that lay across the lower country. The east was fast growing bright.

" 'T will be a beautiful day for the funeral," she said, and turned again, with a sigh, to follow Mrs. Crowe up the stairs.

CHARLES W. CHESNUTT

The Sheriff's Children

"The Sheriff's Children" was originally published in the New York *Independent* in 1889 prior to its inclusion in *The Wife of His Youth and Other Stories of the Color Line* a decade later. A powerful study in miscegenation and moral responsibility, it is set in a South still dealing with a legacy of racial exploitation and distrust, mob violence, and respect for aristocratic character and values. These issues come together in the dilemma of the protagonist, a white sheriff who must confront his past when a group of men come to the jail to lynch his African-

American prisoner. But the greater threat to the sheriff is his own sense of ethical conflict and culpability when he learns that the prisoner is in fact his own son. Despite his courageous determination to save his prisoner, the sheriff cannot easily evade the moral consequences of his treatment of the boy's mother, a former slave, nor his own abdication of parental duties, matters still not resolved at the conclusion of the story. Chesnutt once said that he wrote not for the entertainment of a black audience but for the moral instruction of a white readership, a matter well illustrated by the dramatic issues raised in this story.

*   *   *

Branson County, North Carolina, is in a sequestered district of one of the staidest and most conservative States of the Union. Society in Branson County is almost primitive in its simplicity. Most of the white people own the farms they till, and even before the war there were no very wealthy families to force their neighbors, by comparison, into the category of "poor whites."

To Branson County, as to most rural communities in the South, the war is the one historical event that overshadows all others. It is the era from which all local chronicles are dated,—births, deaths, marriages, storms, freshets. No description of the life of any Southern community would be perfect that failed to emphasize the all pervading influence of the great conflict.

Yet the fierce tide of war that had rushed through the cities and along the great highways of the country had comparatively speaking but slightly disturbed the sluggish current of life in this region, remote from railroads and navigable streams. To the north in Virginia, to the west in Tennessee, and all along the seaboard the war had raged; but the thunder of its cannon had not disturbed the echoes of Branson County, where the loudest sounds heard were the crack of some hunter's rifle, the baying of some deep-mouthed hound, or the yodel of some tuneful negro on his way through the pine forest. To the east, Sherman's army had passed on its march to the sea; but no straggling band of "bummers" had penetrated the confines of Branson County. The war, it is true, had robbed the county of the flower of its young manhood; but the burden of taxation, the doubt and uncertainty of the conflict, and the sting of ultimate defeat, had been borne by the people with an apathy that robbed misfortune of half its sharpness.

The nearest approach to town life afforded by Branson County is found in the little village of Troy, the county seat, a hamlet with a population of four or five hundred.

Ten years make little difference in the appearance of these remote Southern towns. If a railroad is built through one of them, it infuses some enterprise; the social corpse is galvanized by the fresh blood of civilization that pulses along the farthest ramifications of our great system of commercial highways. At the period of which I write, no railroad had come to Troy. If a traveler, accustomed to the bustling life of cities, could have ridden through Troy on a summer day, he might easily have fancied himself in a deserted village. Around him he would have seen weather-beaten houses, innocent of paint, the shingled roofs in many instances covered with a rich growth of moss. Here and there he would have met a razor-backed hog lazily rooting his way along the principal thoroughfare; and more than once be would probably have had to disturb the slumbers of some yellow dog, dozing away the hours in the ardent sunshine, and reluctantly yielding up his place in the middle of the dusty road.

On Saturdays the village presented a somewhat livelier appearance, and the shade trees around the court house square and along Front Street served as hitching-posts for a goodly number of horses and mules and stunted oxen, belonging to the farmer-folk who had come in to trade at the two or three local stores.

A murder was a rare event in Branson County. Every well-informed citizen could tell the number of homicides committed in the county for fifty years back, and whether the slayer, in any given instance, had escaped, either by flight or acquittal, or had suffered the penalty of the law. So, when it became known in Troy early one Friday morning in summer, about ten years after the war, that old Captain Walker, who had served in Mexico under Scott, and had left an arm on the field of Gettysburg, had been foully murdered during the night, there was intense excitement in the village. Business was practically suspended, and the citizens gathered in little groups to discuss the murder, and speculate upon the identity of the murderer. It transpired from testimony at the coroner's inquest, held during the morning, that a strange mulatto had been seen going in the direction of Captain Walker's house the night before, and had been met going away from Troy early Friday morning, by a farmer on his way to town. Other circumstances seemed to connect the stranger with the crime. The sheriff organized a posse to search for him, and early in the evening, when most of the citizens of Troy were at supper, the suspected man was brought in and lodged in the county jail.

By the following morning the news of the capture had spread to the farthest limits of the county. A much larger number of people than usual came to town that Saturday,—bearded men in straw hats and blue homespun shirts, and butternut trousers of great amplitude of material and vagueness of outline; women in homespun frocks and slat-bonnets, with faces as expressionless as the dreary sandhills which gave them a meagre sustenance.

The murder was almost the sole topic of conversation. A steady stream of curious observers visited the house of mourning, and gazed upon the rugged face of the old veteran, now stiff and cold in death; and more than one eye dropped a tear at the remembrance of the cheery smile, and the joke—sometimes superannuated, generally feeble, but always good-natured—with which the captain had been wont to greet his acquaintances. There was a growing sentiment of anger among these stern men, toward the murderer who had thus cut down their friend, and a strong feeling that ordinary justice was too slight a punishment for such a crime.

Toward noon there was an informal gathering of citizens in Dan Tyson's store.

"I hear it 'lowed that Square Kyahtah's too sick ter hol' co'te this evenin'," said one, "an' that the purlim'nary hearin' 'll haf ter go over 'tel nex' week."

A look of disappointment went round the crowd.

"Hit's the durndes', meanes' murder ever committed in this caounty," said another, with moody emphasis.

"I s'pose the nigger 'lowed the Cap'n had some greenbacks," observed a third speaker.

"The Cap'n," said another, with an air of superior information, "has left two bairls of Confedrit money, which he 'spected 'ud be good some day er nuther."

This statement gave rise to a discussion of the speculative value of Confederate money; but in a little while the conversation returned to the murder.

"Hangin' air too good fer the murderer," said one; "he oughter be burnt, stidier bein' hung."

There was an impressive pause at this point, during which a jug of moonlight whiskey went the round of the crowd.

"Well," said a round-shouldered farmer, who, in spite of his peaceable expression and faded gray eye, was known to have been one of the most daring followers of a rebel guerrilla chieftain, "what air yer gwine ter do about it? Ef you fellers air gwine ter set down an' let a wuthless nigger kill the bes' white man in Branson, an' not say nuthin' ner do nuthin', *I'll* move outen the caounty."

This speech gave tone and direction to the rest of the conversation. Whether the fear of losing the round-shouldered farmer operated to bring about the result or not is immaterial to this narrative; but, at all events, the crowd decided to lynch the negro. They agreed that this was the least that could be done to avenge the death of their murdered friend, and that it was a becoming way in which to honor his memory. They had some vague notions of the majesty of the law and the rights of the citizen, but in the passion of the moment these sunk into oblivion; a white man had been killed by a negro.

"The Cap'n was an ole sodger," said one of his friends solemnly. "He'll sleep better when he knows that a co'te-martial has be'n hilt an' jestice done."

By agreement the lynchers were to meet at Tyson's store at five o'clock in the afternoon, and proceed thence to the jail, which was situated down the Lumberton Dirt Road (as the old turnpike antedating the plank-road was called), about half a mile south of the court-house. When the preliminaries of the lynching had been arranged, and a committee appointed to manage the affair, the crowd dispersed, some to go to their dinners, and some to secure recruits for the lynching party.

It was twenty minutes to five o'clock, when an excited negro, panting and perspiring, rushed up to the back door of Sheriff Campbell's dwelling, which stood at a little distance from the jail and somewhat farther than the latter building from the court-house. A turbaned colored woman came to the door in response to the negro's knock.

"Hoddy, Sis' Nance."

"Hoddy, Brer Sam."

"Is de shurff in," inquired the negro.

"Yas, Brer Sam, he's eatin' his dinner," was the answer.

"Will yer ax 'im ter step ter de do' a minute, Sis' Nance?"

The woman went into the dining-room, and a moment later the sheriff came to the door. He was a tall, muscular man, of a ruddier complexion than is usual among Southerners. A pair of keen, deep-set gray eyes looked out from under bushy eyebrows, and about his mouth was a masterful expression, which a full beard, once sandy in color, but now profusely sprinkled with gray, could not entirely conceal. The day was hot; the sheriff had discarded his coat and vest, and had his white shirt open at the throat.

"What do you want, Sam?" he inquired of the negro, who stood hat in hand, wiping the moisture from his face with a ragged shirt-sleeve.

"Shurff, dey gwine ter hang de pris'ner w'at's lock' up in de jail. Dey're comin' dis a-way now. I wuz layin' down on a sack er corn down at de sto', behine a pile er flour-bairls, w'en I hearn Doc' Cain en Kunnel Wright talkin' erbout it. I slip' outen de back do', en run here as fas' as I could. I hearn you say down ter de sto' once't dat you wouldn't let nobody take a pris'ner 'way fum you widout walkin' over yo' dead body, en I thought I'd let you know 'fo' dey come, so yer could pertec' de pris'ner."

The sheriff listened calmly, but his face grew firmer, and a determined gleam lit up his gray eyes. His frame grew more erect, and he unconsciously assumed the attitude of a soldier who momentarily expects to meet the enemy face to face.

"Much obliged, Sam," he answered. "I'll protect the prisoner. Who's coming?"

"I dunno who-all *is* comin'," replied the negro. "Dere's Mistah McSwayne, en Doc' Cain, en Maje' McDonal', en Kunnel Wright, en a heap er yuthers. I wuz so skeered I done furgot mo' d'n half un em. I spec' dey mus' be mos' here by dis time, so I'll git outen de way, fer I don' want nobody fer ter think I wuz mix' up in dis business." The negro glanced nervously down the road toward the town, and made a movement as if to go away.

"Won't you have some dinner first?" asked the sheriff.

The negro looked longingly in at the open door, and sniffed the appetizing odor of boiled pork and collards.

"I ain't got no time fer ter tarry, Shurff," he said, "but Sis' Nance mought gin me sump'n I could kyar in my han' en eat on de way."

A moment later Nancy brought him a huge sandwich of split corn-pone, with a thick slice of fat bacon inserted between the halves, and a couple of baked yams. The negro hastily replaced his ragged hat on his head, dropped the yams in the pocket of his capacious trousers, and, taking the sandwich in his hand, hurried across the road and disappeared in the woods beyond.

The sheriff reentered the house, and put on his coat and hat. He then took down a double-barreled shotgun and loaded it with buckshot. Filling the chambers of a revolver with fresh cartridges, he slipped it into the pocket of the sack-coat which he wore.

A comely young woman in a calico dress watched these proceedings with anxious surprise.

"Where are you going, father?" she asked. She had not heard the conversation with the negro.

"I am goin' over to the jail," responded the sheriff. "There's a mob comin' this way to lynch the nigger we've got locked up. But they won't do it," he added, with emphasis.

"Oh, father! don't go!" pleaded the girl, clinging to his arm; "they'll shoot you if you don't give him up."

"You never mind me, Polly," said her father reassuringly, as he gently unclasped her hands from his arm. "I'll take care of myself and the prisoner, too. There ain't a man in Branson County that would shoot me. Besides, I have faced fire too often to be scared away from my duty. You keep close in the house," he continued, "and if any one disturbs you just use the old horse-pistol in the top bureau drawer. It's a little old-fashioned, but it did good work a few years ago."

The young girl shuddered at this sanguinary allusion, but made no further objection to her father's departure.

The sheriff of Branson was a man far above the average of the community in wealth, education, and social position. His had been one of the few families in the county that before the war had owned large estates and numerous slaves. He had graduated at the State University at Chapel Hill, and had kept up some acquaintance with current literature and advanced thought. He had traveled some in his youth, and was looked up to in the county as an authority on all subjects connected with the outer world. At first an ardent supporter of the Union, he had opposed the secession movement in his native State as long as opposition availed to stem the tide of public opinion. Yielding at last to the force of circumstances, he had entered the Confederate service rather late in the war, and served with distinction through several campaigns, rising in time to the rank of colonel. After the war he had taken the oath of allegiance, and had been chosen by the people as the most available candidate for the office of sheriff, to which he had been elected without opposition. He had filled the office for several terms, and was universally popular with his constituents.

Colonel or Sheriff Campbell, as he was indifferently called, as the military or civil title happened to be most important in the opinion of the person addressing him, had a high sense of the responsibility attaching to his office. He had sworn to do his duty faithfully, and he knew what his duty was, as sheriff, perhaps more clearly than he had apprehended it in other passages of his life. It was, therefore, with no uncertainty in regard to his course that he prepared his weapons and went over to the jail. He had no fears for Polly's safety.

The sheriff had just locked the heavy front door of the jail behind him when a half dozen horsemen, followed by a crowd of men on foot, came round a bend in the road and drew near the jail. They halted in front of the picket fence that surrounded the building, while several of the committee of arrangements rode on a few rods farther to the sheriff's house. One of them dismounted and rapped on the door with his riding-whip.

"Is the sheriff at home?" he inquired.

"No, he has just gone out," replied Polly, who had come to the door.

"We want the jail keys," he continued.

"They are not here," said Polly. "The sheriff has them himself." Then she added, with assumed indifference, "He is at the jail now."

The man turned away, and Polly went into the front room, from which she peered anxiously between the slats of the green blinds of a

window that looked toward the jail. Meanwhile the messenger returned
to his companions and announced his discovery. It looked as though
the sheriff had learned of their design and was preparing to resist it.

One of them stepped forward and rapped on the jail door.

"Well, what is it?" said the sheriff, from within.

"We want to talk to you, Sheriff," replied the spokesman.

There was a little wicket in the door; this the sheriff opened, and
answered through it.

"All right, boys, talk away. You are all strangers to me, and I don't
know what business you can have." The sheriff did not think it necessary to recognize anybody in particular on such an occasion; the question of identity sometimes comes up in the investigation of these
extra-judicial executions.

"We're a committee of citizens and we want to get into the jail."

"What for? It ain't much trouble to get into jail. Most people want
to keep out."

The mob was in no humor to appreciate a joke, and the sheriff's
witticism fell dead upon an unresponsive audience.

"We want to have a talk with the nigger that killed Cap'n Walker."

"You can talk to that nigger in the court-house, when he's brought
out for trial. Court will be in session here next week. I know what you
fellows want, but you can't get my prisoner to-day. Do you want to
take the bread out of a poor man's mouth? I get seventy-five cents a
day for keeping this prisoner, and he's the only one in jail. I can't have
my family suffer just to please you fellows."

One or two young men in the crowd laughed at the idea of Sheriff
Campbell's suffering for want of seventy-five cents a day; but they were
frowned into silence by those who stood near them.

"Ef yer don't let us in," cried a voice, "we'll bu's' the do' open."

"Bust away," answered the sheriff, raising his voice so that all could
hear. "But I give you fair warning. The first man that tries it will be
filled with buckshot. I'm sheriff of this county; I know my duty, and I
mean to do it."

"What's the use of kicking, Sheriff?" argued one of the leaders of the
mob. "The nigger is sure to hang anyhow; he richly deserves it; and
we've got to do something to teach the niggers their places, or white
people won't be able to live in the county."

"There's no use talking, boys," responded the sheriff. "I'm a white
man outside, but in this jail I'm sheriff; and if this nigger's to be hung
in this county, I propose to do the hanging. So you fellows might as
well right-about-face, and march back to Troy. You've had a pleasant
trip, and the exercise will be good for you. You know *me*. I've got
powder and ball, and I've faced fire before now, with nothing between

me and the enemy, and I don't mean to surrender this jail while I'm able to shoot." Having thus announced his determination, the sheriff closed and fastened the wicket, and looked around for the best position from which to defend the building.

The crowd drew off a little, and the leaders conversed together in low tones.

The Branson County jail was a small, two-story brick building, strongly constructed, with no attempt at architectural ornamentation. Each story was divided into two large cells by a passage running from front to rear. A grated iron door gave entrance from the passage to each of the four cells. The jail seldom had many prisoners in it, and the lower windows had been boarded up. When the sheriff had closed the wicket, he ascended the steep wooden stairs to the upper floor. There was no window at the front of the upper passage, and the most available position from which to watch the movements of the crowd below was the front window of the cell occupied by the solitary prisoner.

The sheriff unlocked the door and entered the cell. The prisoner was crouched in a corner, his yellow face, blanched with terror, looking ghastly in the semi-darkness of the room. A cold perspiration had gathered on his forehead, and his teeth were chattering with affright.

"For God's sake, Sheriff," he murmured hoarsely, "don't let 'em lynch me; I didn't kill the old man."

The sheriff glanced at the cowering wretch with a look of mingled contempt and loathing.

"Get up," he said sharply. "You will probably be hung sooner or later, but it shall not be to-day, if I can help it. I'll unlock your fetters, and if I can't hold the jail, you'll have to make the best fight you can. If I'm shot, I'll consider my responsibility at an end."

There were iron fetters on the prisoner's ankles, and handcuffs on his wrists. These the sheriff unlocked, and they fell clanking to the floor.

"Keep back from the window," said the sheriff. "They might shoot if they saw you."

The sheriff drew toward the window a pine bench which formed a part of the scanty furniture of the cell, and laid his revolver upon it. Then he took his gun in hand, and took his stand at the side of the window where he could with least exposure of himself watch the movements of the crowd below.

The lynchers had not anticipated any determined resistance. Of course they had looked for a formal protest, and perhaps a sufficient show of opposition to excuse the sheriff in the eye of any stickler for legal formalities. They had not however come prepared to fight a battle, and no one of them seemed willing to lead an attack upon the jail. The leaders of the party conferred together with a good deal of animated gesticulation, which was visible to the sheriff from his outlook, though the distance was too great for him to hear what was said. At length one of them broke away from the group, and rode back to the main body of the lynchers, who were restlessly awaiting orders.

"Well, boys," said the messenger, "we'll have to let it go for the present. The sheriff says he'll shoot, and he's got the drop on us this time. There ain't any of us that want to follow Cap'n Walker jest yet. Besides, the sheriff is a good fellow, and we don't want to hurt 'im. But," he added, as if to reassure the crowd, which began to show signs of disappointment, "the nigger might as well say his prayers, for he ain't got long to live."

There was a murmur of dissent from the mob, and several voices insisted that an attack be made on the jail. But pacific counsels finally prevailed, and the mob sullenly withdrew.

The sheriff stood at the window until they had disappeared around the bend in the road. He did not relax his watchfulness when the last one was out of sight. Their withdrawal might be a mere feint, to be followed by a further attempt. So closely, indeed, was his attention drawn to the outside, that he neither saw nor heard the prisoner creep stealthily across the floor, reach out his hand and secure the revolver which lay on the bench behind the sheriff, and creep as noiselessly back to his place in the corner of the room.

A moment after the last of the lynching party had disappeared there was a shot fired from the woods across the road; a bullet whistled by the window and buried itself in the wooden casing a few inches from where the sheriff was standing. Quick as thought, with the instinct born of a semi-guerrilla army experience, he raised his gun and fired twice at the point from which a faint puff of smoke showed the hostile bullet to have been sent. He stood a moment watching, and then rested his gun against the window, and reached behind him mechanically for the other weapon. It was not on the bench. As the sheriff realized this fact, he turned his head and looked into the muzzle of the revolver.

"Stay where you are, Sheriff," said the prisoner, his eyes glistening, his face almost ruddy with excitement.

The sheriff mentally cursed his own carelessness for allowing him to be caught in such a predicament. He had not expected anything of the kind. He had relied on the negro's cowardice and subordination in the presence of an armed white man as a matter of course. The sheriff was a brave man, but realized that the prisoner had him at an immense disadvantage. The two men stood thus for a moment, fighting a harmless duel with their eyes.

"Well, what do you mean to do?" asked the sheriff with apparent calmness.

"To get away, of course," said the prisoner, in a tone which caused the sheriff to look at him more closely, and with an involuntary feeling of apprehension; if the man was not mad, he was in a state of mind akin to madness, and quite as dangerous. The sheriff felt that he must speak the prisoner fair, and watch for a chance to turn the tables on him. The keen-eyed, desperate man before him was a different being altogether from the groveling wretch who had begged so piteously for life a few minutes before.

At length the sheriff spoke:—

"Is this your gratitude to me for saving your life at the risk of my own? If I had not done so, you would now be swinging from the limb of some neighboring tree."

"True," said the prisoner, "you saved my life, but for how long? When you came in, you said Court would sit next week. When the crowd went away they said I had not long to live. It is merely a choice of two ropes."

"While there's life there's hope," replied the sheriff. He uttered this commonplace mechanically, while his brain was busy in trying to think out some way of escape. "If you are innocent you can prove it."

The mulatto kept his eye upon the sheriff. "I didn't kill the old man," he replied; "but I shall never be able to clear myself. I was at his house at nine o'clock. I stole from it the coat that was on my back when I was taken. I would be convicted, even with a fair trial, unless the real murderer were discovered beforehand."

The sheriff knew this only too well. While he was thinking what argument next to use, the prisoner continued:—

"Throw me the keys—no, unlock the door."

The sheriff stood a moment irresolute. The mulatto's eye glittered ominously. The sheriff crossed the room and unlocked the door leading into the passage.

"Now go down and unlock the outside door."

The heart of the sheriff leaped within him. Perhaps he might make a dash for liberty, and gain the outside. He descended the narrow stairs, the prisoner keeping close behind him.

The sheriff inserted the huge iron key into the lock. The rusty bolt yielded slowly. It still remained for him to pull the door open.

"Stop!" thundered the mulatto, who seemed to divine the sheriff's purpose. "Move a muscle, and I'll blow your brains out."

The sheriff obeyed; he realized that his chance had not yet come.

"Now keep on that side of the passage, and go back upstairs."

Keeping the sheriff under cover of the revolver, the mulatto followed him up the stairs. The sheriff expected the prisoner to lock him into the cell and make his own escape. He had about come to the conclusion that the best thing he could do under the circumstances was to submit quietly, and take his chances of recapturing the prisoner after the alarm had been given. The sheriff had faced death more than once upon the battlefield. A few minutes before, well armed, and with a brick wall between him and them he had dared a hundred men to fight; but he felt instinctively that the desperate man confronting him was not to be trifled with, and he was too prudent a man to risk his life against such heavy odds. He had Polly to look after, and there was a limit beyond which devotion to duty would be quixotic and even foolish.

"I want to get away," said the prisoner, "and I don't want to be captured; for if I am I know I will be hung on the spot. I am afraid," he added somewhat reflectively, "that in order to save myself I shall have to kill you."

"Good God!" exclaimed the sheriff in involuntary terror; "you would not kill the man to whom you owe your own life."

"You speak more truly than you know," replied the mulatto. "I indeed owe my life to you."

The sheriff started. He was capable of surprise, even in that moment of extreme peril. "Who are you?" he asked in amazement.

"Tom, Cicely's son," returned the other. He had closed the door and stood talking to the sheriff through the grated opening. "Don't you remember Cicely—Cicely whom you sold, with her child, to the speculator on his way to Alabama?"

The sheriff did remember. He had been sorry for it many a time since. It had been the old story of debts, mortgages, and bad crops. He had quarreled with the mother. The price offered for her and her child had been unusually large, and he had yielded to the combination of anger and pecuniary stress.

"Good God!" he gasped, "you would not murder your own father?"

"My father?" replied the mulatto. "It were well enough for me to claim the relationship, but it comes with poor grace from you to ask anything by reason of it. What father's duty have you ever performed for me? Did you give me your name, or even your protection? Other white men gave their colored sons freedom and money, and sent them to the free States. *You* sold *me* to the rice swamps."

"I at least gave you the life you cling to," murmured the sheriff.

"Life?" said the prisoner, with a sarcastic laugh. "What kind of a life? You gave me your own blood, your own features,—no man need look at us together twice to see that,—and you gave me a black mother. Poor wretch! She died under the lash, because she had enough womanhood to call her soul her own. You gave me a white man's spirit, and you made me a slave, and crushed it out."

"But you are free now," said the sheriff. He had not doubted, could not doubt, the mulatto's word. He knew whose passions coursed beneath that swarthy skin and burned in the black eyes opposite his own. He saw in this mulatto what he himself might have become had not the safeguards of parental restraint and public opinion been thrown around him.

"Free to do what?" replied the mulatto. "Free in name, but despised and scorned and set aside by the people to whose race I belong far more than to my mother's."

"There are schools," said the sheriff. "You have been to school." He had noticed that the mulatto spoke more eloquently and used better language than most Branson County people.

"I have been to school, and dreamed when I went that it would work some marvelous change in my condition. But what did I learn? I learned to feel that no degree of learning or wisdom will change the color of my skin and that I shall always wear what in my own country is a badge of degradation. When I think about it seriously I do not care particularly for such a life. It is the animal in me, not the man, that flees the gallows. I owe you nothing," he went on, "and expect nothing of you; and it would be no more than justice if I should avenge upon you my mother's wrongs and my own. But still I hate to shoot you; I have never yet taken human life—for I did *not* kill the old captain. Will you promise to give no alarm and make no attempt to capture me until morning, if I do not shoot?"

So absorbed were the two men in their colloquy and their own tumultuous thoughts that neither of them had heard the door below move upon its hinges. Neither of them had heard a light step come stealthily up the stairs, nor seen a slender form creep along the darkening passage toward the mulatto.

The sheriff hesitated. The struggle between his love of life and his sense of duty was a terrific one. It may seem strange that a man who could sell his own child into slavery should hesitate at such a moment, when his life was trembling in the balance. But the baleful influence of human slavery poisoned the very fountains of life, and created new standards of right. The sheriff was conscientious; his conscience had merely been warped by his environment. Let no one ask what his answer would have been; he was spared the necessity of a decision.

"Stop," said the mulatto, "you need not promise. I could not trust you if you did. It is your life for mine; there is but one safe way for me; you must die."

He raised his arm to fire, when there was a flash—a report from the passage behind him. His arm fell heavily at his side, and the pistol dropped at his feet.

The sheriff recovered first from his surprise, and throwing open the door secured the fallen weapon. Then seizing the prisoner he thrust him into the cell and locked the door upon him; after which he turned to Polly, who leaned half-fainting against the wall, her hands clasped over her heart.

"Oh, father, I was just in time!" she cried hysterically, and, wildly sobbing, threw herself into her father's arms.

"I watched until they all went away," she said. "I heard the shot from the woods and I saw you shoot. Then when you did not come out I feared something had happened, that perhaps you had been wounded. I got out the other pistol and ran over here. When I found the door open, I knew something was wrong, and when I heard voices I crept upstairs, and reached the top just in time to hear him say he would kill you. Oh, it was a narrow escape!"

When she had grown somewhat calmer, the sheriff left her standing there and went back into the cell. The prisoner's arm was bleeding from a flesh wound. His bravado had given place to a stony apathy. There was no sign in his face of fear or disappointment or feeling of any kind. The sheriff sent Polly to the house for cloth, and bound up the prisoner's wound with a rude skill acquired during his army life.

"I'll have a doctor come and dress the wound in the morning," he said to the prisoner. "It will do very well until then, if you will keep quiet. If the doctor asks you how the wound was caused, you can say that you were struck by the bullet fired from the woods. It would do you no good to have it known that you were shot while attempting to escape."

The prisoner uttered no word of thanks or apology, but sat in sullen silence. When the wounded arm had been bandaged, Polly and her father returned to the house.

The sheriff was in an unusually thoughtful mood that evening. He put salt in his coffee at supper, and poured vinegar over his pancakes. To many of Polly's questions he returned random answers. When he had gone to bed he lay awake for several hours.

In the silent watches of the night, when he was alone with God, there came into his mind a flood of unaccustomed thoughts. An hour or two before, standing face to face with death, he had experienced a sensation similar to that which drowning men are said to feel—a kind of clarifying of the moral faculty, in which the veil of the flesh, with its obscuring passions and prejudices, is pushed aside for a moment, and all the acts of one's life stand out, in the clear light of truth, in their correct proportions and relations,—a state of mind in which one sees himself as God may be supposed to see him. In the reaction following his rescue, this feeling had given place for a time to far different emotions. But now, in the silence of midnight, something of this clearness of spirit returned to the sheriff. He saw that he had owed some duty to this son of his,—that neither law nor custom could destroy a responsibility inherent in the nature of mankind. He could not thus, in the eyes of God at least, shake off the consequences of his sin. Had he never sinned, this wayward spirit would never have come back from the vanished past to haunt him. As these thoughts came, his anger against the mulatto died away, and in its place there sprang up a great pity. The hand of parental authority might have restrained the passions he had seen burning in the prisoner's eyes when the desperate man spoke the words which had seemed to doom his father to death. The sheriff felt that he might have saved this fiery spirit from the slough of slavery; that he might have sent him to the free North, and given him there, or in some other land, an opportunity to turn to usefulness and honorable pursuits the talents that had run to crime, perhaps to madness; he might, still less, have given this son of his the poor simulacrum of liberty which men of his caste could possess in a slave-holding community; or least of all, but still something, he might have kept the boy on the plantation, where the burdens of slavery would have fallen lightly upon him.

The sheriff recalled his own youth. He had inherited an honored name to keep untarnished; he had had a future to make; the picture of a fair young bride had beckoned him on to happiness. The poor wretch now stretched upon a pallet of straw between the brick walls of the jail had had none of these things,—no name, no father, no mother—in the true meaning of motherhood,—and until the past few years no possible future, and then one vague and shadowy in its outline, and dependent for form and substance upon the slow solution of a problem in which there were many unknown quantities.

From what he might have done to what he might yet do was an easy transition for the awakened conscience of the sheriff. It occurred to him, purely as a hypothesis, that he might permit his prisoner to escape; but his oath of office, his duty as sheriff, stood in the way of such a course, and the sheriff dismissed the idea from his mind. He could, however, investigate the circumstances of the murder, and move Heaven and earth to discover the real criminal, for he no longer doubted the prisoner's innocence; he could employ counsel for the accused, and perhaps influence public opinion in his favor. An acquittal once secured, some plan could be devised by which the sheriff might in some degree atone for his crime against this son of his—against society—against God.

When the sheriff had reached this conclusion he fell into an unquiet slumber, from which he awoke late the next morning.

He went over to the jail before breakfast and found the prisoner lying on his pallet, his face turned to the wall; he did not move when the sheriff rattled the door.

"Good-morning," said the latter, in a tone intended to waken the prisoner.

There was no response. The sheriff looked more keenly at the recumbent figure; there was an unnatural rigidity about its attitude.

He hastily unlocked the door and, entering the cell, bent over the prostrate form. There was no sound of breathing; he turned the body over—it was cold and stiff. The prisoner had torn the bandage from his wound and bled to death during the night. He had evidently been dead several hours.

HAMLIN GARLAND

The Return of a Private

"The Return of a Private," a story Garland based on his memories of his father's return from the Civil War, was originally published in *Arena* in 1890 and then anthologized in *Main-Travelled Roads* a year later. Although it lacks the stylistic polish of the best fiction of the decade, this story has been one of the most widely read of Garland's early works, in part because of the presentation of Private Edward Smith as a representative soldier, sharing the common lot of rural folk on the middle border. Spurred by idealism about the noble objectives of the war, this private returns home ill, injured, and impoverished, his family diminished by his absence, his future comprised beyond redemption. At once fierce and sentimental, with a dual narrative perspective, this story is one of Garland's most poignant descriptions of characters of great heart and simple dignity who endure the harshness of agrarian life in the Midwest.

* * *

The nearer the train drew toward La Crosse, the soberer the little group of "vets" became. On the long way from New Orleans they had beguiled tedium with jokes and friendly chaff; or with planning with elaborate detail what they were going to do now, after the war. A long journey, slowly, irregularly, yet persistently pushing northward. When they entered on Wisconsin territory they gave a cheer, and another when they reached Madison, but after that they sank into a dumb expectancy.

Comrades dropped off at one or two points beyond, until there were only four or five left who were bound for La Crosse County.

Three of them were gaunt and brown, the fourth was gaunt and pale, with signs of fever and ague upon him. One had a great scar down his temple, one limped, and they all had unnaturally large, bright eyes, showing emaciation. There were no bands greeting them at the station, no banks of gayly dressed ladies waving handkerchiefs and shouting "Bravo!" as they came in on the caboose of a freight train into the towns that had cheered and blared at them on their way to war. As they looked out or stepped upon the platform for a moment, while the train stood at the station, the loafers looked at them indifferently. Their blue coats, dusty and grimy, were too familiar now to excite notice, much less a friendly word. They were the last of the army to return, and the loafers were surfeited with such sights.

The train jogged forward so slowly that it seemed likely to be midnight before they should reach La Crosse. The little squad grumbled and swore, but it was no use; the train would not hurry, and, as a matter of fact, it was nearly two o'clock when the engine whistled "down brakes."

All of the group were farmers, living in districts several miles out of the town, and all were poor.

"Now, boys," said Private Smith, he of the fever and ague, "we are landed in La Crosse in the night. We've got to stay somewhere till mornin'. Now I ain't got no two dollars to waste on a hotel. I've got a wife and children, so I'm goin' to roost on a bench and take the cost of a bed out of my hide."

"Same here," put in one of the other men. "Hide'll grow on again, dollars'll come hard. It's goin' to be mighty hot skirmishin' to find a dollar these days."

"Don't think they'll be a deputation of citizens waitin' to 'scort us to a hotel, eh?" said another. His sarcasm was too obvious to require an answer.

Smith went on, "Then at daybreak we'll start for home—at least, I will."

"Well, I'll be dummed if I'll take two dollars out o' *my* hide," one of the younger men said. "I'm goin' to a hotel, ef I don't never lay up a cent."

"That'll do f'r you," said Smith; "but if you had a wife an' three young uns dependin' on yeh—"

"Which I ain't, thank the Lord! and don't intend havin' while the court knows itself."

The station was deserted, chill, and dark, as they came into it at exactly a quarter to two in the morning. Lit by the oil lamps that flared a dull red light over the dingy benches, the waiting room was not an inviting place. The younger man went off to look up a hotel, while the rest remained and prepared to camp down on the floor and benches. Smith was attended to tenderly by the other men, who spread their blankets on the bench for him, and, by robbing themselves, made quite a comfortable bed, though the narrowness of the bench made his sleeping precarious.

It was chill, though August, and the two men, sitting with bowed heads, grew stiff with cold and weariness, and were forced to rise now and again and walk about to warm their stiffened limbs. It did not occur to them, probably, to contrast their coming home with their going forth, or with the coming home of the generals, colonels, or even captains—but to Private Smith, at any rate, there came a sickness at heart almost deadly as he lay there on his hard bed and went over his situation.

In the deep of the night, lying on a board in the town where he had enlisted three years ago, all elation and enthusiasm gone out of him, he faced the fact that with the joy of home-coming was already mingled the bitter juice of care. He saw himself sick, worn out, taking up the work on his half-cleared farm, the inevitable mortgage standing ready with open jaw to swallow half his earnings. He had given three years of his life for a mere pittance of pay, and now!—

Morning dawned at last, slowly, with a pale yellow dome of light rising silently above the bluffs, which stand like some huge storm-devastated castle, just east of the city. Out to the left the great river swept on its massive yet silent way to the south. Bluejays called across the water from hillside to hillside through the clear, beautiful air, and hawks began to skim the tops of the hills. The older men were astir early, but Private Smith had fallen at last into a sleep, and they went out without waking him. He lay on his knapsack, his gaunt face turned toward the ceiling, his hands clasped on his breast, with a curious pathetic effect of weakness and appeal.

An engine switching near woke him at last, and he slowly sat up and stared about. He looked out of the window and saw that the sun was lightening the hills across the river. He rose and brushed his hair as well as he could, folded his blankets up, and went out to find his companions. They stood gazing silently at the river and at the hills.

"Looks natcher'l, don't it?" they said, as he came out.

"That's what it does," he replied. "An' it looks good. D' yeh see that peak?" He pointed at a beautiful symmetrical peak, rising like a slightly truncated cone, so high that it seemed the very highest of them all. It was touched by the morning sun and it glowed like a beacon, and a light scarf of gray morning fog was rolling up its shadowed side.

"My farm's just beyond that. Now, if I can only ketch a ride, we'll be home by dinner-time."

"I'm talkin' about breakfast," said one of the others.

"I guess it's one more meal o' hardtack f'r me," said Smith.

They foraged around, and finally found a restaurant with a sleepy old German behind the counter, and procured some coffee, which they drank to wash down their hardtack.

"Time'll come," said Smith, holding up a piece by the corner, "when this'll be a curiosity."

"I hope to God it will! I bet I've chawed hardtack enough to shingle every house in the coolly. I've chawed it when my lampers was down, and when they wasn't. I've took it dry, soaked, and mashed. I've had it wormy, musty, sour, and blue-mouldy. I've had it in little bits and big bits; 'fore coffee an' after coffee. I'm ready f'r a change. I'd like t' git holt jest about now o' some of the hot biscuits my wife c'n make when she lays herself out f'r company."

"Well, if you set there gabblin', you'll never *see* yer wife."

"Come on," said Private Smith. "Wait a moment, boys; less take suthin'. It's on me." He led them to the rusty tin dipper which hung on a nail beside the wooden water-pail, and they grinned and drank. Then shouldering their blankets and muskets, which they were "takin' home to the boys," they struck out on their last march.

"They called that coffee Jayvy," grumbled one of them, but it never went by the road where government Jayvy resides. I reckon I know coffee from peas."

They kept together on the road along the turnpike, and up the winding road by the river, which they followed for some miles. The river was very lovely, curving down along its sandy beds, pausing now and then under broad basswood trees, or running in dark, swift, silent currents under tangles of wild grapevines, and drooping alders, and haw trees. At one of these lovely spots the three vets sat down on the thick green sward to rest, "on Smith's account." The leaves of the trees were as fresh and green as in June, the jays called cheery greetings to them, and kingfishers darted to and fro with swooping, noiseless flight.

"I tell yeh, boys, this knocks the swamps of Loueesiana into kingdom come."

"You bet. All they c'n raise down there is snakes, niggers, and p'rticler hell."

"An' fightin' men," put in the older man.

"An' fightin' men. If I had a good hook an' line I'd sneak a pick'rel out o' that pond. Say, remember that time I shot that alligator—"

"I guess we'd better be crawlin' along," interrupted Smith, rising and shouldering his knapsack, with considerable effort, which he tried to hide.

"Say, Smith, lemme give you a lift on that."

"I guess I c'n manage," said Smith, grimly.

"Course. But, yo' see, I may not have a chance right off to pay yeh back for the times you've carried my gun and hull caboodle. Say, now, gimme that gun, anyway."

"All right, if yeh feel like it, Jim," Smith replied, and they trudged along doggedly in the sun, which was getting higher and hotter each half-mile.

"Ain't it queer there ain't no teams comin' along," said Smith, after a long silence.

"Well, no, seein's it's Sunday."

"By jinks, that's a fact. It *is* Sunday. I'll git home in time f'r dinner, sure!" he exulted. "She don't hev dinner usially till about *one* on Sundays." And he fell into a muse, in which he smiled.

"Well, I'll git home jest about six o'clock, jest about when the boys are milkin' the cows," said old Jim Cranby. "I'll step into the barn, an' then I'll say: 'He*ah*! why ain't this milkin' done before this time o' day?' An' then won't they yell!" he added, slapping his thigh in great glee.

Smith went on. "I'll jest go up the path. Old Rover'll come down the road to meet me. He won't bark; he'll know me, an' he'll come down waggin' his tail an' showin' his teeth. That's his way of laughin'. An' so I'll walk up to the kitchen door, an' I'll say, 'Dinner f'r a hungry man!' An' then she'll jump up, an'—"

He couldn't go on. His voice choked at the thought of it. Saunders, the third man, hardly uttered a word, but walked silently behind the others. He had lost his wife the first year he was in the army. She died of pneumonia, caught in the autumn rains while working in the fields in his place.

They plodded along till at last they came to a parting of the ways. To the right the road continued up the main valley; to the left it went over the big ridge.

"Well, boys," began Smith, as they grounded their muskets and looked away up the valley, "here's where we shake hands. We've marched together a good many miles, an' now I s'pose we're done."

"Yes, I don't think we'll do any more of it f'r a while. I don't want to, I know."

"I hope I'll see yeh once in a while, boys, to talk over old times."

"Of course," said Saunders, whose voice trembled a little, too. "It ain't *exactly* like dyin'." They all found it hard to look at each other.

"But we'd ought'r go home with you," said Cranby. "You'll never climb that ridge with all them things on yer back."

"Oh, I'm all right! Don't worry about me. Every step takes me nearer home, yeh see. Well, good-by, boys."

They shook hands. "Good-by. Good luck!"

"Same to you. Lemme know how you find things at home."

"Good-by."

"Good-by."

He turned once before they passed out of sight, and waved his cap, and they did the same, and all yelled. Then all marched away with their long, steady, loping, veteran step. The solitary climber in blue walked on for a time, with his mind filled with the kindness of his comrades, and musing upon the many wonderful days they had had together in camp and field.

He thought of his chum, Billy Tripp. Poor Billy! A "minie" ball fell into his breast one day, fell wailing like a cat, and tore a great ragged hole in his heart. He looked forward to a sad scene with Billy's mother and sweetheart. They would want to know all about it. He tried to recall all that Billy had said, and the particulars of it, but there was little to remember, just that wild wailing sound high in the air, a dull slap, a short, quick, expulsive groan, and the boy lay with his face in the dirt in the ploughed field they were marching across.

That was all. But all the scenes he had since been through had not dimmed the horror, the terror of that moment, when his boy comrade fell, with only a breath between a laugh and a death-groan. Poor handsome Billy! Worth millions of dollars was his young life.

These sombre recollections gave way at length to more cheerful feelings as he began to approach his home coolly. The fields and houses grew familiar, and in one or two he was greeted by people seated in the doorways. But he was in no mood to talk, and pushed on steadily, though he stopped and accepted a drink of milk once at the well-side of a neighbor.

The sun was burning hot on that slope, and his step grew slower, in spite of his iron resolution. He sat down several times to rest. Slowly he crawled up the rough, reddish-brown road, which wound along the hillside, under great trees, through dense groves of jack oaks, with treetops far below him on his left hand, and the hills far above him on his right. He crawled along like some minute, wingless variety of fly.

He ate some hardtack, sauced with wild berries, when he reached the summit of the ridge, and sat there for some time, looking down into his home coolly.

Sombre, pathetic figure! His wide, round, gray eyes gazing down into the beautiful valley, seeing and not seeing, the splendid cloud-shadows sweeping over the western hills and across the green and yellow wheat far below. His head drooped forward on his palm, his shoulders took on a tired stoop, his cheek-bones showed painfully. An observer might have said, "He is looking down upon his own grave."

II

Sunday comes in a Western wheat harvest with such sweet and sudden relaxation to man and beast that it would be holy for that reason, if for no other, and Sundays are usually fair in harvest-time. As one goes out into the field in the hot morning sunshine, with no sound abroad save the crickets and the indescribably pleasant silken rustling of the ripened grain, the reaper and the very sheaves in the stubble seem to be resting, dreaming.

Around the house, in the shade of the trees, the men sit, smoking, dozing, or reading the papers, while the women, never resting, move about at the housework. The men eat on Sundays about the same as on other days, and breakfast is no sooner over and out of the way than dinner begins.

But at the Smith farm there were no men dozing or reading. Mrs. Smith was alone with her three children, Mary, nine, Tommy, six, and little Ted, just past four. Her farm, rented to a neighbor, lay at the head of a coolly or narrow gully, made at some far-off post-glacial period by the vast and angry floods of water which gullied these tremendous furrows in the level prairie—furrows so deep that undisturbed portions of the original level rose like hills on either side, rose to quite considerable mountains.

The chickens wakened her as usual that Sabbath morning from dreams of her absent husband, from whom she had not heard for weeks. The shadows drifted over the hills, down the slopes, across the wheat, and up the opposite wall in leisurely way, as if, being Sunday, they could take it easy also. The fowls clustered about the housewife as she went out into the yard. Fuzzy little chickens swarmed out from the coops, where their clucking and perpetually disgruntled mothers tramped about, petulantly thrusting their heads through the spaces between the slats.

A cow called in a deep, musical bass, and a calf answered from a little pen near by, and a pig scurried guiltily out of the cabbages. Seeing all this, seeing the pig in the cabbages, the tangle of grass in the garden, the broken fence which she had mended again and again—the little woman, hardly more than a girl, sat down and cried. The bright Sabbath morning was only a mockery without him!

A few years ago they had bought this farm, paying part, mortgaging the rest in the usual way. Edward Smith was a man of terrible energy. He worked "nights and Sundays," as the saying goes, to clear the farm of its brush and of its insatiate mortgage! In the midst of his Herculean struggle came the call for volunteers, and with the grim and unselfish devotion to his country which made the Eagle Brigade able to "whip its weight in wild-cats," he threw down his scythe and grub-axe, turned his cattle loose, and became a blue-coated cog in a vast machine for killing men, and not thistles. While the millionaire sent his money to England for safe-keeping, this man, with his girl-wife and three babies, left them on a mortgaged farm, and went away to fight for an idea. It was foolish, but it was sublime for all that.

That was three years before, and the young wife, sitting on the well-curb on this bright Sabbath harvest morning, was righteously rebellious. It seemed to her that she had borne her share of the country's sorrow. Two brothers had been killed, the renter in whose hands her husband had left the farm had proved a villain; one year the farm had been without crops, and now the over-ripe grain was waiting the tardy hand of the neighbor who had rented it, and who was cutting his own grain first.

About six weeks before, she had received a letter saying, "We'll be discharged in a little while." But no other word had come from him. She had seen by the papers that his army was being discharged, and from day to day other soldiers slowly percolated in blue streams back into the State and county, but still *her* hero did not return.

Each week she had told the children that he was coming, and she had watched the road so long that it had become unconscious; and as she stood at the well, or by the kitchen door, her eyes were fixed un-thinkingly on the road that wound down the coolly.

Nothing wears on the human soul like waiting. If the stranded mar-iner, searching the sun-bright seas, could once give up hope of a ship, that horrible grinding on his brain would cease. It was this waiting, hoping, on the edge of despair, that gave Emma Smith no rest.

Neighbors said, with kind intentions: "He's sick, maybe, an' can't start north just yet. He'll come along one o' these days."

"Why don't he write?" was her question, which silenced them all. This Sunday morning it seemed to her as if she could not stand it longer. The house seemed intolerably lonely. So she dressed the little ones in their best calico dresses and home-made jackets, and, closing up the house, set off down the coolly to old Mother Gray's.

"Old Widder Gray" lived at the "mouth of the coolly." She was a widow woman with a large family of stalwart boys and laughing girls. She was the visible incarnation of hospitality and optimistic poverty. With Western open-heartedness she fed every mouth that asked food of her, and worked herself to death as cheerfully as her girls danced in the neighborhood harvest dances.

She waddled down the path to meet Mrs. Smith with a broad smile on her face.

"Oh, you little dears! Come right to your granny. Gimme me a kiss! Come right in, Mis' Smith. How are yeh, anyway? Nice mornin', ain't it? Come in an' set down. Everything's in a clutter, but that won't scare you any."

She led the way into the best room, a sunny, square room, carpeted with a faded and patched rag carpet, and papered with white-and-green-striped wall-paper, where a few faded effigies of dead members of the family hung in variously sized oval walnut frames. The house resounded with singing, laughter, whistling, tramping of heavy boots, and riotous scufflings. Half-grown boys came to the door and crooked their fingers at the children, who ran out, and were soon heard in the midst of the fun.

"Don't s'pose you've heard from Ed?" Mrs. Smith shook her head. "He'll turn up some day, when you ain't lookin' for 'm." The good old soul had said that so many times that poor Mrs. Smith derived no comfort from it any longer.

"Liz heard from Al the other day. He's comin' some day this week. Anyhow, they expect him."

"Did he say anything of—"

"No, he didn't," Mrs. Gray admitted. "But then it was only a short letter, anyhow. Al ain't much for writin', anyhow.—But come out and see my new cheese. I tell yeh, I don't believe I ever had better luck in my life. If Ed should come, I want you should take him up a piece of this cheese."

It was beyond human nature to resist the influence of that noisy, hearty, loving household, and in the midst of the singing and laughing the wife forgot her anxiety, for the time at least, and laughed and sang with the rest.

About eleven o'clock a wagon-load more drove up to the door, and Bill Gray, the widow's oldest son, and his whole family, from Sand Lake Coolly, piled out amid a good-natured uproar. Every one talked at once, except Bill, who sat in the wagon with his wrists on his knees, a straw in his mouth, and an amused twinkle in his blue eyes.

"Ain't heard nothin' o' Ed, I s'pose?" he asked in a kind of bellow. Mrs. Smith shook her head. Bill, with a delicacy very striking in such a great giant, rolled his quid in his mouth, and said:

"Didn't know but you had. I hear two or three of the Sand Lake boys are comin'. Left New Orleenes some time this week. Didn't write nothin' about Ed, but no news is good news in such cases, mother always says."

"Well, go put out yer team," said Mrs. Gray, "an' go 'n bring me in some taters, an', Sim, you go see if you c'n find some corn. Sadie, you put on the water to bile. Come now, hustle yer boots, all o' yeh. If I feed this yer crowd, we've got to have some raw materials. If y' think I'm goin' to feed yeh on pie—you're jest mightily mistaken."

The children went off into the fields, the girls put dinner on to boil, and then went to change their dresses and fix their hair. "Somebody might come," they said.

"Land sakes, I *hope* not! I don't know where in time I'd set 'em, 'less they'd eat at the second table," Mrs. Gray laughed, in pretended dismay.

The two older boys, who had served their time in the army, lay out on the grass before the house, and whittled and talked desultorily about the war and the crops, and planned buying a threshing-machine. The older girls and Mrs. Smith helped enlarge the table and put on the dishes, talking all the time in that cheery, incoherent, and meaningful way a group of such women have,—a conversation to be taken for its spirit rather than for its letter, though Mrs. Gray at last got the ear of them all and dissertated at length on girls.

"Girls in love ain't no use in the whole blessed week," she said. "Sundays they're a-lookin' down the road, expectin' he'll *come.* Sunday afternoons they can't think o' nothin' else, 'cause he's *here.* Monday mornin's they're sleepy and kind o' dreamy and slimpsy, and good f'r nothin' on Tuesday and Wednesday. Thursday they git absent-minded, an' begin to look off toward Sunday agin, an' mope aroun' and let the dishwater git cold, right under their noses. Friday they break dishes, an' go off in the best room an' snivel, an' look out o' the winder. Saturdays they have queer spurts o' workin' like all p'ssessed, an' spurts o' frizzin' their hair. An' Sunday they begin it all over agin."

The girls giggled and blushed, all through this tirade from their mother, their broad faces and powerful frames anything but suggestive of lackadaisical sentiment. But Mrs. Smith said:

"Now, Mrs. Gray, I hadn't ought to stay to dinner. You've got—"

"Now you set right down! If any of them girls' beaus comes, they'll have to take what's left, that's all. They ain't s'posed to have much appetite, nohow. No, you're goin' to stay if they starve, an' they ain't no danger o' that."

At one o'clock the long table was piled with boiled potatoes, cords of boiled corn on the cob, squash and pumpkin pies, hot biscuit, sweet pickles, bread and butter, and honey. Then one of the girls took down a conch-shell from a nail, and going to the door, blew a long, fine, free blast, that showed there was no weakness of lungs in her ample chest.

Then the children came out of the forest of corn, out of the creek, out of the loft of the barn, and out of the garden.

"They come to their feed f'r all the world jest like the pigs when y' holler 'poo-ee!' See 'em scoot!" laughed Mrs. Gray, every wrinkle on her face shining with delight.

The men shut up their jack-knives, and surrounded the horse-trough to souse their faces in the cold, hard water, and in a few moments the table was filled with a merry crowd, and a row of wistful-eyed youngsters circled the kitchen wall, where they stood first on one leg and then on the other, in impatient hunger.

"Now pitch in, Mrs. Smith," said Mrs. Gray, presiding over the table. "You know these men critters. They'll eat every grain of it, if yeh give 'em a chance. I swan, they're made o' India-rubber, their stomachs is, I know it."

"Haf to eat to work," said Bill, gnawing a cob with a swift, circular motion that rivalled a corn-sheller in results.

"More like workin' to eat," put in one of the girls, with a giggle. "More eat 'n work with you."

"*You* needn't say anything, Net. Any one that'll eat seven ears—"

"I didn't, no such thing. You piled your cobs on my plate."

"That'll do to tell Ed Varney. It won't go down here where we know yeh."

"Good land! Eat all yeh want! They's plenty more in the fiel's, but I can't afford to give you young uns tea. The tea is for us women-folks, and 'specially f'r Mis' Smith an' Bill's wife. We're a-goin' to tell fortunes by it."

One by one the men filled up and shoved back, and one by one the children slipped into their places, and by two o'clock the women alone remained around the débris-covered table, sipping their tea and telling fortunes.

As they got well down to the grounds in the cup, they shook them with a circular motion in the hand, and then turned them bottom-side-up quickly in the saucer, then twirled them three or four times one way, and three or four times the other, during a breathless pause. Then Mrs. Gray lifted the cup, and, gazing into it with profound gravity, pronounced the impending fate.

It must be admitted that, to a critical observer, she had abundant preparation for hitting close to the mark, as when she told the girls that "somebody was comin'." "It's a man," she went on gravely. "He is cross-eyed—"

"Oh, you hush!" cried Nettie.

"He has red hair, and is death on b'iled corn and hot biscuit."

The others shrieked with delight.

"But he's goin' to get the mitten, that red-headed feller is, for I see another feller comin' up behind him."

"Oh, lemme see, lemme see!" cried Nettie.

"Keep off," said the priestess, with a lofty gesture. "His hair is black. He don't eat so much, and he works more."

The girls exploded in a shriek of laughter, and pounded their sister on the back.

At last came Mrs. Smith's turn, and she was trembling with excitement as Mrs. Gray again composed her jolly face to what she considered a proper solemnity of expression.

"Somebody is comin' to *you*," she said, after a long pause. "He's got a musket on his back. He's a soldier. He's almost here. See?"

She pointed at two little tea-stems, which really formed a faint suggestion of a man with a musket on his back. He had climbed nearly to the edge of the cup. Mrs. Smith grew pale with excitement. She trembled so she could hardly hold the cup in her hand as she gazed into it.

"It's Ed," cried the old woman. "He's on the way home. Heavens an' earth! There he is now!" She turned and waved her hand out toward the road. They rushed to the door to look where she pointed.

A man in a blue coat, with a musket on his back, was toiling slowly up the hill on the sun-bright, dusty road, toiling slowly, with bent head half hidden by a heavy knapsack. So tired it seemed that walking was indeed a process of falling. So eager to get home he would not stop, would not look aside, but plodded on, amid the cries of the locusts, the welcome of the crickets, and the rustle of the yellow wheat. Getting back to God's country, and his wife and babies!

Laughing, crying, trying to call him and the children at the same time, the little wife, almost hysterical, snatched her hat and ran out into the yard. But the soldier had disappeared over the hill into the hollow beyond, and, by the time she had found the children, he was too far away for her voice to reach him. And, besides, she was not sure it was her husband, for he had not turned his head at their shouts. This seemed so strange. Why didn't he stop to rest at his old neighbor's house? Tortured by hope and doubt, she hurried up the coolly as fast as she could push the baby wagon, the blue-coated figure just ahead pushing steadily, silently forward up the coolly.

When the excited, panting little group came in sight of the gate they saw the blue-coated figure standing, leaning upon the rough rail fence, his chin on his palms, gazing at the empty house. His knapsack, canteen, blankets, and musket lay upon the dusty grass at his feet.

He was like a man lost in a dream. His wide, hungry eyes devoured the scene. The rough lawn, the little unpainted house, the field of clear yellow wheat behind it, down across which streamed the sun, now almost ready to touch the high hill to the west, the crickets crying merrily, a cat on the fence near by, dreaming, unmindful of the stranger in blue—

How peaceful it all was. O God! How far removed from all camps, hospitals, battle lines. A little cabin in a Wisconsin coolly, but it was majestic in its peace. How did he ever leave it for those years of tramping, thirsting, killing?

Trembling, weak with emotion, her eyes on the silent figure, Mrs. Smith hurried up to the fence. Her feet made no noise in the dust and grass, and they were close upon him before he knew of them. The oldest boy ran a little ahead. He will never forget that figure, that face. It will always remain as something epic, that return of the private. He fixed his eyes on the pale face covered with a ragged beard.

"Who *are* you, sir?" asked the wife, or, rather, started to ask, for he turned, stood a moment, and then cried:

"Emma!"

"Edward!"

The children stood in a curious row to see their mother kiss this bearded, strange man, the elder girl sobbing sympathetically with her mother. Illness had left the soldier partly deaf, and this added to the strangeness of his manner.

But the youngest child stood away, even after the girl had recognized her father and kissed him. The man turned then to the baby, and said in a curiously unpaternal tone:

"Come here, my little man; don't you know me?" But the baby backed away under the fence and stood peering at him critically.

"My little man!" What meaning in those words! This baby seemed like some other woman's child, and not the infant he had left in his wife's arms. The war had come between him and his baby—he was only a strange man to him, with big eyes; a soldier, with mother hanging to his arm, and talking in a loud voice.

"And this is Tom," the private said, drawing the oldest boy to him. "*He'll* come and see me. *He* knows his poor old pap when he comes home from the war."

The mother heard the pain and reproach in his voice and hastened to apologize.

"You've changed so, Ed. He can't know yeh. This is papa, Teddy; come and kiss him—Tom and Mary do. Come, won't you?" But Teddy still peered through the fence with solemn eyes, well out of reach. He resembled a half-wild kitten that hesitates, studying the tones of one's voice.

"I'll fix him," said the soldier, and sat down to undo his knapsack, out of which he drew three enormous and very red apples. After giving one to each of the older children, he said:

"*Now* I guess he'll come. Eh, my little man? Now come see your pap."

Teddy crept slowly under the fence, assisted by the overzealous Tommy, and a moment later was kicking and squalling in his father's arms. Then they entered the house, into the sitting room, poor, bare, art-forsaken little room, too, with its rag carpet, its square clock, and its two or three chromos and pictures from *Harper's Weekly* pinned about.

"Emma, I'm all tired out," said Private Smith, as he flung himself down on the carpet as he used to do, while his wife brought a pillow to put under his head, and the children stood about munching their apples.

"Tommy, you run and get me a pan of chips, and Mary, you get the tea-kettle on, and I'll go and make some biscuit."

And the soldier talked. Question after question he poured forth about the crops, the cattle, the renter, the neighbors. He slipped his heavy government brogan shoes off his poor, tired, blistered feet, and lay out with utter, sweet relaxation. He was a free man again, no longer a soldier under command. At supper he stopped once, listened and smiled. "That's old Spot. I know her voice. I s'pose that's her calf out there in the pen. I can't milk her to-night, though. I'm too tired. But I tell you, I'd like a drink o' her milk. What's become of old Rove?"

"He died last winter. Poisoned, I guess." There was a moment of sadness for them all. It was some time before the husband spoke again, in a voice that trembled a little.

"Poor old feller! He'd 'a' known me half a mile away. I expected him to come down the hill to meet me. It 'ud 'a' been more like comin' home if I could 'a' seen him comin' down the road an' waggin' his tail, an' laughin' that way he has. I tell yeh, it kind o' took hold o' me to see the blinds down an' the house shut up."

"But, yeh see, we—we expected you'd write again 'fore you started. And then we thought we'd see you if you *did* come," she hastened to explain.

"Well, I ain't worth a cent on writin'. Besides, it's just as well yeh didn't know when I was comin'. I tell you, it sounds good to hear them chickens out there, an' turkeys, an' the crickets. Do you know they don't have just the same kind o' crickets down South? Who's Sam hired t' help cut yer grain?"

"The Ramsey boys."

"Looks like a good crop; but I'm afraid I won't do much gettin' it cut. This cussed fever an' ague has got me down pretty low. I don't know when I'll get rid of it. I'll bet I've took twenty-five pounds of quinine if I've taken a bit. Gimme another biscuit. I tell yeh, they taste good, Emma. I ain't had anything like it—Say, if you'd 'a' hear'd me braggin' to th' boys about your butter 'n' biscuits I'll bet your ears 'ud 'a' burnt."

The private's wife colored with pleasure. "Oh, you're always a-braggin' about your things. Everybody makes good butter."

"Yes; old lady Snyder, for instance."

"Oh, well, she ain't to be mentioned. She's Dutch."

"Or old Mis' Snively. One more cup o' tea, Mary. That's my girl! I'm feeling better already. I just b'lieve the matter with me is, I'm *starved.*"

This was a delicious hour, one long to be remembered. They were like lovers again. But their tenderness, like that of a typical American family, found utterance in tones, rather than in words. He was praising her when praising her biscuit, and she knew it. They grew soberer when he showed where he had been struck, one ball burning the back of his hand, one cutting away a lock of hair from his temple, and one passing through the calf of his leg. The wife shuddered to think how near she had come to being a soldier's widow. Her waiting no longer seemed hard. This sweet, glorious hour effaced it all.

Then they rose, and all went out into the garden and down to the barn. He stood beside her while she milked old Spot. They began to plan fields and crops for next year.

His farm was weedy and encumbered, a rascally renter had run away with his machinery (departing between two days), his children needed clothing, the years were coming upon him, he was sick and emaciated, but his heroic soul did not quail. With the same courage with which he had faced his Southern march he entered upon a still more hazardous future.

Oh, that mystic hour! The pale man with big eyes standing there by the well, with his young wife by his side. The vast moon swinging above the eastern peaks, the cattle winding down the pasture slopes with jangling bells, the crickets singing, the stars blooming out sweet and far and serene; the katydids rhythmically calling, the little turkeys crying querulously, as they settled to roost in the poplar tree near the open gate. The voices at the well drop lower, the little ones nestle in their father's arms at last, and Teddy falls asleep there.

The common soldier of the American volunteer army had returned. His war with the South was over, and his fight, his daily running fight with nature and against the injustice of his fellow-men, was begun again.

AMBROSE BIERCE

An Occurrence at Owl Creek Bridge

"An Occurrence at Owl Creek Bridge" is one of the most famous works of fiction in American literature and the subject of an award-winning film. Bierce took the name for the title from the Battle of Shiloh, where he had fought near Owl Creek, the western boundary of the battlefield. Later, when he served with Union forces in northern Alabama, one of the principal concerns was that Confederate General Nathan Bedford Forrest's cavalry would destroy the railroad bridge near Decatur, interdicting transportation in four directions. Bierce later used this situation, along with the name of the creek from his earlier experience, for his most important story. First published in the *San Francisco Examiner* in 1890 before its inclusion in *Tales of Soldiers and Civilians* in 1891, the story has attracted attention for its unexpected ending, a device that shocked readers of the day. In literary history, however, "An Occurrence at Owl Creek Bridge" is more important for the artistry of its narration, which limits the data to the sensations of the protagonist in the impressionistic opening, shifts to an expository section explaining how Peyton Farquhar came to be at the bridge, and returns to an identification with the protagonist's mind in the conclusion. The artistry of Bierce's story, as much as its subject, emphasizes the reality of death and its tragic consequences by drawing its readers into the sensations of dying even while the protagonist clings to images of those things he valued most in life. It is a brilliant rendering of a tragic event, one, in the midst of war, so common as to be labeled only an "occurrence."

*   *   *

I

A man stood upon a railroad bridge in Northern Alabama, looking down into the swift waters twenty feet below. The man's hands were behind his back, the wrists bound with a cord. A rope loosely encircled his neck. It was attached to a stout cross-timber above his head, and the slack fell to the level of his knees. Some loose boards laid upon the sleepers supporting the metals of the railway supplied a footing for him, and his executioners—two private soldiers of the Federal army, directed by a sergeant, who in civil life may have been a deputy sheriff. At a short remove upon the same temporary platform was an officer in the uniform of his rank, armed. He was a captain. A sentinel at each end of the bridge stood with his rifle in the position known as "support," that is to say, vertical in front of the left shoulder, the hammer resting on the forearm thrown straight across the chest—a formal and unnatural position, enforcing an erect carriage of the body. It did not appear to be the duty of these two men to know what was occurring at the center of the bridge; they merely blockaded the two ends of the foot plank which traversed it.

Beyond one of the sentinels nobody was in sight; the railroad ran straight away into a forest for a hundred yards, then, curving, was lost to view. Doubtless there was an outpost further along. The other bank of the stream was open ground—a gentle acclivity crowned with a stockade of vertical tree trunks, loop-holed for rifles, with a single embrasure through which protruded the muzzle of a brass cannon commanding the bridge. Midway of the slope between bridge and fort were the spectators—a single company of infantry in line, at "parade rest," the butts of the rifles on the ground, the barrels inclining slightly backward against the right shoulder, the hands crossed upon the stock. A lieutenant stood at the right of the line, the point of his sword upon the ground, his left hand resting upon his right. Excepting the group of four at the center of the bridge not a man moved. The company faced the bridge, staring stonily, motionless. The sentinels, facing the banks of the stream, might have been statues to adorn the bridge. The captain stood with folded arms, silent, observing the work of his subordinates but making no sign. Death is a dignitary who, when he comes announced, is to be received with formal manifestations of respect, even by those most familiar with him. In the code of military etiquette silence and fixity are forms of deference.

The man who was engaged in being hanged was apparently about thirty-five years of age. He was a civilian, if one might judge from his dress, which was that of a planter. His features were good—a straight nose, firm mouth, broad forehead, from which his long, dark hair was combed straight back, falling behind his ears to the collar of his well-fitting frock coat. He wore a mustache and pointed beard but no whiskers; his eyes were large and dark gray and had a kindly expression which one would hardly have expected in one whose neck was in the hemp. Evidently this was no vulgar assassin. The liberal military code makes provision for hanging many kinds of people, and gentlemen are not excluded.

The preparations being complete, the two private soldiers stepped aside and each drew away the plank upon which he had been standing. The sergeant turned to the captain, saluted and placed himself immediately behind that officer, who in turn moved apart one pace. These movements left the condemned man and the sergeant standing on the two ends of the same plank, which spanned three of the cross-ties of the bridge. The end upon which the civilian stood almost, but not quite, reached a fourth. This plank had been held in place by the weight of the captain; it was now held by that of the sergeant. At a signal from the former, the latter would step aside, the plank would tilt and the condemned man go down between two ties. The arrangement commended itself to his judgment as simple and effective. His face had not been covered nor his eyes bandaged. He looked a moment at his "unsteadfast footing," then let his gaze wander to the swirling water of the stream racing madly beneath his feet. A piece of dancing driftwood caught his attention and his eyes followed it down the current. How slowly it appeared to move! What a sluggish stream!

He closed his eyes in order to fix his last thoughts upon his wife and children. The water, touched to gold by the early sun, the brooding mists under the banks at some distance down the stream, the fort, the soldiers, the piece of drift—all had distracted him. And now he became conscious of a new disturbance. Striking through the thought of his dear ones was a sound which he could neither ignore nor understand, a sharp, distinct, metallic percussion like the stroke of a blacksmith's hammer upon the anvil; it had the same ringing quality. He wondered what it was, and whether immeasurably distant or near by—it seemed both. Its recurrence was regular, but as slow as the tolling of a death knell. He awaited each stroke with impatience and—he knew not why—apprehension. The intervals of silence grew progressively longer; the delays became maddening. With their greater infrequency the sounds increased in strength and sharpness. They hurt his ear like the thrust of a knife; he feared he would shriek. What he heard was the ticking of his watch.

He unclosed his eyes and saw again the water below him. "If I could free my hands," he thought, "I might throw off the noose and spring into the stream. By diving I could evade the bullets, and, swimming vigorously, reach the bank, take to the woods, and get away home. My home, thank God, is as yet outside their lines; my wife and little ones are still beyond the invader's farthest advance."

As these thoughts, which have here to be set down in words, were flashed into the doomed man's brain rather than evolved from it, the captain nodded to the sergeant. The sergeant stepped aside.

II

Peyton Farquhar was a well-to-do planter, of an old and highly-respected Alabama family. Being a slave owner, and, like other slave owners, a politician, he was naturally an original secessionist and ardently devoted to the Southern cause. Circumstances of an imperious nature which it is unnecessary to relate here, had prevented him from taking service with the gallant army which had fought the disastrous campaigns ending with the fall of Corinth, and he chafed under the inglorious restraint, longing for the release of his energies, the larger life of the soldier, the opportunity for distinction. That opportunity, he felt, would come, as it comes to all in war time. Meanwhile he did what he could. No service was too humble for him to perform in aid of the South, no adventure too perilous for him to undertake if consistent with the character of a civilian who was at heart a soldier, and who in good faith and without too much qualification assented to at least a part of the frankly villainous dictum that all is fair in love and war.

One evening while Farquhar and his wife were sitting on a rustic bench near the entrance to his grounds, a gray-clad soldier rode up to the gate and asked for a drink of water. Mrs. Farquhar was only too happy to serve him with her own white hands. While she was gone to fetch the water, her husband approached the dusty horseman and inquired eagerly for news from the front.

"The Yanks are repairing the railroads," said the man, "and are getting ready for another advance. They have reached the Owl Creek bridge, put it in order, and built a stockade on the other bank. The commandant has issued an order, which is posted everywhere, declaring that any civilian caught interfering with the railroad, its bridges, tunnels, or trains, will be summarily hanged. I saw the order."

"How far is it to the Owl Creek bridge?" Farquhar asked.

"About thirty miles?"

"Is there no force on this side the creek?"

"Only a picket post half a mile out, on the railroad, and a single sentinel at this end of the bridge."

"Suppose a man—a civilian and student of hanging—should elude the picket post and perhaps get the better of the sentinel," said Farquhar, smiling, "what could he accomplish?"

The soldier reflected. "I was there a month ago," he replied. "I observed that the flood of last winter had lodged a great quantity of driftwood against the wooden pier at this end of the bridge. It is now dry and would burn like tow."

The lady had now brought the water, which the soldier drank. He thanked her ceremoniously, bowed to her husband, and rode away. An hour later, after nightfall, he repassed the plantation, going northward in the direction from which he had come. He was a Federal scout.

III

As Peyton Farquhar fell straight downward through the bridge, he lost consciousness and was as one already dead. From this state he was awakened—ages later, it seemed to him—by the pain of a sharp pressure upon his throat, followed by a sense of suffocation. Keen, poignant agonies seemed to shoot from his neck downward through every fiber of his body and limbs. These pains appeared to flash along well-defined lines of ramification and to beat with an inconceivably rapid periodicity. They seemed like streams of pulsating fire heating him to an intolerable temperature. As to his head, he was conscious of nothing but a feeling of fullness—of congestion. These sensations were unaccompanied by thought. The intellectual part of his nature was already effaced; he had power only to feel, and feeling was torment. He was conscious of motion. Encompassed in a luminous cloud, of which he was now merely the fiery heart, without material substance, he swung through unthinkable arcs of oscillation, like a vast pendulum. Then all at once, with terrible suddenness, the light about him shot upward with the noise of a loud plash; a frightful roaring was in his ears, and all was cold and dark. The power of thought was restored; he knew that the rope had broken and he had fallen into the stream. There was no additional strangulation; the noose about his neck was already suffocating him and kept the water from his lungs. To die of hanging at the bottom of a river!— the idea seemed to him ludicrous. He opened his eyes in the blackness and saw above him a gleam of light, but how distant, how inaccessible! He was still sinking, for the light became fainter and fainter until it was a mere glimmer. Then it began to grow and brighten, and he knew that he was rising toward the surface—knew it with reluctance, for he was now very comfortable. "To be hanged and drowned," he thought, "that is not so bad; but I do not wish to be shot. No; I will not be shot; that is not fair."

He was not conscious of an effort, but a sharp pain in his wrists apprised him that he was trying to free his hands. He gave the struggle his attention, as an idler might observe the feat of a juggler, without interest in the outcome. What splendid effort!—what magnificent, what superhuman strength! Ah, that was a fine endeavor! Bravo! The cord fell away; his arms parted and floated upward, the hands dimly seen on each side in the growing light. He watched them with a new interest as first one and then the other pounced upon the noose at his neck. They tore it away and thrust it fiercely aside, its undulations resembling those of a water snake. "Put it back, put it back!" He thought he shouted these words to his hands, for the undoing of the noose had been succeeded by the direst pang which he had yet experienced. His neck ached horribly; his brain was on fire; his heart, which had been fluttering faintly, gave a great leap, trying to force itself out at his mouth. His whole body was racked and wrenched with an insupportable anguish! But his disobedient hands gave no heed to the command. They beat the water vigorously with quick, downward strokes, forcing him to the surface. He felt his head emerge; his eyes were blinded by the sunlight; his chest expanded convulsively, and with a supreme and crowning agony his lungs engulfed a great draught of air, which instantly he expelled in a shriek!

He was now in full possession of his physical senses. They were, indeed, preternaturally keen and alert. Something in the awful disturbance of his organic system had so exalted and refined them that they made record of things never before perceived. He felt the ripples upon his face and heard their separate sounds as they struck. He looked at the forest on the bank of the stream, saw the individual trees, the leaves and the veining of each leaf—saw the very insects upon them, the locusts, the brilliant-bodied flies, the gray spiders stretching their webs from twig to twig. He noted the prismatic colors in all the dew-drops upon a million blades of grass. The humming of the gnats that danced above the eddies of the stream, the beating of the dragon flies' wings, the strokes of the water spiders' legs, like oars which had lifted their boat—all these made audible music. A fish slid along beneath his eyes and he heard the rush of its body parting the water.

He had come to the surface facing down the stream; in a moment the visible world seemed to wheel slowly round, himself the pivotal point, and he saw the bridge, the fort, the soldiers upon the bridge, the captain, the sergeant, the two privates, his executioners. They were in silhouette against the blue sky. They shouted and gesticulated, pointing at him; the captain had drawn his pistol, but did not fire; the others were unarmed. Their movements were grotesque and horrible, their forms gigantic.

Suddenly he heard a sharp report and something struck the water smartly within a few inches of his head, spattering his face with spray. He heard a second report, and saw one of the sentinels with his rifle at his shoulder, a light cloud of blue smoke rising from the muzzle. The man in the water saw the eye of the man on the bridge gazing into his own through the sights of the rifle. He observed that it was a gray eye, and remembered having read that gray eyes were keenest and that all famous marksmen had them. Nevertheless, this one had missed.

A counter swirl had caught Farquhar and turned him half round; he was again looking into the forest on the bank opposite the fort. The sound of a clear, high voice in a monotonous singsong now rang out behind him and came across the water with a distinctness that pierced and subdued all other sounds, even the beating of the ripples in his ears. Although no soldier, he had frequented camps enough to know the dread significance of that deliberate, drawling, aspirated chant; the lieutenant on shore was taking a part in the morning's work. How coldly and pitilessly—with what an even, calm intonation, presaging and enforcing tranquillity in the men—with what accurately-measured intervals fell those cruel words:

"Attention, company. . . . Shoulder arms. . . . Ready. . . . Aim. . . . Fire."

Farquhar dived—dived as deeply as he could. The water roared in his ears like the voice of Niagara, yet he heard the dulled thunder of the volley, and, rising again toward the surface, met shining bits of metal, singularly flattened, oscillating slowly downward. Some of them touched him on the face and hands, then fell away, continuing their descent. One lodged between his collar and neck; it was uncomfortably warm, and he snatched it out.

As he rose to the surface, gasping for breath, he saw that he had been a long time under water; he was perceptibly farther down stream —nearer to safety. The soldiers had almost finished reloading; the metal ramrods flashed all at once in the sunshine as they were drawn from the barrels, turned in the air, and thrust into their sockets. The two sentinels fired again, independently and ineffectually.

The hunted man saw all this over his shoulder; he was now swimming vigorously with the current. His brain was as energetic as his arms and legs; he thought with the rapidity of lightning.

"The officer," he reasoned, "will not make that martinet's error a second time. It is as easy to dodge a volley as a single shot. He has probably already given the command to fire at will. God help me, I cannot dodge them all!"

An appalling plash within two yards of him, followed by a loud rushing sound, *diminuendo,* which seemed to travel back through the air to the fort and died in an explosion which stirred the very river to its deeps! A rising sheet of water, which curved over him, fell down upon him, blinded him, strangled him! The cannon had taken a hand in the game. As he shook his head free from the commotion of the smitten water, he heard the deflected shot humming through the air ahead, and in an instant it was cracking and smashing the branches in the forest beyond.

"They will not do that again," he thought; "the next time they will use a charge of grape. I must keep my eye upon the gun; the smoke will apprise me—the report arrives too late; it lags behind the missile. It is a good gun."

Suddenly he felt himself whirled round and round—spinning like a top. The water, the banks, the forest, the now distant bridge, fort and men—all were commingled and blurred. Objects were represented by their colors only; circular horizontal streaks of color—that was all he saw. He had been caught in a vortex and was being whirled on with a velocity of advance and gyration which made him giddy and sick. In a few moments he was flung upon the gravel at the foot of the left bank of the stream—the southern bank—and behind a projecting point which concealed him from his enemies. The sudden arrest of his motion, the abrasion of one of his hands on the gravel, restored him and he wept with delight. He dug his fingers into the sand, threw it over himself in handfuls and audibly blessed it. It looked like gold, like diamonds, rubies, emeralds; he could think of nothing beautiful which it did not resemble. The trees upon the bank were giant garden plants; he noted a definite order in their arrangement, inhaled the fragrance of their blooms. A strange, roseate light shone through the spaces among their trunks, and the wind made in their branches the music of æolian harps. He had no wish to perfect his escape, was content to remain in that enchanting spot until retaken.

A whizz and rattle of grapeshot among the branches high above his head roused him from his dream. The baffled cannoneer had fired him a random farewell. He sprang to his feet, rushed up the sloping bank, and plunged into the forest.

All that day he traveled, laying his course by the rounding sun. The forest seemed interminable; nowhere did he discover a break in it, not even a woodman's road. He had not known that he lived in so wild a region. There was something uncanny in the revelation.

By nightfall he was fatigued, footsore, famishing. The thought of his wife and children urged him on. At last he found a road which led him in what he knew to be the right direction. It was as wide and straight as a city street, yet it seemed untraveled. No fields bordered it, no dwelling anywhere. Not so much as the barking of a dog suggested human habitation. The black bodies of the great trees formed a straight wall on both sides, terminating on the horizon in a point, like a diagram in a lesson in perspective. Overhead, as he looked up through this rift in the wood, shone great golden stars looking unfamiliar and grouped in strange constellations. He was sure they were arranged in some order which had a secret and malign significance. The wood on either side was full of singular noises, among which—once, twice, and again—he distinctly heard whispers in an unknown tongue.

His neck was in pain, and, lifting his hand to it, he found it horribly swollen. He knew that it had a circle of black where the rope had bruised it. His eyes felt congested; he could no longer close them. His tongue was swollen with thirst; he relieved its fever by thrusting it forward from between his teeth into the cool air. How softly the turf had carpeted the untraveled avenue! He could no longer feel the roadway beneath his feet!

Doubtless, despite his suffering, he fell asleep while walking, for now he sees another scene—perhaps he has merely recovered from a delirium. He stands at the gate of his own home. All is as he left it, and all bright and beautiful in the morning sunshine. He must have traveled the entire night. As he pushes open the gate and passes up the wide white walk, he sees a flutter of female garments; his wife, looking fresh and cool and sweet, steps down from the veranda to meet him. At the bottom of the steps she stands waiting, with a smile of ineffable joy, an attitude of matchless grace and dignity. Ah, how beautiful she is! He springs forward with extended arms. As he is about to clasp her, he feels a stunning blow upon the back of the neck; a blinding white light blazes all about him, with a sound like the shock of a cannon—then all is darkness and silence!

Peyton Farquhar was dead; his body, with a broken neck, swung gently from side to side beneath the timbers of the Owl Creek bridge.

MARY WILKINS FREEMAN

The Revolt of "Mother"

"The Revolt of 'Mother'," first published in *Harper's Monthly* in 1890 prior to its inclusion in *A New England Nun and Other Stories* the following year, has long been one of Freeman's most widely read stories. Typical of her short fiction, this story contains a swiftly moving plot built on a central conflict, one here involving problems of communication, traditional gender roles, and contrasting responsibilities within the family. From the first sentence onward, the mother's desire for a more comfortable and respectable house clashes with the father's desire to expand the farm to provide for his family, and the resolution of the conflict requires not only her fortitude but his growth to a new level of understanding and sympathy. Interestingly, when this story had become her most famous, Freeman protested that it was not true to New England life and that she was sorry she had written it. The mother would have been as "thrifty" as the father, she maintained, and they would have raised the roof of the old house rather than build a new one. Further, she said, the mother would have "held the household reins" and father would have treated her with "wholesome respect." But whatever Freeman's personal views, her story has long been admired for its skillful presentation of a series of building conflicts within a family, its development of feminist themes, and its artistic rendering of character development and change in a regional setting.

*   *   *

"Father!"

"What is it?"

"What are them men diggin' over there in the field for?"

There was a sudden dropping and enlarging of the lower part of the old man's face, as if some heavy weight had settled therein; he shut his mouth tight, and went on harnessing the great bay mare. He hustled the collar on to her neck with a jerk.

"Father!"

The old man slapped the saddle upon the mare's back.

"Look here, father, I want to know what them men are diggin' over in the field for, an' I'm goin' to know."

"I wish you'd go into the house, mother, an' 'tend to your own affairs," the old man said then. He ran his words together, and his speech was almost as inarticulate as a growl.

But the woman understood; it was her most native tongue. "I ain't goin' into the house till you tell me what them men are doin' over there in the field," said she.

Then she stood waiting. She was a small woman, short and straight-waisted like a child in her brown cotton gown. Her forehead was mild and benevolent between the smooth curves of gray hair; there were meek downward lines about her nose and mouth; but her eyes, fixed upon the old man, looked as if the meekness had been the result of her own will, never of the will of another.

They were in the barn, standing before the wide open doors. The spring air, full of the smell of growing grass and unseen blossoms, came in their faces. The deep yard in front was littered with farm wagons and piles of wood; on the edges, close to the fence and the house, the grass was a vivid green, and there were some dandelions.

The old man glanced doggedly at his wife as he tightened the last buckles on the harness. She looked as immovable to him as one of the rocks in his pasture-land, bound to the earth with generations of blackberry vines. He slapped the reins over the horse, and started forth from the barn.

"*Father!*" said she.

The old man pulled up. "What is it?"

"I want to know what them men are diggin' over there in that field for."

"They're diggin' a cellar, I s'pose, if you've got to know."

"A cellar for what?"

"A barn."

"A barn? You ain't goin' to build a barn over there where we was goin' to have a house, father?"

The old man said not another word. He hurried the horse into the farm wagon, and clattered out of the yard, jouncing as sturdily on his seat as a boy.

The woman stood a moment looking after him, then she went out of the barn across a corner of the yard to the house. The house, standing at right angles with the great barn and a long reach of sheds and out-buildings, was infinitesimal compared with them. It was scarcely as commodious for people as the little boxes under the barn eaves were for doves.

A pretty girl's face, pink and delicate as a flower, was looking out of one of the house windows. She was watching three men who were digging over in the field which bounded the yard near the road line. She turned quietly when the woman entered.

"What are they digging for, mother?" said she. "Did he tell you?"

"They're diggin' for—a cellar for a new barn."

"Oh, mother, he ain't going to build another barn?"

"That's what he says."

A boy stood before the kitchen glass combing his hair. He combed slowly and painstakingly, arranging his brown hair in a smooth hillock over his forehead. He did not seem to pay any attention to the conversation.

"Sammy, did you know father was going to build a new barn?" asked the girl.

The boy combed assiduously.

"Sammy!"

He turned, and showed a face like his father's under his smooth crest of hair. "Yes, I s'pose I did," he said, reluctantly.

"How long have you known it?" asked his mother.

" 'Bout three months, I guess."

"Why didn't you tell of it?"

"Didn't think 'twould do no good."

"I don't see what father wants another barn for," said the girl, in her sweet, slow voice. She turned again to the window, and stared out at the digging men in the field. Her tender, sweet face was full of a gentle distress. Her forehead was as bald and innocent as a baby's, with the light hair strained back from it in a row of curl-papers. She was quite large, but her soft curves did not look as if they covered muscles.

Her mother looked sternly at the boy. "Is he goin' to buy more cows?" said she.

The boy did not reply; he was tying his shoes.

"Sammy, I want you to tell me if he's goin' to buy more cows."

"I s'pose he is."

"How many?"

"Four, I guess."

His mother said nothing more. She went into the pantry, and there was a clatter of dishes. The boy got his cap from a nail behind the door, took an old arithmetic from the shelf, and started for school. He was lightly built, but clumsy. He went out of the yard with a curious spring in the hips, that made his loose home-made jacket tilt up in the rear.

The girl went to the sink, and began to wash the dishes that were piled up there. Her mother came promptly out of the pantry, and shoved her aside. "You wipe 'em," said she; "I'll wash. There's a good many this mornin'."

The mother plunged her hands vigorously into the water, the girl wiped the plates slowly and dreamily. "Mother," said she, "don't you think it's too bad father's going to build that new barn, much as we need a decent house to live in?"

Her mother scrubbed a dish fiercely. "You ain't found out yet we're women-folks, Nanny Penn," said she. "You ain't seen enough of men-folks yet to. One of these days you'll find it out, an' then you'll know that we know only what men-folks think we do, so far as any use of it goes, an' how we'd ought to reckon men-folks in with Providence, an' not complain of what they do any more than we do of the weather."

"I don't care; I don't believe George is anything like that, anyhow," said Nanny. Her delicate face flushed pink, her lips pouted softly, as if she were going to cry.

"You wait an' see. I guess George Eastman ain't no better than other men. You hadn't ought to judge father, though. He can't help it, 'cause he don't look at things jest the way we do. An' we've been pretty comfortable here, after all. The roof don't leak—ain't never but once— that's one thing. Father's kept it shingled right up."

"I do wish we had a parlor."

"I guess it won't hurt George Eastman any to come to see you in a nice clean kitchen. I guess a good many girls don't have as good a place as this. Nobody's ever heard me complain."

"I ain't complained either, mother."

"Well, I don't think you'd better, a good father an' a good home as you've got. S'pose your father made you go out an' work for your livin'? Lots of girls have to that ain't no stronger an' better able to than you be."

Sarah Penn washed the frying-pan with a conclusive air. She scrubbed the outside of it as faithfully as the inside. She was a masterly keeper of her box of a house. Her one living-room never seemed to have in it any of the dust which the friction of life with inanimate matter produces. She swept, and there seemed to be no dirt to go before the broom; she cleaned, and one could see no difference. She was like an artist so perfect that he has apparently no art. To-day she got out a mixing bowl and a board, and rolled some pies, and there was no more flour upon her than upon her daughter who was doing finer work. Nanny was to be married in the fall, and she was sewing on some white cambric and embroidery. She sewed industriously while her mother cooked, her soft milk-white hands and wrists showed whiter than her delicate work.

"We must have the stove moved out in the shed before long," said Mrs. Penn. "Talk about not havin' things, it's been a real blessin' to be able to put a stove up in that shed in hot weather. Father did one good thing when he fixed that stove-pipe out there."

Sarah Penn's face as she rolled her pies had that expression of meek vigor which might have characterized one of the New Testament saints. She was making mince-pies. Her husband, Adoniram Penn, liked them better than any other kind. She baked twice a week. Adoniram often liked a piece of pie between meals. She hurried this morning. It had been later than usual when she began, and she wanted to have a pie baked for dinner. However deep a resentment she might be forced to hold against her husband, she would never fail in sedulous attention to his wants.

Nobility of character manifests itself at loop-holes when it is not provided with large doors. Sarah Penn's showed itself to-day in flaky dishes of pastry. So she made the pies faithfully, while across the table she could see, when she glanced up from her work, the sight that rankled in her patient and steadfast soul—the digging of the cellar of the new barn in the place where Adoniram forty years ago had promised her their new house should stand.

The pies were done for dinner. Adoniram and Sammy were home a few minutes after twelve o'clock. The dinner was eaten with serious haste. There was never much conversation at the table in the Penn family. Adoniram asked a blessing, and they ate promptly, then rose up and went about their work.

Sammy went back to school, taking soft sly lopes out of the yard like a rabbit. He wanted a game of marbles before school, and feared his father would give him some chores to do. Adoniram hastened to the door and called after him, but he was out of sight.

"I don't see what you let him go for, mother," said he. "I wanted him to help me unload that wood."

Adoniram went to work out in the yard unloading wood from the wagon. Sarah put away the dinner dishes, while Nanny took down her curl-papers and changed her dress. She was going down to the store to buy some more embroidery and thread.

When Nanny was gone, Mrs. Penn went to the door. "Father!" she called.

"Well, what is it!"

"I want to see you jest a minute, father."

"I can't leave this wood nohow. I've got to git it unloaded an' go for a load of gravel afore two o'clock. Sammy had ought to helped me. You hadn't ought to let him go to school so early."

"I want to see you jest a minute."

"I tell ye I can't, nohow, mother."

"Father, you come here." Sarah Penn stood in the door like a queen; she held her head as if it bore a crown; there was that patience which makes authority royal in her voice. Adoniram went.

Mrs. Penn led the way into the kitchen, and pointed to a chair. "Sit down, father," said she; "I've got somethin' I want to say to you."

He sat down heavily; his face was quite stolid, but he looked at her with restive eyes. "Well, what is it, mother?"

"I want to know what you're buildin' that new barn for, father?"

"I ain't got nothin' to say about it."

"It can't be you think you need another barn?"

"I tell ye I ain't got nothin' to say about it, mother; an' I ain't goin' to say nothin'."

"Be you goin' to buy more cows?"

Adoniram did not reply; he shut his mouth tight.

"I know you be, as well as I want to. Now, father, look here"— Sarah Penn had not sat down; she stood before her husband in the humble fashion of a Scripture woman—"I'm goin' to talk real plain to you; I never have sence I married you, but I'm goin' to now. I ain't never complained, an' I ain't goin' to complain now, but I'm goin' to talk plain. You see this room here, father; you look at it well. You see there ain't no carpet on the floor, an' you see the paper is all dirty, an' droppin' off the walls. We ain't had no new paper on it for ten year, an' then I put it on myself, an' it didn't cost but ninepence a roll. You see this room, father; it's all the one I've had to work in an' eat in an' sit in sence we was married. There ain't another woman in the whole town whose husband ain't got half the means you have but what's got better. It's all the room Nanny's got to have her company in; an' there ain't one of her mates but what's got better, an' their fathers not so able as hers is. It's all the room she'll have to be married in. What would you have thought, father, if we had had our weddin' in a room no better than this? I was married in my mother's parlor, with a carpet on the floor, an' stuffed furniture, an' a mahogany card-table. An' this is all the room my daughter will have to be married in. Look here, father!"

Sarah Penn went across the room as though it were a tragic stage. She flung open a door and disclosed a tiny bedroom, only large enough

for a bed and bureau, with a path between. "There, father," said she—
"there's all the room I've had to sleep in forty year. All my children
were born there—the two that died, an' the two that's livin'. I was sick
with a fever there."

She stepped to another door and opened it. It led into the small, ill-
lighted pantry. "Here," said she, "is all the buttery I've got—every place
I've got for my dishes, to set away my victuals in, an' to keep my milk-
pans in. Father, I've been takin' care of the milk of six cows in this
place, an' now you're goin' to build a new barn, an' keep more cows,
an' give me more to do in it."

She threw open another door. A narrow crooked flight of stairs
wound upward from it. "There, father," said she, "I want you to look
at the stairs that go up to them two unfinished chambers that are all
the places our son an' daughter have had to sleep in all their lives. There
ain't a prettier girl in town nor a more ladylike one than Nanny, an'
that's the place she has to sleep in. It ain't so good as your horse's stall;
it ain't so warm an' tight."

Sarah Penn went back and stood before her husband. "Now, father," said she, "I want to know if you think you're doin' right an'
accordin' to what you profess. Here, when we was married, forty year
ago, you promised me faithful that we should have a new house built
in that lot over in the field before the year was out. You said you had
money enough, an' you wouldn't ask me to live in no such place as this.
It is forty year now, an' you've been makin' more money, an' I've been
savin' of it for you ever since, an' you ain't built no house yet. You've
built sheds an' cow-houses an' one new barn, an' now you're goin' to
build another. Father, I want to know if you think it's right. You're
lodgin' your dumb beasts better than you are your own flesh an' blood.
I want to know if you think it's right."

"I ain't got nothin' to say."

"You can't say nothin' without ownin' it ain't right, father. An'
there's another thing—I ain't complained; I've got along forty year, an'
I s'pose I should forty more, if it wa'n't for that—if we don't have
another house. Nanny she can't live with us after she's married. She'll
have to go somewheres else to live away from us, an' it don't seem as
if I could have it so, noways, father. She wa'n't ever strong. She's got
considerable color, but there wa'n't never any backbone to her. I've
always took the heft of everything off her, an' she ain't fit to keep house
an' do everything herself. She'll be all worn out inside of a year. Think
of her doin' all the washin' an' ironin' an' bakin' with them soft white
hands an' arms, an' sweepin'! I can't have it so, noways, father."

Mrs. Penn's face was burning; her mild eyes gleamed. She had
pleaded her little cause like a Webster; she had ranged from severity to

pathos; but her opponent employed that obstinate silence which makes eloquence futile with mocking echoes. Adoniram arose clumsily.

"Father, ain't you got nothin' to say?" said Mrs. Penn.

"I've got to go off after that load of gravel. I can't stan' here talkin' all day."

"Father, won't you think it over, an' have a house built there instead of a barn?"

"I ain't got nothin' to say."

Adoniram shuffled out. Mrs. Penn went into her bedroom. When she came out, her eyes were red. She had a roll of unbleached cotton cloth. She spread it out on the kitchen table, and began cutting out some shirts for her husband. The men over in the field had a team to help them this afternoon; she could hear their halloos. She had a scanty pattern for the shirts; she had to plan and piece the sleeves.

Nanny came home with her embroidery, and sat down with her needlework. She had taken down her curl-papers, and there was a soft roll of fair hair like an aureole over her forehead; her face was as delicately fine and clear as porcelain. Suddenly she looked up, and the tender red flamed all over her face and neck. "Mother," said she.

"What say?"

"I've been thinking—I don't see how we're goin' to have any—wedding in this room. I'd be ashamed to have his folks come if we didn't have anybody else."

"Mebbe we can have some new paper before then; I can put it on. I guess you won't have no call to be ashamed of your belongin's."

"We might have the wedding in the new barn," said Nanny, with gentle pettishness. "Why, mother, what makes you look so?"

Mrs. Penn had started, and was staring at her with a curious expression. She turned again to her work, and spread out a pattern carefully on the cloth. "Nothin'," said she.

Presently Adoniram clattered out of the yard in his two-wheeled dump cart, standing as proudly upright as a Roman charioteer. Mrs. Penn opened the door and stood there a minute looking out; the halloos of the men sounded louder.

It seemed to her all through the spring months that she heard nothing but the halloos and the noises of saws and hammers. The new barn grew fast. It was a fine edifice for this little village. Men came on pleasant Sundays, in their meeting suits and clean shirt bosoms, and stood around it admiringly. Mrs. Penn did not speak of it, and Adoniram did not mention it to her, although sometimes, upon a return from inspecting it, he bore himself with injured dignity.

"It's a strange thing how your mother feels about the new barn," he said, confidentially, to Sammy one day.

Sammy only grunted after an odd fashion for a boy; he had learned it from his father.

The barn was all completed ready for use by the third week in July. Adoniram had planned to move his stock in on Wednesday; on Tuesday he received a letter which changed his plans. He came in with it early in the morning. "Sammy's been to the post-office," said he, "an' I've got a letter from Hiram." Hiram was Mrs. Penn's brother, who lived in Vermont.

"Well," said Mrs. Penn, "what does he say about the folks?"

"I guess they're all right. He says he thinks if I come up country right off there's a chance to buy jest the kind of a horse I want." He stared reflectively out of the window at the new barn.

Mrs. Penn was making pies. She went on clapping the rolling-pin into the crust, although she was very pale, and her heart beat loudly.

"I dun' know but what I'd better go," said Adoniram. "I hate to go off jest now, right in the midst of hayin', but the ten-acre lot's cut, an' I guess Rufus an' the others can git along without me three or four days. I can't get a horse round here to suit me, nohow, an' I've got to have another for all that wood-haulin' in the fall. I told Hiram to watch out, an' if he got wind of a good horse to let me know. I guess I'd better go."

"I'll get out your clean shirt an' collar," said Mrs. Penn calmly.

She laid out Adoniram's Sunday suit and his clean clothes on the bed in the little bedroom. She got his shaving-water and razor ready. At last she buttoned on his collar and fastened his black cravat.

Adoniram never wore his collar and cravat except on extra occasions. He held his head high, with a rasped dignity. When he was all ready, with his coat and hat brushed, and a lunch of pie and cheese in a paper bag, he hesitated on the threshold of the door. He looked at his wife, and his manner was defiantly apologetic. "*If* them cows come to-day, Sammy can drive 'em into the new barn," said he; "an' when they bring the hay up, they can pitch it in there."

"Well," replied Mrs. Penn.

Adoniram set his shaven face ahead and started. When he had cleared the door-step, he turned and looked back with a kind of nervous solemnity. "I shall be back by Saturday if nothin' happens," said he.

"Do be careful, father," returned his wife.

She stood in the door with Nanny at her elbow and watched him out of sight. Her eyes had a strange, doubtful expression in them; her peaceful forehead was contracted. She went in, and about her baking again. Nanny sat sewing. Her wedding-day was drawing nearer, and she was getting pale and thin with her steady sewing. Her mother kept glancing at her.

"Have you got that pain in your side this mornin'?" she asked.

"A little."

Mrs. Penn's face, as she worked, changed, her perplexed forehead smoothed, her eyes were steady, her lips firmly set. She formed a maxim for herself, although incoherently with her unlettered thoughts. "Unsolicited opportunities are the guide-posts of the Lord to the new roads of life," she repeated in effect, and she made up her mind to her course of action.

"S'posin' I *had* wrote to Hiram," she muttered once, when she was in the pantry—"s'posin' I had wrote, an' asked him if he knew of any horse? But I didn't, an' father's goin' wa'n't none of my doin'. It looks like a providence." Her voice rang out quite loud at the last.

"What you talkin' about, mother?" called Nanny.

"Nothin'."

Mrs. Penn hurried her baking; at eleven o'clock it was all done. The load of hay from the west field came slowly down the cart track, and drew up at the new barn. Mrs. Penn ran out. "Stop!" she screamed—"stop!"

The men stopped and looked; Sammy upreared from the top of the load, and stared at his mother.

"Stop!" she cried out again. "Don't you put the hay in that barn; put it in the old one."

"Why, he said to put it in here," returned one of the hay-makers, wonderingly. He was a young man, a neighbor's son, whom Adoniram hired by the year to help on the farm.

"Don't you put the hay in the new barn; there's room enough in the old one, ain't there?" said Mrs. Penn.

"Room enough," returned the hired man, in his thick, rustic tones. "Didn't need the new barn, nohow, far as room's concerned. Well, I s'pose he changed his mind." He took hold of the horses' bridles.

Mrs. Penn went back to the house. Soon the kitchen windows were darkened, and a fragrance like warm honey came into the room.

Nanny laid down her work. "I thought father wanted them to put the hay into the new barn?" she said, wonderingly.

"It's all right," replied her mother.

Sammy slid down from the load of hay, and came in to see if dinner was ready.

"I ain't goin' to get a regular dinner to-day, as long as father's gone," said his mother. "I've let the fire go out. You can have some bread an' milk an' pie. I thought we could get along." She set out some bowls of milk, some bread, and a pie on the kitchen table. "You'd better eat your dinner now," said she. "You might jest as well get through with it. I want you to help me afterward."

Nanny and Sammy stared at each other. There was something strange in their mother's manner. Mrs. Penn did not eat anything herself. She went into the pantry, and they heard her moving dishes while they ate. Presently she came out with a pile of plates. She got the clothes-basket out of the shed, and packed them in it. Nanny and Sammy watched. She brought out cups and saucers, and put them in with the plates.

"What you goin' to do, mother?" inquired Nanny, in a timid voice. A sense of something unusual made her tremble, as if it were a ghost. Sammy rolled his eyes over his pie.

"You'll see what I'm goin' to do," replied Mrs. Penn. "If you're through, Nanny, I want you to go up-stairs an' pack up your things; an' I want you, Sammy, to help me take down the bed in the bedroom."

"Oh, mother, what for?" gasped Nanny.

"You'll see."

During the next few hours a feat was performed by this simple, pious New England mother which was equal in its way to Wolfe's storming of the Heights of Abraham. It took no more genius and audacity of bravery for Wolfe to cheer his wondering soldiers up those steep precipices, under the sleeping eyes of the enemy, than for Sarah Penn, at the head of her children, to move all their little household goods into the new barn while her husband was away.

Nanny and Sammy followed their mother's instructions without a murmur; indeed, they were overawed. There is a certain uncanny and superhuman quality about all such purely original undertakings as their mother's was to them. Nanny went back and forth with her light loads, and Sammy tugged with sober energy.

At five o'clock in the afternoon the little house in which the Penns had lived for forty years had emptied itself into the new barn.

Every builder builds somewhat for unknown purposes, and is in a measure a prophet. The architect of Adoniram Penn's barn, while he designed it for the comfort of four-footed animals, had planned better than he knew for the comfort of humans. Sarah Penn saw at a glance its possibilities. Those great box-stalls, with quilts hung before them, would make better bedrooms than the one she had occupied for forty years, and there was a tight carriage-room. The harness-room, with its chimney and shelves, would make a kitchen of her dreams. The great middle space would make a parlor, by-and-by, fit for a palace. Up stairs there was as much room as down. With partitions and windows, what a house would there be! Sarah looked at the row of stanchions before the allotted space for cows, and reflected that she would have her front entry there.

At six o'clock the stove was up in the harness-room, the kettle was boiling, and the table set for tea. It looked almost as home-like as the abandoned house across the yard had ever done. The young hired man milked, and Sarah directed him calmly to bring the milk to the new barn. He came gaping, dropping little blots of foam from the brimming pails on the grass. Before the next morning he had spread the story of Adoniram Penn's wife moving into the new barn all over the little village. Men assembled in the store and talked it over, women with shawls over their heads scuttled into each other's houses before their work was done. Any deviation from the ordinary course of life in this quiet town was enough to stop all progress in it. Everybody paused to look at the staid, independent figure on the side track. There was a difference of opinion with regard to her. Some held her to be insane; some, of a lawless and rebellious spirit.

Friday the minister went to see her. It was in the forenoon, and she was at the barn door shelling pease for dinner. She looked up and returned his salutation with dignity, then she went on with her work. She did not invite him in. The saintly expression of her face remained fixed, but there was an angry flush over it.

The minister stood awkwardly before her, and talked. She handled the pease as if they were bullets. At last she looked up, and her eyes showed the spirit that her meek front had covered for a lifetime.

"There ain't no use talkin', Mr. Hersey," said she. "I've thought it all over an' over, an' I believe I'm doin' what's right. I've made it the subject of prayer, an' it's betwixt me an' the Lord an' Adoniram. There ain't no call for nobody else to worry about it."

"Well, of course, if you have brought it to the Lord in prayer, and feel satisfied that you are doing right, Mrs. Penn," said the minister, helplessly. His thin gray-bearded face was pathetic. He was a sickly man; his youthful confidence had cooled; he had to scourge himself up to some of his pastoral duties as relentlessly as a Catholic ascetic, and then he was prostrated by the smart.

"I think it's right jest as much as I think it was right for our forefathers to come over from the old country 'cause they didn't have what belonged to 'em," said Mrs. Penn. She arose. The barn threshold might have been Plymouth Rock from her bearing. "I don't doubt you mean well, Mr. Hersey," said she, "but there are things people hadn't ought to interfere with. I've been a member of the church for over forty year. I've got my own mind an' my own feet, an' I'm goin' to think my own thoughts an' go my own ways, an' nobody but the Lord is goin' to dictate to me unless I've a mind to have him. Won't you come in an' set down? How is Mis' Hersey?"

"She is well, I thank you," replied the minister. He added some more perplexed apologetic remarks; then he retreated.

He could expound the intricacies of every character study in the Scriptures, he was competent to grasp the Pilgrim Fathers and all historical innovators, but Sarah Penn was beyond him. He could deal with primal cases, but parallel ones worsted him. But, after all, although it was aside from his province, he wondered more how Adoniram Penn would deal with his wife than how the Lord would. Everybody shared the wonder. When Adoniram's four new cows arrived, Sarah ordered three to be put in the old barn, the other in the house shed where the cooking-stove had stood. That added to the excitement. It was whispered that all four cows were domiciled in the house.

Towards sunset on Saturday, when Adoniram was expected home, there was a knot of men in the road near the new barn. The hired man had milked, but he still hung around the premises. Sarah Penn had supper all ready. There were brown-bread and baked beans and a custard pie; it was the supper that Adoniram loved on a Saturday night. She had on a clean calico, and she bore herself imperturbably. Nanny and Sammy kept close at her heels. Their eyes were large, and Nanny was full of nervous tremors. Still there was to them more pleasant excitement than anything else. An inborn confidence in their mother over their father asserted itself.

Sammy looked out of the harness-room window. "There he is," he announced, in an awed whisper. He and Nanny peeped around the casing. Mrs. Penn kept on about her work. The children watched Adoniram leave the new horse standing in the drive while he went to the house door. It was fastened. Then he went around to the shed. That door was seldom locked, even when the family was away. The thought how her father would be confronted by the cow flashed upon Nanny. There was a hysterical sob in her throat. Adoniram emerged from the shed and stood looking about in a dazed fashion. His lips moved; he was saying something, but they could not hear what it was. The hired man was peeping around a corner of the old barn, but nobody saw him.

Adoniram took the new horse by the bridle and led him across the yard to the new barn. Nanny and Sammy slunk close to their mother. The barn doors rolled back, and there stood Adoniram, with the long mild face of the great Canadian farm horse looking over his shoulder.

Nanny kept behind her mother, but Sammy stepped suddenly forward, and stood in front of her.

Adoniram stared at the group. "What on airth you all down here for?" said he. "What's the matter over to the house?"

"We've come here to live, father," said Sammy. His shrill voice quavered out bravely.

"What"—Adoniram sniffed—"what is it smells like cookin?" said he. He stepped forward and looked in the open door of the harness-room. Then he turned to his wife. His old bristling face was pale and frightened. "What on airth does this mean, mother?" he gasped.

"You come in here, father," said Sarah. She led the way into the harness-room and shut the door. "Now, father," said she, "you needn't be scared. I ain't crazy. There ain't nothin' to be upset over. But we've come here to live, an' we're goin' to live here. We've got jest as good a right here as new horses an' cows. The house wa'n't fit for us to live in any longer, an' I made up my mind I wa'n't goin' to stay there. I've done my duty by you forty year, an' I'm goin' to do it now; but I'm goin' to live here. You've got to put in some windows and partitions; an' you'll have to buy some furniture."

"Why, mother!" the old man gasped.

"You'd better take your coat off an' get washed—there's the wash-basin—an' then we'll have supper."

"Why, mother!"

Sammy went past the window, leading the new horse to the old barn. The old man saw him, and shook his head speechlessly. He tried to take off his coat, but his arms seemed to lack the power. His wife helped him. She poured some water into the tin basin, and put in a piece of soap. She got the comb and brush, and smoothed his thin gray hair after he had washed. Then she put the beans, hot bread, and tea on the table. Sammy came in, and the family drew up. Adoniram sat looking dazedly at his plate, and they waited.

"Ain't you goin' to ask a blessin', father?" said Sarah.

And the old man bent his head and mumbled.

All through the meal he stopped eating at intervals, and stared furtively at his wife; but he ate well. The home food tasted good to him, and his old frame was too sturdily healthy to be affected by his mind. But after supper he went out, and sat down on the step of the smaller door at the right of the barn, through which he had meant his Jerseys to pass in stately file, but which Sarah designed for her front house door, and he leaned his head on his hands.

After the supper dishes were cleared away and the milk-pans washed, Sarah went out to him. The twilight was deepening. There was a clear green glow in the sky. Before them stretched the smooth level of field; in the distance was a cluster of hay-stacks like the huts of a village; the air was very cool and calm and sweet. The landscape might have been an ideal one of peace.

Sarah bent over and touched her husband on one of his thin, sinewy shoulders. "Father!"

The old man's shoulders heaved: he was weeping.

"Why, don't do so, father," said Sarah.

"I'll—put up the—partitions, an'—everything you—want, mother." Sarah put her apron up to her face; she was overcome by her own triumph.

Adoniram was like a fortress whose walls had no active resistance, and went down the instant the right besieging tools were used. "Why, mother," he said, hoarsely, "I hadn't no idee you was so set on't as all this comes to."

HAROLD FREDERIC

My Aunt Susan

This story was published in *The Independent* for June 9, 1892. Harold Frederic was living in England at the time he wrote a series of Civil War stories, but they possess the evocative quality of strong memory and the vividness of lived experience. The author would later express a special fondness for his Civil War tales and confess that they were formed, in part, from his own "recollections of that dreadful time—the actual things that a boy from five to nine saw and heard about then, while his own relatives were being killed, and his school-fellows orphaned, and women of his neighborhood forced into mourning and despair—and they had a right to be recorded." Aunt Susan is a latter day Penelope, patiently weaving rugs dominated by the blue and black rags of Union overcoats and widow's mourning garments, and, without realizing it herself, waiting for the return of her soldier lover. The dramatic transformation of Aunt Susan and the town's attitude toward her nephew Ira are filtered through the recollections of a narrator who does not fully understand the story he tells. Ira gives as much attention to the butchering of a pig as he does to the unexpected arrival of his father. In this sense, Frederic was experimenting with the sort of narrative point of view that Sherwood Anderson and Ernest Hemingway would later bring to perfection: one featuring a narrator who comprehends far less about his story and its significance than do his readers.

*   *   *

I held the lamp, while Aunt Susan cut up the pig.

The whole day had been devoted, I remember, to preparations for this great event. Early in the morning I had been to the butcher's to set in train the annual negotiations for a loan of cleaver and meat-saw; and hours afterward had borne these implements proudly homeward through the village street. In the interval I had turned the grindstone, over at the Four Corners, while the grocer's hired man obligingly sharpened our carving-knife. Then there had been the even more back-aching task of clearing away the hard snow from the accustomed site of our wood-pile in the yard, and scraping together a frosted heap of chips and bark for the smudge in the smoke-barrel.

From time to time I sweetened this toil, and helped the laggard hours to a swifter pace, by paying visits to the wood-shed to have still another look at the pig. He was frozen very stiff, and there were small icicles in the crevices whence his eyes had altogether disappeared. My emotions as I viewed his big, cold, pink carcase, with its extended legs, its bland and pasty countenance, and that awful emptiness underneath, were much mixed. Although I was his elder by seven or eight years, we had been close friends during all his life—or all except a very few weeks of his earliest sucking pighood, spent on his native farm. I had fed him daily; I had watched him grow week by week; more than once I had poked him with a stick as he ran around in his sty, to make him squeal for the edification of neighbours' boys who had come into our yard, and would now be sharply ordered out again by Aunt Susan.

As these kindly memories surged over me I could not but feel like a traitor to my old companion, as he lay thus hairless and pallid before my eyes. But then I would remember how good he was going to be to eat—and straightway return with a light heart to the work of kicking up more chips from the ice.

From the living-room in the rear of our little house came the monotonous incessant clatter of Aunt Susan's carpet loom. Through the window I could see the outlines of her figure and the back of her head as she sat on her high bench. It was to me the most familiar of all spectacles, this tireless woman bending resolutely over her work. She was there when I first cautiously ventured my nose out from under the warm blanket of a winter's morning. Very, very often I fell asleep at night in my bed in the recess, lulled off by the murmur of the diligent loom.

Presently I went in to warm myself, and stood with my red fingers over the stove top. She cast but one vague glance at me, through the open frame of the loom between us, and went on with her work. It was not our habit to talk much in that house. She was too busy a woman, for one thing, to have much time for conversation. The impression that she preferred not to talk was always present in my boyish mind. I call up the picture of her still as I saw her then under the top bar of the cumbrous old machine, sitting with lips tight together, and resolute, masterful eyes bent upon the twining intricacy of web and woof before her. At her side were piled a dozen or more big balls of carpet rags, which the village wives and daughters cut up, sewed together and wound in the long winter evenings, while the men-folks sat with their stockinged feet on the stove hearth, and read out the latest "news from the front" in their *Weekly Tribune.*

I knew all these rag balls by the names of their owners. Not only did I often go to their houses for them, upon the strength of the general village rumour that they were ready, and always carry back the finished lengths of carpet; but I had long since unconsciously grown to watch all the varying garments and shifts of fashion in the raiment of our neighbours, with an eye single to the likelihood of their eventually turning up at Aunt Susan's loom. When Hiram Mabie's chequered butternut coat was cut down for his son Roswell, I noted the fact merely as a stage of its progress toward carpet rags. If Mrs. Wilkins concluded to turn her flowered delaine dress a third year, or Sarah Northrup had her bright saffron shawl died black, I was sensible of a wrong having been done our little household. I felt like crossing the street whenever I saw approaching the portly figure of Cyrus Husted's mother, the woman who dragged everybody into her house to show them the ingrain carpet she had bought at Tecumseh, and assured them that it was much cheaper in the long run than the products of my Aunt's industry. I tingled with indignation as she passed me on the side-walk, puffing for breath and stepping mincingly because her shoes were too tight for her.

Nearly all the knowledge of our neighbours' sayings and doings which reached Aunt Susan came to her from me. She kept herself to herself with a vengeance, toiling early and late, rarely going beyond the confines of her yard save on Sunday mornings, when we went to church, and treating with frosty curtness the few people who ventured to come to our house on business or from social curiosity. For one thing, this Juno Mills in which we lived was not really our home. We had only been there for four or five years—a space which indeed spanned all my recollections of life—but left my Aunt more or less a stranger and new-comer. She spared no pains to maintain that condition. I can see now that there were good reasons for this stern aloofness. At the time I thought it was altogether due to the proud and unsociable nature of my Aunt.

In my child's mind I regarded her as distinctly an elderly person. People outside, I know, spoke of her as an old maid, sometimes winking furtively over my head as they did so. But she was not really old at all—was in truth just barely in the thirties. Doubtless the fact that she was tall and dark, with very black hair, and that years of steady concentration of sight upon the strings and threads of the loom had scored a scowling vertical wrinkle between her near-sighted eyes, gave me my notion of her advanced maturity. And in all her ways and words, too, she was so far removed from any idea of youthful softness! I could not remember her having ever kissed me. My imagination never evolved the conceit of her kissing anybody. I had always had at her hands uniformly good treatment, good food, good clothes; after I had learned my letters from the old maroon plush label on the Babbitt's soap box which held the wood behind the stove, and expanded this knowledge by a study of street signs, she had herself taught me how to read, and later provided me with books for the village school. She was my only known relative —the only person in the world who had ever done anything for me. Yet it could not be said that I loved her. Indeed she no more raised the suggestion of tenderness in my mind than did the loom at which she spent her waking hours.

"The Perkinses asked me why you didn't get the butcher to cut up the pig," I remarked at last, rubbing my hands together over the hot stove griddles.

"It's none of their business!" said Aunt Susan, with laconic promptness.

"And Devillo Pollard's got a new overcoat," I added. "He hasn't worn the old army one now for upwards of a week."

"If this war goes on much longer," commented my Aunt, "every carpet in Dearborn County 'll be as blue as a whetstone.

I think that must have been the entire conversation of the afternoon. I especially recall the remark about the overcoat. For two years now the balls of rags had contained an increasing proportion of pale blue woollen strips, as the men of the country round about came home from the South, or bought cheap garments from the second-hand dealers in Tecumseh. All other colours had died out. There was only this light blue, and the black of bombazine or worsted mourning into which the news in each week's papers forced one or another of the neighbouring families. To obviate this monotony, some of the women dyed their white rags with butternut or even cochineal, but this was a mere drop in the bucket, so to speak. The loom spun out only long, depressing rolls of black and blue.

My memory leaps lightly forward now to the early evening, when I held the lamp in the wood-shed, and Aunt Susan cut up the pig.

How joyfully I watched her every operation! Every now and again my interest grew so beyond proper bounds that I held the lamp sidewise, and the flame smoked the chimney. I was in mortal terror over this lamp, even when it was standing on the table quite by itself. We often read in the paper of explosions from this new kerosene, by which people were instantly killed and houses wrapped in an unquenchable fire. Aunt

Susan had stood out against the strange invention, long after most of the other homes of Juno Mills were familiar with the idea of the lamp. Even after she had yielded, and I went to the grocery for more oil and fresh chimneys and wicks, like other boys, she refused to believe that this inflammable fluid was really squeezed out of hard coal, as they said. And for years we lived in momentary belief that our lamp was about to explode.

My fears of sudden death could not, however, for a moment stand up against the delighted excitement with which I viewed the dismemberment of the pig. It was very cold in the shed, but neither of us noticed that. My Aunt attacked the job with skilful resolution and energy, as was her way, chopping small bones, sawing vehemently through big ones, hacking and slicing with the knife, like a strong man in a hurry.

For a long time no word was spoken. I gazed in silence as the head was detached, and then resolved itself slowly into souse—always tacitly set aside as my special portion. In prophecy I saw the big pan, filled with ears, cheeks, snout, feet, and tail, all boiled and allowed to grow cold in their own jelly—that pan to which I was free to repair anytime of day until everything was gone. I thought of myself, too, with apron tied round my neck, and the chopping-bowl on my knees, reducing what remained of the head into small bits, to be seasoned by my Aunt, and then fill other pans as headcheese. The sage and summer-savoury hung in paper flour bags from the rafters overhead. I looked up at them with rapture. It seemed as if my mouth already tasted them in headcheese and sausage, and in the hot gravy which basted the succulent spare-rib. Only the abiding menace of the lamp kept me from dancing with delight.

Gradually, however, as my Aunt passed from the tid-bits to the more substantial portions of her task, getting out the shoulders, the hams for smoking, the pieces for salting down in the brine-barrel, my enthusiasm languished a trifle. The lamp grew heavy as I changed it from hand to hand, holding the free fingers at a respectful distance over the chimney-top for warmth, and shuffling my feet about. It was truly very cold. I strove to divert myself by smiling at the big shadow my bustling Aunt cast against the house side of the shed, and by moving the lamp to affect its proportions, but broke out into yawns instead. A mouse ran swiftly across the scantling just under the lean-to roof. At the same time I thought I caught the muffled sound of distant rapping, as if at our own rarely used front door. I was too sleepy to decide whether I had really heard a noise or not.

All at once I roused myself with a start. The lamp had nearly slipped from my hands, and the horror of what might have happened frightened me into wakefulness.

"The Perkins girls keep on calling me 'wise child.' They yell it after me all the while," I said, desperately clutching at a subject which I hoped would interest my Aunt. I had spoken to her about it a week or so before, and it had stirred her quite out of her wonted stern calm. If anything would induce her to talk now, it would be this.

"They do, eh?" she said, with an alert sharpness of voice which dwindled away into a sigh. Then, after a moment, she added, "Well, never you mind. You just keep right on, tending to your own affairs, and studying your lessons, and in time it'll be you who can laugh at them and all their low down lot. They only do it to make you feel bad. Just don't you humour them."

"But I don't see——" I went on, "why—what do they call me 'wise child' *for?* I asked Hi Budd, up at the Corners, but he only just chuckled and chuckled to himself, and wouldn't say a word."

My Aunt suspended work for the moment, and looked severely down upon me. "Well! Ira Clarence Blodgett!" she said, with grim emphasis, "I am ashamed of you! I thought you had more pride! The idea of talking about things like that with a coarse rough hired man—in a barn!"

To hear my full name thus pronounced, syllable by syllable, sent me fairly weltering, as it were, under Aunt Susan's utmost condemnation. It was the punishment reserved for my gravest crimes. I hung my head, and felt the lamp wagging nervelessly in my hands. I could not deny even her speculative impeachment as to the barn; it was blankly apparent in my mind that the fact of the barn made matters much worse.

"I was helping him wash their two-seated sleigh," I submitted, weakly. "He asked me to."

"What does that matter?" she asked peremptorily. "What business have you got going around talking with men about me?"

"Why, it wasn't about you at all, Aunt Susan," I put in more confidently. "I said the Perkins girls kept calling me 'wise child,' and I asked Hi——"

Aunt Susan sighed once more, and interrupted me to inspect the wick of the lamp. Then she turned again to her work, but less spiritedly now. She took up the cleaver with almost an air of sadness.

"You don't understand—yet," she said. "But don't make it any harder for me by talking. Just go along, and say nothing to nobody. People will think more of you.'

My mind strove in vain to grapple with this suggested picture of myself, moving about in perpetual dumbness, followed everywhere by universal admiration. The lamp would *not* hold itself straight.

All at once we both distinctly heard the sound of footsteps close outside. The noise of crunching on the dry, frozen snow came through the thin clap-boards with sharp resonance. Aunt Susan ceased cutting and listened.

"I heard somebody rapping at the front door a spell ago," I ventured to whisper. My Aunt looked at me, and probably realised that I was too sleepy to be accountable for my actions. At all events, she said nothing, but moved toward the low door of the shed, cleaver in hand.

"Who's there?" she called out in shrill, belligerent tones, and this demand she repeated, after an interval of silence, when an irresolute knocking was heard on the door.

We heard a man coughing immediately outside the door. I saw Aunt Susan start at the sound—almost as if she recognised it. A moment later this man, whoever he was, mastered his cough sufficiently to call out, in a hesitating way:

"Is that you, Susan?"

Aunt Susan raised her chin on the instant, her nostrils drawn in, her eyes flashing like those of a pointer when he sees a gun lifted. I had never seen her so excited. She wheeled round once, and covered me with a swift, penetrating, comprehensive glance, under which my knees smote together, and the lamp lurched perilously. Then she turned again, glided towards the door, halted, moved backward two or three steps—looked again at me, and this time spoke.

"Well, I *swan!*" was what she said, and I felt that she looked it.

"Susan! Is that you?" came the voice again, hoarsely appealing. It was not the voice of any neighbour. I made sure I had never heard it before. I could have smiled to myself at the presumption of any man calling my Aunt by her first name, if I had not been too deeply mystified.

"I've been directed here to find Miss Susan Pike," the man outside explained, between fresh coughings.

"Well, then, mog your boots out of this as quick as ever you can!" my Aunt replied, with great promptitude. "You won't find her here!"

"But I *have* found her!" the stranger protested, with an accent of wearied deprecation. "Don't you know me, Susan? I am not strong, this cold air is very bad for me."

"I say 'get out!' " my Aunt replied sharply, Her tone was unrelenting enough, but I noted that she had tipped her head a little to one side, a clear sign to me that she was opening her mind to argument. I felt certain that presently I should see this man.

And, sure enough, after some further parley, Susan went to the door, and, with a half-defiant gesture, knocked the hook up out of the staple.

"Come along then, if you must!" she said, in scornful tones. Then she marched back till she stood beside me, angry resolution written all over her face, and the cleaver in her hand.

A tall, dark figure, opaque against a gleaming background of moonlight and snowlight, was what I for a moment saw in the frame of the open door-way. Then, as he entered, shut and hooked the door behind him, and stood looking in a dazed way over at our lamplit group, I saw that he was a slender, delicately featured man, with a long beard of yellowish brown, and gentle eyes. He was clad as a soldier, heavy azure-hued caped overcoat and all, and I already knew enough of uniforms —cruel familiarity of my war-time infancy—to tell by his cap that he was an officer. He coughed again, before a word was spoken. He looked the last man in the world to go about routing up peaceful households of a winter's night.

"Well, now—what is your business?" demanded Aunt Susan. She put her hand on my shoulder as she spoke, something I had never known her to do before. I felt confused under this novel caress and it seemed only natural that the stranger, having studied my Aunt's face in a wistful way for a moment, should turn his gaze upon me. I was truly a re-markable object, with Aunt Susan's hand on my shoulder.

"I could make no one hear at the other door. I saw the light through the window here, and came around," the stranger explained. He sent little straying glances at the remains of the pig, and at the weapon my Aunt held at her side, but for the most part looked steadily at me.

"That doesn't matter," said Aunt Susan, coldly. "What do you want, now that you *are* here? Why did you come at all? What business had you to think that I ever wanted to lay eyes on you again? How could you have the courage to show your face here—in *my* house?"

The man's shoulders shivered under their cape, and a wan smile curled in his beard. "You keep your house at a very low temperature," he said with grave pleasantry. He did not seem to mind Aunt Susan's hostile demeanour at all.

"I was badly wounded last September," he went on, quite as if that was what she had asked him, "and lay at the point of death for weeks. Then they sent me North, and I have been in the hospital at Albany ever since. One of the nurses there, struck by my name, asked me if I had any relatives in her village—that is, Juno Mills. In that way I learned where you were living. I suppose I ought not to have come—against doctor's orders—the journey has been too much—I have suf-fered a good deal these last two hours."

I felt my Aunt's hand shake a little on my shoulder. Her voice, though, was as implacable as ever.

"There is a much better reason than that why you should not have come," she said, bitterly.

The stranger was talking to her, but looking at me. He took a step toward me now, with a softened sparkle in his eyes, and an outstretched hand. "This—this then is the boy, is it?" he asked.

With a gesture of amazing swiftness Aunt Susan threw her arm about me, and drew me close to her side, lamp and all. With her other hand she lifted and almost brandished the cleaver.

"No, you don't!" she cried. "You don't touch him! He's mine! I've worked for him day and night, ever since I took him from his dying mother's breast. I closed her eyes. I forgave her. Blood is thicker'n water after all. She was my sister. Yes, I forgave poor Emmeline, and I kissed her before she died. She gave the boy to me, and he's mine! Mine, do you hear?—*mine?*"

"My dear Susan——" our visitor began.

"Don't 'dear Susan' me! I heard it once—once too often. Oh, never again! You left me to run away with her. I don't speak of that. I forgave that when I forgave her. But that was the least of it. You left her to herself for months before she died. You've left the boy to himself ever since. You can't begin now. I've worked my fingers to the bone for him—you can't make me stop, now."

"I went to California," he went on in a low voice, speaking with difficulty. "We didn't get on together as smoothly as we might, perhaps, but I had no earthly notion of deserting her. I was ill myself, laying in yellow-fever quarantine off Key West, at the very time she died. When I finally got back, you and the child were both gone. I could not trace you. I went to the war. I had made money in California. It is trebled now. I rose to be Colonel—I have a Brigadier's brevet in my pocket now. Yet I give you my word I never have desired anything so much, all the time, as to find you again—you and the boy."

My Aunt nodded her head comprehendingly. I felt from the tremor of her hand that she was forcing herself against her own desires to be disagreeable.

"Yes, that war," was what she said. "I know about that war! The honest men that go get killed. But you—*you* come back!"

The man frowned wearily, and gave a little groan of discouragement. "Then this is final, is it? You don't wish to speak with me; you really desire to keep the boy—you are set against my ever seeing him—touching him—why then—of course—of course—excuse my——"

And then for the first time I saw a human being tumble in a dead swoon. My little brain, dazed and bewildered by the strange new things I was hearing, lagged behind my eyes in following the sudden pallor on the man's face—lagged behind my ears in noting the tell-tale quaver and gasp in his voice. Before I comprehended what was toward—lo! there was no man standing in front of me at all.

Like a flash Aunt Susan snatched the lamp from my grasp and flung herself upon her knees beside the limp and huddled figure. After a momentary inspection of the white, bearded face, she set the lamp down on the frozen earth floor and took his head upon her lap.

"Take the lamp, run to the buttery and bring the bottle of hartshorn!" she commanded me, hurriedly. "Or, no—wait—open the door—that's it—walk ahead with the light!"

The strong woman stood upright as she spoke, her shoulders braced against the burden she bore in her arms. Unaided, with slow steps, she carried the senseless form of the soldier into the living room, and held it without rest of any sort, the while I, under her direction, wildly tore off quilts, blankets, sheets and feather-tick from my bed and heaped them up on the floor beside the stove. Then, when I had spread them to her liking, she bent and gently laid him down.

"*Now* get the hartshorn," she said. I heard her putting more wood on the fire, but when I returned with the phial she sat once again with the stranger's head upon her knee. She was softly stroking the fine, waving brown hair upon his brow, but her eyes were lifted, looking dreamily at far-away things. I could have sworn to the beginnings of a smile about her parted lips. It was not like my Aunt Susan at all.

"Come here, Ira," I heard her say at last, after a long time had been spent in silence. I walked over and stood at her shoulder, looking down upon the pale face upturned against the black of her worn dress. The blue veins just discernible in temples and closed eyelids, the delicately-turned features, the way his brown beard curled, the fact that his breathing was gently regular once more—these are what I saw. But my Aunt seemed to demand that I should see more.

"Well?" she asked, in a tone mellowed beyond all recognition. "Don't you—don't you see who it is?"

I suppose I really must have had an idea by this time. But I remember that I shook my head.

My Aunt positively did smile this time. "The Perkins girls were wrong," she said; "there isn't the least smitch of a 'wise child' about *you!*"

There was another pause. Emboldened by consciousness of a change in the emotional atmosphere, I was moved to lay my hand upon my Aunt's shoulder. The action did not seem to displease her, and we remained thus for some minutes, watching together this strange addition to our family party.

Finally she told me to get on my cap, comforter and mittens, and run over to Dr. Peabody's and fetch him back with me. The purport of my mission oppressed me.

"Is he going to die then?" I asked.

Aunt Susan laughed outright. "You little goose," she said; "do you think the doctors kill people *every* time?"

And, laughing again, with a trembling softness in her voice and tears upon her black eye-lashes, she lifted her face to mine—and kissed me!

No fatality dogged good old Doctor Peabody's big footsteps through the snow that night. I fell asleep while he was still at my Aunt's house, but not before the stranger had recovered consciousness, and was sitting up in the large rocking-chair, and it was clearly understood that he was soon to be well again.

The kindly, garrulous doctor did more than reassure our little household. He must have spent most of the night going about reassuring the other households of Juno Mills. At all events, when I first went out next morning—while our neighbours were still eating their buckwheat cakes and pork-fat by lamplight—everybody seemed to know that my father, the distinguished Colonel Blodgett, had returned from the war on sick leave, and was lying ill at the house of his sister-in-law. I felt at once the altered attitude of the village toward me. Important citizens who had never spoken to me before—dignified and portly men in blue cutaway coats with brass buttons, and high stiff hats of shaggy white silk —stopped now to lay their hands on the top of my head and ask me how my father, the Colonel, was getting along. The grocer's hired man gave me a Jackson ball and two molasses cookies the very first time I saw him. Even the Perkins' girls, during the course of the afternoon, strolled over to our front gate, and, instead of hurling enigmatic objurgations at me, invited me to come out and play. The butcher of his own accord came and finished cutting up the pig.

These changes come back to me as one part of the great metamorphosis which the night's events had wrought. Another part was the definite disappearance of the stern-faced, tirelessly toiling old maid I had known all my life as Aunt Susan. In her place there was now a much younger woman, with pleasant lines about her pretty mouth, and eyes that twinkled when they looked at me, and who paid no attention to the loom whatever, but bustled cheerily about the house instead, thinking only of good things for us to eat.

I remember that I marked my sense of the difference by abandoning the old name of Aunt Susan, and calling her now just "Auntie." And one day in the mid-spring, after she and her convalescent patient had returned from their first drive together into the country round about, she told me, as she took off her new bonnet in an absent-minded way, and looked meditatively at the old disused loom, and then bent down to brush my forehead with her warm lips—she told me that henceforth I was to call her Mother.

HENRY JAMES

The Real Thing

"The Real Thing" was first published April 16, 1892, in *Black and White* and was reprinted in *The Real Thing and Other Tales* (1893). The donnée for this tale was a story George du Maurier had related to James some years earlier about a well-born English couple who applied to him for some work modeling. James's notebook entry concerning this story indicates that the author initially had little sympathy for the couple who would become the fictional Monarchs: they "could only *show* themselves, clumsily, for the fine, clean, well-groomed animals that they were." In the printed story, however, they are treated with a great deal of sympathy. The models, Miss Churm and Oronte, are members of a lower social class, but for the artist's purpose they are more adept at modeling for the sort of life the Monarchs had in fact lived. The artist narrator, on the other hand, though generous, is himself on trial as well. He is torn between his personal ambition and his moral sympathy. Oronte and Miss Churm are capable of posing as gentry, and the Monarchs, we learn, are willing to work as servants, but the artist appears to be less flexible. His imagination cannot operate under the stimulus of models who seem to be so self-sufficiently what they are. The story, if it is to succeed, James recorded, must be an "idea," "it must be a picture." That picture occurs in the final scene, when Mrs. Monarch adjusts Miss Churm's hair, and illustrates what the author's brother, William James, would later say in his *Pragmatism* about the nature of reality: that the "real thing" consists in what we perceive and what we imaginatively add to that perception.

* * *

I

When the porter's wife (she used to answer the house-bell), announced "A gentleman—with a lady, sir," I had, as I often had in those days, for the wish was father to the thought, an immediate vision of sitters. Sitters my visitors in this case proved to be; but not in the sense I should have preferred. However, there was nothing at first to indicate that they might not have come for a portrait. The gentleman, a man of fifty, very high and very straight, with a moustache slightly grizzled and a dark grey walking-coat admirably fitted, both of which I noted professionally—I don't mean as a barber or yet as a tailor—would have struck me as a celebrity if celebrities often were striking. It was a truth of which

I had for some time been conscious that a figure with a good deal of frontage was, as one might say, almost never a public institution. A glance at the lady helped to remind me of this paradoxical law: she also looked too distinguished to be a "personality." Moreover one would scarcely come across two variations together.

Neither of the pair spoke immediately—they only prolonged the preliminary gaze which suggested that each wished to give the other a chance. They were visibly shy; they stood there letting me take them in—which, as I afterwards perceived, was the most practical thing they could have done. In this way their embarrassment served their cause. I had seen people painfully reluctant to mention that they desired anything so gross as to be represented on canvas; but the scruples of my new friends appeared almost insurmountable. Yet the gentleman might have said "I should like a portrait of my wife," and the lady might have said "I should like a portrait of my husband." Perhaps they were not husband and wife—this naturally would make the matter more delicate. Perhaps they wished to be done together—in which case they ought to have brought a third person to break the news.

"We come from Mr. Rivet," the lady said at last, with a dim smile which had the effect of a moist sponge passed over a "sunk" piece of painting, as well as of a vague allusion to vanished beauty. She was as tall and straight, in her degree, as her companion, and with ten years less to carry. She looked as sad as a woman could look whose face was not charged with expression; that is her tinted oval mask showed friction as an exposed surface shows it. The hand of time had played over her freely, but only to simplify. She was slim and stiff, and so well-dressed, in dark blue cloth, with lappets and pockets and buttons, that it was clear she employed the same tailor as her husband. The couple had an indefinable air of prosperous thrift—they evidently got a good deal of luxury for their money. If I was to be one of their luxuries it would behove me to consider my terms.

"Ah, Claude Rivet recommended me?" I inquired; and I added that it was very kind of him, though I could reflect that, as he only painted landscape, this was not a sacrifice.

The lady looked very hard at the gentleman, and the gentleman looked round the room. Then staring at the floor a moment and stroking his moustache, he rested his pleasant eyes on me with the remark: "He said you were the right one."

"I try to be, when people want to sit."

"Yes, we should like to," said the lady anxiously.

"Do you mean together?"

My visitors exchanged a glance. "If you could do anything with *me*, I suppose it would be double," the gentleman stammered.

"Oh yes, there's naturally a higher charge for two figures than for one."

"We should like to make it pay," the husband confessed.

"That's very good of you," I returned, appreciating so unwonted a sympathy—for I supposed he meant pay the artist.

A sense of strangeness seemed to dawn on the lady. "We mean for the illustrations—Mr. Rivet said you might put one in."

"Put one in—an illustration?" I was equally confused.

"Sketch her off, you know," said the gentleman, colouring.

It was only then that I understood the service Claude Rivet had rendered me; he had told them that I worked in black and white, for magazines, for story-books, for sketches of contemporary life, and consequently had frequent employment for models. These things were true, but it was not less true (I may confess it now—whether because the aspiration was to lead to everything or to nothing I leave the reader to guess), that I couldn't get the honours, to say nothing of the emoluments, of a great painter of portraits out of my head. My "illustrations" were my pot-boilers; I looked to a different branch of art (far and away the most interesting it had always seemed to me), to perpetuate my fame. There was no shame in looking to it also to make my fortune; but that fortune was by so much further from being made from the moment my visitors wished to be "done" for nothing. I was disappointed; for in the pictorial sense I had immediately *seen* them. I had seized their type—I had already settled what I would do with it. Something that wouldn't absolutely have pleased them, I afterwards reflected.

"Ah, you're—you're—a—?" I began, as soon as I had mastered my surprise. I couldn't bring out the dingy word "models"; it seemed to fit the case so little.

"We haven't had much practice," said the lady.

"We've got to *do* something, and we've thought that an artist in your line might perhaps make something of us," her husband threw off. He further mentioned that they didn't know many artists and that they had gone first, on the off-chance (he painted views of course, but sometimes put in figures—perhaps I remembered), to Mr. Rivet, whom they had met a few years before at a place in Norfolk where he was sketching.

"We used to sketch a little ourselves," the lady hinted.

"It's very awkward, but we absolutely *must* do something," her husband went on.

"Of course, we're not so *very* young," she admitted, with a wan smile.

With the remark that I might as well know something more about them, the husband had handed me a card extracted from a neat new pocket-book (their appurtenances were all of the freshest) and inscribed with the words "Major Monarch." Impressive as these words were they didn't carry my knowledge much further; but my visitor presently added: "I've left the army, and we've had the misfortune to lose our money. In fact our means are dreadfully small."

"It's an awful bore," said Mrs. Monarch.

They evidently wished to be discreet—to take care not to swagger because they were gentlefolks. I perceived they would have been willing to recognise this as something of a drawback, at the same time that I guessed at an underlying sense—their consolation in adversity—that they *had* their points. They certainly had; but these advantages struck me as preponderantly social; such for instance as would help to make a drawing-room look well. However, a drawing-room was always, or ought to be, a picture.

In consequence of his wife's allusion to their age Major Monarch observed: "Naturally, it's more for the figure that we thought of going in. We can still hold ourselves up." On the instant I saw that the figure was indeed their strong point. His "naturally" didn't sound vain, but it lighted up the question. "*She* has got the best," he continued, nodding at his wife, with a pleasant after-dinner absence of circumlocution. I could only reply, as if we were in fact sitting over our wine, that this didn't prevent his own from being very good; which led him in turn to rejoin: "We thought that if you ever have to do people like us, we might be something like it. *She*, particularly—for a lady in a book, you know."

I was so amused by them that, to get more of it, I did my best to take their point of view; and though it was an embarrassment to find myself appraising physically, as if they were animals on hire or useful blacks, a pair whom I should have expected to meet only in one of the relations in which criticism is tacit, I looked at Mrs. Monarch judicially enough to be able to exclaim, after a moment, with conviction: "Oh yes, a lady in a book!" She was singularly like a bad illustration.

"We'll stand up, if you like," said the Major; and he raised himself before me with a really grand air.

I could take his measure at a glance—he was six feet two and a perfect gentleman. It would have paid any club in process of formation and in want of a stamp to engage him at a salary to stand in the principal window. What struck me immediately was that in coming to me they had rather missed their vocation; they could surely have been turned to better account for advertising purposes. I couldn't of course see the thing in detail, but I could see them make someone's fortune— I don't mean their own. There was something in them for a waistcoat-maker, an hotel-keeper or a soap-vendor. I could imagine "We always use it" pinned on their bosoms with the greatest effect; I had a vision of the promptitude with which they would launch a table d'hôte.

Mrs. Monarch sat still, not from pride but from shyness, and presently her husband said to her: "Get up my dear and show how smart you are." She obeyed, but she had no need to get up to show it. She walked to the end of the studio, and then she came back blushing, with her fluttered eyes on her husband. I was reminded of an incident I had accidentally had a glimpse of in Paris—being with a friend there, a dramatist about to produce a play—when an actress came to him to ask to be intrusted with a part. She went through her paces before him, walked up and down as Mrs. Monarch was doing. Mrs. Monarch did it quite as well, but I abstained from applauding. It was very odd to see such people apply for such poor pay. She looked as if she had ten thousand a year. Her husband had used the word that described her: she was, in the London current jargon, essentially and typically "smart." Her figure was, in the same order of ideas, conspicuously and irreproachably "good." For a woman of her age her waist was surprisingly small; her elbow moreover had the orthodox crook. She held her head at the conventional angle; but why did she come to *me*? She ought to have tried on jackets at a big shop. I feared my visitors were not only destitute, but "artistic"—which would be a great complication. When she sat down again I thanked her, observing that what a draughtsman most valued in his model was the faculty of keeping quiet.

"Oh, *she* can keep quiet," said Major Monarch. Then he added, jocosely: "I've always kept her quiet."

"I'm not a nasty fidget, am I?" Mrs. Monarch appealed to her husband.

He addressed his answer to me. "Perhaps it isn't out of place to mention—because we ought to be quite business-like, oughtn't we?—that when I married her she was known as the Beautiful Statue."

"Oh dear!" said Mrs. Monarch, ruefully.

"Of course I should want a certain amount of expression," I rejoined.

"Of *course!*" they both exclaimed.

"And then I suppose you know that you'll get awfully tired."

"Oh, we *never* get tired!" they eagerly cried.

"Have you had any kind of practice?"

They hesitated—they looked at each other. "We've been photographed, *immensely*," said Mrs. Monarch.

"She means the fellows have asked us," added the Major.

"I see—because you're so good-looking."

"I don't know what they thought, but they were always after us."

"We always got our photographs for nothing," smiled Mrs. Monarch.

"We might have brought some, my dear," her husband remarked.

"I'm not sure we have any left. We've given quantities away," she explained to me.

"With our autographs and that sort of thing," said the Major.

"Are they to be got in the shops?" I inquired, as a harmless pleasantry.

"Oh, yes; *hers*—they used to be."

"Not now," said Mrs. Monarch, with her eyes on the floor.

II

I could fancy the "sort of thing" they put on the presentation-copies of their photographs, and I was sure they wrote a beautiful hand. It was odd how quickly I was sure of everything that concerned them. If they were now so poor as to have to earn shillings and pence, they never had had much of a margin. Their good looks had been their capital, and they had good-humouredly made the most of the career that this resource marked out for them. It was in their faces, the blankness, the deep intellectual repose of the twenty years of country-house visiting which had given them pleasant intonations. I could see the sunny drawing-rooms, sprinkled with periodicals she didn't read, in which Mrs. Monarch had continuously sat; I could see the wet shrubberies in which she had walked, equipped to admiration for either exercise. I could see the rich covers the Major had helped to shoot and the wonderful garments in which, late at night, he repaired to the smoking-room to talk about them. I could imagine their leggings and waterproofs, their knowing tweeds and rugs, their rolls of sticks and cases of tackle and neat umbrellas; and I could evoke the exact appearance of their servants and the compact variety of their luggage on the platforms of country stations.

They gave small tips, but they were liked; they didn't do anything themselves, but they were welcome. They looked so well everywhere; they gratified the general relish for stature, complexion and "form." They knew it without fatuity or vulgarity, and they respected themselves in consequence. They were not superficial; they were thorough and kept themselves up—it had been their line. People with such a taste for activity had to have some line. I could feel how, even in a dull house, they could have been counted upon for cheerfulness. At present something had happened—it didn't matter what, their little income had grown less, it had grown least—and they had to do something for pocket-money. Their friends liked them, but didn't like to support them. There was something about them that represented credit—their clothes, their manners, their type; but if credit is a large empty pocket in which an occasional chink reverberates, the chink at least must be audible. What they wanted of me was to help to make it so. Fortunately they had no children—I soon divined that. They would also perhaps wish our relations to be kept secret: this was why it was "for the figure"—the reproduction of the face would betray them.

I liked them—they were so simple; and I had no objection to them if they would suit. But, somehow, with all their perfections I didn't easily believe in them. After all they were amateurs, and the ruling passion of my life was the detestation of the amateur. Combined with this was another perversity—an innate preference for the represented subject over the real one: the defect of the real one was so apt to be a lack of representation. I liked things that appeared; then one was sure. Whether they *were* or not was a subordinate and almost always a profitless question. There were other considerations, the first of which was that I already had two or three people in use, notably a young person with big feet, in alpaca, from Kilburn, who for a couple of years had come to me regularly for my illustrations and with whom I was still—perhaps ignobly—satisfied. I frankly explained to my visitors how the case stood; but they had taken more precautions than I supposed. They had reasoned out their opportunity, for Claude Rivet had told them of the projected *édition de luxe* of one of the writers of our day—the rarest of the novelists—who, long neglected by the multitudinous vulgar and dearly prized by the attentive (need I mention Philip Vincent?) had had the happy fortune of seeing, late in life, the dawn and then the full light of a higher criticism—an estimate in which, on the part of the public, there was something really of expiation. The edition in question, planned by a publisher of taste, was practically an act of high reparation; the wood-cuts with which it was to be enriched were the homage of English art to one of the most independent representatives of English letters. Major and Mrs. Monarch confessed to me that they had hoped I might be able to work *them* into my share of the enterprise. They knew I was to do the first of the books, "Rutland Ramsay," but I had to make clear to them that my participation in the rest of the affair—this first book was to be a test—was to depend on the satisfaction I should give. If this should be limited my employers would drop me without a scruple. It was therefore a crisis for me, and naturally I was making special preparations, looking about for new people, if they should be necessary, and securing the best types. I admitted however that I should like to settle down to two or three good models who would do for everything.

"Should we have often to—a—put on special clothes?" Mrs. Monarch timidly demanded.

"Dear, yes—that's half the business."

"And should we be expected to supply our own costumes?"

"Oh, no; I've got a lot of things. A painter's models put on—or put off—anything he likes."

"And do you mean—a—the same?"

"The same?"

Mrs. Monarch looked at her husband again.

"Oh, she was just wondering," he explained, "if the costumes are in *general* use." I had to confess that they were, and I mentioned further that some of them (I had a lot of genuine, greasy last-century things), had served their time, a hundred years ago, on living, world-stained men and women. "We'll put on anything that *fits*," said the Major.

"Oh, I arrange that—they fit in the pictures."

"I'm afraid I should do better for the modern books. I would come as you like," said Mrs. Monarch.

"She has got a lot of clothes at home: they might do for contemporary life," her husband continued.

"Oh, I can fancy scenes in which you'd be quite natural." And indeed I could see the slipshod rearrangements of stale properties—the stories I tried to produce pictures for without the exasperation of reading them—whose sandy tracts the good lady might help to people. But I had to return to the fact that for this sort of work—the daily mechanical grind—I was already equipped; the people I was working with were fully adequate.

"We only thought we might be more like *some* characters," said Mrs. Monarch mildly, getting up.

Her husband also rose; he stood looking at me with a dim wistfulness that was touching in so fine a man. "Wouldn't it be rather a pull sometimes to have—a—to have—?" He hung fire; he wanted me to help him by phrasing what he meant. But I couldn't—I didn't know. So he brought it out, awkwardly: "The *real* thing; a gentleman, you know, or a lady." I was quite ready to give a general assent—I admitted that there was a great deal in that. This encouraged Major Monarch to say, following up his appeal with an unacted gulp: "It's awfully hard—we've tried everything." The gulp was communicative; it proved too much for his wife. Before I knew it Mrs. Monarch had dropped again upon a divan and burst into tears. Her husband sat down beside her, holding one of her hands; whereupon she quickly dried her eyes with the other, while I felt embarrassed as she looked up at me. "There isn't a confounded job I haven't applied for—waited for—prayed for. You can fancy we'd be pretty bad first. Secretaryships and that sort of thing? You might as well ask for a peerage. I'd be *anything*—I'm strong; a messenger or a coalheaver. I'd put on a gold-laced cap and open carriage-doors in front of the haberdasher's; I'd hang about a station, to carry portmanteaus; I'd be a postman. But they won't *look* at you; there are thousands, as good as yourself, already on the ground. *Gentlemen,* poor beggars, who have drunk their wine, who have kept their hunters!"

I was as reassuring as I knew how to be, and my visitors were presently on their feet again while, for the experiment, we agreed on an hour. We were discussing it when the door opened and Miss Churm came in with a wet umbrella. Miss Churm had to take the omnibus to Maida Vale and then walk half-a-mile. She looked a trifle blowsy and slightly splashed. I scarcely ever saw her come in without thinking afresh how odd it was that, being so little in herself, she should yet be so much in others. She was a meagre little Miss Churm, but she was an ample heroine of romance. She was only a freckled cockney, but she could represent everything, from a fine lady to a shepherdess; she had the faculty, as she might have had a fine voice or long hair. She couldn't spell, and she loved beer, but she had two or three "points," and practice, and a knack, and mother-wit, and a kind of whimsical sensibility, and a love of the theatre, and seven sisters, and not an ounce of respect, especially for the *h.* The first thing my visitors saw was that her umbrella was wet, and in their spotless perfection they visibly winced at it. The rain had come on since their arrival.

"I'm all in a soak; there *was* a mess of people in the 'bus. I wish you lived near a stytion," said Miss Churm. I requested her to get ready as quickly as possible, and she passed into the room in which she always changed her dress. But before going out she asked me what she was to get into this time.

"It's the Russian princess, don't you know?" I answered; "the one with the 'golden eyes,' in black velvet, for the long thing in the *Cheapside.*"

"Golden eyes? I *say!*" cried Miss Churm, while my companions watched her with intensity as she withdrew. She always arranged herself, when she was late, before I could turn round; and I kept my visitors a little, on purpose, so that they might get an idea, from seeing her, what would be expected of themselves. I mentioned that she was quite my notion of an excellent model—she was really very clever.

"Do you think she looks like a Russian princess?" Major Monarch asked, with lurking alarm.

"When I make her, yes."

"Oh, if you have to *make* her—!" he reasoned, acutely.

"That's the most you can ask. There are so many that are not makeable."

"Well now, *here's* a lady"—and with a persuasive smile he passed his arm into his wife's—"who's already made!"

"Oh, I'm not a Russian princess," Mrs. Monarch protested, a little coldly. I could see that she had known some and didn't like them. There, immediately, was a complication of a kind that I never had to fear with Miss Churm.

This young lady came back in black velvet—the gown was rather rusty and very low on her lean shoulders—and with a Japanese fan in her red hands. I reminded her that in the scene I was doing she had to look over someone's head. "I forget whose it is; but it doesn't matter. Just look over a head."

"I'd rather look over a stove," said Miss Churm; and she took her station near the fire. She fell into position, settled herself into a tall attitude, gave a certain backward inclination to her head and a certain forward droop to her fan, and looked, at least to my prejudiced sense, distinguished and charming, foreign and dangerous. We left her looking so, while I went down-stairs with Major and Mrs. Monarch.

"I think I could come about as near it as that," said Mrs. Monarch.

"Oh, you think she's shabby, but you must allow for the alchemy of art."

However, they went off with an evident increase of comfort, founded on their demonstrable advantage in being the real thing. I could fancy them shuddering over Miss Churm. She was very droll about them when I went back, for I told her what they wanted.

"Well, if *she* can sit I'll tyke to bookkeeping," said my model.

"She's very lady-like," I replied, as an innocent form of aggravation.

"So much the worse for *you*. That means she can't turn round."

"She'll do for the fashionable novels."

"Oh yes, she'll *do* for them!" my model humorously declared. "Ain't they bad enough without her?" I had often sociably denounced them to Miss Churm.

III

It was for the elucidation of a mystery in one of these works that I first tried Mrs. Monarch. Her husband came with her, to be useful if necessary—it was sufficiently clear that as a general thing he would prefer to come with her. At first I wondered if this were for "propriety's" sake—if he were going to be jealous and meddling. The idea was too tiresome, and if it had been confirmed it would speedily have brought our acquaintance to a close. But I soon saw there was nothing in it and that if he accompanied Mrs. Monarch it was (in addition to the chance of being wanted), simply because he had nothing else to do. When she was away from him his occupation was gone—she never *had* been away from him. I judged, rightly, that in their awkward situation their close union was their main comfort and that this union had no weak spot. It was a real marriage, an encouragement to the hesitating, a nut for pessimists to crack. Their address was humble (I remember afterwards thinking it had been the only thing about them that was really professional), and I could fancy the lamentable lodgings in which the Major would have been left alone. He could bear them with his wife—he couldn't bear them without her.

He had too much tact to try and make himself agreeable when he couldn't be useful; so he simply sat and waited, when I was too absorbed in my work to talk. But I liked to make him talk—it made my work, when it didn't interrupt it, less sordid, less special. To listen to him was to combine the excitement of going out with the economy of staying at home. There was only one hindrance: that I seemed not to know any of the people he and his wife had known. I think he wondered extremely, during the term of our intercourse, whom the deuce I *did* know. He hadn't a stray sixpence of an idea to fumble for; so we didn't spin it very fine—we confined ourselves to questions of leather and even of liquor (saddlers and breeches-makers and how to get good claret cheap), and matters like "good trains" and the habits of small game. His lore on these last subjects was astonishing, he managed to interweave the station-master with the ornithologist. When he couldn't talk about greater things he could talk cheerfully about smaller, and since I couldn't accompany him into reminiscences of the fashionable world he could lower the conversation without a visible effort to my level.

So earnest a desire to please was touching in a man who could so easily have knocked one down. He looked after the fire and had an opinion on the draught of the stove, without my asking him, and I could see that he thought many of my arrangements not half clever enough. I remember telling him that if I were only rich I would offer him a salary to come and teach me how to live. Sometimes he gave a random sigh, of which the essence was: "Give me even such a bare old barrack as *this,* and I'd do something with it!" When I wanted to use him he came alone; which was an illustration of the superior courage of women. His wife could bear her solitary second floor, and she was in general more discreet; showing by various small reserves that she was alive to the propriety of keeping our relations markedly professional—not letting them slide into sociability. She wished it to remain clear that she and the Major were employed, not cultivated, and if she approved of me as a superior, who could be kept in his place, she never thought me quite good enough for an equal.

She sat with great intensity, giving the whole of her mind to it, and was capable of remaining for an hour almost as motionless as if she were before a photographer's lens. I could see she had been photographed often, but somehow the very habit that made her good for that purpose unfitted her for mine. At first I was extremely pleased with her lady-like air, and it was a satisfaction, on coming to follow her lines, to see how good they were and how far they could lead the pencil. But after a few times I began to find her too insurmountably stiff; do what I would with it my drawing looked like a photograph or a copy of a photograph. Her figure had no variety of expression—she herself had no sense of variety. You may say that this was my business, was only a question of placing her. I placed her in every conceivable position, but she managed to obliterate their differences. She was always a lady certainly, and into the bargain was always the same lady. She was the real thing, but always the same thing. There were moments when I was oppressed by the serenity of her confidence that she *was* the real thing. All her dealings with me and all her husband's were an implication that this was lucky for *me*. Meanwhile I found myself trying to invent types that approached her own, instead of making her own transform itself —in the clever way that was not impossible, for instance, to poor Miss Churm. Arrange as I would and take the precautions I would, she always, in my pictures, came out too tall—landing me in the dilemma of having represented a fascinating woman as seven feet high, which, out of respect perhaps to my own very much scantier inches, was far from my idea of such a personage.

The case was worse with the Major—nothing I could do would keep *him* down, so that he became useful only for the representation of brawny giants. I adored variety and range, I cherished human accidents, the illustrative note; I wanted to characterise closely, and the thing in the world I most hated was the danger of being ridden by a type. I had quarrelled with some of my friends about it—I had parted company with them for maintaining that one *had* to be, and that if the type was beautiful (witness Raphael and Leonardo), the servitude was only a gain. I was neither Leonardo nor Raphael; I might only be a presumptuous young modern searcher, but I held that everything was to be sacrificed sooner than character. When they averred that the haunting type in question could easily *be* character, I retorted, perhaps superficially: "Whose?" It couldn't be everybody's—it might end in being nobody's.

After I had drawn Mrs. Monarch a dozen times I perceived more clearly than before that the value of such a model as Miss Churm resided precisely in the fact that she had no positive stamp, combined of course with the other fact that what she did have was a curious and inexplicable talent for imitation. Her usual appearance was like a curtain which she could draw up at request for a capital performance. This performance was simply suggestive; but it was a word to the wise—it was vivid and pretty. Sometimes, even, I thought it, though she was plain herself, too insipidly pretty; I made it a reproach to her that the figures drawn from her were monotonously (*bêtement,* as we used to say) graceful. Nothing made her more angry: it was so much her pride to feel that she could sit for characters that had nothing in common with each other. She would accuse me at such moments of taking away her "reputytion."

It suffered a certain shrinkage, this queer quantity, from the repeated visits of my new friends. Miss Churm was greatly in demand, never in want of employment, so I had no scruple in putting her off occasionally, to try them more at my ease. It was certainly amusing at first to do the real thing—it was amusing to do Major Monarch's trousers. They *were* the real thing, even if he did come out colossal. It was amusing to do his wife's back hair (it was so mathematically neat,) and the particular "smart" tension of her tight stays. She lent herself especially to positions in which the face was somewhat averted or blurred; she abounded in lady-like back views and *profils perdus.* When she stood erect she took naturally one of the attitudes in which court-painters represent queens and princesses; so that I found myself wondering whether, to draw out this accomplishment, I couldn't get the editor of the *Cheapside* to publish a really royal romance, "A Tale of Buckingham Palace." Sometimes, however, the real thing and the make-believe came into contact; by which I mean that Miss Churm, keeping an appointment or coming to make one on days when I had much work in hand, encountered her invidious rivals. The encounter was not on their part, for they noticed her no more than if she had been the housemaid; not from intentional loftiness, but simply because, as yet, professionally, they didn't know how to fraternise, as I could guess that they would have liked—or at least that the Major would. They couldn't talk about the omnibus— they always walked; and they didn't know what else to try—she wasn't interested in good trains or cheap claret. Besides, they must have felt— in the air—that she was amused at them, secretly derisive of their ever knowing how. She was not a person to conceal her scepticism if she had had a chance to show it. On the other hand Mrs. Monarch didn't think her tidy; for why else did she take pains to say to me (it was going out of the way, for Mrs. Monarch), that she didn't like dirty women?

One day when my young lady happened to be present with my other sitters (she even dropped in, when it was convenient, for a chat), I asked her to be so good as to lend a hand in getting tea—a service with which she was familiar and which was one of a class that, living as I did in a small way, with slender domestic resources, I often appealed to my models to render. They liked to lay hands on my property, to break the sitting, and sometimes the china—I made them feel Bohemian. The next time I saw Miss Churm after this incident she surprised me greatly by making a scene about it—she accused me of having wished to humiliate her. She had not resented the outrage at the time, but had seemed obliging and amused, enjoying the comedy of asking Mrs. Monarch, who sat vague and silent, whether she would have cream and sugar, and putting an exaggerated simper into the question. She had tried intonations—as if she too wished to pass for the real thing; till I was afraid my other visitors would take offence.

Oh, *they* were determined not to do this; and their touching patience was the measure of their great need. They would sit by the hour, uncomplaining, till I was ready to use them; they would come back on the chance of being wanted and would walk away cheerfully if they were not. I used to go to the door with them to see in what magnificent order they retreated. I tried to find other employment for them—I introduced them to several artists. But they didn't "take," for reasons I could appreciate, and I became conscious, rather anxiously, that after such disappointments they fell back upon me with a heavier weight. They did me the honour to think that it was I who was most *their* form. They were not picturesque enough for the painters, and in those days there were not so many serious workers in black and white. Besides, they had an eye to the great job I had mentioned to them—they had secretly set their hearts on supplying the right essence for my pictorial vindication of our fine novelist. They knew that for this undertaking I should want no costume-effects, none of the frippery of past ages—that it was a case in which everything would be contemporary and satirical and, presumably, genteel. If I could work them into it their future would be assured, for the labour would of course be long and the occupation steady.

One day Mrs. Monarch came without her husband—she explained his absence by his having had to go to the City. While she sat there in her usual anxious stiffness there came, at the door, a knock which I immediately recognised as the subdued appeal of a model out of work. It was followed by the entrance of a young man whom I easily perceived to be a foreigner and who proved in fact an Italian acquainted with no English word but my name, which he uttered in a way that made it seem to include all others. I had not then visited his country, nor was I proficient in his tongue; but as he was not so meanly constituted—what Italian is?—as to depend only on that member for expression he conveyed to me, in familiar but graceful mimicry, that he was in search of exactly the employment in which the lady before me was engaged. I was not struck with him at first, and while I continued to draw I emitted rough sounds of discouragement and dismissal. He stood his ground, however, not importunately, but with a dumb, dog-like fidelity in his eyes which amounted to innocent impudence—the manner of a devoted servant (he might have been in the house for years), unjustly suspected. Suddenly I saw that this very attitude and expression made a picture, whereupon I told him to sit down and wait till I should be free. There was another picture in the way he obeyed me, and I observed as I worked that there were others still in the way he looked wonderingly, with his head thrown back, about the high studio. He might have been crossing himself in St. Peter's. Before I finished I said to myself: "The fellow's a bankrupt orange-monger, but he's a treasure."

When Mrs. Monarch withdrew he passed across the room like a flash to open the door for her, standing there with the rapt, pure gaze of the young Dante spellbound by the young Beatrice. As I never insisted, in such situations, on the blankness of the British domestic, I reflected that he had the making of a servant (and I needed one, but couldn't pay him to be only that), as well as of a model; in short I made up my mind to adopt my bright adventurer if he would agree to officiate in the double capacity. He jumped at my offer, and in the event my rashness (for I had known nothing about him), was not brought home to me. He proved a sympathetic though a desultory ministrant, and had in a wonderful degree the *sentiment de la pose*. It was uncultivated, instinctive; a part of the happy instinct which had guided him to my door and helped him to spell out my name on the card nailed to it. He had had no other introduction to me than a guess, from the shape of my high north window, seen outside, that my place was a studio and that as a studio it would contain an artist. He had wandered to England in search of fortune, like other itinerants, and had embarked, with a partner and a small green handcart, on the sale of penny ices. The ices had melted away and the partner had dissolved in their train. My young man wore tight yellow trousers with reddish stripes and his name was Oronte. He was sallow but fair, and when I put him into some old clothes of my own he looked like an Englishman. He was as good as Miss Churm, who could look, when required, like an Italian.

IV

I thought Mrs. Monarch's face slightly convulsed when, on her coming back with her husband, she found Oronte installed. It was strange to have to recognise in a scrap of a lazzarone a competitor to her magnificent Major. It was she who scented danger first, for the Major was anecdotically unconscious. But Oronte gave us tea, with a hundred eager confusions (he had never seen such a queer process), and I think she thought better of me for having at last an "establishment." They saw a couple of drawings that I had made of the establishment, and Mrs. Monarch hinted that it never would have struck her that he had sat for them. "Now the drawings you make from *us,* they look exactly like us," she reminded me, smiling in triumph; and I recognised that this was indeed just their defect. When I drew the Monarchs I couldn't, somehow, get away from them—get into the character I wanted to represent; and I had not the least desire my model should be discoverable in my picture. Miss Churm never was, and Mrs. Monarch thought I hid her, very properly, because she was vulgar; whereas if she was lost it was only as the dead who go to heaven are lost—in the gain of an angel the more.

By this time I had got a certain start with "Rutland Ramsay," the first novel in the great projected series; that is I had produced a dozen drawings, several with the help of the Major and his wife, and I had sent them in for approval. My understanding with the publishers, as I have already hinted, had been that I was to be left to do my work, in this particular case, as I liked, with the whole book committed to me; but my connection with the rest of the series was only contingent. There were moments when, frankly, it *was* a comfort to have the real thing under one's hand; for there were characters in "Rutland Ramsay" that were very much like it. There were people presumably as straight as the Major and women of as good a fashion as Mrs. Monarch. There was a great deal of country-house life—treated, it is true, in a fine, fanciful, ironical, generalised way—and there was a considerable implication of knickerbockers and kilts. There were certain things I had to settle at the outset; such things for instance as the exact appearance of the hero, the particular bloom of the heroine. The author of course gave me a lead, but there was a margin for interpretation. I took the Monarchs into my confidence, I told them frankly what I was about, I mentioned my embarrassments and alternatives. "Oh, take *him!*" Mrs. Monarch murmured sweetly, looking at her husband; and "What could you want better than my wife?" the Major inquired, with the comfortable candour that now prevailed between us.

I was not obliged to answer these remarks—I was only obliged to place my sitters. I was not easy in mind, and I postponed, a little timidly perhaps, the solution of the question. The book was a large canvas, the other figures were numerous, and I worked off at first some of the episodes in which the hero and the heroine were not concerned. When once I had set *them* up I should have to stick to them—I couldn't make my young man seven feet high in one place and five feet nine in another. I inclined on the whole to the latter measurement, though the Major more than once reminded me that *he* looked about as young as anyone. It was indeed quite possible to arrange him, for the figure, so that it would have been difficult to detect his age. After the spontaneous Oronte had been with me a month, and after I had given him to understand several different times that his native exuberance would presently constitute an insurmountable barrier to our further intercourse, I waked to a sense of his heroic capacity. He was only five feet seven, but the remaining inches were latent. I tried him almost secretly at first, for I was really rather afraid of the judgment my other models would pass on such a choice. If they regarded Miss Churm as little better than a snare, what would they think of the representation by a person so little the real thing as an Italian street-vendor of a protagonist formed by a public school?

If I went a little in fear of them it was not because they bullied me, because they had got an oppressive foothold, but because in their really pathetic decorum and mysteriously permanent newness they counted on me so intensely. I was therefore very glad when Jack Hawley came home: he was always of such good counsel. He painted badly himself, but there was no one like him for putting his finger on the place. He had been absent from England for a year; he had been somewhere—I don't remember where—to get a fresh eye. I was in a good deal of dread of any such organ, but we were old friends; he had been away for months and a sense of emptiness was creeping into my life. I hadn't dodged a missile for a year.

He came back with a fresh eye, but with the same old black velvet blouse, and the first evening he spent in my studio we smoked cigarettes till the small hours. He had done no work himself, he had only got the eye; so the field was clear for the production of my little things. He wanted to see what I had done for the *Cheapside*, but he was disappointed in the exhibition. That at least seemed the meaning of two or three comprehensive groans which, as he lounged on my big divan, on a folded leg, looking at my latest drawings, issued from his lips with the smoke of the cigarette.

"What's the matter with you?" I asked.

"What's the matter with *you?*"

"Nothing save that I'm mystified."

"You are indeed. You're quite off the hinge. What's the meaning of this new fad?" And he tossed me, with visible irreverence, a drawing in which I happened to have depicted both my majestic models. I asked if he didn't think it good, and he replied that it struck him as execrable, given the sort of thing I had always represented myself to him as wishing to arrive at; but I let that pass, I was so anxious to see exactly what he meant. The two figures in the picture looked colossal, but I supposed this was *not* what he meant, inasmuch as, for aught he knew to the contrary, I might have been trying for that. I maintained that I was working exactly in the same way as when he last had done me the honour to commend me. "Well, there's a big hole somewhere," he answered; "wait a bit and I'll discover it." I depended upon him to do so: where else was the fresh eye? But he produced at last nothing more luminous than "I don't know—I don't like your types." This was lame, for a critic who had never consented to discuss with me anything but the question of execution, the direction of strokes and the mystery of values.

"In the drawings you've been looking at I think my types are very handsome."

"Oh, they won't do!"

"I've had a couple of new models."

"I see you have. *They* won't do."

"Are you very sure of that?"

"Absolutely—they're stupid."

"You mean *I* am—for I ought to get round that."

"You *can't*—with such people. Who are they?"

I told him, as far as was necessary, and he declared, heartlessly: "*Ce sont des gens qu'il faut mettre à la porte.*"

"You've never seen them; they're awfully good," I compassionately objected.

"Not seen them? Why, all this recent work of yours drops to pieces with them. It's all I want to see of them."

"No one else has said anything against it—the *Cheapside* people are pleased."

"Everyone else is an ass, and the *Cheapside* people the biggest asses of all. Come, don't pretend, at this time of day, to have pretty illusions about the public, especially about publishers and editors. It's not for *such* animals you work—it's for those who know, *coloro che sanno;* so keep straight for *me* if you can't keep straight for yourself. There's a certain sort of thing you tried for from the first—and a very good thing it is. But this twaddle isn't *in* it." When I talked with Hawley later about "Rutland Ramsay" and its possible successors he declared that I must get back into my boat again or I would go to the bottom. His voice in short was the voice of warning.

I noted the warning, but I didn't turn my friends out of doors. They bored me a good deal; but the very fact that they bored me admonished me not to sacrifice them—if there was anything to be done with them —simply to irritation. As I look back at this phase they seem to me to have pervaded my life not a little. I have a vision of them as most of the time in my studio, seated, against the wall, on an old velvet bench to be out of the way, and looking like a pair of patient courtiers in a royal ante-chamber. I am convinced that during the coldest weeks of the winter they held their ground because it saved them fire. Their new-ness was losing its gloss, and it was impossible not to feel that they were objects of charity. Whenever Miss Churm arrived they went away, and after I was fairly launched in "Rutland Ramsay" Miss Churm arrived pretty often. They managed to express to me tacitly that they supposed I wanted her for the low life of the book, and I let them suppose it, since they had attempted to study the work—it was lying about the studio—without discovering that it dealt only with the highest circles. They had dipped into the most brilliant of our novelists without deciphering many passages. I still took an hour from them, now and again, in spite of Jack Hawley's warning: it would be time enough to dismiss them, if dismissal should be necessary, when the rigour of the season was over. Hawley had made their acquaintance—he had met them at my fireside—and thought them a ridiculous pair. Learning that he was a painter they tried to approach him, to show him too that they were the real thing; but he looked at them, across the big room, as if they were miles away: they were a compendium of everything that he most objected to in the social system of his country. Such people as that, all convention and patent-leather, with ejaculations that stopped conversation, had no business in a studio. A studio was a place to learn to see, and how could you see through a pair of feather beds?

The main inconvenience I suffered at their hands was that, at first, I was shy of letting them discover how my artful little servant had begun to sit to me for "Rutland Ramsay." They knew that I had been odd enough (they were prepared by this time to allow oddity to artists,) to pick a foreign vagabond out of the streets, when I might have had a person with whiskers and credentials; but it was some time before they learned how high I rated his accomplishments. They found him in an attitude more than once, but they never doubted I was doing him as an organ-grinder. There were several things they never guessed, and one of them was that for a striking scene in the novel, in which a footman briefly figured, it occurred to me to make use of Major Monarch as the menial. I kept putting this off, I didn't like to ask him to don the livery—besides the difficulty of finding a livery to fit him. At last, one day late in the winter, when I was at work on the despised Oronte (he caught one's idea in an instant), and was in the glow of feeling that I was going very straight, they came in, the Major and his wife, with their society laugh about nothing (there was less and less to laugh at), like country-callers—they always reminded me of that—who have walked across the park after church and are presently persuaded to stay to luncheon. Luncheon was over, but they could stay to tea—I knew they wanted it. The fit was on me, however, and I couldn't let my ardour cool and my work wait, with the fading daylight, while my model prepared it. So I asked Mrs. Monarch if she would mind laying it out—a request which, for an instant, brought all the blood to her face. Her eyes were on her husband's for a second, and some mute telegraphy passed between them. Their folly was over the next instant; his cheerful shrewdness put an end to it. So far from pitying their wounded pride, I must add, I was moved to give it as complete a lesson as I could. They bustled about together and got out the cups and saucers and made the kettle boil. I know they felt as if they were waiting on my servant, and when the tea was prepared I said: "He'll have a cup, please—he's tired." Mrs. Monarch brought him one where he stood, and he took it from her as if he had been a gentleman at a party, squeezing a crush-hat with an elbow.

Then it came over me that she had made a great effort for me—made it with a kind of nobleness—and that I owed her a compensation. Each time I saw her after this I wondered what the compensation could be. I couldn't go on doing the wrong thing to oblige them. Oh, it *was* the wrong thing, the stamp of the work for which they sat—Hawley was not the only person to say it now. I sent in a large number of the drawings I had made for "Rutland Ramsay," and I received a warning that was more to the point than Hawley's. The artistic adviser of the house for which I was working was of opinion that many of my illustrations were not what had been looked for. Most of these illustrations were the subjects in which the Monarchs had figured. Without going into the question of what *had* been looked for, I saw at this rate I shouldn't get the other books to do. I hurled myself in despair upon Miss Churm, I put her through all her paces. I not only adopted Oronte publicly as my hero, but one morning when the Major looked in to see if I didn't require him to finish a figure for the *Cheapside*, for which he had begun to sit the week before, I told him that I had changed my mind—I would do the drawing from my man. At this my visitor turned pale and stood looking at me. "Is *he* your idea of an English gentleman?" he asked.

I was disappointed, I was nervous, I wanted to get on with my work; so I replied with irritation: "Oh, my dear Major—I can't be ruined for *you!*"

He stood another moment; then, without a word, he quitted the studio. I drew a long breath when he was gone, for I said to myself that I shouldn't see him again. I had not told him definitely that I was in danger of having my work rejected, but I was vexed at his not having felt the catastrophe in the air, read with me the moral of our fruitless collaboration, the lesson that, in the deceptive atmosphere of art, even the highest respectability may fail of being plastic.

I didn't owe my friends money, but I did see them again. They reappeared together, three days later, and under the circumstances there was something tragic in the fact. It was a proof to me that they could find nothing else in life to do. They had threshed the matter out in a dismal conference—they had digested the bad news that they were not in for the series. If they were not useful to me even for the *Cheapside* their function seemed difficult to determine, and I could only judge at first that they had come, forgivingly, decorously, to take a last leave. This made me rejoice in secret that I had little leisure for a scene; for I had placed both my other models in position together and I was pegging away at a drawing from which I hoped to derive glory. It had been suggested by the passage in which Rutland Ramsay, drawing up a chair to Artemisia's piano-stool, says extraordinary things to her while she ostensibly fingers out a difficult piece of music. I had done Miss Churm at the piano before—it was an attitude in which she knew how to take on an absolutely poetic grace. I wished the two figures to "compose" together, intensely, and my little Italian had entered perfectly into my conception. The pair were vividly before me, the piano had been pulled out; it was a charming picture of blended youth and murmured love, which I had only to catch and keep. My visitors stood and looked at it, and I was friendly to them over my shoulder.

They made no response, but I was used to silent company and went on with my work, only a little disconcerted (even though exhilarated by the sense that *this* was at least the ideal thing), at not having got rid of them after all. Presently I heard Mrs. Monarch's sweet voice beside, or rather above me: "I wish her hair was a little better done." I looked up and she was staring with a strange fixedness at Miss Churm, whose back was turned to her. "Do you mind my just touching it?" she went on—a question which made me spring up for an instant, as with the instinctive fear that she might do the young lady a harm. But she quieted me with a glance I shall never forget—I confess I should like to have been able to paint *that*—and went for a moment to my model. She spoke to her softly, laying a hand upon her shoulder and bending over her; and as the girl, understanding, gratefully assented, she disposed her rough curls, with a few quick passes, in such a way as to make Miss Churm's head twice as charming. It was one of the most heroic personal services I have ever seen rendered. Then Mrs. Monarch turned away with a low sigh and, looking about her as if for something to do, stooped to the floor with a noble humility and picked up a dirty rag that had dropped out of my paint-box.

The Major meanwhile had also been looking for something to do and, wandering to the other end of the studio, saw before him my breakfast things, neglected, unremoved. "I say, can't I be useful *here?*" he called out to me with an irrepressible quaver. I assented with a laugh that I fear was awkward and for the next ten minutes, while I worked, I heard the light clatter of china and the tinkle of spoons and glass. Mrs.

Monarch assisted her husband—they washed up my crockery, they put it away. They wandered off into my little scullery, and I afterwards found that they had cleaned my knives and that my slender stock of plate had an unprecedented surface. When it came over me, the latent eloquence of what they were doing, I confess that my drawing was blurred for a moment—the picture swam. They had accepted their failure, but they couldn't accept their fate. They had bowed their heads in bewilderment to the perverse and cruel law in virtue of which the real thing could be so much less precious than the unreal; but they didn't want to starve. If my servants were my models, my models might be my servants. They would reverse the parts—the others would sit for the ladies and gentlemen, and *they* would do the work. They would still be in the studio—it was an intense dumb appeal to me not to turn them out. "Take us on," they wanted to say—"we'll do *anything*."

When all this hung before me the *afflatus* vanished—my pencil dropped from my hand. My sitting was spoiled and I got rid of my sitters, who were also evidently rather mystified and awestruck. Then, alone with the Major and his wife, I had a most uncomfortable moment. He put their prayer into a single sentence: "I say, you know—just let *us* do for you, can't you?" I couldn't—it was dreadful to see them emptying my slops; but I pretended I could, to oblige them, for about a week. Then I gave them a sum of money to go away; and I never saw them again. I obtained the remaining books, but my friend Hawley repeats that Major and Mrs. Monarch did me a permanent harm, got me into a second-rate trick. If it be true I am content to have paid the price—for the memory.

CHARLOTTE PERKINS GILMAN

The Yellow Wallpaper

"The Yellow Wallpaper," now one of the most controversial stories in American literature, was first published in *New England Magazine* in 1892 under the name of Charlotte Perkins Stetson. By the 1960s, and with the rise of the feminist movement in America, the story was adopted as an anthem of protest against a patriarchal society that constricts the social, economic, and psychic lives of modern women. Even within this interpretive orthodoxy, however, there were many conflicting readings of whether the narrator of the story is mentally ill, whether she has been driven into pathology by the domination of her husband and physician, and whether the conclusion suggests a positive liberation in which she gains insight into her condition or a descent into the bleakest madness. Perhaps because of the political fervor the story has engendered, there has been little attention paid to its aesthetic elements, to the subtle modulations of its narrative technique, to the progressively fragmented structure that mirrors the mind of the narrator, and to the implications of what the narrator sees in the wallpaper. From a wide variety of perspectives, readers have found Gilman's most famous story to be challenging, rewarding, and an historically valuable revelation of the gender politics of the 1890s.

*   *   *

It is very seldom that mere ordinary people like John and myself secure ancestral halls for the summer.

A colonial mansion, a hereditary estate, I would say a haunted house, and reach the height of romantic felicity—but that would be asking too much of fate!

Still I will proudly declare that there is something queer about it.

Else, why should it be let so cheaply? And why have stood so long untenanted?

John laughs at me, of course, but one expects that in marriage.

John is practical in the extreme. He has no patience with faith, an intense horror of superstition, and he scoffs openly at any talk of things not to be felt and seen and put down in figures.

John is a physician, and *perhaps*—(I would not say it to a living soul, of course, but this is dead paper and a great relief to my mind—) *perhaps* that is one reason I do not get well faster.

You see he does not believe I am sick!

And what can one do?

If a physician of high standing, and one's own husband, assures friends and relatives that there is really nothing the matter with one but temporary nervous depression—a slight hysterical tendency—what is one to do?

My brother is also a physician, and also of high standing, and he says the same thing.

So I take phosphates or phosphites—whichever it is, and tonics, and journeys, and air, and exercise, and am absolutely forbidden to "work" until I am well again.

Personally, I disagree with their ideas.

Personally, I believe that congenial work, with excitement and change, would do me good.

But what is one to do?

I did write for a while in spite of them; but it *does* exhaust me a good deal—having to be so sly about it, or else meet with heavy opposition.

I sometimes fancy that in my condition if I had less opposition and more society and stimulus—but John says the very worst thing I can do is to think about my condition, and I confess it always makes me feel bad.

So I will let it alone and talk about the house.

The most beautiful place! It is quite alone, standing well back from the road, quite three miles from the village. It makes me think of English places that you read about, for there are hedges and walls and gates that lock, and lots of separate little houses for the gardeners and people.

There is a *delicious* garden! I never saw such a garden—large and shady, full of box-bordered paths, and lined with long grape-covered arbors with seats under them.

There were greenhouses, too, but they are all broken now.

There was some legal trouble, I believe, something about the heirs and coheirs; anyhow, the place has been empty for years.

That spoils my ghostliness, I am afraid, but I don't care—there is something strange about the house—I can feel it.

I even said so to John one moonlight evening, but he said what I felt was a *draught,* and shut the window.

I get unreasonably angry with John sometimes. I'm sure I never used to be so sensitive. I think it is due to this nervous condition.

But John says if I feel so, I shall neglect proper self-control; so I take pains to control myself—before him, at least, and that makes me very tired.

I don't like our room a bit. I wanted one downstairs that opened on the piazza and had roses all over the window, and such pretty old-fashioned chintz hangings! but John would not hear of it.

He said there was only one window and not room for two beds, and no near room for him if he took another.

He is very careful and loving, and hardly lets me stir without special direction.

I have a schedule prescription for each hour in the day; he takes all care from me, and so I feel basely ungrateful not to value it more.

He said we came here solely on my account, that I was to have perfect rest and all the air I could get. "Your exercise depends on your strength, my dear," said he, "and your food somewhat on your appetite; but air you can absorb all the time." So we took the nursery at the top of the house.

It is a big, airy room, the whole floor nearly, with windows that look all ways, and air and sunshine galore. It was nursery first and then playroom and gymnasium, I should judge; for the windows are barred for little children, and there are rings and things in the walls.

The paint and paper look as if a boys' school had used it. It is stripped off—the paper—in great patches all around the head of my bed, about as far as I can reach, and in a great place on the other side of the room low down. I never saw a worse paper in my life.

One of those sprawling flamboyant patterns committing every artistic sin.

It is dull enough to confuse the eye in following, pronounced enough to constantly irritate and provoke study, and when you follow the lame uncertain curves for a little distance they suddenly commit suicide— plunge off at outrageous angles, destroy themselves in unheard of contradictions.

The color is repellant, almost revolting; a smouldering unclean yellow, strangely faded by the slow-turning sunlight.

It is a dull yet lurid orange in some places, a sickly sulphur tint in others.

No wonder the children hated it! I should hate it myself if I had to live in this room long.

There comes John, and I must put this away,—he hates to have me write a word.

We have been here two weeks, and I haven't felt like writing before, since that first day.

I am sitting by the window now, up in this atrocious nursery, and there is nothing to hinder my writing as much as I please, save lack of strength.

John is away all day, and even some nights when his cases are serious.

I am glad my case is not serious!

But these nervous troubles are dreadfully depressing.

John does not know how much I really suffer. He knows there is no *reason* to suffer, and that satisfies him.

Of course it is only nervousness. It does weigh on me so not to do my duty in any way!

I meant to be such a help to John, such a real rest and comfort, and here I am a comparative burden already!

Nobody would believe what an effort it is to do what little I am able,—to dress and entertain, and order things.

It is fortunate Mary is so good with the baby. Such a dear baby!

And yet I *cannot* be with him, it makes me so nervous.

I suppose John never was nervous in his life. He laughs at me so about this wall-paper!

At first he meant to repaper the room, but afterwards he said that I was letting it get the better of me, and that nothing was worse for a nervous patient than to give way to such fancies.

He said that after the wall-paper was changed it would be the heavy bedstead, and then the barred windows, and then that gate at the head of the stairs, and so on.

"You know the place is doing you good," he said, "and really, dear, I don't care to renovate the house just for a three months' rental."

"Then do let us go downstairs," I said, "there are such pretty rooms there."

Then he took me in his arms and called me a blessed little goose, and said he would go down cellar, if I wished, and have it whitewashed into the bargain.

But he is right enough about the beds and windows and things.

It is an airy and comfortable room as any one need wish, and, of course, I would not be so silly as to make him uncomfortable just for a whim.

I'm really getting quite fond of the big room, all but that horrid paper.

Out of one window I can see the garden, those mysterious deep-shaded arbors, the riotous old-fashioned flowers, and bushes and gnarly trees.

Out of another I get a lovely view of the bay and a little private wharf belonging to the estate. There is a beautiful shaded lane that runs down there from the house. I always fancy I see people walking in these numerous paths and arbors, but John has cautioned me not to give way to fancy in the least. He says that with my imaginative power and habit of story-making, a nervous weakness like mine is sure to lead to all manner of excited fancies, and that I ought to use my will and good sense to check the tendency. So I try.

I think sometimes that if I were only well enough to write a little it would relieve the press of ideas and rest me.

But I find I get pretty tired when I try.

It is so discouraging not to have any advice and companionship about my work. When I get really well, John says we will ask Cousin Henry and Julia down for a long visit; but he says he would as soon put fireworks in my pillow-case as to let me have those stimulating people about now.

I wish I could get well faster.

But I must not think about that. This paper looks to me as if it *knew* what a vicious influence it had!

There is a recurrent spot where the pattern lolls like a broken neck and two bulbous eyes stare at you upside down.

I get positively angry with the impertinence of it and the everlastingness. Up and down and sideways they crawl, and those absurd, unblinking eyes are everywhere. There is one place where two breaths didn't match, and the eyes go all up and down the line, one a little higher than the other.

I never saw so much expression in an inanimate thing before, and we all know how much expression they have! I used to lie awake as a child and get more entertainment and terror out of blank walls and plain furniture than most children could find in a toy-store.

I remember what a kindly wink the knobs of our big, old bureau used to have, and there was one chair that always seemed like a strong friend.

I used to feel that if any of the other things looked too fierce I could always hop into that chair and be safe.

The furniture in this room is no worse than inharmonious, however, for we had to bring it all from downstairs. I suppose when this was used as a playroom they had to take the nursery things out, and no wonder! I never saw such ravages as the children have made here.

The wall-paper, as I said before, is torn off in spots, and it sticketh closer than a brother—they must have had perseverance as well as hatred.

Then the floor is scratched and gouged and splintered, the plaster itself is dug out here and there, and this great heavy bed which is all we found in the room, looks as if it had been through the wars.

But I don't mind it a bit—only the paper.

There comes John's sister. Such a dear girl as she is, and so careful of me! I must not let her find me writing.

She is a perfect and enthusiastic housekeeper, and hopes for no better profession. I verily believe she thinks it is the writing which made me sick!

But I can write when she is out, and see her a long way off from these windows.

There is one that commands the road, a lovely shaded winding road, and one that just looks off over the country. A lovely country, too, full of great elms and velvet meadows.

This wallpaper has a kind of subpattern in a different shade, a particularly irritating one, for you can only see it in certain lights, and not clearly then.

But in the places where it isn't faded and where the sun is just so—

I can see a strange, provoking, formless sort of figure, that seems to skulk about behind that silly and conspicuous front design.

There's sister on the stairs!

Well, the Fourth of July is over! The people are all gone and I am tired out. John thought it might do me good to see a little company, so we just had mother and Nellie and the children down for a week.

Of course I didn't do a thing. Jennie sees to everything now.

But it tired me all the same.

John says if I don't pick up faster he shall send me to Weir Mitchell in the fall.

But I don't want to go there at all. I had a friend who was in his hands once, and she says he is just like John and my brother, only more so!

Besides, it is such an undertaking to go so far.

I don't feel as if it was worth while to turn my hand over for anything, and I'm getting dreadfully fretful and querulous.

I cry at nothing, and cry most of the time.

Of course I don't when John is here, or anybody else, but when I am alone.

And I am alone a good deal just now. John is kept in town very often by serious cases, and Jennie is good and lets me alone when I want her to.

So I walk a little in the garden or down that lovely lane, sit on the porch under the roses, and lie down up here a good deal.

I'm getting really fond of the room in spite of the wallpaper. Perhaps *because* of the wallpaper.

It dwells in my mind so!

I lie here on this great immovable bed—it is nailed down, I believe —and follow that pattern about by the hour. It it as good as gymnastics, I assure you. I start, we'll say, at the bottom, down in the corner over there where it has not been touched, and I determine for the thousandth time that I *will* follow that pointless pattern to some sort of a conclusion.

I know a little of the principle of design, and I know this thing was not arranged on any laws of radiation, or alternation, or repetition, or symmetry, or anything else that I ever heard of.

It is repeated, of course, by the breadths, but not otherwise.

Looked at in one way each breadth stands alone, the bloated curves and flourishes—a kind of "debased Romanesque" with *delirium tremens*—go waddling up and down in isolated columns of fatuity.

But, on the other hand, they connect diagonally, and the sprawling outlines run off in great slanting waves of optic horror, like a lot of wallowing seaweeds in full chase.

The whole thing goes horizontally, too, at least it seems so, and I exhaust myself in trying to distinguish the order of its going in that direction.

They have used a horizontal breadth for a frieze, and that adds wonderfully to the confusion.

There is one end of the room where it is almost intact, and there, when the crosslights fade and the low sun shines directly upon it, I can almost fancy radiation after all,—the interminable grotesque seem to form around a common centre and rush off in headlong plunges of equal distraction.

It makes me tired to follow it. I will take a nap I guess.

I don't know why I should write this.

I don't want to.

I don't feel able.

And I know John would think it absurd. But I *must* say what I feel and think in some way—it is such a relief!

But the effort is getting to be greater than the relief.

Half the time now I am awfully lazy, and lie down ever so much.

John says I mustn't lose my strength, and has me take cod liver oil and lots of tonics and things, to say nothing of ale and wine and rare meat.

Dear John! He loves me very dearly, and hates to have me sick. I tried to have a real earnest reasonable talk with him the other day, and tell him how I wish he would let me go and make a visit to Cousin Henry and Julia.

But he said I wasn't able to go, nor able to stand it after I got there; and I did not make out a very good case for myself, for I was crying before I had finished.

It is getting to be a great effort for me to think straight. Just this nervous weakness I suppose.

And dear John gathered me up in his arms, and just carried me upstairs and laid me on the bed, and sat by me and read to me till it tired my head.

He said I was his darling and his comfort and all he had, and that I must take care of myself for his sake, and keep well.

He says no one but myself can help me out of it, that I must use my will and self-control and not let any silly fancies run away with me.

There's one comfort, the baby is well and happy, and does not have to occupy this nursery with the horrid wallpaper.

If we had not used it, that blessed child would have! What a fortunate escape! Why, I wouldn't have a child of mine, an impressionable little thing, live in such a room for worlds.

I never thought of it before, but it is lucky that John kept me here after all, I can stand it so much easier than a baby, you see.

Of course I never mention it to them any more—I am too wise,—but I keep watch of it all the same.

There are things in that paper that nobody knows but me, or ever will.

Behind that outside pattern the dim shapes get clearer every day.

It is always the same shape, only very numerous.

And it is like a woman stooping down and creeping about behind that pattern. I don't like it a bit. I wonder—I begin to think—I wish John would take me away from here!

It is so hard to talk with John about my case because he is so wise, and because he loves me so.

But I tried it last night.

It was moonlight. The moon shines in all around just as the sun does.

I hate to see it sometimes, it creeps so slowly, and always comes in by one window or another.

John was asleep and I hated to waken him, so I kept still and watched the moonlight on that undulating wallpaper till I felt creepy.

The faint figure behind seemed to shake the pattern, just as if she wanted to get out.

I got up softly and went to feel and see if the paper *did* move, and when I came back John was awake.

"What is it, little girl?" he said. "Don't go walking about like that—you'll get cold."

I thought it was a good time to talk, so I told him that I really was not gaining here, and that I wished he would take me away.

"Why, darling!" said he, "our lease will be up in three weeks, and I can't see how to leave before.

"The repairs are not done at home, and I cannot possibly leave town just now. Of course if you were in any danger, I could and would, but you really are better, dear, whether you can see it or not. I am a doctor, dear, and I know. You are gaining flesh and color, your appetite is better, I feel really much easier about you."

"I don't weigh a bit more," said I, "nor as much; and my appetite may be better in the evening when you are here, but it is worse in the morning when you are away!"

"Bless her little heart!" said he with a big hug, "she shall be as sick as she pleases! But now let's improve the shining hours by going to sleep, and talk about it in the morning!"

"And you won't go away?" I asked gloomily.

"Why, how can I, dear? It is only three weeks more and then we will take a nice little trip of a few days while Jennie is getting the house ready. Really dear you are better!"

"Better in body perhaps—" I began, and stopped short, for he sat up straight and looked at me with such a stern, reproachful look that I could not say another word.

"My darling," said he, "I beg of you, for my sake and for our child's sake, as well as for your own, that you will never for one instant let that idea enter your mind! There is nothing so dangerous, so fascinating, to a temperament like yours. It is a false and foolish fancy. Can you not trust me as a physician when I tell you so?"

So of course I said no more on that score, and we went to sleep before long. He thought I was asleep first, but I wasn't, and lay there for hours trying to decide whether that front pattern and the back pattern really did move together or separately.

On a pattern like this, by daylight, there is a lack of sequence, a defiance of law, that is a constant irritant to a normal mind.

The color is hideous enough, and unreliable enough, and infuriating enough, but the pattern is torturing.

You think you have mastered it, but just as you get well underway in following, it turns a back-somersault and there you are. It slaps you in the face, knocks you down, and tramples upon you. It is like a bad dream.

The outside pattern is a florid arabesque, reminding one of a fungus. If you can imagine a toadstool in joints, an interminable string of toadstools, budding and sprouting in endless convolutions—why, that is something like it.

That is, sometimes!

There is one marked peculiarity about this paper, a thing nobody seems to notice but myself, and that is that it changes as the light changes.

When the sun shoots in through the east window—I always watch for that first long, straight ray—it changes so quickly that I never can quite believe it.

That is why I watch it always.

By moonlight—the moon shines in all night when there is a moon—I wouldn't know it was the same paper.

At night in any kind of light, in twilight, candlelight, lamplight, and worst of all by moonlight, it becomes bars! The outside pattern I mean, and the woman behind it is as plain as can be.

I didn't realize for a long time what the thing was that showed behind, that dim sub-pattern, but now I am quite sure it is a woman.

By daylight she is subdued, quiet. I fancy it is the pattern that keeps her so still. It is so puzzling. It keeps me quiet by the hour.

I lie down ever so much now. John says it is good for me, and to sleep all I can.

Indeed he started the habit by making me lie down for an hour after each meal.

It is a very bad habit I am convinced, for you see I don't sleep.

And that cultivates deceit, for I don't tell them I'm awake—O no!

The fact is I am getting a little afraid of John.

He seems very queer sometimes, and even Jennie has an inexplicable look.

It strikes me occasionally, just as a scientific hypothesis,—that perhaps it is the paper!

I have watched John when he did not know I was looking, and come into the room suddenly on the most innocent excuses, and I've caught him several times *looking at the paper!* And Jennie too. I caught Jennie with her hand on it once.

She didn't know I was in the room, and when I asked her in a quiet, a very quiet voice, with the most restrained manner possible, what she was doing with the paper—she turned around as if she had been caught stealing, and looked quite angry—asked me why I should frighten her so!

Then she said that the paper stained everything it touched, that she had found yellow smooches on all my clothes and John's, and she wished we would be more careful!

Did not that sound innocent? But I know she was studying that pattern, and I am determined that nobody shall find it out but myself!

Life is very much more exciting now than it used to be. You see I have something more to expect, to look forward to, to watch. I really do eat better, and am more quiet than I was.

John is so pleased to see me improve! He laughed a little the other day, and said I seemed to be flourishing in spite of my wall-paper.

I turned it off with a laugh. I had no intention of telling him it was *because* of the wall-paper—he would make fun of me. He might even want to take me away.

I don't want to leave now until I have found it out. There is a week more, and I think that will be enough.

I'm feeling ever so much better! I don't sleep much at night, for it is so interesting to watch developments; but I sleep a good deal in the daytime.

In the daytime it is tiresome and perplexing.

There are always new shoots on the fungus, and new shades of yellow all over it. I cannot keep count of them, though I have tried conscientiously.

It is the strangest yellow, that wall-paper! It makes me think of all the yellow things I ever saw—not beautiful ones like buttercups, but old foul, bad yellow things.

But there is something else about that paper—the smell! I noticed it the moment we came into the room, but with so much air and sun it was not bad. Now we have had a week of fog and rain, and whether the windows are open or not, the smell is here.

It creeps all over the house.

I find it hovering in the dining-room, skulking in the parlor, hiding in the hall, lying in wait for me on the stairs.

It gets into my hair.

Even when I go to ride, if I turn my head suddenly and surprise it—there is that smell!

Such a peculiar odor, too! I have spent hours in trying to analyze it, to find what it smelled like.

It is not bad—at first, and very gentle, but quite the subtlest, most enduring odor I ever met.

In this damp weather it is awful, I wake up in the night and find it hanging over me.

It used to disturb me at first. I thought seriously of burning the house—to reach the smell.

But now I am used to it. The only thing I can think of that it is like is the *color* of the paper! A yellow smell.

There is a very funny mark on this wall, low down, near the mopboard. A streak that runs round the room. It goes behind every piece of furniture, except the bed, a long, straight, even *smooch*, as if it had been rubbed over and over.

I wonder how it was done and who did it, and what they did it for. Round and round and round—round and round and round—it makes me dizzy!

I really have discovered something at last.

Through watching so much at night, when it changes so, I have finally found out.

The front pattern *does* move—and no wonder! The woman behind shakes it!

Sometimes I think there are a great many women behind, and sometimes only one, and she crawls around fast, and her crawling shakes it all over.

Then in the very bright spots she keeps still, and in the very shady spots she just takes hold of the bars and shakes them hard.

And she is all the time trying to climb through. But nobody could climb through that pattern—it strangles so; I think that is why it has so many heads.

They get through, and then the pattern strangles them off and turns them upside down, and makes their eyes white!

If those heads were covered or taken off it would not be half so bad.

I think that woman gets out in the daytime!

And I'll tell you why—privately—I've seen her!

I can see her out of every one of my windows!

It is the same woman, I know, for she is always creeping, and most women do not creep by daylight.

I see her in that long shaded lane, creeping up and down. I see her in those dark grape arbors, creeping all around the garden.

I see her on that long road under the trees, creeping along, and when a carriage comes she hides under the blackberry vines.

I don't blame her a bit. It must be very humiliating to be caught creeping by daylight!

I always lock the door when I creep by daylight. I can't do it at night, for I know John would suspect something at once.

And John is so queer now, that I don't want to irritate him. I wish he would take another room! Besides, I don't want anybody to get that woman out at night but myself.

I often wonder if I could see her out of all the windows at once.

But, turn as fast as I can, I can only see out of one at one time.

And though I always see her, she *may* be able to creep faster than I can turn!

I have watched her sometimes away off in the open country, creeping as fast as a cloud shadow in a high wind.

If only that top pattern could be gotten off from the under one! I mean to try it, little by little.

I have found out another funny thing, but I shan't tell it this time! It does not do to trust people too much.

There are only two more days to get this paper off, and I believe John is beginning to notice. I don't like the look in his eyes.

And I heard him ask Jennie a lot of professional questions about me. She had a very good report to give.

She said I slept a good deal in the daytime.

John knows I don't sleep very well at night, for all I'm so quiet!

He asked me all sorts of questions, too, and pretended to be very loving and kind.

As if I couldn't see through him!

Still, I don't wonder he acts so, sleeping under this paper for three months.

It only interests me, but I feel sure John and Jennie are secretly affected by it.

Hurrah! This is the last day, but it is enough. John to stay in town over night, and won't be out until this evening.

Jennie wanted to sleep with me—the sly thing! but I told her I should undoubtedly rest better for a night all alone.

That was clever, for really I wasn't alone a bit! As soon as it was moonlight and that poor thing began to crawl and shake the pattern, I got up and ran to help her.

I pulled and she shook, I shook and she pulled, and before morning we had peeled off yards of that paper.

A strip about as high as my head and half around the room.

And then when the sun came and that awful pattern began to laugh at me, I declared I would finish it to-day!

We go away to-morrow, and they are moving all my furniture down again to leave things as they were before.

Jennie looked at the wall in amazement, but I told her merrily that I did it out of pure spite at the vicious thing.

She laughed and said she wouldn't mind doing it herself, but I must not get tired.

How she betrayed herself that time!

But I am here, and no person touches this paper but me,—not *alive!*

She tried to get me out of the room—it was too patent! But I said it was so quiet and empty and clean now that I believed I would lie down again and sleep all I could; and not to wake me even for dinner—I would call when I woke.

So now she is gone, and the servants are gone, and the things are gone, and there is nothing left but that great bedstead nailed down, with the canvas mattress we found on it.

We shall sleep downstairs to-night, and take the boat home to-morrow.

I quite enjoy the room, now it is bare again.

How those children did tear about here!

This bedstead is fairly gnawed!

But I must get to work.

I have locked the door and thrown the key down into the front path.

I don't want to go out, and I don't want to have anybody come in, till John comes.

I want to astonish him.

I've got a rope up here that even Jennie did not find. If that woman does get out, and tries to get away, I can tie her!

But I forgot I could not reach far without anything to stand on!

This bed will *not* move!

I tried to lift and push it until I was lame, and then I got so angry I bit off a little piece at one corner—but it hurt my teeth.

Then I peeled off all the paper I could reach standing on the floor. It sticks horribly and the pattern just enjoys it! All those strangled heads and bulbous eyes and waddling fungus growths just shriek with derision!

I am getting angry enough to do something desperate. To jump out of the window would be admirable exercise, but the bars are too strong even to try.

Besides I wouldn't do it. Of course not. I know well enough that a step like that is improper and might be misconstrued.

I don't like to *look* out of the windows even—there are so many of those creeping women, and they creep so fast.

I wonder if they all come out of that wall-paper as I did?

But I am securely fastened now by my well-hidden rope—you don't get *me* out in the road there!

I suppose I shall have to get back behind the pattern when it comes night, and that is hard!

It is so pleasant to be out in this great room and creep around as I please!

I don't want to go outside. I won't, even if Jennie asks me to.

For outside you have to creep on the ground, and everything is green instead of yellow.

But here I can creep smoothly on the floor, and my shoulder just fits in that long smooch around the wall, so I cannot lose my way.

Why there's John at the door!

It is no use, young man, you can't open it!

How he does call and pound!

Now he's crying for an axe.

It would be a shame to break down that beautiful door!

"John dear!" said I in the gentlest voice, "the key is down by the front steps, under a plaintain leaf!"

That silenced him for a few moments.

Then he said—very quietly indeed, "Open the door, my darling!"

"I can't," said I. "The key is down by the front door under a plantain leaf!"

And then I said it again, several times, very gently and slowly, and said it so often that he had to go and see, and he got it of course, and came in. He stopped short by the door.

"What is the matter?" he cried. "For God's sake, what are you doing!"

I kept on creeping just the same, but I looked at him over my shoulder.

"I've got out at last," said I, "in spite of you and Jane? And I've pulled off most of the paper, so you can't put me back!"

Now why should that man have fainted? But he did, and right across my path by the wall, so that I had to creep over him every time!

KATE CHOPIN

Désirée's Baby

Kate Chopin's most famous story, "Désirée's Baby," was first published in *Vogue* magazine in 1893 prior to its inclusion in *Bayou Folk* a year later. The story was recognized immediately for the power of its anti-racist theme, essentially a portrayal of the destructive inhumanity of ethnic bigotry, here dramatized with stinging irony. The events unfold with Chopin's characteristic subtlety. She describes Désirée in highly idealized terms as "beautiful and gentle, affectionate and sincere" and her husband, Armand, as having a "dark, handsome face" and skin a darker shade than that of his wife; and these observations, which seem initially innocuous, come to have profound, even deadly, implications. The story works through a series of dramatic realizations, from Madame Valmondé's startled recognition of the Negroid features of her grandson, to the mystery among the black servants about the child, to Désirée's blood-chilling epiphany. But it is the dramatic irony of the new awareness in the conclusion that most emphatically establishes the injustice of racism and its devastating consequences. Written with artistic grace and thematic power, this story has deservedly become one of the most celebrated works of short fiction in American literature.

* * *

As the day was pleasant, Madame Valmondé drove over to L'Abri to see Désirée and the baby.

It made her laugh to think of Désirée with a baby. Why, it seemed but yesterday that Désirée was little more than a baby herself; when

Monsieur in riding through the gateway of Valmondé had found her lying asleep in the shadow of the big stone pillar.

The little one awoke in his arms and began to cry for "Dada." That was as much as she could do or say. Some people thought she might have strayed there of her own accord, for she was of the toddling age. The prevailing belief was that she had been purposely left by a party of Texans, whose canvas-covered wagon, late in the day, had crossed the ferry that Coton Maïs kept, just below the plantation. In time Madame Valmondé abandoned every speculation but the one that Désirée had been sent to her by a beneficent Providence to be the child of her affection, seeing that she was without child of the flesh. For the girl grew to be beautiful and gentle, affectionate and sincere,—the idol of Valmondé.

It was no wonder, when she stood one day against the stone pillar in whose shadow she had lain asleep, eighteen years before, that Armand Aubigny riding by and seeing her there, had fallen in love with her. That was the way all the Aubignys fell in love, as if struck by a pistol shot. The wonder was that he had not loved her before; for he had known her since his father brought him home from Paris, a boy of eight, after his mother died there. The passion that awoke in him that day, when he saw her at the gate, swept along like an avalanche, or like a prairie fire, or like anything that drives headlong over all obstacles.

Monsieur Valmondé grew practical and wanted things well considered: that is, the girl's obscure origin. Armand looked into her eyes and did not care. He was reminded that she was nameless. What did it matter about a name when he could give her one of the oldest and proudest in Louisiana? He ordered the *corbeille* from Paris, and contained himself with what patience he could until it arrived; then they were married.

Madame Valmondé had not seen Désirée and the baby for four weeks. When she reached L'Abri she shuddered at the first sight of it, as she always did. It was a sad looking place, which for many years had not known the gentle presence of a mistress, old Monsieur Aubigny having married and buried his wife in France, and she having loved her own land too well ever to leave it. The roof came down steep and black like a cowl, reaching out beyond the wide galleries that encircled the yellow stuccoed house. Big, solemn oaks grew close to it, and their thick-leaved, far-reaching branches shadowed it like a pall. Young Aubigny's rule was a strict one, too, and under it his negroes had forgotten how to be gay, as they had been during the old master's easy-going and indulgent lifetime.

The young mother was recovering slowly, and lay full length, in her soft white muslins and laces, upon a couch. The baby was beside her, upon her arm, where he had fallen asleep, at her breast. The yellow nurse woman sat beside a window fanning herself.

Madame Valmondé bent her portly figure over Désirée and kissed her, holding her an instant tenderly in her arms. Then she turned to the child.

"This is not the baby!" she exclaimed, in startled tones. French was the language spoken at Valmondé in those days.

"I knew you would be astonished," laughed Désirée, "at the way he has grown. The little *cochon de lait!* Look at his legs, mamma, and his hands and finger-nails,—real finger-nails. Zandrine had to cut them this morning. Isn't it true, Zandrine?"

The woman bowed her turbaned head majestically, "Mais si, Madame."

"And the way he cries," went on Désirée, "is deafening. Armand heard him the other day as far away as La Blanche's cabin."

Madame Valmondé had never removed her eyes from the child. She lifted it and walked with it over to the window that was lightest. She scanned the baby narrowly, then looked as searchingly at Zandrine, whose face was turned to gaze across the fields.

"Yes, the child has grown, has changed;" said Madame Valmondé, slowly, as she replaced it beside its mother. "What does Armand say?"

Désirée's face became suffused with a glow that was happiness itself.

"Oh, Armand is the proudest father in the parish, I believe, chiefly because it is a boy, to bear his name; though he says not,—that he would have loved a girl as well. But I know it isn't true. I know he says that to please me. And mamma," she added, drawing Madame Valmondé's head down to her, and speaking in a whisper, "he hasn't punished one of them—not one of them—since baby is born. Even Négrillon, who pretended to have burnt his leg that he might rest from work—he only laughed, and said Négrillon was a great scamp. Oh, mamma, I'm so happy; it frightens me."

What Désirée said was true. Marriage, and later the birth of his son, had softened Armand Aubigny's imperious and exacting nature greatly. This was what made the gentle Désirée so happy, for she loved him desperately. When he frowned she trembled, but loved him. When he smiled, she asked no greater blessing of God. But Armand's dark, handsome face had not often been disfigured by frowns since the day he fell in love with her.

When the baby was about three months old, Désirée awoke one day to the conviction that there was something in the air menacing her peace. It was at first too subtle to grasp. It had only been a disquieting suggestion; an air of mystery among the blacks; unexpected visits from far-off neighbors who could hardly account for their coming. Then a strange, an awful change in her husband's manner, which she dared not ask him to explain. When he spoke to her, it was with averted eyes, from which the old love-light seemed to have gone out. He absented himself from home; and when there, avoided her presence and that of her child, without excuse. And the very spirit of Satan seemed suddenly to take hold of him in his dealings with the slaves. Désirée was miserable enough to die.

She sat in her room, one hot afternoon, in her *peignoir,* listlessly drawing through her fingers the strands of her long, silky brown hair that hung about her shoulders. The baby, half naked, lay asleep upon her own great mahogany bed, that was like a sumptuous throne, with its satin-lined half-canopy. One of La Blanche's little quadroon boys— half naked too—stood fanning the child slowly with a fan of peacock feathers. Désirée's eyes had been fixed absently and sadly upon the baby, while she was striving to penetrate the threatening mist that she felt closing about her. She looked from her child to the boy who stood beside him, and back again; over and over. "Ah!" It was a cry that she could not help; which she was not conscious of having uttered. The blood turned like ice in her veins, and a clammy moisture gathered upon her face.

She tried to speak to the little quadroon boy; but no sound would come, at first. When he heard his name uttered, he looked up, and his mistress was pointing to the door. He laid aside the great, soft fan, and obediently stole away, over the polished floor, on his bare tiptoes.

She stayed motionless, with gaze riveted upon her child, and her face the picture of fright.

Presently her husband entered the room, and without noticing her, went to a table and began to search among some papers which covered it.

"Armand," she called to him, in a voice which must have stabbed him, if he was human. But he did not notice. "Armand," she said again. Then she rose and tottered towards him. "Armand," she panted once more, clutching his arm, "look at our child. What does it mean? tell me."

He coldly but gently loosened her fingers from about his arm and thrust the hand away from him. "Tell me what it means!" she cried despairingly.

"It means," he answered lightly, "that the child is not white; it means that you are not white."

A quick conception of all that this accusation meant for her nerved her with unwonted courage to deny it. "It is a lie; it is not true. I am white! Look at my hair, it is brown; and my eyes are gray, Armand, you know they are gray. And my skin is fair," seizing his wrist. "Look at my hand; whiter than yours, Armand," she laughed hysterically.

"As white as La Blanche's," he returned cruelly; and went away leaving her alone with their child.

When she could hold a pen in her hand, she sent a despairing letter to Madame Valmondé.

"My mother, they tell me I am not white. Armand has told me I am not white. For God's sake tell them it is not true. You must know it is not true. I shall die. I must die. I cannot be so unhappy, and live."

The answer that came was as brief:

"My own Désirée: Come home to Valmondé; back to your mother who loves you. Come with your child."

When the letter reached Désirée she went with it to her husband's study, and laid it open upon the desk before which he sat. She was like a stone image: silent, white, motionless after she placed it there.

In silence he ran his cold eyes over the written words. He said nothing. "Shall I go, Armand?" she asked in tones sharp with agonized suspense.

"Yes, go."

"Do you want me to go?"

"Yes, I want you to go."

He thought Almighty God had dealt cruelly and unjustly with him; and felt, somehow, that he was paying Him back in kind when he stabbed thus into his wife's soul. Moreover he no longer loved her, because of the unconscious injury she had brought upon his home and his name.

She turned away like one stunned by a blow, and walked slowly towards the door, hoping he would call her back.

"Good-by, Armand," she moaned.

He did not answer her. That was his last blow at fate.

Désirée went in search of her child. Zandrine was pacing the sombre gallery with it. She took the little one from the nurse's arms with no word of explanation, and descending the steps, walked away, under the live-oak branches.

It was an October afternoon; the sun was just sinking. Out in the still fields the negroes were picking cotton.

Désirée had not changed the thin white garment nor the slippers which she wore. Her hair was uncovered and the sun's rays brought a golden gleam from its brown meshes. She did not take the broad, beaten road which led to the far-off plantation of Valmondé. She walked across a deserted field, where the stubble bruised her tender feet, so delicately shod, and tore her thin gown to shreds.

274 Madelene Yale Wynne

She disappeared among the reeds and willows that grew thick along the banks of the deep, sluggish bayou; and she did not come back again.

Some weeks later there was a curious scene enacted at L'Abri. In the centre of the smoothly swept back yard was a great bonfire. Armand Aubigny sat in the wide hallway that commanded a view of the spectacle; and it was he who dealt out to a half dozen negroes the material which kept this fire ablaze.

A graceful cradle of willow, with all its dainty furbishings, was laid upon the pyre, which had already been fed with the richness of a priceless *layette*. Then there were silk gowns, and velvet and satin ones added to these; laces, too, and embroideries; bonnets and gloves; for the *corbeille* had been of rare quality.

The last thing to go was a tiny bundle of letters; innocent little scribblings that Désirée had sent to him during the days of their espousal. There was the remnant of one back in the drawer from which he took them. But it was not Désirée's; it was part of an old letter from his mother to his father. He read it. She was thanking God for the blessing of her husband's love:—

"But, above all," she wrote, "night and day, I thank the good God for having so arranged our lives that our dear Armand will never know that his mother, who adores him, belongs to the race that is cursed with the brand of slavery."

MADELENE YALE WYNNE

The Little Room

Madelene Yale Wynne's literary reputation is tied almost exclusively to a single short story, "The Little Room." William Dean Howells published this story in the August 1895 issue of *Harper's Monthly Magazine* and later included it in his anthology *Great Modern American Stories* (1920). The tale was very popular in its day and often reprinted. Much like Frank Stockton's "The Lady and the Tiger," which it resembles in its fusion of an equable, even matter-of-fact tone with a fantastic conception, "The Little Room" also enjoyed widespread celebrity at the end of the nineteenth century. Though Wynne did write "The Sequel to the Little Room," she added nothing to solve its central mystery: was there or was there not a little room in the old Vermont farmhouse? We do know, however, that the comfortably furnished little room seems to exist only when the influence of or attachment to men is absent; otherwise, the door opens to a shallow china closet, a ready emblem of domestic service. In this sense, Wynne's story prefigures, both literally and figuratively, Virginia Woolf's *A Room of One's Own.*

* * *

"How would it do for a smoking-room?"

"Just the very place; only, you know, Roger, you must not think of smoking in the house. I am almost afraid having just a plain common man around, let alone a smoking-man, will upset Aunt Hannah. She is New England—Vermont New England boiled down."

"You leave Aunt Hannah to me; I shall find her tender side. I am going to ask her about the old sea-captain and the yellow calico."

"Not yellow calico—blue chintz."

"Well, yellow *shell*, then."

"No, no! don't mix it up so; you won't know yourself what to expect, and that's half the fun."

"Now you tell me again exactly what to expect; to tell the truth, I didn't half hear about it the other day; I was wool-gathering. It was something queer that happened when you were a child, wasn't it?"

"Something that began to happen long before that, and kept happening, and may happen again; but I hope not."

"What was it?"

"I wonder if the other people in the car can hear us?"

"I fancy not; we don't hear them—not consecutively, at least."

"Well, mother was born in Vermont, you know; she was the only child by a second marriage. Aunt Hannah and Aunt Maria are only half-aunts to me, you know."

"I hope they are half as nice as you are."

"Roger, be still; they certainly will hear us."

"Well, don't you want them to know we are married?"

"Yes, but not just married. There's all the difference in the world."

"You are afraid we look too happy!"

"No; only I want my happiness all to myself."

"Well, the little room?"

"My aunts brought mother up; they were nearly twenty years older than she. I might say Hiram and they brought her up. You see, Hiram was bound out to my grandfather when he was a boy, and when grandfather died Hiram said he 's'posed he went with the farm, 'long o' the critters,' and he has been there ever since. He was my mother's only refuge from the decorum of my aunts. They are simply workers. They make me think of the Maine woman who wanted her epitaph to be, 'She was a *hard* working woman.' "

"They must be almost beyond their working-days. How old are they?"

"Seventy, or thereabouts; but they will die standing; or, at least, on a Saturday night, after all the house-work is done up. They were rather strict with mother, and I think she had a lonely childhood. The house is almost a mile away from any neighbors, and off on top of what they call Stony Hill. It is bleak enough up there even in summer.

"When mamma was about ten years old they sent her to cousins in Brooklyn, who had children of their own, and knew more about bringing them up. She staid there till she was married; she didn't go to Vermont in all that time, and of course hadn't seen her sisters, for they never would leave home for a day. They couldn't even be induced to go to Brooklyn to her wedding, so she and father took their wedding trip up there."

"And that's why we are going up there on our own?"

"Don't, Roger; you have no idea how loud you speak."

"You never say so except when I am going to say that one little word."

"Well, don't say it, then, or say it very, very quietly."

"Well, what was the queer thing?"

"When they got to the house, mother wanted to take father right off into the little room; she had been telling him about it, just as I am going to tell you, and she had said that of all the rooms, that one was the only one that seemed pleasant to her. She described the furniture and the books and paper and everything, and said it was on the north side, between the front and back room. Well, when they went to look for it, there was no little room there; there was only a shallow china-closet. She asked her sisters when the house had been altered and a closet made of the room that used to be there. They both said the house was exactly as it had been built—that they had never made any changes, except to tear down the old wood-shed and build a smaller one.

"Father and mother laughed a good deal over it, and when anything was lost they would always say it must be in the little room, and any exaggerated statement was called 'little-roomy.' When I was a child I thought that was a regular English phrase, I heard it so often.

"Well, they talked it over, and finally they concluded that my mother had been a very imaginative sort of a child, and had read in some book about such a little room, or perhaps even dreamed it, and then had 'made believe,' as children do, till she herself had really thought the room was there."

"Why, of course, that might easily happen."

"Yes, but you haven't heard the queer part yet; you wait and see if you can explain the rest as easily.

"They staid at the farm two weeks, and then went to New York to live. When I was eight years old my father was killed in the war, and mother was broken-hearted. She never was quite strong afterwards, and that summer we decided to go up to the farm for three months.

"I was a restless sort of a child, and the journey seemed very long to me; and finally, to pass the time, mamma told me the story of the little room, and how it was all in her own imagination, and how there really was only a china-closet there.

"She told it with all the particulars; and even to me, who knew beforehand that the room wasn't there, it seemed just as real as could be. She said it was on the north side, between the front and back rooms; that it was very small, and they sometimes called it an entry. There was a door also that opened out-of-doors, and that one was painted green, and was cut in the middle like the old Dutch doors, so that it could be used for a window by opening the top part only. Directly opposite the door was a lounge or couch; it was covered with blue chintz—India chintz—some that had been brought over by an old Salem sea-captain as a 'venture.' He had given it to Maria when she was a young girl. She was sent to Salem for two years to school. Grandfather originally came from Salem."

"I thought there wasn't any room or chintz."

"*That is just it.* They had decided that mother had imagined it all, and yet you see how exactly everything was painted in her mind, for she had even remembered that Hiram had told her that Maria could have married the sea-captain if she had wanted to!

"The India cotton was the regular blue stamped chintz, with the peacock figure on it. The head and body of the bird were in profile, while the tail was full front view behind it. It had seemed to take mamma's fancy, and she drew it for me on a piece of paper as she talked. Doesn't it seem strange to you that she could have made all that up, or even dreamed it?

"At the foot of the lounge were some hanging shelves with some old books on them. All the books were leather-colored except one; that was bright red, and was called the *Ladies' Album*. It made a bright break between the other thicker books.

"On the lower shelf was a beautiful pink sea-shell, lying on a mat made of balls of red shaded worsted. This shell was greatly coveted by mother, but she was only allowed to play with it when she had been particularly good. Hiram had showed her how to hold it close to her ear and hear the roar of the sea in it.

"I know you will like Hiram, Roger, he is quite a character in his way.

"Mamma said she remembered, or *thought* she remembered, having been sick once, and she had to lie quietly for some days on the lounge; then was the time she had become so familiar with everything in the room, and she had been allowed to have the shell to play with all the time. She had had her toast brought to her in there, with make-believe tea. It was one of her pleasant memories of her childhood; it was the first time she had been of any importance to anybody, even herself.

"Right at the head of the lounge was a light-stand, as they called it, and on it was a very brightly polished brass candlestick and a brass tray, with snuffers. That is all I remember of her describing, except that there was a braided rag rug on the floor, and on the wall was a beautiful flowered paper—roses and morning-glories in a wreath on a light blue ground. The same paper was in the front room."

"And all this never existed except in her imagination?"

"She said that when she and father went up there, there wasn't any little room at all like it anywhere in the house; there was a china-closet where she had believed the room to be."

"And your aunts said there had never been any such room."

"That is what they said."

"Wasn't there any blue chintz in the house with a peacock figure?"

"Not a scrap, and Aunt Hannah said there had never been any that she could remember; and Maria just echoed her—she always does that. You see, Aunt Hannah is an up-and-down New England woman. She looks just like herself; I mean, just like her character. Her joints move up and down or backward and forward in a plain square fashion. I don't believe she ever leaned on anything in her life, or sat in an easy-chair. But Maria is different; she is rounder and softer; she hasn't any ideas of her own; she never had any. I don't believe she would think it right or becoming to have one that differed from Aunt Hannah's, so what would be the use of having any? She is an echo, that's all.

"When mamma and I got there, of course I was all excitement to see the china-closet, and I had a sort of feeling that it would be the little room after all. So I ran ahead and threw open the door, crying, 'Come and see the little room.'"

"And, Roger," said Mrs. Grant, laying her hand in his, "there really was a little room there, exactly as mother had remembered it. There was the lounge, the peacock chintz, the green door, the shell, the morning-glory and rose paper, *everything exactly as she had described it to me.*"

"What in the world did the sisters say about it?"

"Wait a minute and I will tell you. My mother was in the front hall still talking with Aunt Hannah. She didn't hear me at first, but I ran out there and dragged her through the front room, saying, 'The room *is* here—it is all right.'"

"It seemed for a minute as if my mother would faint. She clung to me in terror. I can remember now how strained her eyes looked and how pale she was.

"I called out to Aunt Hannah and asked her when they had had the closet taken away and the little room built; for in my excitement I thought that that was what had been done.

" 'That little room has always been there,' said Aunt Hannah, 'ever since the house was built.'

" 'But mamma said there wasn't any little room here, only a china-closet, when she was here with papa,' said I.

" 'No, there has never been any china-closet there; it has always been just as it is now,' said Aunt Hannah.

"Then mother spoke; her voice sounded weak and far off. She said, slowly, and with an effort, 'Maria, don't you remember that you told me that there had *never been any little room here?* and Hannah said so too, and then I said I must have dreamed it?'

" 'No, I don't remember anything of the kind,' said Maria, without the slightest emotion. 'I don't remember you ever said anything about any china-closet. The house has never been altered; you used to play in this room when you were a child, don't you remember?'

" 'I know it,' said mother, in that queer slow voice that made me feel frightened. 'Hannah, don't you remember my finding the china-closet here, with the gilt-edged china on the shelves, and then *you* said that the *china-closet* had always been here?'

" 'No,' said Hannah, pleasantly but unemotionally—'no, I don't think you ever asked me about any china-closet, and we haven't any gilt-edged china that I know of.'

"And that was the strangest thing about it. We never could make them remember that there had ever been any question about it. You would think they could remember how surprised mother had been before, unless she had imagined the whole thing. Oh, it was so queer! They were always pleasant about it, but they didn't seem to feel any interest or curiosity. It was always this answer: 'The house is just as it was built; there have never been any changes, so far as we know.'

"And my mother was in an agony of perplexity. How cold their gray eyes looked to me! There was no reading anything in them. It just seemed to break my mother down, this queer thing. Many times that summer, in the middle of the night, I have seen her get up and take a candle and creep softly down stairs. I could hear the steps creak under her weight. Then she would go through the front room and peer into the darkness, holding her thin hand between the candle and her eyes. She seemed to think the little room might vanish. Then she would come back to bed and toss about all night, or lie still and shiver; it used to frighten me.

"She grew pale and thin, and she had a little cough; then she did not like to be left alone. Sometimes she would make errands in order to send me to the little room for something—a book, or her fan, or her handkerchief; but she would never sit there or let me stay in there long, and sometimes she wouldn't let me go in there for days together. Oh, it was pitiful!"

"Well, don't talk any more about it, Margaret, if it makes you feel so," said Mr. Grant.

"Oh yes, I want you to know all about it, and there isn't much more—no more about the room.

"Mother never got well, and she died that autumn. She used often to sigh, and say, with a wan little laugh, 'There is one thing I am glad of, Margaret: your father knows now all about the little room.' I think she was afraid I distrusted her. Of course, in a child's way, I thought there was something queer about it, but I did not brood over it. I was too young then, and took it as a part of her illness. But, Roger, do you know, it really did affect me. I almost hate to go there after talking about it; I somehow feel as if it might, you know, be a china-closet again."

"That's an absurd idea."

"I know it; of course it can't be. I saw the room, and there isn't any china-closet there, and no gilt-edged china in the house, either."

And then she whispered, "But, Roger, you may hold my hand as you do now, if you will, when we go to look for the little room."

"And you won't mind Aunt Hannah's gray eyes?"

"I won't mind *anything*."

It was dusk when Mr. and Mrs. Grant went into the gate under the two old Lombardy poplars and walked up the narrow path to the door, where they were met by the two aunts.

Hannah gave Mrs. Grant a frigid but not unfriendly kiss; and Maria seemed for a moment to tremble on the verge of an emotion, but she glanced at Hannah, and then gave her greeting in exactly the same repressed and non-committal way.

Supper was waiting for them. On the table was the *gilt-edged china*. Mrs. Grant didn't notice it immediately, till she saw her husband smiling at her over his teacup; then she felt fidgety, and couldn't eat. She was nervous, and kept wondering what was behind her, whether it would be a little room or a closet.

After supper she offered to help about the dishes, but, mercy! she might as well have offered to help bring the seasons round; Maria and Hannah couldn't be helped.

So she and her husband went to find the little room, or closet, or whatever was to be there.

Aunt Maria followed them, carrying the lamp, which she set down, and then went back to the dish-washing.

Margaret looked at her husband. He kissed her, for she seemed troubled; and then, hand in hand, they opened the door. It opened into a *china-closet*. The shelves were neatly draped with scalloped paper; on them was the gilt-edged china, with the dishes missing that had been used at the supper, and which at that moment were being carefully washed and wiped by the two aunts.

Margaret's husband dropped her hand and looked at her. She was trembling a little, and turned to him for help, for some explanation, but in an instant she knew that something was wrong. A cloud had come between them; he was hurt; he was antagonized.

He paused for an appreciable instant, and then said, kindly enough, but in a voice that cut her deeply,

"I am glad this ridiculous thing is ended; don't let us speak of it again."

"Ended!" said she. "How ended?" And somehow her voice sounded to her as her mother's voice had when she stood there and questioned her sisters about the little room. She seemed to have to drag her words out. She spoke slowly: "It seems to me to have only just begun in my case. It was just so with mother when she—"

"I really wish, Margaret, you would let it drop. I don't like to hear you speak of your mother in connection with it. It—" He hesitated, for was not this their wedding-day? "It doesn't seem quite the thing, quite delicate, you know, to use her name in the matter."

She saw it all now: *he didn't believe her*. She felt a chill sense of withering under his glance.

"Come," he added, "let us go out, or into the dining-room, somewhere, anywhere, only drop this nonsense."

He went out; he did not take her hand now—he was vexed, baffled, hurt. Had he not given her his sympathy, his attention, his belief—and his hand?—and she was fooling him. What did it mean?—she so truthful, so free from morbidness—a thing he hated. He walked up and down under the poplars, trying to get into the mood to go and join her in the house.

Margaret heard him go out; then she turned and shook the shelves; she reached her hand behind them and tried to push the boards away; she ran out of the house on to the north side and tried to find in the darkness, with her hands, a door, or some steps leading to one. She tore her dress on the old rose-trees, she fell and rose and stumbled, then she sat down on the ground and tried to think. What could she think—was she dreaming?

She went into the house and out into the kitchen, and begged Aunt Maria to tell her about the little room—what had become of it, when had they built the closet, when had they bought the gilt-edged china?

They went on washing dishes and drying them on the spotless towels with methodical exactness; and as they worked they said that there had never been any little room, so far as they knew; the china-closet had always been there, and the gilt-edged china had belonged to their mother, it had always been in the house.

"No, I don't remember that your mother ever asked about any little room," said Hannah. "She didn't seem very well that summer, but she never asked about any changes in the house; there hadn't ever been any changes."

There it was again: not a sign of interest, curiosity, or annoyance, not a spark of memory.

She went out to Hiram. He was telling Mr. Grant about the farm. She had meant to ask him about the room, but her lips were sealed before her husband.

Months afterwards, when time had lessened the sharpness of their feelings, they learned to speculate reasonably about the phenomenon, which Mr. Grant had accepted as something not to be scoffed away, not to be treated as a poor joke, but to be put aside as something inexplicable on any ordinary theory.

Margaret alone in her heart knew that her mother's words carried a deeper significance than she had dreamed of at the time. "One thing I am glad of, your father knows now," and she wondered if Roger or she would ever know.

Five years later they were going to Europe. The packing was done; the children were lying asleep, with their traveling things ready to be slipped on for an early start.

Roger had a foreign appointment. They were not to be back in America for some years. She had meant to go up to say good-by to her aunts; but a mother of three children intends to do a great many things that never get done. One thing she had done that very day, and as she paused for a moment between the writing of two notes that must be posted before she went to bed, she said:

"Roger, you remember Rita Lash? Well, she and Cousin Nan go up to the Adirondacks every autumn. They are clever girls, and I have intrusted to them something I want done very much."

"They are the girls to do it, then, every inch of them."

"I know it, and they are going to."

"Well?"

"Why, you see, Roger, that little room—"

"Oh—"

"Yes, I was a coward not to go myself, but I didn't find time, because I hadn't the courage."

"Oh! *that* was it, was it?"

"Yes, just that. They are going, and they will write us about it."

"Want to bet?"

"No; I only want to know."

Rita Lash and Cousin Nan planned to go to Vermont on their way to the Adirondacks. They found they would have three hours between trains, which would give them time to drive up to the Keys farm, and they could still get to the camp that night. But, at the last minute, Rita was prevented from going. Nan had to go to meet the Adirondack party, and she promised to telegraph her when she arrived at the camp. Imagine Rita's amusement when she received this message: "Safely arrived; went to the Keys farm; it is a little room."

Rita was amused, because she did not in the least think Nan had been there. She thought it was a hoax; but it put it into her mind to carry the joke further by really stopping herself when she went up, as she meant to do the next week.

She did stop over. She introduced herself to the two maiden ladies, who seemed familiar, as they had been described by Mrs. Grant.

They were, if not cordial, at least not disconcerted at her visit, and willingly showed her over the house. As they did not speak of any other stranger's having been to see them lately, she became confirmed in her belief that Nan had not been there.

In the north room she saw the roses and morning-glory paper on the wall, and also the door that should open into—what?

She asked if she might open it.

"Certainly," said Hannah; and Maria echoed, "Certainly."

She opened it, and found the china-closet. She experienced a certain relief; she at least was not under any spell. Mrs. Grant left it a china-closet; she found it the same. Good.

But she tried to induce the old sisters to remember that there had at various times been certain questions relating to a confusion as to whether the closet had always been a closet. It was no use; their stony eyes gave no sign.

Then she thought of the story of the sea-captain, and said, "Miss Keys, did you ever have a lounge covered with India chintz, with a figure of a peacock on it, given to you in Salem by a sea-captain, who brought it from India?"

"I dun'no' as I ever did," said Hannah. That was all. She thought

Maria's cheeks were a little flushed, but her eyes were like a stone wall. She went on that night to the Adirondacks. When Nan and she were alone in their room she said, "By-the-way, Nan, what did you see at the farm-house? and how did you like Maria and Hannah?"

Nan didn't mistrust that Rita had been there, and she began excitedly to tell her all about her visit. Rita could almost have believed Nan had been there if she hadn't known it was not so. She let her go on for some time, enjoying her enthusiasm, and the impressive way in which she described her opening the door and finding the "little room." Then Rita said: "Now, Nan, that is enough fibbing. I went to the farm myself on my way up yesterday, and there is *no* little room, and there *never* has been any; it is a china-closet, just as Mrs. Grant saw it last."

She was pretending to be busy unpacking her trunk, and did not look up for a moment; but as Nan did not say anything, she glanced at her over her shoulder. Nan was actually pale, and it was hard to say whether she was most angry or frightened. There was something of both in her look. And then Rita began to explain how her telegram had put her in the spirit of going up there alone. She hadn't meant to cut Nan out. She only thought—Then Nan broke in: "It isn't that; I am sure you can't think it is that. But I went myself, and you did not go; you can't have been there, for *it is a little room*."

Oh, what a night they had! They couldn't sleep. They talked and argued, and then kept still for a while, only to break out again, it was so absurd. They both maintained that they had been there, but both felt sure the other one was either crazy or obstinate beyond reason. They were wretched; it was perfectly ridiculous, two friends at odds over such a thing; but there it was—"little room," "china-closet,"—"china-closet," "little room."

The next morning Nan was tacking up some tarlatan at a window to keep the midges out. Rita offered to help her, as she had done for the past ten years. Nan's "No, thanks," cut her to the heart.

"Nan," said she, "come right down from that stepladder and pack your satchel. The stage leaves in just twenty minutes. We can catch the afternoon express train, and we will go together to the farm. I am either going there or going home. You better go with me."

Nan didn't say a word. She gathered up the hammer and tacks, and was ready to start when the stage came round.

It meant for them thirty miles of staging and six hours of train, besides crossing the lake; but what of that, compared with having a lie lying round loose between them! Europe would have seemed easy to accomplish, if it would settle the question.

At the little junction in Vermont they found a farmer with a wagon full of meal-bags. They asked him if he could not take them up to the old Keys farm and bring them back in time for the return train, due in two hours.

They had planned to call it a sketching trip, so they said, "We have been there before, we are artists, and we might find some views worth taking, and we want also to make a short call upon the Misses Keys."

"Did ye calculate to paint the old *house* in the picture?"

They said it was possible they might do so. They wanted to see it, anyway.

"Waal, I guess you are too late. The *house* burnt down last night, and everything in it."

HENRY JAMES

The Beast in the Jungle

James recorded in his notebook in February 1895 this question: "What is there in the idea of *Too late*—of some friendship or passion or bond—some affection long desired and waited for that is formed too late?" This was the germ for the tale of "The Beast in the Jungle," eventually published in the collection *The Better Sort* (1903). Though he never committed his narrative to a full-fledged ghost story, James still achieves ghostly effects. Controlled by an obsessive belief that some momentous destiny awaits him, John Marcher withdraws from the resources of life and affection. As a consequence, he forfeits whatever claim he might have had upon the love of May Bartram, who agrees to wait and watch with him as he embarks on what James called a great "negative adventure." As the woman whom Marcher both rejects and selfishly uses, Bartram provides a second and complementary point of view in the story; and it is she who declares to Marcher that the anxiously awaited event has already occurred, that the beast has already sprung. Marcher's (and the reader's) full comprehension of the remark is deferred until the very end, when it is, indeed, too late.

*   *   *

I

What determined the speech that startled him in the course of their encounter scarcely matters, being probably but some words spoken by himself quite without intention—spoken as they lingered and slowly moved together after their renewal of acquaintance. He had been conveyed by friends, an hour or two before, to the house at which she was staying; the party of visitors at the other house, of whom he was one, and thanks to whom it was his theory, as always, that he was lost in the crowd, had been invited over to luncheon. There had been after luncheon much dispersal, all in the interest of the original motive, a view of Weatherend itself and the fine things, intrinsic features, pictures, heirlooms, treasures of all the arts, that made the place almost famous; and the great rooms were so numerous that guests could wander at their will, hang back from the principal group, and, in cases where they took such matters with the last seriousness, give themselves up to mysterious appreciations and measurements. There were persons to be observed, singly or in couples, bending toward objects in out-of-the-way corners with their hands on their knees and their heads nodding quite as with the emphasis of an excited sense of smell. When they were two they either mingled their sounds of ecstasy or melted into silences of even deeper import, so that there were aspects of the occasion that gave it for Marcher much the air of the "look round," previous to a sale highly advertised, that excites or quenches, as may be, the dream of acquisition. The dream of acquisition at Weatherend would have had to be wild indeed, and John Marcher found himself, among such suggestions, disconcerted almost equally by the presence of those who knew too much and by that of those who knew nothing. The great rooms caused so much poetry and history to press upon him that he needed to wander apart to feel in a proper relation with them, though his doing so was not, as happened, like the gloating of some of his companions, to be compared to the movements of a dog sniffing a cupboard. It had an issue promptly enough in a direction that was not to have been calculated.

It led, in short, in the course of the October afternoon, to his closer meeting with May Bartram, whose face, a reminder, yet not quite a remembrance, as they sat, much separated, at a very long table, had begun merely by troubling him rather pleasantly. It affected him as the sequel of something of which he had lost the beginning. He knew it, and for the time quite welcomed it, as a continuation, but didn't know what it continued, which was an interest, or an amusement, the greater as he was also somehow aware—yet without a direct sign from her— that the young woman herself had not lost the thread. She had not lost it, but she wouldn't give it back to him, he saw, without some putting forth of his hand for it; and he not only saw that, but saw several things more, things odd enough in the light of the fact that at the moment some accident of grouping brought them face to face he was still merely fumbling with the idea that any contact between them in the past would have had no importance. If it had had no importance he scarcely knew why his actual impression of her should so seem to have so much; the answer to which, however, was that in such a life as they all appeared to be leading for the moment one could but take things as they came. He was satisfied, without in the least being able to say why, that this young lady might roughly have ranked in the house as a poor relation; satisfied also that she was not there on a brief visit, but was more or less a part of the establishment—almost a working, a remunerated part. Didn't she enjoy at periods a protection that she paid for by helping, among other services, to show the place and explain it, deal with the tiresome people, answer questions about the dates of the buildings, the styles of the furniture, the authorship of the pictures, the favourite haunts of the ghost? It wasn't that she looked as if you could have given her shillings—it was impossible to look less so. Yet when she finally drifted toward him, distinctly handsome, though ever so much older—older than when he had seen her before—it might have been as an effect of her guessing that he had, within the couple of hours, devoted more imagination to her than to all the others put together, and had thereby penetrated to a kind of truth that the others were too stupid for. She *was* there on harder terms than anyone; she was there as a consequence of things suffered, in one way and another, in the interval of years; and she remembered him very much as she was remembered—only a good deal better.

By the time they at last thus came to speech they were alone in one of the rooms—remarkable for a fine portrait over the chimney-place—out of which their friends had passed, and the charm of it was that even before they had spoken they had practically arranged with each other to stay behind for talk. The charm, happily, was in other things too; it was partly in there being scarce a spot at Weatherend without something to stay behind for. It was in the way the autumn day looked into the high windows as it waned; in the way the red light, breaking at the close from under a low, sombre sky, reached out in a long shaft and played over old wainscots, old tapestry, old gold, old colour. It was most of all perhaps in the way she came to him as if, since she had been turned on to deal with the simpler sort, he might, should he choose to keep the whole thing down, just take her mild attention for a part of her general business. As soon as he heard her voice, however, the gap was filled up and the missing link supplied; the slight irony he divined in her attitude lost its advantage. He almost jumped at it to get there before her. "I met you years and years ago in Rome. I remember all about it." She confessed to disappointment—she had been so sure he didn't; and to prove how well he did he began to pour forth the particular recollections that popped up as he called for them. Her face and her voice, all at his service now, worked the miracle—the impression operating like the torch of a lamplighter who touches into flame, one

by one, a long row of gas jets. Marcher flattered himself that the illumination was brilliant, yet he was really still more pleased on her showing him, with amusement, that in his haste to make everything right he
had got most things rather wrong. It hadn't been at Rome—it had been
at Naples; and it hadn't been seven years before—it had been more
nearly ten. She hadn't been either with her uncle and aunt, but with her
mother and her brother; in addition to which it was not with the Pembles that *he* had been, but with the Boyers, coming down in their company from Rome—a point on which she insisted, a little to his
confusion, and as to which she had her evidence in hand. The Boyers
she had known, but she didn't know the Pembles, though she had heard
of them, and it was the people he was with who had made them acquainted. The incident of the thunderstorm that had raged round them
with such violence as to drive them for refuge into an excavation—this
incident had not occurred at the Palace of the Cæsars, but at Pompeii,
on an occasion when they had been present there at an important find.

He accepted her amendments, he enjoyed her corrections, though the
moral of them was, she pointed out, that he *really* didn't remember the
least thing about her; and he only felt it as a drawback that when all
was made conformable to the truth there didn't appear much of anything left. They lingered together still, she neglecting her office—for
from the moment he was so clever she had no proper right to him—
and both neglecting the house, just waiting as to see if a memory or
two more wouldn't again breathe upon them. It had not taken them
many minutes, after all, to put down on the table, like the cards of a
pack, those that constituted their respective hands; only what came out
was that the pack was unfortunately not perfect—that the past, in-
voked, invited, encouraged, could give them, naturally, no more than it
had. It had made them meet—her at twenty, him at twenty-five; but
nothing was so strange, they seemed to say to each other, as that, while
so occupied, it hadn't done a little more for them. They looked at each
other as with the feeling of an occasion missed; the present one would
have been so much better if the other, in the far distance, in the foreign
land, hadn't been so stupidly meagre. There weren't, apparently, all
counted, more than a dozen little old things that had succeeded in coming to pass between them; trivialities of youth, simplicities of freshness,
stupidities of ignorance, small possible germs, but too deeply buried—
too deeply (didn't it seem?) to sprout after so many years. Marcher said
to himself that he ought to have rendered her some service—saved her
from a capsized boat in the Bay, or at least recovered her dressing-bag,
filched from her cab, in the streets of Naples, by a lazzarone with a
stiletto. Or it would have been nice if he could have been taken with
fever, alone, at his hotel, and she could have come to look after him,

to write to his people, to drive him out in convalescence. *Then* they would be in possession of the something or other that their actual show seemed to lack. It yet somehow presented itself, this show, as too good to be spoiled; so that they were reduced for a few minutes more to wondering a little helplessly why—since they seemed to know a certain number of the same people—their reunion had been so long averted. They didn't use that name for it, but their delay from minute to minute to join the others was a kind of confession that they didn't quite want it to be a failure. Their attempted supposition of reasons for their not having met but showed how little they knew of each other. There came in fact a moment when Marcher felt a positive pang. It was vain to pretend she was an old friend, for all the communities were wanting, in spite of which it was as an old friend that he saw she would have suited him. He had new ones enough—was surrounded with them, for instance, at that hour at the other house; as a new one he probably wouldn't have so much as noticed her. He would have liked to invent something, get her to make-believe with him that some passage of a romantic or critical kind *had* originally occurred. He was really almost reaching out in imagination—as against time—for something that would do, and saying to himself that if it didn't come this new incident would simply and rather awkwardly close. They would separate, and now for no second or for no third chance. They would have tried and not succeeded. Then it was, just at the turn, as he afterwards made it out to himself, that, everything else failing, she herself decided to take up the case and, as it were, save the situation. He felt as soon as she spoke that she had been consciously keeping back what she said and hoping to get on without it; a scruple in her that immensely touched him when, by the end of three or four minutes more, he was able to measure it. What she brought out, at any rate, quite cleared the air and supplied the link—the link it was such a mystery he should frivolously have managed to lose.

"You know you told me something that I've never forgotten and that again and again has made me think of you since; it was that tremendously hot day when we went to Sorrento, across the bay, for the breeze. What I allude to was what you said to me, on the way back, as we sat, under the awning of the boat, enjoying the cool. Have you forgotten?"

He had forgotten, and he was even more surprised than ashamed. But the great thing was that he saw it was no vulgar reminder of any "sweet" speech. The vanity of women had long memories, but she was making no claim on him of a compliment or a mistake. With another woman, a totally different one, he might have feared the recall possibly even some imbecile "offer." So, in having to say that he had indeed forgotten, he was conscious rather of a loss than of a gain; he already saw an interest in the matter of her reference. "I try to think—but I give it up. Yet I remember the Sorrento day."

"I'm not very sure you do," May Bartram after a moment said; "and I'm not very sure I ought to want you to. It's dreadful to bring a person back, at any time, to what he was ten years before. If you've lived away from it," she smiled, "so much the better."

"Ah, if *you* haven't why should I?" he asked.

"Lived away, you mean, from what I myself was?"

"From what *I* was. I was of course an ass," Marcher went on; "but I would rather know from you just the sort of ass I was than—from the moment you have something in your mind—not know anything."

Still, however, she hesitated. "But if you've completely ceased to be that sort——?"

"Why, I can then just so all the more bear to know. Besides, perhaps I haven't."

"Perhaps. Yet if you haven't," she added, "I should suppose you would remember. Not indeed that *I* in the least connect with my impression the invidious name you use. If I had only thought you foolish," she explained, "the thing I speak of wouldn't so have remained with me. It was about yourself." She waited, as if it might come to him; but as, only meeting her eyes in wonder, he gave no sign, she burnt her ships. "Has it ever happened?"

Then it was that, while he continued to stare, a light broke for him and the blood slowly came to his face, which began to burn with recognition. "Do you mean I told you——?" But he faltered, lest what came to him shouldn't be right, lest he should only give himself away.

"It was something about yourself that it was natural one shouldn't forget—that is if one remembered you at all. That's why I ask you," she smiled, "if the thing you then spoke of has ever come to pass?"

Oh, then he saw, but he was lost in wonder and found himself embarrassed. This, he also saw, made her sorry for him, as if her allusion had been a mistake. It took him but a moment, however, to feel that it had not been, much as it had been a surprise. After the first little shock of it her knowledge on the contrary began, even if rather strangely, to taste sweet to him. She was the only other person in the world then who would have it, and she had had it all these years, while the fact of his having so breathed his secret had unaccountably faded from him. No wonder they couldn't have met as if nothing had happened. "I judge," he finally said, "that I know what you mean. Only I had strangely enough lost the consciousness of having taken you so far into my confidence."

"Is it because you've taken so many others as well?"

"I've taken nobody. Not a creature since then."

"So that I'm the only person who knows?"

"The only person in the world."

"Well," she quickly replied, "I myself have never spoken. I've never, never repeated of you what you told me." She looked at him so that he perfectly believed her. Their eyes met over it in such a way that he was without a doubt. "And I never will."

She spoke with an earnestness that, as if almost excessive, put him at ease about her possible derision. Somehow the whole question was a new luxury to him—that is, from the moment she was in possession. If she didn't take the ironic view she clearly took the sympathetic, and that was what he had had, in all the long time, from no one whomsoever. What he felt was that he couldn't at present have begun to tell her and yet could profit perhaps exquisitely by the accident of having done so of old. "Please don't then. We're just right as it is."

"Oh, I am," she laughed, "if you are!" To which she added: "Then you do still feel in the same way?"

It was impossible to him not to take to himself that she was really interested, and it all kept coming as a sort of revelation. He had thought of himself so long as abominably alone, and, lo, he wasn't alone a bit. He hadn't been, it appeared, for an hour—since those moments on the Sorrento boat. It was *she* who had been, he seemed to see as he looked at her—she who had been made so by the graceless fact of his lapse of fidelity. To tell her what he had told her—what had it been but to ask something of her? something that she had given, in her charity, without his having, by a remembrance, by a return of the spirit, failing another encounter, so much as thanked her. What he had asked of her had been simply at first not to laugh at him. She had beautifully not done so for ten years, and she was not doing so now. So he had endless gratitude to make up. Only for that he must see just how he had figured to her. "What, exactly, was the account I gave——?"

"Of the way you did feel? Well, it was very simple. You said you had had from your earliest time, as the deepest thing within you, the sense of being kept for something rare and strange, possibly prodigious and terrible, that was sooner or later to happen to you, that you had in your bones the foreboding and the conviction of, and that would perhaps overwhelm you."

"Do you call that very simple?" John Marcher asked.

She thought a moment. "It was perhaps because I seemed, as you spoke, to understand it."

"You do understand it?" he eagerly asked.

Again she kept her kind eyes on him. "You still have the belief?"

"Oh!" he exclaimed helplessly. There was too much to say.

"Whatever it is to be," she clearly made out, "it hasn't yet come."

He shook his head in complete surrender now. "It hasn't yet come. Only, you know, it isn't anything I'm to *do,* to achieve in the world, to be distinguished or admired for. I'm not such an ass as *that.* It would be much better, no doubt, if I were."

"It's to be something you're merely to suffer?"

"Well, say to wait for—to have to meet, to face, to see suddenly break out in my life; possibly destroying all further consciousness, possibly annihilating me; possibly, on the other hand, only altering everything, striking at the root of all my world and leaving me to the consequences, however they shape themselves."

She took this in, but the light in her eyes continued for him not to be that of mockery. "Isn't what you describe perhaps but the expectation—or, at any rate, the sense of danger, familiar to so many people—of falling in love?"

John Marcher thought. "Did you ask me that before?"

"No—I wasn't so free-and-easy then. But it's what strikes me now."

"Of course," he said after a moment, "it strikes you. Of course it strikes *me.* Of course what's in store for me may be no more than that. The only thing is," he went on, "that I think that if it had been that, I should by this time know."

"Do you mean because you've *been* in love?" And then as he but looked at her in silence: "You've been in love, and it hasn't meant such a cataclysm, hasn't proved the great affair?"

"Here I am, you see. It hasn't been overwhelming."

"Then it hasn't been love," said May Bartram.

"Well, I at least thought it was. I took it for that—I've taken it till now. It was agreeable, it was delightful, it was miserable," he explained. "But it wasn't strange. It wasn't what *my* affair's to be."

"You want something all to yourself—something that nobody else knows or *has* known?"

"It isn't a question of what I 'want'—God knows I don't want anything. It's only a question of the apprehension that haunts me—that I live with day by day."

He said this so lucidly and consistently that, visibly, it further imposed itself. If she had not been interested before she would have been interested now. "Is it a sense of coming violence?"

Evidently now too, again, he liked to talk of it. "I don't think of it as—when it does come—necessarily violent. I only think of it as natural and as of course, above all, unmistakable. I think of it simply as *the* thing. *The* thing will of itself appear natural."

"Then how will it appear strange?"

Marcher bethought himself. "It won't—to *me.*"

"To whom then?"

"Well," he replied, smiling at last, "say to you."

"Oh then, I'm to be present?"

"Why, you *are* present—since you know."

"I see." She turned it over. "But I mean at the catastrophe."

At this, for a minute, their lightness gave way to their gravity; it was as if the long look they exchanged held them together. "It will only depend on yourself—if you'll watch with me."

"Are you afraid?" she asked.

"Don't leave me *now*," he went on.

"Are you afraid?" she repeated.

"Do you think me simply out of my mind?" he pursued instead of answering. "Do I merely strike you as a harmless lunatic?"

"No," said May Bartram. "I understand you. I believe you."

"You mean you feel how my obsession—poor old thing!—may correspond to some possible reality?"

"To some possible reality."

"Then you *will* watch with me?"

She hesitated, then for the third time put her question. "Are you afraid?"

"Did I tell you I was—at Naples?"

"No, you said nothing about it."

"Then I don't know. And I should *like* to know," said John Marcher. "You'll tell me yourself whether you think so. If you'll watch with me you'll see."

"Very good then." They had been moving by this time across the room, and at the door, before passing out, they paused as if for the full wind-up of their understanding. "I'll watch with you," said May Bartram.

II

The fact that she "knew"—knew and yet neither chaffed him nor betrayed him—had in a short time begun to constitute between them a sensible bond, which became more marked when, within the year that followed their afternoon at Weatherend, the opportunities for meeting multiplied. The event that thus promoted these occasions was the death of the ancient lady, her great-aunt, under whose wing, since losing her mother, she had to such an extent found shelter, and who, though but the widowed mother of the new successor to the property, had succeeded—thanks to a high tone and a high temper—in not forfeiting the supreme position at the great house. The deposition of this personage arrived but with her death, which, followed by many changes, made in particular a difference for the young woman in whom Marcher's expert attention had recognised from the first a dependent with a pride that might ache though it didn't bristle. Nothing for a long time had made him easier than the thought that the aching must have been much soothed by Miss Bartram's now finding herself able to set up a small home in London. She had acquired property, to an amount that made that luxury just possible, under her aunt's extremely complicated will, and when the whole matter began to be straightened out, which indeed took time, she let him know that the happy issue was at last in view. He had seen her again before that day, both because she had more than once accompanied the ancient lady to town and because he had paid another visit to the friends who so conveniently made of Weatherend one of the charms of their own hospitality. These friends had taken him back there; he had achieved there again with Miss Bartram some quiet detachment; and he had in London succeeded in persuading her to more than one brief absence from her aunt. They went together, on these latter occasions, to the National Gallery and the South Kensington Museum, where, among vivid reminders, they talked of Italy at large—not now attempting to recover, as at first, the taste of their youth and their ignorance. That recovery, the first day at Weatherend, had served its purpose well, had given them quite enough; so that they were, to Marcher's sense, no longer hovering about the head-waters of their stream, but had felt their boat pushed sharply off and down the current.

They were literally afloat together; for our gentleman this was marked, quite as marked as that the fortunate cause of it was just the buried treasure of her knowledge. He had with his own hands dug up this little hoard, brought to light—that is to within reach of the dim day constituted by their discretions and privacies—the object of value the hiding-place of which he had, after putting it into the ground himself, so strangely, so long forgotten. The exquisite luck of having again just stumbled on the spot made him indifferent to any other question; he would doubtless have devoted more time to the odd accident of his lapse of memory if he had not been moved to devote so much to the sweetness, the comfort, as he felt, for the future, that this accident itself had helped to keep fresh. It had never entered into his plan that anyone should "know," and mainly for the reason that it was not in him to tell anyone. That would have been impossible, since nothing but the amusement of a cold world would have waited on it. Since, however, a mysterious fate had opened his mouth in youth, in spite of him, he would count that a compensation and profit by it to the utmost. That the right person *should* know tempered the asperity of his secret more even than his shyness had permitted him to imagine; and May Bartram was clearly right, because—well, because there she was. Her knowledge simply settled it; he would have been sure enough by this time had she been wrong. There was that in his situation, no doubt, that disposed him too much to see her as a mere confidant, taking all her light for him from the fact—the fact only—of her interest in his predicament, from her mercy, sympathy, seriousness, her consent not to regard him as the funniest of the funny. Aware, in fine, that her price for him was just in her giving him this constant sense of his being admirably spared, he was careful to remember that she had, after all, also a life of her own, with things that might happen to *her*, things that in friendship one should likewise take account of. Something fairly remarkable came to pass with him, for that matter, in this connection—something represented by a certain passage of his consciousness, in the suddenest way, from one extreme to the other.

He had thought himself, so long as nobody knew, the most disinterested person in the world, carrying his concentrated burden, his perpetual suspense, ever so quietly, holding his tongue about it, giving others no glimpse of it nor of its effect upon his life, asking of them no allowance and only making on his side all those that were asked. He had disturbed nobody with the queerness of having to know a haunted man, though he had had moments of rather special temptation on hearing people say that they were "unsettled." If they were as unsettled as he was—he who had never been settled for an hour in his life—they would know what it meant. Yet it wasn't, all the same, for him to make them, and he listened to them civilly enough. This was why he had such good—though possibly such rather colourless—manners; this was why, above all, he could regard himself, in a greedy world, as decently—as, in fact, perhaps even a little sublimely—unselfish. Our point is accordingly that he valued this character quite sufficiently to measure his present danger of letting it lapse, against which he promised himself to be much on his guard. He was quite ready, none the less, to be selfish just a little, since, surely, no more charming occasion for it had come to him. "Just a little," in a word, was just as much as Miss Bartram, taking one day with another, would let him. He never would be in the least coercive, and he would keep well before him the lines on which consideration for her—the very highest—ought to proceed. He would thoroughly establish the heads under which her affairs, her requirements, her peculiarities—he went so far as to give them the latitude of that name—would come into their intercourse. All this naturally was a sign of how much he took the intercourse itself for granted. There was nothing more to be done about *that*. It simply existed; had sprung into being with her first penetrating question to him in the autumn light there at Weatherend. The real form it should have taken on the basis that stood out large was the form of their marrying. But the devil in this was that the very basis itself put marrying out of the question. His conviction, his apprehension, his obsession, in short, was not a condition he could invite a woman to share; and that consequence of it was precisely what was the matter with him. Something or other lay in wait for him, amid the twists and the turns of the months and the years, like a crouching beast in the jungle. It signified little whether the crouching beast were destined to slay him or to be slain. The definite point was the inevitable spring of the creature; and the definite lesson from that was that a man of feeling didn't cause himself to be accompanied by a lady on a tiger-hunt. Such was the image under which he had ended by figuring his life.

They had at first, none the less, in the scattered hours spent together, made no allusion to that view of it; which was a sign he was handsomely ready to give that he didn't expect, that he in fact didn't care always to be talking about it. Such a feature in one's outlook was really like a hump on one's back. The difference it made every minute of the day existed quite independently of discussion. One discussed, of course, *like* a hunchback, for there was always, if nothing else, the hunchback face. That remained, and she was watching him; but people watched best, as a general thing, in silence, so that such would be predominantly the manner of their vigil. Yet he didn't want, at the same time, to be solemn; solemn was what he imagined he too much tended to be with other people. The thing to be, with the one person who knew, was easy and natural—to make the reference rather than be seeming to avoid it, to avoid it rather than be seeming to make it, and to keep it, in any case, familiar, facetious even, rather than pedantic and portentous. Some such consideration as the latter was doubtless in his mind, for instance, when he wrote pleasantly to Miss Bartram that perhaps the great thing he had so long felt as in the lap of the gods was no more than this circumstance, which touched him so nearly, of her acquiring a house in London. It was the first allusion they had yet again made, needing any other hitherto so little; but when she replied, after having given him the news, that she was by no means satisfied with such a trifle, as the climax to so special a suspense, she almost set him wondering if she hadn't even a larger conception of singularity for him than he had for himself. He was at all events destined to become aware little by little, as time went by, that she was all the while looking at his life, judging it, measuring it, in the light of the thing she knew, which grew to be at last, with the consecration of the years, never mentioned between them save as "the real truth" about him. That had always been his own form of reference to it, but she adopted the form so quietly that, looking back at the end of a period, he knew there was no moment at which it was traceable that she had, as he might say, got inside his condition, or exchanged the attitude of beautifully indulging for that of still more beautifully believing him.

It was always open to him to accuse her of seeing him but as the most harmless of maniacs, and this, in the long run—since it covered so much ground—was his easiest description of their friendship. He had a screw loose for her, but she liked him in spite of it, and was practically, against the rest of the world, his kind, wise keeper, unremunerated, but fairly amused and, in the absence of other near ties, not disreputably occupied. The rest of the world of course thought him queer, but she, she only, knew how, and above all why, queer; which was precisely what enabled her to dispose the concealing veil in the right folds. She took his gaiety from him—since it had to pass with them for gaiety— as she took everything else; but she certainly so far justified by her unerring touch his finer sense of the degree to which he had ended by convincing her. *She* at least never spoke of the secret of his life except as "the real truth about you," and she had in fact a wonderful way of making it seem, as such, the secret of her own life too. That was in fine how he so constantly felt her as allowing for him; he couldn't on the whole call it anything else. He allowed for himself, but she, exactly, allowed still more; partly because, better placed for a sight of the matter, she traced his unhappy perversion through portions of its course into which he could scarce follow it. He knew how he felt, but, besides knowing that, she knew how he *looked* as well; he knew each of the things of importance he was insidiously kept from doing, but she could add up the amount they made, understand how much, with a lighter weight on his spirit, he might have done, and thereby establish how, clever as he was, he fell short. Above all she was in the secret of the difference between the forms he went through—those of his little office under Government, those of caring for his modest patrimony, for his library, for his garden in the country, for the people in London whose invitations he accepted and repaid—and the detachment that reigned beneath them and that made of all behaviour, all that could in the least be called behaviour, a long act of dissimulation. What it had come to was that he wore a mask painted with the social simper, out of the eye-holes of which there looked eyes of an expression not in the least matching the other features. This the stupid world, even after years, had never more than half discovered. It was only May Bartram who had, and she achieved, by an art indescribable, the feat of at once—or perhaps it was only alternately—meeting the eyes from in front and mingling her own vision, as from over his shoulder, with their peep through the apertures.

So, while they grew older together, she did watch with him, and so she let this association give shape and colour to her own existence.

Beneath *her* forms as well detachment had learned to sit, and behaviour had become for her, in the social sense, a false account of herself. There was but one account of her that would have been true all the while, and that she could give, directly, to nobody, least of all to John Marcher. Her whole attitude was a virtual statement, but the perception of that only seemed destined to take its place for him as one of the many things necessarily crowded out of his consciousness. If she had, moreover, like himself, to make sacrifices to their real truth, it was to be granted that her compensation might have affected her as more prompt and more natural. They had long periods, in this London time, during which, when they were together, a stranger might have listened to them without in the least pricking up his ears; on the other hand, the real truth was equally liable at any moment to rise to the surface, and the auditor would then have wondered indeed what they were talking about. They had from an early time made up their mind that society was, luckily, unintelligent, and the margin that this gave them had fairly become one of their commonplaces. Yet there were still moments when the situation turned almost fresh—usually under the effect of some expression drawn from herself. Her expressions doubtless repeated themselves, but her intervals were generous. "What saves us, you know, is that we answer so completely to so usual an appearance: that of the man and woman whose friendship has become such a daily habit, or almost, as to be at last indispensable." That, for instance, was a remark she had frequently enough had occasion to make, though she had given it at different times different developments. What we are especially concerned with is the turn it happened to take from her one afternoon when he had come to see her in honour of her birthday. This anniversary had fallen on a Sunday, at a season of thick fog and general outward gloom; but he had brought her his customary offering, having known her now long enough to have established a hundred little customs. It was one of his proofs to himself, the present he made her on her birthday, that he had not sunk into real selfishness. It was mostly nothing more than a small trinket, but it was always fine of its kind, and he was regularly careful to pay for it more than he thought he could afford. "Our habit saves you, at least, don't you see? because it makes you, after all, for the vulgar, indistinguishable from other men. What's the most inveterate mark of men in general? Why, the capacity to spend endless time with dull women—to spend it, I won't say without being bored, but without minding that they are, without being driven off at a tangent by it; which comes to the same thing. I'm your dull woman, a part of the daily bread for which you pray at church. That covers your tracks more than anything."

"And what covers yours?" asked Marcher, whom his dull woman

could mostly to this extent amuse. "I see of course what you mean by your saving me, in one way and another, so far as other people are concerned—I've seen it all along. Only, what is it that saves *you?* I often think, you know, of that."

She looked as if she sometimes thought of that too, but in rather a different way. "Where other people, you mean, are concerned?"

"Well, you're really so in with me, you know—as a sort of result of my being so in with yourself. I mean of my having such an immense regard for you, being so tremendously grateful for all you've done for me. I sometimes ask myself if it's quite fair. Fair I mean to have so involved and—since one may say it—interested you. I almost feel as if you hadn't really had time to do anything else."

"Anything else but be interested?" she asked. "Ah, what else does one ever want to be? If I've been 'watching' with you, as we long ago agreed that I was to do, watching is always in itself an absorption."

"Oh, certainly," John Marcher said, "if you hadn't had your curiosity——! Only, doesn't it sometimes come to you, as time goes on, that your curiosity is not being particularly repaid?"

May Bartram had a pause. "Do you ask that, by any chance, because you feel at all that yours isn't? I mean because you have to wait so long."

Oh, he understood what she meant. "For the thing to happen that never does happen? For the beast to jump out? No, I'm just where I was about it. It isn't a matter as to which I can *choose,* I can decide for a change. It isn't one as to which there *can* be a change. It's in the lap of the gods. One's in the hands of one's law—there one is. As to the form the law will take, the way it will operate, that's its own affair."

"Yes," Miss Bartram replied; "of course one's fate is coming, of course it *has* come, in its own form and its own way, all the while. Only, you know, the form and the way in your case were to have been—well, something so exceptional and, as one may say, so particularly *your* own."

Something in this made him look at her with suspicion. "You say 'were to *have* been,' as if in your heart you had begun to doubt."

"Oh!" she vaguely protested.

"As if you believed," he went on, "that nothing will now take place."

She shook her head slowly, but rather inscrutably. "You're far from my thought."

He continued to look at her. "What then is the matter with you?"

"Well," she said after another wait, "the matter with me is simply that I'm more sure than ever my curiosity, as you call it, will be but too well repaid."

They were frankly grave now; he had got up from his seat, had turned once more about the little drawing-room to which, year after year, he brought his inevitable topic; in which he had, as he might have said, tasted their intimate community with every sauce, where every object was as familiar to him as the things of his own house and the very carpets were worn with his fitful walk very much as the desks in old counting-houses are worn by the elbows of generations of clerks. The generations of his nervous moods had been at work there, and the place was the written history of his whole middle life. Under the impression of what his friend had just said he knew himself, for some reason, more aware of these things, which made him, after a moment, stop again before her. "Is it, possibly, that you've grown afraid?"

"Afraid?" He thought, as she repeated the word, that his question had made her, a little, change colour; so that, lest he should have touched on a truth, he explained very kindly. "You remember that that was what you asked *me* long ago—that first day at Weatherend."

"Oh yes, and you told me you didn't know—that I was to see for myself. We've said little about it since, even in so long a time."

"Precisely," Marcher interposed—"quite as if it were too delicate a matter for us to make free with. Quite as if we might find, on pressure, that I *am* afraid. For then," he said, "we shouldn't, should we? quite know what to do."

She had for the time no answer to this question. "There have been days when I thought you were. Only, of course," she added, "there have been days when we have thought almost anything."

"Everything. Oh!" Marcher softly groaned as with a gasp, half spent, at the face, more uncovered just then than it had been for a long while, of the imagination always with them. It had always had its incalculable moments of glaring out; quite as with the very eyes of the very Beast, and, used as he was to them, they could still draw from him the tribute of a sigh that rose from the depths of his being. All that they had thought, first and last, rolled over him; the past seemed to have been reduced to mere barren speculation. This in fact was what the place had just struck him as so full of—the simplification of everything but the state of suspense. That remained only by seeming to hang in the void surrounding it. Even his original fear, if fear it had been, had lost itself in the desert. "I judge, however," he continued, "that you see I'm not afraid now."

"What I see is, as I make it out, that you've achieved something almost unprecedented in the way of getting used to danger. Living with it so long and so closely, you've lost your sense of it; you know it's there, but you're indifferent, and you cease even, as of old, to have to whistle in the dark. Considering what the danger is," May Bartram wound up, "I'm bound to say that I don't think your attitude could well be surpassed."

John Marcher faintly smiled. "It's heroic?"

"Certainly—call it that."

He considered. "I *am*, then, a man of courage?"

"That's what you were to show me."

He still, however, wondered. "But doesn't the man of courage know what he's afraid of—or *not* afraid of? I don't know *that*, you see. I don't focus it. I can't name it. I only know I'm exposed."

"Yes, but exposed—how shall I say?—so directly. So intimately. That's surely enough."

"Enough to make you feel, then—as what we may call the end of our watch—that I'm not afraid?"

"You're not afraid. But it isn't," she said, "the end of our watch. That is it isn't the end of yours. You've everything still to see."

"Then why haven't *you?*" he asked. He had had, all along, to-day, the sense of her keeping something back, and he still had it. As this was his first impression of that, it made a kind of date. The case was the more marked as she didn't at first answer; which in turn made him go on. "You know something I don't." Then his voice, for that of a man of courage, trembled a little. "You know what's to happen." Her silence, with the face she showed, was almost a confession—it made him sure. "You know, and you're afraid to tell me. It's so bad that you're afraid I'll find out."

All this might be true, for she did look as if, unexpectedly to her, he had crossed some mystic line that she had secretly drawn round her. Yet she might, after all, not have worried; and the real upshot was that he himself, at all events, needn't. "You'll never find out."

III

It was all to have made, none the less, as I have said, a date; as came out in the fact that again and again, even after long intervals, other things that passed between them wore, in relation to this hour, but the character of recalls and results. Its immediate effect had been indeed rather to lighten insistence—almost to provoke a reaction; as if their topic had dropped by its own weight and as if moreover, for that matter, Marcher had been visited by one of his occasional warnings against egotism. He had kept up, he felt, and very decently on the whole, his consciousness of the importance of not being selfish, and it was true that he had never sinned in that direction without promptly enough trying to press the scales the other way. He often repaired his fault, the season permitting, by inviting his friend to accompany him to the opera;

and it not infrequently thus happened that, to show he didn't wish her
to have but one sort of food for her mind, he was the cause of her
appearing there with him a dozen nights in the month. It even happened
that, seeing her home at such times, he occasionally went in with her
to finish, as he called it, the evening, and, the better to make his point,
sat down to the frugal but always careful little supper that awaited his
pleasure. His point was made, he thought, by his not eternally insisting
with her on himself; made for instance, at such hours, when it befell
that, her piano at hand and each of them familiar with it, they went
over passages of the opera together. It chanced to be on one of these
occasions, however, that he reminded her of her not having answered
a certain question he had put to her during the talk that had taken place
between them on her last birthday. "What is it that saves *you?*"—saved
her, he meant, from that appearance of variation from the usual human
type. If he had practically escaped remark, as she pretended, by doing,
in the most important particular, what most men do—find the answer
to life in patching up an alliance of a sort with a woman no better than
himself—how had she escaped it, and how could the alliance, such as
it was, since they must suppose it had been more or less noticed, have
failed to make her rather positively talked about?

"I never said," May Bartram replied, "that it hadn't made me talked
about."

"Ah well then, you're not 'saved.' "

"It has not been a question for me. If you've had your woman, I've
had," she said, "my man."

"And you mean that makes you all right?"

She hesitated. "I don't know why it shouldn't make me—humanly,
which is what we're speaking of—as right as it makes you."

"I see," Marcher returned. " 'Humanly,' no doubt, as showing that
you're living for something. Not, that is, just for me and my secret."

May Bartram smiled. "I don't pretend it exactly shows that I'm not
living for you. It's my intimacy with you that's in question."

He laughed as he saw what she meant. "Yes, but since, as you say,
I'm only, so far as people make out, ordinary, you're—aren't you?—
no more than ordinary either. You help me to pass for a man like
another. So if I *am,* as I understand you, you're not compromised. Is
that it?"

She had another hesitation, but she spoke clearly enough. "That's it.
It's all that concerns me—to help you to pass for a man like another."

He was careful to acknowledge the remark handsomely. "How kind,
how beautiful, you are to me! How shall I ever repay you?"

She had her last grave pause, as if there might be a choice of ways.
But she chose. "By going on as you are."

It was into this going on as he was that they relapsed, and really for so long a time that the day inevitably came for a further sounding of their depths. It was as if these depths, constantly bridged over by a structure that was firm enough in spite of its lightness and of its occasional oscillation in the somewhat vertiginous air, invited on occasion, in the interest of their nerves, a dropping of the plummet and a measurement of the abyss. A difference had been made moreover, once for all, by the fact that she had, all the while, not appeared to feel the need of rebutting his charge of an idea within her that she didn't dare to express, uttered just before one of the fullest of their later discussions ended. It had come up for him then that she "knew" something and that what she knew was bad—too bad to tell him. When he had spoken of it as visibly so bad that she was afraid he might find it out, her reply had left the matter too equivocal to be let alone and yet, for Marcher's special sensibility, almost too formidable again to touch. He circled about it at a distance that alternately narrowed and widened and that yet was not much affected by the consciousness in him that there was nothing she could "know," after all, any better than he did. She had no source of knowledge that he hadn't equally—except of course that she might have finer nerves. That was what women had where they were interested; they made out things, where people were concerned, that the people often couldn't have made out for themselves. Their nerves, their sensibility, their imagination, were conductors and revealers, and the beauty of May Bartram was in particular that she had given herself so to his case. He felt in these days what, oddly enough, he had never felt before, the growth of a dread of losing her by some catastrophe—some catastrophe that yet wouldn't at all be *the* catastrophe: partly because she had, almost of a sudden, begun to strike him as useful to him as never yet, and partly by reason of an appearance of uncertainty in her health, coincident and equally new. It was characteristic of the inner detachment he had hitherto so successfully cultivated and to which our whole account of him is a reference, it was characteristic that his complications, such as they were, had never yet seemed so as at this crisis to thicken about him, even to the point of making him ask himself if he were, by any chance, of a truth, within sight or sound, within touch or reach, within the immediate jurisdiction of the thing that waited.

When the day came, as come it had to, that his friend confessed to him her fear of a deep disorder in her blood, he felt somehow the shadow of a change and the chill of a shock. He immediately began to imagine aggravations and disasters, and above all to think of her peril as the direct menace for himself of personal privation. This indeed gave him one of those partial recoveries of equanimity that were agreeable to him—it showed him that what was still first in his mind was the loss she herself might suffer. "What if she should have to die before knowing, before seeing——?" It would have been brutal, in the early stages of her trouble, to put that question to her; but it had immediately sounded for him to his own concern, and the possibility was what most made him sorry for her. If she did "know," moreover, in the sense of her having had some—what should he think?—mystical, irresistible light, this would make the matter not better, but worse, inasmuch as her original adoption of his own curiosity had quite become the basis of her life. She had been living to see what would *be* to be seen, and it would be cruel to her to have to give up before the accomplishment of the vision. These reflections, as I say, refreshed his generosity; yet, make them as he might, he saw himself, with the lapse of the period, more and more disconcerted. It lapsed for him with a strange, steady sweep, and the oddest oddity was that it gave him, independently of the threat of much inconvenience, almost the only positive surprise his career, if career it could be called, had yet offered him. She kept the house as she had never done; he had to go to her to see her—she could meet him nowhere now, though there was scarce a corner of their loved old London in which she had not in the past, at one time or another, done so; and he found her always seated by her fire in the deep, old-fashioned chair she was less and less able to leave. He had been struck one day, after an absence exceeding his usual measure, with her suddenly looking much older to him than he had ever thought of her being; then he recognised that the suddenness was all on his side—he had just been suddenly struck. She looked older because inevitably, after so many years, she *was* old, or almost; which was of course true in still greater measure of her companion. If she was old, or almost, John Marcher assuredly was, and yet it was her showing of the lesson, not his own, that brought the truth home to him. His surprises began here; when once they had begun they multiplied; they came rather with a rush: it was as if, in the oddest way in the world, they had all been kept back, sown in a thick cluster, for the late afternoon of life, the time at which, for people in general, the unexpected has died out.

One of them was that he should have caught himself—for he *had* so done—*really* wondering if the great accident would take form now as nothing more than his being condemned to see this charming woman, this admirable friend, pass away from him. He had never so unreservedly qualified her as while confronted in thought with such a possibility; in spite of which there was small doubt for him that as an answer to his long riddle the mere effacement of even so fine a feature of his situation would be an abject anticlimax. It would represent, as connected with his past attitude, a drop of dignity under the shadow of which his existence could only become the most grotesque of failures. He had been far from holding it a failure—long as he had waited for the appearance that was to make it a success. He had waited for a quite other thing, not for such a one as that. The breath of his good faith came short, however, as he recognised how long he had waited, or how long, at least, his companion had. That she, at all events, might be recorded as having waited in vain—this affected him sharply, and all the more because of his at first having done little more than amuse himself with the idea. It grew more grave as the gravity of her condition grew, and the state of mind it produced in him, which he ended by watching, himself, as if it had been some definite disfigurement of his outer person, may pass for another of his surprises. This conjoined itself still with another, the really stupefying consciousness of a question that he would have allowed to shape itself had he dared. What did everything mean—what, that is, did *she* mean, she and her vain waiting and her probable death and the soundless admonition of it all—unless that, at this time of day, it was simply, it was overwhelmingly too late? He had never, at any stage of his queer consciousness, admitted the whisper of such a correction; he had never, till within these last few months, been so false to his conviction as not to hold that what was to come to him had time, whether *he* struck himself as having it or not. That at last, at last, he certainly hadn't it, to speak of, or had it but in the scantiest measure—such, soon enough, as things went with him, became the inference with which his old obsession had to reckon: and this it was not helped to do by the more and more confirmed appearance that the great vagueness casting the long shadow in which he had lived had, to attest itself, almost no margin left. Since it was in Time that he was to have met his fate, so it was in Time that his fate was to have acted; and as he waked up to the sense of no longer being young, which was exactly the sense of being stale, just as that, in turn, was the sense of being weak, he waked up to another matter beside. It all hung together; they were subject, he and the great vagueness, to an equal and indivisible law. When the possibilities themselves had, accordingly, turned stale, when the secret of the gods had grown faint, had perhaps even quite evaporated, that, and that only, was failure. It wouldn't have been failure to be bankrupt, dishonoured, pilloried, hanged; it was failure not to be anything. And so, in the dark valley into which his path had taken its unlooked-for twist, he wondered not a little as he groped. He didn't care what awful crash might overtake him, with what ignominy or what monstrosity he might yet be associated—since he wasn't, after all, too utterly old to suffer—if it would only be decently proportionate to the posture he had kept, all his life, in the promised presence of it. He had but one desire left—that he shouldn't have been "sold."

IV

Then it was that one afternoon, while the spring of the year was young and new, she met, all in her own way, his frankest betrayal of these alarms. He had gone in late to see her, but evening had not settled, and she was presented to him in that long, fresh light of waning April days which affects us often with a sadness sharper than the greyest hours of autumn. The week had been warm, the spring was supposed to have begun early, and May Bartram sat, for the first time in the year, without a fire, a fact that, to Marcher's sense, gave the scene of which she formed part a smooth and ultimate look, an air of knowing, in its immaculate order and its cold, meaningless cheer, that it would never see a fire again. Her own aspect—he could scarce have said why—intensified this note. Almost as white as wax, with the marks and signs in her face as numerous and as fine as if they had been etched by a needle, with soft white draperies relieved by a faded green scarf, the delicate tone of which had been consecrated by the years, she was the picture of a serene, exquisite, but impenetrable sphinx, whose head, or indeed all whose person, might have been powdered with silver. She was a sphinx, yet with her white petals and green fronds she might have been a lily too—only an artificial lily, wonderfully imitated and constantly kept, without dust or stain, though not exempt from a slight droop and a complexity of faint creases, under some clear glass bell. The perfection of household care, of high polish and finish, always reigned in her rooms, but they especially looked to Marcher at present as if everything had been wound up, tucked in, put away, so that she might sit with folded hands and with nothing more to do. She was "out of it," to his vision; her work was over; she communicated with him as across some gulf, or from some island of rest that she had already reached, and it made him feel strangely abandoned. Was it—or, rather, wasn't it—that if for so long she had been watching with him the answer to their question had swum into her ken and taken on its name, so that her occupation was verily gone? He had as much as charged her with this in saying to her, many months before, that she even then knew something she was keeping from him. It was a point he had never since ventured to press, vaguely fearing, as he did, that it might become a difference, perhaps a disagreement, between them. He had in short, in this later time, turned nervous, which was what, in all the other years, he had never been; and the oddity was that his nervousness should have waited till he had begun to doubt, should have held off so long as he was sure. There was something, it seemed to him, that the wrong word would bring down on his head, something that would so at least put an end to his suspense. But he wanted not to speak the wrong word; that would make everything ugly. He wanted the knowledge he lacked to drop on him, if drop it could, by its own august weight. If she was to forsake him it was surely for her to take leave. This was why he didn't ask her again, directly, what she knew; but it was also why, approaching the matter from another side, he said to her in the course of his visit: "What do you regard as the very worst that, at this time of day, *can* happen to me?"

He had asked her that in the past often enough; they had, with the odd, irregular rhythm of their intensities and avoidances, exchanged ideas about it and then had seen the ideas washed away by cool intervals, washed like figures traced in sea-sand. It had ever been the mark of their talk that the oldest allusions in it required but a little dismissal and reaction to come out again, sounding for the hour as new. She could thus at present meet his inquiry quite freshly and patiently. "Oh yes, I've repeatedly thought, only it always seemed to me of old that I couldn't quite make up my mind. I thought of dreadful things, between which it was difficult to choose; and so must you have done."

"Rather! I feel now as if I had scarce done anything else. I appear to myself to have spent my life in thinking of nothing *but* dreadful things. A great many of them I've at different times named to you, but there were others I couldn't name."

"They were too, too dreadful?"

"Too, too dreadful—some of them."

She looked at him a minute, and there came to him as he met it an inconsequent sense that her eyes, when one got their full clearness, were still as beautiful as they had been in youth, only beautiful with a strange, cold light—a light that somehow was a part of the effect, if it wasn't rather a part of the cause, of the pale, hard sweetness of the season and the hour. "And yet," she said at last, "there are horrors we have mentioned."

It deepened the strangeness to see her, as such a figure in such a picture, talk of "horrors," but she was to do, in a few minutes, something stranger yet—though even of this he was to take the full measure but afterwards—and the note of it was already in the air. It was, for the matter of that, one of the signs that her eyes were having again such a high flicker of their prime. He had to admit, however, what she said. "Oh yes, there were times when we did go far." He caught himself in the act, speaking as if it all were over. Well, he wished it were; and the consummation depended, for him, clearly, more and more on his companion.

But she had now a soft smile. "Oh, far——!"

It was oddly ironic. "Do you mean you're prepared to go further?"

She was frail and ancient and charming as she continued to look at him, yet it was rather as if she had lost the thread. "Do you consider that we went so far?"

"Why, I thought it the point you were just making—that we *had* looked most things in the face."

"Including each other?" She still smiled. "But you're quite right. We've had together great imaginations, often great fears; but some of them have been unspoken."

"Then the worst—we haven't faced that. I *could* face it, I believe, if I knew what you think it. I feel," he explained, "as if I had lost my power to conceive such things." And he wondered if he looked as blank as he sounded. "It's spent."

"Then why do you assume," she asked, "that mine isn't?"

"Because you've given me signs to the contrary. It isn't a question for you of conceiving, imagining, comparing. It isn't a question now of choosing." At last he came out with it. "You know something that I don't. You've showed me that before."

These last words affected her, he could see in a moment, remarkably, and she spoke with firmness. "I've shown you, my dear, nothing."

He shook his head. "You can't hide it."

"Oh, oh!" May Bartram murmured over what she couldn't hide. It was almost a smothered groan.

"You admitted it months ago, when I spoke of it to you as of something you were afraid I would find out. Your answer was that I couldn't, that I wouldn't, and I don't pretend I have. But you had something therefore in mind, and I see now that it must have been, that it still is, the possibility that, of all possibilities, has settled itself for you as the worst. This," he went on, "is why I appeal to you. I'm only afraid of ignorance now—I'm not afraid of knowledge." And then as for a while she said nothing: "What makes me sure is that I see in your face and feel here, in this air and amid these appearances, that you're out of it. You've done. You've had your experience. You leave me to my fate."

Well, she listened, motionless and white in her chair, as if she had in fact a decision to make, so that her whole manner was a virtual confession, though still with a small, fine, inner stiffness, an imperfect surrender. "It *would* be the worst," she finally let herself say. "I mean the thing that I've never said."

It hushed him a moment. "More monstrous than all the monstrosities we've named?"

"More monstrous. Isn't that what you sufficiently express," she asked, "in calling it the worst?"

Marcher thought. "Assuredly—if you mean, as I do, something that includes all the loss and all the shame that are thinkable."

"It would if it *should* happen," said May Bartram. "What we're speaking of, remember, is only my idea."

"It's your belief," Marcher returned. "That's enough for me. I feel your beliefs are right. Therefore if, having this one, you give me no more light on it, you abandon me."

"No, no!" she repeated. "I'm with you—don't you see?—still." And as if to make it more vivid to him she rose from her chair—a movement she seldom made in these days—and showed herself, all draped and all soft, in her fairness and slimness. "I haven't forsaken you."

It was really, in its effort against weakness, a generous assurance, and had the success of the impulse not, happily, been great, it would have touched him to pain more than to pleasure. But the cold charm in her eyes had spread, as she hovered before him, to all the rest of her person, so that it was, for the minute, almost like a recovery of youth. He couldn't pity her for that; he could only take her as she showed—as capable still of helping him. It was as if, at the same time, her light might at any instant go out; wherefore he must make the most of it. There passed before him with intensity the three or four things he wanted most to know; but the question that came of itself to his lips really covered the others. "Then tell me if I shall consciously suffer."

She promptly shook her head. "Never!"

It confirmed the authority he imputed to her, and it produced on him an extraordinary effect. "Well, what's better than that? Do you call that the worst?"

"You think nothing is better?" she asked.

She seemed to mean something so special that he again sharply wondered, though still with the dawn of a prospect of relief. "Why not, if one doesn't *know?*" After which, as their eyes, over his question, met in a silence, the dawn deepened and something to his purpose came, prodigiously, out of her very face. His own, as he took it in, suddenly flushed to the forehead, and he gasped with the force of a perception to which, on the instant, everything fitted. The sound of his gasp filled the air; then he became articulate. "I see—if I don't suffer!"

In her own look, however, was doubt. "You see what?"

"Why, what you mean—what you've always meant."

She again shook her head. "What I mean isn't what I've always meant. It's different."

"It's something new?"

She hesitated. "Something new. It's not what you think. I see what you think."

His divination drew breath then; only her correction might be wrong. "It isn't that I *am* a donkey?" he asked between faintness and grimness. "It isn't that it's all a mistake?"

"A mistake?" she pityingly echoed. *That* possibility, for her, he saw, would be monstrous; and if she guaranteed him the immunity from pain it would accordingly not be what she had in mind. "Oh, no," she declared; "it's nothing of that sort. You've been right."

Yet he couldn't help asking himself if she weren't, thus pressed, speaking but to save him. It seemed to him he should be most lost if his history should prove all a platitude. "Are you telling me the truth, so that I sha'n't have been a bigger idiot than I can bear to know? I *haven't* lived with a vain imagination, in the most besotted illusion? I haven't waited but to see the door shut in my face?"

She shook her head again. "However the case stands *that* isn't the truth. Whatever the reality, it *is* a reality. The door isn't shut. The door's open," said May Bartram.

"Then something's to come?"

She waited once again, always with her cold, sweet eyes on him. "It's never too late." She had, with her gliding step, diminished the distance between them, and she stood nearer to him, close to him, a minute, as if still full of the unspoken. Her movement might have been for some finer emphasis of what she was at once hesitating and deciding to say. He had been standing by the chimney-piece, fireless and sparely adorned, a small, perfect old French clock and two morsels of rosy Dresden constituting all its furniture; and her hand grasped the shelf while she kept him waiting, grasped it a little as for support and encouragement. She only kept him waiting, however; that is he only waited. It had become suddenly, from her movement and attitude, beautiful and vivid to him that she had something more to give him; her wasted face delicately shone with it, and it glittered, almost as with the white lustre of silver, in her expression. She was right, incontestably, for what he saw in her face was the truth, and strangely, without consequence, while their talk of it as dreadful was still in the air, she appeared to present it as inordinately soft. This, prompting bewilderment, made him but gape the more gratefully for her revelation, so that they continued for some minutes silent, her face shining at him, her contact imponderably pressing, and his stare all kind, but all expectant. The end, none the less, was that what he had expected failed to sound. Something else took place instead, which seemed to consist at first in the mere closing of her eyes. She gave way at the same instant to a slow, fine shudder, and though he remained staring—though he stared, in fact, but the harder—she turned off and regained her chair. It was the end of what she had been intending, but it left him thinking only of that.

"Well, you don't say——?"

She had touched in her passage a bell near the chimney and had sunk back, strangely pale. "I'm afraid I'm too ill."

"Too ill to tell me?" It sprang up sharp to him, and almost to his lips, the fear that she would die without giving him light. He checked himself in time from so expressing his question, but she answered as if she had heard the words.

"Don't you know—now?"

" 'Now'——?" She had spoken as if something that had made a difference had come up within the moment. But her maid, quickly obedient to her bell, was already with them. "I know nothing." And he was afterwards to say to himself that he must have spoken with odious impatience, such an impatience as to show that, supremely disconcerted, he washed his hands of the whole question.

"Oh!" said May Bartram.

"Are you in pain?" he asked, as the woman went to her.

"No," said May Bartram.

Her maid, who had put an arm round her as if to take her to her room, fixed on him eyes that appealingly contradicted her; in spite of which, however, he showed once more his mystification. "What then has happened?"

She was once more, with her companion's help, on her feet, and, feeling withdrawal imposed on him, he had found, blankly, his hat and gloves and had reached the door. Yet he waited for her answer. "What *was* to," she said.

V

He came back the next day, but she was then unable to see him, and as it was literally the first time this had occurred in the long stretch of their acquaintance he turned away, defeated and sore, almost angry— or feeling at least that such a break in their custom was really the beginning of the end—and wandered alone with his thoughts, especially with one of them that he was unable to keep down. She was dying, and he would lose her; she was dying, and his life would end. He stopped in the park, into which he had passed, and stared before him at his recurrent doubt. Away from her the doubt pressed again; in her presence he had believed her, but as he felt his forlornness he threw himself into the explanation that, nearest at hand, had most of a miserable warmth for him and least of a cold torment. She had deceived him to save him—to put him off with something in which he should be able to rest. What could the thing that was to happen to him be, after all, but just this thing that had begun to happen? Her dying, her death, his conse-

quent solitude—*that* was what he had figured as the beast in the jungle,
that was what had been in the lap of the gods. He had had her word
for it as he left her; for what else, on earth, could she have meant? It
wasn't a thing of a monstrous order; not a fate rare and distinguished;
not a stroke of fortune that overwhelmed and immortalised; it had only
the stamp of the common doom. But poor Marcher, at this hour, judged
the common doom sufficient. It would serve his turn, and even as the
consummation of infinite waiting he would bend his pride to accept it.
He sat down on a bench in the twilight. He hadn't been a fool. Something had *been*, as she had said, to come. Before he rose indeed it had
quite struck him that the final fact really matched with the long avenue
through which he had had to reach it. As sharing his suspense, and as
giving herself all, giving her life, to bring it to an end, she had come
with him every step of the way. He had lived by her aid, and to leave
her behind would be cruelly, damnably to miss her. What could be more
overwhelming than that?

Well, he was to know within the week, for though she kept him a
while at bay, left him restless and wretched during a series of days on
each of which he asked about her only again to have to turn away, she
ended his trial by receiving him where she had always received him. Yet
she had been brought out at some hazard into the presence of so many
of the things that were, consciously, vainly, half their past, and there
was scant service left in the gentleness of her mere desire, all too visible,
to check his obsession and wind up his long trouble. That was clearly
what she wanted; the one thing more, for her own peace, while she
could still put out her hand. He was so affected by her state that, once
seated by her chair, he was moved to let everything go; it was she herself
therefore who brought him back, took up again, before she dismissed
him, her last word of the other time. She showed how she wished to
leave their affair in order. "I'm not sure you understood. You've nothing
to wait for more. It *has* come."

Oh, how he looked at her! "Really?"

"Really."

"The thing that, as you said, *was* to?"

"The thing that we began in our youth to watch for."

Face to face with her once more he believed her; it was a claim to
which he had so abjectly little to oppose. "You mean that it has come
as a positive, definite occurrence, with a name and a date?"

"Positive. Definite. I don't know about the 'name,' but, oh, with a
date!"

He found himself again too helplessly at sea. "But come in the
night—come and passed me by?"

May Bartram had her strange, faint smile. "Oh no, it hasn't passed you by!"

"But if I haven't been aware of it, and it hasn't touched me——?"

"Ah, your not being aware of it," and she seemed to hesitate an instant to deal with this—"your not being aware of it is the strangeness *in* the strangeness. It's the wonder *of* the wonder." She spoke as with the softness almost of a sick child, yet now at last, at the end of all, with the perfect straightness of a sybil. She visibly knew that she knew, and the effect on him was of something co-ordinate, in its high character, with the law that had ruled him. It was the true voice of the law; so on her lips would the law itself have sounded. "It *has* touched you," she went on. "It has done its office. It has made you all its own."

"So utterly without my knowing it?"

"So utterly without your knowing it." His hand, as he leaned to her, was on the arm of her chair, and, dimly smiling always now, she placed her own on it. "It's enough if *I* know it."

"Oh!" he confusedly sounded, as she herself of late so often had done.

"What I long ago said is true. You'll never know now, and I think you ought to be content. You've *had* it," said May Bartram.

"But had what?"

"Why, what was to have marked you out. The proof of your law. It has acted. I'm too glad," she then bravely added, "to have been able to see what it's *not*."

He continued to attach his eyes to her, and with the sense that it was all beyond him, and that *she* was too, he would still have sharply challenged her, had he not felt it an abuse of her weakness to do more than take devoutly what she gave him, take it as hushed as to a revelation. If he did speak, it was out of the foreknowledge of his loneliness to come. "If you're glad of what it's 'not,' it might then have been worse?"

She turned her eyes away, she looked straight before her with which, after a moment: "Well, you know our fears."

He wondered. "It's something then we never feared?"

On this, slowly, she turned to him. "Did we ever dream, with all our dreams, that we should sit and talk of it thus?"

He tried for a little to make out if they had; but it was as if their dreams, numberless enough, were in solution in some thick, cold mist, in which thought lost itself. "It might have been that we couldn't talk?"

"Well"—she did her best for him—"not from this side. This, you see," she said, "is the *other* side."

"I think," poor Marcher returned, "that all sides are the same to me." Then, however, as she softly shook her head in correction: "We mightn't, as it were, have got across——?"

"To where we are—no. We're *here*"—she made her weak emphasis.

"And much good does it do us!" was her friend's frank comment.

"It does us the good it can. It does us the good that *it* isn't here. It's past. It's behind," said May Bartram. "Before——" but her voice dropped.

He had got up, not to tire her, but it was hard to combat his yearning. She after all told him nothing but that his light had failed—which he knew well enough without her. "Before——?" he blankly echoed.

"Before, you see, it was always to *come*. That kept it present."

"Oh, I don't care what comes now! Besides," Marcher added, "it seems to me I liked it better present, as you say, than I can like it absent with *your* absence."

"Oh, mine!"—and her pale hands made light of it.

"With the absence of everything." He had a dreadful sense of standing there before her for—so far as anything but this proved, this bottomless drop was concerned—the last time of their life. It rested on him with a weight he felt he could scarce bear, and this weight it apparently was that still pressed out what remained in him of speakable protest. "I believe you; but I can't begin to pretend I understand. *Nothing,* for me, is past; nothing *will* pass until I pass myself, which I pray my stars may be as soon as possible. Say, however," he added, "that I've eaten my cake, as you contend, to the last crumb—how can the thing I've never felt at all be the thing I was marked out to feel?"

She met him, perhaps, less directly, but she met him unperturbed. "You take your 'feelings' for granted. You were to suffer your fate. That was not necessarily to know it."

"How in the world—when what is such knowledge but suffering?"

She looked up at him a while, in silence. "No—you don't understand."

"I suffer," said John Marcher.

"Don't, don't!"

"How can I help at least *that?*"

"*Don't!*" May Bartram repeated.

She spoke it in a tone so special, in spite of her weakness, that he stared an instant—stared as if some light, hitherto hidden, had shimmered across his vision. Darkness again closed over it, but the gleam had already become for him an idea. "Because I haven't the right——?"

"Don't *know*—when you needn't," she mercifully urged. "You needn't—for we shouldn't."

"Shouldn't?" If he could but know what she meant!

"No—it's too much."

"Too much?" he still asked—but with a mystification that was the next moment, of a sudden, to give way. Her words, if they meant something, affected him in this light—the light also of her wasted face—as meaning *all,* and the sense of what knowledge had been for herself came over him with a rush which broke through into a question. "Is it of that, then, you're dying?"

She but watched him, gravely at first, as if to see, with this, where he was, and she might have seen something, or feared something, that moved her sympathy. "I would live for you still—if I could." Her eyes closed for a little, as if, withdrawn into herself, she were, for a last time, trying. "But I can't!" she said as she raised them again to take leave of him.

She couldn't indeed, as but too promptly and sharply appeared, and he had no vision of her after this that was anything but darkness and doom. They had parted forever in that strange talk; access to her chamber of pain, rigidly guarded, was almost wholly forbidden him; he was feeling now moreover, in the face of doctors, nurses, the two or three relatives attracted doubtless by the presumption of what she had to "leave," how few were the rights, as they were called in such cases, that he had to put forward, and how odd it might even seem that their intimacy shouldn't have given him more of them. The stupidest fourth cousin had more, even though she had been nothing in such a person's life. She had been a feature of features in *his,* for what else was it to have been so indispensable? Strange beyond saying were the ways of existence, baffling for him the anomaly of his lack, as he felt it to be, of producible claim. A woman might have been, as it were, everything to him, and it might yet present him in no connection that anyone appeared obliged to recognise. If this was the case in these closing weeks it was the case more sharply on the occasion of the last offices rendered, in the great grey London cemetery, to what had been mortal, to what had been precious, in his friend. The concourse at her grave was not numerous, but he saw himself treated as scarce more nearly concerned with it than if there had been a thousand others. He was in short from this moment face to face with the fact that he was to profit extraordinarily little by the interest May Bartram had taken in him. He couldn't quite have said what he expected, but he had somehow not expected this approach to a double privation. Not only had her interest failed him, but he seemed to feel himself unattended—and for a reason he couldn't sound—by the distinction, the dignity, the propriety, if nothing else, of the man markedly bereaved. It was as if, in the view of society, he had not *been* markedly bereaved, as if there still failed some sign or proof of it, and as if, none the less, his character could never be affirmed, nor the deficiency ever made up. There were moments, as the weeks went by, when he would have liked, by some almost aggressive act, to take his stand on the intimacy of his loss, in order that it *might* be questioned and his retort, to the relief of his spirit, so recorded; but the moments of an irritation more helpless followed fast on these, the moments during which, turning things over with a good conscience but with a bare horizon, he found himself wondering if he oughtn't to have begun, so to speak, further back.

He found himself wondering indeed at many things, and this last speculation had others to keep it company. What could he have done, after all, in her lifetime, without giving them both, as it were, away? He couldn't have made it known she was watching him, for that would have published the superstition of the Beast. This was what closed his mouth now—now that the Jungle had been threshed to vacancy and that the Beast had stolen away. It sounded too foolish and too flat; the difference for him in this particular, the extinction in his life of the element of suspense, was such in fact as to surprise him. He could scarce have said what the effect resembled; the abrupt cessation, the positive prohibition, of music perhaps, more than anything else, in some place all adjusted and all accustomed to sonoriety and to attention. If he could at any rate have conceived lifting the veil from his image at some moment of the past (what had he done, after all, if not lift it to *her?*) so to do this to-day, to talk to people at large of the jungle cleared and confide to them that he now felt it as safe, would have been not only to see them listen as to a goodwife's tale, but really to hear himself tell one. What it presently came to in truth was that poor Marcher waded through his beaten grass, where no life stirred, where no breath sounded, where no evil eye seemed to gleam from a possible lair, very much as if vaguely looking for the Beast, and still more as if missing it. He walked about in an existence that had grown strangely more spacious, and, stopping fitfully in places where the undergrowth of life struck him as closer, asked himself yearningly, wondered secretly and sorely, if it would have lurked here or there. It would have at all events *sprung;* what was at least complete was his belief in the truth itself of the assurance given him. The change from his old sense to his new was absolute and final: what was to happen *had* so absolutely and finally happened that he was as little able to know a fear for his future as to know a hope; so absent in short was any question of anything still to come. He was to live entirely with the other question, that of his unidentified past, that of his having to see his fortune impenetrably muffled and masked.

The torment of this vision became then his occupation; he couldn't perhaps have consented to live but for the possibility of guessing. She had told him, his friend, not to guess; she had forbidden him, so far as he might, to know, and she had even in a sort denied the power in him to learn: which were so many things, precisely, to deprive him of rest. It wasn't that he wanted, he argued for fairness, that anything that had happened to him should happen over again; it was only that he shouldn't, as an anticlimax, have been taken sleeping so sound as not to be able to win back by an effort of thought the lost stuff of consciousness. He declared to himself at moments that he would either win it back or have done with consciousness for ever; he made this idea his one motive, in fine, made it so much his passion that none other, to compare with it, seemed ever to have touched him. The lost stuff of consciousness became thus for him as a strayed or stolen child to an unappeasable father; he hunted it up and down very much as if he were knocking at doors and inquiring of the police. This was the spirit in which, inevitably, he set himself to travel; he started on a journey that was to be as long as he could make it; it danced before him that, as the other side of the globe couldn't possibly have less to say to him, it might, by a possibility of suggestion, have more. Before he quitted London, however, he made a pilgrimage to May Bartram's grave, took his way to it through the endless avenues of the grim suburban necropolis, sought it out in the wilderness of tombs, and, though he had come but for the renewal of the act of farewell, found himself, when he had at last stood by it, beguiled into long intensities. He stood for an hour, powerless to turn away and yet powerless to penetrate the darkness of death; fixing with his eyes her inscribed name and date, beating his forehead against the fact of the secret they kept, drawing his breath, while he waited as if, in pity of him, some sense would rise from the stones. He kneeled on the stones, however, in vain; they kept what they concealed; and if the face of the tomb did become a face for him it was because her two names were like a pair of eyes that didn't know him. He gave them a last long look, but no palest light broke.

VI

He stayed away, after this, for a year; he visited the depths of Asia, spending himself on scenes of romantic interest, of superlative sanctity; but what was present to him everywhere was that for a man who had known what *he* had known the world was vulgar and vain. The state of mind in which he had lived for so many years shone out to him, in reflection, as a light that coloured and refined, a light beside which the glow of the East was garish, cheap and thin. The terrible truth was that he had lost—with everything else—a distinction as well; the things he

saw couldn't help being common when he had become common to look
at them. He was simply now one of them himself—he was in the dust,
without a peg for the sense of difference; and there were hours when,
before the temples of gods and the sepulchres of kings, his spirit turned,
for nobleness of association, to the barely discriminated slab in the London suburb. That had become for him, and more intensely with time
and distance, his one witness of a past glory. It was all that was left to
him for proof or pride, yet the past glories of Pharaohs were nothing
to him as he thought of it. Small wonder then that he came back to it
on the morrow of his return. He was drawn there this time as irresistibly
as the other, yet with a confidence, almost, that was doubtless the effect
of the many months that had elapsed. He had lived, in spite of himself,
into his change of feeling, and in wandering over the earth had wandered, as might be said, from the circumference to the centre of his
desert. He had settled to his safety and accepted perforce his extinction;
figuring to himself, with some colour, in the likeness of certain little old
men he remembered to have seen, of whom, all meagre and wizened as
they might look, it was related that they had in their time fought twenty
duels or been loved by ten princesses. They indeed had been wondrous
for others, while he was but wondrous for himself; which, however, was
exactly the cause of his haste to renew the wonder by getting back, as
he might put it, into his own presence. That had quickened his steps
and checked his delay. If his visit was prompt it was because he had
been separated so long from the part of himself that alone he now
valued.

It is accordingly not false to say that he reached his goal with a
certain elation, and stood there again with a certain assurance. The
creature beneath the sod *knew* of his rare experience, so that, strangely
now, the place had lost for him its mere blankness of expression. It met
him in mildness—not, as before, in mockery; it wore for him the air of
conscious greeting that we find, after absence, in things that have closely
belonged to us and which seem to confess of themselves to the connection. The plot of ground, the graven tablet, the tended flowers affected
him so as belonging to him that he quite felt for the hour like a contented landlord reviewing a piece of property. Whatever had happened—well, had happened. He had not come back this time with the
vanity of that question, his former worrying, "What, *what?*" now practically so spent. Yet he would, none the less, never again so cut himself
off from the spot; he would come back to it every month, for if he did
nothing else by its aid he at least held up his head. It thus grew for him,
in the oddest way, a positive resource; he carried out his idea of periodical returns, which took their place at last among the most inveterate
of his habits. What it all amounted to, oddly enough, was that, in his

now so simplified world, this garden of death gave him the few square feet of earth on which he could still most live. It was as if, being nothing anywhere else for anyone, nothing even for himself, he were just everything here, and if not for a crowd of witnesses, or indeed for any witness but John Marcher, then by clear right of the register that he could scan like an open page. The open page was the tomb of his friend, and *there* were the facts of the past, there the truth of his life, there the backward reaches in which he could lose himself. He did this, from time to time, with such effect that he seemed to wander through the old years with his hand in the arm of a companion who was, in the most extraordinary manner, his other, his younger self; and to wander, which was more extraordinary yet, round and round a third presence—not wandering she, but stationary, still, whose eyes, turning with his revolution, never ceased to follow him, and whose seat was his point, so to speak, of orientation. Thus in short he settled to live—feeding only on the sense that he once *had* lived, and dependent on it not only for a support but for an identity.

It sufficed him, in its way, for months, and the year elapsed; it would doubtless even have carried him further but for an accident, superficially slight, which moved him, in a quite other direction, with a force beyond any of his impressions of Egypt or of India. It was a thing of the merest chance—the turn, as he afterwards felt, of a hair, though he was indeed to live to believe that if light hadn't come to him in this particular fashion it would still have come in another. He was to live to believe this, I say, though he was not to live, I may not less definitely mention, to do much else. We allow him at any rate the benefit of the conviction, struggling up for him at the end, that, whatever might have happened or not happened, he would have come round of himself to the light. The incident of an autumn day had put the match to the train laid from of old by his misery. With the light before him he knew that even of late his ache had only been smothered. It was strangely drugged, but it throbbed; at the touch it began to bleed. And the touch, in the event, was the face of a fellow-mortal. This face, one grey afternoon when the leaves were thick in the alleys, looked into Marcher's own, at the cemetery, with an expression like the cut of a blade. He felt it, that is, so deep down that he winced at the steady thrust. The person who so mutely assaulted him was a figure he had noticed, on reaching his own goal, absorbed by a grave a short distance away, a grave apparently fresh, so that the emotion of the visitor would probably match it for frankness. This fact alone forbade further attention, though during the time he stayed he remained vaguely conscious of his neighbour, a middle-aged man apparently, in mourning, whose bowed back, among the clustered monuments and mortuary yews, was constantly presented.

Marcher's theory that these were elements in contact with which he himself revived, had suffered, on this occasion, it may be granted, a sensible though inscrutable check. The autumn day was dire for him as none had recently been, and he rested with a heaviness he had not yet known on the low stone table that bore May Bartram's name. He rested without power to move, as if some spring in him, some spell vouchsafed, had suddenly been broken forever. If he could have done that moment as he wanted he would simply have stretched himself on the slab that was ready to take him, treating it as a place prepared to receive his last sleep. What in all the wide world had he now to keep awake for? He stared before him with the question, and it was then that, as one of the cemetery walks passed near him, he caught the shock of the face.

His neighbour at the other grave had withdrawn, as he himself, with force in him to move, would have done by now, and was advancing along the path on his way to one of the gates. This brought him near, and his pace was slow, so that—and all the more as there was a kind of hunger in his look—the two men were for a minute directly confronted. Marcher felt him on the spot as one of the deeply stricken—a perception so sharp that nothing else in the picture lived for it, neither his dress, his age, nor his presumable character and class; nothing lived but the deep ravage of the features that he showed. He *showed* them— that was the point; he was moved, as he passed, by some impulse that was either a signal for sympathy or, more possibly, a challenge to another sorrow. He might already have been aware of our friend, might, at some previous hour, have noticed in him the smooth habit of the scene, with which the state of his own senses so scantly consorted, and might thereby have been stirred as by a kind of overt discord. What Marcher was at all events conscious of was, in the first place, that the imaged of scarred passion presented to him was conscious too—of something that profaned the air; and, in the second, that, roused, startled, shocked, he was yet the next moment looking after it, as it went, with envy. The most extraordinary thing that had happened to him— though he had given that name to other matters as well—took place, after his immediate vague stare, as a consequence of this impression. The stranger passed, but the raw glare of his grief remained, making our friend wonder in pity what wrong, what wound it expressed, what injury not to be healed. What had the man *had* to make him, by the loss of it, so bleed and yet live?

Something—and this reached him with a pang—that *he*, John Marcher, hadn't; the proof of which was precisely John Marcher's arid end. No passion had ever touched him, for this was what passion meant; he had survived and maundered and pined, but where had been *his* deep

ravage? The extraordinary thing we speak of was the sudden rush of
the result of this question. The sight that had just met his eyes named
to him, as in letters of quick flame, something he had utterly, insanely
missed, and what he had missed; made these things a train of fire, made
them mark themselves in an anguish of inward throbs. He had seen
outside of his life, not learned it within, the way a woman was mourned
when she had been loved for herself; such was the force of his conviction
of the meaning of the stranger's face, which still flared for him like a
smoky torch. It had not come to him, the knowledge, on the wings of
experience; it had brushed him, jostled him, upset him, with the disrespect of chance, the insolence of an accident. Now that the illumination
had begun, however, it blazed to the zenith, and what he presently stood
there gazing at was the sounded void of his life. He gazed, he drew
breath, in pain; he turned in his dismay, and, turning, he had before
him in sharper incision than ever the open page of his story. The name
on the table smote him as the passage of his neighbour had done, and
what it said to him, full in the face, was that *she* was what he had
missed. This was the awful thought, the answer to all the past, the vision
at the dread clearness of which he turned as cold as the stone beneath
him. Everything fell together, confessed, explained, overwhelmed; leaving him most of all stupefied at the blindness he had cherished. The fate
he had been marked for he had met with a vengeance—he had emptied
the cup to the lees; he had been the man of his time, *the* man, to whom
nothing on earth was to have happened. That was the rare stroke—that
was his visitation. So he saw it, as we say, in pale horror, while the
pieces fitted and fitted. So *she* had seen it, while he didn't, and so she
served at this hour to drive the truth home. It was the truth, vivid and
monstrous, that all the while he had waited the wait was itself his portion. This the companion of his vigil had at a given moment perceived,
and she had then offered him the chance to baffle his doom. One's
doom, however, was never baffled, and on the day she had told him
that his own had come down she had seen him but stupidly stare at the
escape she offered him.

The escape would have been to love her; then, *then* he would have
lived. *She* had lived—who could say now with what passion?—since
she had loved him for himself; whereas he had never thought of her (ah,
how it hugely glared at him!) but in the chill of his egotism and the
light of her use. Her spoken words came back to him, and the chain
stretched and stretched. The beast had lurked indeed, and the beast, at
its hour, had sprung; it had sprung in that twilight of the cold April
when, pale, ill, wasted, but all beautiful, and perhaps even then recov-
erable, she had risen from her chair to stand before him and let him

imaginably guess. It had sprung as he didn't guess; it had sprung as she hopelessly turned from him, and the mark, by the time he left her, had fallen where it *was* to fall. He had justified his fear and achieved his fate; he had failed, with the last exactitude, of all he was to fail of; and a moan now rose to his lips as he remembered she had prayed he mightn't know. This horror of waking—*this* was knowledge, knowledge under the breath of which the very tears in his eyes seemed to freeze. Through them, none the less, he tried to fix it and hold it; he kept it there before him so that he might feel the pain. That at least, belated and bitter, had something of the taste of life. But the bitterness suddenly sickened him, and it was as if, horribly, he saw, in the truth, in the cruelty of his image, what had been appointed and done. He saw the Jungle of his life and saw the lurking Beast; then, while he looked, perceived it, as by a stir of the air, rise, huge and hideous, for the leap that was to settle him. His eyes darkened—it was close; and, instinctively turning, in his hallucination, to avoid it, he flung himself, on his face, on the tomb.

STEPHEN CRANE

The Blue Hotel

"The Blue Hotel," first published in *Collier's Weekly* in 1896, is one of the most celebrated stories in American literature, one that has been the subject of a wide array of interpretations. It is based on Crane's experiences on a journalistic trip through the West, particularly on his stop in Lincoln, Nebraska, where he saw a blue hotel. In the century since its publication, the story has been regarded as representative of a number of literary movements, most often as a naturalistic story depicting inexorable deterministic forces that impel the death of the Swede. Other readers have seen "The Blue Hotel" as a realistic story focused on the issue of moral responsibility, the subject of the conclusion. And still others have put the emphasis on the impressionistic growth of insight on the part of the Easterner, who comes to a realization of the role he has played in the tragic events. Part of the richness of the story is that it can be read from all of these perspectives, and it has captivated readers and fueled international critical controversy, testimony to the power and significance of Crane's artistic legacy.

*   *   *

I

The Palace Hotel at Fort Romper was painted a light blue, a shade that is on the legs of a kind of heron, causing the bird to declare its position against any background. The Palace Hotel, then, was always screaming and howling in a way that made the dazzling winter landscape of Nebraska seem only a gray swampish hush. It stood alone on the prairie, and when the snow was falling the town two hundred yards away was not visible. But when the traveller alighted at the railway station he was obliged to pass the Palace Hotel before he could come upon the company of low clapboard houses which composed Fort Romper, and it was not to be thought that any traveller could pass the Palace Hotel without looking at it. Pat Scully, the proprietor, had proved himself a master of strategy when he chose his paints. It is true that on clear days, when the great trans-continental expresses, long lines of swaying Pullmans, swept through Fort Romper, passengers were overcome at the sight, and the cult that knows the brown-reds and the subdivisions of the dark greens of the East expressed shame, pity, horror, in a laugh. But to the citizens of this prairie town and to the people who would naturally stop there, Pat Scully had performed a feat. With this opulence and splendor, these creeds, classes, egotisms, that streamed through Romper on the rails day after day, they had no color in common.

As if the displayed delights of such a blue hotel were not sufficiently enticing, it was Scully's habit to go every morning and evening to meet the leisurely trains that stopped at Romper and work his seductions upon any man that he might see wavering, gripsack in hand.

One morning, when a snow-crusted engine dragged its long string of freight cars and its one passenger coach to the station, Scully performed the marvel of catching three men. One was a shaky and quick-eyed Swede, with a great shining cheap valise; one was a tall bronzed cowboy, who was on his way to a ranch near the Dakota line; one was a little silent man from the East, who didn't look it, and didn't announce it. Scully practically made them prisoners. He was so nimble and merry and kindly that each probably felt it would be the height of brutality to try to escape. They trudged off over the creaking board sidewalks in the wake of the eager little Irishman. He wore a heavy fur cap squeezed tightly down on his head. It caused his two red ears to stick out stiffly, as if they were made of tin.

At last, Scully, elaborately, with boisterous hospitality, conducted them through the portals of the blue hotel. The room which they entered was small. It seemed to be merely a proper temple for an enormous stove, which, in the centre, was humming with godlike violence. At various points on its surface the iron had become luminous and glowed

yellow from the heat. Beside the stove Scully's son Johnnie was playing
High-Five with an old farmer who had whiskers both gray and sandy.
They were quarrelling. Frequently the old farmer turned his face towards a box of sawdust—colored brown from tobacco juice—that was
behind the stove, and spat with an air of great impatience and irritation.
With a loud flourish of words Scully destroyed the game of cards, and
bustled his son up-stairs with part of the baggage of the new guests. He
himself conducted them to three basins of the coldest water in the world.
The cowboy and the Easterner burnished themselves fiery-red with this
water, until it seemed to be some kind of a metal polish. The Swede,
however, merely dipped his fingers gingerly and with trepidation. It was
notable that throughout this series of small ceremonies the three trav-
ellers were made to feel that Scully was very benevolent. He was conferring great favors upon them. He handed the towel from one to the
other with an air of philanthropic impulse.

Afterwards they went to the first room, and, sitting about the stove,
listened to Scully's officious clamor at his daughters, who were preparing the mid-day meal. They reflected in the silence of experienced men
who tread carefully amid new people. Nevertheless, the old farmer, stationary, invincible in his chair near the warmest part of the stove, turned
his face from the sawdust box frequently and addressed a glowing commonplace to the strangers. Usually he was answered in short but adequate sentences by either the cowboy or the Easterner. The Swede said
nothing. He seemed to be occupied in making furtive estimates of each
man in the room. One might have thought that he had the sense of silly
suspicion which comes to guilt. He resembled a badly frightened man.

Later, at dinner, he spoke a little, addressing his conversation entirely
to Scully. He volunteered that he had come from New York, where for
ten years he had worked as a tailor. These facts seemed to strike Scully
as fascinating, and afterwards he volunteered that he had lived at
Romper for fourteen years. The Swede asked about the crops and the
price of labor. He seemed barely to listen to Scully's extended replies.
His eyes continued to rove from man to man.

Finally, with a laugh and a wink, he said that some of these Western
communities were very dangerous; and after his statement he straightened his legs under the table, tilted his head, and laughed again, loudly.
It was plain that the demonstration had no meaning to the others. They
looked at him wondering and in silence.

II

As the men trooped heavily back into the front-room, the two little
windows presented views of a turmoiling sea of snow. The huge arms

of the wind were making attempts—mighty, circular, futile—to embrace the flakes as they sped. A gate-post like a still man with a blanched face stood aghast amid this profligate fury. In a hearty voice Scully announced the presence of a blizzard. The guests of the blue hotel, lighting their pipes, assented with grunts of lazy masculine contentment. No island of the sea could be exempt in the degree of this little room with its humming stove. Johnnie, son of Scully, in a tone which defined his opinion of his ability as a card-player, challenged the old farmer of both gray and sandy whiskers to a game of High-Five. The farmer agreed with a contemptuous and bitter scoff. They sat close to the stove, and squared their knees under a wide board. The cowboy and the Easterner watched the game with interest. The Swede remained near the window, aloof, but with a countenance that showed signs of an inexplicable excitement.

The play of Johnnie and the gray-beard was suddenly ended by another quarrel. The old man arose while casting a look of heated scorn at his adversary. He slowly buttoned his coat, and then stalked with fabulous dignity from the room. In the discreet silence of all other men the Swede laughed. His laughter rang somehow childish. Men by this time had begun to look at him askance, as if they wished to inquire what ailed him.

A new game was formed jocosely. The cowboy volunteered to become the partner of Johnnie, and they all then turned to ask the Swede to throw in his lot with the little Easterner. He asked some questions about the game, and, learning that it wore many names, and that he had played it when it was under an alias, he accepted the invitation. He strode towards the men nervously, as if he expected to be assaulted. Finally, seated, he gazed from face to face and laughed shrilly. This laugh was so strange that the Easterner looked up quickly, the cowboy sat intent and with his mouth open, and Johnnie paused, holding the cards with still fingers.

Afterwards there was a short silence. Then Johnnie said, "Well, let's get at it. Come on now!" They pulled their chairs forward until their knees were bunched under the board. They began to play, and their interest in the game caused the others to forget the manner of the Swede.

The cowboy was a board-whacker. Each time that he held superior cards he whanged them, one by one, with exceeding force, down upon the improvised table, and took the tricks with a glowing air of prowess and pride that sent thrills of indignation into the hearts of his opponents. A game with a board-whacker in it is sure to become intense. The countenances of the Easterner and the Swede were miserable whenever the cowboy thundered down his aces and kings, while Johnnie, his eyes gleaming with joy, chuckled and chuckled.

Because of the absorbing play none considered the strange ways of
the Swede. They paid strict heed to the game. Finally, during a lull
caused by a new deal, the Swede suddenly addressed Johnnie: "I suppose
there have been a good many men killed in this room." The jaws of the
others dropped and they looked at him.

"What in hell are you talking about?" said Johnnie.

The Swede laughed again his blatant laugh, full of a kind of false
courage and defiance. "Oh, you know what I mean all right," he
answered.

"I'm a liar if I do!" Johnnie protested. The card was halted, and the
men stared at the Swede. Johnnie evidently felt that as the son of the
proprietor he should make a direct inquiry. "Now, what might you
be drivin' at, mister?" he asked. The Swede winked at him. It was a
wink full of cunning. His fingers shook on the edge of the board. "Oh,
maybe you think I have been to nowheres. Maybe you think I'm a
tenderfoot?"

"I don't know nothin' about you," answered Johnnie, "and I don't
give a damn where you've been. All I got to say is that I don't know
what you're driving at. There hain't never been nobody killed in this
room."

The cowboy, who had been steadily gazing at the Swede, then spoke:
"What's wrong with you, mister?"

Apparently it seemed to the Swede that he was formidably menaced.
He shivered and turned white near the corners of his mouth. He sent
an appealing glance in the direction of the little Easterner. During these
moments he did not forget to wear his air of advanced pot-valor. "They
say they don't know what I mean," he remarked mockingly to the
Easterner.

The latter answered after prolonged and cautious reflection. "I don't
understand you," he said, impassively.

The Swede made a movement then which announced that he thought
he had encountered treachery from the only quarter where he had
expected sympathy, if not help. "Oh, I see you are all against me.
I see—"

The cowboy was in a state of deep stupefaction. "Say," he cried, as
he tumbled the deck violently down upon the board "—say, what are
you gittin' at, hey?"

The Swede sprang up with the celerity of a man escaping from a
snake on the floor. "I don't want to fight!" he shouted. "I don't want
to fight!"

The cowboy stretched his long legs indolently and deliberately. His
hands were in his pockets. He spat into the sawdust box. "Well, who
the hell thought you did?" he inquired.

The Swede backed rapidly towards a corner of the room. His hands were out protectingly in front of his chest, but he was making an obvious struggle to control his fright. "Gentlemen," he quavered, "I suppose I am going to be killed before I can leave this house! I suppose I am going to be killed before I can leave this house!" In his eyes was the dying-swan look. Through the windows could be seen the snow turning blue in the shadow of dusk. The wind tore at the house and some loose thing beat regularly against the clap-boards like a spirit tapping.

A door opened, and Scully himself entered. He paused in surprise as he noted the tragic attitude of the Swede. Then he said, "What's the matter here?"

The Swede answered him swiftly and eagerly: "These men are going to kill me."

"Kill you!" ejaculated Scully. "Kill you! What are you talkin'?"

The Swede made the gesture of a martyr.

Scully wheeled sternly upon his son. "What is this, Johnnie?"

The lad had grown sullen. "Damned if I know," he answered. "I can't make no sense to it." He began to shuffle the cards, fluttering them together with an angry snap. "He says a good many men have been killed in this room, or something like that. And he says he's goin' to be killed here too. I don't knows what ails him. He's crazy, I shouldn't wonder."

Scully then looked for explanation to the cowboy, but the cowboy simply shrugged his shoulders.

"Kill you?" said Scully again to the Swede. "Kill you? Man, you're off your nut."

"Oh, I know," burst out the Swede. "I know what will happen. Yes, I'm crazy—yes. Yes, of course, I'm crazy—yes. But I know one thing—" There was a sort of sweat of misery and terror upon his face. "I know I won't get out of here alive."

The cowboy drew a deep breath, as if his mind was passing into the last stages of dissolution. "Well, I'm dog-goned," he whispered to himself.

Scully wheeled suddenly and faced his son. "You've been troublin' this man!"

Johnnie's voice was loud with its burden of grievance. "Why, good Gawd, I ain't done nothin' to 'im."

The Swede broke in. "Gentlemen, do not disturb yourselves. I will leave this house. I will go away because"—he accused them dramatically with his glance—"because I do not want to be killed."

Scully was furious with his son. "Will you tell me what is the matter, you young divil? What's the matter, anyhow? Speak out!"

"Blame it!" cried Johnnie in despair, "don't I tell you I don't know.

He—he says we want to kill him, and that's all I know. I can't tell what ails him."

The Swede continued to repeat: "Never mind, Mr. Scully; never mind. I will leave this house. I will go away, because I do not wish to be killed. Yes, of course, I am crazy—yes. But I know one thing! I will go away. I will leave this house. Never mind, Mr. Scully; never mind. I will go away."

"You will not go 'way," said Scully. "You will not go 'way until I hear the reason of this business. If anybody has troubled you I will take care of him. This is my house. You are under my roof, and I will not allow any peaceable man to be troubled here." He cast a terrible eye upon Johnnie, the cowboy, and the Easterner.

"Never mind, Mr. Scully; never mind. I will go away. I do not wish to be killed." The Swede moved towards the door, which opened upon the stairs. It was evidently his intention to go at once for his baggage.

"No, no," shouted Scully peremptorily; but the white-faced man slid by him and disappeared. "Now," said Scully severely, "what does this mane?"

Johnnie and the cowboy cried together: "Why, we didn't do nothin' to 'im!"

Scully's eyes were cold. "No," he said, "you didn't?"

Johnnie swore a deep oath. "Why, this is the wildest loon I ever see. We didn't do nothin' at all. We were jest sittin' here playin' cards, and he—"

The father suddenly spoke to the Easterner. "Mr. Blanc," he asked, "what has these boys been doin'?"

The Easterner reflected again. "I didn't see anything wrong at all," he said at last, slowly.

Scully began to howl. "But what does it mane?" He stared ferociously at his son. "I have a mind to lather you for this, me boy."

Johnnie was frantic. "Well, what have I done?" he bawled at his father.

III

"I think you are tongue-tied," said Scully finally to his son, the cowboy, and the Easterner; and at the end of this scornful sentence he left the room.

Up-stairs the Swede was swiftly fastening the straps of his great valise. Once his back happened to be half turned towards the door, and, hearing a noise there, he wheeled and sprang up, uttering a loud cry. Scully's wrinkled visage showed grimly in the light of the small lamp he carried. This yellow effulgence, streaming upward, colored only his prominent features, and left his eyes, for instance, in mysterious shadow. He resembled a murderer.

"Man! man!" he exclaimed, "have you gone daffy?"

"Oh, no! Oh, no!" rejoined the other. "There are people in this world who know pretty nearly as much as you do—understand?"

For a moment they stood gazing at each other. Upon the Swede's deathly pale cheeks were two spots brightly crimson and sharply edged, as if they had been carefully painted. Scully placed the light on the table and sat himself on the edge of the bed. He spoke ruminatively. "By cracky, I never heard of such a thing in my life. It's a complete muddle. I can't, for the soul of me, think how you ever got this idea into your head." Presently he lifted his eyes and asked: "And did you sure think they were going to kill you?"

The Swede scanned the old man as if he wished to see into his mind. "I did," he said at last. He obviously suspected that this answer might precipitate an outbreak. As he pulled on a strap his whole arm shook, the elbow wavering like a bit of paper.

Scully banged his hand impressively on the foot-board of the bed. "Why, man, we're goin' to have a line of ilictric street-cars in this town next spring."

" 'A line of electric street-cars,' " repeated the Swede, stupidly.

"And," said Scully, "there's a new railroad goin' to be built down from Broken Arm to here. Not to mintion the four churches and the smashin' big brick school-house. Then there's the big factory, too. Why, in two years Romper'll be a met-tro-*pol*-is."

Having finished the preparation of his baggage, the Swede straightened himself. "Mr. Scully," he said, with sudden hardihood, "how much do I owe you?"

"You don't owe me anythin'," said the old man, angrily.

"Yes, I do," retorted the Swede. He took seventy-five cents from his pocket and tendered it to Scully; but the latter snapped his fingers in disdainful refusal. However, it happened that they both stood gazing in a strange fashion at three silver pieces on the Swede's open palm.

"I'll not take your money," said Scully at last. "Not after what's been goin' on here." Then a plan seemed to strike him. "Here," he cried, picking up his lamp and moving towards the door. "Here! Come with me a minute."

"No," said the Swede, in overwhelming alarm.

"Yes," urged the old man. "Come on! I want you to come and see a picter—just across the hall—in my room."

The Swede must have concluded that his hour was come. His jaw dropped and his teeth showed like a dead man's. He ultimately followed Scully across the corridor, but he had the step of one hung in chains.

Scully flashed the light high on the wall of his own chamber. There was revealed a ridiculous photograph of a little girl. She was leaning against a balustrade of gorgeous decoration, and the formidable bang to her hair was prominent. The figure was as graceful as an upright sled-stake, and, withal, it was of the hue of lead. "There," said Scully, tenderly, "that's the picter of my little girl that died. Her name was Carrie. She had the purtiest hair you ever saw! I was that fond of her, she—"

Turning then, he saw that the Swede was not contemplating the picture at all, but, instead, was keeping keen watch on the gloom in the rear.

"Look, man!" cried Scully, heartily. "That's the picter of my little gal that died. Her name was Carrie. And then here's the picter of my oldest boy, Michael. He's a lawyer in Lincoln, an' doin' well. I gave that boy a grand eddycation, and I'm glad for it now. He's a fine boy. Look at 'im now. Ain't he bold as blazes, him there in Lincoln, an honored an' respicted gintleman. An honored an' respicted gintleman," concluded Scully with a flourish. And, so saying, he smote the Swede jovially on the back.

The Swede faintly smiled.

"Now," said the old man, "there's only one more thing." He dropped suddenly to the floor and thrust his head beneath the bed. The Swede could hear his muffled voice. "I'd keep it under me piller if it wasn't for that boy Johnnie. Then there's the old woman—Where is it now? I never put it twice in the same place. Ah, now come out with you!"

Presently he backed clumsily from under the bed, dragging with him an old coat rolled into a bundle. "I've fetched him," he muttered. Kneeling on the floor, he unrolled the coat and extracted from its heart a large yellow-brown whiskey bottle.

His first manœuvre was to hold the bottle up to the light. Reassured, apparently, that nobody had been tampering with it, he thrust it with a generous movement towards the Swede.

The weak-kneed Swede was about to eagerly clutch this element of strength, but he suddenly jerked his hand away and cast a look of horror upon Scully.

"Drink," said the old man affectionately. He had risen to his feet, and now stood facing the Swede.

There was a silence. Then again Scully said: "Drink!"

The Swede laughed wildly. He grabbed the bottle, put it to his mouth, and as his lips curled absurdly around the opening and his throat worked, he kept his glance, burning with hatred, upon the old man's face.

IV

After the departure of Scully the three men, with the card-board still upon their knees, preserved for a long time an astounded silence. Then Johnnie said: "That's the dod-dangest Swede I ever see."

"He ain't no Swede," said the cowboy, scornfully.

"Well, what is he then?" cried Johnnie. "What is he then?"

"It's my opinion," replied the cowboy deliberately, "he's some kind of a Dutchman." It was a venerable custom of the country to entitle as Swedes all light-haired men who spoke with a heavy tongue. In consequence the idea of the cowboy was not without its daring. "Yes, sir," he repeated. "It's my opinion this feller is some kind of a Dutchman."

"Well, he says he's a Swede, anyhow," muttered Johnnie, sulkily. He turned to the Easterner: "What do you think, Mr. Blanc?"

"Oh, I don't know," replied the Easterner.

"Well, what do you think makes him act that way?" asked the cowboy.

"Why, he's frightened." The Easterner knocked his pipe against a rim of the stove. "He's clear frightened out of his boots."

"What at?" cried Johnnie and cowboy together.

The Easterner reflected over his answer.

"What at?" cried the others again.

"Oh, I don't know, but it seems to me this man has been read-ing dime-novels, and he thinks he's right out in the middle of it—the shootin' and stabbin' and all."

"But," said the cowboy, deeply scandalized, "this ain't Wyoming, ner none of them places. This is Nebrasker."

"Yes," added Johnnie, "an' why don't he wait till he gits *out West?*"

The travelled Easterner laughed. "It isn't different there even—not in these days. But he thinks he's right in the middle of hell."

Johnnie and the cowboy mused long.

"It's awful funny," remarked Johnnie at last.

"Yes," said the cowboy. "This is a queer game. I hope we don't git snowed in, because then we'd have to stand this here man bein' around with us all the time. That wouldn't be no good."

"I wish pop would throw him out," said Johnnie.

Presently they heard a loud stamping on the stairs, accompanied by ringing jokes in the voice of old Scully, and laughter, evidently from the Swede. The men around the stove stared vacantly at each other. "Gosh!" said the cowboy. The door flew open, and old Scully, flushed and anecdotal, came into the room. He was jabbering at the Swede, who followed him, laughing bravely. It was the entry of two roisterers from a banquet-hall.

"Come now," said Scully sharply to the three seated men, "move up and give us a chance at the stove." The cowboy and the Easterner obediently sidled their chairs to make room for the new-comers. Johnnie, however, simply arranged himself in a more indolent attitude, and then remained motionless.

"Come! Git over, there," said Scully.

"Plenty of room on the other side of the stove," said Johnnie.

"Do you think we want to sit in the draught?" roared the father.

But the Swede here interposed with a grandeur of confidence. "No, no. Let the boy sit where he likes," he cried in a bullying voice to the father.

"All right! All right!" said Scully, deferentially. The cowboy and the Easterner exchanged glances of wonder.

The five chairs were formed in a crescent about one side of the stove. The Swede began to talk; he talked arrogantly, profanely, angrily. Johnnie, the cowboy, and the Easterner maintained a morose silence, while old Scully appeared to be receptive and eager, breaking in constantly with sympathetic ejaculations.

Finally the Swede announced that he was thirsty. He moved in his chair, and said that he would go for a drink of water.

"I'll git it for you," cried Scully at once.

"No," said the Swede, contemptuously. "I'll get it for myself." He arose and stalked with the air of an owner off into the executive parts of the hotel.

As soon as the Swede was out of hearing Scully sprang to his feet and whispered intensely to the others: "Up-stairs he thought I was tryin' to poison 'im."

"Say," said Johnnie, "this makes me sick. Why don't you throw 'im out in the snow?"

"Why, he's all right now," declared Scully. "It was only that he was from the East, and he thought this was a tough place. That's all. He's all right now."

The cowboy looked with admiration upon the Easterner. "You were straight," he said. "You were on to that there Dutchman."

"Well," said Johnnie to his father, "he may be all right now, but I don't see it. Other time he was scared, but now he's too fresh."

Scully's speech was always a combination of Irish brogue and idiom, Western twang and idiom, and scraps of curiously formal diction taken from the story-books and newspapers. He now hurled a strange mass of language at the head of his son. "What do I keep? What do I keep? What do I keep?" he demanded, in a voice of thunder. He slapped his knee impressively, to indicate that he himself was going to make reply, and that all should heed. "I keep a hotel," he shouted. "A hotel, do you mind? A guest under my roof has sacred privileges. He is to be intimidated by none. Not one word shall he hear that would prijudice him in favor of goin' away. I'll not have it. There's no place in this here town where they can say they iver took in a guest of mine because he was afraid to stay here." He wheeled suddenly upon the cowboy and the Easterner. "Am I right?"

"Yes, Mr. Scully," said the cowboy, "I think you're right."

"Yes, Mr. Scully," said the Easterner, "I think you're right."

V

At six-o'clock supper, the Swede fizzed like a fire-wheel. He sometimes seemed on the point of bursting into riotous song, and in all his madness he was encouraged by old Scully. The Easterner was incased in reserve; the cowboy sat in wide-mouthed amazement, forgetting to eat, while Johnnie wrathily demolished great plates of food. The daughters of the house, when they were obliged to replenish the biscuits, approached as warily as Indians, and, having succeeded in their purpose, fled with ill-concealed trepidation. The Swede domineered the whole feast, and he gave it the appearance of a cruel bacchanal. He seemed to have grown suddenly taller; he gazed, brutally disdainful, into every face. His voice rang through the room. Once when he jabbed out harpoon-fashion with his fork to pinion a biscuit, the weapon nearly impaled the hand of the Easterner which had been stretched quietly out for the same biscuit.

After supper, as the men filed towards the other room, the Swede smote Scully ruthlessly on the shoulder. "Well, old boy, that was a good, square meal." Johnnie looked hopefully at his father; he knew that shoulder was tender from an old fall; and, indeed, it appeared for a moment as if Scully was going to flame out over the matter, but in the end he smiled a sickly smile and remained silent. The others understood from his manner that he was admitting his responsibility for the Swede's new view-point.

Johnnie, however, addressed his parent in an aside. "Why don't you license somebody to kick you down-stairs?" Scully scowled darkly by way of reply.

When they were gathered about the stove, the Swede insisted on another game of High-Five. Scully gently deprecated the plan at first, but the Swede turned a wolfish glare upon him. The old man subsided, and the Swede canvassed the others. In his tone there was always a great threat. The cowboy and the Easterner both remarked indifferently that they would play. Scully said that he would presently have to go to meet the 6.58 train, and so the Swede turned menacingly upon Johnnie. For a moment their glances crossed like blades, and then Johnnie smiled and said, "Yes, I'll play."

They formed a square, with the little board on their knees. The Easterner and the Swede were again partners. As the play went on, it was noticeable that the cowboy was not board-whacking as usual. Meanwhile, Scully, near the lamp, had put on his spectacles and, with an appearance curiously like an old priest, was reading a newspaper. In time he went out to meet the 6.58 train, and, despite his precautions, a gust of polar wind whirled into the room as he opened the door. Besides scattering the cards, it chilled the players to the marrow. The Swede cursed frightfully. When Scully returned, his entrance disturbed a cosey and friendly scene. The Swede again cursed. But presently they were once more intent, their heads bent forward and their hands moving swiftly. The Swede had adopted the fashion of board-whacking.

Scully took up his paper and for a long time remained immersed in matters which were extraordinarily remote from him. The lamp burned badly, and once he stopped to adjust the wick. The newspaper, as he turned from page to page, rustled with a slow and comfortable sound. Then suddenly he heard three terrible words: "You are cheatin'!"

Such scenes often prove that there can be little of dramatic import in environment. Any room can present a tragic front; any room can be comic. This little den was now hideous as a torture-chamber. The new faces of the men themselves had changed it upon the instant. The Swede held a huge fist in front of Johnnie's face, while the latter looked steadily over it into the blazing orbs of his accuser. The Easterner had grown pallid; the cowboy's jaw had dropped in that expression of bovine amazement which was one of his important mannerisms. After the three words, the first sound in the room was made by Scully's paper as it floated forgotten to his feet. His spectacles had also fallen from his nose, but by a clutch he had saved them in air. His hand, grasping the spectacles, now remained poised awkwardly and near his shoulder. He stared at the card-players.

Probably the silence was while a second elapsed. Then, if the floor had been suddenly twitched out from under the men they could not have moved quicker. The five had projected themselves headlong towards a common point. It happened that Johnnie, in rising to hurl himself upon the Swede, had stumbled slightly because of his curiously instinctive care for the cards and the board. The loss of the moment allowed time for the arrival of Scully, and also allowed the cowboy time to give the Swede a great push which sent him staggering back. The men found tongue together, and hoarse shouts of rage, appeal, or fear burst from every throat. The cowboy pushed and jostled feverishly at the Swede, and the Easterner and Scully clung wildly to Johnnie; but, through the smoky air, above the swaying bodies of the peace-compellers, the eyes of the two warriors ever sought each other in glances of challenge that were at once hot and steely.

Of course the board had been overturned, and now the whole company of cards was scattered over the floor, where the boots of the men trampled the fat and painted kings and queens as they gazed with their silly eyes at the war that was waging above them.

Scully's voice was dominating the yells. "Stop now? Stop, I say! Stop, now——"

Johnnie, as he struggled to burst through the rank formed by Scully and the Easterner, was crying, "Well, he says I cheated! He says I cheated! I won't allow no man to say I cheated! If he says I cheated, he's a —— ——!"

The cowboy was telling the Swede, "Quit, now! Quit, d'ye hear——"

The screams of the Swede never ceased: "He did cheat! I saw him! I saw him——"

As for the Easterner, he was importuning in a voice that was not heeded: "Wait a moment, can't you? Oh, wait a moment. What's the good of a fight over a game of cards? Wait a moment——"

In this tumult no complete sentences were clear. "Cheat"—"Quit"—"He says"—these fragments pierced the uproar and rang out sharply. It was remarkable that, whereas Scully undoubtedly made the most noise, he was the least heard of any of the riotous band.

Then suddenly there was a great cessation. It was as if each man had paused for breath; and although the room was still lighted with the anger of men, it could be seen that there was no danger of immediate conflict, and at once Johnnie, shouldering his way forward, almost succeeded in confronting the Swede. "What did you say I cheated for? What did you say I cheated for? I don't cheat, and I won't let no man say I do!"

The Swede said, "I saw you! I saw you!"

"Well," cried Johnnie, "I'll fight any man what says I cheat!"

"No, you won't," said the cowboy. "Not here."

"Ah, be still, can't you?" said Scully, coming between them.

The quiet was sufficient to allow the Easterner's voice to be heard. He was repeating, "Oh, wait a moment, can't you? What's the good of a fight over a game of cards? Wait a moment!"

Johnnie, his red face appearing above his father's shoulder, hailed the Swede again. "Did you say I cheated?"

The Swede showed his teeth. "Yes."

"Then," said Johnnie, "we must fight."

"Yes, fight," roared the Swede. He was like a demoniac. "Yes fight!

I'll show you what kind of a man I am! I'll show you who you want to fight! Maybe you think I can't fight! Maybe you think I can't! I'll show you, you skin, you card-sharp! Yes, you cheated! You cheated! You cheated!"

"Well, let's go at it, then, mister," said Johnnie, coolly.

The cowboy's brow was beaded with sweat from his efforts in intercepting all sorts of raids. He turned in despair to Scully. "What are you goin' to do now?"

A change had come over the Celtic visage of the old man. He now seemed all eagerness; his eyes glowed.

"We'll let them fight," he answered, stalwartly. "I can't put up with it any longer. I've stood this damned Swede till I'm sick. We'll let them fight."

VI

The men prepared to go out-of-doors. The Easterner was so nervous that he had great difficulty in getting his arms into the sleeves of his new leather coat. As the cowboy drew his fur cap down over his ears his hands trembled. In fact, Johnnie and old Scully were the only ones who displayed no agitation. These preliminaries were conducted without words.

Scully threw open the door. "Well, come on," he said. Instantly a terrific wind caused the flame of the lamp to struggle at its wick, while a puff of black smoke sprang from the chimney-top. The stove was in mid-current of the blast, and its voice swelled to equal the roar of the storm. Some of the scarred and bedabbled cards were caught up from the floor and dashed helplessly against the farther wall. The men lowered their heads and plunged into the tempest as into a sea.

No snow was falling, but great whirls and clouds of flakes, swept up from the ground by the frantic winds, were streaming southward with the speed of bullets. The covered land was blue with the sheen of an unearthly satin, and there was no other hue save where, at the low, black railway station—which seemed incredibly distant—one light gleamed like a tiny jewel. As the men floundered into a thigh-deep drift, it was known that the Swede was bawling out something. Scully went to him, put a hand on his shoulder and projected an ear. "What's that you say?" he shouted.

"I say," bawled the Swede again, "I won't stand much show against this gang. I know you'll all pitch on me."

Scully smote him reproachfully on the arm. "Tut, man!" he yelled. The wind tore the words from Scully's lips and scattered them far alee.

"You are all a gang of—" boomed the Swede, but the storm also seized the remainder of this sentence.

Immediately turning their backs upon the wind, the men had swung around a corner to the sheltered side of the hotel. It was the function of the little house to preserve here, amid this great devastation of snow, an irregular V-shape of heavily incrusted grass, which crackled beneath the feet. One could imagine the great drifts piled against the windward side. When the party reached the comparative peace of this spot it was found that the Swede was still bellowing.

"Oh, I know what kind of a thing this is! I know you'll all pitch on me. I can't lick you all!"

Scully turned upon him panther fashion. "You'll not have to whip all of us. You'll have to whip my son Johnnie. An' the man what troubles you durin' that time will have me to dale with."

The arrangements were swiftly made. The two men faced each other, obedient to the harsh commands of Scully, whose face, in the subtly luminous gloom, could be seen set in the austere impersonal lines that are pictured on the countenances of the Roman veterans. The Easterner's teeth were chattering, and he was hopping up and down like a mechanical toy. The cowboy stood rock-like.

The contestants had not stripped off any clothing. Each was in his ordinary attire. Their fists were up, and they eyed each other in a calm that had the elements of leonine cruelty in it.

During this pause, the Easterner's mind, like a film, took lasting impressions of three men—the iron-nerved master of the ceremony; the Swede, pale, motionless, terrible; and Johnnie, serene yet ferocious, brutish yet heroic. The entire prelude had in it a tragedy greater than the tragedy of action, and this aspect was accentuated by the long, mellow cry of the blizzard, as it sped the tumbling and wailing flakes into the black abyss of the south.

"Now!" said Scully.

The two combatants leaped forward and crashed together like bullocks. There was heard the cushioned sound of blows, and of a curse squeezing out from between the tight teeth of one.

As for the spectators, the Easterner's pent-up breath exploded from him with a pop of relief, absolute relief from the tension of the preliminaries. The cowboy bounded into the air with a yowl. Scully was immovable as from supreme amazement and fear at the fury of the fight which he himself had permitted and arranged.

For a time the encounter in the darkness was such a perplexity of flying arms that it presented no more detail than would a swiftly revolving wheel. Occasionally a face, as if illumined by a flash of light, would shine out, ghastly and marked with pink spots. A moment later, the men might have been known as shadows, if it were not for the involuntary utterance of oaths that came from them in whispers.

Suddenly a holocaust of warlike desire caught the cowboy, and he bolted forward with the speed of a broncho. "Go it, Johnnie! go it! Kill him! Kill him!"

Scully confronted him. "Kape back," he said; and by his glance the cowboy could tell that this man was Johnnie's father.

To the Easterner there was a monotony of unchangeable fighting that was an abomination. This confused mingling was eternal to his sense, which was concentrated in a longing for the end, the priceless end. Once the fighters lurched near him, and as he scrambled hastily backward he heard them breathe like men on the rack.

"Kill him, Johnnie! Kill him! Kill him! Kill him!" The cowboy's face was contorted like one of those agony masks in museums.

"Keep still," said Scully, icily.

Then there was a sudden loud grunt, incomplete, cut short, and Johnnie's body swung away from the Swede and fell with sickening heaviness to the grass. The cowboy was barely in time to prevent the mad Swede from flinging himself upon his prone adversary. "No, you don't," said the cowboy, interposing an arm. "Wait a second."

Scully was at his son's side. "Johnnie! Johnnie, me boy!" His voice had a quality of melancholy tenderness. "Johnnie! Can you go on with it?" He looked anxiously down into the bloody, pulpy face of his son.

There was a moment of silence, and then Johnnie answered in his ordinary voice, "Yes, I—it—yes."

Assisted by his father he struggled to his feet. "Wait a bit now till you git your wind," said the old man.

A few paces away the cowboy was lecturing the Swede. "No, you don't! Wait a second!"

The Easterner was plucking at Scully's sleeve. "Oh, this is enough," he pleaded. "This is enough! Let it go as it stands. This is enough!"

"Bill," said Scully, "git out of the road." The cowboy stepped aside. "Now." The combatants were actuated by a new caution as they advanced towards collision. They glared at each other, and then the Swede aimed a lightning blow that carried with it his entire weight. Johnnie was evidently half stupid from weakness, but he miraculously dodged, and his fist sent the over-balanced Swede sprawling.

The cowboy, Scully, and the Easterner burst into a cheer that was like a chorus of triumphant soldiery, but before its conclusion the Swede had scuffled agilely to his feet and come in berserk abandon at his foe. There was another perplexity of flying arms, and Johnnie's body again swung away and fell, even as a bundle might fall from a roof. The Swede instantly staggered to a little wind-waved tree and leaned upon it, breathing like an engine, while his savage and flame-lit eyes roamed from face to face as the men bent over Johnnie. There was a splendor of isolation in his situation at this time which the Easterner felt once when, lifting his eyes from the man on the ground, he beheld that mysterious and lonely figure, waiting.

"Are you any good yet, Johnnie?" asked Scully in a broken voice.

The son gasped and opened his eyes languidly. After a moment he answered, "No—I ain't—any good—any—more." Then, from shame and bodily ill, he began to weep, the tears furrowing down through the blood-stains on his face. "He was too—too—too heavy for me."

Scully straightened and addressed the waiting figure. "Stranger," he said, evenly, "it's all up with our side." Then his voice changed into that vibrant huskiness which is commonly the tone of the most simple and deadly announcements. "Johnnie is whipped."

Without replying, the victor moved off on the route to the front door of the hotel.

The cowboy was formulating new and unspellable blasphemies. The Easterner was startled to find that they were out in a wind that seemed to come direct from the shadowed arctic floes. He heard again the wail of the snow as it was flung to its grave in the south. He knew now that all this time the cold had been sinking into him deeper and deeper, and he wondered that he had not perished. He felt indifferent to the condition of the vanquished man.

"Johnnie, can you walk?" asked Scully.

"Did I hurt—hurt him any?" asked the son.

"Can you walk, boy? Can you walk?"

Johnnie's voice was suddenly strong. There was a robust impatience in it. "I asked you whether I hurt him any!"

"Yes, yes, Johnnie," answered the cowboy, consolingly; "he's hurt a good deal."

They raised him from the ground, and as soon as he was on his feet he went tottering off, rebuffing all attempts at assistance. When the party rounded the corner they were fairly blinded by the pelting of the snow. It burned their faces like fire. The cowboy carried Johnnie through the drift to the door. As they entered some cards again rose from the floor and beat against the wall.

The Easterner rushed to the stove. He was so profoundly chilled that he almost dared to embrace the glowing iron. The Swede was not in the room. Johnnie sank into a chair, and, folding his arms on his knees, buried his face in them. Scully, warming one foot and then the other at a rim of the stove, muttered to himself with Celtic mournfulness. The cowboy had removed his fur cap, and with a dazed and rueful air he was running one hand through his tousled locks. From overhead they could hear the creaking of boards, as the Swede tramped here and there in his room.

The sad quiet was broken by the sudden flinging open of a door that led towards the kitchen. It was instantly followed by an inrush of women. They precipitated themselves upon Johnnie amid a chorus of lamentation. Before they carried their prey off to the kitchen, there to be bathed and harangued with that mixture of sympathy and abuse which is a feat of their sex, the mother straightened herself and fixed old Scully with an eye of stern reproach. "Shame be upon you, Patrick Scully!" she cried. "Your own son, too. Shame be upon you!"

"There now! Be quiet, now!" said the old man, weakly.

"Shame be upon you, Patrick Scully!" The girls, rallying to this slogan, sniffed disdainfully in the direction of those trembling accomplices, the cowboy and the Easterner. Presently they bore Johnnie away, and left the three men to dismal reflection.

VII

"I'd like to fight this here Dutchman myself," said the cowboy, breaking a long silence.

Scully wagged his head sadly. "No, that wouldn't do. It wouldn't be right. It wouldn't be right."

"Well, why wouldn't it?" argued the cowboy. "I don't see no harm in it."

"No," answered Scully, with mournful heroism. "It wouldn't be right. It was Johnnie's fight, and now we mustn't whip the man just because he whipped Johnnie."

"Yes, that's true enough," said the cowboy; "but—he better not get fresh with me, because I couldn't stand no more of it."

"You'll not say a word to him," commanded Scully, and even then they heard the tread of the Swede on the stairs. His entrance was made theatric. He swept the door back with a bang and swaggered to the middle of the room. No one looked at him. "Well," he cried, insolently, at Scully, "I s'pose you'll tell me now how much I owe you?"

The old man remained stolid. "You don't owe me nothin'."

"Huh!" said the Swede, "huh! Don't owe 'im nothin'."

The cowboy addressed the Swede. "Stranger, I don't see how you come to be so gay around here."

Old Scully was instantly alert. "Stop!" he shouted, holding his hand forth, fingers upward. "Bill, you shut up!"

The cowboy spat carelessly into the sawdust-box. "I didn't say a word, did I?" he asked.

"Mr. Scully," called the Swede, "how much do I owe you?" It was seen that he was attired for departure, and that he had his valise in his hand.

"You don't owe me nothin'," repeated Scully in his same imperturbable way.

"Huh!" said the Swede. "I guess you're right. I guess if it was any way at all, you'd owe me somethin'. That's what I guess." He turned to the cowboy. " 'Kill him! Kill him! Kill him!' " he mimicked, and then guffawed victoriously. " 'Kill him!' " He was convulsed with ironical humor.

But he might have been jeering the dead. The three men were immovable and silent, staring with glassy eyes at the stove.

The Swede opened the door and passed into the storm, giving one derisive glance backward at the still group.

As soon as the door was closed, Scully and the cowboy leaped to their feet and began to curse. They trampled to and fro, waving their arms and smashing into the air with their fists. "Oh, but that was a hard minute!" wailed Scully. "That was a hard minute! Him there leerin' and scoffin'! One bang at his nose was worth forty dollars to me that minute! How did you stand it, Bill?"

"How did I stand it?" cried the cowboy in a quivering voice. "How did I stand it? Oh!"

The old man burst into sudden brogue. "I'd like to take that Swade," he wailed, "and hould 'im down on a shtone flure and bate 'im to a jelly wid a shtick!"

The cowboy groaned in sympathy. "I'd like to git him by the neck and ha-ammer him"—he brought his hand down on a chair with a noise like a pistol-shot—"hammer that there Dutchman until he couldn't tell himself from a dead coyote!"

"I'd bate 'im until he—"

"I'd show *him* some things—"

And then together they raised a yearning, fanatic cry—"Oh-o-oh! if we only could—"

"Yes!"

"Yes!"

"And then I'd—"

"O-o-oh!"

VIII

The Swede, tightly gripping his valise, tacked across the face of the storm as if he carried sails. He was following a line of little naked, gasping trees, which he knew must mark the way of the road. His face, fresh from the pounding of Johnnie's fists, felt more pleasure than pain in the wind and the driving snow. A number of square shapes loomed upon him finally, and he knew them as the houses of the main body of the town. He found a street and made travel along it, leaning heavily upon the wind whenever, at a corner, a terrific blast caught him.

He might have been in a deserted village. We picture the world as thick with conquering and elate humanity, but here, with the bugles of the tempest pealing, it was hard to imagine a peopled earth. One viewed the existence of man then as a marvel, and conceded a glamour of wonder to these lice which were caused to cling to a whirling, fire-smote, ice-locked, disease-stricken, space-lost bulb. The conceit of man was explained by this storm to be the very engine of life. One was a coxcomb not to die in it. However, the Swede found a saloon.

In front of it an indomitable red light was burning, and the snow-flakes were made blood-color as they flew through the circumscribed territory of the lamp's shining. The Swede pushed open the door of the saloon and entered. A sanded expanse was before him, and at the end of it four men sat about a table drinking. Down one side of the room extended a radiant bar, and its guardian was leaning upon his elbows listening to the talk of the men at the table. The Swede dropped his valise upon the floor, and, smiling fraternally upon the barkeeper, said, "Gimme some whiskey, will you?" The man placed a bottle, a whiskey-glass, and a glass of ice-thick water upon the bar. The Swede poured himself an abnormal portion of whiskey and drank it in three gulps. "Pretty bad night," remarked the bartender, indifferently. He was making the pretension of blindness which is usually a distinction of his class; but it could have been seen that he was furtively studying the half-erased blood-stains on the face of the Swede. "Bad night," he said again.

"Oh, it's good enough for me," replied the Swede, hardily, as he poured himself some more whiskey. The barkeeper took his coin and manœuvred it through its reception by the highly nickelled cash-machine. A bell rang; a card labelled "20 cts." had appeared.

"No," continued the Swede, "this isn't too bad weather. It's good enough for me."

"So?" murmured the barkeeper, languidly.

The copious drams made the Swede's eyes swim, and he breathed a trifle heavier. "Yes, I like this weather. I like it. It suits me." It was apparently his design to impart a deep significance to these words.

"So?" murmured the bartender again. He turned to gaze dreamily at the scroll-like birds and bird-like scrolls which had been drawn with soap upon the mirrors back of the bar.

"Well, I guess I'll take another drink," said the Swede, presently. "Have something?"

"No, thanks; I'm not drinkin'," answered the bartender. Afterwards he asked, "How did you hurt your face?"

The Swede immediately began to boast loudly. "Why, in a fight. I thumped the soul out of a man down here at Scully's hotel."

The interest of the four men at the table was at last aroused.

"Who was it?" said one.

"Johnnie Scully," blustered the Swede. "Son of the man what runs it. He will be pretty near dead for some weeks, I can tell you. I made a nice thing of him, I did. He couldn't get up. They carried him in the house. Have a drink?"

Instantly the men in some subtle way incased themselves in reserve. "No, thanks," said one. The group was of curious formation. Two were prominent local business men; one was the district-attorney; and one was a professional gambler of the kind known as "square." But a scrutiny of the group would not have enabled an observer to pick the gambler from the men of more reputable pursuits. He was, in fact, a man so delicate in manner, when among people of fair class, and so judicious in his choice of victims, that in the strictly masculine part of the town's life he had come to be explicitly trusted and admired. People called him a thoroughbred. The fear and contempt with which his craft was regarded was undoubtedly the reason that his quiet dignity shone conspicuous above the quiet dignity of men who might be merely hatters, billiard-makers, or grocery-clerks. Beyond an occasional unwary traveller, who came by rail, this gambler was supposed to prey solely upon reckless and senile farmers, who, when flush with good crops, drove into town in all the pride and confidence of an absolutely invulnerable stupidity. Hearing at times in circuitous fashion of the despoilment of such a farmer, the important men of Romper invariably laughed in contempt of the victim, and, if they thought of the wolf at all, it was with a kind of pride at the knowledge that he would never dare think of attacking their wisdom and courage. Besides, it was popular that this gambler had a real wife and two real children in a neat cottage in a suburb, where he led an exemplary home life; and when any one even suggested a discrepancy in his character, the crowd immediately vociferated descriptions of this virtuous family circle. Then men who led exemplary home lives, and men who did not lead exemplary home lives, all subsided in a bunch, remarking that there was nothing more to be said.

However, when a restriction was placed upon him—as, for instance, when a strong clique of members of the new Pollywog Club refused to permit him, even as a spectator, to appear in the rooms of the organization—the candor and gentleness with which he accepted the

judgment disarmed many of his foes and made his friends more desperately partisan. He invariably distinguished between himself and a
respectable Romper man so quickly and frankly that his manner actually
appeared to be a continual broadcast compliment.

And one must not forget to declare the fundamental fact of his entire
position in Romper. It is irrefutable that in all affairs outside of his
business, in all matters that occur eternally and commonly between man
and man, this thieving card-player was so generous, so just, so moral,
that, in a contest, he could have put to flight the consciences of nine-
tenths of the citizens of Romper.

And so it happened that he was seated in this saloon with the two
prominent local merchants and the district-attorney.

The Swede continued to drink raw whiskey, meanwhile babbling at
the barkeeper and trying to induce him to indulge in potations. "Come
on. Have a drink. Come on. What—no? Well, have a little one, then.
By gawd, I've whipped a man tonight, and I want to celebrate. I
whipped him good, too. Gentlemen," the Swede cried to the men at the
table, "have a drink?"

"Ssh!" said the barkeeper.

The group at the table, although furtively attentive, had been pretending to be deep in talk, but now a man lifted his eyes towards the
Swede and said, shortly, "Thanks. We don't want any more."

At this reply the Swede ruffled out his chest like a rooster. "Well,"
he exploded, "it seems I can't get anybody to drink with me in this
town. Seems so, don't it? Well!"

"Ssh!" said the barkeeper.

"Say," snarled the Swede, "don't you try to shut me up. I won't have
it. I'm a gentleman, and I want people to drink with me. And I want
'em to drink with me now. *Now*—do you understand?" He rapped the
bar with his knuckles.

Years of experience had calloused the bartender. He merely grew
sulky. "I hear you," he answered.

"Well," cried the Swede, "listen hard then. See those men over there?
Well, they're going to drink with me, and don't you forget it. Now you
watch."

"Hi!" yelled the barkeeper, "this won't do!"

"Why won't it?" demanded the Swede. He stalked over to the table,
and by chance laid his hand upon the shoulder of the gambler. "How
about this?" he asked, wrathfully. "I asked you to drink with me."

The gambler simply twisted his head and spoke over his shoulder.
"My friend, I don't know you."

"Oh, hell!" answered the Swede, "come and have a drink."

"Now, my boy," advised the gambler, kindly, "take your hand off my shoulder and go 'way and mind your own business." He was a little, slim man, and it seemed strange to hear him use this tone of heroic patronage to the burly Swede. The other men at the table said nothing.

"What! You won't drink with me, you little dude? I'll make you then! I'll make you!" The Swede had grasped the gambler frenziedly at the throat, and was dragging him from his chair. The other men sprang up. The barkeeper dashed around the corner of his bar. There was a great tumult, and then was seen a long blade in the hand of the gambler. It shot forward, and a human body, this citadel of virtue, wisdom, power, was pierced as easily as if it had been a melon. The Swede fell with a cry of supreme astonishment.

The prominent merchants and the district-attorney must have at once tumbled out of the place backward. The bartender found himself hanging limply to the arm of a chair and gazing into the eyes of a murderer.

"Henry," said the latter, as he wiped his knife on one of the towels that hung beneath the bar-rail, "you tell 'em where to find me. I'll be home, waiting for 'em." Then he vanished. A moment afterwards the barkeeper was in the street dinning through the storm for help, and, moreover, companionship.

The corpse of the Swede, alone in the saloon, had its eyes fixed upon a dreadful legend that dwelt atop of the cash-machine: "This registers the amount of your purchase."

IX

Months later, the cowboy was frying pork over the stove of a little ranch near the Dakota line, when there was a quick thud of hoofs outside, and presently the Easterner entered with the letters and the papers.

"Well," said the Easterner at once, "the chap that killed the Swede has got three years. Wasn't much, was it?"

"He has? Three years?" The cowboy poised his pan of pork, while he ruminated upon the news. "Three years. That ain't much."

"No. It was a light sentence," replied the Easterner as he unbuckled his spurs. "Seems there was a good deal of sympathy for him in Romper."

"If the bartender had been any good," observed the cowboy, thoughtfully, "he would have gone in and cracked that there Dutchman on the head with a bottle in the beginnin' of it and stopped all this here murderin'."

"Yes, a thousand things might have happened," said the Easterner, tartly.

The cowboy returned his pan of pork to the fire, but his philosophy continued. "It's funny, ain't it? If he hadn't said Johnnie was cheatin' he'd be alive this minute. He was an awful fool. Game played for fun, too. Not for money. I believe he was crazy."

"I feel sorry for that gambler," said the Easterner.

"Oh, so do I," said the cowboy. "He don't deserve none of it for killin' who he did."

"The Swede might not have been killed if everything had been square."

"Might not have been killed?" exclaimed the cowboy. "Everythin' square? Why, when he said that Johnnie was cheatin' and acted like such a jackass? And then in the saloon he fairly walked up to git hurt?" With these arguments the cowboy browbeat the Easterner and reduced him to rage.

"You're a fool!" cried the Easterner, viciously. "You're a bigger jack-ass than the Swede by a million majority. Now let me tell you one thing. Let me tell you something. Listen! Johnnie *was* cheating!"

" 'Johnnie,' " said the cowboy, blankly. There was a minute of silence, and then he said, robustly, "Why, no. The game was only for fun."

"Fun or not," said the Easterner, "Johnnie was cheating. I saw him. I know it. I saw him. And I refused to stand up and be a man. I let the Swede fight it out alone. And you—you were simply puffing around the place and wanting to fight. And then old Scully himself! We are all in it! This poor gambler isn't even a noun. He is kind of an adverb. Every sin is the result of a collaboration. We, five of us, have collaborated in the murder of this Swede. Usually there are from a dozen to forty women really involved in every murder, but in this case it seems to be only five men—you, I, Johnnie, old Scully, and that fool of an unfortunate gambler came merely as a culmination, the apex of a human movement, and gets all the punishment."

The cowboy, injured and rebellious, cried out blindly into this fog of mysterious theory: "Well, I didn't do anythin', did I?"

STEPHEN CRANE

The Bride Comes to Yellow Sky

"The Bride Comes to Yellow Sky" was first published in *McClure's Magazine* in 1898 and quickly reprinted in *The Open Boat and Other Tales of Adventure* the same year. Essentially a parody of the standard western story, which traditionally featured a dashing sheriff, a beautiful ingenue, a dangerous villain in a black hat, and a dramatic gunfight in the conclusion, Crane's story presents a newly married marshal, a dowdy bride, a harmless and aging desperado, and a deflating confrontation. Beyond parody, however, there is much in the story to admire, including a complex structural organization, a pattern of ironic imagery, and the historically significant portrayal of a western town at the moment of transition to a more "civilized" status. It is also important for its demonstration of Crane's skill in the comic mode, particularly in the handling of his characteristic irony.

*   *   *

I

The great Pullman was whirling onward with such dignity of motion that a glance from the window seemed simply to prove that the plains of Texas were pouring eastward. Vast flats of green grass, dull-hued spaces of mesquite and cactus, little groups of frame houses, woods of light and tender trees, all were sweeping into the east, sweeping over the horizon, a precipice.

A newly married pair had boarded this coach at San Antonio. The man's face was reddened from many days in the wind and sun, and a direct result of his new black clothes was that his brick-colored hands were constantly performing in a most conscious fashion. From time to time he looked down respectfully at his attire. He sat with a hand on each knee, like a man waiting in a barber's shop. The glances he devoted to other passengers were furtive and shy.

The bride was not pretty, nor was she very young. She wore a dress of blue cashmere, with small reservations of velvet here and there and with steel buttons abounding. She continually twisted her head to regard her puff sleeves, very stiff, straight, and high. They embarrassed her. It was quite apparent that she had cooked, and that she expected to cook, dutifully. The blushes caused by the careless scrutiny of some passengers as she had entered the car were strange to see upon this plain, underclass countenance, which was drawn in placid, almost emotionless lines.

They were evidently very happy. "Ever been in a parlor-car before?" he asked, smiling with delight.

"No," she answered. "I never was. It's fine, ain't it?"

"Great! And then after a while we'll go forward to the diner and get a big layout. Finest meal in the world. Charge a dollar."

"Oh, do they?" cried the bride. "Charge a dollar? Why, that's too much—for us—ain't it, Jack?"

"Not this trip, anyhow," he answered bravely. "We're going to go the whole thing."

Later, he explained to her about the trains. "You see, it's a thousand miles from one end of Texas to the other, and this train runs right across it and never stops but four times." He had the pride of an owner. He pointed out to her the dazzling fittings of the coach, and in truth her eyes opened wider as she contemplated the sea-green figured velvet, the shining brass, silver, and glass, the wood that gleamed as darkly brilliant as the surface of a pool of oil. At one end a bronze figure sturdily held a support for a separated chamber, and at convenient places on the ceiling were frescoes in olive and silver.

To the minds of the pair, their surroundings reflected the glory of their marriage that morning in San Antonio. This was the environment of their new estate, and the man's face in particular beamed with an elation that made him appear ridiculous to the negro porter. This individual at times surveyed them from afar with an amused and superior grin. On other occasions he bullied them with skill in ways that did not make it exactly plain to them that they were being bullied. He subtly used all the manners of the most unconquerable kind of snobbery. He oppressed them, but of this oppression they had small knowledge, and they speedily forgot that infrequently a number of travelers covered them with stares of derisive enjoyment. Historically there was supposed to be something infinitely humorous in their situation.

"We are due in Yellow Sky at 3.42," he said, looking tenderly into her eyes.

"Oh, are we?" she said, as if she had not been aware of it. To evince surprise at her husband's statement was part of her wifely amiability. She took from a pocket a little silver watch, and as she held it before her and stared at it with a frown of attention, the new husband's face shone.

"I bought it in San Anton' from a friend of mine," he told her gleefully.

"It's seventeen minutes past twelve," she said, looking up at him with a kind of shy and clumsy coquetry. A passenger, noting this play, grew excessively sardonic, and winked at himself in one of the numerous mirrors.

At last they went to the dining-car. Two rows of negro waiters, in glowing white suits, surveyed their entrance with the interest and also the equanimity of men who had been forewarned. The pair fell to the lot of a waiter who happened to feel pleasure in steering them through their meal. He viewed them with the manner of a fatherly pilot, his countenance radiant with benevolence. The patronage, entwined with the ordinary deference, was not plain to them. And yet, as they returned to their coach, they showed in their faces a sense of escape.

To the left, miles down a long purple slope, was a little ribbon of mist where moved the keening Rio Grande. The train was approaching it at an angle, and the apex was Yellow Sky. Presently it was apparent that, as the distance from Yellow Sky grew shorter, the husband became commensurately restless. His brick-red hands were more insistent in their prominence. Occasionally he was even rather absent-minded and far-away when the bride leaned forward and addressed him.

As a matter of truth, Jack Potter was beginning to find the shadow of a deed weigh upon him like a leaden slab. He, the town marshal of Yellow Sky, a man known, liked, and feared in his corner, a prominent person, had gone to San Antonio to meet a girl he believed he loved, and there, after the usual prayers, had actually induced her to marry him, without consulting Yellow Sky for any part of the transaction. He was now bringing his bride before an innocent and unsuspecting community.

Of course, people in Yellow Sky married as it pleased them, in accordance with a general custom; but such was Potter's thought of his duty to his friends, or of their idea of his duty, or of an unspoken form which does not control men in these matters, that he felt he was heinous. He had committed an extraordinary crime. Face to face with this girl in San Antonio, and spurred by his sharp impulse, he had gone headlong over all the social hedges. At San Antonio he was like a man hidden in the dark. A knife to sever any friendly duty, any form, was easy to his hand in that remote city. But the hour of Yellow Sky, the hour of daylight, was approaching.

He knew full well that his marriage was an important thing to his town. It could only be exceeded by the burning of the new hotel. His friends could not forgive him. Frequently he had reflected on the advisability of telling them by telegraph, but a new cowardice had been upon him. He feared to do it. And now the train was hurrying him toward a scene of amazement, glee, and reproach. He glanced out of the window at the line of haze swinging slowly in towards the train.

Yellow Sky had a kind of brass band, which played painfully, to the delight of the populace. He laughed without heart as he thought of it. If the citizens could dream of his prospective arrival with his bride, they would parade the band at the station and escort them, amid cheers and laughing congratulations, to his adobe home.

He resolved that he would use all the devices of speed and plainscraft in making the journey from the station to his house. Once within that safe citadel, he could issue some sort of a vocal bulletin, and then not go among the citizens until they had time to wear off a little of their enthusiasm.

The bride looked anxiously at him. "What's worrying you, Jack?"
He laughed again. "I'm not worrying, girl. I'm only thinking of Yellow Sky."

She flushed in comprehension.

A sense of mutual guilt invaded their minds and developed a finer tenderness. They looked at each other with eyes softly aglow. But Potter often laughed the same nervous laugh. The flush upon the bride's face seemed quite permanent.

The traitor to the feelings of Yellow Sky narrowly watched the speeding landscape. "We're nearly there," he said.

Presently the porter came and announced the proximity of Potter's home. He held a brush in his hand and, with all his airy superiority gone, he brushed Potter's new clothes as the latter slowly turned this way and that way. Potter fumbled out a coin and gave it to the porter, as he had seen others do. It was a heavy and muscle-bound business, as that of a man shoeing his first horse.

The porter took their bag, and as the train began to slow they moved forward to the hooded platform of the car. Presently the two engines and their long string of coaches rushed into the station of Yellow Sky.

"They have to take water here," said Potter, from a constricted throat and in mournful cadence, as one announcing death. Before the train stopped, his eye had swept the length of the platform, and he was glad and astonished to see there was none upon it but the station-agent, who, with a slightly hurried and anxious air, was walking toward the water-tanks. When the train had halted, the porter alighted first and placed in position a little temporary step.

"Come on, girl," said Potter hoarsely. As he helped her down they each laughed on a false note. He took the bag from the negro, and bade his wife cling to his arm. As they slunk rapidly away, his hang-dog glance perceived that they were unloading the two trunks, and also that the station-agent far ahead near the baggage-car had turned and was running toward him, making gestures. He laughed, and groaned as he laughed, when he noted the first effect of his marital bliss upon Yellow Sky. He gripped his wife's arm firmly to his side, and they fled. Behind them the porter stood chuckling fatuously.

II

The California Express on the Southern Railway was due at Yellow Sky in twenty-one minutes. There were six men at the bar of the "Weary Gentleman" saloon. One was a drummer who talked a great deal and rapidly; three were Texans who did not care to talk at that time; and

two were Mexican sheep-herders who did not talk as a general practice
in the "Weary Gentleman" saloon. The barkeeper's dog lay on the board
walk that crossed in front of the door. His head was on his paws, and
he glanced drowsily here and there with the constant vigilance of a dog
that is kicked on occasion. Across the sandy street were some vivid green
grass plots, so wonderful in appearance amid the sands that burned near
them in a blazing sun that they caused a doubt in the mind. They exactly
resembled the grass mats used to represent lawns on the stage. At the
cooler end of the railway station a man without a coat sat in a tilted
chair and smoked his pipe. The fresh-cut bank of the Rio Grande circled
near the town, and there could be seen beyond it a great, plum-colored
plain of mesquite.

Save for the busy drummer and his companions in the saloon, Yellow
Sky was dozing. The new-comer leaned gracefully upon the bar, and
recited many tales with the confidence of a bard who has come upon a
new field.

"——and at the moment that the old man fell down stairs with the
bureau in his arms, the old woman was coming up with two scuttles of
coal, and, of course——"

The drummer's tale was interrupted by a young man who suddenly
appeared in the open door. He cried: "Scratchy Wilson's drunk, and has
turned loose with both hands." The two Mexicans at once set down
their glasses and faded out of the rear entrance of the saloon.

The drummer, innocent and jocular, answered: "All right, old man.
S'pose he has. Come in and have a drink, anyhow."

But the information had made such an obvious cleft in every skull
in the room that the drummer was obliged to see its importance. All
had become instantly solemn. "Say," said he, mystified, "what is this?"
His three companions made the introductory gesture of eloquent speech,
but the young man at the door forestalled them.

"It means, my friend," he answered, as he came into the saloon,
"that for the next two hours this town won't be a health resort."

The barkeeper went to the door and locked and barred it. Reaching
out of the window, he pulled in heavy wooden shutters and barred
them. Immediately a solemn, chapel-like gloom was upon the place. The
drummer was looking from one to another.

"But, say," he cried, "what is this, anyhow? You don't mean there
is going to be a gun-fight?"

"Don't know whether there'll be a fight or not," answered one man
grimly. "But there'll be some shootin'—some good shootin'."

The young man who had warned them waved his hand. "Oh, there'll
be a fight fast enough, if anyone wants it. Anybody can get a fight out
there in the street. "There's a fight just waiting."

The drummer seemed to be swayed between the interest of a foreigner and a perception of personal danger.

"What did you say his name was?" he asked.

"Scratchy Wilson," they answered in chorus.

"And will he kill anybody? What are you going to do? Does this happen often? Does he rampage around like this once a week or so? Can he break in that door?"

"No, he can't break down that door," replied the barkeeper. "He's tried it three times. But when he comes you'd better lay down on the floor, stranger. He's dead sure to shoot at it, and a bullet may come through."

Thereafter the drummer kept a strict eye upon the door. The time had not yet been called for him to hug the floor, but, as a minor precaution, he sidled near to the wall. "Will he kill anybody?" he said again.

The men laughed low and scornfully at the question.

"He's out to shoot, and he's out for trouble. Don't see any good in experimentin' with him."

"But what do you do in a case like this? What do you do?"

A man responded: "Why, he and Jack Potter——"

"But," in chorus, the other men interrupted, "Jack Potter's in San Anton'."

"Well, who is he? What's he got to do with it?"

"Oh, he's the town marshal. He goes out and fights Scratchy when he gets on one of these tears."

"Wow," said the drummer, mopping his brow. "Nice job he's got."

The voices had toned away to mere whisperings. The drummer wished to ask further questions which were born of an increasing anxiety and bewilderment; but when he attempted them, the men merely looked at him in irritation and motioned him to remain silent. A tense waiting hush was upon them. In the deep shadows of the room their eyes shone as they listened for sounds from the street. One man made three gestures at the barkeeper, and the latter, moving like a ghost, handed him a glass and a bottle. The man poured a full glass of whisky, and set down the bottle noiselessly. He gulped the whisky in a swallow, and turned again toward the door in immovable silence. The drummer saw that the barkeeper, without a sound, had taken a Winchester from beneath the bar. Later he saw this individual beckoning to him, so he tiptoed across the room.

"You better come with me back of the bar."

"No, thanks," said the drummer, perspiring. "I'd rather be where I can make a break for the back door."

Whereupon the man of bottles made a kindly but peremptory gesture. The drummer obeyed it, and finding himself seated on a box with his head below the level of the bar, balm was laid upon his soul at sight of various zinc and copper fittings that bore a resemblance to armor-plate. The barkeeper took a seat comfortably upon an adjacent box.

"You see," he whispered, "this here Scratchy Wilson is a wonder with a gun—a perfect wonder—and when he goes on the war trail, we hunt our holes—naturally. He's about the last one of the old gang that used to hang out along the river here. He's a terror when he's drunk. When he's sober he's all right—kind of simple—wouldn't hurt a fly—nicest fellow in town. But when he's drunk—whoo!"

There were periods of stillness. "I wish Jack Potter was back from San Anton'," said the barkeeper. "He shot Wilson up once—in the leg —and he would sail in and pull out the kinks in this thing."

Presently they heard from a distance the sound of a shot, followed by three wild yowls. It instantly removed a bond from the men in the darkened saloon. There was a shuffling of feet. They looked at each other. "Here he comes," they said.

III

A man in a maroon-colored flannel shirt, which had been purchased for purposes of decoration and made, principally, by some Jewish women on the east side of New York, rounded a corner and walked into the middle of the main street of Yellow Sky. In either hand the man held a long, heavy, blue-black revolver. Often he yelled, and these cries rang through a semblance of a deserted village, shrilly flying over the roofs in a volume that seemed to have no relation to the ordinary vocal strength of a man. It was as if the surrounding stillness formed the arch of a tomb over him. These cries of ferocious challenge rang against walls of silence. And his boots had red tops with gilded imprints, of the kind beloved in winter by little sledding boys on the hillsides of New England.

The man's face flamed in a rage begot of whisky. His eyes, rolling and yet keen for ambush, hunted the still doorways and windows. He walked with the creeping movement of the midnight cat. As it occurred to him, he roared menacing information. The long revolvers in his hands were as easy as straws; they were moved with an electric swiftness. The little fingers of each hand played sometimes in a musician's way. Plain from the low collar of the shirt, the cords of his neck straightened and sank, straightened and sank, as passion moved him. The only sounds were his terrible invitations. The calm adobes preserved their demeanor at the passing of this small thing in the middle of the street.

There was no offer of fight; no offer of fight. The man called to the sky. There were no attractions. He bellowed and fumed and swayed his revolvers here and everywhere.

The dog of the barkeeper of the "Weary Gentleman" saloon had not appreciated the advance of events. He yet lay dozing in front of his master's door. At sight of the dog, the man paused and raised his revolver humorously. At sight of the man, the dog sprang up and walked diagonally away, with a sullen head, and growling. The man yelled, and the dog broke into a gallop. As it was about to enter an alley, there was a loud noise, a whistling, and something spat the ground directly before it. The dog screamed, and, wheeling in terror, galloped headlong in a new direction. Again there was a noise, a whistling, and sand was kicked viciously before it. Fear-stricken, the dog turned and flurried like an animal in a pen. The man stood laughing, his weapons at his hips.

Ultimately the man was attracted by the closed door of the "Weary Gentleman" saloon. He went to it, and hammering with a revolver, demanded drink.

The door remaining imperturbable, he picked a bit of paper from the walk and nailed it to the framework with a knife. He then turned his back contemptuously upon this popular resort, and walking to the opposite side of the street, and spinning there on his heel quickly and lithely, fired at the bit of paper. He missed it by a half inch. He swore at himself, and went away. Later, he comfortably fusil-laded the windows of his most intimate friend. The man was playing with this town. It was a toy for him.

But still there was no offer of fight. The name of Jack Potter, his ancient antagonist, entered his mind, and he concluded that it would be a glad thing if he should go to Potter's house and by bombardment induce him to come out and fight. He moved in the direction of his desire, chanting Apache scalp-music.

When he arrived at it, Potter's house presented the same still front as had the other adobes. Taking up a strategic position, the man howled a challenge. But this house regarded him as might a great stone god. It gave no sign. After a decent wait, the man howled further challenges, mingling with them wonderful epithets.

Presently there came the spectacle of a man churning himself into deepest rage over the immobility of a house. He fumed at it as the winter wind attacks a prairie cabin in the North. To the distance there should have gone the sound of a tumult like the fighting of 200 Mexicans. As necessity bade him, he paused for breath or to reload his revolvers.

IV

Potter and his bride walked sheepishly and with speed. Sometimes they laughed together shamefacedly and low.

"Next corner, dear," he said finally.

They put forth the efforts of a pair walking bowed against a strong wind. Potter was about to raise a finger to point the first appearance of the new home when, as they circled the corner, they came face to face with a man in a maroon-colored shirt who was feverishly pushing cartridges into a large revolver. Upon the instant the man dropped his revolver to the ground, and, like lightning, whipped another from its holster. The second weapon was aimed at the bridegroom's chest.

There was a silence. Potter's mouth seemed to be merely a grave for his tongue. He exhibited an instinct to at once loosen his arm from the woman's grip, and he dropped the bag to the sand. As for the bride, her face had gone as yellow as old cloth. She was a slave to hideous rites gazing at the apparitional snake.

The two men faced each other at a distance of three paces. He of the revolver smiled with a new and quiet ferocity.

"Tried to sneak up on me," he said. "Tried to sneak up on me!" His eyes grew more baleful. As Potter made a slight movement, the man thrust his revolver venomously forward. "No, don't you do it, Jack Potter. Don't you move a finger toward a gun just yet. Don't you move an eyelash. The time has come for me to settle with you, and I'm goin' to do it my own way and loaf along with no interferin'. So if you don't want a gun bent on you, just mind what I tell you."

Potter looked at his enemy. "I ain't got a gun on me, Scratchy," he said. "Honest, I ain't." He was stiffening and steadying, but yet somewhere at the back of his mind a vision of the Pullman floated, the seagreen figured velvet, the shining brass, silver, and glass, the wood that gleamed as darkly brilliant as the surface of a pool of oil—all the glory of the marriage, the environment of the new estate. "You know I fight when it comes to fighting, Scratchy Wilson, but I ain't got a gun on me. You'll have to do all the shootin' yourself."

His enemy's face went livid. He stepped forward and lashed his weapon to and fro before Potter's chest. "Don't you tell me you ain't got no gun on you, you whelp. Don't tell me no lie like that. There ain't a man in Texas ever seen you without no gun. Don't take me for no kid." His eyes blazed with light, and his throat worked like a pump.

"I ain't takin' you for no kid," answered Potter. His heels had not moved an inch backward. "I'm takin' you for a——fool. I tell you I ain't got a gun, and I ain't. If you're goin' to shoot me up, you better begin now. You'll never get a chance like this again."

So much enforced reasoning had told on Wilson's rage. He was calmer. "If you ain't got a gun, why ain't you got a gun?" he sneered. "Been to Sunday-school?"

"I ain't got a gun because I've just come from San Anton' with my wife. I'm married," said Potter. "And if I'd thought there was going to be any galoots like you prowling around when I brought my wife home, I'd had a gun, and don't you forget it."

"Married!" said Scratchy, not at all comprehending.

"Yes, married. I'm married," said Potter distinctly.

"Married?" said Scratchy. Seemingly for the first time he saw the drooping, drowning woman at the other man's side. "No!" he said. He was like a creature allowed a glimpse of another world. He moved a pace backward, and his arm with the revolver dropped to his side. "Is this the lady?" he asked.

"Yes, this is the lady," answered Potter.

There was another period of silence.

"Well," said Wilson at last, slowly, "I s'pose it's all off now."

"It's all off if you say so, Scratchy. You know I didn't make the trouble." Potter lifted his valise.

"Well, I 'low it's off, Jack," said Wilson. He was looking at the ground. "Married!" He was not a student of chivalry; it was merely that in the presence of this foreign condition he was a simple child of the earlier plains. He picked up his starboard revolver, and placing both weapons in their holsters, he went away. His feet made funnel-shaped tracks in the heavy sand.

ABRAHAM CAHAN

A Providential Match

"A Providential Match" appeared in *The Imported Bridegroom and Other Stories* (1898). William Dean Howells, in his review of this collection, marveled at Cahan's ability to hold the reader suspended "between a laugh and a heartache." Certainly the taut poise between the affectingly tragic and the grotesquely comic is sustained in the character of Robert Friedman (née Rouvke Arbel), who in his native Russia is eagerly servile but in America is financially successful if socially awkward. Rouvke, the immigrant, desires most of all not to be seen as a "greener" in the New World, but his thoughts often drift back to his native land. The misfortunes of his former master, his own relative success as a pedlar, and the intervention of a matchmaker combine to make the unthinkable seem well within Rouvke's grasp. He will marry a true daughter of Israel, the lovely Hanele; it will be a providential match. But Cahan's wry humor gives the story an unexpected twist and discloses that providence works more easily in the moonlight on the ocean (even though below deck there is stench and squalor) than it does through tradition-bound arrangements and negotiations.

*   *   *

He is still known among his townspeople as Rouvke Arbel. Rouvke they call him, because this name, in its more respectful form of Rouven, was bestowed upon him on the eighth day of his life, at the ceremony which initiated him into Israel. As to the nickname of Arbel, which is Yiddish for "sleeve," he is indebted for it to the apparently never-to-be-forgotten fact that before he came to America, and when he still drove horses and did all sorts of work for Peretz the distiller, he was in the habit of assigning to the sleeves of his sheep-skin coat such duties as generally devolve upon a pocket-handkerchief.

That was only about four years ago; and yet Rouvke is now quite a different young man in quite a different coat and with a handkerchief in its side-pocket. The face is precisely the same: the same everlasting frown, the same pockmarks, hollow yet ruddy cheeks, snub nose, and little gray eyes, at once timid and sly. But for all that, such is the dissimilarity between the Rouvke of four years ago and the Rouvke of to-day that recently, when his mother, who still peddles boiled potatoes in Kropovetz, Government of Kovno, had been surprised by a photograph of her son, her first impulse was to spit at the portrait and to repudiate it as the ungodly likeness of some unknown gentile. But then this photograph, which, by the way, Rouvke had taken by mere chance and for the sole reason that it was no use trying to get any cash from the Bowery photographer, to whom he had sold, on the installment plan, "a pair of pants made to order"—this photograph fully establishes its original's claim of not being a "greener" in the New World. For this is what the portrait reveals. Rouvke's hair is now entirely free from the pair of sidelocks, or *peieths,* which dangled over his ears when he first set foot on American soil; it is parted in the middle and combed on either side in the shape of a curled ostrich-feather. He wears a collar; and this collar is so high and so much below the size of his neck that it gives you the uncomfortable idea of its owner having swallowed the handle of the whip with which he used to rule over Peretz the distiller's mare. The flannel muffler, which seemed never to part company with him while he lived in Kropovetz, has been supplanted by a gay necktie, and the sheepskin by a diagonal "cut-away."

Now, if you were conversant with the business of "custom-peddling," you might perhaps conjecture, upon inspecting Rouvke's photograph, that his cut-away, which seems to be at least one size too large for him, had formerly encased the portly figure of a bartender. And so it had, although for no length of time; for finding the bartender as backward in his payments as the photographer had been, Rouvke soon contrived to prevail upon his delinquent customer to exchange the cut-away for a "mishfeet corkshcrew Printz Albert," which would "feet him like a glove," and carrying off the diagonal in advance he let the bartender wait for the glove-like garment until doomsday.

But "bishness is bishness," as Rouvke would put it. Otherwise he is quite a fine fellow. His bills he pays promptly. On the Eve of the Day of Atonement he subscribes a dollar or two to the funds of the synagogue "Sons of Kropovetz," and has been known to start a newly arrived townsman in business by standing his security in a perforated chair-seat store to the amount of two dollars and a half. Nevertheless, since he visits the Bowery Savings Bank on Saturdays with the same punctuality with which he puts on his phylacteries and prays in his room every morning on week-days, and since his townsfolk, who, unlike him, are blessed with families, cannot afford such excursions to the Bowery institution, these latter Kropovetz Americans begrudge him his bank account, as well as his credit in the peddler-supply stores, and out of sheer envy like to refer to him, not as Robert Friedman, as his business-card reads, but as "Rouvke Arbel—what do you think of that slouch!"

Let us hope, however, that these invidious references never reach Rouvke's ears; for his susceptibilities in this direction are, it must be owned, rather keen. Indeed, if there be a weakness of which he is guilty, it is a rather intense love of approbation and a slight proneness to parade himself. I do not know what he would not give to have people say: "Robert is a smart fellow! Robert is no greenhorn! Robert is the best soul in the world!" It was this foible which, in translating his first name into English, caused him to prefer Robert to Reuben, on the ground that the former appellation seemed to have less of Kropovetz and more of a "tzibilized" sound to it.

The feminine element was until recently absent from Rouvke's life. True, while at home, in the domestic employ of Peretz, the distiller, he would bestow an occasional pinch on Leike the servant maid's cheek. But that was by no means a pinch of gallantry; it was never one of those pinches which a Kropovetz lad will accompany with a look of ostensible mock admiration in his half-shut eyes, and with the exclamation: "Capital stuff, that! as sure as I am a Jew!" No! Leike the lame devil, Leike the scold, Rouvke hated from the deepest recesses of his driver's soul;

and when he pinched her, as he often did in the kitchen, he did it, not from love, but simply that she might smart and "jump to heaven, the scarecrow." And Leike would so amply repay him with the ladle, that there would ensue a series of the most complex and the most ingenious oaths, attended by hair-tearing and by squeaking, till the mistress would come rushing in and terminate the war by boxing the ears of both belligerent parties.

To Hanele, his master's only daughter, Rouvke used to serve tea with more alacrity than to the rest of the family; and when Feive, the matchmaker, made his first appearance and the first suitor was introduced, Rouvke's appetite for sour cream and rye bread somehow disappeared for a few days, while Rouvke himself moved about as if out of gear, and on one occasion caught a slap in the face, because, upon being ordered to fetch a pail of water, he stood staring as if he did not understand Yiddish. But this seemed of no consequence, and Rouvke himself could not, for the life of him, explain this sudden disappearance both of his appetite and presence of mind. Indeed, how could he have dared to connect Hanele with it? What could there have been in common between the relish for sour cream of a mere driver, and the pet daughter of Reb[1] Peretz, the distiller, the son of Rabbi Berele, and the first citizen of Kropovetz?

The negotiations of which Hanele was the object were soon broken off, and Rouvke's truant appetite again fell into the line of drivers' appetites; with this difference, however, that, when Hanele asked for a glass of tea, he would now run to serve her with still more eagerness than before.

Suitor after suitor called and was dismissed, until a year rolled by, when Rouvke's name appeared in the military service-roll, and he packed off for America.

In America he passed his first four years in the school of peddling, among the most diligent and most successful of its students, and so had no mind for anything else in the world. Only during the first few months his heart would almost unremittingly be pining and yearning after Kropovetz—after his mother, his master's family, his master's appletree, under which he had loved to steal a nap on summer days; the raised lawn in front of the house, where he would sit down of a Friday evening and show off his enormous top-boots, just after he had given them a fresh coat of tar, "in honor of the Sabbath;" the well by the synagogue, where on Saturdays, during the intermission in the morning prayer, he used to indulge in a lark with his chums, while the elder members of the congregation were attending the reading of the scrolls. But of all the memories which at this early period of his life in New York troubled his busy mind and gnawed at his enterprising heart that of Hanele was the most excruciating and the most persistent. In due course, however, the waves of time drowned in his mind and in his heart Hanele as well as the apple-tree, the lawn in front of the house, and the well by the synagogue. Only at rare intervals, when plying a new arrival from Kropovetz with questions as to the place where his cradle had been rocked, Rouvke would, after a cursory inquiry concerning the health of his mother and of the Peretz family in general, exact the most minute information about Hanele; and then he would for some time feel as if his heart was "stretching," as he himself would mentally define the effect of his stirred-up recollections.

For the rest, Rouvke followed the regular peddler course with undisturbed assiduity. From a handkerchief peddler he was promoted to "basket-peddling"—that is to say, his stock became plentiful enough and heterogeneous enough to call for a portable store in the shape of a basket. After a while he joined the class where the peddling is done on the "stairses" of tenement-houses. The curriculum of this class includes the occasional experience of being sent head foremost down all the "stairses," of then picking one's self up and imperturbably knocking at some door on the ground-floor, only to come face to face with the janitor and thus get into fresh trouble, and so on. Finally, Rouvke reached the senior grade of the institution, and graduated with the degree of custom peddler, and with the following business card for his diploma: "Robert Friedman, Dealer in Furniture, Carpets, Jewelry, Clothing, Ladies' Dress Goods, etc. Weekly Payments Taken."

As has been said, Rouvke was a stranger to the feminine world. He met a good many members of the gentle sex, but that was exclusively in a business way. The other peddlers he would often encounter on the street in company with nicely dressed "yoong laddas," with whom they loudly spoke in English. He also knew that these fellows attended dancing academies, balls, and picnics; but to him himself these entertainments were a *terra incognita*. And sometimes when Rouvke entered the house of a fellow countryman on business (Rouvke never visited his fellow countrymen except on business), and there happening to be an English-speaking young woman, the host said: "Miss Goldberg—Mr. Friedman; Mr. Friedman—Miss Goldberg," Mr. Friedman would blush crimson at the transaction, while the sentence, "I'm pleashed to meech you," which he well knew was then in order, stuck in his throat and would not budge. This, however, was no common occurrence, for Rouvke took care to avoid such predicaments. At all events, he never allowed these things to bother his head.

After a while, however, by the time the peddlers and his townsfolk estimated his capital in cash at five thousand dollars, and when he actually had over three thousand dollars in bank deposits and twenty-five summers behind his back, his heart somehow resumed its old stretching process. He was at a loss to account for it; but he became aware that each time he passed by a pretty young woman this stretching sensation forced him to outrun her, and, making a show of stopping to look at a window display, to allow his eyes to stray off under the brim of the fair one's hat.

He gradually became a new sort of Rouvke. Formerly, when he was subjected to the tortures of an introduction to a "yoong ladda," the ordeal would result in a mere blush, accompanied by one or two minutes' violent throbbing. Whereas now, every time a similar accident befell him, he would, after the calamity was over, hasten to find himself in front of a looking-glass, and fall to inspecting his glaring necktie and more particularly the pockmarks on his nose. In times past he was hardly ever conscious of these traces of smallpox on his face; now they dwelt in his mind with such pertinacity that one night he dreamed of seeing a watermelon, which was somehow at the same time a dog with a huge nose all covered with pocks. And when he awoke in the morning he felt so sick at heart that he could not relish his breakfast, and was so dazed all that day that he had a carpet sent to an Irishwoman who had ordered some satin for a dress.

Rouvke enrolled in a public evening school for immigrants, and when he had achieved the wisdom of piecing together the letters in "cat," "rat," "mat," of the First Reader, he one afternoon bought a newspaper, and applied himself to looking for an advertisement of some physician who would undertake to remove the footprints of smallpox. He had an idea that the papers contained kindred advertisements. The undertaking proved a failure, however, for Rouvke could detect in the paper neither "cat" nor "rat," while the other words only swam before his eyes. And his heart was "stretching" and "stretching."

It would be unfair to Rouvke, however, to ascribe his attending evening school to the sole purpose of being able to make out a medical advertisement. His chief motive therefor was twofold: In the first place, he would often say to himself: "Robert, bear in mind that you are Rouvke no longer; the chances are that in a year or two you may open a peddler's supply-store of your own: now, you know that the owner of a store who cannot read and write is in danger of being robbed by his bookkeeper." In the second place, his "stretching" heart seemed to whisper: "Robert, remember those ladies have nothing but sneers for a gentleman who does not know how to read a newspaper."

Moreover, those of his fellow peddlers who had studied the Talmud in Russia, and having, therefore, some mental training, found no trouble in picking up some crumbs of broken English in its written form, would often rally him on the "iron head" he must possess to retain the ponderous load of the addresses and accounts of his numerous customers without committing them to writing. These pleasantries pierced Rouvke to the heart; but the pain they gave him was not half so cruel as his moral pangs at the jokes which were showered at him on the subject of his shyness in the presence of ladies. Often he would be entrapped into the company of a "nearly American-born" daughter of Israel; but a still more frequent prank at his expense was for a facetious fellow to drag him out to the middle of the floor in a peddler-supply store, and to force him into a waltz, or to jestingly measure his legs, by way of ascertaining their potential adroitness in a dancing-hall. "Eh, Robert!" they would torment him, "buy a teecket for a ball, veel you? A ball fi'sht clesh, I tell you. Come, ven the laddas veel shee you, dey veel get shtuck— in de co'ners." Robert would struggle, scream, swear, and, after all, steal up to the front of the looking-glass. And his heart would be "stretching" and "stretching."

Whenever he heard of a new marriage, he would apply for details as to the bride and the bridegroom—how much he earned a week, how they came to be engaged, what space of time interposed between the engagement and the wedding. One Saturday morning, while mounting the stairs which led to his miniature hall bedroom, he saw through an open door a young woman buttoning the shirt-collar for her husband; whereupon his heart swelled with a feeling of mixed envy and extreme friendliness for the young couple. "Who is he?" he remarked to himself, on reaching his room, which now seemed to him desolate and lonely. "Only a tailor, a penniless workman. When I am married I shall not live in a tenement house." And at this his fancy unfolded a picture: A parlor with bronze clock on the mantelpiece; a mirror between two lace window-curtains; a dark-eyed little woman in a chocolate-colored wrapper sweeping a carpet of flaming red and yellow; and, behold! he, Robert, comes in from business, and the young woman addresses him in a piping little voice: "Hello, Rob! Will you have dinner?" just as he had the day before seen in the house of a newly married custom-peddler.

And it came to pass, in those days of "heart-stretching," that one Saturday morning Robert met at the "Sons of Kropovetz" Synagogue a new arrival from his native place in the person of Feive the *melamed.* As the Hebrew term implies, this tall and bony old gentleman, with the face of a martyr, had at home conducted one of the schools in which a Jewish boy passes the day, learning the Word of God. As is not unusual with melameds, Feive's profession yielded him an income which made it necessary for him to devote his spare hours to the business of *shadchen,* or *shidech* agent—that is, of matchmaker in the matrimonial sense of the word. In course of time the shadchen spirit had become so deeply imbedded in Reb Feive's soul that even on finding himself in

New York, and before his draggling satin coat had had time to exhale its lingering traces of steerage odors, his long and snuff-stocked nose fell to smelling for shidechs.

"Ah, Reb Feive!" Rouvke accosted his townsman, "how do you do? Quite an unexpected guest, as sure as I am a Jew! When did you arrive?"

And after a perfunctory catechism upon the health of his mother and Kropovetz matters in general, he inquired about his old master.

"Peretz?" the old man echoed Rouvke's interrogation. "May the Uppermost have mercy on him! You have heard that he is now in reduced circumstances, have you not? The distillery is closed."

"You don't say so!"

"Yes, he is in a very bad way," Reb Feive resumed, curling one of his long yellowish-gray side-locks. "You know what hard times the Jews are now having in Russia. Things are getting from bad to worse—may He whom I dare not mention without washing my hands deliver us and preserve!—a Jew can nowadays hardly engage in any business, much less in the liquor line. Poor Peretz, he looks so careworn!"

"Can it be true that the distillery has been closed? I am *very* sorry."

Rouvke was moved with profound pity for his old employer, who had been kind to him, and to whom he had been devoted. But this feeling of commiseration was instantly succeeded by a vague sense of triumph. "What have I lived to see!" Rouvke seemed to exclaim. "I am now richer than Reb Peretz, as sure as I am a Jew!" And at this he became aware of the bank-book in his breast-pocket.

"Oh, I am *very, very* sorry for him!" he added, with renewed sincerity, after a slight pause. "Why, such an honest Jew! And how is Hanele?"

"As usual," the shadchen rejoined—"still unmarried. But it serves Peretz right (may God not punish me for my hard words!). When I offered her the best matches in the world, he was hard to please. Nothing short of a king would have suited his ambition."

As the old shadchen spoke his right arm, hand, and fingers were busily engaged punctuating his words with a system of the most intricate and most diversified evolutions in the air.

"And how does she look?" Rouvke again broke in. "Is she still as pretty as she used to be?"

"That she is," the matchmaker returned grimly. "But all the worse for her. Would she were plainer looking, for then her father would not have been so fastidious about a young man for her, and she might be a mother of three children by this time."

"Oh, she will have no trouble in making a match; such a beauty!" Rouvke observed.

In the afternoon of the same day, Rouvke lay across his bed with his legs stretched on a chair, after his wont, and his head lost in recollections of Hanele. She had recently all but faded away from his memory, and when he did have occasion to recall her, her portrait before his mind's eye would be a mere faint-drawn outline. But now, singularly enough, he could somehow again vividly see her good-natured, deep, dark eyes, and her rosy lips perpetually exposing the dazzling whiteness of her teeth and illuminating her pallid face with inextinguishable good humor; he could hear the rustle of her fresh calico dress as she friskily ran up to answer her father's solemnly affectionate "Good Sabbath," on Reb Peretz's return from synagogue, the last Saturday before Rouvke's departure.

The image did not send a yearning thrill through Rouvke, as it would have done during his first few months in America; still, on the other hand, it now had for his wearied soul a quieting, benign charm, which it had never exercised before, and the more deeply to indulge in its soothing effect, he shut his eyes. "Suppose I marry her." The thought flashed through his mind, but was instantly dismissed as an absurdity too gross to be indulged even for a pastime. But the thought carried him back to his old days in Kropovetz, and he wished he could go there in flesh for a visit. What a glorious time it would be to let them see his stylish American dress, his business-like manners and general air of prosperity and "echucation"! Ah, how they would be stupefied to see the once Rouvke Arbel thus elegantly attired, "like a regula' dood"! For who in all Kropovetz wears a cut-away, a brown derby, a necktie, and a collar like his? And would it not be lovely to donate a round sum to the synagogue? Oh, how he would be sought after and paraded!

"Poor Reb Peretz!" he said to himself, transferring his thoughts to the news of his old employer's adversity. "Poor Hanele!" Whereat the Kropovetz girl loomed up, her head lowered and tears trickling down her cheeks, as he had once seen her when she sat quietly lamenting her defeated expectation of a new dress. Rouvke conceived the vague idea of sending Reb Peretz fifty dollars, which would make the respectable sum of one hundred rubles. But the generous plan was presently lost in a labyrinth of figures, accounts of his customers, and reflections upon his prospective store, which the notion of fifty dollars called forth in his dollar-ridden brain.

He thus lay plunged in meditation until his reverie was broken by the door flying open.

"Good Sabbath! Good Sabbath!" Reb Feive greeted his young townsman with his martyr-like features relaxed into a significant smile, as he squeezed himself through the narrow space between the half-opened door and the foot of the bedstead. "Do not take ill my not knocking at

the door first. I am not yet used to your customs here, greenhorn that
I am."

"Ah, Reb Feive! Good Sabbath!" Rouvke returned, starting up with
an anxious air and foreboding an appeal for pecuniary assistance.

"Guess what brings me, Rouven."

"How can I tell?" the host rejoined, with a forced simper. "And why
should you not call just for a visit in honor of the Sabbath? You are a
welcome guest. Be seated," he added, indicating his solitary chair and
himself keeping his seat on the bed, which rendered the additional service of lounge.

"How dare these beggarly greenhorns beset me in this manner?" he
left unsaid. "Indeed, what business have they to come to America
at all?"

"Well, how are things going on in Kropovetz?" he asked, audibly.
"Business is very dull *here—very* dull, indeed—may I not be punished
for talking business on Sabbath"—

"Well, *do* leave business alone! You had better hear my errand,
Rouven," the matchmaker said, working his fingers. "Suppose I had a
shidech for you, eh?"

"A shidech?" Rouvke ejaculated, much relieved from his misgivings,
only to become all of a flutter with delicious surprise.

"Yes, a shidech; and what sort of a one! You never dreamed of such
a shidech, I can assure you. Never mind blushing like that. Why, is it
not high time for a young man like you to get married?"

"I am not blushing at all," Rouvke protested, coloring still more
deeply, and missing the sentence by which he had been about to inform
himself of the fair one's name without betraying his feverish impatience.

"Well," Reb Feive resumed, with a smile, and twisting his side-lock
into a corkscrew, "it would be too cruel to try your patience. Let us
come straight to the point, then. I mean—guess whom—well, I mean
Hanele, Peretz the distiller's Hanele! What do you think of that?" the
shadchen added in a whisper, as he let go of his corkscrew, and started
back in well-acted ecstasy to watch the produced effect.

Rouvke flushed up to the roots of his hair, while his mouth opened
in one of those embarrassed grins which seem to be especially adapted
to the mouths of Kropovetz horse-drivers,—one which makes the general expression of the face such that you are at a loss whether to take
it for a smile or for the preliminary to a cry.

"You must be joking, Reb Feive. Why I a-a-a-I am not thinking of
getting married as yet; a-a-you had better tell me some news," he
faltered.

The fact is that the shadchen's attack had taken him so unawares
that it gave him no time to analyze his own mind, and although the

subject thrilled his soul with delightful curiosity, he dreaded the risk of committing himself. But Feive was not the man to let himself be put off so easily in matters of a professional nature; and so, warming up to the beloved topic, he launched out in a flood of garrulity, emphasizing his speech now by striking some figure in space, now by an energetic twirl of his yellowish gray appendages. He enlarged with real shadchenlike gusto on the prospective bride's virtues and accomplishments; on the love which, according to him, she had always professed for Rouvke; on the frivolity of American girls; on the honor it would confer upon his listener to marry into the family of Reb Peretz the distiller.

Rouvke followed Reb Feive with breathless attention, but never uttered a word or a gesture which might be interpreted into an encouragement. This, however, mattered but little to the old matrimonial commission agent, for, carried away with his own eloquence, he talked himself into the impression that Rouvke "was willing," if I may be permitted to borrow a phrase from a more famous horse-driver. At any rate, when Reb Feive suddenly bethought himself that he came near missing the afternoon service at the synagogue, and abruptly got up from his seat, Rouvke seemed anxious to detain him; and as he returned "What is your hurry, Reb Feive?" to his departing visitor's "Good-pie! —is that the way you say here on leaving?" he felt for the old man a kind of filial tenderness.

Choson is a term applied to a Jewish young man, embracing the period from the time he is placed on the matrimonial market down to the termination of the nuptial festivities. There is all the difference in the world between a choson and a common unmarried mortal of the male sex, who is left to the bare designation of *bocher,* the very sound of the hymeneal title possessing an indefinable charm, an element of solemnity, which seems to invest its bearer with a glittering halo.

Reb Feive thus suddenly, as if by a magic wand, converted Rouvke from a simple bocher into a choson. And so keenly alive was Rouvke to his unexpected transformation, that for some time after the wizard's departure his face was wreathed in bashful smiles, as if his new self, by its dazzling presence, embarrassed him. He felt the change in himself in a general way, however, and quite apart from the idea of Hanele. As to Pertez's daughter, the notion of her assenting to marry him again seemed preposterous. Besides, admitting for argument's sake, as the phrase goes, that she would accept him, Rouvke reflected that he would then not be fool enough to enter into wedlock with a portionless girl; that if he waited a year or two longer (although it seemed much too long to wait), that is, until he was a prospering storekeeper, he could get for a wife the daughter of some Division Street merchant with two or three thousand dollars into the bargain.

So he relinquished the thought of Hanele as a thing out of the question and proceeded to picture himself the choson of some American girl. But as he was making that effort, the image of the Kropovetz maiden kept intruding upon his imagination, interfering with the mental process, and his heart seemed all the while to be longing after the dismissed subject and filled with the desire that he might have both matches to choose from. Finally, he yielded and resumed the discussion of Reb Feive's project. The idea of a Division Street business man for a father-in-law, beside the assumption of becoming the son-in-law of Reb Peretz, appeared prosaic and vulgar. Those New York merchants had risen from the mire, like himself, while his old master looked at the world from the lofty height of distinguished birth, added to Talmudical learning and exceeding social importance. And here the ties of traditional reverence and adoration which bound Rouvke to his former employer made themselves keenly felt in his heart. Ah, for the privilege of calling Reb Peretz father-in-law! To think of the stir the news would make among his townsfolk, both in Kropovetz and here in New York! Besides, the American-born or "nearly American-born" girls inspire him with fear. These young ladies are brought up at picnics and balls, while to him the very thought of inviting a lady for a dance is embarrassing. What are they good for, anyway? They look more Christian than Jewish, and are only great hands at squandering their husbands' money on candy, dresses, and theatres. A woman like that would domineer over him, treat him haughtily, and generally make life a burden to him. Hanele, dear Hanele, on the other hand, is a true daughter of Israel. She would make a good housekeeper; would occasionally also mind the store; would accompany him to synagogue every Saturday; and that is just what a man like him wants in a wife. An English-speaking Mrs. Friedman he would have to call "darling," a word barren of any charm or meaning for his heart, whereas Hanele he would address in the melodious terms of "*Kreinele meine! Gold meine!*"[1] Ah, the very music of these sounds would make him cry with happiness!

The thought of a walk to synagogue with Hanele, dressed in a plush cloak and an enormous hat, by his side, and of whispering these words of endearment in her ear was enchanting enough; but then, enchantment-like, the spectacle soon faded away before the hard, retrospective fact of Rouvke, the horse-driver, in top-boots, serving tea to Hanele, the only daughter of Reb Peretz the distiller. "Oh, it cannot be! Feive *is a greener* to take such a match into his head!" he mentally exclaimed in black despair. And forthwith he once more sought consolation in the prospect of a marriage portion which a New York wife would bring

---

[1] "My little crown! My gold!"

him, and fell to adding the probable amount to his own future capital. Hanele will reject him? Why, so much the better! That makes it impossible for him to commit the folly of sacrificing at least two thousand dollars. And his spirits rose at the narrow escape he was having from a ruinous temptation. Still, lurking in a deeper corner of his heart, there lingered something which wounded his pride and made him feel as if he would much rather have *that* means of escape cut off from him and the temptation left for himself to grapple with.

Feive, the melamed, had another talk with Rouvke; but although he did not hesitate to speak authoritatively of Reb Peretz's and Hanele's assent, he utterly failed to elicit from his interlocutor any positive hint. Nothing daunted, however, the shadchen despatched a lengthy epistle to Reb Peretz. He went off in raptures over Rouvke's wealth, social rank in America, and religious habits, and gave him credit for newly acquired education. "It is not the Rouvke of yore," read at least one line on each of the ten pages of the letter. The installment peddling business was elevated to the dignity of a combination of large concerns in furniture, jewelry, and clothing. The owner of this thriving establishment was depicted as panting with love for Hanele, and this again was pointed out as proof that the match had been foreordained by Providence.

Reb Peretz's answer had not reached its destination when in New York there occurred two events which came to the daring matchmaker's assistance.

The daughter of a Seventh Ward landlord had been betrothed to a successful custom peddler, her father promising one thousand dollars in cash, in addition to a complete household outfit, as her marriage portion. As the fixed wedding-day drew near, the choson was one day shocked to receive from his would-be father-in-law the intimation that his girl and the household outfit were good enough on their own merits, and that the thousand dollars would have to be dispensed with. The young man immediately cut short his visits to the landlord's daughter; but a fortnight had hardly elapsed before he found himself behind prison bars on an action brought in the name of his broken-hearted sweetheart. How the matter was compromised does not concern our story; but the news, which for several days was the main topic of gossip in the peddler stores, reached Rouvke; and the effect it had on him the reader may well imagine: it riddled to pieces the only unfavorable argument in his discussion of Feive's offer.

A still more powerful element in reaching a conclusion was with Rouvke the following incident:—

One day he went to see the shadchen, who had his lodging in the house of a fellow townsman. While he stood behind the door adjusting his necktie, as he now invariably did before entering a house, he over-heard a loud dialogue between the housewife and her boarder. Catching his own name, Rouvke paused with bated breath to listen.

"Pray, don't be talking nonsense, Reb Feive," came to the ears of our eavesdropper. "Peretz the distiller give his Hanele in marriage to Rouvke Arbel!—That pock-pitted bugbear and Hanele! Such a beauty, such a pampered child! Why, anybody would be glad to marry her, penniless as she may be. She marry that horrid thing, slop-tub, cholera that he is!"

Rouvke was cut to the quick; and shivering before the prospect of hearing some further uncomplimentary allusions to himself, he was on the point of beating retreat; but the very thought of those epithets con-tinuing to be uttered at his expense, even though beyond his hearing, was too painful to bear; and so he put a stop to them by a knock at the door.

"But are you really sure, Reb Feive, that Reb Peretz will have me?" he queried, after a little, all of a flutter, in a private conversation with the shadchen, in the bedroom.

"Leave it to me," the marriage-broker replied. "I have managed greater things in my lifetime. It is as good as settled."

"See if I do not marry Hanele after all, if only to spite you, grudging witch that you are!" Rouvke, in his heart, addressed to his towns-woman, on emerging from the pitchy darkness of the little bedroom.

"Good-by, Mrs. Kohen!" his tongue then said, as his eyes looked daggers at her.

Reb Peretz concluded the reading of Reb Feive's letter by good na-turedly calling him "foolish melamed." Little by little, however, the very fact that the shadchen could now dare conceive such a match at all began to mortify him. It took him back to the time when Rouvke used to sit behind his mare, and when he, Reb Peretz, was the most pros-perous Jew for miles around, and it wrung his heart with pity both for himself and for Hanele. He became aware that it was over a year since a young man had come to offer himself, and instead of becoming irri-tated with his daughter, as had latterly been frequently the case with him, he was overpowered by an acute twinge of hurt pride, as well as by compunction for the splendid matrimonial opportunities which he had brushed aside from her. It occurred to Reb Peretz that Hanele was now in her twenty-fifth year, whereupon his fancy reproachfully pointed at his cherished child in the form of a gray-haired old maid. A shudder ran through his veins at the vision, and he began to seek refuge in commercial air castles, but the aërial structures were presently blown away, only to leave him face to face with the wretched ramshackle edifice of his actual affairs. His attention reverted to the American letter, but the collocation of Rouvke Arbel with Hanele sickened Reb Peretz. His self-respect suddenly rushed back upon him, and he felt like "tearing out the beard and sidelocks" of the impudent shadchen.

Nevertheless, he took up the letter once more. This time the match-maker's eulogies of Rouvke's flourishing business made a deeper impression on him, and brought the indistinct reflection that in course of time he might have to emigrate to America himself with his whole family.

"Pooh, nonsense!" he ultimately concluded, after a third or fourth reading of Reb Feive's missive. "America makes a new man of every young fellow. There had not been a more miserable wretch than Tevke, the watchman; and yet when he recently came back from America for a visit, he looked like a prince. Let her go and be a mother of children, as behooves a daughter of Israel. We must trust to God. The match does look like a Providential affair."

Reb Peretz was a whole day in mustering courage for an explanation with Hanele. But when he had at last broached the subject to her, by means of rendering Feive's Hebrew letter into Yiddish, his undertaking proved easier of achievement than he had anticipated.

Hanele was really a "true daughter of Israel," and this implies that her education was limited to the reading of a Yiddish version of the Five Books of Moses, and that her knowledge of the world did not extend beyond "Kropovetz and its goats," as the phrase runs in her native town. She was a taciturn, good-natured, and tractable girl, and her greatest pleasure was to be knitting fancy table-cloths and brooding over day-dreams. Moreover, the repeated appearance and disappearance of chosons, by recurrently unsettling her hitherto calm and easy heart, had left it in a state of perpetual unrest. She had not fallen in love with any of the young men who had sought her hand and her marriage portion, for, according to a rigid old rule of propriety to which her father clung, she never had been allowed the chance of interchanging a word with any of them, even while the suit was pending. Still, when a month passed without a shadchen putting in an appearance, she would often, when the latch gave a click, raise her eyes to the door in the eager hope that it would admit a member of that profession. In her reveries she now frequently dwelt on her girl friends who had married out of Kropovetz, and then her soul would be yearning and longing, she knew not after what. With all the tender affection which tied her to her family, with all her attachment to her native surroundings, her father's house became dreary and lonely to her; she grew tired of her home and home-sick after the rest of the world.

To be sure, the first intimation as to her marrying Rouvke Arbel shocked her, and on realizing the full meaning of the offer she dropped her head on her father's shoulder and burst into tears. But as Reb Peretz stroked her hair, while he presented the matter in an aspect which was even an improvement on Feive's plea, he gradually hypnotized her into a lighter mood, and she recalled Rouvke's photograph, which his mother had on several occasions flaunted before her. The match now assumed a somewhat romantic phase. She let her jaded imagination waft her away to an unknown far-off land, where she saw herself glittering with gold and pearls and nestling up to a masculine figure in sumptuous attire. It was a bewitching, thrilling scene only slightly marred by the dim outline of Rouvke in top-boots and sheepskin rising in the background. Ah, it was such a pity to have that taint on the otherwise fascinating picture! And, in order to remove the sickly blotch, Hanele essayed to rig Rouvke out in a "cut-away," stand-up collar, and necktie after the model of the photograph. But then her effort produced a total stranger with features she could not make out, while Rouvke Arbel, top-boots, sheepskin and all, seemed to have dodged the elegant attire and to remain aloof both from the stranger and the photograph. Well, it is not Rouvke, then, who is proposed to her, she settled, with the three images crowding each other in her mind. It is an entirely new man. Besides, who can tell what may transpire? Let her first get to America and then—who knows, but she may in truth marry another man, a nice young fellow who had never been her father's servant? And Hanele felt that such would be the case. At all events, did not Baske David, the flour merchant's daughter, marry a former blacksmith in America, and is she not happy? Ah, the letters she writes to her!

"Say yes or no. Speak out, my little dove," Reb Peretz insisted, in conclusion of a second conversation on the same subject. "It is not my destiny which is to be decided. It is for you to say," he added, feeling that Hanele had no business to render any but an affirmative decision.

"Yes," she at last whispered, drooping her head and bursting into a cry.

The shadchen gave himself no rest, and letters sailed over the Atlantic by the dozen. In his first reply Reb Peretz took care to appear oscillating. His second contained a hint as to the attachment which Hanele had always felt for Rouvke, whom they had treated like one of the family. There were also letters with remote allusions to money which Hanele would want for some dresses and to pay her way. And thus, with every message he penned, the conviction gained on Reb Peretz that his daughter would be happy in America, and that the match was really of Providential origin.

These letters operated on Rouvke's heart as an ointment does on a wound, to cite his own illustration; and in spite of the money hints, which constituted the fly in this ointment, he felt happy. He thought of

Hanele; he dreamed of her; and, above all, he thought and dreamed of the sensation which her departure from home would create at Kropovetz, and of his glory on her arrival in New York. "Good luck to you, Robert!" the peddlers repeatedly congratulated him. "Have you ever dreamed of becoming the son-in-law of Peretz the distiller? There should be no end to the treats which you ought to stand now." And Robert stood treat and was wreathed in chosonlike smiles.

It was a busy day at Castle Garden. Several transatlantic steamers had arrived, and the railed inclosure within the vast shed was alive with a motley crowd of freshly landed steerage passengers. Outside, there was a cluster of empty merchandise trucks waiting for their human loads, while at a haughty distance from these stood a pair of highly polished carriages—quite a rare sight in front of the immigrant landing station. It was Rouvke who had engaged these superior vehicles. He had come in them with Reb Feive, and with two or three others of his fellow countrymen and brothers in business, to meet Hanele. He was dressed in his Saturday clothes and in a brand-new brown derby hat, and even wore a huge red rose which one of the party, a gallant custom peddler, had stuck into the lapel of his "cut-away" before starting.

The atmosphere of the barn-like garden was laden with nauseating odors of steerage and of carbolic acid, and reeking with human wretchedness. Leaning against the railing or sitting on their baggage, there were bevies of unkempt men and women in shabby dress of every cut and color, holding on to ragged, bulging parcels, baskets, or sacks, and staring at space with a look of forlorn, stupefied, and cowed resignation. The cry of children in their mothers' arms, blending in jarring discord with the gruff yells of the uniformed officers, jostling their way through the crowd, and with the general hum and buzz inside and outside the inclosure, made the scene as painful to the ear as it was to the eye and nostrils, and completed the impression of misery and desolation.

Rouvke and his companions, among a swarm of other residents of the East Side, who, like themselves, had come to meet newly landed friends, stood gazing through the railing. Rouvke was nervously biting his finger-nails, and now and then brushing his new derby with his coat-sleeve or adjusting his necktie. Reb Feive was winding his side-lock about his finger, while the young peddlers were vying with each other in pleasantries appropriate to the situation. Our choson was lost in a tumult of emotions. He made repeated attempts at collecting his wits and devising a befitting form of welcome; he tried to figure to himself Hanele's present appearance and to forecast her conduct on first catching sight of him; he also essayed to analyze the whole situation and to think out a plan for the immediate future. But all his efforts fell flat.

His thoughts were fragmentary, and no sooner had he laid hold of an idea or an image than it would flee from his mind again and his attention would, for spite, as it were, occupy itself with the merest trifle, such as the size of the whiskers of one of the officers or the sea-biscuit at which an immigrant urchin was nibbling.

At last Rouvke's heart gave a leap. His eyes had fallen on Hanele. She was still more beautiful and charming than before. Instead of the spare and childish-looking girl whom he had left at Kropovetz, there stood before him a stately, well-formed young woman of twenty-five.

"Ha—Ha—Hanele!" he gasped out, all but melting away with emotion, and suddenly feeling, not like Robert Friedman, but like Rouvke Arbel.

Hanele turned her head toward him, but she did not see him. So at least it seemed, for instead of pushing her way to the part of the railing where he stood, she started back and obliterated herself in the crowd.

Presently her name was called, together with other names, and she emerged from a stream of fellow immigrants. More dead than alive, Rouvke ran forward to meet her; but he had advanced two steps when his legs refused to proceed, and his face became blank with amazement. For, behold, snugly supporting Hanele's arm, there was a young man in spectacles and in a seedy gray uniform overcoat of a Russian collegian, with its brass buttons superseded by new ones of black celluloid.

The pair marched up to Rouvke, she with her eyes fixed at the floor, as she clung to her companion, and the collegian with his head raised in timid defiance.

"How do you do, Rouven?" she began. "This is *Gospodin*[1] Levinsky—my choson. Do not take it ill, Rouven. I am not to blame, as true as I am a child of Israel. You see, it is my Providential match, and I could not help it," she rattled off in a trembling voice and like an embarrassed schoolboy reciting a lesson which he has gotten well by heart.

"I'll pay you every copeck, you can rest assured," the collegian interposed, turning as white as a sheet. "I have a rich brother in Buffalo."

Hanele had met the young man in the steerage of the Dutch vessel which brought them across the ocean; and they passed a fortnight there, walking or sitting together on deck, and sharing the weird over-awing whispers of the waves, the stern thumping of the engine, and the soothing smiles of the moon—that skillfulest of shadchens in general, and on ship's deck in particular. The long and short of it is that the match-making luminary had cut Reb Feive out of his job.

[1]Russian for Mister.

Hanele's explanation at first stunned Rouvke, and he stood for some time eyeing her with a grin of stupid distraction. But presently, upon recovering his senses, he turned as red as fire, and making a face like that of a child when suddenly robbed of its toy, he wailed out in a husky voice:

"I want my hundred and fifty dollars back!" And then in English:—
"I call a politzman. I vant my hoondered an' fifty dollar!"

"*Ai, ai*—murderess! murderess!" Reb Feive burst out at Hanele. "I am going to get your father to come over here, *ai, ai!*" he lamented, all but bursting into tears with rage. And presently, in caressing tones:—

"Listen to me, Hanele! I know you are a good and God-fearing Jewish girl. Fie! drop that abominable beggar. Leave that gentile-like shaven mug, I tell you. Rouven is your Providential match. Look at him, the prince that he is! You will live like a queen with him, you will roll in gold and jewels, Hanele!"

But Hanele only clung to the collegian's arm the faster, and the two were about to leave the Garden, when Rouvke grasped his successful rival by the lapels of his overcoat, crying as he did so: "Politzman! Politzman!"

The young couple looked a picture of helplessness. But at this juncture a burly shaven-faced "runner" of an immigrant hotel, who had been watching the scene, sprang to their rescue. Brushing Rouvke aside with a thrust of his mighty arm, accompanied by a rasping "Git out, or I'll punch your pockmarked nose, ye monkey!" he marched Hanele and her *choson* away, leaving Rouvke staring as if he were at a loss to realize the situation, while Reb Feive, violently wringing his hands, gasped, "Ai! ai! ai!" and the young peddlers bandied whispered jokes.

ALICE DUNBAR-NELSON

Sister Josepha

This story was first published in *The Goodness of St. Rocque and Other Stories* (1899). The local-color elements in "Sister Josepha" are muted, and the story of the orphan Camille appears at first glance to be a classic examination of the opposing claims of the spirit and the flesh. Camille is a willful and vivacious girl whose force of personality dominates the other children. As she grows older her beauty becomes her distinction and her curse. Camille's instincts tell her that the motives of a prospective foster father are more likely to be sexual than compassionate, and she resolves to take the veil and to become Sister Josepha. The change of names is significant, for the biblical Joseph was sold into slavery by his own family; similarly, Camille's abandonment to the orphanage results in another form of bondage. Life in the convent is secure but also confining and provides no release for what is best in her. The world outside the heavy door of the convent is inviting, but, as Sister Dominica remarks, it is not meant for one "with no name but Camille, no friends," and nothing but her beauty to recommend her. What is more, she has no "nationality," by which Dunbar-Nelson seems to mean Josepha has no discernible racial identity. Ultimately, "Sister Josepha" is a story about the tragic consequences for a woman without an identity in a hard world.

*   *   *

Sister Josepha told her beads mechanically, her fingers numb with the accustomed exercise. The little organ creaked a dismal "O Salutaris," and she still knelt on the floor, her white-bonneted head nodding suspiciously. The Mother Superior gave a sharp glance at the tired figure; then, as a sudden lurch forward brought the little sister back to consciousness, Mother's eyes relaxed into a genuine smile.

The bell tolled the end of vespers, and the sombre-robed nuns filed out of the chapel to go about their evening duties. Little Sister Josepha's work was to attend to the household lamps, but there must have been as much oil spilled upon the table to-night as was put in the vessels. The small brown hands trembled so that most of the wicks were trimmed with points at one corner which caused them to smoke that night.

"Oh, cher Seigneur," she sighed, giving an impatient polish to a refractory chimney, "it is wicked and sinful, I know, but I am so tired. I can't be happy and sing any more. It doesn't seem right for le bon Dieu to have me all cooped up here with nothing to see but stray visitors, and always the same old work, teaching those mean little girls to sew, and washing and filling the same old lamps. Pah!" And she polished the chimney with a sudden vigorous jerk which threatened destruction.

They were rebellious prayers that the red mouth murmured that night, and a restless figure that tossed on the hard dormitory bed. Sister Dominica called from her couch to know if Sister Josepha were ill.

"No," was the somewhat short response; then a muttered, "Why can't they let me alone for a minute? That pale-eyed Sister Dominica never sleeps; that's why she is so ugly."

About fifteen years before this night some one had brought to the orphan asylum connected with this convent, du Sacré Cœur, a round, dimpled bit of three-year-old humanity, who regarded the world from a pair of gravely twinkling black eyes, and only took a chubby thumb out of a rosy mouth long enough to answer in monosyllabic French. It was a child without an identity; there was but one name that any one seemed to know, and that, too, was vague,—Camille.

She grew up with the rest of the waifs; scraps of French and American civilization thrown together to develop a seemingly inconsistent miniature world. Mademoiselle Camille was a queen among them, a pretty little tyrant who ruled the children and dominated the more timid sisters in charge.

One day an awakening came. When she was fifteen, and almost fully ripened into a glorious tropical beauty of the type that matures early, some visitors to the convent were fascinated by her and asked the Mother Superior to give the girl into their keeping.

Camille fled like a frightened fawn into the yard, and was only unearthed with some difficulty from behind a group of palms. Sulky and pouting, she was led into the parlour, picking at her blue pinafore like a spoiled infant.

"The lady and gentleman wish you to go home with them, Camille," said the Mother Superior, in the language of the convent. Her voice was kind and gentle apparently; but the child, accustomed to its various inflections, detected a steely ring behind its softness, like the proverbial iron hand in the velvet glove.

"You must understand, madame," continued Mother, in stilted English, "that we never force children from us. We are ever glad to place them in comfortable—how you say that?—quarters—maisons—homes—bien! But we will not make them go if they do not wish."

Camille stole a glance at her would-be guardians, and decided instantly, impulsively, finally. The woman suited her; but the man! It was doubtless intuition of the quick, vivacious sort which belonged to her blood that served her. Untutored in worldly knowledge, she could not divine the meaning of the pronounced leers and admiration of her physical charms which gleamed in the man's face, but she knew it made her feel creepy, and stoutly refused to go.

Next day Camille was summoned from a task to the Mother Superior's parlour. The other girls gazed with envy upon her as she dashed down the courtyard with impetuous movement. Camille, they decided crossly, received too much notice. It was Camille this, Camille that; she was pretty, it was to be expected. Even Father Ray lingered longer in his blessing when his hands pressed her silky black hair.

As she entered the parlour, a strange chill swept over the girl. The room was not an unaccustomed one, for she had swept it many times, but to-day the stiff black chairs, the dismal crucifixes, the gleaming whiteness of the walls, even the cheap lithograph of the Madonna which

Camille had always regarded as a perfect specimen of art, seemed cold and mean.

"Camille, ma chère," said Mother, "I am extremely displeased with you. Why did you not wish to go with Monsieur and Madame Lafayé yesterday?"

The girl uncrossed her hands from her bosom, and spread them out in a deprecating gesture.

"Mais, ma mère, I was afraid."

Mother's face grew stern. "No foolishness now," she exclaimed.

"It is not foolishness, ma mère; I could not help it, but that man looked at me so funny, I felt all cold chills down my back. Oh, dear Mother, I love the convent and the sisters so, I just want to stay and be a sister too, may I?"

And thus it was that Camille took the white veil at sixteen years. Now that the period of novitiate was over, it was just beginning to dawn upon her that she had made a mistake.

"Maybe it would have been better had I gone with the funny-looking lady and gentleman," she mused bitterly one night. "Oh, Seigneur, I'm so tired and impatient; it's so dull here, and, dear God, I'm so young."

There was no help for it. One must arise in the morning, and help in the refectory with the stupid Sister Francesca, and go about one's duties with a prayerful mien, and not even let a sigh escape when one's head ached with the eternal telling of beads.

A great fête day was coming, and an atmosphere of preparation and mild excitement pervaded the brown walls of the convent like a delicate aroma. The old Cathedral around the corner had stood a hundred years, and all the city was rising to do honour to its age and time-softened beauty. There would be a service, oh, but such a one! with two Cardinals, and Archbishops and Bishops, and all the accompanying glitter of soldiers and orchestras. The little sisters of the Convent du Sacré Cœur clasped their hands in anticipation of the holy joy. Sister Josepha curled her lip, she was so tired of churchly pleasures.

The day came, a gold and blue spring day, when the air hung heavy with the scent of roses and magnolias, and the sunbeams fairly laughed as they kissed the houses. The old Cathedral stood gray and solemn, and the flowers in Jackson Square smiled cheery birthday greetings across the way. The crowd around the door surged and pressed and pushed in its eagerness to get within. Ribbons stretched across the banquette were of no avail to repress it, and important ushers with cardinal colours could do little more.

The Sacred Heart sisters filed slowly in at the side door, creating a momentary flutter as they paced reverently to their seats, guarding the blue-bonneted orphans. Sister Josepha, determined to see as much of the world as she could, kept her big black eyes opened wide, as the church rapidly filled with the fashionably dressed, perfumed, rustling, and self-conscious throng.

Her heart beat quickly. The rebellious thoughts that will arise in the most philosophical of us surged in her small heavily gowned bosom. For her were the gray things, the neutral tinted skies, the ugly garb, the coarse meats; for them the rainbow, the ethereal airiness of earthly joys, the bonbons and glacés of the world. Sister Josepha did not know that the rainbow is elusive, and its colours but the illumination of tears; she had never been told that earthly ethereality is necessarily ephemeral, nor that bonbons and glacés, whether of the palate or of the soul, nauseate and pall upon the taste. Dear God, forgive her, for she bent with contrite tears over her worn rosary, and glanced no more at the worldly glitter of femininity.

The sunbeams streamed through the high windows in purple and crimson lights upon a veritable fugue of colour. Within the seats, crush upon crush of spring millinery; within the aisles erect lines of gold-braided, gold-buttoned military. Upon the altar, broad sweeps of golden robes, great dashes of crimson skirts, mitres and gleaming crosses, the soft neutral hue of rich lace vestments; the tender heads of childhood in picturesque attire; the proud, golden magnificence of the domed altar with its weighting mass of lilies and wide-eyed roses, and the long candles that sparkled their yellow star points above the reverent throng within the altar rails.

The soft baritone of the Cardinal intoned a single phrase in the suspended silence. The censer took up the note in its delicate clink clink, as it swung to and fro in the hands of a fair-haired child. Then the organ, pausing an instant in a deep, mellow, long-drawn note, burst suddenly into a magnificent strain, and the choir sang forth, "Kyrie Eleïson, Christe Eleïson." One voice, flute-like, piercing, sweet, rang high over the rest. Sister Josepha heard and trembled, as she buried her face in her hands, and let her tears fall, like other beads, through her rosary.

It was when the final word of the service had been intoned, the last peal of the exit march had died away, that she looked up meekly, to encounter a pair of youthful brown eyes gazing pityingly upon her. That was all she remembered for a moment, that the eyes were youthful and handsome and tender. Later, she saw that they were placed in a rather beautiful boyish face, surmounted by waves of brown hair, curling and soft, and that the head was set on a pair of shoulders decked in military uniform. Then the brown eyes marched away with the rest of the rear guard, and the white-bonneted sisters filed out the side door, through the narrow court, back into the brown convent.

That night Sister Josepha tossed more than usual on her hard bed, and clasped her fingers often in prayer to quell the wickedness in her heart. Turn where she would, pray as she might, there was ever a pair of tender, pitying brown eyes, haunting her persistently. The squeaky organ at vespers intoned the clank of military accoutrements to her ears, the white bonnets of the sisters about her faded into mists of curling brown hair. Briefly, Sister Josepha was in love.

The days went on pretty much as before, save for the one little heart that beat rebelliously now and then, though it tried so hard to be submissive. There was the morning work in the refectory, the stupid little girls to teach sewing, and the insatiable lamps that were so greedy for oil. And always the tender, boyish brown eyes, that looked so sorrowfully at the fragile, beautiful little sister, haunting, following, pleading.

Perchance, had Sister Josepha been in the world, the eyes would have been an incident. But in this home of self-repression and retrospection, it was a life-story. The eyes had gone their way, doubtless forgetting the little sister they pitied; but the little sister?

The days glided into weeks, the weeks into months. Thoughts of escape had come to Sister Josepha, to flee into the world, to merge in the great city where recognition was impossible, and, working her way like the rest of humanity, perchance encounter the eyes again.

It was all planned and ready. She would wait until some morning when the little band of black-robed sisters wended their way to mass at the Cathedral. When it was time to file out the side-door into the courtway, she would linger at prayers, then slip out another door, and unseen glide up Chartres Street to Canal, and once there, mingle in the throng that filled the wide thoroughfare. Beyond this first plan she could think no further. Penniless, garbed, and shaven though she would be, other difficulties never presented themselves to her. She would rely on the mercies of the world to help her escape from this torturing life of inertia. It seemed easy now that the first step of decision had been taken.

The Saturday night before the final day had come, and she lay feverishly nervous in her narrow little bed, wondering with wide-eyed fear at the morrow. Pale-eyed Sister Dominica and Sister Francesca were whispering together in the dark silence, and Sister Josepha's ears pricked up as she heard her name.

"She is not well, poor child," said Francesca. "I fear the life is too confining."

"It is best for her," was the reply. "You know, sister, how hard it would be for her in the world, with no name but Camille, no friends, and her beauty; and then—"

Sister Josepha heard no more, for her heart beating tumultously in her bosom drowned the rest. Like the rush of the bitter salt tide over a drowning man clinging to a spar, came the complete submerging of her hopes of another life. No name but Camille, that was true; no nationality, for she could never tell from whom or whence she came; no friends, and a beauty that not even an ungainly bonnet and shaven head could hide. In a flash she realised the deception of the life she would lead, and the cruel self-torture of wonder at her own identity. Already, as if in anticipation of the world's questionings, she was asking herself, "Who am I? What am I?"

The next morning the sisters du Sacré Cœur filed into the Cathedral at High Mass, and bent devout knees at the general confession. "Confiteor Deo omnipotenti," murmured the priest; and tremblingly one little sister followed the words, "Je confesse à Dieu, tout puissant—que j'ai beaucoup péché par pensées—c'est ma faute—c'est ma faute—c'est ma très grande faute."

The organ pealed forth as mass ended, the throng slowly filed out, and the sisters paced through the courtway back into the brown convent walls. One paused at the entrance, and gazed with swift longing eyes in the direction of narrow, squalid Chartres Street, then, with a gulping sob, followed the rest, and vanished behind the heavy door.

CHARLES W. CHESNUTT

The Wife of His Youth

"The Wife of His Youth" was originally published in the *Atlantic Monthly*, the leading literary magazine in the country at the time, prior to its inclusion in *The Wife of His Youth and Other Stories of the Color Line* in 1899. Its significance in American literary history derives from its portrayal of an ethical dilemma within its African-American protagonist, one driven not by simple racial injustice but informed by the more complex history of slavery and racism in the nineteenth century and the legacy of attitudes about ethnicity that permeated the social fabric after the Civil War. In this instance, the central character, Mr. Ryder, must decide whether to move forward morally at the cost of sacrificing wealth, social position, and a beautiful young wife, a judgment he shares with a group of assembled friends. His decision provides the crux of the plot, but the skill with which Chesnutt presents the problem, and the artistry of his style, as well as a believable psychological flow, make the story significant as art quite beyond its didactic social function. Frequently anthologized, this story is one of the most significant of the turn

of the century, a period in which issues of race began to come into focus
in the best of American fiction.

*   *   *

I

Mr. Ryder was going to give a ball. There were several reasons why
this was an opportune time for such an event.

Mr. Ryder might aptly be called the dean of the Blue Veins. The
original Blue Veins were a little society of colored persons organized in
a certain Northern city shortly after the war. Its purpose was to establish
and maintain correct social standards among a people whose social condition presented almost unlimited room for improvement. By accident,
combined perhaps with some natural affinity, the society consisted of
individuals who were, generally speaking, more white than black. Some
envious outsider made the suggestion that no one was eligible for membership who was not white enough to show blue veins. The suggestion
was readily adopted by those who were not of the favored few, and
since that time the society, though possessing a longer and more pretentious name, had been known far and wide as the "Blue Vein
Society," and its members as the "Blue Veins."

The Blue Veins did not allow that any such requirement existed for
admission to their circle, but, on the contrary, declared that character
and culture were the only things considered; and that if most of their
members were light-colored, it was because such persons, as a rule, had
had better opportunities to qualify themselves for membership. Opinions differed, too, as to the usefulness of the society. There were those
who had been known to assail it violently as a glaring example of the
very prejudice from which the colored race had suffered most; and later,
when such critics had succeeded in getting on the inside, they had been
heard to maintain with zeal and earnestness that the society was a life-
boat, an anchor, a bulwark and a shield,—a pillar of cloud by day and
of fire by night, to guide their people through the social wilderness.
Another alleged prerequisite for Blue Vein membership was that of free
birth; and while there was really no such requirement, it is doubtless
true that very few of the members would have been unable to meet it
if there had been. If there were one or two of the older members who
had come up from the South and from slavery, their history presented
enough romantic circumstances to rob their servile origin of its grosser
aspects.

While there were no such tests of eligibility, it is true that the Blue
Veins had their notions on these subjects, and that not all of them were
equally liberal in regard to the things they collectively disclaimed. Mr.

Ryder was one of the most conservative. Though he had not been among the founders of the society, but had come in some years later, his genius for social leadership was such that he had speedily become its recognized adviser and head, the custodian of its standards, and the preserver of its traditions. He shaped its social policy, was active in providing for its entertainment, and when the interest fell off, as it sometimes did, he fanned the embers until they burst again into a cheerful flame.

There were still other reasons for his popularity. While he was not as white as some of the Blue Veins, his appearance was such as to confer distinction upon them. His features were of a refined type, his hair was almost straight; he was always neatly dressed; his manners were irreproachable, and his morals above suspicion. He had come to Groveland a young man, and obtaining employment in the office of a railroad company as messenger had in time worked himself up to the position of stationery clerk, having charge of the distribution of the office supplies for the whole company. Although the lack of early training had hindered the orderly development of a naturally fine mind, it had not prevented him from doing a great deal of reading or from forming decidedly literary tastes. Poetry was his passion. He could repeat whole pages of the great English poets; and if his pronunciation was sometimes faulty, his eye, his voice, his gestures, would respond to the changing sentiment with a precision that revealed a poetic soul and disarmed criticism. He was economical, and had saved money; he owned and occupied a very comfortable house on a respectable street. His residence was handsomely furnished, containing among other things a good library, especially rich in poetry, a piano, and some choice engravings. He generally shared his house with some young couple, who looked after his wants and were company for him; for Mr. Ryder was a single man. In the early days of his connection with the Blue Veins he had been regarded as quite a catch, and young ladies and their mothers had manœuvred with much ingenuity to capture him. Not, however, until Mrs. Molly Dixon visited Groveland had any woman ever made him wish to change his condition to that of a married man.

Mrs. Dixon had come to Groveland from Washington in the spring, and before the summer was over she had won Mr. Ryder's heart. She possessed many attractive qualities. She was much younger than he; in fact, he was old enough to have been her father, though no one knew exactly how old he was. She was whiter than he, and better educated. She had moved in the best colored society of the country, at Washington, and had taught in the schools of that city. Such a superior person had been eagerly welcomed to the Blue Vein Society, and had taken a leading part in its activities. Mr. Ryder had at first been attracted by her charms of person, for she was very good looking and not over twenty-five; then by her refined manners and the vivacity of her wit. Her husband had been a government clerk, and at his death had left a considerable life insurance. She was visiting friends in Groveland, and, finding the town and the people to her liking, had prolonged her stay indefinitely. She had not seemed displeased at Mr. Ryder's attentions, but on the contrary had given him every proper encouragement; indeed, a younger and less cautious man would long since have spoken. But he had made up his mind, and had only to determine the time when he would ask her to be his wife. He decided to give a ball in her honor, and at some time during the evening of the ball to offer her his heart and hand. He had no special fears about the outcome, but, with a little touch of romance, he wanted the surroundings to be in harmony with his own feelings when he should have received the answer he expected.

Mr. Ryder resolved that this ball should mark an epoch in the social history of Groveland. He knew, of course,—no one could know better,—the entertainments that had taken place in past years, and what must be done to surpass them. His ball must be worthy of the lady in whose honor it was to be given, and must, by the quality of its guests, set an example for the future. He had observed of late a growing liberality, almost a laxity, in social matters, even among members of his own set, and had several times been forced to meet in a social way persons whose complexions and callings in life were hardly up to the standard which he considered proper for the society to maintain. He had a theory of his own.

"I have no race prejudice," he would say, "but we people of mixed blood are ground between the upper and the nether millstone. Our fate lies between absorption by the white race and extinction in the black. The one doesn't want us yet, but may take us in time. The other would welcome us, but it would be for us a backward step. 'With malice towards none, with charity for all,' we must do the best we can for ourselves and those who are to follow us. Self-preservation is the first law of nature."

His ball would serve by its exclusiveness to counteract leveling tendencies, and his marriage with Mrs. Dixon would help to further the upward process of absorption he had been wishing and waiting for.

II

The ball was to take place on Friday night. The house had been put in order, the carpets covered with canvas, the halls and stairs decorated with palms and potted plants; and in the afternoon Mr. Ryder sat on his front porch, which the shade of a vine running up over a wire netting

made a cool and pleasant lounging place. He expected to respond to
the toast "The Ladies" at the supper, and from a volume of Tennyson
—his favorite poet—was fortifying himself with apt quotations. The
volume was open at "A Dream of Fair Women." His eyes fell on these
lines, and he read them aloud to judge better of their effect:—

> *"At length I saw a lady within call,*
> *Stiller than chisell'd marble, standing there;*
> *A daughter of the gods, divinely tall,*
> *And most divinely fair."*

He marked the verse, and turning the page read the stanza beginning,—

> *"O sweet pale Margaret,*
> *O rare pale Margaret."*

He weighed the passage a moment, and decided that it would not do.
Mrs. Dixon was the palest lady he expected at the ball, and she was of
a rather ruddy complexion, and of lively disposition and buxom build.
So he ran over the leaves until his eye rested on the description of Queen
Guinevere:—

> *"She seem'd a part of joyous Spring:*
> *A gown of grass-green silk she wore,*
> *Buckled with golden clasps before;*
> *A light-green tuft of plumes she bore*
> *Closed in a golden ring.*

> *"She look'd so lovely, as she sway'd*
> *The rein with dainty finger-tips,*
> *A man had given all other bliss,*
> *And all his worldly worth for this,*
> *To waste his whole heart in one kiss*
> *Upon her perfect lips."*

As Mr. Ryder murmured these words audibly, with an appreciative
thrill, he heard the latch of his gate click, and a light footfall sounding
on the steps. He turned his head, and saw a woman standing before his
door.

She was a little woman, not five feet tall, and proportioned to her
height. Although she stood erect, and looked around her with very

bright and restless eyes, she seemed quite old; for her face was crossed and recrossed with a hundred wrinkles, and around the edges of her bonnet could be seen protruding here and there a tuft of short gray wool. She wore a blue calico gown of ancient cut, a little red shawl fastened around her shoulders with an old-fashioned brass brooch, and a large bonnet profusely ornamented with faded red and yellow artificial flowers. And she was very black,—so black that her toothless gums, revealed when she opened her mouth to speak, were not red, but blue. She looked like a bit of the old plantation life, summoned up from the past by the wave of a magician's wand, as the poet's fancy had called into being the gracious shapes of which Mr. Ryder had just been reading.

He rose from his chair and came over to where she stood.

"Good-afternoon, madam," he said.

"Good-evenin', suh," she answered, ducking suddenly with a quaint curtsy. Her voice was shrill and piping, but softened somewhat by age. "Is dis yere whar Mistuh Ryduh lib, suh?" she asked, looking around her doubtfully, and glancing into the open windows, through which some of the preparations for the evening were visible.

"Yes," he replied, with an air of kindly patronage, unconsciously flattered by her manner, "I am Mr. Ryder. Did you want to see me?"

"Yas, suh, ef I ain't 'sturbin' of you too much."

"Not at all. Have a seat over here behind the vine, where it is cool. What can I do for you?"

" 'Scuse me, suh," she continued, when she had sat down on the edge of a chair, " 'scuse me, suh, I's lookin' for my husban'. I heerd you wuz a big man an' had libbed heah a long time, an' I 'lowed you wouldn't min' ef I'd come roun' an' ax you ef you'd ever heerd of a merlatter man by de name er Sam Taylor 'quirin' roun' in de chu'ches ermongs' de people fer his wife 'Liza Jane?"

Mr. Ryder seemed to think for a moment.

"There used to be many such cases right after the war," he said, "but it has been so long that I have forgotten them. There are very few now. But tell me your story, and it may refresh my memory."

She sat back farther in her chair so as to be more comfortable, and folded her withered hands in her lap.

"My name's 'Liza," she began, " 'Liza Jane. W'en I wuz young I us'ter b'long ter Marse Bob Smif, down in ole Missoura. I wuz bawn down dere. W'en I wuz a gal I wuz married ter a man named Jim. But Jim died, an' after dat I married a merlatter man named Sam Taylor. Sam wuz free-bawn, but his mammy and daddy died, an' de w'ite folks 'prenticed him ter my marster fer ter work fer 'im 'tel he wuz growed up. Sam worked in de fiel', an' I wuz de cook. One day Ma'y Ann, ole miss's maid, came rushin' out ter de kitchen, an' says she, "Liza Jane, ole marse gwine sell yo' Sam down de ribber.'

" 'Go way f'm yere,' says I; 'my husban's free!'

" 'Don' make no diff'ence. I heerd ole marse tell ole miss he wuz gwine take yo' Sam 'way wid 'im ter-morrow, fer he needed money, an' he knowed whar he could git a t'ousan' dollars fer Sam an' no questions axed.'

"W'en Sam come home f'm de fiel' dat night, I tole him 'bout ole marse gwine steal 'im, an' Sam run erway. His time wuz mos' up, an' he swo' dat w'en he wuz twenty-one he would come back an' he'p me run erway, er else save up de money ter buy my freedom. An' I know he'd'a' done it, fer he thought a heap er me, Sam did. But w'en he come back he didn' fin' me, fer I wuzn' dere. Ole marse had heerd dat I warned Sam, so he had me whip' an' sol' down de ribber.

"Den de wah broke out, an' w'en it wuz ober de cullud folks wuz scattered. I went back ter de ole home; but Sam wuzn' dere, an' I couldn' l'arn nuffin' 'bout 'im. But I knowed he'd be'n dere to look fer me an' hadn' foun' me, an' had gone erway ter hunt fer me.

"I's be'n lookin' fer 'im eber sence," she added simply, as though twenty-five years were but a couple of weeks, "an' I knows he's be'n lookin' fer me. Fer he sot a heap er sto' by me, Sam did, an' I know he's be'n huntin' fer me all dese years,—'less'n he's be'n sick er sump'n, so he couldn' work, er out'n his head, so he couldn' 'member his promise. I went back down de ribber, fer I 'lowed he'd gone down dere lookin' fer me. I's be'n ter Noo Orleans, an' Atlanty, an' Charleston, an' Richmon'; an' w'en I'd be'n all ober de Souf I come ter de Norf. Fer I knows I'll fin' 'im some er dese days," she added softly, "er he'll fin' me, an' den we'll bofe be as happy in freedom as we wuz in de ole days befo' de wah." A smile stole over her withered countenance as she paused a moment, and her bright eyes softened into a faraway look.

This was the substance of the old woman's story. She had wandered a little here and there. Mr. Ryder was looking at her curiously when she finished.

"How have you lived all these years?" he asked.

"Cookin', suh. I's a good cook. Does you know anybody w'at needs a good cook, suh? I's stoppin' wid a cullud fam'ly roun' de corner yonder 'tel I kin git a place."

"Do you really expect to find your husband? He may be dead long ago."

She shook her head emphatically. "Oh no, he ain' dead. De signs an' de tokens tells me. I dremp three nights runnin' on'y dis las' week dat I foun' him."

"He may have married another woman. Your slave marriage would not have prevented him, for you never lived with him after the war, and without that your marriage doesn't count."

"Wouldn' make no diff'ence wid Sam. He wouldn' marry no yuther 'ooman 'tel he foun' out 'bout me. I knows it," she added. "Sump'n's be'n tellin' me all dese years dat I's gwine fin' Sam 'fo' I dies."

"Perhaps he's outgrown you, and climbed up in the world where he wouldn't care to have you find him."

"No, indeed, suh," she replied, "Sam ain' dat kin' er man. He wuz good ter me, Sam wuz, but he wuzn' much good ter nobody e'se, fer he wuz one er de triflin'es' han's on de plantation. I 'spec's ter haf ter suppo't 'im w'en I fin' 'im, fer he nebber would work 'less'n he had ter. But den he wuz free, an' he didn' git no pay fer his work, an' I don' blame 'im much. Mebbe he's done better sence he run erway, but I ain' 'spectin' much."

"You may have passed him on the street a hundred times during the twenty-five years, and not have known him; time works great changes."

She smiled incredulously. "I'd know 'im 'mongs' a hund'ed men. Fer dey wuzn' no yuther merlatter man like my man Sam, an' I couldn' be mistook. I's toted his picture roun' wid me twenty-five years."

"May I see it?" asked Mr. Ryder. "It might help me to remember whether I have seen the original."

As she drew a small parcel from her bosom he saw that it was fastened to a string that went around her neck. Removing several wrappers, she brought to light an old-fashioned daguerreotype in a black case. He looked long and intently at the portrait. It was faded with time, but the features were still distinct, and it was easy to see what manner of man it had represented.

He closed the case, and with a slow movement handed it back to her.

"I don't know of any man in town who goes by that name," he said, "nor have I heard of any one making such inquiries. But if you will leave me your address, I will give the matter some attention, and if I find out anything I will let you know."

She gave him the number of a house in the neighborhood, and went away, after thanking him warmly.

He wrote the address on the fly-leaf of the volume of Tennyson, and, when she had gone, rose to his feet and stood looking after her curiously. As she walked down the street with mincing step, he saw several persons whom she passed turn and look back at her with a smile of kindly amusement. When she had turned the corner, he went upstairs to his bedroom, and stood for a long time before the mirror of his dressing-case, gazing thoughtfully at the reflection of his own face.

III

At eight o'clock the ballroom was a blaze of light and the guests had begun to assemble; for there was a literary programme and some routine business of the society to be gone through with before the dancing. A black servant in evening dress waited at the door and directed the guests to the dressing-rooms.

The occasion was long memorable among the colored people of the city; not alone for the dress and display, but for the high average of intelligence and culture that distinguished the gathering as a whole. There were a number of school-teachers, several young doctors, three or four lawyers, some professional singers, an editor, a lieutenant in the United States army spending his furlough in the city, and others in various polite callings; these were colored, though most of them would not have attracted even a casual glance because of any marked difference from white people. Most of the ladies were in evening costume, and dress coats and dancing pumps were the rule among the men. A band of string music, stationed in an alcove behind a row of palms, played popular airs while the guests were gathering.

The dancing began at half past nine. At eleven o'clock supper was served. Mr. Ryder had left the ballroom some little time before the intermission, but reappeared at the supper-table. The spread was worthy of the occasion, and the guests did full justice to it. When the coffee had been served, the toast-master, Mr. Solomon Sadler, rapped for order. He made a brief introductory speech, complimenting host and guests, and then presented in their order the toasts of the evening. They were responded to with a very fair display of after-dinner wit.

"The last toast," said the toast-master, when he reached the end of the list, "is one which must appeal to us all. There is no one of us of the sterner sex who is not at some time dependent upon woman,— in infancy for protection, in manhood for companionship, in old age for care and comforting. Our good host has been trying to live alone, but the fair faces I see around me to-night prove that he too is largely dependent upon the gentler sex for most that makes life worth living, —the society and love of friends,—and rumor is at fault if he does not soon yield entire subjection to one of them. Mr. Ryder will now respond to the toast,—The Ladies."

There was a pensive look in Mr. Ryder's eyes as he took the floor and adjusted his eyeglasses. He began by speaking of woman as the gift of Heaven to man, and after some general observations on the relations of the sexes he said: "But perhaps the quality which most distinguishes woman is her fidelity and devotion to those she loves. History is full of examples, but has recorded none more striking than one which only to-day came under my notice."

He then related, simply but effectively, the story told by his visitor of the afternoon. He gave it in the same soft dialect, which came readily to his lips, while the company listened attentively and sympathetically. For the story had awakened a responsive thrill in many hearts. There were some present who had seen, and others who had heard their fathers and grandfathers tell, the wrongs and sufferings of this past generation, and all of them still felt, in their darker moments, the shadow hanging over them. Mr. Ryder went on:—

"Such devotion and confidence are rare even among women. There are many who would have searched a year, some who would have waited five years, a few who might have hoped ten years; but for twenty-five years this woman has retained her affection for and her faith in a man she has not seen or heard of in all that time.

"She came to me to-day in the hope that I might be able to help her find this long-lost husband. And when she was gone I gave my fancy rein, and imagined a case I will put to you.

"Suppose that this husband, soon after his escape, had learned that his wife had been sold away, and that such inquiries as he could make brought no information of her whereabouts. Suppose that he was young, and she much older than he; that he was light, and she was black; that their marriage was a slave marriage, and legally binding only if they chose to make it so after the war. Suppose, too, that he made his way to the North, as some of us have done, and there, where he had larger opportunities, had improved them, and had in the course of all these years grown to be as different from the ignorant boy who ran away from fear of slavery as the day is from the night. Suppose, even, that he had qualified himself, by industry, by thrift, and by study, to win the friendship and be considered worthy the society of such people as these I see around me to-night, gracing my board and filling my heart with gladness; for I am old enough to remember the day when such a gathering would not have been possible in this land. Suppose, too, that, as the years went by, this man's memory of the past grew more and more indistinct, until at last it was rarely, except in his dreams, that any image of this bygone period rose before his mind. And then suppose that accident should bring to his knowledge the fact that the wife of his youth, the wife he had left behind him,—not one who had walked by his side and kept pace with him in his upward struggle, but one upon whom advancing years and a laborious life had set their mark,—was alive and seeking him, but that he was absolutely safe from recognition or discovery, unless he chose to reveal himself. My friends, what would the man do? I will presume that he was one who loved honor, and tried to deal justly with all men. I will even carry the case further, and suppose that perhaps he had set his heart upon another, whom he had hoped to call his own. What would he do, or rather what ought he to do, in such a crisis of a lifetime?

"It seemed to me that he might hesitate, and I imagined that I was an old friend, a near friend, and that he had come to me for advice; and I argued the case with him. I tried to discuss it impartially. After we had looked upon the matter from every point of view, I said to him, in words that we all know:—

> *'This above all: to thine own self be true,*
> *And it must follow, as the night the day,*
> *Thou canst not then be false to any man.'*

Then, finally, I put the question to him, 'Shall you acknowledge her?'

"And now, ladies and gentlemen, friends and companions, I ask you, what should he have done?"

There was something in Mr. Ryder's voice that stirred the hearts of those who sat around him. It suggested more than mere sympathy with an imaginary situation; it seemed rather in the nature of a personal appeal. It was observed, too, that his look rested more especially upon Mrs. Dixon, with a mingled expression of renunciation and inquiry.

She had listened, with parted lips and streaming eyes. She was the first to speak: "He should have acknowledged her."

"Yes," they all echoed, "he should have acknowledged her."

"My friends and companions," responded Mr. Ryder, "I thank you, one and all. It is the answer I expected, for I knew your hearts."

He turned and walked toward the closed door of an adjoining room, while every eye followed him in wondering curiosity. He came back in a moment, leading by the hand his visitor of the afternoon, who stood startled and trembling at the sudden plunge into this scene of brilliant gayety. She was neatly dressed in gray, and wore the white cap of an elderly woman.

"Ladies and gentlemen," he said, "this is the woman, and I am the man, whose story I have told you. Permit me to introduce to you the wife of my youth."

ZITKALA-SÄ

The Trial Path

"The Trial Path" was first published in *Harper's Monthly* in October 1901 and later collected in *American Indian Stories* (1921). This brief tale evokes the cultural dislocation its author undoubtedly felt most of her adult life at the same time that it retrieves in the memory of the grandmother a traditional form of heroism, justice, and forgiveness. When the young girl observes that the star peeping through the smoke-hole of the tepee must be the soul of her dead grandfather, the grandmother is instantly transported to her own youth. The tale she tells of the trial her lover must face is cast in the present tense and makes dramatically vivid a tribal custom that has passed away. By bringing the woman's memory of the past into the palpable present, the author conveys that the "sacred knowledge" the grandmother wishes to impart to her granddaughter has a special urgency. But the child has fallen asleep, and the old woman's knowledge will likely die when she dies. "Asleep!" she laments. "I have been talking in the dark, unheard. I did wish the girl would plant in her heart this sacred tale."

* * *

It was an autumn night on the plain. The smoke-lapels of the cone-shaped tepee flapped gently in the breeze. From the low night sky, with its myriad fire points, a large bright star peeped in at the smoke-hole of the wigwam between its fluttering lapels, down upon two Dakotas talking in the dark. The mellow stream from the star above, a maid of twenty summers, on a bed of sweetgrass, drank in with her wakeful eyes. On the opposite side of the tepee, beyond the centre fireplace, the grandmother spread her rug. Though once she had lain down, the telling of a story has aroused her to a sitting posture.

Her eyes are tight closed. With a thin palm she strokes her wind-shorn hair.

"Yes, my grandchild, the legend says the large bright stars are wise old warriors, and the small dim ones are handsome young braves," she reiterates, in a high, tremulous voice.

"Then this one peeping in at the smoke-hole yonder is my dear old grandfather," muses the young woman, in long-drawn-out words.

Her soft rich voice floats through the darkness within the tepee, over the cold ashes heaped on the centre fire, and passes into the ear of the toothless old woman, who sits dumb in silent reverie. Thence it flies on swifter wing over many winter snows, till at last it cleaves the warm light atmosphere of her grandfather's youth. From there her grandmother made answer:

"Listen! I am young again. It is the day of your grandfather's death. The elder one, I mean, for there were two of them. They were like twins, though they were not brothers. They were friends, inseparable! All things, good and bad, they shared together, save one, which made them mad. In that heated frenzy the younger man slew his most intimate friend. He killed his elder brother, for long had their affection made them kin."

The voice of the old woman broke. Swaying her stooped shoulders to and fro as she sat upon her feet, she muttered vain exclamations beneath her breath. Her eyes, closed tight against the night, beheld behind them the light of bygone days. They saw again a rolling black cloud spread itself over the land. Her ear heard the deep rumbling of a tempest in the west. She bent low a cowering head, while angry thunderbirds shrieked across the sky. "Heyä! heyä!" (No! no!) groaned the toothless grandmother at the fury she had awakened. But the glorious peace afterward, when yellow sunshine made the people glad, now lured her memory onward through the storm.

"How fast, how loud my heart beats as I listen to the messenger's horrible tale!" she ejaculates. "From the fresh grave of the murdered man he hurried to our wigwam. Deliberately crossing his bare shins, he sat down unbidden beside my father, smoking a long-stemmed pipe. He had scarce caught his breath when, panting, he began:

" 'He was an only son, and a much-adored brother.'

"With wild, suspecting eyes he glanced at me as if I were in league with the man-killer, my lover. My father, exhaling sweet-scented smoke, assented—'How.' Then interrupting the 'Eya' on the lips of the round-eyed tale-bearer, he asked, 'My friend, will you smoke?' He took the pipe by its red-stone bowl, and pointed the long slender stem toward the man. 'Yes, yes, my friend,' replied he, and reached out a long brown arm.

"For many heart-throbs he puffed out the blue smoke, which hung like a cloud between us. But even through the smoke-mist I saw his sharp black eyes glittering toward me. I longed to ask what doom awaited the young murderer, but dared not open my lips, lest I burst forth into screams instead. My father plied the question. Returning the pipe, the man replied: 'Oh, the chieftain and his chosen men have had counsel together. They have agreed it is not safe to allow a man-killer loose in our midst. He who kills one of our tribe is an enemy, and must suffer the fate of a foe.'

"My temples throbbed like a pair of hearts!

"While I listened, a crier passed by my father's tepee. Mounted, and swaying with his pony's steps, he proclaimed in a loud voice these words (hark! I hear them now!): 'Ho-po! Give ear, all you people. A terrible deed is done. Two friends—ay, brothers in heart—have quarrelled together. Now one lies buried on the hill, while the other sits, a dreaded man-killer, within his dwelling. Says our chieftain: "He who kills one of our tribe commits the offence of an enemy. As such he must be tried. Let the father of the dead man choose the mode of torture or taking of life. He has suffered livid pain, and he alone can judge how great the punishment must be to avenge his wrong." It is done.

" 'Come, every one, to witness the judgment of a father upon him who was once his son's best friend. A wild pony is now lassoed. The man-killer must mount and ride the ranting beast. Stand you all in two parallel lines from the centre tepee of the bereaved family to the wigwam opposite in the great outer ring. Between you, in the wide space, is the given trialway. From the outer circle the rider must mount and guide his pony toward the centre tepee. If, having gone the entire distance, the man-killer gains the centre tepee still sitting on the pony's back, his life is spared and pardon given. But should he fall, then he himself has chosen death.'

"The crier's words now cease. A lull holds the village breathless. Then hurrying feet tear along, swish, swish, through the tall grass. Sobbing women hasten toward the trialway. The muffled groan of the round camp-ground is unbearable. With my face hid in the folds of my blanket, I run with the crowd toward the open place in the outer circle of our village. In a moment the two long files of solemn-faced people mark the path of the public trial. Ah! I see strong men trying to lead the lassoed pony, pitching and rearing, with white foam flying from his mouth. I choke with pain as I recognize my handsome lover desolately alone, striding with set face toward the lassoed pony. 'Do not fall! Choose life and me!' I cry in my breast, but over my lips I hold my thick blanket.

"In an instant he has leaped astride the frightened beast, and the men have let go their hold. Like an arrow sprung from a strong bow, the pony, with extended nostrils, plunges halfway to the centre tepee. With all his might the rider draws the strong reins in. The pony halts with wooden legs. The rider is thrown forward by force, but does not fall. Now the maddened creature pitches, with flying heels. The line of men and women sways outward. Now it is back in place, safe from the kicking, snorting thing.

"The pony is fierce, with its large black eyes bulging out of their sockets. With humped back and nose to the ground, it leaps into the air. I shut my eyes. I cannot see him fall.

"A loud shout goes up from the hoarse throats of men and women. I look. So! The wild horse is conquered. My lover dismounts at the doorway of the centre wigwam. The pony, wet with sweat and shaking with exhaustion, stands like a guilty dog at his master's side. Here at the entranceway of the tepee sit the bereaved father, mother, and sister. The old warrior father rises. Stepping forward two long strides, he grasps the hand of the murderer of his only son. Holding it so the people can see, he cries, with compassionate voice, 'My son!' A murmur of surprise sweeps like a puff of sudden wind along the lines.

"The mother, with swollen eyes, with her hair cut square with her shoulders, now rises. Hurrying to the young man, she takes his right hand. 'My son!' she greets him. But on the second word her voice shook, and she turned away in sobs.

"The young people rivet their eyes upon the young woman. She does not stir. With bowed head, she sits motionless. The old warrior speaks to her. 'Shake hands with the young brave, my little daughter. He was your brother's friend for many years. Now he must be both friend and brother to you.'

"Hereupon the girl rises. Slowly reaching out her slender hand, she cries, with twitching lips, 'My brother!' The trial ends."

"Grandmother!" exploded the girl on the bed of sweet-grass. "Is this true?"

"Tosh!" answered the grandmother, with a warmth in her voice. "It is all true. During the fifteen winters of our wedded life many ponies passed from our hands, but this little winner, Ohiyesa, was a constant member of our family. At length, on that sad day your grandfather died, Ohiyesa was killed at the grave."

Though the various groups of stars which move across the sky, marking the passing of time, told how the night was in its zenith, the old Dakota woman ventured an explanation of the burial ceremony.

"My grandchild, I have scarce ever breathed the sacred knowledge in my heart. To-night I must tell you one of them. Surely you are old enough to understand.

"Our wise medicine-man said I did well to hasten Ohiyesa after his master. Perchance on the journey along the ghost-path your grandfather will weary, and in his heart wish for his pony. The creature, already bound on the spirit-trail, will be drawn by that subtle wish. Together master and beast will enter the next camp-ground."

The woman ceased her talking. But only the deep breathing of the girl broke the quiet, for now the night wind had lulled itself to sleep.

"Hinnu! hinnu! Asleep! I have been talking in the dark, unheard. I did wish the girl would plant in her heart this sacred tale," muttered she, in a querulous voice.

Nestling into her bed of sweet-scented grass, she dozed away into another dream. Still the guardian star in the night sky beamed compassionately down upon the little tepee on the plain.

EDITH WHARTON

The Other Two

"The Other Two," Edith Wharton's masterpiece of the comedy of manners, was published in *The Descent of Man and Other Stories* in 1904. In accord with much of her fiction of this period, it explores the issues surrounding a woman's role in a society controlled by men, especially the "modern" issue of a divorced woman in polite society. Much of the brilliance of the story derives from the device of identifying the narrative intelligence not with the woman but with her third husband, Waythorn, so that the plot involves not so much the resolution of an external conflict but the subtle adjustment of his perception of his new wife, whom he comes to see as an "old shoe" that "too many feet had worn." His encounters with the two previous husbands lead to his growing awareness that they are not altogether as "brutish" as his wife had described them and that her social advancement had come at their expense—uncomfortable realizations that force him to reassess his own situation. The artistic skill of the story, along with its gentle humor and psychological insight, combine to make it a "shaft driven straight into the heart of human experience," Wharton's definition of the objective of modern fiction.

*   *   *

I

Waythorn, on the drawing-room hearth, waited for his wife to come down to dinner.

It was their first night under his own roof, and he was surprised at his thrill of boyish agitation. He was not so old, to be sure—his glass gave him little more than the five-and-thirty years to which his wife confessed—but he had fancied himself already in the temperate zone; yet here he was listening for her step with a tender sense of all it symbolised, with some old trail of verse about the garlanded nuptial doorposts floating through his enjoyment of the pleasant room and the good dinner just beyond it.

They had been hastily recalled from their honeymoon by the illness

of Lily Haskett, the child of Mrs. Waythorn's first marriage. The little
girl, at Waythorn's desire, had been transferred to his house on the day
of her mother's wedding, and the doctor, on their arrival, broke the
news that she was ill with typhoid, but declared that all the symptoms
were favourable. Lily could show twelve years of unblemished health,
and the case promised to be a light one. The nurse spoke as reassuringly,
and after a moment of alarm Mrs. Waythorn had adjusted herself to
the situation. She was very fond of Lily—her affection for the child had
perhaps been her decisive charm in Waythorn's eyes—but she had the
perfectly balanced nerves which her little girl had inherited, and no
woman ever wasted less tissue in unproductive worry. Waythorn was
therefore quite prepared to see her come in presently, a little late because
of a last look at Lily, but as serene and well-appointed as if her good-
night kiss had been laid on the brow of health. Her composure was
restful to him; it acted as ballast to his somewhat unstable sensibilities.
As he pictured her bending over the child's bed he thought how soothing
her presence must be in illness: her very step would prognosticate
recovery.

His own life had been a gray one, from temperament rather than
circumstance, and he had been drawn to her by the unperturbed gaiety
which kept her fresh and elastic at an age when most women's activities
are growing either slack or febrile. He knew what was said about her;
for, popular as she was, there had always been a faint undercurrent of
detraction. When she had appeared in New York, nine or ten years
earlier, as the pretty Mrs. Haskett whom Gus Varick had unearthed
somewhere—was it in Pittsburg or Utica?—society, while promptly accepting her, had reserved the right to cast a doubt on its own indiscrim-
ination. Enquiry, however, established her undoubted connection with
a socially reigning family, and explained her recent divorce as the natural result of a runaway match at seventeen; and as nothing was known
of Mr. Haskett it was easy to believe the worst of him.

Alice Haskett's remarriage with Gus Varick was a passport to the
set whose recognition she coveted, and for a few years the Varicks were
the most popular couple in town. Unfortunately the alliance was brief
and stormy, and this time the husband had his champions. Still, even
Varick's stanchest supporters admitted that he was not meant for mat-
rimony, and Mrs. Varick's grievances were of a nature to bear the inspection of the New York courts. A New York divorce is in itself a
diploma of virtue, and in the semi-widowhood of this second separation
Mrs. Varick took on an air of sanctity, and was allowed to confide her
wrongs to some of the most scrupulous ears in town. But when it was
known that she was to marry Waythorn there was a momentary reaction. Her best friends would have preferred to see her remain in the rôle

of the injured wife, which was as becoming to her as crape to a rosy complexion. True, a decent time had elapsed, and it was not even suggested that Waythorn had supplanted his predecessor. People shook their heads over him, however, and one grudging friend, to whom he affirmed that he took the step with his eyes open, replied oracularly: "Yes—and with your ears shut."

Waythorn could afford to smile at these innuendoes. In the Wall Street phrase, he had "discounted" them. He knew that society has not yet adapted itself to the consequences of divorce, and that till the adaptation takes place every woman who uses the freedom the law accords her must be her own social justification. Waythorn had an amused confidence in his wife's ability to justify herself. His expectations were fulfilled, and before the wedding took place Alice Varick's group had rallied openly to her support. She took it all imperturbably: she had a way of surmounting obstacles without seeming to be aware of them, and Waythorn looked back with wonder at the trivialities over which he had worn his nerves thin. He had the sense of having found refuge in a richer, warmer nature than his own, and his satisfaction, at the moment, was humourously summed up in the thought that his wife, when she had done all she could for Lily, would not be ashamed to come down and enjoy a good dinner.

The anticipation of such enjoyment was not, however, the sentiment expressed by Mrs. Waythorn's charming face when she presently joined him. Though she had put on her most engaging teagown she had neglected to assume the smile that went with it, and Waythorn thought he had never seen her look so nearly worried.

"What is it?" he asked. "Is anything wrong with Lily?"

"No; I've just been in and she's still sleeping." Mrs. Waythorn hesitated. "But something tiresome has happened."

He had taken her two hands, and now perceived that he was crushing a paper between them.

"This letter?"

"Yes—Mr. Haskett has written—I mean his lawyer has written."

Waythorn felt himself flush uncomfortably. He dropped his wife's hands.

"What about?"

"About seeing Lily. You know the courts—"

"Yes, yes," he interrupted nervously.

Nothing was known about Haskett in New York. He was vaguely supposed to have remained in the outer darkness from which his wife had been rescued, and Waythorn was one of the few who were aware that he had given up his business in Utica and followed her to New York in order to be near his little girl. In the days of his wooing, Waythorn had often met Lily on the doorstep, rosy and smiling, on her way "to see papa."

"I am so sorry," Mrs. Waythorn murmured.

He roused himself. "What does he want?"

"He wants to see her. You know she goes to him once a week."

"Well—he doesn't expect her to go to him now, does he?"

"No—he has heard of her illness; but he expects to come here."

"Here?"

Mrs. Waythorn reddened under his gaze. They looked away from each other.

"I'm afraid he has the right. . . . You'll see. . . ." She made a proffer of the letter.

Waythorn moved away with a gesture of refusal. He stood staring about the softly lighted room, which a moment before had seemed so full of bridal intimacy.

"I'm so sorry," she repeated. "If Lily could have been moved—"

"That's out of the question," he returned impatiently.

"I suppose so."

Her lip was beginning to tremble, and he felt himself a brute.

"He must come, of course," he said. "When is—his day?"

"I'm afraid—to-morrow."

"Very well. Send a note in the morning."

The butler entered to announce dinner.

Waythorn turned to his wife. "Come—you must be tired. It's beastly, but try to forget about it," he said, drawing her hand through his arm.

"You're so good, dear. I'll try," she whispered back.

Her face cleared at once, and as she looked at him across the flowers, between the rosy candle-shades, he saw her lips waver back into a smile.

"How pretty everything is!" she sighed luxuriously.

He turned to the butler. "The champagne at once, please. Mrs. Waythorn is tired."

In a moment or two their eyes met above the sparkling glasses. Her own were quite clear and untroubled: he saw that she had obeyed his injunction and forgotten.

II

Waythorn, the next morning, went down town earlier than usual. Haskett was not likely to come till the afternoon, but the instinct of flight drove him forth. He meant to stay away all day—he had thoughts of dining at his club. As his door closed behind him he reflected that before he opened it again it would have admitted another man who had as much right to enter it as himself, and the thought filled him with a physical repugnance.

He caught the "elevated" at the employés' hour, and found himself crushed between two layers of pendulous humanity. At Eighth Street the man facing him wriggled out, and another took his place. Waythorn glanced up and saw that it was Gus Varick. The men were so close together that it was impossible to ignore the smile of recognition on Varick's handsome overblown face. And after all—why not? They had always been on good terms, and Varick had been divorced before Waythorn's attentions to his wife began. The two exchanged a word on the perennial grievance of the congested trains, and when a seat at their side was miraculously left empty the instinct of self-preservation made Waythorn slip into it after Varick.

The latter drew the stout man's breath of relief. "Lord—I was beginning to feel like a pressed flower." He leaned back, looking unconcernedly at Waythorn. "Sorry to hear that Sellers is knocked out again."

"Sellers?" echoed Waythorn, starting at his partner's name.

Varick looked surprised. "You didn't know he was laid up with the gout?"

"No. I've been away—I only got back last night." Waythorn felt himself reddening in anticipation of the other's smile.

"Ah—yes; to be sure. And Sellers's attack came on two days ago. I'm afraid he's pretty bad. Very awkward for me, as it happens, because he was just putting through a rather important thing for me."

"Ah?" Waythorn wondered vaguely since when Varick had been dealing in "important things." Hitherto he had dabbled only in the shallow pools of speculation, with which Waythorn's office did not usually concern itself.

It occurred to him that Varick might be talking at random, to relieve the strain of their propinquity. That strain was becoming momentarily more apparent to Waythorn, and when, at Cortlandt Street, he caught sight of an acquaintance and had a sudden vision of the picture he and Varick must present to an initiated eye, he jumped up with a muttered excuse.

"I hope you'll find Sellers better," said Varick civilly, and he stammered back: "If I can be of any use to you—" and let the departing crowd sweep him to the platform.

At his office he heard that Sellers was in fact ill with the gout, and would probably not be able to leave the house for some weeks.

"I'm sorry it should have happened so, Mr. Waythorn," the senior clerk said with affable significance. "Mr. Sellers was very much upset at the idea of giving you such a lot of extra work just now."

"Oh, that's no matter," said Waythorn hastily. He secretly welcomed the pressure of additional business, and was glad to think that, when the day's work was over, he would have to call at his partner's on the way home.

He was late for luncheon, and turned in at the nearest restaurant instead of going to his club. The place was full, and the waiter hurried him to the back of the room to capture the only vacant table. In the cloud of cigar-smoke Waythorn did not at once distinguish his neighbours; but presently, looking about him, he saw Varick seated a few feet off. This time, luckily, they were too far apart for conversation, and Varick, who faced another way, had probably not even seen him; but there was an irony in their renewed nearness.

Varick was said to be fond of good living, and as Waythorn sat despatching his hurried luncheon he looked across half enviously at the other's leisurely degustation of his meal. When Waythorn first saw him he had been helping himself with critical deliberation to a bit of Camembert at the ideal point of liquefaction, and now, the cheese removed, he was just pouring his *café double* from its little two-storied earthen pot. He poured slowly, his ruddy profile bent above the task, and one beringed white hand steadying the lid of the coffee-pot; then he stretched his other hand to the decanter of cognac at his elbow, filled a liqueur-glass, took a tentative sip, and poured the brandy into his coffee-cup.

Waythorn watched him in a kind of fascination. What was he thinking of—only of the flavour of the coffee and the liqueur? Had the morning's meeting left no more trace in his thoughts than on his face? Had his wife so completely passed out of his life that even this odd encounter with her present husband, within a week after her remarriage, was no more than an incident in his day? And as Waythorn mused, another idea struck him: had Haskett ever met Varick as Varick and he had just met? The recollection of Haskett perturbed him, and he rose and left the restaurant, taking a circuitous way out to escape the placid irony of Varick's nod.

It was after seven when Waythorn reached home. He thought the footman who opened the door looked at him oddly.

"How is Miss Lily?" he asked in haste.

"Doing very well, sir. A gentleman—"

"Tell Barlow to put off dinner for half an hour," Waythorn cut him off, hurrying upstairs.

He went straight to his room and dressed without seeing his wife. When he reached the drawing-room she was there, fresh and radiant. Lily's day had been good; the doctor was not coming back that evening.

At dinner Waythorn told her of Sellers's illness and of the resulting complications. She listened sympathetically, adjuring him not to let himself be overworked, and asking vague feminine questions about the routine of the office. Then she gave him the chronicle of Lily's day; quoted the nurse and doctor, and told him who had called to inquire. He had never seen her more serene and unruffled. It struck him, with a curious pang, that she was very happy in being with him, so happy that she found a childish pleasure in rehearsing the trivial incidents of her day.

After dinner they went to the library, and the servant put the coffee and liqueurs on a low table before her and left the room. She looked singularly soft and girlish in her rosy pale dress, against the dark leather of one of his bachelor armchairs. A day earlier the contrast would have charmed him.

He turned away now, choosing a cigar with affected deliberation.

"Did Haskett come?" he asked, with his back to her.

"Oh, yes—he came."

"You didn't see him, of course?"

She hesitated a moment. "I let the nurse see him."

That was all. There was nothing more to ask. He swung round toward her, applying a match to his cigar. Well, the thing was over for a week, at any rate. He would try not to think of it. She looked up at him, a trifle rosier than usual, with a smile in her eyes.

"Ready for your coffee, dear?"

He leaned against the mantelpiece, watching her as she lifted the coffee-pot. The lamplight struck a gleam from her bracelets and tipped her soft hair with brightness. How light and slender she was, and how each gesture flowed into the next! She seemed a creature all compact of harmonies. As the thought of Haskett receded, Waythorn felt himself yielding again to the joy of possessorship. They were his, those white hands with their flitting motions, his the light haze of hair, the lips and eyes. . . .

She set down the coffee-pot, and reaching for the decanter of cognac, measured off a liqueur-glass and poured it into his cup.

Waythorn uttered a sudden exclamation.

"What is the matter?" she said, startled.

"Nothing; only—I don't take cognac in my coffee."

"Oh, how stupid of me," she cried.

Their eyes met, and she blushed a sudden agonised red.

III

Ten days later, Mr. Sellers, still house-bound, asked Waythorn to call on his way down town.

The senior partner, with his swaddled foot propped up by the fire, greeted his associate with an air of embarrassment.

"I'm sorry, my dear fellow; I've got to ask you to do an awkward thing for me."

Waythorn waited, and the other went on, after a pause apparently given to the arrangement of his phrases: "The fact is, when I was knocked out I had just gone into a rather complicated piece of business for—Gus Varick."

"Well?" said Waythorn, with an attempt to put him at his ease.

"Well—it's this way: Varick came to me the day before my attack. He had evidently had an inside tip from somebody, and had made about a hundred thousand. He came to me for advice, and I suggested his going in with Vanderlyn."

"Oh, the deuce!" Waythorn exclaimed. He saw in a flash what had happened. The investment was an alluring one, but required negotiation. He listened quietly while Sellers put the case before him, and, the statement ended, he said: "You think I ought to see Varick?"

"I'm afraid I can't as yet. The doctor is obdurate. And this thing can't wait. I hate to ask you, but no one else in the office knows the ins and outs of it."

Waythorn stood silent. He did not care a farthing for the success of Varick's venture, but the honour of the office was to be considered, and he could hardly refuse to oblige his partner.

"Very well," he said, "I'll do it."

That afternoon, apprised by telephone, Varick called at the office. Waythorn, waiting in his private room, wondered what the others thought of it. The newspapers, at the time of Mrs. Waythorn's marriage, had acquainted their readers with every detail of her previous matrimonial ventures, and Waythorn could fancy the clerks smiling behind Varick's back as he was ushered in.

Varick bore himself admirably. He was easy without being undignified, and Waythorn was conscious of cutting a much less impressive figure. Varick had no experience of business, and the talk prolonged itself for nearly an hour while Waythorn set forth with scrupulous precision the details of the proposed transaction.

"I'm awfully obliged to you," Varick said as he rose. "The fact is I'm not used to having much money to look after, and I don't want to make an ass of myself—" He smiled, and Waythorn could not help noticing that there was something pleasant about his smile. "It feels uncommonly queer to have enough cash to pay one's bills. I'd have sold my soul for it a few years ago!"

Waythorn winced at the allusion. He had heard it rumoured that a lack of funds had been one of the determining causes of the Varick separation, but it did not occur to him that Varick's words were intentional. It seemed more likely that the desire to keep clear of embarrassing topics had fatally drawn him into one. Waythorn did not wish to be outdone in civility.

"We'll do the best we can for you," he said. "I think this is a good thing you're in."

"Oh, I'm sure it's immense. It's awfully good of you—" Varick broke off, embarrassed. "I suppose the thing's settled now—but if—"

"If anything happens before Sellers is about, I'll see you again," said Waythorn quietly. He was glad, in the end, to appear the more self-possessed of the two.

The course of Lily's illness ran smooth, and as the days passed Waythorn grew used to the idea of Haskett's weekly visit. The first time the day came round, he stayed out late, and questioned his wife as to the visit on his return. She replied at once that Haskett had merely seen the nurse downstairs, as the doctor did not wish any one in the child's sick-room till after the crisis.

The following week Waythorn was again conscious of the recurrence of the day, but had forgotten it by the time he came home to dinner. The crisis of the disease came a few days later, with a rapid decline of fever, and the little girl was pronounced out of danger. In the rejoicing which ensued the thought of Haskett passed out of Waythorn's mind, and one afternoon, letting himself into the house with a latch-key, he went straight to his library without noticing a shabby hat and umbrella in the hall.

In the library he found a small effaced-looking man with a thinnish gray beard sitting on the edge of a chair. The stranger might have been a piano-tuner, or one of those mysteriously efficient persons who are summoned in emergencies to adjust some detail of the domestic machinery. He blinked at Waythorn through a pair of gold-rimmed spectacles and said mildly: "Mr. Waythorn, I presume? I am Lily's father."

Waythorn flushed. "Oh—" he stammered uncomfortably. He broke off, disliking to appear rude. Inwardly he was trying to adjust the actual Haskett to the image of him projected by his wife's reminiscences. Waythorn had been allowed to infer that Alice's first husband was a brute.

"I am sorry to intrude," said Haskett, with his over-the-counter politeness.

"Don't mention it," returned Waythorn, collecting himself. "I suppose the nurse has been told?"

"I presume so. I can wait," said Haskett. He had a resigned way of speaking, as though life had worn down his natural powers of resistance.

Waythorn stood on the threshold, nervously pulling off his gloves.

"I'm sorry you've been detained. I will send for the nurse," he said;

and as he opened the door he added with an effort: "I'm glad we can give you a good report of Lily." He winced as the *we* slipped out, but Haskett seemed not to notice it.

"Thank you, Mr. Waythorn. It's been an anxious time for me."

"Ah, well, that's past. Soon she'll be able to go to you." Waythorn nodded and passed out.

In his own room he flung himself down with a groan. He hated the womanish sensibility which made him suffer so acutely from the grotesque chances of life. He had known when he married that his wife's former husbands were both living, and that amid the multiplied contacts of modern existence there were a thousand chances to one that he would run against one or the other, yet he found himself as much disturbed by his brief encounter with Haskett as though the law had not obligingly removed all difficulties in the way of their meeting.

Waythorn sprang up and began to pace the room nervously. He had not suffered half as much from his two meetings with Varick. It was Haskett's presence in his own house that made the situation so intolerable. He stood still, hearing steps in the passage.

"This way, please," he heard the nurse say. Haskett was being taken upstairs, then: not a corner of the house but was open to him. Waythorn dropped into another chair, staring vaguely ahead of him. On his dressing-table stood a photograph of Alice, taken when he had first known her. She was Alice Varick then—how fine and exquisite he had thought her! Those were Varick's pearls about her neck. At Waythorn's instance they had been·returned before her marriage. Had Haskett ever given her any trinkets—and what had become of them, Waythorn wondered? He realised suddenly that he knew very little of Haskett's past or present situation; but from the man's appearance and manner of speech he could reconstruct with curious precision the surroundings of Alice's first marriage. And it startled him to think that she had, in the background of her life, a phase of existence so different from anything with which he had connected her. Varick, whatever his faults, was a gentleman, in the conventional, traditional sense of the term: the sense which at that moment seemed, oddly enough, to have most meaning to Waythorn. He and Varick had the same social habits, spoke the same language, understood the same allusions. But this other man . . . it was grotesquely uppermost in Waythorn's mind that Haskett had worn a made-up tie attached with an elastic. Why should that ridiculous detail symbolise the whole man? Waythorn was exasperated by his own paltriness, but the fact of the tie expanded, forced itself on him, became as it were the key to Alice's past. He could see her, as Mrs. Haskett, sitting in a "front parlour" furnished in plush, with a pianola, and a copy of "Ben Hur" on the centre-table. He could see her going to the theatre with Haskett—or perhaps even to a "Church Sociable"—she in a "picture hat" and Haskett in a black frock-coat, a little creased, with the made-up tie on an elastic. On the way home they would stop and look at the illuminated shop-windows, lingering over the photographs of New York actresses. On Sunday afternoons Haskett would take her for a walk, pushing Lily ahead of them in a white enamelled perambulator, and Waythorn had a vision of the people they would stop and talk to. He could fancy how pretty Alice must have looked, in a dress adroitly constructed from the hints of a New York fashion-paper, and how she must have looked down on the other women, chafing at her life, and secretly feeling that she belonged in a bigger place.

For the moment his foremost thought was one of wonder at the way in which she had shed the phase of existence which her marriage with Haskett implied. It was as if her whole aspect, every gesture, every inflection, every allusion, were a studied negation of that period of her life. If she had denied being married to Haskett she could hardly have stood more convicted of duplicity than in this obliteration of the self which had been his wife.

Waythorn started up, checking himself in the analysis of her motives. What right had he to create a fantastic effigy of her and then pass judgment on it? She had spoken vaguely of her first marriage as unhappy, had hinted, with becoming reticence, that Haskett had wrought havoc among her young illusions. . . . It was a pity for Waythorn's peace of mind that Haskett's very inoffensiveness shed a new light on the nature of those illusions. A man would rather think that his wife has been brutalised by her first husband than that the process has been reversed.

WILLA CATHER

A Wagner Matinée

"A Wagner Matinée" was originally published in *Everybody's Magazine* in 1904 before it was revised and reprinted in *The Troll Garden* in 1905 and again revised and published in *Youth and the Bright Medusa* in 1920, each revision softening somewhat the harshness of Aunt Georgiana's thoughts about life on the prairie. Part of the brilliance of the story is that it is narrated by Georgiana's nephew Clark, a young student in Boston, so that his psychological movement is Westward, back to detailed memories of his agrarian past in Nebraska, while her reflections are Eastward, to her youth in Boston and a life of culture and sensitivity. Through his contemplation, and his sharp memories of music on the plains, Clark comes to understand what the last thirty years must have been like for his aunt and what their afternoon together at a Wagner concert can mean. At first rigid, a "granite Rameses in a museum," she is transformed by the music to a deeper sensitivity, regaining the humanity she had known in her earlier life. The story thus ends with Georgiana's poignant expression of need and desire, the tragic hopelessness of which is fully understood by her nephew.

*   *   *

I received one morning a letter, written in pale ink on glassy, blue-lined note-paper, and bearing the postmark of a little Nebraska village. This communication, worn and rubbed, looking as if it had been carried for some days in a coat pocket that was none too clean, was from my uncle Howard, and informed me that his wife had been left a small legacy by a bachelor relative, and that it would be necessary for her to go to Boston to attend to the settling of the estate. He requested me to meet her at the station and render her whatever services might be necessary. On examining the date indicated as that of her arrival, I found it to be no later than tomorrow. He had characteristically delayed writing until, had I been away from home for a day, I must have missed my aunt altogether.

The name of my Aunt Georgiana opened before me a gulf of recollection so wide and deep that, as the letter dropped from my hand, I felt suddenly a stranger to all the present conditions of my existence, wholly ill at ease and out of place amid the familiar surroundings of my study. I became, in short, the gangling farmer-boy my aunt had known, scourged with chilblains and bashfulness, my hands cracked and sore from the corn husking. I sat again before her parlour organ, fumbling the scales with my stiff, red fingers, while she, beside me, made canvas mittens for the huskers.

The next morning, after preparing my landlady for a visitor, I set out for the station. When the train arrived I had some difficulty in finding my aunt. She was the last of the passengers to alight, and it was not until I got her into the carriage that she seemed really to recognize me. She had come all the way in a day coach; her linen duster had become black with soot and her black bonnet grey with dust during the journey. When we arrived at my boarding-house the landlady put her to bed at once and I did not see her again until the next morning.

Whatever shock Mrs. Springer experienced at my aunt's appearance, she considerately concealed. As for myself, I saw my aunt's battered figure with that feeling of awe and respect with which we behold explorers who have left their ears and fingers north of Franz-Joseph-Land, or their health somewhere along the Upper Congo. My Aunt Georgiana had been a music teacher at the Boston Conservatory, somewhere back in the latter sixties. One summer, while visiting in the little village among the Green Mountains where her ancestors had dwelt for generations, she had kindled the callow fancy of my uncle, Howard Carpenter, then an idle, shiftless boy of twenty-one. When she returned to her duties in Boston, Howard followed her, and the upshot of this infatuation was that she eloped with him, eluding the reproaches of her family and the criticism of her friends by going with him to the Nebraska frontier. Carpenter, who, of course, had no money, took up a homestead in Red Willow County, fifty miles from the railroad. There they had measured off their land themselves, driving across the prairie in a wagon, to the wheel of which they had tied a red cotton handkerchief, and counting its revolutions. They built a dug-out in the red hillside, one of those cave dwellings whose inmates so often reverted to primitive conditions. Their water they got from the lagoons where the buffalo drank, and their slender stock of provisions was always at the mercy of bands of roving Indians. For thirty years my aunt had not been farther than fifty miles from the homestead.

I owed to this woman most of the good that ever came my way in my boyhood, and had a reverential affection for her. During the years when I was riding herd for my uncle, my aunt, after cooking the three meals—the first of which was ready at six o'clock in the morning—and putting the six children to bed, would often stand until midnight at her ironing-board, with me at the kitchen table beside her, hearing me recite Latin declensions and conjugations, gently shaking me when my drowsy head sank down over a page of irregular verbs. It was to her, at her ironing or mending, that I read my first Shakspere, and her old textbook on mythology was the first that ever came into my empty hands. She taught me my scales and exercises on the little parlour organ which her husband had bought her after fifteen years during which she had not so much as seen a musical instrument. She would sit beside me by the hour, darning and counting, while I struggled with the "Joyous Farmer." She seldom talked to me about music, and I understood why. Once when I had been doggedly beating out some easy passages from an old score of *Euryanthe* I had found among her music books, she came up to me and, putting her hands over my eyes, gently drew my head back upon her shoulder, saying tremulously, "Don't love it so well, Clark, or it may be taken from you."

When my aunt appeared on the morning after her arrival in Boston, she was still in a semi-somnambulant state. She seemed not to realize that she was in the city where she had spent her youth, the place longed for hungrily half a lifetime. She had been so wretchedly train-sick throughout the journey that she had no recollection of anything but her discomfort, and, to all intents and purposes, there were but a few hours of nightmare between the farm in Red Willow County and my study on Newbury Street. I had planned a little pleasure for her that after-noon, to repay her for some of the glorious moments she had given me when we used to milk together in the straw-thatched cowshed and she, because I was more than usually tired, or because her husband had spoken sharply to me, would tell me of the splendid performance of the *Huguenots* she had seen in Paris, in her youth.

At two o'clock the Symphony Orchestra was to give a Wagner pro-gram, and I intended to take my aunt; though, as I conversed with her, I grew doubtful about her enjoyment of it. I suggested our visiting the Conservatory and the Common before lunch, but she seemed altogether too timid to wish to venture out. She questioned me absently about various changes in the city, but she was chiefly concerned that she had forgotten to leave instructions about feeding half-skimmed milk to a certain weakling calf, "old Maggie's calf, you know, Clark," she ex-plained, evidently having forgotten how long I had been away. She was further troubled because she had neglected to tell her daughter about the freshly-opened kit of mackerel in the cellar, which would spoil if it were not used directly.

I asked her whether she had ever heard any of the Wagnerian operas, and found that she had not, though she was perfectly familiar with their respective situations, and had once possessed the piano score of *The Flying Dutchman*. I began to think it would be best to get her back to Red Willow County without waking her, and regretted having suggested the concert.

From the time we entered the concert hall, however, she was a trifle less passive and inert, and for the first time seemed to perceive her surroundings. I had felt some trepidation lest she might become aware of her queer, country clothes, or might experience some painful embar-rassment at stepping suddenly into the world to which she had been dead for a quarter of a century. But, again, I found how superficially I had judged her. She sat looking about her with eyes as impersonal, almost as stony, as those with which the granite Rameses in a museum watches the froth and fret that ebbs and flows about his pedestal. I have seen this same aloofness in old miners who drift into the Brown hotel at Denver, their pockets full of bullion, their linen soiled, their haggard faces unshaven; standing in the thronged corridors as solitary as though they were still in a frozen camp on the Yukon.

The matinée audience was made up chiefly of women. One lost the contour of faces and figures, indeed any effect of line whatever, and there was only the colour of bodices past counting, the shimmer of fabrics soft and firm, silky and sheer; red, mauve, pink, blue, lilac, purple, écru, rose, yellow, cream, and white, all the colours that an impressionist finds in a sunlit landscape, with here and there the dead shadow of a frock coat. My Aunt Georgiana regarded them as though they had been so many daubs of tube-paint on a palette.

When the musicians came out and took their places, she gave a little stir of anticipation, and looked with quickening interest down over the rail at that invariable grouping, perhaps the first wholly familiar thing that had greeted her eye since she had left old Maggie and her weakling calf. I could feel how all those details sank into her soul, for I had not forgotten how they had sunk into mine when I came fresh from ploughing forever and forever between green aisles of corn, where, as in a treadmill, one might walk from daybreak to dusk without perceiving a shadow of change. The clean profiles of the musicians, the gloss of their linen, the dull black of their coats, the beloved shapes of the instruments, the patches of yellow light on the smooth, varnished bellies of the 'cellos and the bass viols in the rear, the restless, wind-tossed forest of fiddle necks and bows—I recalled how, in the first orchestra I ever heard, those long bow-strokes seemed to draw the heart out of me, as a conjurer's stick reels out yards of paper ribbon from a hat.

The first number was the *Tannhäuser* overture. When the horns drew out the first strain of the Pilgrim's chorus, Aunt Georgiana clutched my coat sleeve. Then it was I first realized that for her this broke a silence of thirty years. With the battle between the two motives, with the frenzy of the Venusberg theme and its ripping of strings, there came to me an overwhelming sense of the waste and wear we are so powerless to combat; and I saw again the tall, naked house on the prairie, black and grim as a wooden fortress; the black pond where I had learned to swim, its margin pitted with sun-dried cattle tracks; the rain gullied clay banks about the naked house, the four dwarf ash seedlings where the dishcloths were always hung to dry before the kitchen door. The world there was the flat world of the ancients; to the east, a cornfield that stretched to daybreak; to the west, a corral that reached to sunset; between, the conquests of peace, dearer-bought than those of war.

The overture closed, my aunt released my coat sleeve, but she said nothing. She sat staring dully at the orchestra. What, I wondered, did she get from it? She had been a good pianist in her day, I knew, and her musical education had been broader than that of most music teachers of a quarter of a century ago. She had often told me of Mozart's operas and Meyerbeer's, and I could remember hearing her sing, years ago, certain melodies of Verdi. When I had fallen ill with a fever in her house she used to sit by my cot in the evening—when the cool, night wind blew in through the faded mosquito netting tacked over the window and I lay watching a certain bright star that burned red above the cornfield—and sing "Home to our mountains, O, let us return!" in a way fit to break the heart of a Vermont boy near dead of homesickness already.

I watched her closely through the prelude to *Tristan and Isolde*, trying vainly to conjecture what that seething turmoil of strings and winds might mean to her, but she sat mutely staring at the violin bows that drove obliquely downward, like the pelting streaks of rain in a summer shower. Had this music any message for her? Had she enough left to at all comprehend this power which had kindled the world since she had left it? I was in a fever of curiosity, but Aunt Georgiana sat silent upon her peak in Darien. She preserved this utter immobility throughout the number from *The Flying Dutchman*, though her fingers worked mechanically upon her black dress, as if, of themselves, they were recalling the piano score they had once played. Poor hands! They had been stretched and twisted into mere tentacles to hold and lift and knead with;—on one of them a thin, worn band that had once been a wedding ring. As I pressed and gently quieted one of those groping hands, I remembered with quivering eyelids their services for me in other days.

Soon after the tenor began the "Prize Song," I heard a quick drawn breath and turned to my aunt. Her eyes were closed, but the tears were glistening on her cheeks, and I think, in a moment more, they were in my eyes as well. It never really died, then—the soul which can suffer so excruciatingly and so interminably; it withers to the outward eye only; like that strange moss which can lie on a dusty shelf half a century and yet, if placed in water, grows green again. She wept so throughout the development and elaboration of the melody.

During the intermission before the second half, I questioned my aunt and found that the "Prize Song" was not new to her. Some years before there had drifted to the farm in Red Willow County a young German, a tramp cow-puncher, who had sung in the chorus at Bayreuth when he was a boy, along with the other peasant boys and girls. Of a Sunday morning he used to sit on his gingham-sheeted bed in the hands' bedroom which opened off the kitchen, cleaning the leather of his boots and saddle, singing the "Prize Song," while my aunt went about her work in the kitchen. She had hovered over him until she had prevailed upon him to join the country church, though his sole fitness for this step, in so far as I could gather, lay in his boyish face and his possession of this divine melody. Shortly afterward, he had gone to town on the Fourth of July, been drunk for several days, lost his money at a faro table, ridden a saddled Texas steer on a bet, and disappeared with a fractured collar-bone. All this my aunt told me huskily, wanderingly, as though she were talking in the weak lapses of illness.

"Well, we have come to better things than the old *Trovatore* at any rate, Aunt Georgie?" I queried, with a well meant effort at jocularity. Her lip quivered and she hastily put her handkerchief up to her mouth. From behind it she murmured, "And you have been hearing this ever since you left me, Clark?" Her question was the gentlest and saddest of reproaches.

The second half of the program consisted of four numbers from the *Ring*, and closed with Siegfried's funeral march. My aunt wept quietly, but almost continuously, as a shallow vessel overflows in a rain-storm. From time to time her dim eyes looked up at the lights, burning softly under their dull glass globes.

The deluge of sound poured on and on; I never knew what she found in the shining current of it; I never knew how far it bore her, or past what happy islands. From the trembling of her face I could well believe that before the last number she had been carried out where the myriad graves are, into the grey, nameless burying grounds of the sea; or into some world of death vaster yet, where, from the beginning of the world, hope has lain down with hope and dream with dream and, renouncing, slept.

The concert was over; the people filed out of the hall chattering and laughing, glad to relax and find the living level again, but my kinswoman made no effort to rise. The harpist slipped the green felt cover over his instrument; the flute-players shook the water from their mouthpieces; the men of the orchestra went out one by one, leaving the stage to the chairs and music stands, empty as a winter cornfield.

I spoke to my aunt. She burst into tears and sobbed pleadingly. "I don't want to go, Clark, I don't want to go!"

I understood. For her, just outside the concert hall, lay the black pond with the cattle-tracked bluffs; the tall, unpainted house, with weather-curled boards, naked as a tower; the crook-backed ash seedlings where the dish-cloths hung to dry; the gaunt, moulting turkeys picking up refuse about the kitchen door.

WILLIAM DEAN HOWELLS

Editha

"Editha" was published in *Harper's Monthly* for January 1905. This compact story is a perfect illustration of Howellsian realism and, at the same time, reflects the anti-imperialism and Christian socialism of the author's later years. The ironic inversions of the tale are salient but not bitter, and they permit Howells to analyze rather than simply condemn the social and psychological forces at work in the country just prior to its involvement in the Spanish-American War. Newspaper publishers (particularly William Randolph Hearst and Joseph Pulitzer) ran sensationalistic stories and jingoistically promoted the fear of a Spanish force "at our very gates." But Howells's interest here is less in the manipulation of public opinion than in the perverted and corrupting influences of a timid attachment to sentimental prejudices. Editha Balcom urges her fiancé, George Gearson, to become a manly figure worthy of her love and sacrifice, only to find that she has created a stranger who slightly frightens her. Gearson, a would-be minister and a pacifist, becomes a fallen military hero because he is, at bottom, a moral coward. The story is an intricate and effective dramatization of what Howells called a "moral complicity" that implicates men and women in their relations to one another and to the national life. That point is made powerfully clear at the end with Mrs. Gearson's angry refusal to endorse Editha's romantic demonstrations of grief and loss.

*   *   *

The air was thick with the war feeling, like the electricity of a storm which has not yet burst. Editha sat looking out into the hot spring afternoon, with her lips parted, and panting with the intensity of the question whether she could let him go. She had decided that she could not let him stay, when she saw him at the end of the still leafless avenue, making slowly up toward the house, with his head down, and his figure relaxed. She ran impatiently out on the veranda, to the edge of the steps, and imperatively demanded greater haste of him with her will before she called aloud to him, "George!"

He had quickened his pace in mystical response to her mystical urgence, before he could have heard her; now he looked up and answered, "Well?"

"Oh, how united we are!" she exulted, and then she swooped down the steps to him. "What is it?" she cried.

"It's war," he said, and he pulled her up to him, and kissed her.

She kissed him back intensely, but irrelevantly, as to their passion, and uttered from deep in her throat, "How glorious!"

"It's war," he repeated, without consenting to her sense of it; and she did not know just what to think at first. She never knew what to think of him; that made his mystery, his charm. All through their courtship, which was contemporaneous with the growth of the war feeling, she had been puzzled by his want of seriousness about it. He seemed to despise it even more than he abhorred it. She could have understood his abhorring any sort of bloodshed; that would have been a survival of his old life when he thought he would be a minister, and before he changed and took up the law. But making light of a cause so high and noble seemed to show a want of earnestness at the core of his being. Not but that she felt herself able to cope with a congenital defect of that sort, and make his love for her save him from himself. Now perhaps the miracle was already wrought in him. In the presence of the tremendous fact that he announced, all triviality seemed to have gone out of him; she began to feel that. He sank down on the top step, and wiped his forehead with his handkerchief, while she poured out upon him her question of the origin and authenticity of his news.

All the while, in her duplex emotioning, she was aware that now at the very beginning she must put a guard upon herself against urging him, by any word or act, to take the part that her whole soul willed him to take, for the completion of her ideal of him. He was very nearly perfect as he was, and he must be allowed to perfect himself. But he was peculiar, and he might very well be reasoned out of his peculiarity. Before her reasoning went her emotioning: her nature pulling upon his nature, her womanhood upon his manhood, without her knowing the means she was using to the end she was willing. She had always supposed that the man who won her would have done something to win her; she did not know what, but something. George Gearson had simply asked her for her love, on the way home from a concert, and she gave her love to him, without, as it were, thinking. But now, it flashed upon her, if he could do something worthy to *have* won her—be a hero, *her* hero—it would be even better than if he had done it before asking her; it would be grander. Besides, she had believed in the war from the beginning.

"But don't you see, dearest," she said, "that it wouldn't have come to this, if it hadn't been in the order of Providence? And I call any war glorious that is for the liberation of people who have been struggling for years against the cruelest oppression. Don't you think so too?"

"I suppose so," he returned, languidly. "But war! Is it glorious to break the peace of the world?"

"That ignoble peace! It was no peace at all, with that crime and shame at our very gates." She was conscious of parroting the current phrases of the newspapers, but it was no time to pick and choose her words. She must sacrifice anything to the high ideal she had for him, and after a good deal of rapid argument she ended with the climax: "But now it doesn't matter about the how or why. Since the war has come, all that is gone. There are no two sides, any more. There is nothing now but our country."

He sat with his eyes closed and his head leant back against the veranda, and he said with a vague smile, as if musing aloud, "Our country—right or wrong."

"Yes, right or wrong!" she returned fervidly. "I'll go and get you some lemonade." She rose rustling, and whisked away; when she came back with two tall glasses of clouded liquid, on a tray, and the ice clucking in them, he still sat as she had left him, and she said as if there had been no interruption: "But there is no question of wrong in this case. I call it a sacred war. A war for liberty, and humanity, if ever there was one. And I know you will see it just as I do, yet."

He took half the lemonade at a gulp, and he answered as he set the glass down: "I know you always have the highest ideal. When I differ from you, I ought to doubt myself."

A generous sob rose in Editha's throat for the humility of a man, so very nearly perfect, who was willing to put himself below her.

Besides, she felt, more subliminally, that he was never so near slipping through her fingers as when he took that meek way.

"You shall not say that! Only, for once I happen to be right." She seized his hand in her two hands, and poured her soul from her eyes into his. "Don't you think so?" she entreated him.

He released his hand and drank the rest of his lemonade, and she added, "Have mine, too," but he shook his head in answering, "I've no business to think so, unless I act so, too."

Her heart stopped a beat before it pulsed on with leaps that she felt in her neck. She had noticed that strange thing in men; they seemed to feel bound to do what they believed, and not think a thing was finished when they said it, as girls did. She knew what was in his mind, but she pretended not, and she said, "Oh, I am not sure," and then faltered.

He went on as if to himself without apparently heeding her, "There's only one way of proving one's faith in a thing like this."

She could not say that she understood; but she did understand.

He went on again. "If I believed—if I felt as you do about this war —Do you wish me to feel as you do?"

Now she was really not sure; so she said, "George, I don't know what you mean."

He seemed to muse away from her as before. "There is a sort of fascination in it. I suppose that at the bottom of his heart every man would like at times to have his courage tested; to see how he would act."

"How can you talk in that ghastly way!"

"It *is* rather morbid. Still, that's what it comes to, unless you're swept away by ambition, or driven by conviction. I haven't the conviction or the ambition, and the other thing is what it comes to with me. I ought to have been a preacher, after all; then I couldn't have asked it of myself, as I must, now I'm a lawyer. And you believe it's a holy war, Editha?" he suddenly addressed her. "Or, I know you do! But you wish me to believe so, too?"

She hardly knew whether he was mocking or not, in the ironical way he always had with her plainer mind. But the only thing was to be outspoken with him.

"George, I wish you to believe whatever you think is true, at any and every cost. If I've tried to talk you into anything, I take it all back."

"Oh, I know that, Editha. I know how sincere you are, and how— I wish I had your undoubting spirit! I'll think it over; I'd like to believe as you do. But I don't, now; I don't, indeed. It isn't this war alone; though this seems peculiarly wanton and needless; but it's every war— so stupid; it makes me sick. Why shouldn't this thing have been settled reasonably?"

"Because," she said, very throatily again, "God meant it to be war."

"You think it was God? Yes, I suppose that is what people will say."

"Do you suppose it would have been war if God hadn't meant it?"

"I don't know. Sometimes it seems as if God had put this world into men's keeping to work it as they pleased."

"Now, George, that is blasphemy."

"Well, I won't blaspheme. I'll try to believe in your pocket Providence," he said, and then he rose to go.

"Why don't you stay to dinner?" Dinner at Balcom's Works was at one o'clock.

"I'll come back to supper, if you'll let me. Perhaps I shall bring you a convert."

"Well, you may come back, on that condition."

"All right. If I don't come, you'll understand."

He went away without kissing her, and she felt it a suspension of their engagement. It all interested her intensely; she was undergoing a tremendous experience, and she was being equal to it. While she stood looking after him, her mother came out through one of the long windows, on to the veranda, with a catlike softness and vagueness.

"Why didn't he stay to dinner?"

"Because—because—war has been declared," Editha pronounced, without turning.

Her mother said, "Oh, my!" and then said nothing more until she had sat down in one of the large Shaker chairs, and rocked herself for some time. Then she closed whatever tacit passage of thought there had been in her mind with the spoken words, "Well, I hope *he* won't go."

"And *I* hope he *will,*" the girl said, and confronted her mother with a stormy exaltation that would have frightened any creature less unimpressionable than a cat.

Her mother rocked herself again for an interval of cogitation. What she arrived at in speech was, "Well, I guess you've done a wicked thing, Editha Balcom."

The girl said, as she passed indoors through the same window her mother had come out by, "I haven't done anything—yet."

In her room, she put together all her letters and gifts from Gearson, down to the withered petals of the first flower he had offered, with that timidity of his veiled in that irony of his. In the heart of the packet she enshrined her engagement ring which she had restored to the pretty box he had brought it her in. Then she sat down, if not calmly yet strongly, and wrote:

> "GEORGE: I understood—when you left me. But I think we had better emphasize your meaning that if we cannot be one in everything we had better be one in nothing. So I am sending these things for your keeping till you have made up your mind.
>
> "I shall always love you, and therefore I shall never marry any one else. But the man I marry must love his country first of all, and be able to say to me,
>
> > '*I could not love thee, dear, so much,*
> > *Loved I not honor more.*'
>
> "There is no honor above America with me. In this great hour there is no other honor.
>
> "Your heart will make my words clear to you. I had never expected to say so much, but it has come upon me that I must say the utmost.
>
> > EDITHA."

She thought she had worded her letter well, worded it in a way that could not be bettered; all had been implied and nothing expressed.

She had it ready to send with the packet she had tied with red, white, and blue ribbon, when it occurred to her that she was not just to him, that she was not giving him a fair chance. He had said he would go and think it over, and she was not waiting. She was pushing, threatening, compelling. That was not a woman's part. She must leave him free, free, free. She could not accept for her country or herself a forced sacrifice.

In writing her letter she had satisfied the impulse from which it sprang; she could well afford to wait till he had thought it over. She put the packet and the letter by, and rested serene in the consciousness of having done what was laid upon her by her love itself to do, and yet used patience, mercy, justice.

She had her reward. Gearson did not come to tea, but she had given him till morning, when, late at night there came up from the village the sound of a fife and drum with a tumult of voices, in shouting, singing, and laughing. The noise drew nearer and nearer; it reached the street end of the avenue; there it silenced itself, and one voice, the voice she knew best, rose over the silence. It fell; the air was filled with cheers; the fife and drum struck up, with the shouting, singing, and laughing again, but now retreating; and a single figure came hurrying up the avenue.

She ran down to meet her lover and clung to him. He was very gay, and he put his arm round her with a boisterous laugh. "Well, you must call me Captain, now; or Cap, if you prefer; that's what the boys call me. Yes, we've had a meeting at the town hall, and everybody has volunteered; and they selected me for captain, and I'm going to the war, the big war, the glorious war, the holy war ordained by the pocket Providence that blesses butchery. Come along; let's tell the whole family about it. Call them from their downy beds, father, mother, Aunt Hitty, and all the folks!"

But when they mounted the veranda steps he did not wait for a larger audience; he poured the story out upon Editha alone.

"There was a lot of speaking, and then some of the fools set up a shout for me. It was all going one way, and I thought it would be a good joke to sprinkle a little cold water on them. But you can't do that with a crowd that adores you. The first thing I knew I was sprinkling hell-fire on them. 'Cry havoc, and let slip the dogs of war.' That was the style. Now that it had come to the fight, there were no two parties; there was one country, and the thing was to fight the fight to a finish as quick as possible. I suggested volunteering then and there, and I wrote my name first of all on the roster. Then they elected me—that's all. I wish I had some ice-water!"

She left him walking up and down the veranda, while she ran for the ice-pitcher and a goblet, and when she came back he was still walking up and down, shouting the story he had told her to her father and mother, who had come out more sketchily dressed than they commonly were by day. He drank goblet after goblet of the ice-water without noticing who was giving it, and kept on talking, and laughing through his talk wildly. "It's astonishing," he said, "how well the worse reason looks when you try to make it appear the better. Why, I believe I was the first convert to the war in that crowd to-night! I never thought I should like to kill a man; but now, I shouldn't care; and the smokeless powder lets you see the man drop that you kill. It's all for the country! What a thing it is to have a country that *can't* be wrong, but if it is, is right anyway!"

Editha had a great, vital thought, an inspiration. She set down the ice-pitcher on the veranda floor, and ran up-stairs and got the letter she had written him. When at last he noisily bade her father and mother, "Well, good night. I forgot I woke you up; I sha'n't want any sleep myself," she followed him down the avenue to the gate. There, after the whirling words that seemed to fly away from her thoughts and refuse to serve them, she made a last effort to solemnize the moment that seemed so crazy, and pressed the letter she had written upon him.

"What's this?" he said. "Want me to mail it?"

"No, no. It's for you. I wrote it after you went this morning. Keep it—keep it—and read it sometime—" She thought, and then her inspiration came: "Read it if ever you doubt what you've done, or fear that I regret your having done it. Read it after you've started."

They strained each other in embraces that seemed as ineffective as their words, and he kissed her face with quick, hot breaths that were so unlike him, that made her feel as if she had lost her old lover and found a stranger in his place. The stranger said, "What a gorgeous flower you are, with your red hair, and your blue eyes that look black now, and your face with the color painted out by the white moonshine! Let me hold you under my chin, to see whether I love blood, you tiger-lily!" Then he laughed Gearson's laugh, and released her, scared and giddy. Within her wilfulness she had been frightened by a sense of subtler force in him, and mystically mastered as she had never been before.

She ran all the way back to the house, and mounted the steps panting. Her mother and father were talking of the great affair. Her mother said: "Wa'n't Mr. Gearson in rather of an excited state of mind? Didn't you think he acted curious?"

"Well, not for a man who'd just been elected captain and had to set 'em up for the whole of Company A," her father chuckled back.

"What in the world do you mean, Mr. Balcom? Oh! There's Editha!" She offered to follow the girl indoors.

"Don't come, mother!" Editha called, vanishing.

Mrs. Balcom remained to reproach her husband. "I don't see much of anything to laugh at."

"Well, it's catching. Caught it from Gearson. I guess it won't be much of a war, and I guess Gearson don't think so, either. The other fellows will back down as soon as they see we mean it. I wouldn't lose any sleep over it. I'm going back to bed, myself."

Gearson came again next afternoon, looking pale, and rather sick, but quite himself, even to his languid irony. "I guess I'd better tell you, Editha, that I consecrated myself to your god of battles last night by pouring too many libations to him down my own throat. But I'm all right, now. One has to carry off the excitement, somehow."

"Promise me," she commanded, "that you'll never touch it again!"

"What! Not let the cannikin clink? Not let the soldier drink? Well, I promise."

"You don't belong to yourself now; you don't even belong to *me*. You belong to your country, and you have a sacred charge to keep yourself strong and well for your country's sake. I have been thinking, thinking all night and all day long."

"You look as if you had been crying a little, too," he said with his queer smile.

"That's all past. I've been thinking, and worshipping *you*. Don't you suppose I know all that you've been through, to come to this? I've followed you every step from your old theories and opinions."

"Well, you've had a long row to hoe."

"And I know you've done this from the highest motives—"

"Oh, there won't be much pettifogging to do till this cruel war is—"

"And you haven't simply done it for my sake. I couldn't respect you if you had."

"Well, then we'll say I haven't. A man that hasn't got his own respect intact wants the respect of all the other people he can corner. But we won't go into that. I'm in for the thing now, and we've got to face our future. My idea is that this isn't going to be a very protracted struggle; we shall just scare the enemy to death before it comes to a fight at all. But we must provide for contingencies, Editha. If anything happens to me—"

"Oh, George!" She clung to him sobbing.

"I don't want you to feel foolishly bound to my memory. I should hate that, wherever I happened to be."

"I am yours, for time and eternity—time and eternity." She liked the words; they satisfied her famine for phrases.

"Well, say eternity; that's all right; but time's another thing; and I'm talking about time. But there is something! My mother! If anything happens—"

She winced, and he laughed. "You're not the bold soldier-girl of yesterday!" Then he sobered. "If anything happens, I want you to help my mother out. She won't like my doing this thing. She brought me up to think war a fool thing as well as a bad thing. My father was in the civil war; all through it; lost his arm in it." She thrilled with the sense of the arm round her; what if that should be lost? He laughed as if divining her: "Oh, it doesn't run in the family, as far as I know!" Then he added, gravely, "He came home with misgivings about war, and they grew on him. I guess he and mother agreed between them that I was to be brought up in his final mind about it; but that was before my time. I only knew him from my mother's report of him and his opinions; I don't know whether they were hers first; but they were hers last. This will be a blow to her. I shall have to write and tell her—"

He stopped, and she asked, "Would you like me to write too, George?"

"I don't believe that would do. No, I'll do the writing. She'll understand a little if I say that I thought the way to minimize it was to make war on the largest possible scale at once—that I felt I must have been helping on the war somehow if I hadn't helped keep it from coming, and I knew I hadn't; when it came, I had no right to stay out of it."

Whether his sophistries satisfied him or not, they satisfied her. She clung to his breast, and whispered, with closed eyes and quivering lips, "Yes, yes, yes!"

"But if anything should happen, you might go to her, and see what you could do for her. You know? It's rather far off; she can't leave her chair—"

"Oh, I'll go, if it's the ends of the earth! But nothing will happen! Nothing *can!* I—"

She felt herself lifted with his rising, and Gearson was saying, with his arm still round her, to her father: "Well, we're off at once, Mr. Balcom. We're to be formally accepted at the capital, and then bunched up with the rest somehow, and sent into camp somewhere, and got to the front as soon as possible. We all want to be in the van, of course; we're the first company to report to the Governor. I came to tell Editha, but I hadn't got round to it."

She saw him again for a moment at the capital, in the station, just before the train started southward with his regiment. He looked well, in his uniform, and very soldierly, but somehow girlish, too, with his clean-shaven face and slim figure. The manly eyes and the strong voice satisfied her, and his preoccupation with some unexpected details of duty flattered her. Other girls were weeping and bemoaning themselves, but she felt a sort of noble distinction in the abstraction, the almost unconsciousness, with which they parted. Only at the last moment he said, "Don't forget my mother. It mayn't be such a walk-over as I supposed," and he laughed at the notion.

He waved his hand to her, as the train moved off—she knew it among a score of hands that were waved to other girls from the platform of the car, for it held a letter which she knew was hers. Then he went inside the car to read it, doubtless, and she did not see him again. But she felt safe for him through the strength of what she called her love. What she called her God, always speaking the name in a deep voice and with the implication of a mutual understanding, would watch over him and keep him and bring him back to her. If with an empty sleeve, then he should have three arms instead of two, for both of hers should be his for life. She did not see, though, why she should always be thinking of the arm his father had lost.

There were not many letters from him, but they were such as she could have wished, and she put her whole strength into making hers such as she imagined he could have wished, glorifying and supporting him. She wrote to his mother glorifying him as their hero, but the brief answer she got was merely to the effect that Mrs. Gearson was not well enough to write herself, and thanking her for her letter by the hand of some one who called herself "Yrs truly, Mrs. W. J. Andrews."

Editha determined not to be hurt, but to write again quite as if the answer had been all she expected. But before it seemed as if she could have written, there came news of the first skirmish, and in the list of the killed which was telegraphed as a trifling loss on our side, was Gearson's name. There was a frantic time of trying to make out that it might be, must be, some other Gearson; but the name, and the company and the regiment, and the State were too definitely given.

Then there was a lapse into depths out of which it seemed as if she never could rise again; then a lift into clouds far above all grief, black clouds, that blotted out the sun, but where she soared with him, with George, George! She had the fever that she expected of herself, but she did not die in it; she was not even delirious, and it did not last long. When she was well enough to leave her bed, her one thought was of George's mother, of his strangely worded wish that she should go to her and see what she could do for her. In the exaltation of the duty laid upon her—it buoyed her up instead of burdening her—she rapidly recovered.

Her father went with her on the long railroad journey from northern

New York to western Iowa; he had business out at Davenport, and he said he could just as well go then as any other time; and he went with her to the little country town where George's mother lived in a little house on the edge of illimitable corn-fields, under trees pushed to a top of the rolling prairie. George's father had settled there after the civil war, as so many other old soldiers had done; but they were Eastern people, and Editha fancied touches of the East in the June rose over-hanging the front door, and the garden with early summer flowers stretching from the gate of the paling fence.

It was very low inside the house, and so dim, with the closed blinds, that they could scarcely see one another: Editha tall and black in her crapes which filled the air with the smell of their dyes; her father standing decorously apart with his hat on his forearm, as at funerals; a woman rested in a deep armchair, and the woman who had let the strangers in stood behind the chair.

The seated woman turned her head round and up, and asked the woman behind her chair, "*Who* did you say?"

Editha, if she had done what she expected of herself, would have gone down on her knees at the feet of the seated figure and said, "I am George's Editha," for answer.

But instead of her own voice she heard that other woman's voice, saying, "Well, I don't know as I *did* get the name just right. I guess I'll have to make a little more light in here," and she went and pushed two of the shutters ajar.

Then Editha's father said in his public will-now-address-a-few-remarks tone, "My name is Balcom, ma'am; Junius H. Balcom, of Balcom's Works, New York; my daughter—"

"Oh!" The seated woman broke in, with a powerful voice, the voice that always surprised Editha from Gearson's slender frame. "Let me see you! Stand round where the light can strike on your face," and Editha dumbly obeyed. "So, you're Editha Balcom," she sighed.

"Yes," Editha said, more like a culprit than a comforter.

"What did you come for?" Mrs. Gearson asked.

Editha's face quivered, and her knees shook. "I came—because—because George—" She could go no farther.

"Yes," the mother said, "he told me he had asked you to come if he got killed. You didn't expect that, I suppose, when you sent him."

"I would rather have died myself than done it!" Editha said with more truth in her deep voice than she ordinarily found in it. "I tried to leave him free—"

"Yes, that letter of yours, that came back with his other things, left him free."

Editha saw now where George's irony came from.

"It was not to be read before—unless—until—I told him so," she faltered.

"Of course, he wouldn't read a letter of yours, under the circumstances, till he thought you wanted him to. Been sick?" the woman abruptly demanded.

"Very sick," Editha said, with self-pity.

"Daughter's life," her father interposed, "was almost despaired of, at one time."

Mrs. Gearson gave him no heed. "I suppose you would have been glad to die, such a brave person as you! I don't believe *he* was glad to die. He was always a timid boy, that way; he was afraid of a good many things; but if he was afraid he did what he made up his mind to. I suppose he made up his mind to go, but I knew what it cost him, by what it cost me when I heard of it. I had been through *one* war before. When you sent him you didn't expect he would get killed."

The voice seemed to compassionate Editha, and it was time. "No," she huskily murmured.

"No, girls don't; women don't, when they give their men up to their country. They think they'll come marching back, somehow, just as gay as they went, or if it's an empty sleeve, or even an empty pantaloon, it's all the more glory, and they're so much the prouder of them, poor things."

The tears began to run down Editha's face; she had not wept till then; but it was now such a relief to be understood that the tears came.

"No, you didn't expect him to get killed," Mrs. Gearson repeated in a voice which was startlingly like George's again. "You just expected him to kill some one else, some of those foreigners, that weren't there because they had any say about it, but because they had to be there, poor wretches—conscripts, or whatever they call 'em. You thought it would be all right for my George, *your* George, to kill the sons of those miserable mothers and the husbands of those girls that you would never see the faces of." The woman lifted her powerful voice in a psalmlike note. "I thank my God he didn't live to do it! I thank my God they killed him first, and that he ain't livin' with their blood on his hands!" She dropped her eyes which she had raised with her voice, and glared at Editha. "What you got that black on for?" She lifted herself by her powerful arms so high that her helpless body seemed to hang limp its full length. "Take it off, take it off, before I tear it from your back!"

The lady who was passing the summer near Balcom's Works was sketching Editha's beauty, which lent itself wonderfully to the effects of a colorist. It had come to that confidence which is rather apt to grow between artist and sitter, and Editha had told her everything.

"To think of your having such a tragedy in your life!" the lady said. She added: "I suppose there are people who feel that way about war. But when you consider the good this war has done—how much it has done for the country! I can't understand such people, for my part. And when you had come all the way out there to console her—got up out of a sick bed! Well!"

"I think," Editha said, magnanimously, "she wasn't quite in her right mind; and so did papa."

"Yes," the lady said, looking at Editha's lips in nature and then at her lips in art, and giving an empirical touch to them in the picture. "But how dreadful of her! How perfectly—excuse me—how *vulgar!*"

A light broke upon Editha in the darkness which she felt had been without a gleam of brightness for weeks and months. The mystery that had bewildered her was solved by the word; and from that moment she rose from grovelling in shame and self-pity, and began to live again in the ideal.

MARY AUSTIN

The Walking Woman

This story was first published in the *Atlantic Monthly* for August 1907 and later collected in *Lost Borders* (1909). As with many of Austin's stories and sketches, "The Walking Woman" is written in a style as lean and spare as its desert setting. The resulting effect, however, is neither a sense of austerity nor of a cruel and indifferent landscape. Instead, the simplicity of her style and the lives she describes serve as tonic counterstatements to the artificiality and complexity of the times. The mysterious title character is a woman without a name, though she is sometimes called Mrs. Walker because she has walked the region without apparent purpose and without protection or friends for so very long. She is a familiar figure to the men and women who live in the area, but they disagree about her in nearly every particular: Is she attractive or ugly? Wise or mad? Healthy or lame? The narrator comes to understand the woman largely through an instinctive sympathy and understanding, for the walking woman tells her very little; even her words seem mere punctuation for deeper thoughts and feelings. The walking woman has come to know and to treasure in her memory three important things: "To work and to love and to bear children." These are natural values, "society-made values," the woman has rejected, or rather has quite literally walked away from.

* * *

The first time of my hearing of her was at Temblor. We had come all one day between blunt, whitish bluffs rising from mirage water, with a thick, pale wake of dust billowing from the wheels, all the dead wall of the foothills sliding and shimmering with heat, to learn that the Walking Woman had passed us somewhere in the dizzying dimness, going down to the Tulares on her own feet. We heard of her again in the Carrisal, and again at Adobe Station, where she had passed a week before the shearing, and at last I had a glimpse of her at the Eighteen-Mile House as I went hurriedly northward on the Mojave stage; and afterward sheepherders at whose camps she slept, and cowboys at rodeos, told me as much of her way of life as they could understand. Like enough they told her as much of mine. That was very little. She was the Walking Woman, and no one knew her name, but because she was a sort of whom men speak respectfully, they called her to her face Mrs. Walker, and she answered to it if she was so inclined. She came and went about our western world on no discoverable errand, and whether she had some place of refuge where she lay by in the interim, or whether between her seldom, unaccountable appearances in our quarter she went on steadily walking, was never learned. She came and went, oftenest in a kind of muse of travel which the untrammelled space begets, or at rare intervals flooding wondrously with talk, never of herself, but of things she had known and seen. She must have seen some rare happenings, too—by report. She was at Maverick the time of the Big Snow, and at Tres Piños when they brought home the body of Morena; and if anybody could have told whether De Borba killed Mariana for spite or defence, it would have been she, only she could not be found when most wanted. She was at Tunawai at the time of the cloud-burst, and if she had cared for it could have known most desirable things of the ways of trail-making, burrow-habiting small things.

All of which should have made her worth meeting, though it was not, in fact, for such things I was wishful to meet her; and as it turned out, it was not of these things we talked when at last we came together. For one thing, she was a woman, not old, who had gone about alone in a country where the number of women is as one in fifteen. She had eaten and slept at the herder's camps, and laid by for days at one-man stations whose masters had no other touch of human kind than the passing of chance prospectors, or the halting of the tri-weekly stage. She had been set on her way by teamsters who lifted her out of white, hot desertness and put her down at the crossing of unnamed ways, days distant from anywhere. And through all this she passed unarmed and unoffended. I had the best testimony to this, the witness of the men themselves. I think they talked of it because they were so much surprised at it. It was not, on the whole, what they expected of themselves.

Well I understand that nature which wastes its borders with too eager burning, beyond which rim of desolation it flares forever quick and white, and have had some inkling of the isolating calm of a desire too high to stoop to satisfaction. But you could not think of these things pertaining to the Walking Woman; and if there were ever any truth in the exemption from offence residing in a frame of behavior called ladylike, it should have been inoperative here. What this really means is that you get no affront so long as your behavior in the estimate of the particular audience invites none. In the estimate of the immediate audience—conduct which affords protection in Mayfair gets you no consideration in Maverick. And by no canon could it be considered ladylike to go about on your own feet, with a blanket and a black bag and almost no money in your purse, in and about the haunts of rude and solitary men.

There were other things that pointed the wish for a personal encounter with the Walking Woman. One of them was the contradiction of reports of her—as to whether she was comely, for example. Report said yes, and again, plain to the point of deformity. She had a twist to her face, some said; a hitch to one shoulder; they averred she limped as she walked. But by the distance she covered she should have been straight and young. As to sanity, equal incertitude. On the mere evidence of her way of life she was cracked; not quite broken, but unserviceable. Yet in her talk there was both wisdom and information, and the word she brought about trails and water-holes was as reliable as an Indian's.

By her own account she had begun by walking off an illness. There had been an invalid to be taken care of for years, leaving her at last broken in body, and with no recourse but her own feet to carry her out of that predicament. It seemed there had been, besides the death of her invalid, some other worrying affairs, upon which, and the nature of her illness, she was never quite clear, so that it might very well have been an unsoundness of mind which drove her to the open, sobered and healed at last by the large soundness of nature. It must have been about that time that she lost her name. I am convinced that she never told it because she did not know it herself. She was the Walking Woman, and the country people called her Mrs. Walker. At the time I knew her, though she wore short hair and a man's boots, and had a fine down over all her face from exposure to the weather, she was perfectly sweet and sane.

I had met her occasionally at ranch-houses and road-stations, and had got as much acquaintance as the place allowed; but for the things I wished to know there wanted a time of leisure and isolation. And when the occasion came we talked altogether of other things.

It was at Warm Spring in the Little Antelope I came upon her in the heart of a clear forenoon. The spring lies off a mile from the main trail, and has the only trees about it known in that country. First you come upon a pool of waste full of weeds of a poisonous dark green, every reed ringed about the water-level with a muddy white incrustation. Then the three oaks appear staggering on the slope, and the spring sobs and blubbers below them in ashy-colored mud. All the hills of that country have the down plunge toward the desert and back abruptly toward the Sierra. The grass is thick and brittle and bleached straw-color toward the end of the season. As I rode up the swale of the spring I saw the Walking Woman sitting where the grass was deepest, with her black bag and blanket, which she carried on a stick, beside her. It was one of those days when the genius of talk flows as smoothly as the rivers of mirage through the blue hot desert morning.

You are not to suppose that in my report of a Borderer I give you the words only, but the full meaning of the speech. Very often the words are merely the punctuation of thought; rather, the crests of the long waves of inter-communicative silences. Yet the speech of the Walking Woman was fuller than most.

The best of our talk that day began in some dropped word of hers from which I inferred that she had had a child. I was surprised at that, and then wondered why I should have been surprised, for it is the most natural of all experiences to have children. I said something of that purport, and also that it was one of the perquisites of living I should be least willing to do without. And that led to the Walking Woman saying that there were three things which if you had known you could cut out all the rest, and they were good any way you got them, but best if, as in her case, they were related to and grew each one out of the others. It was while she talked that I decided that she really did have a twist to her face, a sort of natural warp or skew into which it fell when it was worn merely as a countenance, but which disappeared the moment it became the vehicle of thought or feeling.

The first of the experiences the Walking Woman had found most worth while had come to her in a sand-storm on the south slope of Tehachapi in a dateless spring. I judged it should have been about the time she began to find herself, after the period of worry and loss in which her wandering began. She had come, in a day pricked full of intimations of a storm, to the camp of Filon Geraud, whose companion shepherd had gone a three days' *pasear* to Mojave for supplies. Geraud was of great hardihood, red-blooded, of a full laughing eye, and an indubitable spark for women. It was the season of the year when there is a soft bloom on the days, but the nights are cowering cold and the lambs tender, not yet flockwise. At such times a sand-storm works incalculable disaster. The lift of the wind is so great that the whole surface of the ground appears to travel upon it slantwise, thinning out miles high in air. In the intolerable smother the lambs are lost from the ewes; neither dogs nor man make headway against it.

The morning flared through a horizon of yellow smudge, and by mid-forenoon the flock broke.

"There were but the two of us to deal with the trouble," said the Walking Woman. "Until that time I had not known how strong I was, nor how good it is to run when running is worth while. The flock travelled down the wind, the sand bit our faces; we called, and after a time heard the words broken and beaten small by the wind. But after a little we had not to call. All the time of our running in the yellow dusk of day and the black dark of night, I knew where Filon was. A flock-length away, I knew him. Feel? What should I feel? I knew. I ran with the flock and turned it this way and that as Filon would have.

"Such was the force of the wind that when we came together we held by one another and talked a little between pantings. We snatched and ate what we could as we ran. All that day and night until the next afternoon the camp kit was not out of the cayaques. But we held the flock. We herded them under a butte when the wind fell off a little, and the lambs sucked; when the storm rose they broke, but we kept upon their track and brought them together again. At night the wind quieted, and we slept by turns; at least Filon slept. I lay on the ground when my turn was and beat with the storm. I was no more tired than the earth was. The sand filled in the creases of the blanket, and where I turned, dripped back upon the ground. But we saved the sheep. Some ewes there were that would not give down their milk because of the worry of the storm, and the lambs died. But we kept the flock together. And I was not tired."

The Walking Woman stretched out her arms and clasped herself, rocking in them as if she would have hugged the recollection to her breast.

"For you see," said she, "I worked with a man, without excusing, without any burden on me of looking or seeming. Not fiddling or fumbling as women work, and hoping it will all turn out for the best. It was not for Filon to ask, Can you, or Will you. He said, Do, and I did. And my work was good. We held the flock. And that," said the Walking Woman, the twist coming in her face again, "is one of the things that make you able to do without the others."

"Yes," I said; and then, "What others?"

"Oh," she said, as if it pricked her, "the looking and the seeming."

And I had not thought until that time that one who had the courage to be the Walking Woman would have cared! We sat and looked at the pattern of the thick crushed grass on the slope, wavering in the fierce noon like the waterings in the coat of a tranquil beast; the ache of a world-old bitterness sobbed and whispered in the spring. At last—

"It is by the looking and the seeming," said I, "that the opportunity finds you out."

"Filon found out," said the Walking Woman. She smiled; and went on from that to tell me how, when the wind went down about four o'clock and left the afternoon clear and tender, the flock began to feed, and they had out the kit from the cayaques, and cooked a meal. When it was over, and Filon had his pipe between his teeth, he came over from his side of the fire, of his own notion, and stretched himself on the ground beside her. Of his own notion. There was that in the way she said it that made it seem as if nothing of the sort had happened before to the Walking Woman, and for a moment I thought she was about to tell me one of the things I wished to know; but she went on to say what Filon had said to her of her work with the flock. Obvious, kindly things, such as any man in sheer decency would have said, so that there must have something more gone with the words to make them so treasured of the Walking Woman.

"We were very comfortable," said she, "and not so tired as we expected to be. Filon leaned up on his elbow. I had not noticed until then how broad he was in the shoulders, and how strong in the arms. And we had saved the flock together. We felt that. There was something that said together, in the slope of his shoulders toward me. It was around his mouth and on the cheek high up under the shine of his eyes. And under the shine the look—the look that said, 'We are of one sort and one mind'—his eyes that were the color of the flat water in the toulares—do you know the look?"

"I know it."

"The wind was stopped and all the earth smelled of dust, and Filon understood very well that what I had done with him I could not have done so well with another. And the look—the look in the eyes—"

"Ah-ah—!"

I have always said, I will say again, I do not know why at this point the Walking Woman touched me. If it were merely a response to my unconscious throb of sympathy, or the unpremeditated way of her heart to declare that this, after all, was the best of all indispensable experiences; or if in some flash of forward vision, encompassing the unimpassioned years, the stir, the movement of tenderness were for *me*—but no; as often as I have thought of it, I have thought of a different reason, but no conclusive one, why the Walking Woman should have put out her hand and laid it on my arm.

"To work together, to love together," said the Walking Woman, withdrawing her hand again; "there you have two of the things; the other you know."

"The mouth at the breast," said I.

"The lips and the hands," said the Walking Woman. "The little, pushing hands and the small cry." There ensued a pause of fullest understanding, while the land before us swam in the noon, and a dove in the oaks behind the spring began to call. A little red fox came out of the hills and lapped delicately at the pool.

"I stayed with Filon until the fall," said she. "All that summer in the Sierras, until it was time to turn south on the trail. It was a good time, and longer than he could be expected to have loved one like me. And besides, I was no longer able to keep the trail. My baby was born in October."

Whatever more there was to say to this, the Walking Woman's hand said it, straying with remembering gesture to her breast. There are so many ways of loving and working, but only one way of the first-born. She added after an interval, that she did not know if she would have given up her walking to keep at home and tend him, or whether the thought of her son's small feet running beside her in the trails would have driven her to the open again. The baby had not stayed long enough for that. "And whenever the wind blows in the night," said the Walking Woman, "I wake and wonder if he is well covered."

She took up her black bag and her blanket; there was the ranch-house of Dos Palos to be made before night, and she went as outliers do, without a hope expressed of another meeting and no word of good-bye. She was the Walking Woman. That was it. She had walked off all sense of society-made values, and, knowing the best when the best came to her, was able to take it. Work—as I believed; love—as the Walking Woman had proved it; a child—as you subscribe to it. But look you: it was the naked thing the Walking Woman grasped, not dressed and tricked out, for instance, by prejudices in favor of certain occupations; and love, man love, taken as it came, not picked over and rejected if it carried no obligation of permanency; and a child; *any* way you get it, a child is good to have, say nature and the Walking Woman; to have it and not to wait upon a proper concurrence of so many decorations that the event may not come at all.

At least one of us is wrong. To work and to love and to bear children. *That* sounds easy enough. But the way we live establishes so many things of much more importance.

Far down the dim, hot valley I could see the Walking Woman with her blanket and black bag over her shoulder. She had a queer, sidelong gait, as if in fact she had a twist all through her.

Recollecting suddenly that people called her lame, I ran down to the open place below the spring where she had passed. There in the bare, hot sand the track of her two feet bore evenly and white.

ZONA GALE

Nobody Rich, Nobody Poor

"Nobody Rich, Nobody Poor" was included in Zona Gale's collection of stories *Friendship Village* (1909). Gale used the imaginary citizens of Friendship Village in more than eighty stories appearing in five separate volumes; a novel entitled *From Mothers to Men* (1911), a novella, *Christmas* (1912), and a play, *The Neighbors* (1914). The setting was based on Gale's native Portage, Wisconsin, but as she said in the preface to her first collection, the community and its inhabitants were figures of the imagination, known only by the sympathetic "comradeship" she felt for them. Gale thought of her tales as a "kind of middle door to experience, minus the fuss of official arriving"; as such, at their best Gale's stories convey a cordial immediacy free from the contrivance that strives for dramatic effect. Calliope Marsh, the dominant character in this and most of the other Friendship Village tales, is a sly and knowing woman who shrewdly manages to convert individual grief, despair, and cynicism into communal happiness. The conception of the story is comic, and it is rendered with a splendid eye for telling, realistic detail, but the author's final purpose is to dramatize a transcendent and democratically available realm of experience that lies nearby in the commonplace. Gale herself believed that the fiction of the future "will clarify the beauty of much that we are accustomed to pass by."

*   *   *

Two days before Thanksgiving the air was already filled with white turkey feathers, and I stood at a window and watched until the loneliness of my still house seemed like something pointing a mocking finger at me. When I could bear it no longer I went out in the snow, and through the soft drifts I fought my way up the Plank Road toward the village.

I had almost passed the little bundled figure before I recognized Calliope. She was walking in the middle of the road, as in Friendship we all walk in winter; and neither of us had umbrellas. I think that I distrust people who put up umbrellas on a country road in a fall of friendly flakes.

Instead of inquiring perfunctorily how I did, she greeted me with a fragment of what she had been thinking—which is always as if one were to open a door of his mind to you instead of signing you greeting from a closed window.

"I just been tellin' myself," she looked up to say without preface, "that if I could see one more good old-fashion' Thanksgivin', life'd sort o' smooth out. An' land knows, it needs some smoothin' out for me."

With this I remember that it was as if my own loneliness spoke for me. At my reply Calliope looked at me quickly—as if I, too, had opened a door.

"Sometimes Thanksgivin' *is* some like seein' the sun shine when you're feelin' rill rainy yourself," she said thoughtfully.

She held out her blue-mittened hand and let the flakes fall on it in stars and coronets.

"I wonder," she asked evenly, "if you'd help me get up a Thanksgivin' dinner for a few poor sick folks here in Friendship?"

In order to keep my self-respect, I recall that I was as ungracious as possible. I think I said that the day meant so little to me that I was willing to do anything to avoid spending it alone. A statement which seems to me now not to bristle with logic.

"That's nice of you," Calliope replied genially. Then she hesitated, looking down Daphne Street, which the Plank Road had become, toward certain white houses. There were the homes of Mis' Mayor Uppers, Mis' Holcomb-that-was-Mame-Bliss, and the Liberty sisters,—all substantial dignified houses, typical of the simple prosperity of the countryside.

"The only trouble," she added simply, "is that in Friendship I don't know of a soul rill sick, nor a soul what you might call poor."

At this I laughed, unwillingly enough. Dear Calliope! Here indeed was a drawback to her project.

"Honestly," she said reflectively, "Friendship can't seem to do anything like any other town. When the new minister come here, he give out he was goin' to do settlement work. An' his second week in the place he come to me with a reg'lar hang-dog look. 'What kind of a town is this?' he says to me, disgusted. 'They ain't nobody sick in it an' they ain't nobody poor!' I guess he could 'a' got along without the poor—most of us can. But we mostly like to hev a few sick to carry the flowers off our house plants to, an' now an' then a tumbler o' jell. An' yet I've known weeks at a time when they wasn't a soul rill flat down sick in Friendship. It's so now. An' that's hard, when you're young an' enthusiastic, like the minister."

"But where are you going to find your guests then, Calliope?" I asked curiously.

"Well," she said brightly, "I was just plannin' as you come up with me. An' I says to myself: 'God give me to live in a little bit of a place where we've all got enough to get along on, an' Thanksgivin' finds us all in health. It looks like He'd afflicted us by lettin' us hev nobody to do for.' An' then it come to me that if we was to get up the dinner,— with all the misery an' hunger they is in the world,—God in His goodness would let some of it come our way to be fed. 'In the wilderness a cedar,' you know—as Liddy Ember an' I was always tellin' each other when we kep' shop together. An' so to-day I said to myself I'd go to work an' get up the dinner an' trust there'd be eaters for it."

"Why, Calliope," I said, "Calliope!"

"I ain't got much to do with, myself," she added apologetically; "the most I've got in my sullar, I guess, is a gallon jar o' watermelon pickles. I could give that. You don't think it sounds irreverent—connectin' God with a big dinner, so?" she asked anxiously.

And, at my reply:—

"Well, then," she said briskly, "let's step in an' see a few folks that might be able to tell us of somebody to do for. Let's ask Mis' Mayor Uppers an' Mis' Holcomb-that-was-Mame-Bliss, an' the Liberty girls."

Because I was lonely and idle, and because I dreaded inexpressibly going back to my still house, I went with her. Her ways were a kind of entertainment, and I remember that I believed my leisure to be infinite.

We turned first toward the big shuttered house of Mis' Mayor Uppers, to whom, although her husband had been a year ago removed from office, discredited, and had not since been seen in Friendship, we yet gave her old proud title, as if she had been Former Lady Mayoress. For the present mayor, Authority Hubblethwaite, was, as Calliope said, "unconnect'."

I watched Mis' Uppers in some curiosity while Calliope explained that she was planning a dinner for the poor and sick,—"the lame and the sick that's comfortable enough off to eat,"—and could she suggest some poor and sick to ask? Mis' Uppers was like a vinegar cruet of mine, slim and tall, with a little grotesquely puckered face for a stopper, as if the whole known world were sour.

"I'm sure," she said humbly, "it's a nice i-dea. But I declare, I'm put to it to suggest. We ain't got nobody sick nor nobody poor in Friendship, you know."

"Don't you know of anybody kind o' hard up? Or somebody that, if they ain't down sick, feels sort o' spindlin'?" Calliope asked anxiously.

Mis' Uppers thought, rocking a little and running a pin in and out of a fold of her skirt.

"No," she said at length, "I don't know a soul. I think the church'd give a good deal if a real poor family'd come here to do for. Since the Cadozas went, we ain't known which way to look for poor. Mis' Ricker gettin' her fortune so puts her beyond the wolf. An' Peleg Bemus, you can't *get* him to take anything. No, I don't know of anybody real decently poor."

"An' nobody sick?" Calliope pressed her wistfully.

"Well, there's Mis' Crawford," admitted Mis' Uppers; "she had a spell o' lumbago two weeks ago, but I see her pass the house to-day. Mis' Brady was laid up with toothache, too, but the *Daily* last night said she'd had it out. An' Mis' Doctor Helman did have one o' her stomach attacks this week, an' Elzabella got out her dyin' dishes an' her dyin' linen from the still-room—you know how Mis' Doctor always brings out her nice things when she's sick, so't if she should die an' the neighbours come in, it'd all be shipshape. But she got better this time an' helped put 'em back. I declare it's hard to get up anything in the charity line here."

Calliope sat smiling a little, and I knew that it was because of her secret certainty that "some o' the hunger" would come her way, to be fed.

"I can't help thinkin'," she said quietly, "that we'll find somebody. An' I tell you what: if we do, can I count on you to help some?"

Mis' Mayor Uppers flushed with quick pleasure.

"Me, Calliope?" she said. And I remembered that they had told me how the Friendship Married Ladies' Cemetery Improvement Sodality had been unable to tempt Mis' Uppers to a single meeting since the mayor ran away. "Oh, but I couldn't though," she said wistfully.

"No need to go to the table if you don't want," Calliope told her. "Just bake up something' for us an' bring it over. Make a couple o' your cherry pies—did you get hold of any cherries to put up this year? Well, a couple o' your cherry pies an' a batch o' your nice drop sponge cakes," she directed. "Could you?"

Mis' Mayor Uppers looked up with a kind of light in her eyes.

"Why, yes," she said, "I could, I guess. I'll bake 'em Thanksgivin' mornin'. I—I was wonderin' how I'd put in the day."

When we stepped out in the snow again, Calliope's face was shining. Sometimes now, when my faith is weak in any good thing, I remember her look that November morning. But all that I thought then was how I was being entertained that lonely day.

The dear Liberty sisters were next, Lucy and Viny and Libbie Liberty.

We went to the side door,—there were houses in Friendship whose front doors we tacitly understood that we were never expected to use,—and we found the sisters down cellar, with shawls over their heads, feeding their hens through the cellar window, opening on the glassed-in coop under the porch.

In Friendship it is a point of etiquette for a morning caller never to interrupt the employment of a hostess. So we obeyed the summons of the Liberty sisters to "come right down"; and we sat on a firkin and an inverted tub while Calliope told her plan and the hens fought for delectable morsels.

"My grief!" said Libbie Liberty, tartly, "where you goin' to *get* your sick an' poor?"

Mis' Viny, balancing on the window ledge to reach for eggs, looked back at us.

"Friendship's so comfortable that way," she said, "I don't see how you can get up much of anything."

And little Miss Lucy, kneeling on the floor of the cellar to measure more feed, said without looking up:—

"You know, since mother died we ain't never done anything for holidays. No—we can't seem to want to think about Thanksgiving or Christmas or like that."

They all turned their grave lined faces toward us.

"We want to let the holidays just slip by without noticin'," Miss Viny told us. "Seems like it hurts less that way."

Libbie Liberty smiled wanly.

"Don't you know," she said, "when you hold your hand still in hot water, you don't feel how hot the water really is? But when you move around in it some, it begins to burn you. Well, when we let Thanksgiving an' Christmas alone, it ain't so bad. But when we start to move around in 'em—"

Her voice faltered and stopped.

"We miss mother terrible," Miss Lucy said simply.

Calliope put her blue mitten to her mouth, but her eyes she might not hide, and they were soft with sympathy.

"I know—I know," she said. "I remember the first Christmas after my mother died—I ached like the toothache all over me, an' I couldn't bear to open my presents. Nor the next year I couldn't either—I couldn't open my presents with any heart. But—" Calliope hesitated, "that second year," she said, "I found somethin' I could do. I saw I could fix up little things for other folks an' take some comfort in it. Like mother would of."

She was silent for a moment, looking thoughtfully at the three lonely figures in the dark cellar of their house.

"Your mother," she said abruptly, "stuffed the turkey for a year ago the last harvest home."

"Yes," they said.

"Look here," said Calliope; "if I can get some poor folks together, —or even *one* poor folk, or hungry,—will you three come over to my house an' stuff the turkey? The way—I can't help thinkin' the way your mother would of, if she'd been here. An' then," Calliope went on briskly, "could you bring some fresh eggs an' make a pan o' custard over to my house? An' mebbe one o' you'd stir up a sunshine cake. You must know how to make your mother's sunshine cake?"

There was another silence in the cellar when Calliope had done, and for a minute I wondered if, after all, she had not failed, and if the bleeding of the three hearts might be so stanched. It was not self-reliant Libbie Liberty who spoke first; it was gentle Miss Lucy.

"I guess," she said, "I could, if we all do it. I know mother would of."

"Yes," Miss Viny nodded, "mother would of."

Libbie Liberty stood for a moment with compressed lips.

"It seems like not payin' respect to mother," she began; and then shook her head. "It ain't that," she said; "it's only missin' her when we begin to step around the kitchen, bakin' up for a holiday."

"I know—I know," Calliope said again. "That's why I said for you to come over in my kitchen. You come over there an' stir up the sunshine cake, too, an' bake it in my oven, so's we can hev it et hot. Will you do that?"

And after a little time they consented. If Calliope found any sick or poor, they would do that.

"We ain't gettin' many i-dees for guests," Calliope said, as we reached the street, "but we're gettin' helpers, anyway. An' some dinner, too."

Then we went to the house of Mis' Holcomb-that-was-Mame-Bliss—called so, of course, to distinguish her from the "Other" Holcombs.

"Don't you be shocked at her," Calliope warned me, as we closed Mis' Holcomb's gate behind us; "she's dreadful diff'r'nt an' bitter since Abigail was married last month. She's got hold o' some kind of a Persian book, in a decorated cover, from the City; an' now she says your soul is like when you look in a lookin'-glass—that there ain't really nothin' there. An' that the world's some wind an' the rest water, an' they ain't no God only your own breath—oh, poor Mis' Holcomb!" said Calliope. "I guess she ain't rill balanced. But we ought to go to see her. We always consult Mis' Holcomb about everything."

Poor Mis' Holcomb-that-was-Mame-Bliss! I can see her now in her comfortable dining room, where she sat cleaning her old silver, her thin, veined hands as fragile as her grandmother's spoons.

"Of course, you don't know," she said, when Calliope had unfolded her plans, "how useless it all seems to me. What's the use—I keep sayin' to myself now'-days; what's the use? You put so much pains on some-thing', an' then it goes off an' leaves you. Mebbe it dies, an' everything's all wasted. There ain't anything to tie to. It's like lookin' in a glass all the while. It's seemin',' it ain't bein'. We ain't certain o' nothin' but our breath, an' when that goes, what hev you got? What's the use o' plan-nin' Thanksgivin' for anybody?"

"Well, if you're hungry, it's kind o' nice to get fed up," said Calliope, crisply. "Don't you know a soul that's hungry, Mame Bliss?"

She shook her head.

"No," she said, "I don't. Nor nobody sick in body."

"Nobody sick in body," Calliope repeated absently.

"Soul-sick an' soul-hungry you can't feed up," Mis' Holcomb added.

"I donno," said Calliope, thoughtfully, "I donno but you can."

"No," Mis' Holcomb went on; "your soul's like yourself in the glass: they ain't anything there."

"I donno," Calliope said again; "some mornin's when I wake up with the sun shinin' in, I can feel my soul in me just as plain as plain."

Mis' Holcomb sighed.

"Life looks dreadful footless to me," she said.

"Well," said Calliope, "sometimes life *is* some like hearin' firecrackers go off when you don't feel up to shootin' 'em yourself. When I'm like that, I always think if I'd go out an' buy a bunch or two, an' get some-body to give me a match, I could see more sense to things. Look here, Mame Bliss; if I get hold o' any folks to give the dinner for, will you help me some?"

"Yes," Mis' Holcomb assented half-heartedly, "I'll help you. I ain't nobody much in family, now Abigail's done what she has. They's only Eppleby, an' he won't be home Thanksg'vin this year. So I ain't nothin' else to do."

"That's the *i*-dee," said Calliope, heartily; "if everything's foolish, it's just as foolish doin' nothin' as doin' somethin'. Will you bring over a kettleful o' boiled potatoes to my house Thanksgivin' noon? An' mash 'em an' whip 'em in my kitchen? I'll hev the milk to put in. You—you don't cook as much as some, do you, Mame?"

Did Calliope ask her that purposely? I am almost sure that she did. Mis' Holcomb's neck stiffened a little.

"I guess I can cook a thing or two beside mash' potatoes," she said, and thought for a minute. "How'd you like a pan o' 'scalloped oysters an' some baked marcaroni with plenty o' cheese?" she demanded.

"Sounds like it'd go down awful easy," admitted Calliope, smiling. "It's just what we need to carry the dinner off full sail," she added earnestly.

"Well, I ain't nothin' else to do an' I'll make 'em," Mis' Holcomb promised. "Only it beats me who you can find to do for. If you don't get anybody, let me know before I order the oysters."

Calliope stood up, her little wrinkled face aglow; and I wondered at her confidence.

"You just go ahead an' order your oysters," she said. "That dinner's goin' to come off Thanksgivin' noon at twelve o'clock. An' you be there to help feed the hungry, Mame."

When we were on the street again, Calliope looked at me with her way of shy eagerness.

"Could you hev the dinner up to your house," she asked me, "if I do every bit o' the work?"

"Why, Calliope," I said, amazed at her persistence, "have it there, of course. But you haven't any guests yet."

She nodded at me through the falling flakes.

"You say you ain't got much to be thankful for," she said, "so I thought mebbe you'd put in the time that way. Don't you worry about folks to eat the dinner. I'll tell Mis' Holcomb an' the others to come to your house—an' I'll get the food an' the folks. Don't you worry! An' I'll bring my watermelon pickles an' a bowl o' cream for Mis' Holcomb's potatoes, an' I'll furnish the turkey—a big one. The rest of us'll get the dinner in your kitchen Thanksgivin' mornin'. My!" she said, "seems though life's smoothin' out fer me a'ready. Good-by—it's 'most noon."

She hurried up Daphne Street in the snow, and I turned toward my lonely house. But I remember that I was planning how I would make my table pretty, and how I would add a delicacy or two from the City for this strange holiday feast. And I found myself hurrying to look over certain long-disused linen and silver, and to see whether my Cloth-o'-Gold rose might be counted on to bloom by Thursday noon.

SUI SIN FAR

Mrs. Spring Fragrance

"Mrs. Spring Fragrance," the title story of Sui Sin Far's only volume of fiction, presents a Chinese-American protagonist in the process of assimilating into the values and courtship traditions of a new culture. A story of immense charm and subtle humor, with a strong plot and fascinating conversations, it reveals the complex manipulations of a well-intentioned woman who attempts to "assist" in the romantic struggles of her friends and their children. In the process, much is revealed about the differing assumptions of Mrs. Spring Fragrance and her husband, their deep and abiding love for each other, the complexity of their roles in an alien culture, and her attempt to remain a properly subordinate Asian woman while at the same time assuming control of family affairs. Originally published in *Hampton's Magazine* in 1910, the story has been admired for its realistic depiction of a Chinese-American woman who quickly adopts new ideas of love and individual fulfillment, as opposed to her husband, who maintains conservative Chinese values regarding the family.

*   *   *

When Mrs. Spring Fragrance first arrived in Seattle, she was unacquainted with even one word of the American language. Five years later, her husband, speaking of her, said: "There are no more American words for her learning." And everyone who knew Mrs. Spring Fragrance agreed with Mr. Spring Fragrance. This gentleman, whose business name was Sing Yook, was a young curio merchant. Though conservatively Chinese in many respects, he was at the same time what is called by the Westerners "Americanized." Mrs. Spring Fragrance was even more so—"Americanized."

Next door to the Spring Fragrances lived the Chin Yuens. Mrs. Chin Yuen was much older than Mrs. Spring Fragrance; but she had a daughter of eighteen with whom Mrs. Spring Fragrance was great friends. The daughter was a pretty girl, whose Chinese name was Mai Gwi Far (a rose), and whose American name was Laura. This daughter had a sweetheart, a youth named Kai Tzu. Kai Tzu, who was American born, and as ruddy and stalwart as any young Westerner, was noted among baseball players as one of the finest pitchers on the Coast. He could also sing "Drink to me only with thine eyes," to Laura's piano accompaniment.

Now, the only person who knew that Kai Tzu loved Laura and that Laura loved Kai Tzu was Mrs. Spring Fragrance. For though the Chin Yuen parents lived in a house furnished in American style and wore American clothes, they religiously observed many Chinese customs and their ideals of life were the ideals of their Chinese forefathers. Therefore, they had betrothed their daughter, Laura, at the age of fifteen, to the eldest son of the Chinese Government school-teacher in San Francisco. The time for the consummation of the betrothal was approaching.

"I have just had such a pretty walk," said Mrs. Spring Fragrance to Laura one day when the girl was very depressed. "I crossed the banks above the beach and came back by the long road. In the green grass the daffodils were blowing; in the cottage gardens the currant bushes were flowering, and in the air was the perfume of the wall flower. I wished, Laura, that you were with me."

Laura burst into tears. "That is the walk Kai Tzu and I so love," she sobbed, "but never, ah, never, can we take it together again."

"Now, Little Sister," comforted Mrs. Spring Fragrance, "you really must not grieve like that. Is there not a beautiful American poem written by a noble American named Tennyson which says: ' 'Tis better to have loved and lost, than never to have loved at all'?"

Mrs. Spring Fragrance was unaware that Mr. Spring Fragrance had returned from the city, tired with the day's business, and had thrown himself down on the bamboo settee on the veranda, and that though his eyes were engaged in scanning the pages of the *Chinese World*, his ears could not help receiving the words which were borne to him through the open window.

> " 'Tis better to have loved and lost,
> Than never to have loved at all,"

repeated Mr. Spring Fragrance. Not wishing to hear more of the secret talk of women, he arose and sauntered around the veranda to the other side of the house. Two pigeons circled around his head. He felt in his pocket for a li-chi which he usually carried for their picking. His fingers touched a little box. It contained a jade pendant which Mrs. Spring Fragrance had particularly admired the last time she was downtown. It was the fifth anniversary of Mr. and Mrs. Spring Fragrance's wedding day. Mr. Spring Fragrance pressed the little box down into the depths of his pocket.

A young man came out of the back door of the house on Mr. Spring Fragrance's left-hand side.

"Good evening," said the young man.

"Good evening," returned Mr. Spring Fragrance.

"Will you please tell me," said Mr. Spring Fragrance, "the meaning of two lines of an American verse which I have heard?"

"Certainly," returned the young man with a genial smile. He was a star student at the University of Washington, and had not the slightest doubt that he could explain the meaning of all things in the universe.

"Well," said Mr. Spring Fragrance, "it is this:

> " 'Tis better to have loved and lost,
> Than never to have loved at all."

"Ah!" responded the young man with an air of profound wisdom. "That, Mr. Spring Fragrance, means that it is a good thing to love anyway—even if we can't get what we love, or, as the poet tells us, lose what we love. Of course one needs some experience to feel the truth of this teaching."

"The truth of the teaching," echoed Mr. Spring Fragrance a little testily; "there is no truth in it whatever. It is disobedient to reason. Is it not better to have what you do not love than to love what you do not have?"

"That depends," answered the young man, "upon temperament."

"I thank you. Good evening," said Mr. Spring Fragrance. While he was musing upon the unwisdom of the American way of looking at things, inside the house Laura was refusing to be comforted.

"Ah, no! No!" cried she. "If I had not gone to school with Kai Tzu, nor talked and walked with him, nor played the accompaniments to his songs, then I might consider with complacency, or at least without horror, my approaching marriage with the son of Man You. But as it is, oh, as it is——"

Mrs. Spring Fragrance knelt down beside the girl, who was rocking herself to and fro in heartfelt grief; clasping her arms around her neck, she cried in sympathy:

"Little Sister, O Little Sister! Dry your tears—do not despair. A moon has yet to pass before the marriage can take place. Who knows what the stars may have to say to one another during its passing. A little bird has whispered to me——"

For a long time Mrs. Spring Fragrance talked. For a long time Laura listened. When the girl arose to go, there was a bright light in her eyes.

Mrs. Spring Fragrance, in San Francisco on a visit to her cousin, the wife of the herb doctor of Clay Street, was having a good time. She was invited everywhere that the wife of an honorable Chinese merchant could go. There was much to see and hear, including more than a dozen babies who had been born in the families of her friends since she last visited the city of the Golden Gate. Mrs. Spring Fragrance loved babies. She had had two herself, but both had been transplanted into the spirit land before the completion of even one moon.

There were also many dinners and theater parties given in her honor. It was at one of the theater parties that Mrs. Spring Fragrance met Ah Oi, a young girl who had the reputation of being the prettiest Chinese girl in San Francisco and, according to Chinese gossip, the naughtiest.

In spite of all the gossip, however, Mrs. Spring Fragrance took a great fancy to Ah Oi, and invited her to a *tête-à-tête* picnic on the following day. This invitation Ah Oi joyfully accepted. She was really a sort of bird girl and never felt so happy as when out in the park or woods.

On the day after the picnic Mrs. Spring Fragrance wrote to Laura Chin Yuen thus:

MY PRECIOUS LAURA:

May the bamboo ever wave. Next week I accompany Ah Oi to the beauteous town of San Jose. There will we be met by the son of the Illustrious Teacher, and in a little Mission, presided over by a benevolent American priest, the little Ah Oi and the son of the Illustrious Teacher will be joined together in love and harmony—two pieces of music made to complete one another.

The son of the Illustrious Teacher, having been through an American Hall of Learning, is well able to provide for his orphan bride, and fears not the displeasure of his parents, now that he is assured that your grief at his loss will not be inconsolable. He wishes me to waft to you and to Kai Tzu, and the little Ah Oi joins with him, ten thousand rainbow wishes for your happiness.

My respects to your honorable parents, and to yourself the heart of your loving friend,

JADE SPRING FRAGRANCE.

To Mr. Spring Fragrance Mrs. Spring Fragrance also indited a letter, which read:

GREAT AND HONORED MAN:

Greeting from your plum blossom, who is desirous of hiding herself from the sun of your presence for a week of seven days more. My honorable cousin is preparing for the Fifth Moon Festival, and wishes me to compound for the occasion some American "fudge," for which delectable sweet, made by my clumsy hands, you have sometimes shown a slight prejudice. I am enjoying a most agreeable visit, and American friends, as also our own, strive benevolently for the accomplishment of my pleasure. Mrs. Samuel Smith, an American lady, known to my cousin, asked for my accompaniment to a magniloquent lecture the other evening. The subject was "America, the Protector of China"! It was most exhilarating, and the effect of so much expression of benevolence leads me to beg of you to forget to remember that the barber charges you one dollar for a shave while he humbly submits to the American man a bill of fifteen cents. And murmur no more because your honored elder brother, on a visit to this country, is detained under the rooftree of this great Government instead of under your own humble roof. Console him with the reflection that he is protected under the wing of the Eagle, the Emblem of Liberty. What is the loss of ten hundred years or ten thousand times ten dollars compared with the happiness of knowing oneself so securely sheltered? All of this I have learned from Mrs. Samuel Smith, who is as brilliant and great of mind as one of your own superior sex.

For me, it is sufficient to know that the Golden Gate Park is most enchanting and the seals on the rock at the Cliff House extremely entertaining and amiable. There is much feasting and merrymaking under the lanterns, in honor of your Stupid Thorn.

I have purchased for your smoking a pipe with an amber mouth. It is said to be very sweet to the lips and to emit a cloud of smoke fit for the gods to inhale.

Awaiting by the wonderful wire of the telegram message your gracious permission to remain for the celebration of the Fifth Moon Festival and the making of American fudge, I continue for ten thousand times ten thousand years,

Your ever loving and obedient woman,

JADE.

P.S. Forget not to care for the cat, the birds, and the flowers. Do not eat too quickly nor fan too vigorously now that the weather is warming.

Mrs. Spring Fragrance smiled as she folded this last epistle. Even if he were old-fashioned, there was never a husband so good and kind as hers. Only on one occasion since their marriage had he slighted her wishes. That was when, on the last anniversary of their wedding, she had signified a desire for a certain jade pendant, and he had failed to satisfy that desire.

But Mrs. Spring Fragrance, being of a happy nature and disposed to look upon the bright side of things, did not allow her mind to dwell upon the jade pendant. Instead, she gazed complacently down upon her bejeweled fingers and folded in with her letter to Mr. Spring Fragrance a bright little sheaf of condensed love.

Mr. Spring Fragrance sat on his doorstep reading his letters; there was one from Mrs. Spring Fragrance, and another from an elderly bachelor cousin in San Francisco. The one from the elderly bachelor cousin was a business letter, but it contained the following postscript:

"Tsen Hing, the son of the Government school-master, seems to be much in the company of your young wife. He is a good-looking youth. Pardon me, my dear cousin, but if women are allowed to stray at will from under their husband's mulberry roofs, what is to prevent them from becoming butterflies?"

"Sing Foon is old and cynical," said Mr. Spring Fragrance to himself. "Why should I pay any attention to him? This is America, where a man may speak to a woman, and a woman listen, without any thought of evil."

He destroyed his cousin's letter and reread his wife's. Then he became very thoughtful. Was the making of American fudge sufficient reason for a wife to wish to remain a week longer in a city where her husband was not?

The young man who lived in the next house came out to water the lawn.

"Good evening," said he. "Any news from Mrs. Spring Fragrance?"

"She is having a very good time," returned Mr. Spring Fragrance.

"Glad to hear it. I think you told me she was to return the end of this week."

"I have changed my mind about her," said Mr. Spring Fragrance. "I am bidding her remain a week longer, as I wish to give a smoking party during her absence. I hope I may have the pleasure of your company."

"I shall be delighted," returned the other. "But, Mr. Spring Fragrance, don't invite any other white fellows. If you do not, I shall be able to get in a scoop. You know, I'm a sort of honorary reporter for the *Gleaner*. I shall call it a high-class Chinese stag party!"

In spite of his melancholy mood, Mr. Spring Fragrance smiled.

"Everything is 'high class' in America," he observed.

"Sure!" cheerfully assented the young man. "Haven't you ever heard that all Americans are princes and princesses, and just as soon as a foreigner puts his foot upon our shores he also becomes of the nobility—I mean, the royal family."

Mr. Spring Fragrance puffed his pipe in silence for some moments. Weightier matters were troubling his mind.

At last he spoke. "Love," said he slowly and distinctly, "comes before the wedding in this country, does it not?"

"Yes, certainly."

"Presuming," continued Mr. Spring Fragrance, "presuming that some friend of your father's—living, presuming, in England—has a daughter that he arranges with your father to be your wife. Presuming that you have never seen that daughter, but that you marry her, knowing her not. Presuming that she marries you, knowing you not. After she marries you and knows you, will that woman love you?"

"Emphatically, no!" answered the young man.

"That is the way it would be in America—that the woman who marries the man like that would not love him?"

"Yes, that is the way it would be in America. Love, in this country, must be free, or it is not love at all."

"In China it is different!" mused Mr. Spring Fragrance.

"Oh, yes, I have no doubt that in China it is different."

"But the love is in the heart all the same," went on Mr. Spring Fragrance.

"Yes, all the same. Everybody falls in love some time or another. Some"—pensively—"many times."

Mr. Spring Fragrance arose.

"I must go downtown," said he.

As he walked down the street, he recalled the remark of a business acquaintance who had met his wife and had had some conversation with her: "She is just like an American woman."

He had felt somewhat flattered when this remark had been made. He looked upon it as a compliment to his wife's cleverness; but it rankled in his mind as he entered the telegraph office. If his wife was becoming like an American woman, would it not be possible for her to love, as an American woman, a man to whom she was not married? There also floated in his memory the verse which his wife had quoted to the daughter of Chin Yuen. Yet, when the telegraph clerk handed him a blank, he wrote this message:

"Remain as you wish, but remember that ''Tis better to have loved and lost, than never to have loved at all.' "

When Mrs. Spring Fragrance received this message, her laughter tinkled like falling water. How droll! How delightful! Here was her husband quoting American poetry in a telegram. Perhaps he had been reading her American poetry books since she had left him! She hoped so. They would lead him to understand her sympathy for her dear Laura and Kai Tzu. She need no longer keep from him their secret. How joyful! It had been such a hardship to refrain from confiding in him before. But discreetness had been most necessary, because Mr. Spring Fragrance entertained as old-fashioned notions concerning marriage as did the Chin Yuen parents. Strange that that should be so, since he had fallen in love with her picture before ever he had seen her, just as she had fallen in love with his! And when the marriage veil was lifted and each saw the other for the first time in the flesh, there had been no disillusion, no lessening of the respect and affection which those who had brought about the marriage had inspired in each young heart.

Mrs. Spring Fragrance began to wish she could fall asleep and wake to find herself, the week flown, in her own little home, pouring tea for Mr. Spring Fragrance.

Mr. Spring Fragrance was walking to business with Mr. Chin Yuen. As they walked they talked.

"Yes," said Mr. Chin Yuen, "the old order is passing away and the new order is taking its place, even with us who are Chinese. I have finally consented to give my daughter in marriage to young Kai Tzu."

Mr. Spring Fragrance expressed surprise. He had understood that the marriage between his neighbor's daughter and the San Francisco school-teacher's son was all arranged.

"So 'twas," answered Mr. Chin Yuen; "but it seems the young renegade, without consultation or advice, has placed his affections upon some untrustworthy female, and is so under her influence that he refuses to fulfill his parents' promise to me for him."

"So!" said Mr. Spring Fragrance. The shadow on his brow deepened.

"But," said Mr. Chin Yuen with affable resignation, "it is all ordained by Heaven. Our daughter, as the wife of Kai Tzu, for whom she has long had a loving feeling, will not now be compelled to dwell with a mother-in-law and where her own mother is not. For that we are thankful, as she is our only one, and the conditions of life in this Western country are not as in China. Moreover, Kai Tzu, though not so much of a scholar as the teacher's son, has a keen eye for business and that, in America, is certainly much more desirable than scholarship. What do you think?"

"Eh! What!" exclaimed Mr. Spring Fragrance. The latter part of his companion's remarks had been lost upon him.

That day the shadow which had been following Mr. Spring Fragrance ever since he had heard his wife quote " 'Tis better to have loved" became so heavy and deep that he quite lost himself within it. At home, in the evening, he fed the cat, the bird, and the flowers. Then, seating himself in a carved black chair—a present from his wife on his last birthday—he took out his pipe and smoked. The cat jumped into his lap. He stroked it softly and tenderly. It had been much fondled by Mrs. Spring Fragrance, and Mr. Spring Fragrance was under the impression that it missed her. "Poor thing!" said he, "I suppose you want her back." When he arose to go to bed he placed the animal carefully on the floor, and thus apostrophised it:

"O Wise and Silent One, your mistress returns to you, but her heart she leaves behind her with the Tommies in San Francisco."

The Wise and Silent One made no reply. He was not a jealous cat.

Mr. Spring Fragrance slept not that night; the next morning he ate not. Three days and three nights without sleep and food passed.

There was a springlike freshness in the air on the day that Mrs. Spring Fragrance came home. The skies overhead were as blue as Puget Sound stretching its gleaming length toward the mighty Pacific, and all the beautiful green world seemed to be throbbing with springing life. Mrs. Spring Fragrance was never so radiant.

"Oh," she cried light-heartedly, "is it not lovely to see the sun shining so clear and everything so bright to welcome me?"

Mr. Spring Fragrance did not smile. It was the morning after the fourth sleepless night.

"Everything—everyone is glad to see me but you," she declared, smiling up into his face.

"If my wife is glad to see me," quietly replied Mr. Spring Fragrance, "I also am glad to see her!"

Mrs. Spring Fragrance looked up into his face with honest and earnest eyes. There was something in his manner which touched her heart.

"Yen," said she, "you do not look well. You are not well. What is it?"

Something arose in Mr. Spring Fragrance's throat which prevented him from replying.

"O darling one! O sweetest one!" cried a girl's joyous voice. Laura Chin Yuen ran into the room and threw her arms around Mrs. Spring Fragrance's neck.

"I spied you from the window," said Laura, "and I couldn't rest until I told you. We are to be married next week, Kai Tzu and I. And all through you; all through you—the sweetest jade jewel in the world!"

"I must be downtown in half an hour," said Mr. Spring Fragrance, looking at his watch. Then he passed out of the room.

"So the son of the Government teacher and little Happy Love are already married," Laura cried, as she relieved Mrs. Spring Fragrance of her cloak, her hat, and her folding fan.

Mr. Spring Fragrance paused upon the doorstep.

"Sit down, Little Sister, and I will tell you all about it," said Mrs. Spring Fragrance, forgetting her husband for the moment.

When Laura Chin Yuen had danced away, Mr. Spring Fragrance came in and hung up his hat.

"You got back very soon," said Mrs. Spring Fragrance, covertly wiping away the tears which had begun to fall as soon as she thought herself alone. She could not understand being left at the moment of her arrival.

"I did not go," answered Mr. Spring Fragrance. "I have been listening to you and Laura."

"But if the business is very important, do not you think you should attend to it?" anxiously queried Mrs. Spring Fragrance.

"It is not important to me now," returned Mr. Spring Fragrance. "I would prefer to hear again about Ah Oi and Tsen Hing and Laura and Kai Tzu."

"How lovely of you to say that!" exclaimed Mrs. Spring Fragrance, who was easily made happy. And she began to chat away to her husband in the friendliest and wifeliest fashion possible. When she had finished she asked him if he were not glad to hear that those who loved as did the young lovers whose secrets she had been keeping were to be united; and he replied that indeed he was; that he would like every man to be as happy with his wife as he himself had ever been and ever would be.

"You did not always talk like that," said Mrs. Spring Fragrance slyly. "You must have been reading my American poetry books!"

"American poetry!" ejaculated Mr. Spring Fragrance almost fiercely. "American poetry is detestable, abhorrible!"

"Why! why!" exclaimed Mrs. Spring Fragrance, more and more surprised.

But the only explanation which Mr. Spring Fragrance vouchsafed was a jadestone pendant.

Part III

NATURALISM

STEPHEN CRANE

The Men in the Storm

"The Men in the Storm" was first published in *Arena* magazine in 1894, part of Crane's growing body of naturalistic work about urban poverty in the Bowery, a subject that had the year before been the subject of his first novel, *Maggie: A Girl of the Streets*. This story is significant for its portrayal of the desperation of the impoverished men who wait in a storm for a "charitable house" to open for the evening. It depicts not only the hopelessness of poverty but the hostility of nature as well, for the snow beats on the men with "stinging flakes" that cut "like knives and needles." The story makes clear, however, that the men themselves are not degraded creatures, for they are "strong, healthy, clear-skinned fellows." Rather, they have been reduced to abject humiliation in society, and they are left "trying to perceive where they had failed, what they had lacked, to be thus vanquished in the race." It is a profound inquiry, one that was consistent with the aims of the reformist magazine in which the story appeared, and one that has sustained critical attention for more than a century.

*   *   *

At about three o'clock of the February afternoon, the blizzard began to swirl great clouds of snow along the streets, sweeping it down from the roofs and up from the pavements until the faces of pedestrians tingled and burned as from a thousand needle-prickings. Those on the walks huddled their necks closely in the collars of their coats and went along stooping like a race of aged people. The drivers of vehicles hurried their horses furiously on their way. They were made more cruel by the exposure of their positions, aloft on high seats. The street cars, bound uptown, went slowly, the horses slipping and straining in the spongy brown mass that lay between the rails. The drivers, muffled to the eyes, stood erect and facing the wind, models of grim philosophy. Overhead the trains rumbled and roared, and the dark structure of the elevated railroad, stretching over the avenue, dripped little streams and drops of water upon the mud and snow beneath it.

All the clatter of the street was softened by the masses that lay upon the cobbles until, even to one who looked from a window, it became important music, a melody of life made necessary to the ear by the dreariness of the pitiless beat and sweep of the storm. Occasionally one could see black figures of men busily shovelling the white drifts from the walks. The sounds from their labor created new recollections of rural experiences which every man manages to have in a measure. Later, the immense windows of the shops became aglow with light, throwing great beams of orange and yellow upon the pavement. They were infinitely cheerful, yet in a way they accented the force and discomfort of the storm, and gave a meaning to the pace of the people and the vehicles, scores of pedestrians and drivers, wretched with cold faces, necks and feet, speeding for scores of unknown doors and entrances, scattering to an infinite variety of shelters, to places which the imagination made warm with the familiar colors of home.

There was an absolute expression of hot dinners in the pace of the people. If one dared to speculate upon the destination of those who came trooping, he lost himself in a maze of social calculations; he might fling a handful of sand and attempt to follow the flight of each particular grain. But as to the suggestion of hot dinners, he was in firm lines of thought, for it was upon every hurrying face. It is a matter of tradition; it is from the tales of childhood. It comes forth with every storm.

However, in a certain part of a dark West-side street, there was a collection of men to whom these things were as if they were not. In this street was located a charitable house where for five cents the homeless of the city could get a bed at night and, in the morning, coffee and bread.

During the afternoon of the storm, the whirling snows acted as drivers, as men with whips, and at half-past three, the walk before the closed doors of the house was covered with wanderers of the street, waiting. For some distance on either side of the place they could be seen lurking in doorways and behind projecting parts of buildings, gathering in close bunches in an effort to get warm. A covered wagon drawn up near the curb sheltered a dozen of them. Under the stairs that led to the elevated railway station, there were six or eight, their hands stuffed deep in their pockets, their shoulders stooped, jiggling their feet. Others always could be seen coming, a strange procession, some slouching along with the characteristic hopeless gait of professional strays, some coming with hesitating steps wearing the air of men to whom this sort of thing was new.

It was an afternoon of incredible length. The snow, blowing in twisting clouds, sought out the men in their meager hiding-places and skilfully beat in among them, drenching their persons with showers of fine, stinging flakes. They crowded together, muttering, and fumbling in their pockets to get their red, inflamed wrists covered by the cloth.

Newcomers usually halted at one of the groups and addressed a question, perhaps much as a matter of form, "Is it open yet?"

Those who had been waiting inclined to take the questioner seriously and become contemptuous. "No; do yeh think we'd be standin' here?" The gathering swelled in numbers steadily and persistently. One could always see them coming, trudging slowly through the storm.

Finally, the little snow plains in the street began to assume a leaden hue from the shadows of evening. The buildings upreared gloomily save where various windows became brilliant figures of light that made shimmers and splashes of yellow on the snow. A street lamp on the curb struggled to illuminate, but it was reduced to impotent blindness by the swift gusts of sleet crusting its panes.

In this half-darkness, the men began to come from their shelter places and mass in front of the doors of charity. They were of all types, but the nationalities were mostly American, German and Irish. Many were strong, healthy, clear-skinned fellows with that stamp of countenance which is not frequently seen upon seekers after charity. There were men of undoubted patience, industry and temperance, who in time of ill-fortune, do not habitually turn to rail at the state of society, snarling at the arrogance of the rich and bemoaning the cowardice of the poor, but who at these times are apt to wear a sudden and singular meekness, as if they saw the world's progress marching from them and were trying to perceive where they had failed, what they had lacked, to be thus vanquished in the race. Then there were others of the shifting, Bowery lodging-house element who were used to paying ten cents for a place to sleep, but who now came here because it was cheaper.

But they were all mixed in one mass so thoroughly that one could not have discerned the different elements but for the fact that the laboring men, for the most part, remained silent and impassive in the blizzard, their eyes fixed on the windows of the house, statues of patience.

The sidewalk soon became completely blocked by the bodies of the men. They pressed close to one another like sheep in a winter's gale, keeping one another warm by the heat of their bodies. The snow came down upon this compressed group of men until, directly from above, it might have appeared like a heap of snow-covered merchandise, if it were not for the fact that the crowd swayed gently with a unanimous, rhythmical motion. It was wonderful to see how the snow lay upon the heads and shoulders of these men, in little ridges an inch thick perhaps in places, the flakes steadily adding drop and drop, precisely as they fall upon the unresisting grass of the fields. The feet of the men were all wet and cold and the wish to warm them accounted for the slow, gentle, rhythmical motion. Occasionally some man whose ears or nose tingled acutely from the cold winds would wriggle down until his head was protected by the shoulders of his companions.

There was a continuous murmuring discussion as to the probability of the doors being speedily opened. They persistently lifted their eyes toward the windows. One could hear little combats of opinion.

"There's a light in th' winder!"

"Naw; it's a reflection f'm across th' way."

"Well, didn't I see 'em lite it?"

"You did?"

"I did!"

"Well, then, that settles it!"

As the time approached when they expected to be allowed to enter, the men crowded to the doors in an unspeakable crush, jamming and wedging in a way that it seemed would crack bones. They surged heavily against the building in a powerful wave of pushing shoulders. Once a rumor flitted among all the tossing heads.

"They can't open th' doors! Th' fellers er smack up ag'in 'em."

Then a dull roar of rage came from the men on the outskirts; but all the time they strained and pushed until it appeared to be impossible for those that they cried out against to do anything but be crushed to pulp.

"Ah, git away f'm th' door!"

"Git outa that!"

"Throw 'em out!"

"Kill 'em!"

"Say, fellers, now, what th' 'ell? Give 'em a chanct t' open th' door!"

"Yeh damned pigs, give 'em a chanct t' open th' door!"

Men in the outskirts of the crowd occasionally yelled when a boot-heel of one of frantic trampling feet crushed on their freezing extremities.

"Git off me feet, yeh clumsy tarrier!"

"Say, don't stand on me feet! Walk on th' ground!"

A man near the doors suddenly shouted: "O-o-oh! Le' me out—le' me out!" And another, a man of infinite valor, once twisted his head so as to half face those who were pushing behind him. "Quit yer shovin', yeh"—and he delivered a volley of the most powerful and singular invective straight into the faces of the men behind him. It was as if he was hammering the noses of them with curses of triple brass. His face, red with rage, could be seen; upon it, an expression of sublime disregard of consequences. But nobody cared to reply to his imprecations; it was too cold. Many of them snickered and all continued to push.

In occasional pauses of the crowd's movement the men had opportunity to make jokes; usually grim things, and no doubt very uncouth. Nevertheless, they are notable—one does not expect to find the quality of humor in a heap of old clothes under a snowdrift.

The winds seemed to grow fiercer as time wore on. Some of the gusts of snow that came down on the close collection of heads cut like knives and needles, and the men huddled, and swore, not like dark assassins, but in a sort of an American fashion, grimly and desperately, it is true, but yet with a wondrous under-effect, indefinable and mystic, as if there was some kind of humor in this catastrophe, in this situation in a night of snow-laden winds.

Once, the window of the huge dry-goods shop across the street furnished material for a few moments of forgetfulness. In the brilliantly-lighted space appeared the figure of a man. He was rather stout and very well clothed. His whiskers were fashioned charmingly after those of the Prince of Wales. He stood in an attitude of magnificent reflection. He slowly stroked his moustache with a certain grandeur of manner, and looked down at the snow-encrusted mob. From below, there was denoted a supreme complacence in him. It seemed that the sight operated inversely, and enabled him to more clearly regard his own environment, delightful relatively.

One of the mob chanced to turn his head and perceive the figure in the window. "Hello, lookit 'is whiskers," he said genially.

Many of the men turned then, and a shout went up. They called to him in all strange keys. They addressed him in every manner, from familiar and cordial greetings to carefully-worded advice concerning changes in his personal appearance. The man presently fled, and the mob chuckled ferociously like ogres who had just devoured something.

They turned then to serious business. Often they addressed the stolid front of the house.

"Oh, let us in fer Gawd's sake!"

"Let us in or we'll all drop dead!"

"Say, what's th' use o' keepin' all us poor Indians out in th' cold?"

And always some one was saying, "Keep off me feet."

The crushing of the crowd grew terrific toward the last. The men, in keen pain from the blasts, began almost to fight. With the pitiless whirl of snow upon them, the battle for shelter was going to the strong. It became known that the basement door at the foot of a little steep flight of stairs was the one to be opened, and they jostled and heaved in this direction like laboring fiends. One could hear them panting and groaning in their fierce exertion.

Usually some one in the front ranks was protesting to those in the rear: "O—o—ow! Oh, say, now, fellers, let up, will yeh? Do yeh wanta kill somebody?"

A policeman arrived and went into the midst of them, scolding and berating, occasionally threatening, but using no force but that of his hands and shoulders against these men who were only struggling to get in out of the storm. His decisive tones rang out sharply: "Stop that pushin' back there! Come, boys, don't push! Stop that! Here, you, quit yer shovin'! Cheese that!"

When the door below was opened, a thick stream of men forced a way down the stairs, which were of an extraordinary narrowness and seemed only wide enough for one at a time. Yet they somehow went down almost three abreast. It was a difficult and painful operation. The crowd was like a turbulent water forcing itself through one tiny outlet. The men in the rear, excited by the success of the others, made frantic exertions, for it seemed that this large band would more than fill the quarters and that many would be left upon the pavements. It would be disastrous to be of the last, and accordingly men with the snow biting their faces, writhed and twisted with their might. One expected that from the tremendous pressure, the narrow passage to the basement door would be so choked and clogged with human limbs and bodies that movement would be impossible. Once indeed the crowd was forced to stop, and a cry went along that a man had been injured at the foot of the stairs. But presently the slow movement began again, and the policeman fought at the top of the flight to ease the pressure on those who were going down.

A reddish light from a window fell upon the faces of the men when they, in turn, arrived at the last three steps and were about to enter. One could then note a change of expression that had come over their features. As they thus stood upon the threshold of their hopes, they looked suddenly content and complacent. The fire had passed from their eyes and the snarl had vanished from their lips. The very force of the crowd in the rear, which had previously vexed them, was regarded from another point of view, for it now made it inevitable that they should go through the little doors into the place that was cheery and warm with light.

The tossing crowd on the sidewalk grew smaller and smaller. The snow beat with merciless persistence upon the bowed heads of those who waited. The wind drove it up from the pavements in frantic forms of winding white, and it seethed in circles about the huddled forms, passing in, one by one, three by three, out of the storm.

STEPHEN CRANE

An Experiment in Misery

When "An Experiment in Misery" was first published in the *New York Press* in 1894, it contained an explanatory "frame" in the introduction and conclusion that established the experiment in the story. Two men are looking at a tramp in New York City when the younger man suggests that he wants to understand how the tramp feels and that, in search of insight, he will adopt ragged clothes and spend a day and a night living the life of the downtrodden. The story as it now stands then unfolds, followed by a concluding section in which the two men from the opening discuss the lessons learned in the experiment, especially the young man's change of attitude—his development of a social consciousness. When Crane published the story in book form in 1898, the explanatory frame had been deleted, but the central themes of economic degradation and inherent nobility remain, making this story part of Crane's naturalistic exploration of urban poverty in the 1890s.

*   *   *

It was late at night, and a fine rain was swirling softly down, causing the pavements to glisten with hue of steel and blue and yellow in the rays of the innumerable lights. A youth was trudging slowly, without enthusiasm, with his hands buried deep in his trouser's pockets, towards the down-town places where beds can be hired for coppers. He was clothed in an aged and tattered suit, and his derby was a marvel of dust-covered crown and torn rim. He was going forth to eat as the wanderer may eat, and sleep as the homeless sleep. By the time he had reached City Hall Park he was so completely plastered with yells of "bum" and "hobo," and with various unholy epithets that small boys had applied to him at intervals, that he was in a state of the most profound dejection. The sifting rain saturated the old velvet collar of his overcoat, and as the wet cloth pressed against his neck, he felt that there no longer could be pleasure in life. He looked about him searching for an outcast of highest degree that they too might share miseries, but the lights threw a quivering glare over rows and circles of deserted benches that glistened damply, showing patches of wet sod behind them. It seemed that their usual freights had fled on this night to better things. There were only squads of well-dressed Brooklyn people who swarmed towards the bridge.

The young man loitered about for a time and then went shuffling off down Park Row. In the sudden descent in style of the dress of the crowd he felt relief, and as if he were at last in his own country. He began to see tatters that matched his tatters. In Chatham Square there were aimless men strewn in front of saloons and lodging-houses, standing sadly, patiently, reminding one vaguely of the attitudes of chickens in a storm. He aligned himself with these men, and turned slowly to occupy himself with the flowing life of the great street.

Through the mists of the cold and storming night, the cable cars went in silent procession, great affairs shining with red and brass, moving with formidable power, calm and irresistible, dangerful and gloomy, breaking silence only by the loud fierce cry of the gong. Two rivers of people swarmed along the side walks, spattered with black mud, which made each shoe leave a scar-like impression. Overhead elevated trains with a shrill grinding of the wheels stopped at the station, which upon its leg-like pillars seemed to resemble some monstrous kind of crab squatting over the street. The quick fat puffings of the engines could be heard. Down an alley there were sombre curtains of purple and black, on which street lamps dully glittered like embroidered flowers.

A saloon stood with a voracious air on a corner. A sign leaning against the front of the door-post announced "Free hot soup to-night!" The swing doors, snapping to and fro like ravenous lips, made gratified smacks as the saloon gorged itself with plump men, eating with astounding and endless appetite, smiling in some indescribable manner as the men came from all directions like sacrifices to a heathenish superstition.

Caught by the delectable sign the young man allowed himself to be swallowed. A bar-tender placed a schooner of dark and portentous beer on the bar. Its monumental form up-reared until the froth a-top was above the crown of the young man's brown derby.

"Soup over there, gents," said the bar-tender affably. A little yellow man in rags and the youth grasped their schooners and went with speed toward a lunch counter, where a man with oily but imposing whiskers ladled genially from a kettle until he had furnished his two mendicants with a soup that was steaming hot, and in which there were little floating suggestions of chicken. The young man, sipping his broth, felt the cordiality expressed by the warmth of the mixture, and he beamed at the man with oily but imposing whiskers, who was presiding like a priest behind an altar. "Have some more, gents?" he inquired of the two sorry figures before him. The little yellow man accepted with a swift gesture, but the youth shook his head and went out, following a man whose wondrous seediness promised that he would have a knowledge of cheap lodging-houses.

On the side-walk he accosted the seedy man. "Say, do you know a cheap place to sleep?"

The other hesitated for a time gazing sideways. Finally he nodded in the direction of the street, "I sleep up there," he said, "when I've got the price."

"How much?"

"Ten cents."

The young man shook his head dolefully. "That's too rich for me."

At that moment there approached the two a reeling man in strange garments. His head was a fuddle of bushy hair and whiskers, from which his eyes peered with a guilty slant. In a close scrutiny it was possible to distinguish the cruel lines of a mouth which looked as if its lips had just closed with satisfaction over some tender and piteous morsel. He appeared like an assassin steeped in crimes performed awkwardly.

But at this time his voice was tuned to the coaxing key of an affectionate puppy. He looked at the men with wheedling eyes, and began to sing a little melody for charity.

"Say, gents, can't yeh give a poor feller a couple of cents t' git a bed. I got five, and I gits anudder two I gits me a bed. Now, on th' square, gents, can't yeh jest gimme two cents t' git a bed? Now, yeh know how a respecter'ble gentlem'n feels when he's down on his luck, an' I——"

The seedy man, staring with imperturbable countenance at a train which clattered overhead, interrupted in an expressionless voice—"Ah, go t' h—!"

But the youth spoke to the prayerful assassin in tones of astonishment and inquiry. "Say, you must be crazy! Why don't yeh strike somebody that looks as if they had money?"

The assassin, tottering about on his uncertain legs, and at intervals brushing imaginary obstacles from before his nose, entered into a long explanation of the psychology of the situation. It was so profound that it was unintelligible.

When he had exhausted the subject, the young man said to him—

"Let's see th' five cents."

The assassin wore an expression of drunken woe at this sentence, filled with suspicion of him. With a deeply pained air he began to fumble in his clothing, his red hands trembling. Presently he announced in a voice of bitter grief, as if he had been betrayed—"There's on'y four."

"Four," said the young man thoughtfully. "Well, look-a-here, I'm a stranger here, an' if ye'll steer me to your cheap joint I'll find the other three."

The assassin's countenance became instantly radiant with joy. His whiskers quivered with the wealth of his alleged emotions. He seized the young man's hand in a transport of delight and friendliness.

"B' Gawd," he cried, "if ye'll do that, b' Gawd, I'd say yeh was a damned good fellow, I would, an' I'd remember yeh all m' life, I would, b' Gawd, an' if I ever got a chance I'd return the compliment"—he spoke with drunken dignity,—"b' Gawd, I'd treat yeh white, I would, an' I'd allus remember yeh."

The young man drew back, looking at the assassin coldly. "Oh, that's all right," he said. "You show me th' joint—that's all you've got t' do."

The assassin, gesticulating gratitude, led the young man along a dark street. Finally he stopped before a little dusty door. He raised his hand impressively. "Look-a-here," he said, and there was a thrill of deep and ancient wisdom upon his face, "I've brought yeh here, an' that's my part, ain't it? If th' place don't suit yeh, yeh needn't git mad at me, need yeh? There won't be no bad feelin', will there?"

"No," said the young man.

The assassin waved his arm tragically, and led the march up the steep stairway. On the way the young man furnished the assassin with three pennies. At the top a man with benevolent spectacles looked at them through a hole in a board. He collected their money, wrote some names on a register, and speedily was leading the two men along a gloom-shrouded corridor.

Shortly after the beginning of this journey the young man felt his liver turn white, for from the dark and secret places of the building there suddenly came to his nostrils strange and unspeakable odours, that assailed him like malignant diseases with wings. They seemed to be from human bodies closely packed in dens; the exhalations from a hundred pairs of reeking lips; the fumes from a thousand bygone debauches; the expression of a thousand present miseries.

A man, naked save for a little snuff-coloured undershirt, was parading sleepily along the corridor. He rubbed his eyes, and, giving vent to a prodigious yawn, demanded to be told the time.

"Half-past one."

The man yawned again. He opened a door, and for a moment his form was outlined against a black, opaque interior. To this door came the three men, and as it was again opened the unholy odours rushed out like fiends, so that the young man was obliged to struggle as against an overpowering wind.

It was some time before the youth's eyes were good in the intense gloom within, but the man with benevolent spectacles led him skilfully, pausing but a moment to deposit the limp assassin upon a cot. He took the youth to a cot that lay tranquilly by the window, and showing him a tall locker for clothes that stood near the head with the ominous air of a tombstone, left him.

The youth sat on his cot and peered about him. There was a gas-jet in a distant part of the room, that burned a small flickering orange-hued flame. It caused vast masses of tumbled shadows in all parts of the place, save where, immediately about it, there was a little grey haze. As the young man's eyes became used to the darkness, he could see upon the cots that thickly littered the floor the forms of men sprawled out, lying in death-like silence, or heaving and snoring with tremendous effort, like stabbed fish.

The youth locked his derby and his shoes in the mummy case near him, and then lay down with an old and familiar coat around his shoulders. A blanket he handed gingerly, drawing it over part of the coat. The cot was covered with leather, and as cold as melting snow. The youth was obliged to shiver for some time on this affair, which was like a slab. Presently, however, his chill gave him peace, and during this period of leisure from it he turned his head to stare at his friend the assassin, whom he could dimly discern where he lay sprawled on a cot in the abandon of a man filled with drink. He was snoring with incredible vigour. His wet hair and beard dimly glistened, and his inflamed nose shone with subdued lustre like a red light in a fog.

Within reach of the youth's hand was one who lay with yellow breast and shoulders bare to the cold drafts. One arm hung over the side of the cot, and the fingers lay full length upon the wet cement floor of the room. Beneath the inky brows could be seen the eyes of the man exposed by the partly opened lids. To the youth it seemed that he and this corpselike being were exchanging a prolonged stare, and that the other threatened with his eyes. He drew back watching his neighbour from the shadows of his blanket edge. The man did not move once through the night, but lay in this stillness as of death like a body stretched out expectant of the surgeon's knife.

And all through the room could be seen the tawny hues of naked flesh, limbs thrust into the darkness, projecting beyond the cots; upreared knees, arms hanging long and thin over the cot edges. For the most part they were statuesque, carven, dead. With the curious lockers standing all about like tombstones, there was a strange effect of a graveyard where bodies were merely flung.

Yet occasionally could be seen limbs wildly tossing in fantastic nightmare gestures, accompanied by guttural cries, grunts, oaths. And there was one fellow off in a gloomy corner, who in his dreams was oppressed by some frightful calamity, for of a sudden he began to utter long wails that went almost like yells from a hound, echoing wailfully and weird through this chill place of tombstones where men lay like the dead.

The sound in its high piercing beginnings, that dwindled to final melancholy moans, expressed a red and grim tragedy of the unfathomable possibilities of the man's dreams. But to the youth these were not merely the shrieks of a vision-pierced man: they were an utterance of the meaning of the room and its occupants. It was to him the protest of the wretch who feels the touch of the imperturbable granite wheels, and who then cries with an impersonal eloquence, with a strength not from him, giving voice to the wail of a whole section, a class, a people. This, weaving into the young man's brain, and mingling with his views of the vast and sombre shadows that, like mighty black fingers, curled around the naked bodies, made the young man so that he did not sleep, but lay carving the biographies for these men from his meagre experience. At times the fellow in the corner howled in a writhing agony of his imaginations.

Finally a long lance-point of grey light shot through the dusty panes of the window. Without, the young man could see roofs drearily white in the dawning. The point of light yellowed and grew brighter, until the golden rays of the morning sun came in bravely and strong. They touched with radiant colour the form of a small fat man, who snored in stuttering fashion. His round and shiny bald head glowed suddenly with the valour of a decoration. He sat up, blinked at the sun, swore fretfully, and pulled his blanket over the ornamental splendours of his head.

The youth contentedly watched this rout of the shadows before the bright spears of the sun, and presently he slumbered. When he awoke he heard the voice of the assassin raised in valiant curses. Putting up his head, he perceived his comrade seated on the side of the cot engaged in scratching his neck with long finger-nails that rasped like files.

"Hully Jee, dis is a new breed. They've got can-openers on their feet." He continued in a violent tirade.

The young man hastily unlocked his closet and took out his shoes and hat. As he sat on the side of the cot lacing his shoes, he glanced about and saw that daylight had made the room comparatively commonplace and uninteresting. The men, whose faces seemed stolid, serene or absent, were engaged in dressing, while a great crackle of bantering conversation arose.

A few were parading in unconcerned nakedness. Here and there were men of brawn, whose skins shone clear and ruddy. They took splendid poses, standing massively like chiefs. When they had dressed in their ungainly garments there was an extraordinary change. They then showed bumps and deficiencies of all kinds.

There were others who exhibited many deformities. Shoulders were slanting, humped, pulled this way and pulled that way. And notable among these latter men was the little fat man, who had refused to allow his head to be glorified. His pudgy form, builded like a pear, bustled to and fro, while he swore in fishwife fashion. It appeared that some article of his apparel had vanished.

The young man attired speedily, and went to his friend the assassin. At first the latter looked dazed at the sight of the youth. This face seemed to be appealing to him through the cloud wastes of his memory. He scratched his neck and reflected. At last he grinned, a broad smile gradually spreading until his countenance was a round illumination. "Hello, Willie," he cried cheerily.

"Hello," said the young man. "Are yeh ready t' fly?"

"Sure." The assassin tied his shoe carefully with some twine and came ambling.

When he reached the street the young man experienced no sudden relief from unholy atmospheres. He had forgotten all about them, and had been breathing naturally, and with no sensation of discomfort or distress.

He was thinking of these things as he walked along the street, when he was suddenly startled by feeling the assassin's hand, trembling with excitement, clutching his arm, and when the assassin spoke, his voice went into quavers from a supreme agitation.

"I'll be hully, bloomin' blowed if there wasn't a feller with a night-shirt on up there in that joint."

The youth was bewildered for a moment, but presently he turned to smile indulgently at the assassin's humour.

"Oh, you're a d——d liar," he merely said.

Whereupon the assassin began to gesture extravagantly, and take oath by strange gods. He frantically placed himself at the mercy of remarkable fates if his tale were not true.

"Yes, he did! I cross m'heart thousan' times!" he protested, and at the moment his eyes were large with amazement, his mouth wrinkled in unnatural glee.

"Yessir! A nightshirt! A hully white nightshirt!"

"You lie!"

"No, sir! I hope ter die b'fore I kin git anudder ball if there wasn't a jay wid a hully, bloomin' white nightshirt!"

His face was filled with the infinite wonder of it. "A hully white nightshirt," he continually repeated.

The young man saw the dark entrance to a basement restaurant. There was a sign which read "No mystery about our hash"! and there were other age-stained and world-battered legends which told him that the place was within his means. He stopped before it and spoke to the assassin. "I guess I'll git somethin' t' eat."

At this the assassin, for some reason, appeared to be quite embarrassed. He gazed at the seductive front of the eating place for a moment. Then he started slowly up the street. "Well, good-bye, Willie," he said bravely.

For an instant the youth studied the departing figure. Then he called out, "Hol' on a minnet." As they came together he spoke in a certain fierce way, as if he feared that the other would think him to be charitable. "Look-a-here, if yeh wanta git some breakfas' I'll lend yeh three cents t' do it with. But say, look-a-here, you've gota git out an' hustle. I ain't goin' t' support yeh, or I'll go broke b'fore night. I ain't no millionaire."

"I take me oath, Willie," said the assassin earnestly, "th' on'y thing I really needs is a ball. Me t'roat feels like a fryin'-pan. But as I can't get a ball, why, th' next bes' thing is breakfast, an' if yeh do that for me, b' Gawd, I say yeh was th' whitest lad I ever see."

They spent a few moments in dexterous exchanges of phrases, in which they each protested that the other was, as the assassin had originally said, "a respecter'ble gentlem'n." And they concluded with mutual assurances that they were the souls of intelligence and virtue. Then they went into the restaurant.

There was a long counter, dimly lighted from hidden sources. Two or three men in soiled white aprons rushed here and there.

The youth bought a bowl of coffee for two cents and a roll for one cent. The assassin purchased the same. The bowls were webbed with brown seams, and the tin spoons wore an air of having emerged from the first pyramid. Upon them were black mosslike encrustations of age, and they were bent and scarred from the attacks of long-forgotten teeth. But over their repast the wanderers waxed warm and mellow. The assassin grew affable as the hot mixture went soothingly down his parched throat, and the young man felt courage flow in his veins.

Memories began to throng in on the assassin, and he brought forth long tales, intricate, incoherent, delivered with a chattering swiftness as from an old woman. "——great job out'n Orange. Boss keep yeh hustlin' though all time. I was there three days, and then I went an' ask 'im t' lend me a dollar. 'G-g-go ter the devil,' he ses, an' I lose me job."

"South no good. Damn niggers work for twenty-five an' thirty cents a day. Run white man out. Good grub though. Easy livin'."

"Yas; useter work little in Toledo, raftin' logs. Make two or three dollars er day in the spring. Lived high. Cold as ice though in the winter."

"I was raised in northern N'York. O-o-oh, yeh jest oughto live there. No beer ner whisky though, way off in the woods. But all th' good hot grub yeh can eat. B' Gawd, I hung around there long as I could till th' ol' man fired me. 'Git t' hell outa here, yeh wuthless skunk, git t' hell outa here, an' go die,' he ses. 'You're a hell of a father,' I ses, 'you are,' an' I quit 'im."

As they were passing from the dim eating place, they encountered an old man who was trying to steal forth with a tiny package of food, but a tall man with an indomitable moustache stood dragon fashion, barring the way of escape. They heard the old man raise a plaintive protest. "Ah, you always want to know what I take out, and you never see that I usually bring a package in here from my place of business."

As the wanderers trudged slowly along Park Row, the assassin began to expand and grow blithe. "B' Gawd, we've been livin' like kings," he said, smacking appreciative lips.

"Look out, or we'll have t' pay fer it t'night," said the youth with gloomy warning.

But the assassin refused to turn his gaze toward the future. He went with a limping step, into which he injected a suggestion of lamblike gambols. His mouth was wreathed in a red grin.

In the City Hall Park the two wanderers sat down in the little circle of benches sanctified by traditions of their class. They huddled in their old garments, slumbrously conscious of the march of the hours which for them had no meaning.

The people of the street hurrying hither and thither made a blend of black figures changing yet frieze-like. They walked in their good clothes as upon important missions, giving no gaze to the two wanderers seated upon the benches. They expressed to the young man his infinite distance from all that he valued. Social position, comfort, the pleasures of living, were unconquerable kingdoms. He felt a sudden awe.

And in the background a multitude of buildings, of pitiless hues and sternly high, were to him emblematic of a nation forcing its regal head into the clouds, throwing no downward glances; in the sublimity of its aspirations ignoring the wretches who may flounder at its feet. The roar of the city in his ear was to him the confusion of strange tongues, babbling heedlessly; it was the clink of coin, the voice of the city's hopes which were to him no hopes.

He confessed himself an outcast, and his eyes from under the lowered rim of his hat began to glance guiltily, wearing the criminal expression that comes with certain convictions.

STEPHEN CRANE

The Open Boat

"The Open Boat" is one of the most widely read stories in American literature. Ever since its initial publication in *Scribner's Magazine* in June of 1897, this story of the struggle for survival of four men at sea in an open dinghy has been the subject of intense interest and broadly divergent interpretations, ranging from assertions that Crane depicted nature as a malevolent entity, to assumptions that the author portrayed nature as indifferent, to studies that focus on the psychological growth of the men through the experience, as they form a brotherhood on the seas with greater compassion and understanding than the men had known before the sinking of their ship. Based on Crane's personal experience following the sinking of the *Commodore* on December 31, 1896, about which he wrote a celebrated journalistic account, the transformation of the events into a "story" allowed for greater thematic development, for the contemplation of the meaning of Caroline S. Norton's poem "A Soldier of the Legion" as well as the high, cold star that shines above them, and for the collective protest against "this old ninny-woman, Fate." More than perhaps any other pairing of a journalistic account with fiction depicting the same events, this story demonstrates the efficacy of the art of the short story in English.

*   *   *

A TALE INTENDED TO BE AFTER THE FACT. BEING THE EXPERIENCE OF FOUR MEN FROM THE SUNK STEAMER COMMODORE

I

None of them knew the color of the sky. Their eyes glanced level, and were fastened upon the waves that swept toward them. These waves were of the hue of slate, save for the tops, which were of foaming white, and all of the men knew the colors of the sea. The horizon narrowed and widened, and dipped and rose, and at all times its edge was jagged with waves that seemed thrust up in points like rocks.

Many a man ought to have a bath-tub larger than the boat which here rode upon the sea. These waves were most wrongfully and bar-

barously abrupt and tall, and each froth-top was a problem in small boat navigation.

The cook squatted in the bottom and looked with both eyes at the six inches of gunwale which separated him from the ocean. His sleeves were rolled over his fat forearms, and the two flaps of his unbuttoned vest dangled as he bent to bail out the boat. Often he said: "Gawd! That was a narrow clip." As he remarked it he invariably gazed eastward over the broken sea.

The oiler, steering with one of the two oars in the boat, sometimes raised himself suddenly to keep clear of water that swirled in over the stern. It was a thin little oar and it seemed often ready to snap.

The correspondent, pulling at the other oar, watched the waves and wondered why he was there.

The injured captain, lying in the bow, was at this time buried in that profound dejection and indifference which comes, temporarily at least, to even the bravest and most enduring when, willy nilly, the firm fails, the army loses, the ship goes down. The mind of the master of a vessel is rooted deep in the timbers of her, though he command for a day or a decade, and this captain had on him the stern impression of a scene in the grays of dawn of seven turned faces, and later a stump of a topmast with a white ball on it that slashed to and fro at the waves, went low and lower, and down. Thereafter there was something strange in his voice. Although steady, it was deep with mourning, and of a quality beyond oration or tears.

"Keep'er a little more south, Billie," said he.

" 'A little more south,' sir," said the oiler in the stern.

A seat in this boat was not unlike a seat upon a bucking broncho, and, by the same token, a broncho is not much smaller. The craft pranced and reared, and plunged like an animal. As each wave came, and she rose for it, she seemed like a horse making at a fence outrageously high. The manner of her scramble over these walls of water is a mystic thing, and, moreover, at the top of them were ordinarily these problems in white water, the foam racing down from the summit of each wave, requiring a new leap, and a leap from the air. Then, after scornfully bumping a crest, she would slide, and race, and splash down a long incline and arrive bobbing and nodding in front of the next menace.

A singular disadvantage of the sea lies in the fact that after successfully surmounting one wave you discover that there is another behind it just as important and just as nervously anxious to do something effective in the way of swamping boats. In a ten-foot dingey one can get an idea of the resources of the sea in the line of waves that is not probable to the average experience, which is never at sea in a dingey.

As each slaty wall of water approached, it shut all else from the view of the men in the boat, and it was not difficult to imagine that this particular wave was the final outburst of the ocean, the last effort of the grim water. There was a terrible grace in the move of the waves, and they came in silence, save for the snarling of the crests.

In the wan light, the faces of the men must have been gray. Their eyes must have glinted in strange ways as they gazed steadily astern. Viewed from a balcony, the whole thing would doubtlessly have been weirdly picturesque. But the men in the boat had no time to see it, and if they had had leisure there were other things to occupy their minds. The sun swung steadily up the sky, and they knew it was broad day because the color of the sea changed from slate to emerald-green, streaked with amber lights, and the foam was like tumbling snow. The process of the breaking day was unknown to them. They were aware only of this effect upon the color of the waves that rolled toward them.

In disjointed sentences the cook and the correspondent argued as to the differebetween a life-saving station and a house of refuge. The cook had said: "There's a house of refuge just north of the Mosquito Inlet Light, and as soon as they see us, they'll come off in their boat and pick us up."

"As soon as who see us?" said the correspondent.

"The crew," said the cook.

"Houses of refuge don't have crews," said the correspondent. "As I understand them, they are only places where clothes and grub are stored for the benefit of shipwrecked people. They don't carry crews."

"Oh, yes, they do," said the cook.

"No, they don't," said the correspondent.

"Well, we're not there yet, anyhow," said the oiler, in the stern.

"Well," said the cook, "perhaps it's not a house of refuge that I'm thinking of as being near Mosquito Inlet Light. Perhaps it's a life-saving station."

"We're not there yet," said the oiler, in the stern.

II

As the boat bounced from the top of each wave, the wind tore through the hair of the hatless men, and as the craft plopped her stern down again the spray slashed past them. The crest of each of these waves was a hill, from the top of which the men surveyed, for a moment, a broad tumultuous expanse; shining and windriven. It was probably splendid. It was probably glorious, this play of the free sea, wild with lights of emerald and white and amber.

"Bully good thing it's an on-shore wind," said the cook. "If not, where would we be? Wouldn't have a show."

"That's right," said the correspondent.

The busy oiler nodded his assent.

Then the captain, in the bow, chuckled in a way that expressed humor, contempt, tragedy, all in one. "Do you think we've got much of a show, now, boys?" said he.

Whereupon the three were silent, save for a trifle of hemming and hawing. To express any particular optimism at this time they felt to be childish and stupid, but they all doubtless possessed this sense of the situation in their mind. A young man thinks doggedly at such times. On the other hand, the ethics of their condition was decidedly against any open suggestion of hopelessness. So they were silent.

"Oh, well," said the captain, soothing his children, "we'll get ashore all right."

But there was that in his tone which made them think, so the oiler quoth: "Yes! If this wind holds!"

The cook was bailing: "Yes! If we don't catch hell in the surf."

Canton flannel gulls flew near and far. Sometimes they sat down on the sea, near patches of brown sea-weed that rolled over the waves with a movement like carpets on a line in a gale. The birds sat comfortably in groups, and they were envied by some in the dingey, for the wrath of the sea was no more to them than it was to a covey of prairie chickens a thousand miles inland. Often they came very close and stared at the men with black beadlike eyes. At these times they were uncanny and sinister in their unblinking scrutiny, and the men hooted angrily at them, telling them to be gone. One came, and evidently decided to alight on the top of the captain's head. The bird flew parallel to the boat and did not circle, but made short sidelong jumps in the air in chicken-fashion. His black eyes were wistfully fixed upon the captain's head. "Ugly brute," said the oiler to the bird. "You look as if you were made with a jack-knife." The cook and the correspondent swore darkly at the creature. The captain naturally wished to knock it away with the end of the heavy painter, but he did not dare do it, because anything resembling an emphatic gesture would have capsized this freighted boat, and so with his open hand, the captain gently and carefully waved the gull away. After it had been discouraged from the pursuit the captain breathed easier on account of his hair, and others breathed easier because the bird struck their minds at this time as being somehow grewsome and ominous.

In the meantime the oiler and the correspondent rowed. And also they rowed.

They sat together in the same seat, and each rowed an oar. Then the oiler took both oars; then the correspondent took both oars; then the oiler; then the correspondent. They rowed and they rowed. The very ticklish part of the business was when the time came for the reclining one in the stern to take his turn at the oars. By the very last star of truth, it is easier to steal eggs from under a hen than it was to change seats in the dingey. First the man in the stern slid his hand along the thwart and moved with care, as if he were of Sèvres. Then the man in the rowing seat slid his hand along the other thwart. It was all done with the most extraordinary care. As the two sidled past each other, the whole party kept watchful eyes on the coming wave, and the captain cried: "Look out now! Steady there!"

The brown mats of sea-weed that appeared from time to time were like islands, bits of earth. They were travelling, apparently, neither one way nor the other. They were, to all intents, stationary. They informed the men in the boat that it was making progress slowly toward the land.

The captain, rearing cautiously in the bow, after the dingey soared on a great swell, said that he had seen the lighthouse at Mosquito Inlet. Presently the cook remarked that he had seen it. The correspondent was at the oars, then, and for some reason he too wished to look at the lighthouse, but his back was toward the far shore and the waves were important, and for some time he could not seize an opportunity to turn his head. But at last there came a wave more gentle than the others, and when at the crest of it he swiftly scoured the western horizon.

"See it?" said the captain.

"No," said the correspondent, slowly, "I didn't see anything."

"Look again," said the captain. He pointed. "It's exactly in that direction."

At the top of another wave, the correspondent did as he was bid, and this time his eyes chanced on a small still thing on the edge of the swaying horizon. It was precisely like the point of a pin. It took an anxious eye to find a lighthouse so tiny.

"Think we'll make it, captain?"

"If this wind holds and the boat don't swamp, we can't do much else," said the captain.

The little boat, lifted by each towering sea, and splashed viciously by the crests, made progress that in the absence of seaweed was not apparent to those in her. She seemed just a wee thing wallowing, miraculously, top-up, at the mercy of five oceans. Occasionally, a great spread of water, like white flames, swarmed into her.

"Bail her, cook," said the captain, serenely.

"All right, captain," said the cheerful cook.

III

It would be difficult to describe the subtle brotherhood of men that was here established on the seas. No one said that it was so. No one mentioned it. But it dwelt in the boat, and each man felt it warm him. They were a captain, an oiler, a cook, and a correspondent, and they were friends, friends in a more curiously iron-bound degree than may be common. The hurt captain, lying against the water-jar in the bow, spoke always in a low voice and calmly, but he could never command a more ready and swiftly obedient crew than the motley three of the dingey. It was more than a mere recognition of what was best for the common safety. There was surely in it a quality that was personal and heartfelt. And after this devotion to the commander of the boat there was this comradeship that the correspondent, for instance, who had been taught to be cynical of men, knew even at the time was the best experience of his life. But no one said that it was so. No one mentioned it.

"I wish we had a sail," remarked the captain. "We might try my overcoat on the end of an oar and give you two boys a chance to rest." So the cook and the correspondent held the mast and spread wide the overcoat. The oiler steered, and the little boat made good way with her new rig. Sometimes the oiler had to scull sharply to keep a sea from breaking into the boat, but otherwise sailing was a success.

Meanwhile the light-house had been growing slowly larger. It had now almost assumed color, and appeared like a little gray shadow on the sky. The man at the oars could not be prevented from turning his head rather often to try for a glimpse of this little gray shadow.

At last, from the top of each wave the men in the tossing boat could see land. Even as the light-house was an upright shadow on the sky, this land seemed but a long black shadow on the sea. It certainly was thinner than paper. "We must be about opposite New Smyrna," said the cook, who had coasted this shore often in schooners. "Captain, by the way, I believe they abandoned that life-saving station there about a year ago."

"Did they?" said the captain.

The wind slowly died away. The cook and the correspondent were not now obliged to slave in order to hold high the oar. But the waves continued their old impetuous swooping at the dingey, and the little craft, no longer under way, struggled woundily over them. The oiler or the correspondent took the oars again.

Shipwrecks are *apropos* of nothing. If men could only train for them and have them occur when the men had reached pink condition, there would be less drowning at sea. Of the four in the dingey none had slept any time worth mentioning for two days and two nights previous to embarking in the dingey, and in the excitement of clambering about the deck of a foundering ship they had also forgotten to eat heartily.

For these reasons, and for others, neither the oiler nor the correspondent was fond of rowing at this time. The correspondent wondered ingenuously how in the name of all that was sane could there be people who thought it amusing to row a boat. It was not an amusement; it was a diabolical punishment, and even a genius of mental aberrations could never conclude that it was anything but a horror to the muscles and a crime against the back. He mentioned to the boat in general how the amusement of rowing struck him, and the weary-faced oiler smiled in full sympathy. Previously to the foundering, by the way, the oiler had worked double-watch in the engine-room of the ship.

"Take her easy, now, boys," said the captain. "Don't spend yourselves. If we have to run a surf you'll need all your strength, because we'll sure have to swim for it. Take your time."

Slowly the land arose from the sea. From a black line it became a line of black and a line of white, trees, and sand. Finally, the captain said that he could make out a house on the shore. "That's the house of refuge, sure," said the cook. "They'll see us before long, and come out after us."

The distant light-house reared high. "The keeper ought to be able to make us out now, if he's looking through a glass," said the captain. "He'll notify the life-saving people."

"None of those other boats could have got ashore to give word of the wreck," said the oiler, in a low voice. "Else the life-boat would be out hunting us."

Slowly and beautifully the land loomed out of the sea. The wind came again. It had veered from the northeast to the southeast. Finally, a new sound struck the ears of the men in the boat. It was the low thunder of the surf on the shore. "We'll never be able to make the lighthouse now," said the captain. "Swing her head a little more north, Billie," said the captain.

" 'A little more north,' sir," said the oiler.

Whereupon the little boat turned her nose once more down the wind, and all but the oarsman watched the shore grow. Under the influence of this expansion doubt and direful apprehension was leaving the minds of the men. The management of the boat was still most absorbing, but it could not prevent a quiet cheerfulness. In an hour, perhaps, they would be ashore.

Their back-bones had become thoroughly used to balancing in the boat and they now rode this wild colt of a dingey like circus men. The correspondent thought that he had been drenched to the skin, but happening to feel in the top pocket of his coat, he found therein eight cigars.

Four of them were soaked with sea-water; four were perfectly scatheless. After a search, somebody produced three dry matches, and thereupon the four waifs rode in their little boat, and with an assurance of an impending rescue shining in their eyes, puffed at the big cigars and judged well and ill of all men. Everybody took a drink of water.

IV

"Cook," remarked the captain, "there don't seem to be any signs of life about your house of refuge."

"No," replied the cook. "Funny they don't see us!"

A broad stretch of lowly coast lay before the eyes of the men. It was of low dunes topped with dark vegetation. The roar of the surf was plain, and sometimes they could see the white lip of a wave as it spun up the beach. A tiny house was blocked out black upon the sky. Southward, the slim light-house lifted its little gray length.

Tide, wind, and waves were swinging the dingey northward. "Funny they don't see us," said the men.

The surf's roar was here dulled, but its tone was, nevertheless, thunderous and mighty. As the boat swam over the great rollers, the men sat listening to this roar. "We'll swamp sure," said everybody.

It is fair to say here that there was not a life-saving station within twenty miles in either direction, but the men did not know this fact and in consequence they made dark and opprobrious remarks concerning the eyesight of the nation's life-savers. Four scowling men sat in the dingey and surpassed records in the invention of epithets.

"Funny they don't see us."

The light-heartedness of a former time had completely faded. To their sharpened minds it was easy to conjure pictures of all kinds of incompetency and blindness and, indeed, cowardice. There was the shore of the populous land, and it was bitter and bitter to them that from it came no sign.

"Well," said the captain, ultimately, "I suppose we'll have to make a try for ourselves. If we stay out here too long, we'll none of us have strength left to swim after the boat swamps."

And so the oiler, who was at the oars, turned the boat straight for the shore. There was a sudden tightening of muscles. There was some thinking.

"If we don't all get ashore—" said the captain. "If we don't all get ashore, I suppose you fellows know where to send news of my finish?"

They then briefly exchanged some addresses and admonitions. As for the reflections of the men, there was a great deal of rage in them. Perchance they might be formulated thus: "If I am going to be drowned—

if I am going to be drowned—if I am going to be drowned, why, in the name of the seven mad gods who rule the sea, was I allowed to come thus far and contemplate sand and trees? Was I brought here merely to have my nose dragged away as I was about to nibble the sacred cheese of life? It is preposterous. If this old ninny-woman, Fate, cannot do better than this, she should be deprived of the management of men's fortunes. She is an old hen who knows not her intention. If she has decided to drown me, why did she not do it in the beginning and save me all this trouble. The whole affair is absurd. . . . But, no, she cannot mean to drown me. She dare not drown me. She cannot drown me. Not after all this work." Afterward the man might have had an impulse to shake his fist at the clouds: "Just you drown me, now, and then hear what I call you!"

The billows that came at this time were more formidable. They seemed always just about to break and roll over the little boat in a turmoil of foam. There was a preparatory and long growl in the speech of them. No mind unused to the sea would have concluded that the dingey could ascend these sheer heights in time. The shore was still afar. The oiler was a wily surfman. "Boys," he said, swiftly, "she won't live three minutes more and we're too far out to swim. Shall I take her to sea again, captain?"

"Yes! Go ahead!" said the captain.

This oiler, by a series of quick miracles, and fast and steady oarsmanship, turned the boat in the middle of the surf and took her safely to sea again.

There was a considerable silence as the boat bumped over the furrowed sea to deeper water. Then somebody in gloom spoke. "Well, anyhow, they must have seen us from the shore by now."

The gulls went in slanting flight up the wind toward the gray desolate east. A squall, marked by dingy clouds, and clouds brick-red, like smoke from a burning building, appeared from the southeast.

"What do you think of those life-saving people? Ain't they peaches?"

"Funny they haven't seen us."

"Maybe they think we're out here for sport! Maybe they think we're fishin'. Maybe they think we're damned fools."

It was a long afternoon. A changed tide tried to force them southward, but wind and wave said northward. Far ahead, where coast-line, sea, and sky formed their mighty angle, there were little dots which seemed to indicate a city on the shore.

"St. Augustine?"

The captain shook his head. "Too near Mosquito Inlet."

And the oiler rowed, and then the correspondent rowed. Then the

oiler rowed. It was a weary business. The human back can become the
seat of more aches and pains than are registered in books for the com-
posite anatomy of a regiment. It is a limited area, but it can become the
theatre of innumerable muscular conflicts, tangles, wrenches, knots, and
other comforts.

"Did you ever like to row, Billie?" asked the correspondent.

"No," said the oiler. "Hang it."

When one exchanged the rowing-seat for a place in the bottom of
the boat, he suffered a bodily depression that caused him to be careless
of everything save an obligation to wiggle one finger. There was cold
sea-water swashing to and fro in the boat, and he lay in it. His head,
pillowed on a thwart, was within an inch of the swirl of a wave crest,
and sometimes a particularly obstreperous sea came in-board and
drenched him once more. But these matters did not annoy him. It is
almost certain that if the boat had capsized he would have tumbled
comfortably out upon the ocean as if he felt sure that it was a great soft
mattress.

"Look! There's a man on the shore!"

"Where?"

"There! See 'im? See 'im?"

"Yes, sure! He's walking along."

"Now he's stopped. Look! He's facing us!"

"He's waving at us!"

"So he is! By thunder!"

"Ah, now, we're all right! Now we're all right! There'll be a boat
out here for us in half an hour."

"He's going on. He's running. He's going up to that house there."

The remote beach seemed lower than the sea, and it required a
searching glance to discern the little black figure. The captain saw a
floating stick and they rowed to it. A bath-towel was by some weird
chance in the boat, and, tying this on the stick, the captain waved it.
The oarsman did not dare turn his head, so he was obliged to ask
questions.

"What's he doing now?"

"He's standing still again. He's looking, I think. . . . There he goes
again. Toward the house. . . . Now he's stopped again."

"Is he waving at us?"

"No, not now! he was, though."

"Look! There comes another man!"

"He's running."

"Look at him go, would you."

"Why, he's on a bicycle. Now he's met the other man. They're both
waving at us. Look!"

"There comes something up the beach."

"What the devil is that thing?"

"Why, it looks like a boat."

"Why, certainly it's a boat."

"No, it's on wheels."

"Yes, so it is. Well, that must be the life-boat. They drag them along shore on a wagon."

"That's the life-boat, sure."

"No, by——, it's—it's an omnibus."

"I tell you it's a life-boat."

"It is not! It's an omnibus. I can see it plain. See? One of these big hotel omnibuses."

"By thunder, you're right. It's an omnibus, sure as fate. What do you suppose they are doing with an omnibus? Maybe they are going around collecting the lifecrew, hey?"

"That's it, likely. Look! There's a fellow waving a little black flag. He's standing on the steps of the omnibus. There come those other two fellows. Now they're all talking together. Look at the fellow with the flag. Maybe he ain't waving it."

"That ain't a flag, is it? That's his coat. Why, certainly, that's his coat."

"So it is. It's his coat. He's taken it off and is waving it around his head. But would you look at him swing it."

"Oh, say, there isn't any life-saving station there. That's just a winter resort hotel omnibus that has brought over some of the boarders to see us drown."

"What's that idiot with the coat mean? What's he signaling, anyhow?"

"It looks as if he were trying to tell us to go north. There must be a life-saving station up there."

"No! He thinks we're fishing. Just giving us a merry hand. See? Ah, there, Willie."

"Well, I wish I could make something out of those signals. What do you suppose he means?"

"He don't mean anything. He's just playing."

"Well, if he'd just signal us to try the surf again, or to go to sea and wait, or go north, or go south, or go to hell—there would be some reason in it. But look at him. He just stands there and keeps his coat revolving like a wheel. The ass!"

"There come more people."

"Now there's quite a mob. Look! Isn't that a boat?"

"Where? Oh, I see where you mean. No, that's no boat."

"That fellow is still waving his coat."

"He must think we like to see him do that. Why don't he quit it. It don't mean anything."

"I don't know. I think he is trying to make us go north. It must be that there's a life-saving station there somewhere."

"Say, he ain't tired yet. Look at 'im wave."

"Wonder how long he can keep that up. He's been revolving his coat ever since he caught sight of us. He's an idiot. Why aren't they getting men to bring a boat out. A fishing boat—one of those big yawls—could come out here all right. Why don't he do something?"

"Oh, it's all right, now."

"They'll have a boat out here for us in less than no time, now that they've seen us."

A faint yellow tone came into the sky over the low land. The shadows on the sea slowly deepened. The wind bore coldness with it, and the men began to shiver.

"Holy smoke!" said one, allowing his voice to express his impious mood, "if we keep on monkeying out here! If we've got to flounder out here all night!"

"Oh, we'll never have to stay here all night! Don't you worry. They've seen us now, and it won't be long before they'll come chasing out after us."

The shore grew dusky. The man waving a coat blended gradually into this gloom, and it swallowed in the same manner the omnibus and the group of people. The spray, when it dashed uproariously over the side, made the voyagers shrink and swear like men who were being branded.

"I'd like to catch the chump who waved the coat. I feel like soaking him one, just for luck."

"Why? What did he do?"

"Oh, nothing, but then he seemed so damned cheerful."

In the meantime the oiler rowed, and then the correspondent rowed, and then the oiler rowed. Gray-faced and bowed forward, they mechanically, turn by turn, plied the leaden oars. The form of the lighthouse had vanished from the southern horizon, but finally a pale star appeared, just lifting from the sea. The streaked saffron in the west passed before the all-merging darkness, and the sea to the east was black. The land had vanished, and was expressed only by the low and drear thunder of the surf.

"If I am going to be drowned—if I am going to be drowned—if I am going to be drowned, why, in the name of the seven mad gods, who rule the sea, was I allowed to come thus far and contemplate sand and trees? Was I brought here merely to have my nose dragged away as I was about to nibble the sacred cheese of life?"

The patient captain, drooped over the water-jar, was sometimes obliged to speak to the oarsman.

"Keep her head up! Keep her head up!"

" 'Keep her head up,' sir." The voices were weary and low.

This was surely a quiet evening. All save the oarsman lay heavily and listlessly in the boat's bottom. As for him, his eyes were just capable of noting the tall black waves that swept forward in a most sinister silence, save for an occasional subdued growl of a crest.

The cook's head was on a thwart, and he looked without interest at the water under his nose. He was deep in other scenes. Finally he spoke. "Billie," he murmured, dreamfully, "what kind of pie do you like best?"

V

"Pie," said the oiler and the correspondent, agitatedly. "Don't talk about those things, blast you!"

"Well," said the cook, "I was just thinking about ham sandwiches, and——"

A night on the sea in an open boat is a long night. As darkness settled finally, the shine of the light, lifting from the sea in the south, changed to full gold. On the northern horizon a new light appeared, a small bluish gleam on the edge of the waters. These two lights were the furniture of the world. Otherwise there was nothing but waves.

Two men huddled in the stern, and distances were so magnificent in the dingey that the rower was enabled to keep his feet partly warmed by thrusting them under his companions. Their legs indeed extended far under the rowing-seat until they touched the feet of the captain forward. Sometimes, despite the efforts of the tired oarsman, a wave came piling into the boat, an icy wave of the night, and the chilling water soaked them anew. They would twist their bodies for a moment and groan, and sleep the dead sleep once more, while the water in the boat gurgled about them as the craft rocked.

The plan of the oiler and the correspondent was for one to row until he lost the ability, and then arouse the other from his sea-water couch in the bottom of the boat.

The oiler plied the oars until his head drooped forward, and the overpowering sleep blinded him. And he rowed yet afterward. Then he touched a man in the bottom of the boat, and called his name. "Will you spell me for a little while?" he said, meekly.

"Sure, Billie," said the correspondent, awakening and dragging himself to a sitting position. They exchanged places carefully, and the oiler, cuddling down in the sea-water at the cook's side, seemed to go to sleep instantly.

The particular violence of the sea had ceased. The waves came without snarling. The obligation of the man at the oars was to keep the boat headed so that the tilt of the rollers would not capsize her, and to preserve her from filling when the crests rushed past. The black waves were silent and hard to be seen in the darkness. Often one was almost upon the boat before the oarsman was aware.

In a low voice the correspondent addressed the captain. He was not sure that the captain was awake, although this iron man seemed to be always awake. "Captain, shall I keep her making for that light north, sir?"

The same steady voice answered him. "Yes. Keep it about two points off the port bow."

The cook had tied a life-belt around himself in order to get even the warmth which this clumsy cork contrivance could donate, and he seemed almost stove-like when a rower, whose teeth invariably chattered wildly as soon as he ceased his labor, dropped down to sleep.

The correspondent, as he rowed, looked down at the two men sleeping under foot. The cook's arm was around the oiler's shoulders, and, with their fragmentary clothing and haggard faces, they were the babes of the sea, a grotesque rendering of the old babes in the wood.

Later he must have grown stupid at his work, for suddenly there was a growling of water, and a crest came with a roar and a swash into the boat, and it was a wonder that it did not set the cook afloat in his life-belt. The cook continued to sleep, but the oiler sat up, blinking his eyes and shaking with the new cold.

"Oh, I'm awful sorry, Billie," said the correspondent, contritely.

"That's all right, old boy," said the oiler, and lay down again and was asleep.

Presently it seemed that even the captain dozed, and the correspondent thought that he was the one man afloat on all the oceans. The wind had a voice as it came over the waves, and it was sadder than the end.

There was a long, loud swishing astern of the boat, and a gleaming trail of phosphorescence, like blue flame, was furrowed on the black waters. It might have been made by a monstrous knife.

Then there came a stillness, while the correspondent breathed with the open mouth and looked at the sea.

Suddenly there was another swish and another long flash of bluish light, and this time it was alongside the boat, and might almost have been reached with an oar. The correspondent saw an enormous fin speed like a shadow through the water, hurling the crystalline spray and leaving the long glowing trail.

The correspondent looked over his shoulder at the captain. His face was hidden, and he seemed to be asleep. He looked at the babes of the sea. They certainly were asleep. So, being bereft of sympathy, he leaned a little way to one side and swore softly into the sea.

But the thing did not then leave the vicinity of the boat. Ahead or astern, on one side or the other, at intervals long or short, fled the long sparkling streak, and there was to be heard the whiroo of the dark fin. The speed and power of the thing was greatly to be admired. It cut the water like a gigantic and keen projectile.

The presence of this biding thing did not affect the man with the same horror that it would if he had been a picnicker. He simply looked at the sea dully and swore in an undertone.

Nevertheless, it is true that he did not wish to be alone with the thing. He wished one of his companions to awaken by chance and keep him company with it. But the captain hung motionless over the water-jar and the oiler and the cook in the bottom of the boat were plunged in slumber.

VI

"If I am going to be drowned—if I am going to be drowned—if I am going to be drowned, why, in the name of the seven mad gods, who rule the sea, was I allowed to come thus far and contemplate sand and trees?"

During this dismal night, it may be remarked that a man would conclude that it was really the intention of the seven mad gods to drown him, despite the abominable injustice of it. For it was certainly an abominable injustice to drown a man who had worked so hard, so hard. The man felt it would be a crime most unnatural. Other people had drowned at sea since galleys swarmed with painted sails, but still——

When it occurs to a man that nature does not regard him as important, and that she feels she would not maim the universe by disposing of him, he at first wishes to throw bricks at the temple, and he hates deeply the fact that there are no bricks and no temples. Any visible expression of nature would surely be pelleted with his jeers.

Then, if there be no tangible thing to hoot he feels, perhaps, the desire to confront a personification and indulge in pleas, bowed to one knee, and with hands supplicant, saying: "Yes, but I love myself."

A high cold star on a winter's night is the word he feels that she says to him. Thereafter he knows the pathos of his situation.

The men in the dingey had not discussed these matters, but each had, no doubt, reflected upon them in silence and according to his mind. There was seldom any expression upon their faces save the general one of complete weariness. Speech was devoted to the business of the boat.

To chime the notes of his emotion, a verse mysteriously entered the correspondent's head. He had even forgotten that he had forgotten this verse, but it suddenly was in his mind.

> A soldier of the Legion lay dying in Algiers,
> There was lack of woman's nursing, there was dearth of woman's
>   tears;
> But a comrade stood beside him, and he took that comrade's hand
> And he said: "I shall never see my own, my native land."

In his childhood, the correspondent had been made acquainted with the fact that a soldier of the Legion lay dying in Algiers, but he had never regarded the fact as important. Myriads of his school-fellows had informed him of the soldier's plight, but the dinning had naturally ended by making him perfectly indifferent. He had never considered it his affair that a soldier of the Legion lay dying in Algiers, nor had it appeared to him as a matter for sorrow. It was less to him than breaking of a pencil's point.

Now, however, it quaintly came to him as a human, living thing. It was no longer merely a picture of a few throes in the breast of a poet, meanwhile drinking tea and warming his feet at the grate; it was an actuality—stern, mournful, and fine.

The correspondent plainly saw the soldier. He lay on the sand with his feet out straight and still. While his pale left hand was upon his chest in an attempt to thwart the going of his life, the blood came between his fingers. In the far Algerian distance, a city of low square forms was set against a sky that was faint with the last sunset hues. The correspondent, plying the oars and dreaming of the slow and slower movements of the lips of the soldier, was moved by a profound and perfectly impersonal comprehension. He was sorry for the soldier of the Legion who lay dying in Algiers.

The thing which had followed the boat and waited had evidently grown bored at the delay. There was no longer to be heard the slash of the cut-water, and there was no longer the flame of the long trail. The light in the north still glimmered, but it was apparently no nearer to the boat. Sometimes the boom of the surf rang in the correspondent's ears, and he turned the craft seaward then and rowed harder. Southward, someone had evidently built a watch-fire on the beach. It was too low and too far to be seen, but it made a shimmering, roseate reflection upon the bluff back of it, and this could be discerned from the boat.

The wind came stronger, and sometimes a wave suddenly raged out like a mountain-cat and there was to be seen the sheen and sparkle of a broken crest.

The captain, in the bow, moved on his water-jar and sat erect. "Pretty long night," he observed to the correspondent. He looked at the shore. "Those life-saving people take their time."

"Did you see that shark playing around?"

"Yes, I saw him. He was a big fellow, all right."

"Wish I had known you were awake."

Later the correspondent spoke into the bottom of the boat.

"Billie!" There was a slow and gradual disentanglement. "Billie, will you spell me?"

"Sure," said the oiler.

As soon as the correspondent touched the cold comfortable sea-water in the bottom of the boat, and had huddled close to the cook's life-belt he was deep in sleep, despite the fact that his teeth played all the popular airs. This sleep was so good to him that it was but a moment before he heard a voice call his name in a tone that demonstrated the last stages of exhaustion. "Will you spell me?"

"Sure, Billie."

The light in the north had mysteriously vanished, but the correspondent took his course from the wide-awake captain.

Later in the night they took the boat farther out to sea, and the captain directed the cook to take one oar at the stern and keep the boat facing the seas. He was to call out if he should hear the thunder of the surf. This plan enabled the oiler and the correspondent to get respite together. "We'll give those boys a chance to get into shape again," said the captain. They curled down and, after a few preliminary chatterings and trembles, slept once more the dead sleep. Neither knew they had bequeathed to the cook the company of another shark, or perhaps the same shark.

As the boat caroused on the waves, spray occasionally bumped over the side and gave them a fresh soaking, but this had no power to break their repose. The ominous slash of the wind and the water affected them as it would have affected mummies.

"Boys," said the cook, with the notes of every reluctance in his voice, "she's drifted in pretty close. I guess one of you had better take her to sea again." The correspondent, aroused, heard the crash of the toppled crests.

As he was rowing, the captain gave him some whiskey and water, and this steadied the chills out of him. "If I ever get ashore and anybody shows me even a photograph of an oar——"

At last there was a short conversation.

"Billie. . . . Billie, will you spell me?"

"Sure," said the oiler.

VII

When the correspondent again opened his eyes, the sea and the sky were each of the gray hue of the dawning. Later, carmine and gold was painted upon the waters. The morning appeared finally, in its splendor, with a sky of pure blue, and the sunlight flamed on the tips of the waves.

On the distant dunes were set many little black cottages, and a tall white wind-mill reared above them. No man, nor dog, nor bicycle appeared on the beach. The cottages might have formed a deserted village.

The voyagers scanned the shore. A conference was held in the boat. "Well," said the captain, "if no help is coming, we might better try a run through the surf right away. If we stay out here much longer we will be too weak to do anything for ourselves at all." The others silently acquiesced in this reasoning. The boat was headed for the beach. The correspondent wondered if none ever ascended the tall wind-tower, and if then they never looked seaward. This tower was a giant, standing with its back to the plight of the ants. It represented in a degree, to the correspondent, the serenity of nature amid the struggles of the individual—nature in the wind, and nature in the vision of men. She did not seem cruel to him then, nor beneficent, nor treacherous, nor wise. But she was indifferent, flatly indifferent. It is, perhaps, plausible that a man in this situation, impressed with the unconcern of the universe, should see the innumerable flaws of his life and have them taste wickedly in his mind and wish for another chance. A distinction between right and wrong seems absurdly clear to him, then, in this new ignorance of the grave-edge, and he understands that if he were given another opportunity he would mend his conduct and his words, and be better and brighter during an introduction, or at a tea.

"Now, boys," said the captain, "she is going to swamp sure. All we can do is to work her in as far as possible, and then when she swamps, pile out and scramble for the beach. Keep cool now and don't jump until she swamps sure."

The oiler took the oars. Over his shoulders he scanned the surf. "Captain," he said, "I think I'd better bring her about, and keep her head-on to the seas and back her in."

"All right, Billie," said the captain. "Back her in." The oiler swung the boat then and, seated in the stern, the cook and the correspondent were obliged to look over their shoulders to contemplate the lonely and indifferent shore.

The monstrous inshore rollers heaved the boat high until the men were again enabled to see the white sheets of water scudding up the slanted beach. "We won't get in very close," said the captain. Each time a man could wrest his attention from the rollers, he turned his glance toward the shore, and in the expression of the eyes during this contemplation there was a singular quality. The correspondent, observing the others, knew that they were not afraid, but the full meaning of their glances was shrouded.

As for himself, he was too tired to grapple fundamentally with the fact. He tried to coerce his mind into thinking of it, but the mind was dominated at this time by the muscles, and the muscles said they did not care. It merely occurred to him that if he should drown it would be a shame.

There were no hurried words, no pallor, no plain agitation. The men simply looked at the shore. "Now, remember to get well clear of the boat when you jump," said the captain.

Seaward the crest of a roller suddenly fell with a thunderous crash, and the long white comber came roaring down upon the boat.

"Steady now," said the captain. The men were silent. They turned their eyes from the shore to the comber and waited. The boat slid up the incline, leaped at the furious top, bounced over it, and swung down the long back of the waves. Some water had been shipped and the cook bailed it out.

But the next crest crashed also. The tumbling boiling flood of white water caught the boat and whirled it almost perpendicular. Water swarmed in from all sides. The correspondent had his hands on the gunwale at this time, and when the water entered at that place he swiftly withdrew his fingers, as if he objected to wetting them.

The little boat, drunken with this weight of water, reeled and snuggled deeper into the sea.

"Bail her out, cook! Bail her out," said the captain.

"All right, captain," said the cook.

"Now, boys, the next one will do for us, sure," said the oiler. "Mind to jump clear of the boat."

The third wave moved forward, huge, furious, implacable. It fairly swallowed the dingey, and almost simultaneously the men tumbled into the sea. A piece of life-belt had lain in the bottom of the boat, and as the correspondent went overboard he held this to his chest with his left hand.

The January water was icy, and he reflected immediately that it was colder than he had expected to find it off the coast of Florida. This appeared to his dazed mind as a fact important enough to be noted at the time. The coldness of the water was sad; it was tragic. This fact was somehow mixed and confused with his opinion of his own situation that it seemed almost a proper reason for tears. The water was cold.

When he came to the surface he was conscious of little but the noisy water. Afterward he saw his companions in the sea. The oiler was ahead in the race. He was swimming strongly and rapidly. Off to the correspondent's left, the cook's great white and corked back bulged out of the water, and in the rear the captain was hanging with his one good hand to the keel of the overturned dingey.

There is a certain immovable quality to a shore, and the correspondent wondered at it amid the confusion of the sea.

It seemed also very attractive, but the correspondent knew that it was a long journey, and he paddled leisurely. The piece of life-preserver lay under him, and sometimes he whirled down the incline of a wave as if he were on a hand-sled.

But finally he arrived at a place in the sea where travel was beset with difficulty. He did not pause swimming to inquire what manner of current had caught him, but there his progress ceased. The shore was set before him like a bit of scenery on a stage, and he looked at it and understood with his eyes each detail of it.

As the cook passed, much farther to the left, the captain was calling to him, "Turn over on your back, cook! Turn over on your back and use the oar."

"All right, sir." The cook turned on his back, and, paddling with an oar, went ahead as if he were a canoe.

Presently the boat also passed to the left of the correspondent with the captain clinging with one hand to the keel. He would have appeared like a man raising himself to look over a board fence, if it were not for the extraordinary gymnastics of the boat. The correspondent marvelled that the captain could still hold to it.

They passed on, nearer to shore—the oiler, the cook, the captain— and following them went the water-jar, bouncing gayly over the seas.

The correspondent remained in the grip of this strange new enemy —a current. The shore, with its white slope of sand and its green bluff, topped with little silent cottages, was spread like a picture before him. It was very near to him then, but he was impressed as one who in a gallery looks at a scene from Brittany or Algiers.

He thought: "I am going to drown? Can it be possible? Can it be possible? Can it be possible? Perhaps an individual must consider his own death to be the final phenomenon of nature.

But later a wave perhaps whirled him out of this small deadly current, for he found suddenly that he could again make progress toward the shore. Later still, he was aware that the captain, clinging with one hand to the keel of the dingey, had his face turned away from the shore and toward him, and was calling his name. "Come to the boat! Come to the boat!"

In his struggle to reach the captain and the boat, he reflected that when one gets properly wearied, drowning must really be a comfortable arrangement, a cessation of hostilities accompanied by a large degree of relief, and he was glad of it, for the main thing in his mind for some moments had been horror of the temporary agony. He did not wish to be hurt.

Presently he saw a man running along the shore. He was undressing with most remarkable speed. Coat, trousers, shirt, everything flew magically off him.

"Come to the boat," called the captain.

"All right, captain." As the correspondent paddled, he saw the captain let himself down to bottom and leave the boat. Then the correspondent performed his one little marvel of the voyage. A large wave caught him and flung him with ease and supreme speed completely over the boat and far beyond it. It struck him even then as an event in gymnastics, and a true miracle of the sea. An overturned boat in the surf is not a plaything to a swimming man.

The correspondent arrived in water that reached only to his waist, but his condition did not enable him to stand for more than a moment. Each wave knocked him into a heap, and the under-tow pulled at him.

Then he saw the man who had been running and undressing, and undressing and running, come bounding into the water. He dragged ashore the cook, and then waded toward the captain, but the captain waved him away, and sent him to the correspondent. He was naked, naked as a tree in winter, but a halo was about his head, and he shone like a saint. He gave a strong pull, and a long drag, and a bully heave at the correspondent's hand. The correspondent, schooled in the minor formulæ, said: "Thanks, old man." But suddenly the man cried: "What's that?" He pointed a swift finger. The correspondent said: "Go."

In the shallows, face downward, lay the oiler. His forehead touched sand that was periodically, between each wave, clear of the sea.

The correspondent did not know all that transpired afterward. When he achieved safe ground he fell, striking the sand with each particular part of his body. It was as if he had dropped from a roof, but the thud was grateful to him.

It seems that instantly the beach was populated with men with blankets, clothes, and flasks, and women with coffee-pots and all the remedies sacred to their minds. The welcome of the land to the men from the sea was warm and generous, but a still and dripping shape was carried slowly up the beach, and the land's welcome for it could only be the different and sinister hospitality of the grave.

When it came night, the white waves paced to and fro in the moonlight, and the wind brought the sound of the great sea's voice to the men on shore, and they felt that they could then be interpreters.

HAMLIN GARLAND

Under the Lion's Paw

One of the stories in *Main-Travelled Roads*, "Under The Lion's Paw," which originally appeared in *Harper's Weekly* in 1899, is an example of Garland's naturalistic emphasis on the need for economic reform. Inspired by Henry George's *Progress and Poverty* (1879), which mounted an argument for the "single tax" to end land speculation, Garland gave this idea fictional form in a story that shows the human toll of the fiscal policies of the late nineteenth century. In 1892 Garland read this story before the national convention of the People's Party to a rousing reception, and he became known as a spokesman for the Populists. But beyond its political dimension, this story is also an excellent evocation of the rural ethic of the Midwest, particularly in the warm hospitality of the Councils, who have known their own share of hardship, and the dogged determination of Timothy Haskins to make a life for his family. Its dramatic conclusion, turning on tragic resignation, demonstrates Garland's ability to create stories that are artistically skillful as well as socially powerful, traits that have drawn readers to this story for more than a century.

* * *

It was the last of autumn and first day of winter coming together. All day long the ploughmen on their prairie farms had moved to and fro in their wide level fields through the falling snow, which melted as it fell, wetting them to the skin—all day, notwithstanding the frequent squalls of snow, the dripping, desolate clouds, and the muck of the furrows, black and tenacious as tar.

Under their dripping harness the horses swung to and fro silently, with that marvellous uncomplaining patience which marks the horse. All day the wild geese, honking wildly, as they sprawled sidewise down the wind, seemed to be fleeing from an enemy behind, and with neck outthrust and wings extended, sailed down the wind, soon lost to sight.

Yet the ploughman behind his plough, though the snow lay on his ragged great-coat, and the cold clinging mud rose on his heavy boots, fettering him like gyves, whistled in the very beard of the gale. As day passed, the snow, ceasing to melt, lay along the ploughed land, and lodged in the depth of the stubble, till on each slow round the last furrow stood out black and shining as jet between the ploughed land and the gray stubble.

When night began to fall, and the geese, flying low, began to alight invisibly in the near corn-field, Stephen Council was still at work "finishing a land." He rode on his sulky plough when going with the wind, but walked when facing it. Sitting bent and cold but cheery under his slouch hat, he talked encouragingly to his four-in-hand.

"Come round there, boys!—Round agin! We got t' finish this land. Come in there, Dan! *Stiddy,* Kate,—stiddy! None o' y'r tantrums, Kittie. It's purty tuff, but got a be did. *Tchk! tchk!* Step along, Pete! Don't let Kate git y'r single-tree on the wheel. *Once* more!"

They seemed to know what he meant, and that this was the last round, for they worked with greater vigor than before.

"Once more, boys, an' then, sez I, oats an' a nice warm stall, an' sleep f'r all."

By the time the last furrow was turned on the land it was too dark to see the house, and the snow was changing to rain again. The tired and hungry man could see the light from the kitchen shining through the leafless hedge, and he lifted a great shout, "Supper f'r a half a dozen!"

It was nearly eight o'clock by the time he had finished his chores and started for supper. He was picking his way carefully through the mud, when the tall form of a man loomed up before him with a premonitory cough.

"Waddy ye want?" was the rather startled question of the farmer.

"Well, ye see," began the stranger, in a deprecating tone, "we'd like t' git in f'r the night. We've tried every house f'r the last two miles, but they hadn't any room f'r us. My wife's jest about sick, 'n' the children are cold and hungry—"

"Oh, y' want 'o stay all night, eh?"

"Yes, sir; it 'ud be a great accom—"

"Waal, I don't make it a practice t' turn anybuddy way hungry, not on sech nights as this. Drive right in. We ain't got much, but sech as it is—"

But the stranger had disappeared. And soon his steaming, weary team, with drooping heads and swinging single-trees, moved past the well to the block beside the path. Council stood at the side of the "schooner" and helped the children out—two little half-sleeping children—and then a small woman with a babe in her arms.

"There ye go!" he shouted jovially, to the children. "*Now* we're all right! Run right along to the house there, an' tell Mam' Council you wants sumpthin' t' eat. Right this way, Mis'—keep right off t' the right there. I'll go an' git a lantern. Come," he said to the dazed and silent group at his side.

"Mother," he shouted, as he neared the fragrant and warmly lighted kitchen, "here are some wayfarers an' folks who need sumpthin' t' eat an' a place t' snooze." He ended by pushing them all in.

Mrs. Council, a large, jolly, rather coarse-looking woman, took the children in her arms. "Come right in, you little rabbits. 'Most asleep, hey? Now here's a drink o' milk f'r each o' ye. I'll have s'm tea in a minute. Take off y'r things and set up t' the fire."

While she set the children to drinking milk, Council got out his lantern and went out to the barn to help the stranger about his team, where his loud, hearty voice could be heard as it came and went between the haymow and the stalls.

The woman came to light as a small, timid, and discouraged-looking woman, but still pretty, in a thin and sorrowful way.

"Land sakes! An' you've travelled all the way from Clear Lake t'-day in this mud! Waal! waal! No wonder you're all tired out. Don't wait f'r the men, Mis'—" She hesitated, waiting for the name.

"Haskins."

"Mis' Haskins, set right up to the table an' take a good swig o' tea whilst I make y' s'm toast. It's green tea, an' it's good. I tell Council as I git older I don't seem to enjoy Young Hyson n'r Gunpowder. I want the reel green tea, jest as it comes off'n the vines. Seems t' have more heart in it, some way. Don't s'pose it has. Council says it's all in m' eye."

Going on in this easy way, she soon had the children filled with bread and milk and the woman thoroughly at home, eating some toast and sweet-melon pickles, and sipping the tea.

"See the little rats!" she laughed at the children. "They're full as they can stick now, and they want to go to bed. Now, don't git up, Mis' Haskins; set right where you are an' let me look after 'em. I know all about young ones, though I'm all alone now. Jane went an' married last fall. But, as I tell Council, it's lucky we keep our health. Set right there, Mis' Haskins; I won't have you stir a finger."

It was an unmeasured pleasure to sit there in the warm, homely kitchen, the jovial chatter of the housewife driving out and holding at bay the growl of the impotent, cheated wind.

The little woman's eyes filled with tears which fell down upon the sleeping baby in her arms. The world was not so desolate and cold and hopeless, after all.

"Now I hope Council won't stop out there and talk politics all night. He's the greatest man to talk politics an' read the *Tribune*—How old is it?"

She broke off and peered down at the face of the babe.

"Two months 'n' five days," said the mother, with a mother's exactness.

"Ye don't say! I want 'o know! The dear little pudzy-wudzy!" she went on, stirring it up in the neighborhood of the ribs with her fat forefinger.

"Pooty tough on 'oo to go gallivant'n' 'cross lots this way—"

"Yes, that's so; a man can't lift a mountain," said Council, entering the door. "Mother, this is Mr. Haskins, from Kansas. He's been eat up 'n' drove out by grasshoppers."

"Glad t' see yeh!—Pa, empty that wash-basin 'n' give him a chance t' wash."

Haskins was a tall man, with a thin, gloomy face. His hair was a reddish brown, like his coat, and seemed equally faded by the wind and sun, and his sallow face, though hard and set, was pathetic somehow. You would have felt that he had suffered much by the line of his mouth showing under his thin, yellow mustache.

"Hain't Ike got home yet, Sairy?"

"Hain't seen 'im."

"W-a-a-l, set right up, Mr. Haskins; wade right into what we've got; 'tain't much, but we manage to live on it—she gits fat on it," laughed Council, pointing his thumb at his wife.

After supper, while the women put the children to bed, Haskins and Council talked on, seated near the huge cooking-stove, the steam rising from their wet clothing. In the Western fashion Council told as much of his own life as he drew from his guest. He asked but few questions, but by and by the story of Haskins' struggles and defeat come out. The story was a terrible one, but he told it quietly, seated with his elbows on his knees, gazing most of the time at the hearth.

"I didn't like the looks of the country, anyhow," Haskins said, partly rising and glancing at his wife. "I was ust t' northern Ingyannie, where we have lots o' timber 'n lots o' rain, 'n' I didn't like the looks o' that dry prairie. What galled me the worst was goin' s' far away acrosst so much fine land layin' all through here vacant."

"And the 'hoppers eat ye four years, hand runnin', did they?"

"Eat! They wiped us out. They chawed everything that was green. They jest set around waitin' f'r us to die t' eat us, too. My God! I ust t' dream of 'em sittin' 'round on the bedpost, six feet long, workin' their jaws. They eet the fork-handles. They got worse 'n' worse till they jest rolled on one another, piled up like snow in winter. Well, it ain't no use. If I was t' talk all winter I couldn't tell nawthin'. But all the while I couldn't help thinkin' of all that land back here that nobuddy was usin' that I ought 'o had 'stead o' bein' out there in that cussed country."

"Waal, why didn't ye stop an' settle here?" asked Ike, who had come in and was eating his supper.

"Fer the simple reason that you fellers wantid ten 'r fifteen dollars an acre fer the bare land, and I hadn't no money fer that kind o' thing."

"Yes, I do my own work," Mrs. Council was heard to say in the pause which followed. "I'm a gettin' purty heavy t' be on m' laigs all day, but we can't afford t' hire, so I keep rackin' around somehow, like a foundered horse. S' lame—I tell Council he can't tell how lame I am, f'r I'm jest as lame in one laig as t'other." And the good soul laughed at the joke on herself as she took a handful of flour and dusted the biscuit-board to keep the dough from sticking.

"Well, I hain't *never* been very strong," said Mrs. Haskins. "Our folks was Canadians an' small-boned, and then since my last child I hain't got up again fairly. I don't like t' complain. Tim has about all he can bear now—but they was days this week when I jest wanted to lay right down an' die."

"Waal, now, I'll tell ye," said Council, from his side of the stove, silencing everybody with his good-natured roar, "I'd go down and *see* Butler, *anyway*, if I was you. I guess he'd let you have his place purty cheap; the farm's all run down. He's ben anxious t' let t' somebuddy next year. It 'ud be a good chance fer you. Anyhow, you go to bed and sleep like a babe. I've got some ploughin' t' do, anyhow, an' we'll see if somethin' can't be done about your case. Ike, you go out an' see if the horses is all right, an' I'll show the folks t' bed."

When the tired husband and wife were lying under the generous quilts of the spare bed, Haskins listened a moment to the wind in the eaves, and then said, with a slow and solemn tone,

"There are people in this world who are good enough t' be angels, an' only haff t' die to *be* angels."

II

Jim Butler was one of those men called in the West "land poor." Early in the history of Rock River he had come into the town and started in the grocery business in a small way, occupying a small building in a mean part of the town. At this period of his life he earned all he got,

and was up early and late sorting beans, working over butter, and cart-
ing his goods to and from the station. But a change came over him at
the end of the second year, when he sold a lot of land for four times
what he paid for it. From that time forward he believed in land speculation as the surest way of getting rich. Every cent he could save or
spare from his trade he put into land at forced sale, or mortgages on
land, which were "just as good as the wheat," he was accustomed
to say.

Farm after farm fell into his hands, until he was recognized as one
of the leading landowners of the county. His mortgages were scattered
all over Cedar County, and as they slowly but surely fell in he sought
usually to retain the former owner as tenant.

He was not ready to foreclose; indeed, he had the name of being one
of the "easiest" men in the town. He let the debtor off again and again,
extending the time whenever possible.

"I don't want y'r land," he said. "All I'm after is the int'rest on my
money—that's all. Now, if y' want 'o stay on the farm, why, I'll give
y' a good chance. I can't have the land layin' vacant." And in many
cases the owner remained as tenant.

In the meantime he had sold his store; he couldn't spend time in it;
he was mainly occupied now with sitting around town on rainy days
smoking and "gassin' with the boys," or in riding to and from his farms.
In fishing-time he fished a good deal. Doc Grimes, Ben Ashley, and Cal
Cheatham were his cronies on these fishing excursions or hunting trips
in the time of chickens or partridges. In winter they went to Northern
Wisconsin to shoot deer.

In spite of all these signs of easy life Butler persisted in saying he
"hadn't enough money to pay taxes on his land," and was careful to
convey the impression that he was poor in spite of his twenty farms. At
one time he was said to be worth fifty thousand dollars, but land had
been a little slow of sale of late, so that he was not worth so much.

A fine farm, known as the Higley place, had fallen into his hands in
the usual way the previous year, and he had not been able to find a
tenant for it. Poor Higley, after working himself nearly to death on it
in the attempt to lift the mortgage, had gone off to Dakota, leaving the
farm and his curse to Butler.

This was the farm which Council advised Haskins to apply for; and
the next day Council hitched up his team and drove down town to see
Butler.

"You jest let *me* do the talkin'," he said. "We'll find him wearin'
out his pants on some salt barrel somew'ers; and if he thought you
wanted a place he'd sock it to you hot and heavy. You jest keep quiet;
I'll fix 'im."

Butler was seated in Ben Ashley's store telling fish yarns when Council sauntered in casually.

"Hello, But; lyin' agin, hey?"

"Hello, Steve! how goes it?"

"Oh, so-so. Too dang much rain these days. I thought it was goin' t' freeze up f'r good last night. Tight squeak if I get m' ploughin' done. How's farmin' with *you* these days?"

"Bad. Ploughin' ain't half done."

"It 'ud be a religious idee f'r you t' go out an' take a hand y'rself."

"I don't haff to," said Butler, with a wink.

"Got anybody on the Higley place?"

"No. Know of anybody?"

"Waal, no; not eggsackly. I've got a relation back t' Michigan who's ben hot an' cold on the idee o' comin' West f'r some time. *Might* come if he could get a good lay-out. What do you talk on the farm?"

"Well, I d' know. I'll rent it on shares or I'll rent it money rent."

"Waal, how much money, say?"

"Well, say ten per cent, on the price—two-fifty."

"Waal, that ain't bad. Wait on 'im till 'e thrashes?"

Haskins listened eagerly to his important question, but Council was coolly eating a dried apple which he had speared out of a barrel with his knife. Butler studied him carefully.

"Well, knocks me out of twenty-five dollars interest."

"My relation'll need all he's got t' git his crops in," said Council, in the safe, indifferent way.

"Well, all right; *say* wait," concluded Butler.

"All right; this is the man. Haskins, this is Mr. Butler—no relation to Ben—the hardest-working man in Cedar County."

On the way home Haskins said: "I ain't much better off. I'd like that farm; it's a good farm, but it's all run down, an' so 'm I. I could make a good farm of it if I had half a show. But I can't stock it n'r seed it."

"Waal, now, don't you worry," roared Council in his ear. "We'll pull y' through somehow till next harvest. He's agreed t' hire it ploughed, an' you can earn a hundred dollars ploughin' an' y' c'n git the seed o' me, an' pay me back when y' can."

Haskins was silent with emotion, but at last he said, "I ain't got nothin' t' live on."

"Now, don't you worry 'bout that. You jest make your headquarters at ol' Steve Council's. Mother'll take a pile o' comfort in havin' y'r wife an' children 'round. Y' see, Jane's married off lately, an' Ike's away a good 'eal, so we'll be darn glad t' have y' stop with us this winter. Nex' spring we'll see if y' can't git a start agin." And he chirruped to the team, which sprang forward with the rumbling, clattering wagon.

"Say, looky here, Council, you can't do this. I never saw—" shouted Haskins in his neighbor's ear.

Council moved about uneasily in his seat and stopped his stammering gratitude by saying: "Hold on, now; don't make such a fuss over a little thing. When I see a man down, an' things all on top of 'm, I jest like t' kick 'em off an' help 'm up. That's the kind of religion I got, an' it's about the *only* kind."

They rode the rest of the way home in silence. And when the red light of the lamp shone out into the darkness of the cold and windy night, and he thought of this refuge for his children and wife, Haskins could have put his arm around the neck of his burly companion and squeezed him like a lover. But he contented himself with saying, "Steve Council, you'll git y'r pay f'r this some day."

"Don't want any pay. My religion ain't run on such business principles."

The wind was growing colder, and the ground was covered with a white frost, as they turned into the gate of the Council farm, and the children came rushing out, shouting, "Papa's come!" They hardly looked like the same children who had sat at the table the night before. Their torpidity, under the influence of sunshine and Mother Council, had given way to a sort of spasmodic cheerfulness, as insects in winter revive when laid on the hearth.

III

Haskins worked like a fiend, and his wife, like the heroic woman that she was, bore also uncomplainingly the most terrible burdens. They rose early and toiled without intermission till the darkness fell on the plain, then tumbled into bed, every bone and muscle aching with fatigue, to rise with the sun next morning to the same round of the same ferocity of labor.

The eldest boy drove a team all through the spring, ploughing and seeding, milked the cows, and did chores innumerable, in most ways taking the place of a man.

An infinitely pathetic but common figure—this boy on the American farm, where there is no law against child labor. To see him in his coarse clothing, his huge boots, and his ragged cap, as he staggered with a pail of water from the well, or trudged in the cold and cheerless dawn out into the frosty field behind his team, gave the city-bred visitor a sharp pang of sympathetic pain. Yet Haskins loved his boy, and would have saved him from this if he could, but he could not.

By June the first year the result of such Herculean toil began to show on the farm. The yard was cleaned up and sown to grass, the garden ploughed and planted, and the house mended.

Council had given them four of his cows. "Take 'em an' run 'em on shares. I don't want 'o milk s' many. Ike's away s' much now, Sat'd'ys an' Sund'ys, I can't stand the bother anyhow."

Other men, seeing the confidence of Council in the newcomer, had sold him tools on time; and as he was really an able farmer, he soon had round him many evidences of his care and thrift. At the advice of Council he had taken the farm for three years, with the privilege of re-renting or buying at the end of the term.

"It's a good bargain, an' y' want 'o nail it," said Council. "If you have any kind ov a crop, you c'n pay y'r debts, an' keep seed an' bread."

The new hope which now sprang up in the heart of Haskins and his wife grew great almost as a pain by the time the wide field of wheat began to wave and rustle and swirl in the winds of July. Day after day he would snatch a few moments after supper to go and look at it.

"Have ye seen the wheat t'-day, Nettie?" he asked one night as he rose from supper.

"No, Tim, I ain't had time."

"Well, take time now. Le's go look at it."

She threw an old hat on her head—Tommy's hat—and looking almost pretty in her thin, sad way, went out with her husband to the hedge.

"Ain't it grand, Nettie? Just look at it."

It was grand. Level, russet here and there, heavy-headed, wide as a lake, and full of multitudinous whispers and gleams of wealth, it stretched away before the gazers like the fabled field of the cloth of gold.

"Oh, I think—I *hope* we'll have a good crop, Tim; and oh, how good the people have been to us!"

"Yes; I don't know where we'd be t'-day if it hadn't ben f'r Council and his wife."

"They're the best people in the world," said the little woman, with a great sob of gratitude.

"We'll be in the field on Monday, sure," said Haskins, gripping the rail on the fence as if already at the work of the harvest.

The harvest came, bounteous, glorious, but the winds came and blew it into tangles, and the rain matted it here and there close to the ground, increasing the work of gathering it threefold.

Oh, how they toiled in those glorious days! Clothing dripping with sweat, arms aching, filled with briers, fingers raw and bleeding, backs broken with the weight of heavy bundles, Haskins and his man toiled on. Tommy drove the harvester, while his father and a hired man bound on the machine. In this way they cut ten acres every day, and almost every night after supper, when the hand went to bed, Haskins returned to the field shocking the bound grain in the light of the moon. Many a night he worked till his anxious wife came out at ten o'clock to call him in to rest and lunch.

At the same time she cooked for the men, took care of the children, washed and ironed, milked the cows at night, made the butter, and sometimes fed the horses and watered them while her husband kept at the shocking.

No slave in the Roman galleys could have toiled so frightfully and lived, for this man thought himself a free man, and that he was working for his wife and babes.

When he sank into his bed with a deep groan of relief, too tired to change his grimy, dripping clothing, he felt that he was getting nearer and nearer to a home of his own, and pushing the wolf of want a little farther from his door.

There is no despair so deep as the despair of a homeless man or woman. To roam the roads of the country or the streets of the city, to feel there is no rood of ground on which the feet can rest, to halt weary and hungry outside lighted windows and hear laughter and song within,—these are the hungers and rebellions that drive men to crime and women to shame.

It was the memory of this homelessness, and the fear of its coming again, that spurred Timothy Haskins and Nettie, his wife, to such ferocious labor during that first year.

IV

" 'M, yes; 'm, yes; first-rate," said Butler, as his eye took in the neat garden, the pig-pen, and the well-filled barnyard. "You're gitt'n' quite a stock around yeh. Done well, eh?"

Haskins was showing Butler around the place. He had not seen it for a year, having spent the year in Washington and Boston with Ashley, his brother-in-law, who had been elected to Congress.

"Yes, I've laid out a good deal of money durin' the last three years. I've paid out three hundred dollars f'r fencin'."

"Um—h'm! I see, I see," said Butler, while Haskins went on:

"The kitchen there cost two hundred; the barn ain't cost much in money, but I've put a lot o' time on it. I've dug a new well, and I—"

"Yes, yes, I see. You've done well. Stock worth a thousand dollars," said Butler, picking his teeth with a straw.

"About that," said Haskins, modestly. "We begin to feel 's if we was gitt'n' a home f'r ourselves; but we've worked hard. I tell you we begin to feel it, Mr. Butler, and we're goin' t' begin to ease up purty soon. We've been kind o' plannin' a trip back t' *her* folks after the fall ploughin's done."

"*Eggs*-actly!" said Butler, who was evidently thinking of something else. "I suppose you've kind o' calc'lated on stayin' here three years more?"

"Well, yes. Fact is, I think I c'n buy the farm this fall, if you'll give me a reasonable show."

"Um—m! What do you call a reasonable show?"

"Well, say a quarter down and three years' time."

Butler looked at the huge stacks of wheat, which filled the yard, over which the chickens were fluttering and crawling, catching grasshoppers, and out of which the crickets were singing innumerably. He smiled in a peculiar way as he said, "Oh, I won't be hard on yeh. But what did you expect to pay f'r the place?"

"Why, about what you offered it for before, two thousand five hundred, or *possibly* three thousand dollars," he added quickly, as he saw the owner shake his head.

"This farm is worth five thousand and five hundred dollars," said Butler, in a careless and decided voice.

"*What!*" almost shrieked the astounded Haskins. "What's that? Five thousand? Why, that's double what you offered it for three years ago."

"Of course, and it's worth it. It was all run down then; now it's in good shape. You've laid out fifteen hundred dollars in improvements, according to your own story."

"But *you* had nothin' t' do about that. It's my work an' my money."

"You bet it was; but it's my land."

"But what's to pay me for all my—"

"Ain't you had the use of 'em?" replied Butler, smiling calmly into his face.

Haskins was like a man struck on the head with a sandbag; he couldn't think; he stammered as he tried to say: "But—I never'd git the use—You'd rob me! More 'n that: you agreed—you promised that I could buy or rent at the end of three years at—"

"That's all right. But I didn't say I'd let you carry off the improvements, nor that I'd go on renting the farm at two-fifty. The land is doubled in value, it don't matter how; it don't enter into the question; an' now you can pay me five hundred dollars a year rent, or take it on your own terms at fifty-five hundred, or—git out."

He was turning away when Haskins, the sweat pouring from his face, fronted him, saying again:

"But *you've* done nothing to make it so. You hain't added a cent. I put it all there myself, expectin' to buy. I worked an' sweat to improve it. I was workin' for myself an' babes—"

"Well, why didn't you buy when I offered to sell? What y' kickin' about?"

"I'm kickin' about payin' you twice f'r my own things,—my own fences, my own kitchen, my own garden."

Butler laughed. "You're too green t' eat, young feller. *Your* improvements! The law will sing another tune."

"But I trusted your word."

"Never trust anybody, my friend. Besides, I didn't promise not to do this thing. Why, man, don't look at me like that. Don't take me for a thief. It's the law. The reg'lar thing. Everybody does it."

"I don't care if they do. It's stealin' jest the same. You take three thousand dollars of my money—the work o' my hands and my wife's." He broke down at this point. He was not a strong man mentally. He could face hardship, ceaseless toil, but he could not face the cold and sneering face of Butler.

"But I don't take it," said Butler, coolly. "All you've got to do is to go on jest as you've been a-doin', or give me a thousand dollars down, and a mortgage at ten per cent on the rest.

Haskins sat down blindly on a bundle of oats near by, and with staring eyes and drooping head went over the situation. He was under the lion's paw. He felt a horrible numbness in his heart and limbs. He was hid in a mist, and there was no path out.

Butler walked about, looking at the huge stacks of grain, and pulling now and again a few handfuls out, shelling the heads in his hands and blowing the chaff away. He hummed a little tune as he did so. He had an accommodating air of waiting.

Haskins was in the midst of the terrible toil of the last year. He was walking again in the rain and the mud behind his plough; he felt the dust and dirt of the threshing. The ferocious husking-time, with its cutting wind and biting, clinging snows, lay hard upon him. Then he thought of his wife, how she had cheerfully cooked and baked, without holiday and without rest.

"Well, what do you think of it?" inquired the cool, mocking, insinuating voice of Butler.

"I think you're a thief and a liar!" shouted Haskins, leaping up. "A black-hearted houn'!" Butler's smile maddened him; with a sudden leap he caught a fork in his hands, and whirled it in the air. "You'll never rob another man, damn ye!" he grated through his teeth, a look of pitiless ferocity in his accusing eyes.

Butler shrank and quivered, expecting the blow; stood, held hypnotized by the eyes of the man he had a moment before despised—a man transformed into an avenging demon. But in the deadly hush between the lift of the weapon and its fall there came a gush of faint, childish laughter and then across the range of his vision, far away and dim, he saw the sun-bright head of his baby girl, as, with the pretty, tottering run of a two-year-old, she moved across the grass of the dooryard. His hands relaxed; the fork fell to the ground; his head lowered.

"Make out y'r deed an' mor'gage, an' git off'n my land, an' don't ye never cross my line agin; if y' do, I'll kill ye."

Butler backed away from the man in wild haste, and climbing into his buggy with trembling limbs drove off down the road, leaving Haskins seated dumbly on the sunny pile of sheaves, his head sunk into his hands.

THEODORE DREISER

Curious Shifts of the Poor

"Curious Shifts of the Poor" was published in *Demorest's* magazine in November 1899. Dreiser later recognized the atmospheric appropriateness of the piece to the decline of George Hurstwood in *Sister Carrie* and worked these sketches into the final chapters of that novel. The unperturbed tone of this story contributes to the sense of poverty and misery as a sociological curiosity and controls the fierce indignation the author reserves for the final paragraphs. The poor are anonymous, almost ghostly figures who appear at the street corner and disappear into flop houses for the night. The self-appointed soldier of charity approaches his business without passion or pity, sure of his duty and of Providence, but he is as misguided as any other figure in the tale. The elegance of carriages and clubs, enthusiastic theatergoers and wealthy loungers, contrasts sharply with the vacant faces and the stupid silences of the "flotsam and jetsam of society." However, Dreiser's inventory of extremes is not intended to elicit pity so much as it is to expose the ignorance and error of a complacent city, proud of its progress and improvements and indifferent to its poor.

*   *   *

At the hour when Broadway assumes its most interesting aspect, a peculiar individual takes his stand at the corner of Twenty-sixth street. It
is the hour when the theatres are just beginning to receive their patrons.
Fire signs, announcing the night's amusements, blaze on every hand.
Cabs and carriages, their lamps gleaming like yellow eyes, patter by.
Couples and parties of three and four are freely mingled in the common
crowd which passes by in a thick stream, laughing and jesting. On Fifth
avenue are loungers, a few wealthy strollers, a gentleman in evening
dress with a lady at his side, some clubmen, passing from one smoking
room to another. Across the way the great hotels, the Hoffman House
and the Fifth Avenue, show a hundred gleaming windows, their cafés
and billiard rooms filled with a pleasure-loving throng. All about, the
night has a feeling of pleasure and exhilaration, the curious enthusiasm
of a great city, bent upon finding joy in a thousand different ways.

In the midst of this lightsome atmosphere a short, stocky-built soldier, in a great cape-overcoat and soft felt hat, takes his stand at the
corner. For a while he is alone, gazing like any idler upon an ever-
fascinating scene. A policeman passes, saluting him as Captain, in a
friendly way. An urchin, who has seen him there before, stops and gazes.
To all others he is nothing out of the ordinary save in dress, a stranger,
whistling for his own amusement.

As the first half hour wanes, certain characters appear. Here and
there in the passing crowd one may see now and then a loiterer, edging
interestedly near. A slouchy figure crosses the opposite corner and
glances furtively in his direction. Another comes down Fifth avenue to
the corner of Twenty-sixth street, takes a general survey and hobbles
off again. Two or three noticeable Bowery types edge along the Fifth
avenue side of Madison Square, but do not venture over. The soldier in
his cape-overcoat walks a line of ten feet at his corner, to and fro,
whistling.

As nine o'clock approaches, some of the hubbub of the earlier hour
passes. On Broadway the crowd is neither so thick nor so gay. There are
fewer cabs passing. The atmosphere of the hotels is not so youthful. The
air, too, is colder. On every hand move curious figures, watchers and
peepers without an imaginary circle, which they are afraid to enter—
dozens in all. Presently, with the arrival of a keener sense of cold, one
figure comes forward. It crosses Broadway from out the shadow of
Twenty-sixth street, and, in a halting, circuitous way, arrives close to the
waiting figure. There is something shamefaced, a diffident air about the
movement, as if the intention were to conceal any idea of stopping until
the very last moment. Then, suddenly, close to the soldier comes the

halt. The Captain looks in recognition, but there is no especial greeting. The newcomer nods slightly, and murmurs something, like one who waits for gifts. The other simply motions toward the edge of the walk.

"Stand over there."

The spell is broken. Even while the soldier resumes his short, solemn walk, other figures shuffle forward. They do not so much as greet the leader, but join the one, shuffling and hitching and scraping their feet.

"Cold, isn't it?"

"I don't like winter."

"Looks as though it might snow."

The motley company has increased to ten. One or two know each other and converse. Others stand off a few feet, not wishing to be in the crowd, and yet not counted out. They are peevish, crusty, silent, eying nothing in particular, and moving their feet. The soldier, counting sufficient to begin, comes forward.

"Beds, eh, all of you?"

There is a general shuffle and murmur of approval.

"Well, line up here. I'll see what I can do. I haven't a cent myself."

They fall into a sort of broken, ragged line. One sees now some of the chief characteristics by contrast. There is a wooden leg in the line. Hats are all drooping, a collection that would ill become a second-hand Hester street basement collection. Trousers are all warped and frayed at the bottom, and coats worn and faded. In the glare of the street lights, some of the faces look dry and chalky. Others are red with blotches, and puffed in the cheeks and under the eyes. One or two are raw-boned and remind one of railroad hands. A few spectators come near, drawn by the seemingly conferring group, then more and more, and quickly there is a pushing, gaping crowd. Someone in the line begins to talk.

"Silence!" exclaims the Captain. "Now, then, gentlemen, these men are without beds. They have got to have some place to sleep to-night. They can't lie out in the street. I need twelve cents to put one to bed. Who will give it to me?"

No reply.

"Well, we'll have to wait here, boys, until someone does. Twelve cents isn't so very much for one man."

"Here is fifteen," exclaims a young man, who is peering forward with strained eyes. "It's all I can afford."

"All right; now I have fifteen. Step out of the line," and seizing the one at the end of the line nearest him by the shoulder, the Captain marches him off a little way and stands him up alone.

Coming back, he resumes his place before the little line and begins again.

"I have three cents here. These men must be put to bed somehow.

There are," counting, "one, two, three, four, five, six, seven, eight, nine, ten, eleven, twelve men. Nine cents more will put the next man to bed, give him a good, comfortable bed for the night. I go right along and look after that myself. Who will give me nine cents?"

One of the watchers, this time a middle-aged man, hands in a five-cent piece.

"Good. Now I have eight cents. Four more will give this man a bed. Come, gentlemen, we are going very slow this evening. You all have good beds. How about these?"

"Here you are," remarked a bystander, putting a coin into his hand.

"That," says the Captain, looking at the coin, "pays for two beds for two men and leaves five for the next one. Who will give seven cents more?"

On the one hand the little line of those whose beds are secure is growing, but on the other the bedless waxes long. Silently the queer drift of poverty washes in, and they take their places at the foot of the line unnoticed. Ever and anon the Captain counts and announces the number remaining. Its growth neither dismays nor interests him. He does not even speak of it. His concern is wholly over the next man, and the securing of twelve cents. Strangers, gazing out of mere curiosity, find their sympathies enlisted, and pay into the hands of the Captain dimes and quarters, as he states in a short, brusque, unaffected way, the predicament of the men.

In the line of men whose beds are secure, a relaxed air is apparent. The strain of uncertainty being removed, there is moderate good feeling, and some leaning toward sociability. Those nearest one another begin to talk. Politics, religion, the state of the government, some newspaper sensations, and the more notorious facts of the world find mouth-pieces and auditors here. Vague and rambling are the discussions. Cracked and husky voices pronounce forcibly on odd things. There are squints and leers and dull ox-like stares from those who are too dull or too weary to converse.

Standing tells. In the course of time the earliest arrivals become weary and uneasy. There is a constant shifting from one foot to the other, a leaning out and looking back to see how many more must be provided for before the company can march away. Comments are made and crude wishes for the urging forward of things.

"Huh! There's a lot back there yet."

"Yes, must be over a hundred to-night."

"Look at the guy in the cab."

"Captain's a great fellow, ain't he?"

A cab has stopped. Some gentleman in evening dress reaches out a bill to the Captain, who takes it with simple thanks, and turns away to his line. There is a general craning of necks as the jewel in the broad white shirt-front sparkles and the cab moves off. Even the crowd gapes in awe.

"That fixes up nine men for the night," says the Captain, counting out as many of the line near him. "Line up over there. Now, then, there are only seven. I need twelve cents."

Money comes slow. In the course of time the crowd thins out to a meagre handful. Fifth avenue, save for an occasional cab or foot-passenger, is bare. Broadway is thinly peopled with pedestrians. Only now and then a stranger passing notices the small group, hands out a coin and goes away, unheeding.

The Captain is stolid and determined. He talks on, very slowly, uttering the fewest words, and with a certain assurance, as though he could not fail.

"Come, I can't stay out here all night. These men are getting tired and cold. Someone give me four cents."

There comes a time when he says nothing at all. Money is handed him, and for each twelve cents he singles out a man and puts him in the other line. Then he walks up and down as before, looking at the ground.

The theatres let out. Fire signs disappear. A clock strikes eleven. Another half hour, and he is down to the last two men.

A lady in opera cape and rustling silk skirt comes down Fifth avenue, supported by her escort. The latter glances at the line and comes over. There is a bill in his fingers.

"Here you are," he says.

"Thanks," says the Captain. "Now we have some for to-morrow night."

The last two are lined up. The soldier walks along, studying his line and counting.

"One hundred and thirty-seven," he exclaims, when he reaches the head.

"Now, boys, line up there. Steady now, we'll be off in a minute."

He places himself at the head and calls out, "Forward, march!" and away they go.

Across Fifth avenue, through Madison Square, by the winding path, east on Twenty-third street, and down Third avenue trudges the long, serpentine company.

Below Tenth street is a lodging house, and here the queer, ragamuffin line brings up, while the Captain enters in to arrange. In a few minutes the deal is consummated, and the line marches slowly in, each being provided with a key as the Captain looks on. When the last one has disappeared up the dingy stairway, he comes out, muffles his great coat closer in the cold air, pulls down his slouch brim, and tramps, a solitary, silent figure, into the night.

Such is the Captain's idea of his duty to his fellow man. He is a strange man, with a strange bias. Utter confidence in Providence, perfectly sure that he deals direct with God, he takes this means of fulfilling his own destiny.

Outside the door of what was once a row of red brick family dwellings, in Fifteenth street, but what is now a mission or convent house of the Sisters of Mercy, hangs a plain wooden contribution box, on which is painted the statement that every noon a meal is given free to all those who apply and ask for aid. This simple announcement is modest in the extreme, covering, as it does, a charity so broad. Unless one were looking up this matter in particular, he could stand at Sixth avenue and Fifteenth street for days, around the noon hour, and never notice that, out of the vast crowd that surges along that busy thoroughfare, there turned out, every few seconds, some weather-beaten, heavy-footed specimen of humanity, gaunt in countenance, and dilapidated in the matter of clothes. The fact is true, however, and the colder the day the more apparent it becomes. Space and lack of culinary room compels an arrangement which permits of only twenty-five or thirty eating at one time, so that a line has to be formed outside, and an orderly entrance effected.

One such line formed on a January day last year. It was peculiarly cold. Already, at eleven in the morning, several shambled forward out of Sixth avenue, their thin clothes flapping and fluttering in the wind, and leaned up against the iron fence. One came up from the west out of Seventh avenue and stopped close to the door, nearer than all the others. Those who had been waiting before him, but farther away, now drew near, and by a certain stolidity of demeanor, no words being spoken, indicated that they were first. The newcomer looked sullenly along the line and then moved out, taking his place at the foot. When order had been restored, the animal feeling of opposition relaxed.

"Must be pretty near noon," ventured one.

"It is," said another; "I've been waitin' nearly an hour."

"Gee, but it's cold."

The line was growing rapidly. Those at the head evidently congratulated themselves upon not having long to wait. There was much jerking of heads and looking down the line.

"It don't matter much how near you get to the front, so long as you're in the first twenty-five. You all go in together," commented one of the first twenty-five.

"This here Single Tax is the thing. There ain't goin' to be no order till it comes," said another, discussing that broader topic.

At last the door opened and the motherly Sister looked out. Slowly the line moved up, and one by one thirty men passed in. Then she interposed a stout arm and the line halted with six men on the steps. In this position they waited. After a while one of the earliest to go in came out, and then another. Every time one came out the line moved up. And this continued until two o'clock, when the last hungry dependent crossed the threshold, and the door was closed.

It was a winter evening. Already at four o'clock, the sombre hue of night was thickening the air. A heavy snow was falling—a fine, picking, whipping snow, borne forward by a swift wind in long, thin lines. The street was bedded with it, six inches of cold, soft carpet, churned brown by the crush of teams and the feet of men. Along the Bowery, men slouched through it with collars up and hats pulled over their ears.

Before a dirty four-story building gathered a crowd of men. It began with the approach of two or three, who hung about the closed wooden doors, and beat their feet to keep them warm. They made no effort to go in, but shifted ruefully about, digging their hands deep in their pockets, and leering at the crowd and the increasing lamps. There were old men with grizzled beards and sunken eyes; men who were comparatively young, but shrunken by disease; men who were middle-aged.

With the growth of the crowd about the door came a murmur. It was not conversation, but a running comment directed at anyone in general. It contained oaths and slang phrases.

"I wisht they'd hurry up."

"Look at the copper watchin'."

"Maybe it ain't winter, nuther."

"I wisht I was with Otis."

Now a sharper lash of wind cut down, and they huddled closer. There was no anger, no threatening words. It was all sullen endurance, unlightened by either wit or good fellowship.

A carriage went jingling by with some reclining figure in it. One of the members nearest the door saw it.

"Look at the bloke ridin'."

"He ain't so cold."

"Eh! Eh! Eh!" yelled another, the carriage having long since passed out of hearing.

Little by little the night crept on. Along the walk a crowd turned out on its way home. Still the men hung around the door, unwavering.

"Ain't they ever goin' to open up?" queried a hoarse voice suggestively.

This seemed to renew general interest in the closed door, and many gazed in that direction. They looked at it as dumb brutes look, as dogs paw and whine and study the knob. They shifted and blinked and muttered, now a curse, now a comment. Still they waited, and still the snow whirled and cut them.

A glimmer appeared through the transom overhead, where someone was lighting the gas. It sent a thrill of possibility through the watcher. On the old hats and peaked shoulders snow was piling. It gathered in little heaps and curves, and no one brushed it off. In the center of the crowd the warmth and steam melted it, and water trickled off hat-rims and down noses which the owners could not reach to scratch. On the outer rim the piles remained unmelted. Those who could not get in the center lowered their heads to the weather and bent their forms.

At last the bars grated inside and the crowd pricked up its ears. There was someone who called, "Slow up there now!" and then the door opened. It was push and jam for a minute, with grim, beast silence to prove its quality, and then the crowd lessened. It melted inward like logs floating, and disappeared. There were wet hats and shoulders, a cold, shrunken, disgruntled mass, pouring in between bleak walls. It was just six o'clock, and there was supper in every hurrying pedestrian's face.

"Do you sell anything to eat here?" questioned one of the grizzled old carpet-slippers who opened the door.

"No; nothin' but beds."

The waiting throng had been housed.

For nearly a quarter of a century Fleischman, the caterer, has given a loaf of bread to anyone who will come for it to the rear door of his restaurant, on the corner of Broadway and Ninth street, at midnight. Every night, during twenty-three years, about three hundred men have formed in line, and, at the appointed time, marched past the doorway, picked their loaf from a great box placed just outside, and vanished again into the night. From the beginning to the present time there has been little change in the character or number of these men. There are two or three figures that have grown familiar to those who have seen this little procession pass year after year. Two of them have missed scarcely a night in fifteen years. There are about forty, more or less, regular callers. The remainder of the line is formed of strangers every night.

The line is not allowed to form before eleven o'clock. At this hour, perhaps a single figure shambles around the corner and halts on the edge of the sidewalk. Other figures appear and fall in behind. They come almost entirely one at a time. Haste is seldom manifest in their approach. Figures appear from every direction, limping slowly, slouching stupidly, or standing with assumed or real indifference, until the end of the line is reached, when they take their places and wait. Most of those in the line are over thirty. There is seldom one under twenty. A low murmur of conversation is heard, but for the most part the men stand in stupid, unbroken silence. Here and there are two or three talkative ones, and if you pass close enough you will hear every topic of the times discussed or referred to, except those which are supposed to interest the poor. Wretchedness, poverty, hunger and distress are never mentioned. The possibilities of a match between prize-ring favorites, the day's evidence in the latest murder trial, the chance of war in Africa, the latest improvements in automobiles, the prosperity or depression of some other portion of the world, or the mistakes of the Government, from Washington to the campaign in Manila. These, or others like them, are the topics of whatever conversation is held. It is for the most part a rambling, disconnected conversation.

"Wait until Dreyfus gets out of prison," said one to his little black-eyed neighbor one night, "and you'll see them guys fallin' on his neck."

"Maybe they will and maybe they won't," the other muttered. "You needn't think, just because you see dagoes selling violets on Broadway, that the spring is here."

The passing of a Broadway car awakens a vague idea of progress, and some one remarks: "They'll have them things running by liquid air before we know it."

"I've driv mule cars by here myself," replies another.

A few moments before twelve a great box of bread is pushed outside the door, and exactly on the hour a portly round-faced German takes his position by it, and calls "Ready." The whole line at once, like a well-drilled company of regulars, moves swiftly, in good marching time, diagonally across the sidewalk to the inner edge and pushes, with only the noise of tramping feet, past the box. Each man reaches for a loaf, and, breaking line, wanders off by himself. Most of them do not even glance at their bread, but put it indifferently under their coats or in their pockets.

In the great sea of men here are these little eddies of driftwood, a hundred nightly in Madison Square, 300 outside a bakery at midnight, crowds without the lodging-houses in stormy weather, and all this day after day. These are the poor in body and in spirit. The lack of houses and lands and fine clothing is nothing. Many have these and are equally wretched. The cause of misery lies elsewhere. The attitude of pity which the world thinks proper to hold toward poverty is misplaced—a result of the failure to see and to realize. Poverty of worldly goods is not in itself pitiful. A sickly body, an ignorant mind, a narrow spirit, brutal impulses and perverted appetites are the pitiful things. The adding of material riches to one thus afflicted would not remove him from out the pitiful. On the other hand, there are so-called poor people in every community among its ornaments. There is no pity for them, but rather love and honor. They are rich in wisdom and influence.

The individuals composing this driftwood are no more miserable than others. Most of them would be far more uncomfortable if compelled to lead respectable lives. They cannot be benefited by money. There may be a class of poor for whom a little money judiciously expended would result in good, but these are the lifeless flotsam and jetsam of society without vitality to ever revive. Few among them would survive a month if they should come suddenly into the possession of a fortune.

Their parade before us should not appeal to our pity, but should awaken us to what we are—for society is no better than its poorest type. They expose what is present, though better concealed, everywhere. They are the few skeletons of the sunlight—types of these with which society's closets are full. Civilization, in spite of its rapid progress, is still in profound ignorance of the things essential to a healthy, happy and prosperous life. Ignorance and error are everywhere manifest in the miseries and sufferings of men. Wealth may create an illusion, or modify a ghastly appearance of ignorance and error, but it cannot change the effect. The result is as real in the mansions of Fifth avenue as in the midnight throng outside a baker's door.

The livid-faced dyspeptic who rides from his club to his apartments and pauses on the way to hand his dollar to the Captain should awaken the same pity as the shivering applicant for a free bed whom his dollar aids—pity for the ignorance and error that cause the distress of the world.

JACK LONDON

The Law of Life

"The Law of Life" was published in *McClure's Magazine* in March 1901 and was later included in the collection *Children of the Frost* (1902). London's Darwinian premises for this tale are explicit: "Nature was not kindly to the flesh. She had no concern for that concrete thing called the individual. Her interest lay in the species, the race." The task of life is to create more life, and its officer is the law of death. Human bonds and affections dissolve, bit by bit, under the ministry of this fundamental law—the love and respect of children, the odd and ineffectual message of the missionary's "talking books," the stature of a chief, the heroism of a hunter—and old Koskoosh is left to die on the frozen tundra. Somewhat paradoxically, London's management of the story compels a sympathy for the dying man at the same that it requires acknowledgment of the necessity of his situation. The old man is blind, and the narrator creates a sense of his diminished world and his imminent death by addressing the reader's ear, not the eye. He hears his tribe breaking camp, preparing to leave him behind; he hears the whimpering of a child and the grunt of the Shaman. The cold darkness and foreboding silence, occasionally punctuated by the howls of wolverines, the dying fire and memories of a vigorous past, create a surreal and unforgiving world. Nevertheless, Koskoosh accepts the law of life as finally rational, and he meets his death with a resigned dignity.

* * *

Old Koskoosh listened greedily. Though his sight had long since faded, his hearing was still acute, and the slightest sound penetrated to the glimmering intelligence which yet abode behind the withered forehead, but which no longer gazed forth upon the things of the world. Ah! that was Sit-cum-to-ha, shrilly anathematizing the dogs as she cuffed and beat them into the harnesses. Sit-cum-to-ha was his daughter's daughter, but she was too busy to waste a thought upon her broken grandfather, sitting alone there in the snow, forlorn and helpless. Camp must be broken. The long trail waited while the short day refused to linger. Life called her, and the duties of life, not death. And he was very close to death now.

The thought made the old man panicky for the moment, and he stretched forth a palsied hand which wandered tremblingly over the small heap of dry wood beside him. Reassured that it was indeed there, his hand returned to the shelter of his mangy furs, and he again fell to listening. The sulky crackling of half-frozen hides told him that the chief's moose-skin lodge had been struck, and even then was being rammed and jammed into portable compass. The chief was his son, stalwart and strong, head man of the tribesmen, and a mighty hunter. As the women toiled with the camp luggage, his voice rose, chiding them for their slowness. Old Koskoosh strained his ears. It was the last time he would hear that voice. There went Geehow's lodge! And Tusken's! Seven, eight, nine; only the Shaman's could be still standing. There! They were at work upon it now. He could hear the Shaman grunt as he piled it on the sled. A child whimpered, and a woman soothed it with soft, crooning gutturals. Little Koo-tee, the old man thought, a fretful child, and not over strong. It would die soon, perhaps, and they would burn a hole through the frozen tundra and pile rocks above to keep the wolverines away. Well, what did it matter? A few years at best, and as many an empty belly as a full one. And in the end, Death waited, ever-hungry and hungriest of them all.

What was that? Oh, the men lashing the sleds and drawing tight the thongs. He listened, who would listen no more. The whip-lashes snarled and bit among the dogs. Hear them whine! How they hated the work and the trail! They were off! Sled after sled churned slowly away into the silence. They were gone. They had passed out of his life, and he faced the last bitter hour alone. No. The snow crunched beneath a moccasin; a man stood beside him; upon his head a hand rested gently. His son was good to do this thing. He remembered other old men whose sons had not waited after the tribe. But his son had. He wandered away into the past, till the young man's voice brought him back.

"Is it well with you?" he asked.

And the old man answered, "It is well."

"There be wood beside you," the younger man continued, "and the fire burns bright. The morning is gray, and the cold has broken. It will snow presently. Even now is it snowing."

"Ay, even now is it snowing."

"The tribesmen hurry. Their bales are heavy, and their bellies flat with lack of feasting. The trail is long and they travel fast. I go now. It is well?"

"It is well. I am as a last year's leaf, clinging lightly to the stem. The first breath that blows, and I fall. My voice is become like an old woman's. My eyes no longer show me the way of my feet, and my feet are heavy, and I am tired. It is well."

He bowed his head in content till the last noise of the complaining snow had died away, and he knew his son was beyond recall. Then his hand crept out in haste to the wood. It alone stood betwixt him and the eternity which yawned in upon him. At last the measure of his life was a handful of fagots. One by one they would go to feed the fire, and just so, step by step, death would creep upon him. When the last stick had surrendered up its heat, the frost would begin to gather strength. First his feet would yield, then his hands; and the numbness would travel, slowly, from the extremities to the body. His head would fall forward upon his knees, and he would rest. It was easy. All men must die.

He did not complain. It was the way of life, and it was just. He had been born close to the earth, close to the earth had he lived, and the law thereof was not new to him. It was the law of all flesh. Nature was not kindly to the flesh. She had no concern for that concrete thing called the individual. Her interest lay in the species, the race. This was the deepest abstraction old Koskoosh's barbaric mind was capable of, but he grasped it firmly. He saw it exemplified in all life. The rise of the sap, the bursting greenness of the willow bud, the fall of the yellow leaf—in this alone was told the whole history. But one task did nature set the individual. Did he not perform it, he died. Did he perform it, it was all the same, he died. Nature did not care; there were plenty who were obedient, and it was only the obedience in this matter, not the obedient, which lived and lived always. The tribe of Koskoosh was very old. The old men he had known when a boy, had known old men before them. Therefore it was true that the tribe lived, that it stood for the obedience of all its members, way down into the forgotten past, whose very resting places were unremembered. They did not count; they were episodes. They had passed away like clouds from a summer sky. He also was an episode, and would pass away. Nature did not care. To life she set one task, gave one law. To perpetuate was the task of life, its law was death. A maiden was a good creature to look upon, full-breasted and strong, with spring to her step and light in her eyes. But her task was yet before her. The light in her eyes brightened, her step quickened, she was now bold with the young men, now timid, and she gave them of her own unrest. And ever she grew fairer and yet fairer to look upon, till some hunter, able no longer to withhold himself, took her to his lodge to cook and toil for him and to become the mother of his children. And with the coming of her offspring her looks left her. Her limbs dragged and shuffled, her eyes dimmed and bleared, and only the little children found joy against the withered cheek of the old squaw by the fire. Her task was done. But a little while, on the first pinch of famine or the first long trail, and she would be left, even as he had been left, in the snow, with a little pile of wood. Such was the law.

He placed a stick carefully upon the fire and resumed his meditations. It was the same everywhere, with all things. The mosquitos vanished with the first frost. The little tree-squirrel crawled away to die. When age settled upon the rabbit it became slow and heavy, and could no longer outfoot its enemies. Even the big bald-face grew clumsy and blind and quarrelsome, in the end to be dragged down by a handful of yelping huskies. He remembered how he had abandoned his own father on an upper reach of the Klondike one winter, the winter before the missionary came with his talk-books and his box of medicines. Many a time had Koskoosh smacked his lips over the recollection of that box, though now his mouth refused to moisten. The "painkiller" had been especially good. But the missionary was a bother after all, for he brought no meat into the camp, and he ate heartily, and the hunters grumbled. But he chilled his lungs on the divide by the Mayo, and the dogs afterwards nosed the stones away and fought over his bones.

Koskoosh placed another stick on the fire and harked back deeper into the past. There was the time of the Great Famine, when the old men crouched empty-bellied to the fire, and from their lips fell dim traditions of the ancient day when the Yukon ran wide open for three winters, and then lay frozen for three summers. He had lost his mother in that famine. In the summer the salmon run had failed, and the tribe looked forward to the winter and the coming of the caribou. Then the winter came, but with it there were no caribou. Never had the like been known, not even in the lives of the old men. But the caribou did not come, and it was the seventh year, and the rabbits had not replenished, and the dogs were naught but bundles of bones. And through the long darkness the children wailed and died, and the women, and the old men; and not one in ten of the tribe lived to meet the sun when it came back in the spring. That *was* a famine!

But he had seen times of plenty, too, when the meat spoiled on their hands, and the dogs were fat and worthless with overeating—times when they let the game go unkilled, and the women were fertile, and the lodges were cluttered with sprawling men-children and women-children. Then it was the men became high-stomached, and revived ancient quarrels, and crossed the divides to the south to kill the Pellys, and to the west that they might sit by the dead fires of the Tananas. He remembered, when a boy, during a time of plenty, when he saw a moose pulled down by the wolves. Zing-ha lay with him in the snow and watched—Zing-ha, who later became the craftiest of hunters, and who, in the end, fell through an air-hole on the Yukon. They found him, a month afterward, just as he had crawled half-way out and frozen stiff to the ice.

But the moose. Zing-ha and he had gone out that day to play at hunting after the manner of their fathers. On the bed of the creek they struck the fresh track of a moose, and with it the tracks of many wolves. "An old one," Zing-ha, who was quicker at reading the sign, said—"an old one who cannot keep up with the herd. The wolves have cut him out from his brothers, and they will never leave him." And it was so. It was their way. By day and by night, never resting, snarling on his heels, snapping at his nose, they would stay by him to the end. How Zing-ha and he felt the blood-lust quicken! The finish would be a sight to see!

Eager-footed, they took the trail, and even he, Koskoosh, slow of sight and an unversed tracker, could have followed it blind, it was so wide. Hot were they on the heels of the chase, reading the grim tragedy, fresh-written, at every step. Now they came to where the moose had made a stand. Thrice the length of a grown man's body, in every direction, had the snow been stamped about and uptossed. In the midst were the deep impressions of the splay-hoofed game, and all about, everywhere, were the lighter footmarks of the wolves. Some, while their brothers harried the kill, had lain to one side and rested. The full-stretched impress of their bodies in the snow was as perfect as though made the moment before. One wolf had been caught in a wild lunge of the maddened victim and trampled to death. A few bones, well picked, bore witness.

Again, they ceased the uplift of their snowshoes at a second stand. Here the great animal had fought desperately. Twice had he been dragged down, as the snow attested, and twice had he shaken his assailants clear and gained footing once more. He had done his task long since, but none the less was life dear to him. Zing-ha said it was a strange thing, a moose once down to get free again; but this one certainly had. The Shaman would see signs and wonders in this when they told him.

And yet again, they came to where the moose had made to mount the bank and gain the timber. But his foes had laid on from behind, till he reared and fell back upon them, crushing two deep into the snow. It was plain the kill was at hand, for their brothers had left them untouched. Two more stands were hurried past, brief in time-length and very close together. The trail was red now, and the clean stride of the great beast had grown short and slovenly. Then they heard the first sounds of the battle—not the full-throated chorus of the chase, but the short, snappy bark which spoke of close quarters and teeth to flesh. Crawling up the wind, Zing-ha bellied it through the snow, and with him crept he, Koskoosh, who was to be chief of the tribesmen in the years to come. Together they shoved aside the under branches of a young spruce and peered forth. It was the end they saw.

The picture, like all of youth's impressions, was still strong with him, and his dim eyes watched the end played out as vividly as in that far-off time. Koskoosh marveled at this, for in the days which followed, when he was a leader of men and a head of councilors, he had done great deeds and made his name a curse in the mouths of the Pellys, to say naught of the strange white man he had killed, knife to knife, in open fight.

For long he pondered on the days of his youth, till the fire died down and the frost bit deeper. He replenished it with two sticks this time, and gauged his grip on life by what remained. If Sit-cum-to-ha had only remembered her grandfather, and gathered a larger armful, his hours would have been longer. It would have been easy. But she was ever a careless child, and honored not her ancestors from the time the Beaver, son of the son of Zing-ha, first cast eyes upon her. Well, what mattered it? Had he not done likewise in his own quick youth? For a while he listened to the silence. Perhaps the heart of his son might soften, and he would come back with the dogs to take his old father on with the tribe to where the caribou ran thick and the fat hung heavy upon them.

He strained his ears, his restless brain for the moment stilled. Not a stir, nothing. He alone took breath in the midst of the great silence. It was very lonely, Hark! What was that? A chill passed over his body. The familiar, long-drawn howl broke the void, and it was close at hand. Then on his darkened eyes was projected the vision of the moose—the old bull moose—the torn flanks and bloody sides, the riddled mane, and the great branching horns, down low and tossing to the last. He saw the flashing forms of gray, the gleaming eyes, the lolling tongues, the slavered fangs. And he saw the inexorable circle close in till it became a dark point in the midst of the stamped snow.

A cold muzzle thrust against his cheek, and at its touch his soul leaped back to the present. His hand shot into the fire and dragged out a burning faggot. Overcome for the nonce by his hereditary fear of man, the brute retreated, raising a prolonged call to his brothers; and greedily they answered, till a ring of crouching, jaw-slobbered gray was stretched round about. The old man listened to the drawing in of this circle. He waved his brand wildly, and sniffs turned to snarls; but the panting brutes refused to scatter. Now one wormed his chest forward, dragging his haunches after, now a second, now a third; but never a one drew back. Why should he cling to life? he asked, and dropped the blazing stick into the snow. It sizzled and went out. The circle grunted uneasily, but held its own. Again he saw the last stand of the old bull moose, and Koskoosh dropped his head wearily upon his knees. What did it matter after all? Was it not the law of life?

FRANK NORRIS

A Deal in Wheat

"A Deal in Wheat" was first published in the San Francisco magazine *The Wave* in 1902 and collected in *A Deal in Wheat and Other Stories of the New and Old West* in 1903. Norris published in *The Responsibilities of the Novelist* (1903) and elsewhere statements of his artistic credo. He thought the realist writer was primarily concerned with "accuracy" and therefore obliged to deal in the mere surfaces of life. The naturalist writer, by contrast, was devoted to dramatizing the "truth" of life and as a consequence needed to penetrate beneath ordinary experience and to find larger generalizations that helped explain the true relations that exist between and among people from various classes and sections of the country. "A Deal in Wheat" illustrates this naturalist premise perfectly. "Bears" are financial speculators who sell stock for delivery in the future, believing, and sometimes knowing, that prices will fall; "bulls" buy low, hoping to sell at a higher price. Both are profittakers, not above manipulating the market for personal gain. For the bear Truslow and the bull Hornung, stock manipulation is thrilling and hilarious theater. The real victims of these transactions do not trade in stocks, however. Sam Lewiston is luckier than most, but he, too, has been caught in the "cogs and wheels of a great and terrible engine." Due to falling wheat prices, he loses his ranch in Kansas and, due to rising wheat prices, he and many others in a bread line on Chicago's South Side are denied food. Lewiston manages to survive, but he also dimly perceives beneath the surface of common experience the true "significance of things."

*   *   *

1

THE BEAR—WHEAT AT SIXTY-TWO

As Sam Lewiston backed the horse into the shafts of his buckboard and began hitching the tugs to the whiffletree, his wife came out from the kitchen door of the house and drew near, and stood for some time at the horse's head, her arms folded and her apron rolled around them. For a long moment neither spoke. They had talked over the situation so long and so comprehensively the night before that there seemed to be nothing more to say.

The time was late in the summer, the place a ranch in southwestern Kansas, and Lewiston and his wife were two of a vast population of farmers, wheat growers, who at that moment were passing through a crisis—a crisis that at any moment might culminate in tragedy. Wheat was down to sixty-six.

At length Emma Lewiston spoke.

"Well," she hazarded, looking vaguely out across the ranch toward the horizon, leagues distant; "well, Sam, there's always that offer of brother Joe's. We can quit—and go to Chicago—if the worst comes."

"And give up!" exclaimed Lewiston, running the lines through the torets. "Leave the ranch! Give up! After all these years!"

His wife made no reply for the moment. Lewiston climbed into the buckboard and gathered up the lines. "Well, here goes for the last try, Emmie," he said. "Good-by, girl. Maybe things will look better in town to-day."

"Maybe," she said gravely. She kissed her husband good-by and stood for some time looking after the buckboard traveling toward the town in a moving pillar of dust.

"I don't know," she murmured at length; "I don't know just how we're going to make out."

When he reached town, Lewiston tied the horse to the iron railing in front of the Odd Fellows' Hall, the ground floor of which was occupied by the post-office, and went across the street and up the stairway of a building of brick and granite—quite the most pretentious structure of the town—and knocked at a door upon the first landing. The door was furnished with a pane of frosted glass, on which, in gold letters, was inscribed, "Bridges & Co., Grain Dealers."

Bridges himself, a middle-aged man who wore a velvet skull-cap and who was smoking a Pittsburg stogie, met the farmer at the counter and the two exchanged perfunctory greetings.

"Well," said Lewiston, tentatively, after awhile.

"Well, Lewiston," said the other, "I can't take that wheat of yours at any better than sixty-two."

"Sixty-*two*."

"It's the Chicago price that does it, Lewiston. Truslow is bearing the stuff for all he's worth. It's Truslow and the bear clique that stick the knife into us. The price broke again this morning. We've just got a wire."

"Good heavens," murmured Lewiston, looking vaguely from side to side. "That—that ruins me. I *can't* carry my grain any longer—what with storage charges and—and——Bridges, I don't see just how I'm going to make out. Sixty-two cents a bushel! Why, man, what with this and with that it's cost me nearly a dollar a bushel to raise that wheat, and now Truslow——"

He turned away abruptly with a quick gesture of infinite discouragement.

He went down the stairs, and making his way to where his buckboard was hitched, got in, and, with eyes vacant, the reins slipping and sliding in his limp, half-open hands, drove slowly back to the ranch. His wife had seen him coming, and met him as he drew up before the barn.

"Well?" she demanded.

"Emmie," he said as he got out of the buckboard, laying his arm across her shoulder, "Emmie, I guess we'll take up with Joe's offer. We'll go to Chicago. We're cleaned out!"

II

THE BULL—WHEAT AT A DOLLAR-TEN

... ——*and said Party of the Second Part further covenants and agrees to merchandise such wheat in foreign ports, it being understood and agreed between the Party of the First Part and the Party of the Second Part that the wheat hereinbefore mentioned is released and sold to the Party of the Second Part for export purposes only, and not for consumption or distribution within the boundaries of the United States of America or of Canada.*

"Now, Mr. Gates, if you will sign for Mr. Truslow I guess that'll be all," remarked Hornung when he had finished reading.

Hornung affixed his signature to the two documents and passed them over to Gates, who signed for his principal and client, Truslow—or, as he had been called ever since he had gone into the fight against Hornung's corner—the Great Bear. Hornung's secretary was called in and witnessed the signatures, and Gates thrust the contract into his Gladstone bag and stood up, smoothing his hat.

"You will deliver the warehouse receipts for the grain," began Gates.

"I'll send a messenger to Truslow's office before noon," interrupted Hornung. "You can pay by certified check through the Illinois Trust people."

When the other had taken himself off, Hornung sat for some moments gazing abstractedly toward his office windows, thinking over the whole matter. He had just agreed to release to Truslow, at the rate of one dollar and ten cents per bushel, one hundred thousand out of the two million and odd bushels of wheat that he, Hornung, controlled, or actually owned. And for the moment he was wondering if, after all, he had done wisely in not goring the Great Bear to actual financial death. He had made him pay one hundred thousand dollars. Truslow was good for this amount. Would it not have been better to have put a prohibitive figure on the grain and forced the Bear into bankruptcy? True, Hornung would then be without his enemy's money, but Truslow would have been eliminated from the situation, and that—so Hornung told himself—was always a consummation most devoutly, strenuously and diligently to be striven for. Truslow once dead was dead, but the Bear was never more dangerous than when desperate.

"But so long as he can't get *wheat*," muttered Hornung at the end of his reflections, "he can't hurt me. And he can't get it. That I *know*."

For Hornung controlled the situation. So far back as the February of that year an "unknown bull" had been making his presence felt on the floor of the Board of Trade. By the middle of March the commercial reports of the daily press had begun to speak of "the powerful bull clique"; a few weeks later that legendary condition of affairs implied and epitomized in the magic words "Dollar Wheat" had been attained, and by the first of April, when the price had been boosted to one dollar and ten cents a bushel, Hornung had disclosed his hand, and in place of mere rumours, the definite and authoritative news that May wheat had been cornered in the Chicago pit went flashing around the world from Liverpool to Odessa and from Duluth to Buenos Ayres.

It was—so the veteran operators were persuaded—Truslow himself who had made Hornung's corner possible. The Great Bear had for once over-reached himself, and, believing himself all-powerful, had hammered the price just the fatal fraction too far down. Wheat had gone to sixty-two—for the time, and under the circumstances, an abnormal price. When the reaction came it was tremendous. Hornung saw his chance, seized it, and in a few months had turned the tables, had cornered the product, and virtually driven the bear clique out of the pit.

On the same day that the delivery of the hundred thousand bushels was made to Truslow, Hornung met his broker at his lunch club.

"Well," said the latter, "I see you let go that line of stuff to Truslow."

Hornung nodded; but the broker added:

"Remember, I was against it from the very beginning. I know we've cleared up over a hundred thou'. I would have fifty times preferred to have lost twice that and *smashed Truslow dead*. Bet you what you like he makes us pay for it somehow."

"Huh!" grunted his principal. "How about insurance, and warehouse charges, and carrying expenses on that lot? Guess we'd have had to pay those, too, if we'd held on."

But the other put up his chin, unwilling to be persuaded. "I won't sleep easy," he declared, "till Truslow is busted."

III

THE PIT

Just as Going mounted the steps on the edge of the pit the great gong struck, a roar of a hundred voices developed with the swiftness of successive explosions, the rush of a hundred men surging downward to the centre of the pit filled the air with the stamp and grind of feet, a hundred hands in eager strenuous gestures tossed upward from out the brown of the crowd, the official reporter in his cage on the margin of the pit leaned far forward with straining ear to catch the opening bid, and another day of battle was begun.

Since the sale of the hundred thousand bushels of wheat to Truslow the "Hornung crowd" had steadily shouldered the price higher until on this particular morning it stood at one dollar and a half. That was Hornung's price. No one else had any grain to sell.

But not ten minutes after the opening, Going was surprised out of all countenance to hear shouted from the other side of the pit these words:

"Sell May at one-fifty."

Going was for the moment touching elbows with Kimbark on one side and with Merriam on the other, all three belonging to the "Hornung crowd." Their answering challenge of "*Sold*" was as the voice of one man. They did not pause to reflect upon the strangeness of the circumstance. (That was for afterward.) Their response to the offer was as unconscious as reflex action and almost as rapid, and before the pit was well aware of what had happened the transaction of one thousand bushels was down upon Going's trading-card and fifteen hundred dollars had changed hands. But here was a marvel—the whole available supply of wheat cornered, Hornung master of the situation, invincible, unassailable; yet behold a man willing to sell, a Bear bold enough to raise his head.

"That was Kennedy, wasn't it, who made that offer?" asked Kimbark, as Going noted down the trade—"Kennedy, that new man?"

"Yes; who do you suppose he's selling for; who's willing to go short at this stage of the game?"

"Maybe he ain't short."

"Short! Great heavens, man; where'd he get the stuff?"

"Blamed if I know. We can account for every handful of May. Steady! Oh, there he goes again."

"Sell a thousand May at one-fifty," vociferated the bear-broker, throwing out his hand, one finger raised to indicate the number of "contracts" offered. This time it was evident that he was attacking the Hornung crowd deliberately, for, ignoring the jam of traders that swept toward him, he looked across the pit to where Going and Kimbark were shouting "*Sold! Sold!*" and nodded his head.

A second time Going made memoranda of the trade, and either the Hornung holdings were increased by two thousand bushels of May wheat or the Hornung bank account swelled by at least three thousand dollars of some unknown short's money.

Of late—so sure was the bull crowd of its position—no one had even thought of glancing at the inspection sheet on the bulletin board. But now one of Going's messengers hurried up to him with the announcement that this sheet showed receipts at Chicago for that morning of twenty-five thousand bushels, and not credited to Hornung. Some one had got hold of a line of wheat overlooked by the "clique" and was dumping it upon them.

"Wire the Chief," said Going over his shoulder to Merriam. This one struggled out of the crowd, and on a telegraph blank scribbled:

> "Strong bear movement—New man—Kennedy—Selling in lots of five contracts—Chicago receipts twenty-five thousand."

The message was despatched, and in a few moments the answer came back, laconic, of military terseness:

> "Support the market."

And Going obeyed, Merriam and Kimbark following, the new broker fairly throwing the wheat at them in thousand-bushel lots.

"Sell May at 'fifty; sell May; sell May." A moment's indecision, an instant's hesitation, the first faint suggestion of weakness, and the market would have broken under them. But for the better part of four hours they stood their ground, taking all that was offered, in constant communication with the Chief, and from time to time stimulated and steadied by his brief, unvarying command:

"Support the market."

At the close of the session they had bought in the twenty-five thousand bushels of May. Hornung's position was as stable as a rock, and the price closed even with the opening figure—one dollar and a half.

But the morning's work was the talk of all La Salle Street. Who was back of the raid? What was the meaning of this unexpected selling? For weeks the pit trading had been merely nominal. Truslow, the Great Bear, from whom the most serious attack might have been expected, had gone to his country seat at Geneva Lake, in Wisconsin, declaring himself to be out of the market entirely. He went bass-fishing every day.

IV

THE BELT LINE

On a certain day toward the middle of the month, at a time when the mysterious Bear had unloaded some eighty thousand bushels upon Hornung, a conference was held in the library of Hornung's home. His broker attended it, and also a clean-faced, bright-eyed individual whose name of Cyrus Ryder might have been found upon the pay-roll of a rather well-known detective agency. For upward of half an hour after the conference began the detective spoke, the other two listening attentively, gravely.

"Then, last of all," concluded Ryder, "I made out I was a hobo, and began stealing rides on the Belt Line Railroad. Know the road? It just circles Chicago. Truslow owns it. Yes? Well, then I began to catch on. I noticed that cars of certain numbers—thirty-one nought thirty-four, thirty-two one ninety—well, the numbers don't matter, but anyhow, these cars were always switched onto the sidings by Mr. Truslow's main elevator D soon as they came in. The wheat was shunted in, and they were pulled out again. Well, I spotted one car and stole a ride on her. Say, look here, *that car went right around the city on the Belt, and came back to D again, and the same wheat in her all the time.* The grain was reinspected—it was raw, I tell you—and the warehouse receipts made out just as though the stuff had come in from Kansas or Iowa."

"The same wheat all the time!" interrupted Hornung.

"The same wheat—your wheat, that you sold to Truslow."

"Great snakes!" ejaculated Hornung's broker. "Truslow never took it abroad at all."

"Took it abroad! Say, he's just been running it around Chicago, like the supers in 'Shenandoah,' round an' round, so you'd think it was a new lot, an' selling it back to you again."

"No wonder we couldn't account for so much wheat."

"Bought it from us at one-ten, and made us buy it back—our own wheat—at one-fifty."

Hornung and his broker looked at each other in silence for a moment. Then all at once Hornung struck the arm of his chair with his fist and exploded in a roar of laughter. The broker stared for one bewildered moment, then followed his example.

"Sold! Sold!" shouted Hornung almost gleefully. "Upon my soul it's as good as a Gilbert and Sullivan show. And we——Oh, Lord! Billy, shake on it, and hats off to my distinguished friend, Truslow. He'll be President some day. Hey! What? Prosecute him? Not I."

"He's done us out of a neat hatful of dollars for all that," observed the broker, suddenly grave.

"Billy, it's worth the price."

"We've got to make it up somehow."

"Well, tell you what. We were going to boost the price to one seventy-five next week, and make that our settlement figure."

"Can't do it now. Can't afford it."

"No. Here; we'll let out a big link; we'll put wheat at two dollars, and let it go at that."

"Two it is, then," said the broker.

V

THE BREAD LINE

The street was very dark and absolutely deserted. It was a district on the "South Side," not far from the Chicago River, given up largely to wholesale stores, and after nightfall was empty of all life. The echoes slept but lightly hereabouts, and the slightest footfall, the faintest noise, woke them upon the instant and sent them clamouring up and down the length of the pavement between the iron shuttered fronts. The only light visible came from the side door of a certain "Vienna" bakery, where at one o'clock in the morning loaves of bread were given away to any who should ask. Every evening about nine o'clock the outcasts began to gather about the side door. The stragglers came in rapidly, and the line—the "bread line," as it was called—began to form. By midnight it was usually some hundred yards in length, stretching almost the entire length of the block.

Toward ten in the evening, his coat collar turned up against the fine drizzle that pervaded the air, his hands in his pockets, his elbows gripping his sides, Sam Lewiston came up and silently took his place at the end of the line.

Unable to conduct his farm upon a paying basis at the time when Truslow, the "Great Bear," had sent the price of grain down to sixty-two cents a bushel, Lewiston had turned over his entire property to his creditors, and, leaving Kansas for good, had abandoned farming, and had left his wife at her sister's boarding-house in Topeka with the understanding that she was to join him in Chicago so soon as he had found a steady job. Then he had come to Chicago and had turned workman. His brother Joe conducted a small hat factory on Archer Avenue, and for a time he found there a meager employment. But difficulties had occurred, times were bad, the hat factory was involved in debts, the repealing of a certain import duty on manufactured felt overcrowded the home market with cheap Belgian and French products, and in the end his brother had assigned and gone to Milwaukee.

Thrown out of work, Lewiston drifted aimlessly about Chicago, from pillar to post, working a little, earning here a dollar, there a dime, but always sinking, sinking, till at last the ooze of the lowest bottom dragged at his feet and the rush of the great ebb went over him and engulfed him and shut him out from the light, and a park bench became his home and the "bread line" his chief makeshift of subsistence.

He stood now in the enfolding drizzle, sodden, stupefied with fatigue. Before and behind stretched the line. There was no talking. There was no sound. The street was empty. It was so still that the passing of a cable-car in the adjoining thoroughfare grated like prolonged rolling explosions, beginning and ending at immeasurable distances. The drizzle descended incessantly. After a long time midnight struck.

There was something ominous and gravely impressive in this interminable line of dark figures, close-pressed, soundless; a crowd, yet absolutely still; a close-packed, silent file, waiting, waiting in the vast deserted night-ridden street; waiting without a word, without a movement, there under the night and under the slow-moving mists of rain.

Few in the crowd were professional beggars. Most of them were workmen, long since out of work, forced into idleness by long-continued "hard times," by ill luck, by sickness. To them the "bread line" was a godsend. At least they could not starve. Between jobs here in the end was something to hold them up—a small platform, as it were, above the sweep of black water, where for a moment they might pause and take breath before the plunge.

The period of waiting on this night of rain seemed endless to those silent, hungry men; but at length there was a stir. The line moved. The side door opened. Ah, at last! They were going to hand out the bread.

But instead of the usual white-aproned undercook with his crowded hampers there now appeared in the doorway a new man—a young fellow who looked like a bookkeeper's assistant. He bore in his hand a placard, which he tacked to the outside of the door. Then he disappeared within the bakery, locking the door after him.

A shudder of poignant despair, an unformed, inarticulate sense of calamity, seemed to run from end to end of the line. What had happened? Those in the rear, unable to read the placard, surged forward, a sense of bitter disappointment clutching at their hearts.

The line broke up, disintegrated into a shapeless throng—a throng that crowded forward and collected in front of the shut door whereon the placard was affixed. Lewiston, with the others, pushed forward. On the placard he read these words:

"Owing to the fact that the price of grain has been increased to two dollars a bushel, there will be no distribution of bread from this bakery until further notice."

Lewiston turned away, dumb, bewildered. Till morning he walked the streets, going on without purpose, without direction. But now at last his luck had turned. Overnight the wheel of his fortunes had creaked and swung upon its axis, and before noon he had found a job in the street-cleaning brigade. In the course of time he rose to be first shift-boss, then deputy inspector, then inspector, promoted to the dignity of driving in a red wagon with rubber tires and drawing a salary instead of mere wages. The wife was sent for and a new start made.

But Lewiston never forgot. Dimly he began to see the significance of things. Caught once in the cogs and wheels of a great and terrible engine, he had seen—none better—its workings. Of all the men who had vainly stood in the "bread line" on that rainy night in early summer, he, perhaps, had been the only one who had struggled up to the surface again. How many others had gone down in the great ebb? Grim question; he dared not think how many.

He had seen the two ends of a great wheat operation—a battle between Bear and Bull. The stories (subsequently published in the city's press) of Truslow's countermove in selling Hornung his own wheat, supplied the unseen section. The farmer—he who raised the wheat— was ruined upon one hand; the working-man—he who consumed it— was ruined upon the other. But between the two, the great operators, who never saw the wheat they traded in, bought and sold the world's food, gambled in the nourishment of entire nations, practised their tricks, their chicanery and oblique shifty "deals," were reconciled in their differences, and went on through their appointed way, jovial, contented, enthroned, and unassailable.

PAUL LAURENCE DUNBAR

The Lynching of Jube Benson

"The Lynching of Jube Benson" was first published in Dunbar's collection of stories *The Heart of Happy Hollow* (1902). That a lynching story should be included in a volume bearing such a seemingly benign pastoral title suggests something of the fierce, if disguised, irony in much of Dunbar's fiction and verse. In 1903, he expressed his anger more openly in the widely reprinted essay "The Fourth of July and Race Outrages": "Every wire, no longer in the South alone, brings us news of a new hanging or a new burning, some recent outrage against a helpless people, some fresh degradation of an already degraded race." Dunbar was not exaggerating; between 1889 and 1918, more than 2,500 lynchings of African Americans occurred, principally but not exclusively in the South. Given the political urgency of the situation and the outrageous nature of the crime, Dunbar's careful modulation of this narrative demonstrates remarkable artistic control of his material. The white narrator speaks out of a well of unwanted recollection and sad acquaintance with his own barbarity, and the consequences of his "blood guilt" are betrayed by the gray hair and lined face of a man barely thirty years old. Jube Benson is lynched by ordinary citizens who too casually disregard common virtue and whose racism stems from a perversely easy and traditional way of thinking about blacks. This seems to be the understanding the narrator wishes to convey when he says, "All human love and gratitude are damned poor things. . . . The truth is a nasty thing to stand."

* * *

Gordon Fairfax's library held but three men, but the air was dense with clouds of smoke. The talk had drifted from one topic to another much as the smoke wreaths had puffed, floated, and thinned away. Then Handon Gay, who was an ambitious young reporter, spoke of a lynching story in a recent magazine, and the matter of punishment without trial put new life into the conversation.

"I should like to see a real lynching," said Gay rather callously.

"Well, I should hardly express it that way," said Fairfax, "but if a real, live lynching were to come my way, I should not avoid it."

"I should," spoke the other from the depths of his chair, where he had been puffing in moody silence. Judged by his hair, which was freely sprinkled with gray, the speaker might have been a man of forty-five or fifty, but his face, though lined and serious, was youthful, the face of a man hardly past thirty.

"What, you, Dr. Melville? Why, I thought that you physicians wouldn't weaken at anything."

"I have seen one such affair," said the doctor gravely, "in fact, I took a prominent part in it."

"Tell us about it," said the reporter, feeling for his pencil and note-book, which he was, nevertheless, careful to hide from the speaker.

The men drew their chairs eagerly up to the doctor's, but for a minute he did not seem to see them, but sat gazing abstractedly into the fire, then he took a long draw upon his cigar and began:

"I can see it all very vividly now. It was in the summer time and about seven years ago. I was practicing at the time down in the little town of Bradford. It was a small and primitive place, just the location for an impecunious medical man, recently out of college.

"In lieu of a regular office, I attended to business in the first of two rooms which I rented from Hiram Daly, one of the more prosperous of the townsmen. Here I boarded and here also came my patients—white and black—whites from every section, and blacks from 'nigger town,' as the west portion of the place was called.

"The people about me were most of them coarse and rough, but they were simple and generous, and as time passed on I had about abandoned my intention of seeking distinction in wider fields and determined to settle into the place of a modest country doctor. This was rather a strange conclusion for a young man to arrive at, and I will not deny that the presence in the house of my host's beautiful young daughter, Annie, had something to do with my decision. She was a beautiful young girl of seventeen or eighteen, and very far superior to her surroundings. She had a native grace and a pleasing way about her that made everybody that came under her spell her abject slave. White and black who knew her loved her, and none, I thought, more deeply and respectfully than Jube Benson, the black man of all work about the place.

"He was a fellow whom everybody trusted; an apparently steady-going, grinning sort, as we used to call him. Well, he was completely under Miss Annie's thumb, and would fetch and carry for her like a faithful dog. As soon as he saw that I began to care for Annie, and anybody could see that, he transferred some of his allegiance to me and became my faithful servitor also. Never did a man have a more devoted adherent in his wooing than did I, and many a one of Annie's tasks which he volunteered to do gave her an extra hour with me. You can imagine that I liked the boy and you need not wonder any more than as both wooing and my practice waxed apace, I was content to give up my great ambitions and stay just where I was.

"It wasn't a very pleasant thing, then, to have an epidemic of typhoid break out in the town that kept me going so that I hardly had time for the courting that a fellow wants to carry on with his sweetheart while he is still young enough to call her his girl. I fumed, but duty was duty, and I kept to my work night and day. It was now that Jube proved how invaluable he was as a coadjutor. He not only took messages to Annie, but brought sometimes little ones from her to me, and he would tell me little secret things that he had overheard her say that made me throb with joy and swear at him for repeating his mistress's conversation. But best of all, Jube was a perfect Cerberus, and no one on earth could have been more effective in keeping away or deluding the other young fellows who visited the Dalys. He would tell me of it afterward, chuckling softly to himself. 'An,' Doctah, I say to Mistah Hemp Stevens, " 'Scuse us, Mistah Stevens, but Miss Annie, she des gone out," an' den he go outer de gate lookin' moughty lonesome. When Sam Elkins come, I say, "Sh, Mistah Elkins, Miss Annie, she done tuk down," an' he say, "What, Jube, you don' reckon hit de——" Den he stop an' look skeert, an' I say, "I feared hit is, Mistah Elkins," an' sheks my haid ez solemn. He goes outer de gate lookin' lak his bes' frien' done daid, an' all de time Miss Annie behine de cu'tain ovah de po'ch des' a laffin' fit to kill.'

"Jube was a most admirable liar, but what could I do? He knew that I was a young fool of a hypocrite, and when I would rebuke him for these deceptions, he would give way and roll on the floor in an excess of delighted laughter until from very contagion I had to join him—and, well, there was no need of my preaching when there had been no beginning to his repentance and when there must ensue a continuance of his wrongdoing.

"This thing went on for over three months, and then, pouf! I was down like a shot. My patients were nearly all up, but the reaction from overwork made me an easy victim of the lurking germs. Then Jube loomed up as a nurse. He put everyone else aside, and with the doctor, a friend of mine from a neighboring town, took entire charge of me. Even Annie herself was put aside, and I was cared for as tenderly as a baby. Tom, that was my physician and friend, told me all about it afterward with tears in his eyes. Only he was a big, blunt man and his expressions did not convey all that he meant. He told me how my nigger had nursed me as if I were a sick kitten and he my mother. Of how fiercely he guarded his right to be the sole one to 'do' for me, as he called it, and how, when the crisis came, he hovered, weeping, but hopeful, at my bedside, until it was safely passed, when they drove him, weak and exhausted, from the room. As for me, I knew little about it at the time, and cared less. I was too busy in my fight with death. To my chimerical vision there was only a black but gentle demon that came and went, alternating with a white fairy, who would insist on coming in on her head, growing larger and larger and then dissolving. But the pathos and devotion in the story lost nothing in my blunt friend's telling.

"It was during the period of a long convalescence, however, that I came to know my humble ally as he really was, devoted to the point of abjectness. There were times when for very shame at his goodness to me, I would beg him to go away, to do something else. He would go, but before I had time to realize that I was not being ministered to, he would be back at my side, grinning and pottering just the same. He manufactured duties for the joy of performing them. He pretended to see desires in me that I never had, because he liked to pander to them, and when I became entirely exasperated, and ripped out a good round oath, he chuckled with the remark, 'Dah, now, you sholy is gittin' well. Nevah did hyeah a man anywhaih nigh Jo'dan's sho' cuss lak dat.'

"Why, I grew to love him, love him, oh, yes, I loved him as well— oh, what am I saying? All human love and gratitude are damned poor things; excuse me, gentlemen, this isn't a pleasant story. The truth is usually a nasty thing to stand.

"It was not six months after that that my friendship to Jube, which he had been at such great pains to win, was put to too severe a test.

"It was in the summer again, and as business was slack, I had ridden over to see my friend, Dr. Tom. I had spent a good part of the day there, and it was past four o'clock when I rode leisurely into Bradford.

I was in a particularly joyous mood and no premonition of the impending catastrophe oppressed me. No sense of sorrow, present or to come forced itself upon me, even when I saw men hurrying through the almost deserted streets. When I got within sight of my home and saw a crowd surrounding it, I was only interested sufficiently to spur my horse into a jog trot, which brought me up to the throng, when something in the sullen, settled horror in the men's faces gave me a sudden, sick thrill. They whispered a word to me, and without a thought, save for Annie, the girl who had been so surely growing into my heart, I leaped from the saddle and tore my way through the people to the house.

"It was Annie, poor girl, bruised and bleeding, her face and dress torn from struggling. They were gathered round her with white faces, and, oh, with what terrible patience they were trying to gain from her fluttering lips the name of her murderer. They made way for me and I knelt at her side. She was beyond my skill, and my will merged with theirs. One thought was in our minds.

" 'Who?' I asked.

"Her eyes half opened, 'That black——' She fell back into my arms dead.

"We turned and looked at each other. The mother had broken down and was weeping, but the face of the father was like iron.

" 'It is enough,' he said; 'Jube has disappeared.' He went to the door and said to the expectant crowd, 'She is dead.'

"I heard the angry roar without swelling up like the noise of a flood, and then I heard the sudden movement of many feet as the men separated into searching parties, and laying the dead girl back upon her couch, I took my rifle and went out to join them.

"As if by intuition the knowledge had passed among the men that Jube Benson had disappeared, and he, by common consent, was to be the object of our search. Fully a dozen of the citizens had seen him hastening toward the woods and noted his skulking air, but as he had grinned in his old good-natured way, they had, at the time, thought nothing of it. Now, however, the diabolical reason of his slyness was apparent. He had been shrewd enough to disarm suspicion, and by now was far away. Even Mrs. Daly, who was visiting with a neighbor, had seen him stepping out a back way, and had said with a laugh, 'I reckon that black rascal's a-running off somewhere.' Oh, if she had only known.

" 'To the woods! To the woods!' that was the cry, and away we went, each with the determination not to shoot, but to bring the culprit alive into town, and then to deal with him as his crime deserved.

"I cannot describe the feelings I experienced as I went out that night to beat the woods for this human tiger. My heart smoldered within me like a coal, and I went forward under the impulse of a will that was half my own, half some more malignant power's. My throat throbbed dryly, but water nor whiskey would not have quenched my thirst. The thought has come to me since that now I could interpret the panther's desire for blood and sympathize with it, but then I thought nothing. I simply went forward, and watched, watched with burning eyes for a familiar form that I had looked for as often before with such different emotions.

"Luck or ill-luck, which you will, was with our party, and just as dawn was graying the sky, we came upon our quarry crouched in the corner of a fence. It was only half light, and we might have passed, but my eyes had caught sight of him, and I raised the cry. We leveled our guns and he rose and came toward us.

" 'I t'ought you wa'n't gwine see me,' he said sullenly, 'I didn't mean no harm.'

" 'Harm!'

"Some of the men took the word up with oaths, others were ominously silent.

"We gathered around him like hungry beasts, and I began to see terror dawning in his eyes. He turned to me, 'I's moughty glad you's hyeah, doc,' he said, 'you ain't gwine let 'em whup me.'

" 'Whip you, you hound,' I said, 'I'm going to see you hanged,' and in the excess of my passion I struck him full on the mouth. He made a motion as if to resent the blow against even such odds, but controlled himself.

" 'W'y, doctah,' he exclaimed in the saddest voice I have ever heard, 'w'y, doctor! I ain't stole nuffin' o' yo'n, an' I was comin' back. I only run off to see my gal, Lucy, ovah to de Centah.'

" 'You lie!' I said, and my hands were busy helping the others bind him upon a horse. Why did I do it? I don't know. A false education, I reckon, one false from the beginning. I saw his black face glooming there in the half light, and I could only think of him as a monster. It's tradition. At first I was told that the black man would catch me, and when I got over that, they taught me that the devil was black, and when I had recovered from the sickness of that belief, here were Jube and his fellows with faces of menacing blackness. There was only one conclusion: This black man stood for all the powers of evil, the result of whose machinations had been gathering in my mind from childhood up. But this has nothing to do with what happened.

"After firing a few shots to announce our capture, we rode back into town with Jube. The ingathering parties from all directions met us as we made our way up to the house. All was very quiet and orderly. There

was no doubt that it was as the papers would have said, a gathering of
the best citizens. It was a gathering of stern, determined men, bent on
a terrible vengeance.

"We took Jube into the house, into the room where the corpse lay.
At sight of it, he gave a scream like an animal's and his face went the
color of storm-brown water. This was enough to condemn him. We
divined, rather than heard, his cry of 'Miss Ann, Miss Ann, oh, my
God, doc, you don't t'ink I done it?'

"Hungry hands were ready. We hurried him out into the yard. A
rope was ready. A tree was at hand. Well, that part was the least of it,
save that Hiram Daly stepped aside to let me be the first to pull upon
the rope. It was lax at first, and I felt the quivering soft weight resist
my muscles. Other hands joined, and Jube swung off his feet.

"No one was masked. We knew each other. Not even the culprit's
face was covered, and the last I remember of him as he went into the
air was a look of sad reproach that will remain with me until I meet
him face to face again.

"We were tying the end of the rope to a tree, where the dead man
might hang as a warning to his fellows, when a terrible cry chilled us
to the marrow.

" 'Cut 'im down, cut 'im down, he ain't guilty. We got de one. Cut
him down, fu' Gawd's sake. Here's de man, we foun' him hidin' in de
barn!'

"Jube's brother, Ben, and another Negro, came rushing toward us,
half dragging, half carrying a miserable-looking wretch between them.
Someone cut the rope and Jube dropped lifeless to the ground.

" 'Oh, my Gawd, he's daid, he's daid!' wailed the brother, but with
blazing eyes he brought his captive into the center of the group, and we
saw in the full light the scratched face of Tom Skinner—the worst white
ruffian in the town—but the face we saw was not as we were accustomed to see it, merely smeared with dirt. It was blackened to imitate
a Negro's.

"God forgive me; I could not wait to try to resuscitate Jube. I knew
he was already past help, so I rushed into the house and to the dead
girl's side. In the excitement they had not yet washed or laid her out.
Carefully, carefully, I searched underneath her broken finger nails. There
was skin there. I took it out, the little curled pieces, and went with it
to my office.

"There, determinedly, I examined it under a powerful glass, and read
my own doom. It was the skin of a white man, and in it were embedded
strands of short, brown hair or beard.

"How I went out to tell the waiting crowd I do not know, for something kept crying in my ears, 'Blood guilty! Blood guilty!'

"The men went away stricken into silence and awe. The new prisoner attempted neither denial nor plea. When they were gone I would have helped Ben carry his brother in, but he waved me away fiercely, 'You he'ped murder my brotha, you dat was *his* frien', go 'way, go 'way! I'll tek him home myse'f.' I could only respect his wish, and he and his comrade took up the dead man and between them bore him up the street on which the sun was now shining full.

"I saw the few men who had not skulked indoors uncover as they passed, and I—I—stood there between the two murdered ones, while all the while something in my ears kept crying, 'Blood guilty! Blood guilty!' "

The doctor's head dropped into his hands and he sat for some time in silence, which was broken by neither of the men, then he rose, saying, "Gentlemen, that was my last lynching."

JOHN M. OSKISON

The Problem of Old Harjo

"The Problem of Old Harjo," John M. Oskison's best-known short story, was published in *The Southern Workman* in 1907. It is an intriguing study in cultural anthropology documenting the conflict of values when two cultures interact. In this case, a dominant Christian society attempts to impose its traditions and religious prescriptions upon Old Harjo and his two wives. Indeed, Harjo is described, imagistically, as a patriarch comparable to Abraham, the father of the ancient Hebrews. The Christian missionaries in this story have no regard for Harjo's Cherokee religious customs but seek to force him to conform to their values or face eternal damnation. They are initially oblivious to the loving and mutually supportive relationship Harjo exhibits with his two wives, but eventually the idealistic Miss Evans comes to realize that there is no compelling reason to interfere with a happy domestic arrangement, one that may even be better than that of many traditional Christian families.

*   *   *

The Spirit of the Lord had descended upon old Harjo. From the new missionary, just out from New York, he had learned that he was a sinner. The fire in the new missionary's eyes and her gracious appeal had convinced old Harjo that this was the time to repent and be saved.

He was very much in earnest, and he assured Miss Evans that he wanted to be baptized and received into the church at once. Miss Evans was enthusiastic and went to Mrs. Rowell with the news. It was Mrs. Rowell who had said that it was no use to try to convert the older Indians, and she, after fifteen years of work in Indian Territory missions, should have known. Miss Evans was pardonably proud of her conquest.

"Old Harjo converted!" exclaimed Mrs. Rowell. "Dear Miss Evans, do you know that old Harjo has two wives?" To the older woman it was as if some one had said to her "Madame, the Sultan of Turkey wishes to teach one of your mission Sabbath school classes."

"But," protested the younger woman, "he is really sincere, and—

"Then ask him," Mrs. Rowell interrupted a bit sternly, "if he will put away one of his wives. Ask him, before he comes into the presence of the Lord, if he is willing to conform to the laws of the country in which he lives, the country that guarantees his idle existence. Miss Evans, your work is not even begun." No one who knew Mrs. Rowell would say that she lacked sincerity and patriotism. Her own cousin was an earnest crusader against Mormonism, and had gathered a goodly share of that wagonload of protests that the Senate had been asked to read when it was considering whether a certain statesman of Utah should be allowed to represent his state at Washington.

In her practical, tactful way, Mrs. Rowell had kept clear of such embarrassments. At first, she had written letters of indignant protest to the Indian Office against the toleration of bigamy amongst the tribes. A wise inspector had been sent to the mission, and this man had pointed out that it was better to ignore certain things, "deplorable, to be sure," than to attempt to make over the habits of the old men. Of course, the young Indians would not be permitted to take more than one wife each."

So Mrs. Rowell had discreetly limited her missionary efforts to the young, and had exercised toward the old and bigamous only that strict charity which even a hopeless sinner might claim.

Miss Evans, it was to be regretted, had only the vaguest notions about "expediency;" so weak on matters of doctrine was she that the news that Harjo was living with two wives didn't startle her. She was young and possessed of but one enthusiasm—that for saving souls.

"I suppose," she ventured, "that old Harjo *must* put away one wife before he can join the church?"

"There can be no question about it, Miss Evans."

"Then I shall have to ask him to do it." Miss Evans regretted the necessity for forcing this sacrifice, but had no doubt that the Indian would make it an order to accept the gift of salvation which she was commissioned to bear to him.

Harjo lived in a "double" log cabin three miles from the mission. His ten acres of corn had been gathered into its fence-rail crib; four hogs that were to furnish his winter's bacon had been brought in from the woods and penned conveniently near to the crib; out in a corner of the garden, a fat mound of dirt rose where the crop of turnips and potatoes had been buried against the corrupting frost; and in the hayloft of his log stable were stored many pumpkins, dried corn, onions (suspended in bunches from the rafters) and the varied forage that Mrs. Harjo number one and Mrs. Harjo number two had thriftily provided. Three cows, three young heifers, two colts, and two patient, capable mares bore the Harjo brand, a fantastic "H—I" that the old man had designed. Materially, Harjo was solvent; and if the Government had ever come to his aid he could not recall the date.

This attempt to rehabilitate old Harjo morally, Miss Evans felt, was not one to be made at the mission; it should be undertaken in the Creek's own home where the evidences of his sin should confront him as she explained.

When Miss Evans rode up to the block in front of Harjo's cabin, the old Indian came out, slowly and with a broadening smile of welcome on his face. A clean gray flannel shirt had taken the place of the white collarless garment, with crackling stiff bosom, that he had worn to the mission meetings. Comfortable, well-patched moccasins had been substituted for creaking boots, and brown corduroys, belted in at the waist, for tight black trousers. His abundant gray hair fell down on his shoulders. In his eyes, clear and large and black, glowed the light of true hospitality. Miss Evans thought of the patriarchs as she saw him lead her horse out to the stable; thus Abraham might have looked and lived.

"Harjo," began Miss Evans before following the old man to the covered passageway between the disconnected cabins, "is it true that you have two wives?" Her tone was neither stern nor accusatory. The Creek had heard that question before, from scandalized missionaries and perplexed registry clerks when he went to Muscogee to enroll himself and his family in one of the many "final" records ordered to be made by the Government preparatory to dividing the Creek lands among the individual citizens.

For answer, Harjo called, first into the cabin that was used as a kitchen and then, in a loud, clear voice, toward the small field, where Miss Evans saw a flock of half-grown turkeys running about in the corn stubble. From the kitchen emerged a tall, thin Indian woman of fifty-five, with a red handkerchief bound severely over her head. She spoke to Miss Evans and sat down in the passageway. Presently, a clear, sweet voice was heard in the field; a stout, handsome woman, about the same age as the other, climbed the rail fence and came up to the house. She, also, greeted Miss Evans briefly. Then she carried a tin basin to the well near by, where she filled it to the brim. Setting it down on the horse block, she rolled back her sleeves, tucked in the collar of her gray blouse, and plunged her face in the water. In a minute she came out of the kitchen freshened and smiling. 'Liza Harjo had been pulling dried bean stalks at one end of the field, and it was dirty work. At last old Harjo turned to Miss Evans and said, "These two my wife—this one 'Liza, this one Jennie."

It was done with simple dignity. Miss Evans bowed and stammered. Three pairs of eyes were turned upon her in patient, courteous inquiry.

It was hard to state the case. The old man was so evidently proud of his women, and so flattered by Miss Evans' interest in them, that he would find it hard to understand. Still, it had to be done, and Miss Evans took the plunge.

"Harjo, you want to come into our church?" The old man's face lighted.

"Oh, yes, I would come to Jesus, please, my friend."

"Do you know, Harjo, that the Lord commanded that one man should mate with but one woman? The question was stated again in simpler terms, and the Indian replied, "Me know that now, my friend. Long time ago"—Harjo plainly meant the whole period previous to his conversion—"me did not know. The Lord Jesus did not speak to me in that time and so I was blind. I do what blind man do."

"Harjo, you must have only one wife when you come into our church. Can't you give up one of these women?" Miss Evans glanced at the two, sitting by with smiles of polite interest on their faces, understanding nothing. They had not shared Harjo's enthusiasm either for the white man's God or his language.

"Give up my wife?" A sly smile stole over his face. He leaned closer to Miss Evans. "You tell me, my friend, which one I give up." He glanced from 'Liza to Jennie as if to weigh their attractions, and the two rewarded him with their pleasantest smiles. "You tell me which one," he urged.

"Why, Harjo, how can I tell you!" Miss Evans had little sense of humor; she had taken the old man seriously.

"Then," Harjo sighed, continuing the comedy, for surely the missionary was jesting with him, " 'Liza and Jennie must say." He talked to the Indian women for a time, and they laughed heartily. 'Liza, pointing to the other, shook her head. At length Harjo explained, "My friend, they cannot say. Jennie, she would run a race to see which one stay, but 'Liza, she say no, she is fat and cannot run."

Miss Evans comprehended at last. She flushed angrily, and protested,

"Harjo, you are making a mock of a sacred subject; I cannot allow you to talk like this."

"But did you not speak in fun, my friend?" Harjo queried, sobering. "Surely you have just said what your friend, the white woman at the mission (he meant Mrs. Rowell) would say, and you do not mean what you say."

"Yes, Harjo, I mean it. It is true that Mrs. Rowell raised the point first, but I agree with her. The church cannot be defiled by receiving a bigamist into its membership." Harjo saw that the young woman was serious, distressingly serious. He was silent for a long time, but at last he raised his head and spoke quietly, "It is not good to talk like that if it is not in fun."

He rose and went to the stable. As he led Miss Evans' horse up to the block it was champing a mouthful of corn, the last of a generous portion that Harjo had put before it. The Indian held the bridle and waited for Miss Evans to mount. She was embarrassed, humiliated, angry. It was absurd to be dismissed in this way by—"by an ignorant old bigamist!" Then the humor of it burst upon her, and its human aspect. In her anxiety concerning the spiritual welfare of the sinner Harjo, she had insulted the man Harjo. She began to understand why Mrs. Rowell had said that the old Indians were hopeless.

"Harjo," she begged, coming out of the passageway, "please forgive me. I do not want you to give up one of your wives. Just tell me why you took them."

"I will tell you that, my friend." The old Creek looped the reins over his arm and sat down on the block. "For thirty years Jennie has lived with me as my wife. She is of the Bear people, and she came to me when I was thirty-five and she was twenty-five. She could not come before, for her mother was old, very old, and Jennie, she stay with her and feed her.

"So, when I was thirty years old I took 'Liza for my woman. She is of the Crow people. She help me make this little farm here when there was no farm for many miles around.

"Well, five years 'Liza and me, we live here and work hard. But there was no child. Then the old mother of Jennie she died, and Jennie got no family left in this part of the country. So 'Liza say to me, 'Why don't you take Jennie in here?' I say, 'You don't care?' and she say, 'No, maybe we have children here then.' But we have no children—never have children. We do not like that, but God He would not let it be. So, we have lived here thirty years very happy. Only just now you make me sad."

"Harjo," cried Miss Evans, "forget what I said. Forget that you wanted to join the church." For a young mission worker with a single purpose always before her, Miss Evans was saying a strange thing. Yet she couldn't help saying it; all of her zeal seemed to have been dissipated by a simple statement of the old man.

"I cannot forget to love Jesus, and I want to be saved." Old Harjo spoke with solemn earnestness. The situation was distracting. On one side stood a convert eager for the protection of the church, asking only that he be allowed to fulfill the obligations of humanity and on the other stood the church, represented by Mrs. Rowell, that set an impossible condition on receiving old Harjo to itself. Miss Evans wanted to cry; prayer, she felt, would be entirely inadequate as a means of expression.

"Oh! Harjo," she cried out, "I don't know what to do. I must think it over and talk with Mrs. Rowell again."

But Mrs. Rowell could suggest no way out; Miss Evans' talk with her only gave the older woman another opportunity to preach the folly of wasting time on the old and "unreasonable" Indians. Certainly the church could not listen even to a hint of a compromise in this case. If Harjo wanted to be saved there was one way and only one—unless—

"Is either of the two women old? I mean, so old that she is—an—"

"Not at all," answered Miss Evans. "They're both strong and—yes, happy. I think they will outlive Harjo."

"Can't you appeal to one of the women to go away? I dare say we could provide for her." Miss Evans, incongruously, remembered Jennie's jesting proposal to race for the right to stay with Harjo. What could the mission provide as a substitute for the little home that 'Liza had helped to create there in the edge of the woods? What other home would satisfy Jennie?

"Mrs. Rowell, are you sure that we ought to try to take one of Harjo's women from him? I'm not sure that it would in the least advance morality amongst the tribe, but I'm certain that it would make three gentle people unhappy for the rest of their lives."

"You may be right, Miss Evans." Mrs. Rowell was not seeking to create unhappiness, for enough of it inevitably came to be pictured in the little mission building. "You may be right," she repeated, "but it is a grievous misfortune that old Harjo should wish to unite with the church."

No one was more regular in his attendance at the mission meetings than old Harjo. Sitting well forward, he was always in plain view of Miss Evans at the organ. Before the service began, and after it was over, the old man greeted the young woman. There was never a spoken question, but in the Creek's eyes was always a mute inquiry.

Once Miss Evans ventured to write to her old pastor in New York, and explain her trouble. This was what he wrote in reply: "I am surprised that you are troubled, for I should have expected you to rejoice, as I do, over this new and wonderful evidence of the Lord's reforming power. Though the church cannot receive the old man so long as he is confessedly a bigamist and violator of his country's just laws, you should be greatly strengthened in your work through bringing him to desire salvation."

"Oh! it's easy to talk when you're free from responsibility!" cried out Miss Evans. "But I woke him up to a desire for this water of salvation that he cannot take. I have seen Harjo's home, and I know how cruel and useless it would be to urge him to give up what he loves— for he does love those two women who have spent half their lives and more with him. What, what can be done!"

Month after month, as old Harjo continued to occupy his seat in the mission meetings, with that mute appeal in his eyes and a persistent light of hope on his face, Miss Evans repeated the question, "What can be done?" If she was sometimes tempted to say to the old man, "Stop worrying about your soul; you'll get to Heaven as surely as any of us," there was always Mrs. Rowell to remind her that she was not a Mormon missionary. She could not run away from her perplexity. If she should secure a transfer to another station, she felt that Harjo would give up coming to the meetings, and in his despair become a positive influence for evil amongst his people. Mrs. Rowell would not waste her energy on an obstinate old man. No, Harjo was her creation, her impossible convert, and throughout the years, until death—the great solvent which is not always a solvent—came to one of them, would continue to haunt her.

And meanwhile, what?

JACK LONDON

To Build a Fire

"To Build a Fire" was first published in *The Century Magazine* in August 1908 and later included in the volume of short stories *Lost Face* (1910); an earlier and happier version written for young readers was published in *Youth's Companion* in May 1902. Unlike Twain's tenderfoot, who is almost always a comic figure, London's *chechaquo*, or newcomer to the Yukon, is a tragic figure and something of an Everyman. And unlike his fellow naturalist, Theodore Dreiser, who tends to fill his narratives with an abundance of "things," London so severely reduces his landscapes to bare essentials that virtually every object and feature functions symbolically. That London conceived of his protagonist as a representative, even allegorical figure is evidenced by the fact that, in revision, he deleted all references to the prospector's name and substituted the phrase "the man." This man's tragic flaw resides in his own high opinion of his capacities, and his actual limitations are dramatically highlighted by the narrative shifts between a vulnerable human consciousness and that of a dog ruled by sure instinct. He is the tragic victim of the harsh environment he fatally underestimates, but the quality of detachment in the narrator creates a dramatic tension that sustains the narrative and serves to underscore London's Darwinian vision of life.

*   *   *

He travels fastest who travels alone . . . but not after the
frost has dropped below zero fifty degrees or more.
—*Yukon Code.*

Day had broken cold and gray, exceedingly cold and gray, when the man turned aside from the main Yukon trail and climbed the high earthbank, where a dim and little-traveled trail led eastward through the fat spruce timberland. It was a steep bank, and he paused for breath at the top, excusing the act to himself by looking at his watch. It was nine o'clock. There was no sun or hint of sun, though there was not a cloud in the sky. It was a clear day, and yet there seemed an intangible pall over the face of things, a subtle gloom that made the day dark, and that was due to the absence of sun. This fact did not worry the man. He was used to the lack of sun. It had been days since he had seen the sun, and he knew that a few more days must pass before that cheerful orb, due south, would just peep above the sky-line and dip immediately from view.

The man flung a look back along the way he had come. The Yukon lay a mile wide and hidden under three feet of ice. On top of this ice were as many feet of snow. It was all pure white, rolling in gentle, snow-covered undulations where the ice-jams of the freeze-up had formed. North and south, as far as his eye could see, it was unbroken white, save for a dark hair-line that curved and twisted from around the spruce-covered island to the south, and that curved and twisted away into the north, where it disappeared behind another spruce-covered island. This dark hair-line was the trail—the main trail—that led south five hundred miles to the Chilcoot Pass, Dyea, and salt water; and that led north seventy miles to Dawson, and still on to the north a thousand miles to Nulato, and finally to St. Michael on Bering Sea, a thousand miles and half a thousand more.

But all this—the mysterious, far-reaching hair-line trail, the absence of sun from the sky, the tremendous cold, and the strangeness and weirdness of it all—made no impression on the man. It was not because he was long used to it. He was a new-comer in the land, a *chechaquo,* and this was his first winter. The trouble with him was that he was without imagination. He was quick and alert in the things of life, but only in the things, and not in the significances. Fifty degrees below zero meant eighty-odd degrees of frost. Such fact impressed him as being cold and uncomfortable, and that was all. It did not lead him to meditate upon his frailty as a creature of temperature, and upon man's frailty in general, able only to live within certain narrow limits of temperature; and from there on it did not lead him to the conjectural field of immortality and man's place in the universe. Fifty degrees below zero stood for a bite of frost that hurt and that must be guarded against by the use of mittens, ear-flaps, warm moccasins, and thick socks. Fifty degrees below zero was to him just precisely fifty degrees below zero. That there should be anything more to it than that was a thought that never entered his head.

As he turned to go on, he spat speculatively. There was a sharp, explosive crackle that startled him. He spat again. And again, in the air, before it could fall to the snow, the spittle crackled. He knew that at fifty below spittle crackled on the snow, but this spittle had crackled in the air. Undoubtedly it was colder than fifty below—how much colder he did not know. But the temperature did not matter. He was bound for the old claim on the left fork of Henderson Creek, where the boys were already. They had come over across the divide from the Indian Creek country while he had come the round-about way to take a look at the possibilities of getting out logs in the spring from the islands in the Yukon. He would be in to camp by six o'clock; a bit after dark, it was true, but the boys would be there, a fire would be going, and a hot supper would be ready. As for lunch, he pressed his hand against the protruding bundle under his jacket. It was also under his shirt, wrapped up in a handkerchief, and lying against the naked skin. It was the only way to keep the biscuits from freezing. He smiled agreeably to himself as he thought of those biscuits, each cut open and sopped in bacon grease, and each inclosing a generous slice of fried bacon.

He plunged in among the big spruce-trees. The trail was faint. A foot of snow had fallen since the last sled had passed over, and he was glad he was without a sled, traveling light. In fact, he carried nothing but the lunch wrapped in the handkerchief. He was surprised, however, at the cold. It certainly was cold, he concluded, as he rubbed his numb nose and cheek-bones with his mittened hand. He was a warm-whiskered man, but the hair on his face did not protect the high cheek-bones and the eager nose that thrust itself aggressively into the frosty air.

At the man's heels trotted a dog, a big native husky, the proper wolf-dog, gray-coated and without any visible or temperamental difference from its brother, the wild wolf. The animal was depressed by the tremendous cold. It knew that it was no time for traveling. Its instinct told it a truer tale than was told to the man by the man's judgment. In reality, it was not merely colder than fifty below zero; it was colder than sixty below, than seventy below. It was seventy-five below zero. Since the freezing-point is thirty-two above zero, it meant that one hundred and seven degrees of frost obtained. The dog did not know anything about thermometers. Possibly in its brain there was no sharp consciousness of a condition of very cold such as was in the man's brain. But the brute had its instinct. It experienced a vague but menacing apprehension that subdued it and made it shrink along at the man's heels, and that made it question eagerly every unwonted movement of the man as if expecting him to go into camp or to seek shelter somewhere and build a fire. The dog had learned fire, and it wanted fire, or else to burrow under the snow and cuddle its warmth in the confined space.

The frozen moisture of its breathing had settled on its fur in a fine powder of frost, and especially were its jowls, muzzle, and eyelashes whitened by its crystalled breath. The man's red beard and mustache were likewise frosted, but more solidly, the deposit taking the form of ice, and increasing with every warm, moist breath he exhaled. Also, the man was chewing tobacco, and the muzzle of ice held his lips so rigidly that he was unable to clear his chin when he expelled the juice. The result was that a crystal beard of the color and solidity of amber was increasing its length on his chin. If he fell down it would shatter itself, like glass, into brittle fragments. But he did not mind the appendage. It was the penalty all tobacco-chewers paid in that country, and he had been out before in two cold snaps. They had not been so cold as this, he knew, but by the spirit thermometer at Sixty Mile he knew they had been registered at fifty below and at fifty-five.

He held on through the level stretch of woods for several miles, crossed a wide flat of nigger-heads, and dropped down a bank to the frozen bed of a small stream. This was Henderson Creek, and he knew he was ten miles from the forks. He looked at his watch. It was ten o'clock. He was making four miles an hour, and he calculated that he would arrive at the forks at half-past twelve. He decided to celebrate that event by eating his lunch there.

The dog dropped in again at his heels with a tail drooping discouragement as the man swung along the creek-bed. The furrow of the old sled-trail was plainly visible, but a dozen inches of snow covered the marks of the last runners. In a month no man had come up or down that silent creek. The man held steadily on. He was not much given to thinking, and just then particularly he had nothing to think about save that he would eat lunch at the forks and that at six o'clock he would be in camp with the boys. There was nobody to talk to; and, had there been, speech would have been impossible because of the ice-muzzle on his mouth. So he continued monotonously to chew tobacco and to increase the length of his amber beard.

Once in a while the thought reiterated itself that it was very cold and that he had never experienced such cold. As he walked along he rubbed his cheek-bones and nose with the back of his mittened hand. He did this automatically, now and again changing hands. But rub as he would, the instant he stopped, his cheek-bones went numb, and the following instant the end of his nose went numb. He was sure to frost his cheeks; he knew that, and experienced a pang of regret that he had not devised a nose-strap of the sort Bud wore in cold snaps. Such a strap passed across the cheeks, as well, and saved them. But it didn't matter much, after all. What were frosted cheeks? A bit painful, that was all; they were never serious.

Empty as the man's mind was of thoughts, he was keenly observant, and he noticed the changes in the creek, the curves and bends and timber-jams, and always he sharply noted where he placed his feet. Once, coming around a bend, he shied abruptly, like a startled horse, curved away from the place where he had been walking, and retreated several paces back along the trail. The creek he knew was frozen clear to the bottom,—no creek could contain water in that arctic winter,—but he knew also that there were springs that bubbled out from the hillsides and ran along under the snow and on top the ice of the creek. He knew that the coldest snaps never froze these springs, and he knew likewise their danger. They were traps. They hid pools of water under the snow that might be three inches deep, or three feet. Sometimes a skin of ice half an inch thick covered them, and in turn was covered by the snow. Sometimes there were alternate layers of water and ice-skin, so that when one broke through he kept on breaking through for a while, sometimes wetting himself to the waist.

That was why he had shied in such panic. He had felt the give under his feet and heard the crackle of a snow-hidden ice-skin. And to get his feet wet in such a temperature meant trouble and danger. At the very least it meant delay, for he would be forced to stop and build a fire, and under its protection to bare his feet while he dried his socks and moccasins. He stood and studied the creek-bed and its banks, and decided that the flow of water came from the right. He reflected awhile, rubbing his nose and cheeks, then skirted to the left, stepping gingerly and testing the footing for each step. Once clear of the danger, he took a fresh chew of tobacco, and swung along at his four-mile gait.

In the course of the next two hours he came upon several similar traps. Usually the snow above the hidden pools had a sunken, candied appearance that advertised the danger. Once again, however, he had a close call; and once, suspecting danger, he compelled the dog to go on in front. The dog did not want to go. It hung back until the man shoved it forward, and then it went quickly across the white, unbroken surface. Suddenly it broke through, floundered to one side, and got away to firmer footing. It had wet its forefeet and legs, and almost immediately the water that clung to it turned to ice. It made quick efforts to lick the ice off its legs, then dropped down in the snow, and began to bite out the ice that had formed between the toes. This was a matter of instinct. To permit the ice to remain would mean sore feet. It did not know this. It merely obeyed the mysterious prompting that arose from the deep crypts of its being. But the man knew, having achieved a judgment on the subject, and he removed the mitten from his right hand and helped tear out the ice-particles. He did not expose his fingers more than a minute, and was astonished at the swift numbness that smote them. It certainly was cold. He pulled on the mitten hastily, and beat the hand savagely across his chest.

At twelve o'clock the day was at its brightest. Yet the sun was too far south on its winter journey to clear the horizon. The bulge of the earth intervened between it and Henderson Creek, where the man walked under a clear sky at noon and cast no shadow. At half past twelve to the minute he arrived at the forks of the creek. He was pleased at the speed he had made. If he kept it up, he would certainly be with the boys by six. He unbuttoned his jacket and shirt and drew forth his lunch. The action consumed no more than a quarter of a minute, yet in that brief moment the numbness laid hold of the exposed fingers. He did not put the mitten on, but, instead, struck the fingers a dozen sharp smashes against his leg. Then he sat down on a snow-covered log to eat. The sting that followed upon the striking of his fingers against his leg ceased so quickly that he was startled. He had had no chance to take a bite of biscuit. He struck the fingers repeatedly and returned them to the mitten, baring the other hand for the purpose of eating. He tried to take a mouthful, but the ice-muzzle prevented. He had forgotten to build a fire and thaw out. He chuckled at his foolishness, and as he chuckled he noted the numbness creeping into the exposed fingers. Also, he noted that the stinging which had first come to his toes when he sat down was already passing away. He wondered whether the toes were warm or numb. He moved them inside the moccasins and decided that they were numb.

He pulled the mitten on hurriedly and stood up. He was a bit frightened. He stamped up and down until the stinging returned into the feet. It certainly was cold, was his thought. That man from Sulphur Creek had spoken the truth when telling how cold it sometimes got in the country. And he had laughed at him at the time! That showed one must not be too sure of things. There was no mistake about it, it *was* cold. He strode up and down, stamping his feet and threshing his arms, until reassured by the returning warmth. Then he got out matches and proceeded to make a fire. From the undergrowth, where high water of the previous spring had lodged a supply of seasoned twigs, he got his fire-wood. Working carefully from a small beginning, he soon had a roaring fire, over which he thawed the ice from his face, and in the protection of which he ate his biscuits. For the moment the cold of space was outwitted. The dog took satisfaction in the fire, stretching out close enough for warmth and far enough away to escape being singed.

When the man had finished, he filled his pipe and took his comfortable time over a smoke. Then he pulled on his mittens, settled the earflaps of his cap firmly about his ears, and took the creek trail up the left fork. The dog was disappointed and yearned back toward the fire. This man did not know cold. Possibly all the generations of his ancestry had been ignorant of cold, of real cold, of cold one hundred and seven degrees below freezing-point. But the dog knew; all its ancestry knew, and it had inherited the knowledge. And it knew that it was not good to walk abroad in such fearful cold. It was the time to lie snug in a hole in the snow and wait for a curtain of cloud to be drawn across the face of outer space whence this cold came. On the other hand, there was no keen intimacy between the dog and the man. The one was the toil-slave of the other, and the only caresses it had ever received were the caresses of the whip-lash and of harsh and menacing throat-sounds that threatened the whip-lash. So the dog made no effort to communicate its apprehension to the man. It was not concerned in the welfare of the man; it was for its own sake that it yearned back toward the fire. But the man whistled, and spoke to it with the sound of whip-lashes, and the dog swung in at the man's heels and followed after.

The man took a chew of tobacco, and proceeded to start a new amber beard. Also, his moist breath quickly powdered with white his mustache, eyebrows, and lashes. There did not seem to be so many springs on the left fork of the Henderson, and for half an hour the man

saw no signs of any. And then it happened. At a place where there were
no signs, where the soft, unbroken snow seemed to advertise solidity
beneath, the man broke through. It was not deep. He wet himself half-
way to the knees before he floundered out to the firm crust.
He was angry, and cursed his luck aloud. He had hoped to get into
camp with the boys at six o'clock, and this would delay him an hour;
for he would have to build a fire and dry out his foot-gear. This was
imperative at that low temperature—he knew that much; and he turned
aside to the bank, which he climbed. On top, tangled in the underbrush
about the trunks of several small spruce-trees, was a high-water deposit
of dry fire-wood—sticks and twigs, principally, but also larger portions
of seasoned branches and fine, dry, last-year's grasses. He threw down
several large pieces on top of the snow. This served for a foundation,
and prevented the young flame from drowning itself in the snow it otherwise would melt. The flame he got by touching a match to a small
shred of birch-bark that he took from his pocket. This burned even more
readily than paper. Placing it on the foundation, he fed the young flame
with wisps of dry grass and with the tiniest dry twigs.

He worked slowly and carefully, keenly aware of his danger. Gradually, as the flame grew stronger, he increased the size of the twigs with
which he fed it. He squatted in the snow, pulling the twigs out from
their entanglement in the brush, and feeding directly to the flame. He
knew there must be no failure. When it is seventy-five below zero a man
must not fail in his first attempt to build a fire—that is, if his feet are
wet. If his feet are dry, and he fails, he can run along the trail for half
a mile and restore his circulation. But the circulation of wet and freezing
feet cannot be restored by running when it is seventy-five below. No
matter how fast he runs, the wet feet will freeze the harder.

All this the man knew. The old-timer on Sulphur Creek had told him
about it the previous fall, and now he was appreciating the advice.
Already all sensation had gone out of his feet. To build the fire he had
been forced to remove his mittens, and the fingers had quickly gone
numb. His pace of four miles an hour had kept his heart pumping blood
to the surface of his body and to all the extremities. But the instant he
stopped, the action of the pump eased down. The cold of space smote
the unprotected tip of the planet, and he, being on that unprotected tip,
received the full force of the blow. The blood of his body recoiled before
it. The blood was alive, like the dog, and like the dog it wanted to hide
away and cover itself up from the fearful cold. So long as he walked
four miles an hour, he pumped that blood, willy-nilly, to the surface;
but now it ebbed away and sank down into the recesses of his body.
The extremities were the first to feel its absence. His wet feet froze the
faster, and his exposed fingers numbed the faster, though they had not

yet begun to freeze. Nose and cheeks were already freezing, while the skin of all his body chilled as it lost its blood.

But he was safe. Toes and nose and cheeks would be only touched by the frost, for the fire was beginning to burn with strength. He was feeding it with twigs the size of his finger. In another minute he would be able to feed it with branches the size of his wrist, and then he could remove his wet foot-gear, and while it dried, he could keep his naked feet warm by the fire, rubbing them at first, of course, with snow. The fire was a success. He was safe. He remembered the advice of the old-timer on Sulphur Creek and smiled. The old-timer had been very serious in laying down the law that no man must travel alone in the Klondike after fifty below. Well, here he was; he had had the accident; he was alone; and he had saved himself. Those old-timers were rather womanish, some of them, he thought. All a man had to do was to keep his head, and he was all right. Any man who was a man could travel alone. But it was surprising, the rapidity with which his cheeks and nose were freezing. And he had not thought his fingers could go lifeless in so short a time. Lifeless they were, for he could scarcely make them move together to grip a twig, and they seemed remote from his body and from him. When he touched a twig he had to look and see whether or not he had hold of it. The wires were pretty well down between him and his finger-ends.

All of which counted for little. There was the fire, snapping and crackling and promising life with every dancing flame. He started to untie his moccasins. They were coated with ice; the thick German socks were like sheaths of iron half-way to the knees; and the moccasin-strings were like rods of steel all twisted and knotted as by some conflagration. For a moment he tugged with his numb fingers, then, realizing the folly of it, he drew his sheath-knife.

But before he could cut the strings, it happened. It was his own fault, or, rather, his mistake. He should not have built the fire under the spruce-tree. He should have built it in the open. But it had been easier to pull the twigs from the brush and drop them directly on the fire. Now the tree under which he had done this carried a weight of snow on its boughs. No wind had blown for weeks, and each bough was fully freighted. Each time he had pulled a twig he had communicated a slight agitation to the tree—an imperceptible agitation, so far as he was concerned, but an agitation sufficient to bring about the disaster. High up in the tree one bough capsized its load of snow. This fell on the boughs beneath, capsizing them. This process continued, spreading out and involving the whole tree. It grew like an avalanche, and it descended without warning upon the man and the fire, and the fire was blotted out! Where it had burned was a mantle of fresh and disordered snow.

The man was shocked. It was as though he had just heard his own sentence of death. For a moment he sat and stared at the spot where the fire had been. Then he grew very calm. Perhaps the old-timer on Sulphur Creek was right. If he had only had a trail-mate he would have been in no danger now. The trail-mate could have built the fire. Well, it was up to him to build the fire over again, and this second time there must be no failure. Even if he succeeded, he would most likely lose some toes. His feet must be badly frozen by now, and there would be some time before the second fire was ready.

Such were his thoughts, but he did not sit and think them. He was busy all the time they were passing through his mind. He made a new foundation for a fire, this time in the open, where no treacherous tree could blot it out. Next, he gathered dry grasses and tiny twigs from the high-water flotsam. He could not bring his fingers together to pull them out, but he was able to gather them by the handful. In this way he got many rotten twigs and bits of green moss that were undesirable, but it was the best he could do. He worked methodically, even collecting an armful of the larger branches to be used later when the fire gathered strength. And all the while the dog sat and watched him, a certain yearning wistfulness in its eyes, for it looked upon him as the fire-provider, and the fire was slow in coming.

When all was ready, the man reached in his pocket for a second piece of birch-bark. He knew the bark was there, and, though he could not feel it with his fingers, he could hear its crisp rustling as he fumbled for it. Try as he would, he could not clutch hold of it. And all the time, in his consciousness, was the knowledge that each instant his feet were freezing. This thought tended to put him in a panic, but he fought against it and kept calm. He pulled on his mittens with his teeth, and threshed his arms back and forth, beating his hands with all his might against his sides. He did this sitting down, and he stood up to do it; and all the while the dog sat in the snow, its wolf-brush of a tail curled around warmly over its forefeet, its sharp wolf-ears pricked forward intently as it watched the man. And the man, as he beat and threshed with his arms and hands, felt a great surge of envy as he regarded the creature that was warm and secure in its natural covering.

After a time he was aware of the first far-away signals of sensation in his beaten fingers. The faint tingling grew stronger till it evolved into a stinging ache that was excruciating, but which the man hailed with satisfaction. He stripped the mitten from his right hand and fetched forth the birch-bark. The exposed fingers were quickly going numb again. Next he brought out his bunch of sulphur matches. But the tremendous cold had already driven the life out of his fingers. In his effort to separate one match from the others, the whole bunch fell in the snow.

He tried to pick it out of the snow, but failed. The dead fingers could neither touch nor clutch. He was very careful. He drove the thought of his freezing feet, and nose, and cheeks, out of his mind, devoting his whole soul to the matches. He watched, using the sense of vision in place of that of touch, and when he saw his fingers on each side the bunch, he closed them—that is, he willed to close them, for the wires were down, and the fingers did not obey. He pulled the mitten on the right hand and beat it fiercely against his knee. Then, with both mittened hands, he scooped the bunch of matches, along with much snow, into his lap. Yet he was no better off.

After some manipulation he managed to get the bunch between the heels of his mittened hands. In this fashion he carried it to his mouth. The ice crackled and snapped when by a violent effort he opened his mouth. He drew the lower jaw in, curled the upper lip out of the way, and scraped the bunch with his upper teeth in order to separate a match. He succeeded in getting one, which he dropped on his lap. He was no better off. He could not pick it up. Then he devised a way. He picked it up in his teeth and scratched it on his leg. Twenty times he scratched before he succeeded in lighting it. As it flamed he held it with his teeth to the birch-bark. But the burning brimstone went up his nostrils and into his lungs, causing him to cough spasmodically. The match fell into the snow and went out.

The old-timer on Sulphur Creek was right, he thought in the moment of controlled despair that ensued: after fifty below a man should travel with a partner. He beat his hands, but failed in exciting any sensation. Suddenly he bared both hands, removing the mittens with his teeth. He caught the whole bunch between the heels of his hands. His arm-muscles not being frozen enabled him to press the hand-heels tightly against the matches. Then he scratched the bunch along his leg. It flared into flame, seventy sulphur matches at once! There was no wind to blow them out. He kept his head to one side to escape the strangling fumes, and held the blazing bunch to the birch-bark. As he so held it, he became aware of sensation in his hand. His flesh was burning. He could smell it. Deep down below the surface he could feel it. The sensation developed into pain that grew acute. And still he endured it, holding the flame of the matches clumsily to the bark that would not light readily because his own burning hands were in the way, absorbing most of the flame.

At last, when he could endure no more, he jerked his hands apart. The blazing matches fell sizzling into the snow, but the birch-bark was alight. He began laying dry grasses and the tiniest twigs on the flame. He could not pick and choose, for he had to lift the fuel between the heels of his hands. Small pieces of rotten wood and green moss clung to the twigs, and he bit them off as well as he could with his teeth. He cherished the flame carefully and awkwardly. It meant life, and it must not perish. The withdrawal of blood from the surface of his body now made him begin to shiver, and he grew more awkward. A large piece of green moss fell squarely on the little fire. He tried to poke it out with his fingers, but his shivering frame made him poke too far, and he disrupted the nucleus of the little fire, the burning grasses and tiny twigs separating and scattering. He tried to poke them together again, but in spite of the tenseness of the effort, his shivering got away with him, and the twigs were hopelessly scattered. Each twig gushed a puff of smoke and went out. The fire-provider had failed. As he looked apathetically about him, his eyes chanced on the dog, sitting across the ruins of the fire from him, in the snow, making restless, hunching movements, slightly lifting one forefoot and then the other, shifting its weight back and forth on them with wistful eagerness.

The sight of the dog put a wild idea into his head. He remembered the tale of the man, caught in a blizzard, who killed a steer and crawled inside the carcass, and so was saved. He would kill the dog and bury his hands in the warm body until the numbness went out of them. Then he could build another fire. He spoke to the dog, calling it to him; but in his voice was a strange note of fear that frightened the animal, who had never known the man to speak in such way before. Something was the matter, and its suspicious nature sensed danger—it knew not what danger, but somewhere, somehow, in its brain arose an apprehension of the man. It flattened its ears down at the sound of the man's voice, and its restless, hunching movements and the liftings and shiftings of its forefeet became more pronounced; but it would not come to the man. He got on his hands and knees and crawled toward the dog. This unusual posture again excited suspicion, and the animal sidled mincingly away.

The man sat up in the snow for a moment and struggled for calmness. Then he pulled on his mittens, by means of his teeth, and got upon his feet. He glanced down at first in order to assure himself that he was really standing up, for the absence of sensation in his feet left him unrelated to the earth. His erect position in itself started to drive the webs of suspicion from the dog's mind; and when he spoke peremptorily, with the sound of whip-lashes in his voice, the dog rendered its customary allegiance and came to him. As it came within reaching distance the man lost his control. His arms flashed out to the dog, and he experienced genuine surprise when he discovered that his hands could not clutch, that there was neither bend nor feeling in the fingers. He had forgotten for the moment that they were frozen and that they were freezing more and more. All this happened quickly, and before the an-

imal could get away he encircled its body with his arms. He sat down
in the snow, and in this fashion held the dog, while it snarled and
whined and struggled.

But it was all he could do, hold its body encircled in his arms and
sit there. He realized that he could not kill the dog. There was no way
to do it. With his helpless hands he could neither draw nor hold his
sheath-knife nor throttle the animal. He released it, and it plunged
wildly away, with tail between its legs, and still snarling. It halted forty
feet away and surveyed him curiously, with ears sharply pricked forward. The man looked down at his hands in order to locate them, and
found them hanging on the ends of his arms. It struck him as curious
that one should have to use his eyes in order to find out where his hands
were. He began threshing his arms back and forth, beating the mittened
hands against his sides. He did this for five minutes, violently, and his
heart pumped enough blood up to the surface to put a stop to his shivering. But no sensation was aroused in the hands. He had an impression
that they hung like weights on the ends of his arms, but when he tried
to run the impression down, he could not find it.

A certain fear of death, dull and oppressive, came to him. This fear
quickly became poignant as he realized that it was no longer a mere
matter of freezing his fingers and toes, or of losing his hands and feet,
but that it was a matter of life and death with the chances against him.
This threw him into a panic, and he turned and ran up the creek-bed
along the old, dim trail. The dog joined in behind and kept up with
him. He ran blindly, without intention, in fear such as he had never
known in his life. Slowly, as he plowed and floundered through the
snow, he began to see things again,—the banks of the creek, the old
timber-jams, the leafless aspens, and the sky. The running made him
feel better. He did not shiver. Maybe, if he ran on, his feet would thaw
out; and, anyway, if he ran far enough he would reach camp and the
boys. Without doubt he would lose some fingers and toes and some of
his face; but the boys would take care of him, and save the rest of him
when he got there. And at the same time there was another thought in
his mind that said he would never get to the camp and the boys; that
it was too many miles away, that the freezing had too great a start on
him, and that he would soon be stiff and dead. This thought he kept in
the background, and refused to consider. Sometimes it pushed itself forward and demanded to be heard, but he thrust it back and strove to
think of other things.

It struck him as curious that he could run at all on feet so frozen
that he could not feel them when they struck the earth and took the
weight of his body. He seemed to himself to skim along above the sur-

face, and to have no connection with the earth. Somewhere he had once seen a winged Mercury, and he wondered if Mercury felt as he felt when skimming over the earth.

His theory of running until he reached camp and the boys had one flaw in it: he lacked the endurance. Several times he stumbled, and finally he tottered, crumpled up, and fell. When he tried to rise, he failed. He must sit and rest, he decided, and next time he would merely walk and keep on going. As he sat and regained his breath, he noted that he was feeling quite warm and comfortable. He was not shivering, and it even seemed that a warm glow had come to his chest and trunk. And yet, when he touched his nose or cheeks, there was no sensation. Running would not thaw them out. Nor would it thaw out his hands and feet. Then the thought came to him that the frozen portions of his body must be extending. He tried to keep this thought down, to forget it, to think of something else; he was aware of the panicky feeling that it caused, and he was afraid of the panic. But the thought asserted itself, and persisted, until it produced a vision of his body totally frozen. This was too much, and he made another wild run along the trail. Once he slowed down to a walk, but the thought of the freezing extending itself made him run again.

And all the time the dog ran with him, at his heels. When he fell down a second time, it curled its tail over its forefeet and sat in front of him, facing him, curiously eager and intent. The warmth and security of the animal angered him, and he cursed it till it flattened down its ears appeasingly. This time the shivering came more quickly upon the man. He was losing in his battle with the frost. It was creeping into his body from all sides. The thought of it drove him on, but he ran no more than a hundred feet, when he staggered and pitched headlong. It was his last panic. When he had recovered his breath and control, he sat up and entertained in his mind the conception of meeting death with dignity. However, the conception did not come to him in such terms. His idea of it was that he had been making a fool of himself, running around like a chicken with its head cut off—such was the simile that occurred to him. Well, he was bound to freeze anyway, and he might as well take it decently. With this new-found peace of mind came the first glimmerings of drowsiness. A good idea, he thought, to sleep off to death. It was like taking an anesthetic. Freezing was not so bad as people thought. There were lots worse ways to die.

He pictured the boys finding his body next day. Suddenly he found himself with them, coming along the trail and looking for himself. And, still with them, he came around a turn in the trail and found himself lying in the snow. He did not belong with himself any more, for even then he was out of himself, standing with the boys and looking at himself in the snow. It certainly was cold, was his thought. When he got back to the States he could tell the folks what real cold was. He drifted on from this to a vision of the old-timer on Sulphur Creek. He could see him quite clearly, warm, and comfortable, and smoking a pipe.

"You were right, old hoss; you were right," the man mumbled to the old-timer of Sulphur Creek.

Then the man drowsed off into what seemed to him the most comfortable and satisfying sleep he had ever known. The dog sat facing him and waiting. The brief day drew to a close in a long, slow twilight. There were no signs of a fire to be made, and, besides, never in the dog's experience had it known a man to sit like that in the snow and make no fire. As the twilight drew on, its eager yearning for the fire mastered it, and with a great lifting and shifting of forefeet, it whined softly, then flattened its ears down in anticipation of being chidden by the man. But the man remained silent. Later, the dog whined loudly. And still later it crept close to the man and caught the scent of death. This made the animal bristle and back away. A little longer it delayed, howling under the stars that leaped and danced and shone brightly in the cold sky. Then it turned and trotted up the trail in the direction of the camp it knew, where were the other food-providers and the fire-providers.

THEODORE DREISER

The Second Choice

"The Second Choice" was first published in *Cosmopolitan* magazine in February 1918 and collected that same year in *Free and Other Stories*. Dreiser takes for the premise of his story the melodramatic and hackneyed plot device of a love triangle, but he achieves something moving and quite original with such threadbare materials. It is the quality of pity, in the author, combined with a steadfast, almost relentless depiction of the monotonous destiny of his characters that gives the story such a creative tension. Arthur Bristow plays the figure of the "cad," of the conventional melodrama, and Shirley the innocent victim. However, the reader is not likely to find Arthur particularly villainous, merely restless and frivolous. And the sympathy we have for Shirley has little or nothing to do with her lost virtue. Barton Williams is loyal and true, but in Shirley's eyes he is docile and predictable—in a word, boring. Barton is Shirley's "second choice," but her resignation to this fact suggests that she has few choices at all. The houses that line Bethune street and the families that live in them are replicas of one another, and they map out Shirley's fate with a dull and implacable logic. Within this context, Shirley is both ordinary and tragic, and her willingness to help her mother set the table at the end of the story is an almost heroic gesture of her acceptance of her compromised life.

*   *   *

Shirley Dear:

You don't want the letters. There are only six of them, anyhow, and think, they're all I have of you to cheer me on my travels. What good would they be to you—little bits of notes telling me you're sure to meet me—but me—think of me! If I send them to you, you'll tear them up, whereas if you leave them with me I can dab them with musk and ambergris and keep them in a little silver box, always beside me.

Ah, Shirley dear, you really don't know how sweet I think you are, how dear! There isn't a thing we have ever done together that isn't as clear in my mind as this great big skyscraper over the way here in Pittsburgh, and far more pleasing. In fact, my thoughts of you are the most precious and delicious things I have, Shirley.

But I'm too young to marry now. You know that, Shirley, don't you? I haven't placed myself in any way yet, and I'm so restless that I don't know whether I ever will, really. Only yesterday, old Roxbaum—that's my new employer here—came to me and wanted to know if I would like an assistant overseership on one of his coffee plantations in Java, said there would not be much money in it for a year or two, a bare living, but later there would be more—and I jumped at it. Just the thought of Java and going there did that, although I knew I could make more staying right here. Can't you see how it is with me, Shirl? I'm too restless and too young. I couldn't take care of you right, and you wouldn't like me after a while if I didn't.

But ah, Shirley sweet, I think the dearest things of you! There isn't an hour, it seems, but some little bit of you comes back—a dear, sweet bit—the night we sat on the grass in Tregore Park and counted the stars through the trees; that first evening at Sparrows Point when we missed the last train and had to walk to Langley. Remember the tree-toads, Shirl? And then that warm April Sunday in Atholby woods! Ah, Shirl, you don't want the six notes! Let me keep them. But think of me, will you, sweet, wherever you go and whatever you do? I'll always think of you, and wish that you had met a better, saner man than me, and that I really could have married you and been all you wanted me to be.

By-by, sweet. I may start for Java within the month. If so, and you would want them, I'll send you some cards from there—if they have any.

Your worthless,
ARTHUR.

She sat and turned the letter in her hand, dumb with despair. It was the very last letter she would ever get from him. Of that she was certain. He was gone now, once and for all. She had written him only once, not making an open plea but asking him to return her letters, and then there had come this tender but evasive reply, saying nothing of a possible return but desiring to keep her letters for old times' sake—the happy hours they had spent together.

The happy hours! Oh, yes, yes, yes—the happy hours!

In her memory now, as she sat here in her home after the day's work, meditating on all that had been in the few short months since he had come and gone, was a world of color and light—a color and a light so transfiguring as to seem celestial, but now, alas, wholly dissipated. It had contained so much of all she had desired—love, romance, amusement, laughter. He had been so gay and thoughtless, or headstrong, so youthfully romantic, and with such a love of play and change and to be saying and doing anything and everything. Arthur could dance in a gay way, whistle, sing after a fashion, play. He could play cards and do tricks, and he had such a superior air, so genial and brisk, with a kind of innate courtesy in it and yet an intolerance for slowness and stodginess or anything dull or dingy, such as characterized——But here her thoughts fled from him. She refused to think of any one but Arthur.

Sitting in her little bedroom now, off the parlor on the ground floor in her home in Bethune Street, and looking out over the Kessels' yard, and beyond that—there being no fences in Bethune Street—over the "yards" or lawns of the Pollards, Bakers, Cryders, and others, she thought of how dull it must all have seemed to him, with his fine imaginative mind and experiences, his love of change and gayety, his atmosphere of something better than she had ever known. How little she had been fitted, perhaps, by beauty or temperament to overcome this— the something—dullness in her work or her home, which possibly had driven him away. For, although many had admired her to date, and she was young and pretty in her simple way and constantly receiving suggestions that her beauty was disturbing to some, still, he had not cared for her—he had gone.

And now, as she meditated, it seemed that this scene, and all that it stood for—her parents, her work, her daily shuttling to and fro between the drug company for which she worked and this street and house—

was typical of her life and what she was destined to endure always. Some girls were so much more fortunate. They had fine clothes, fine homes, a world of pleasure and opportunity in which to move. They did not have to scrimp and save and work to pay their own way. And yet she had always been compelled to do it, but had never complained until now—or until he came, and after. Bethune Street, with its commonplace front yards and houses nearly all alike, and this house, so like the others, room for room and porch for porch, and her parents, too, really like all the others, had seemed good enough, quite satisfactory, indeed, until then. But now, now!

Here, in their kitchen, was her mother, a thin, pale, but kindly woman, peeling potatoes and washing lettuce, and putting a bit of steak or a chop or a piece of liver in a frying-pan day after day, morning and evening, month after month, year after year. And next door was Mrs. Kessel doing the same thing. And next door Mrs. Cryder. And next door Mrs. Pollard. But, until now, she had not thought it so bad. But now—now—oh! And on all the porches or lawns all along this street were the husbands and fathers, mostly middle-aged or old men like her father, reading their papers or cutting the grass before dinner, or smoking and meditating afterward. Her father was out in front now, a stooped, forbearing, meditative soul, who had rarely anything to say— leaving it all to his wife, her mother, but who was fond of her in his dull, quiet way. He was a pattern-maker by trade, and had come into possession of this small, ordinary home via years of toil and saving, her mother helping him. They had no particular religion, as he often said, thinking reasonably human conduct a sufficient passport to heaven, but they had gone occasionally to the Methodist Church over in Nicholas Street, and she had once joined it. But of late she had not gone, weaned away by the other commonplace pleasures of her world.

And then in the midst of it, the dull drift of things, as she now saw them to be, he had come—Arthur Bristow—young, energetic, good-looking, ambitious, dreamful, and instanter, and with her never knowing quite how, the whole thing had been changed. He had appeared so swiftly—out of nothing, as it were.

Previous to him had been Barton Williams, stout, phlegmatic, good-natured, well-meaning, who was, or had been before Arthur came, asking her to marry him, and whom she allowed to half assume that she would. She had liked him in a feeble, albeit, as she thought, tender way, thinking him the kind, according to the logic of her neighborhood, who would make her a good husband, and, until Arthur appeared on the scene, had really intended to marry him. It was not really a love-match, as she saw now, but she thought it was, which was much the same thing, perhaps. But, as she now recalled, when Arthur came, how the scales fell from her eyes! In a trice, as it were, nearly, there was a new heaven and a new earth. Arthur had arrived, and with him a sense of something different.

Mabel Gove had asked her to come over to her house in Westleigh, the adjoining suburb, for Thanksgiving eve and day, and without a thought of anything, and because Barton was busy handling a part of the work in the despatcher's office of the Great Eastern and could not see her, she had gone. And then, to her surprise and strange, almost ineffable delight, the moment she had seen him, he was there—Arthur, with his slim, straight figure and dark hair and eyes and clean-cut features, as clean and attractive as those of a coin. And as he had looked at her and smiled and narrated humorous bits of things that had happened to him, something had come over her—a spell—and after dinner they had all gone round to Edith Barringer's to dance, and there as she had danced with him, somehow, without any seeming boldness on his part, he had taken possession of her, as it were, drawn her close, and told her she had beautiful eyes and hair and such a delicately rounded chin, and that he thought she danced gracefully and was sweet. She had nearly fainted with delight.

"Do you like me?" he had asked in one place in the dance, and, in spite of herself, she had looked up into his eyes, and from that moment she was almost mad over him, could think of nothing else but his hair and eyes and his smile and his graceful figure.

Mabel Gove had seen it all, in spite of her determination that no one should, and on their going to bed later, back at Mabel's home, she had whispered:

"Ah, Shirley, I saw. You like Arthur, don't you?"

"I think he's very nice," Shirley recalled replying, for Mabel knew of her affair with Barton and liked him, "but I'm not crazy over him." And for this bit of treason she had sighed in her dreams nearly all night.

And the next day, true to a request and a promise made by him, Arthur had called again at Mabel's to take her and Mabel to a "movie" which was not so far away, and from there they had gone to an ice-cream parlor, and during it all, when Mabel was not looking, he had squeezed her arm and hand and kissed her neck, and she had held her breath, and her heart had seemed to stop.

"And now you're going to let me come out to your place to see you, aren't you?" he had whispered.

And she had replied, "Wednesday evening," and then written the address on a little piece of paper and given it to him.

But now it was all gone, gone!

This house, which now looked so dreary—how romantic it had seemed that first night *he* called—the front room with its commonplace furniture, and later in the spring, the veranda, with its vines just sprouting, and the moon in May. Oh, the moon in May, and June and July, when he was here! How she had lied to Barton to make evenings for Arthur, and occasionally to Arthur to keep him from contact with Barton. She had not even mentioned Barton to Arthur because—because —well, because Arthur was so much better, and somehow (she admitted it to herself now) she had not been sure that Arthur would care for her long, if at all, and then—well, and then, to be quite frank, Barton might be good enough. She did not exactly hate him because she had found Arthur—not at all. She still liked him in a way—he was so kind and faithful, so very dull and straightforward and thoughtful of her, which Arthur was certainly not. Before Arthur had appeared, as she well remembered, Barton had seemed to be plenty good enough—in fact, all that she desired in a pleasant, companionable way, calling for her, taking her places, bringing her flowers and candy, which Arthur rarely did, and for that, if nothing more, she could not help continuing to like him and to feel sorry for him, and, besides, as she had admitted to herself before, if Arthur left her—* * * * * Weren't his parents better off than hers—and hadn't he a good position for such a man as he—one hundred and fifty dollars a month and the certainty of more later on? A little while before meeting Arthur, she had thought this very good, enough for two to live on at least, and she had thought some of trying it at some time or other—but now—now——

And that first night he had called—how well she remembered it— how it had transfigured the parlor next this in which she was now, filling it with something it had never had before, and the porch outside, too, for that matter, with its gaunt, leafless vine, and this street, too, even— dull, commonplace Bethune Street. There had been a flurry of snow during the afternoon while she was working at the store, and the ground was white with it. All the neighboring homes seemed to look sweeter and happier and more inviting than ever they had as she came past them, with their lights peeping from under curtains and drawn shades. She had hurried into hers and lighted the big red-shaded parlor lamp, her one artistic treasure, as she thought, and put it near the piano, between it and the window, and arranged the chairs, and then bustled to the task of making herself as pleasing as she might. For him she had gotten out her one best filmy house dress and done up her hair in the fashion she thought most becoming—and that he had not seen before —and powdered her cheeks and nose and darkened her eyelashes, as some of the girls at the store did, and put on her new gray satin slippers, and then, being so arrayed, waited nervously, unable to eat anything or to think of anything but him.

And at last, just when she had begun to think he might not be coming, he had appeared with that arch smile and a "Hello! It's here you live, is it? I was wondering. George, but you're twice as sweet as I thought you were, aren't you?" And then, in the little entryway, behind the closed door, he had held her and kissed her on the mouth a dozen times while she pretended to push against his coat and struggle and say that her parents might hear.

And, oh, the room afterward, with him in it in the red glow of the lamp, and with his pale handsome face made handsomer thereby, as she thought! He had made her sit near him and had held her hands and told her about his work and his dreams—all that he expected to do in the future—and then she had found herself wishing intensely to share just such a life—his life—anything that he might wish to do; only, she kept wondering, with a slight pain, whether he would want her to—he was so young, dreamful, ambitious, much younger and more dreamful than herself, although, in reality, he was several years older.

And then followed that glorious period from December to this late September, in which everything which was worth happening in love had happened. Oh, those wondrous days the following spring, when, with the first burst of buds and leaves, he had taken her one Sunday to Atholby, where all the great woods were, and they had hunted spring beauties in the grass, and sat on a slope and looked at the river below and watched some boys fixing up a sailboat and setting forth in it quite as she wished she and Arthur might be doing—going somewhere together—far, far away from all commonplace things and life! And then he had slipped his arm about her and kissed her cheek and neck, and tweaked her ear and smoothed her hair—and oh, there on the grass, with the spring flowers about her and a canopy of small green leaves above, the perfection of love had come—love so wonderful that the mere thought of it made her eyes brim now! And then had been days, Saturday afternoons and Sundays, at Atholby and Sparrows Point, where the great beach was, and in lovely Tregore Park, a mile or two from her home, where they could go of an evening and sit in or near the pavilion and have ice-cream and dance or watch the dancers. Oh, the stars, the winds, the summer breath of those days! Ah, me! Ah, me!

Naturally, her parents had wondered from the first about her and Arthur, and her and Barton, since Barton had already assumed a proprietary interest in her and she had seemed to like him. But then she was an only child and a pet, and used to presuming on that, and they could not think of saying anything to her. After all, she was young and pretty and was entitled to change her mind; only, only—she had had to indulge in a career of lying and subterfuge in connection with Barton,

since Arthur was headstrong and wanted every evening that he chose—
to call for her at the store and keep her down-town to dinner and a
show.

Arthur had never been like Barton, shy, phlegmatic, obedient, waiting
long and patiently for each little favor, but, instead, masterful and eager,
rifling her of kisses and caresses and every delight of love, and teasing
and playing with her as a cat would a mouse. She could never resist
him. He demanded of her her time and her affection without let or
hindrance. He was not exactly selfish or cruel, as some might have been,
but gay and unthinking at times, unconsciously so, and yet loving and
tender at others—nearly always so. But always he would talk of things
in the future as if they really did not include her—and this troubled her
greatly—of places he might go, things he might do, which, somehow,
he seemed to think or assume that she could not or would not do with
him. He was always going to Australia sometime, he thought, in a business way, or to South Africa, or possibly to India. He never seemed to
have any fixed clear future for himself in mind.

A dreadful sense of helplessness and of impending disaster came over
her at these times, of being involved in some predicament over which
she had no control, and which would lead her on to some sad end.
Arthur, although plainly in love, as she thought, and apparently delighted with her, might not always love her. She began, timidly at first
(and always, for that matter), to ask him pretty, seeking questions about
himself and her, whether their future was certain to be together, whether
he really wanted her—loved her—whether he might not want to marry
some one else or just her, and whether she wouldn't look nice in a pearl
satin wedding-dress with a long creamy veil and satin slippers and a
bouquet of bridal-wreath. She had been so slowly but surely saving to
that end, even before he came, in connection with Barton; only, after
he came, all thought of the import of it had been transferred to him.
But now, also, she was beginning to ask herself sadly, "Would it ever
be?" He was so airy, so inconsequential, so ready to say: "Yes, yes,"
and "Sure, sure! That's right! Yes, indeedy; you bet! Say, kiddie, but
you'll look sweet!" but, somehow, it had always seemed as if this whole
thing were a glorious interlude and that it could not last. Arthur was
too gay and ethereal and too little settled in his own mind. His ideas of
travel and living in different cities, finally winding up in New York or
San Francisco, but never with her exactly until she asked him, was too
ominous, although he always reassured her gaily: "Of course! Of
course!" But somehow she could never believe it really, and it made her
intensely sad at times, horribly gloomy. So often she wanted to cry, and
she could scarcely tell why.

And then, because of her intense affection for him, she had finally quarreled with Barton, or nearly that, if one could say that one ever really quarreled with him. It had been because of a certain Thursday evening a few weeks before about which she had disappointed him. In a fit of generosity, knowing that Arthur was coming Wednesday, and because Barton had stopped in at the store to see her, she had told him that he might come, having regretted it afterward, so enamored was she of Arthur. And then when Wednesday came, Arthur had changed his mind, telling her he would come Friday instead, but on Thursday evening he had stopped in at the store and asked her to go to Sparrows Point, with the result that she had no time to notify Barton. He had gone to the house and sat with her parents until ten-thirty, and then, a few days later, although she had written him offering an excuse, had called at the store to complain slightly.

"Do you think you did just right, Shirley? You might have sent word, mightn't you? Who was it—the new fellow you won't tell me about?"

Shirley flared on the instant.

"Supposing it was? What's it to you? I don't belong to you yet, do I? I told you there wasn't any one, and I wish you'd let me alone about that. I couldn't help it last Thursday—that's all—and I don't want you to be fussing with me—that's all. If you don't want to, you needn't come any more, anyhow."

"Don't say that, Shirley," pleaded Barton. "You don't mean that. I won't bother you, though, if you don't want me any more."

And because Shirley sulked, not knowing what else to do, he had gone and she had not seen him since.

And then sometime later when she had thus broken with Barton, avoiding the railway station where he worked, Arthur had failed to come at his appointed time, sending no word until the next day, when a note came to the store saying that he had been out of town for his firm over Sunday and had not been able to notify her, but that he would call Tuesday. It was an awful blow. At the time, Shirley had a vision of what was to follow. It seemed for the moment as if the whole world had suddenly been reduced to ashes, that there was nothing but black charred cinders anywhere—she felt that about all life. Yet it all came to her clearly then that this was but the beginning of just such days and just such excuses, and that soon, soon, he would come no more. He was beginning to be tired of her and soon he would not even make excuses. She felt it, and it froze and terrified her.

And then, soon after, the indifference which she feared did follow— almost created by her own thoughts, as it were. First, it was a meeting he had to attend somewhere one Wednesday night when he was to have come for her. Then he was going out of town again, over Sunday. Then he was going away for a whole week—it was absolutely unavoidable, he said, his commercial duties were increasing—and once he had casually remarked that nothing could stand in the way where she was concerned—never! She did not think of reproaching him with this; she was too proud. If he was going, he must go. She would not be willing to say to herself that she had ever attempted to hold any man. But, just the same, she was agonized by the thought. When he was with her, he seemed tender enough; only, at times, his eyes wandered and he seemed slightly bored. Other girls, particularly pretty ones, seemed to interest him as much as she did.

And the agony of the long days when he did not come any more for a week or two at a time! The waiting, the brooding, the wondering, at the store and here in her home—in the former place making mistakes at times because she could not get her mind off him and being reminded of them, and here at her own home at nights, being so absent-minded that her parents remarked on it. She felt sure that her parents must be noticing that Arthur was not coming any more, or as much as he had —for she pretended to be going out with him, going to Mabel Gove's instead—and that Barton had deserted her too, he having been driven off by her indifference, never to come any more, perhaps, unless she sought him out.

And then it was that the thought of saving her own face by taking up with Barton once more occurred to her, of using him and his affections and faithfulness and dulness, if you will, to cover up her own dilemma. Only, this ruse was not to be tried until she had written Arthur this one letter—a pretext merely to see if there was a single ray of hope, a letter to be written in a gentle-enough way and asking for the return of the few notes she had written him. She had not seen him now in nearly a month, and the last time she had, he had said he might soon be compelled to leave her awhile—to go to Pittsburgh to work. And it was his reply to this that she now held in her hand—from Pittsburgh! It was frightful! The future without him!

But Barton would never know really what had transpired, if she went back to him. In spite of all her delicious hours with Arthur, she could call him back, she felt sure. She had never really entirely dropped him, and he knew it. He had bored her dreadfully on occasion, arriving on off days when Arthur was not about, with flowers or candy, or both, and sitting on the porch steps and talking of the railroad business and of the whereabouts and doings of some of their old friends. It was shameful, she had thought at times, to see a man so patient, so hopeful, so good-natured as Barton, deceived in this way, and by her, who was so miserable over another. Her parents must see and know, she had thought at these times, but still, what else was she to do?

"I'm a bad girl," she kept telling herself. "I'm all wrong. What right have I to offer Barton what is left?" But still, somehow, she realized that Barton, if she chose to favor him, would only to be too grateful for even the leavings of others where she was concerned, and that even yet, if she but deigned to crook a finger, she could have him. He was so simple, so good-natured, so stolid and matter of fact, so different to Arthur whom (she could not help smiling at the thought of it) she was loving now about as Barton loved her—slavishly, hopelessly.

And then, as the days passed and Arthur did not write any more—just this one brief note—she at first grieved horribly, and then in a fit of numb despair attempted, bravely enough from one point of view, to adjust herself to the new situation. Why should she despair? Why die of agony where there were plenty who would still sigh for her—Barton among others? She was young, pretty, very—many told her so. She could, if she chose, achieve a vivacity which she did not feel. Why should she brook this unkindness without a thought of retaliation? Why shouldn't she enter upon a gay and heartless career, indulging in a dozen flirtations at once—dancing and killing all thoughts of Arthur in a round of frivolities? There were many who beckoned to her. She stood at her counter in the drug store on many a day and brooded over this, but at the thought of which one to begin with, she faltered. After her late love, all were so tame, for the present anyhow.

And then—and then—always there was Barton, the humble or faithful, to whom she had been so unkind and whom she had used and whom she still really liked. So often self-reproaching thoughts in connection with him crept over her. He must have known, must have seen how badly she was using him all this while, and yet he had not failed to come and come, until she had actually quarreled with him, and any one would have seen that it was literally hopeless. She could not help remembering, especially now in her pain, that he adored her. He was not calling on her now at all—by her indifference she had finally driven him away—but a word, a word—She waited for days, weeks, hoping against hope, and then——

The office of Barton's superior in the Great Eastern terminal had always made him an easy object for her blandishments, coming and going, as she frequently did, via this very station. He was in the office of the assistant train-despatcher on the ground floor, where passing to and from the local, which, at times, was quicker than a street-car, she could easily see him by peering in; only, she had carefully avoided him for nearly a year. If she chose now, and would call for a message-blank at the adjacent telegraph-window which was a part of his room, and raised her voice as she often had in the past, he could scarcely fail to hear, if he did not see her. And if he did, he would rise and come over—of that she was sure, for he never could resist her. It had been a wile of hers in the old days to do this or to make her presence felt by idling outside. After a month of brooding, she felt that she must act—her position as a deserted girl was too much. She could not stand it any longer really —the eyes of her mother, for one.

It was six-fifteen one evening when, coming out of the store in which she worked, she turned her step disconsolately homeward. Her heart was heavy, her face rather pale and drawn. She had stopped in the store's retiring-room before coming out to add to her charms as much as possible by a little powder and rouge and to smooth her hair. It would not take much to reallure her former sweetheart, she felt sure— and yet it might not be so easy after all. Suppose he had found another? But she could not believe that. It had scarcely been long enough since he had last attempted to see her, and he was really so very, very fond of her and so faithful. He was too slow and certain in his choosing— he had been so with her. Still, who knows? With this thought, she went forward in the evening, feeling for the first time the shame and pain that comes of deception, the agony of having to relinquish an ideal and the feeling of despair that comes to those who find themselves in the position of suppliants, stooping to something which in better days and better fortune they would not know. Arthur was the cause of this.

When she reached the station, the crowd that usually filled it at this hour was swarming. There were so many pairs like Arthur and herself laughing and hurrying away or so she felt. First glancing in the small mirror of a weighing scale to see if she were still of her former charm, she stopped thoughtfully at a little flower stand which stood outside, and for a few pennies purchased a tiny bunch of violets. She then went inside and stood near the window, peering first furtively to see if he were present. He was. Bent over his work, a green shade over his eyes, she could see his stolid, genial figure at a table. Stepping back a moment to ponder, she finally went forward and, in a clear voice, asked,

"May I have a blank, please?"

The infatuation of the discarded Barton was such that it brought him instantly to his feet. In his stodgy, stocky way he rose, his eyes glowing with a friendly hope, his mouth wreathed in smiles, and came over. At the sight of her, pale, but pretty—paler and prettier, really, than he had ever seen her—he thrilled dumbly.

"How are you, Shirley?" he asked sweetly, as he drew near, his eyes searching her face hopefully. He had not seen her for so long that he was intensely hungry, and her paler beauty appealed to him more than ever. Why wouldn't she have him? he was asking himself. Why wouldn't his persistent love yet win her? Perhaps it might. "I haven't seen you in a month of Sundays, it seems. How are the folks?"

"They're all right, Bart," she smiled archly, "and so am I. How have you been? It has been a long time since I've seen you. I've been wondering how you were. Have you been all right? I was just going to send a message."

As he had approached, Shirley had pretended at first not to see him, a moment later to affect surprise, although she was really suppressing a heavy sigh. The sight of him, after Arthur, was not reassuring. Could she really interest herself in him any more? Could she?

"Sure, sure," he replied genially; "I'm always all right. You couldn't kill me, you know. Not going away, are you, Shirl?" he queried interestedly.

"No; I'm just telegraphing to Mabel. She promised to meet me tomorrow, and I want to be sure she will."

"You don't come past here as often as you did, Shirley," he complained tenderly. "At least, I don't seem to see you so often," he added with a smile. "It isn't anything I have done, is it?" he queried, and then, when she protested quickly, added: "What's the trouble, Shirl? Haven't been sick, have you?"

She affected all her old gaiety and ease, feeling as though she would like to cry.

"Oh, no," she returned; "I've been all right. I've been going through the other door, I suppose, or coming in and going out on the Langdon Avenue car." (This was true, because she had been wanting to avoid him.) "I've been in such a hurry, most nights, that I haven't had time to stop, Bart. You know how late the store keeps us at times."

He remembered, too, that in the old days she had made time to stop or meet him occasionally.

"Yes, I know," he said tactfully. "But you haven't been to any of our old card-parties either of late, have you? At least, I haven't seen you. I've gone to two or three, thinking you might be there."

That was another thing Arthur had done—broken up her interest in these old store and neighborhood parties and a banjo-and-mandolin club to which she had once belonged. They had all seemed so pleasing and amusing in the old days—but now—* * * * In those days Bart had been her usual companion when his work permitted.

"No," she replied evasively, but with a forced air of pleasant remembrance; "I have often thought of how much fun we had at those, though. It was a shame to drop them. You haven't seen Harry Stull or Trina Task recently, have you?" she inquired, more to be saying something than for any interest she felt.

He shook his head negatively, then added:

"Yes, I did, too; here in the waiting-room a few nights ago. They were coming down-town to a theater, I suppose."

His face fell slightly as he recalled how it had been their custom to do this, and what their one quarrel had been about. Shirley noticed it. She felt the least bit sorry for him, but much more for herself, coming back so disconsolately to all this.

"Well, you're looking as pretty as ever, Shirley," he continued, noting that she had not written the telegram and that there was something wistful in her glance. "Prettier, I think," and she smiled sadly. Every word that she tolerated from him was as so much gold to him, so much of dead ashes to her. "You wouldn't like to come down some evening this week and see 'The Mouse-Trap,' would you? We haven't been to a theater together in I don't know when." His eyes sought hers in a hopeful, doglike way.

So—she could have him again—that was the pity of it! To have what she really did not want, did not care for! At the least nod now he would come, and this very devotion made it all but worthless, and so sad. She ought to marry him now for certain, if she began in this way, and could in a month's time if she chose, but oh, oh—could she? For the moment she decided that she could not, would not. If he had only repulsed her —told her to go—ignored her—but no; it was her fate to be loved by him in this moving, pleading way, and hers not to love him as she wished to love—to be loved. Plainly, he needed some one like her, whereas she, she——. She turned a little sick, a sense of the sacrilege of gaiety at this time creeping into her voice, and exclaimed:

"No, no!" Then seeing his face change, a heavy sadness come over it, "Not this week, anyhow, I mean" ("Not so soon," she had almost said). "I have several engagements this week and I'm not feeling well. But"—seeing his face change, and the thought of her own state returning—"you might come out to the house some evening instead, and then we can go some other time."

His face brightened intensely. It was wonderful how he longed to be with her, how the least favor from her comforted and lifted him up. She could see also now, however, how little it meant to her, how little it could ever mean, even if to him it was heaven. The old relationship would have to be resumed in toto, once and for all, but did she want it that way now that she was feeling so miserable about this other affair? As she meditated, these various moods racing to and fro in her mind, Barton seemed to notice, and now it occurred to him that perhaps he had not pursued her enough—was too easily put off. She probably did like him yet. This evening, her present visit, seemed to prove it.

"Sure, sure!" he agreed. "I'd like that. I'll come out Sunday, if you say. We can go any time to the play. I'm sorry, Shirley, if you're not feeling well. I've thought of you a lot these days. I'll come out Wednesday, if you don't mind."

She smiled a wan smile. It was all so much easier than she had expected—her triumph—and so ashenlike in consequence, a flavor of dead-sea fruit and defeat about it all, that it was pathetic. How could she, after Arthur? How could he, really?

"Make it Sunday," she pleaded, naming the farthest day off, and then hurried out.

Her faithful lover gazed after her, while she suffered an intense nausea. To think—to think—it should all be coming to this! She had not used her telegraph-blank, and now had forgotten all about it. It was not the simple trickery that discouraged her, but her own future which could find no better outlet than this, could not rise above it apparently, or that she had no heart to make it rise above it. Why couldn't she interest herself in some one different to Barton? Why did she have to return to him? Why not wait and meet some other—ignore him as before? But no, no; nothing mattered now—no one—it might as well be Barton really as any one, and she would at least make him happy and at the same time solve her own problem. She went out into the train-shed and climbed into her train. Slowly, after the usual pushing and jostling of a crowd, it drew out toward Latonia, that suburban region in which her home lay. As she rode, she thought.

"What have I just done? What am I doing?" she kept asking herself as the clacking wheels on the rails fell into a rhythmic dance and the houses of the brown, dry, endless city fled past in a maze. "Severing myself decisively from the past—the happy past—for supposing, once I am married, Arthur should return and want me again—suppose! Suppose!"

Below at one place, under a shed, were some market-gardeners disposing of the last remnants of their day's wares—a sickly, dull life, she thought. Here was Rutgers Avenue, with its line of red street-cars, many wagons and tracks and counter-streams of automobiles—how often had she passed it morning and evening in a shuttle-like way, and how often would, unless she got married! And here, now, was the river flowing smoothly between its banks lined with coal-pockets and wharves—away, away to the huge deep sea which she and Arthur had enjoyed so much. Oh, to be in a small boat and drift out, out into the endless, restless, pathless deep! Somehow the sight of this water, to-night and every night, brought back those evenings in the open with Arthur at Sparrows Point, the long line of dancers in Eckert's Pavilion, the woods at Atholby, the park, with the dancers in the pavilion—she choked back a sob. Once Arthur had come this way with her on just such an evening as this, pressing her hand and saying how wonderful she was. Oh,

Arthur! Arthur! And now Barton was to take his old place again—
forever, no doubt. She could not trifle with her life longer in this foolish
way, or his. What was the use? But think of it!

Yes, it must be—forever now, she told herself. She must marry. Time
would be slipping by and she would become too old. It was her only
future—marriage. It was the only future she had ever contemplated
really, a home, children, the love of some man whom she could love as
she loved Arthur. Ah, what a happy home that would have been for
her! But now, now——

But there must be no turning back now, either. There was no other
way. If Arthur ever came back—but fear not, he wouldn't! She had
risked so much and lost—lost him. Her little venture into true love had
been such a failure. Before Arthur had come all had been well enough.
Barton, stout and simple and frank and direct, had in some way—how,
she could scarcely realize now—offered sufficient of a future. But now,
now! He had enough money, she knew, to build a cottage for the two
of them. He had told her so. He would do his best always to make her
happy, she was sure of that. They could live in about the state her
parents were living in—or a little better, not much—and would never
want. No doubt there would be children, because he craved them—
several of them—and that would take up her time, long years of it—
the sad, gray years! But then Arthur, whose children she would have
thrilled to bear, would be no more, a mere memory—think of that!—
and Barton, the dull, the commonplace, would have achieved his finest
dream—and why?

Because love was a failure for her—that was why—and in her life
there could be no more true love. She would never love any one again
as she had Arthur. It could not be, she was sure of it. He was too
fascinating, too wonderful. Always, always, wherever she might be,
whoever she might marry, he would be coming back, intruding between
her and any possible love, receiving any possible kiss. It would be Arthur
she would be loving or kissing. She dabbed at her eyes with a tiny
handkerchief, turned her face close to the window and stared out, and
then as the environs of Latonia came into view, wondered (so deep is
romance): What if Arthur should come back at some time—or now!
Supposing he should be here at the station now, accidentally or on
purpose, to welcome her, to soothe her weary heart. He had met her
here before. How she would fly to him, lay her head on his shoulder,
forget forever that Barton ever was, that they had ever separated for an
hour. Oh, Arthur! Arthur!

But no, no; here was Latonia—here the viaduct over her train, the
long business street and the cars marked "Center" and "Langdon
Avenue" running back into the great city. A few blocks away in tree-

shaded Bethune Street, duller and plainer than ever, was her parents' cottage and the routine of that old life which was now, she felt, more fully fastened upon her than ever before—the lawn-mowers, the lawns, the front porches all alike. Now would come the going to and fro of Barton to business as her father and she now went to business, her keeping house, cooking, washing, ironing, sewing for Barton as her mother now did these things for her father and herself. And she would not be in love really, as she wanted to be. Oh, dreadful! She could never escape it really, now that she could endure it less, scarcely for another hour. And yet she must, must, for the sake of—for the sake of—she closed her eyes and dreamed.

She walked up the street under the trees, past the houses and lawns all alike to her own, and found her father on their veranda reading the evening paper. She sighed at the sight.

"Back, daughter?" he called pleasantly.

"Yes."

"Your mother is wondering if you would like steak or liver for dinner. Better tell her."

"Oh, it doesn't matter."

She hurried into her bedroom, threw down her hat and gloves, and herself on the bed to rest silently, and groaned in her soul. To think that it had all come to this!—Never to see him any more!—To see only Barton, and marry him and live in such a street, have four or five children, forget all her youthful companionships—and all to save her face before her parents, and her future. Why must it be? Should it be, really? She choked and stifled. After a little time her mother, hearing her come in, came to the door—thin, practical, affectionate, conventional.

"What's wrong, honey? Aren't you feeling well to-night? Have you a headache? Let me feel."

Her thin cool fingers crept over her temples and hair. She suggested something to eat or a headache powder right away.

"I'm all right, mother. I'm just not feeling well now. Don't bother. I'll get up soon. Please don't."

"Would you rather have liver or steak to-night, dear?"

"Oh, anything—nothing—please don't bother—steak will do—anything"—if only she could get rid of her and be at rest!

Her mother looked at her and shook her head sympathetically, then retreated quietly, saying no more. Lying so, she thought and thought—grinding, destroying thoughts about the beauty of the past, the darkness of the future—until able to endure them no longer she got up and, looking distractedly out of the window into the yard and the house next door, stared at her future fixedly. What should she do? What should she really do? There was Mrs. Kessel in her kitchen getting her dinner as usual, just as her own mother was now, and Mr. Kessel out on the front porch in his shirt-sleeves reading the evening paper. Beyond was Mr. Pollard in his yard, cutting the grass. All along Bethune Street were such houses and such people—simple, commonplace souls all—clerks, managers, fairly successful craftsmen, like her father and Barton, excellent in their way but not like Arthur the beloved, the lost—and here was she, perforce, or by decision of necessity, soon to be one of them, in some such street as this no doubt, forever and—. For the moment it choked and stifled her.

She decided that she would not. No, no, no! There must be some other way—many ways. She did not have to do this unless she really wished to—would not—only—. Then going to the mirror she looked at her face and smoothed her hair.

"But what's the use?" she asked of herself wearily and resignedly after a time. "Why should I cry? Why shouldn't I marry Barton? I don't amount to anything, anyhow. Arthur wouldn't have me. I wanted him, and I am compelled to take some one else—or no one—what difference does it really make who? My dreams are too high, that's all. I wanted Arthur, and he wouldn't have me. I don't want Barton, and he crawls at my feet. I'm a failure, that's what's the matter with me."

And then, turning up her sleeves and removing a fichu which stood out too prominently from her breast, she went into the kitchen and, looking about for an apron, observed:

"Can't I help? Where's the tablecloth?" and finding it among napkins and silverware in a drawer in the adjoining room, proceeded to set the table.

BIOGRAPHICAL NOTES

Mary Austin

Mary Austin was born in Carlinville, Illinois, in 1868. She moved to California at the age of nineteen and lived for many years on or near the Mojave desert. In 1906, she joined the artist colony of Carmel, California. In 1924, she moved to Santa Fe, New Mexico. Her first book, *Land of Little Rain* (1903), a collection of sketches, and *The Basket Woman* (1904) and *Lost Borders* (1909), collections of short stories, deal with the landscape and people of the California desert. Later she was to write novels and short fiction dealing with a remarkable variety of subjects and settings. In 1918, she published *The Young Woman Citizen*, a political handbook addressed to the newly enfranchised woman voter; her autobiography, *Earth Horizon* (1932), was well received and widely read. Despite her various talents and wide-ranging interests, she returned again and again to Western and Southwestern subjects. She published *The American Rhythm* (1923), a study of American Indian verse and song, and *Children Sing in the Far West* (1928), a collection of Indian songs written with the children she was teaching at the time. *The Arrow Maker* (1911) is a play about Indian life. She died in August 1934.

Ambrose Bierce

Ambrose Bierce was born on a farm in Ohio in 1842, but he grew up in northern Indiana before studying surveying and engineering at the Kentucky Military Institute (1859–1860). With the outbreak of the Civil War, he enlisted as a private in the Ninth Indiana Infantry, eventually rising to the rank of lieutenant and serving as the regimental cartographer. He was at the battles of Shiloh, Chickamauga, and Kennesaw Mountain, among others, and these events served as the background for his most important stories of war, published in *Tales of Soldiers and Civilians* (1891). After the war he worked as an editor and journalist for newspapers in California, including the *San Francisco Examiner*, while publishing fiction in magazines. His sardonic humor, misanthropic themes, and predilection for Gothic horror earned him the epithet "bitter Bierce," and his essays and stories underscore the tragic elements of human existence. His best fiction, however, is essentially impressionistic, recording the sensory experiences of the central character with extraordinary clarity and verisimilitude, as he does in his masterpiece, "An Occurrence at Owl Creek Bridge." He died in Mexico under mysterious circumstances, having disappeared in 1914 while on a trip to observe the insurrection by Pancho Villa.

George Washington Cable

George Washington Cable was born in New Orleans in 1844 to parents who were originally from the North and who had freed their slaves well before the Civil War. At the age of nineteen he enlisted in the Confederate cavalry and was wounded in battle. After the war, he began his writing career as a journalist for the *New Orleans Picayune* but soon moved to local-color fiction, capturing the dialects and rich social texture of his native city. His first collection of stories, *Old Creole Days* (1879), established his reputation as a Southern writer, and his masterpiece, a complex novel of New Orleans entitled *The Grandissimes*, followed in 1880. His subsequent works, including *Doctor Sevier* (1884), a realistic novel of plague in Louisiana, *John March, Southerner* (1894), a romantic exposé of Reconstruction economics and politics, and *The Cavalier* (1901), a historical novel of the Civil War, were not nearly so successful and did not find a wide audience. *The Silent South* (1885) and *The Negro Question* (1890) revealed his deep concern for African Americans and the fundamental need for racial justice. The social and psychological depth of his local-color realism, the accuracy of his descriptions, and his willingness to confront reformist social issues made him one of the most important Southern writers of the late nineteenth century. He died in Florida in 1925.

Abraham Cahan

Abraham Cahan was born in a village near Vilna, Lithuania, in 1860 into an Orthodox Jewish family. He learned Russian and became a teacher in a secular Jewish school as well as a member of a revolutionary study circle. He fled Russia for the United States in 1882 after the assassination of Czar Alexander II. During the 1880s and 1890s he taught English, was active in radical politics, helped organize the first Jewish trade unions, and wrote for newspapers and journals in three languages. In 1897 he helped found the *Jewish Daily Forward*, the great Yiddish-language social-democratic newspaper, which he edited from 1902 until his death in 1951. He wrote fiction in English for twenty-five years (and some in Yiddish), from his first published story in 1892 to his last and best-known work, *The Rise of David Levinsky*, in 1917. He wrote two other novels, *Yekl: A Tale of the New York Ghetto* (1896) and *The White Terror and the Red: A Novel of Revolutionary Russia* (1905), and numerous short stories, some of which are collected in *The Imported Bridegroom and Other Stories* (1898).

Willa Cather

Willa Cather was born in 1873 in Virginia, the eldest child of Charles and Mary Cather, both descendants of established families of the Commonwealth. In 1883 the family moved to Nebraska, joining relatives who had earlier settled on the prairie. This crucial move, dislocating and dramatic, introduced her to a landscape and a way of life that she would later memorialize in a series of novels of the plains, *O Pioneers!*, *My Ántonia*, and *A Lost Lady*. Energetic, intelligent, outspoken, Cather grew up in Red Cloud before moving on to the University of Nebraska, where she began her journalistic career writing for local newspapers. After graduation she worked as a teacher and journalist in Pittsburgh before moving to New York to become an editor at *McClure's Magazine*. With the appearance of *O Pioneers!* in 1913 she was able to devote her life to her own fiction, publishing *Death Comes for the Archbishop*, *The Professor's House*, and *Shadows on the Rock*. Her short stories, which explore basic themes of the barrenness of rural life on the plains, the need for aesthetic fulfillment, and the role of memory as an ongoing part of the present, filled several volumes, the most remarkable of which are *The Troll Garden* (1905) and *Youth and the Bright Medusa* (1920). She received the Pulitzer Prize in 1923 for *One of Ours*, a novel about a soldier in World War I. She died in New York in 1947.

Charles Waddell Chesnutt

Charles W. Chesnutt was the first African-American writer to create a substantial body of fiction read and admired by readers of all races. Born in Cleveland in 1858, Chesnutt moved as a young man to Fayetteville, North Carolina, the region that provides the setting for many of his stories. Schooled in Latin as well as English and American literature, he was drawn early to journalism, then to law, and then to the life of an author. His first important book was *The Conjure Woman* (1899), a collection of black folk tales told by Uncle Julius, a ranconteur and manipulator who uses stories as a means to personal rewards. Also that year Chesnutt published a biography of Frederick Douglass and another volume of short fiction, *The Wife of His Youth and Other Stories of the Color Line*, which explores issues of race, justice, and moral responsibility. This volume contained his most successful fiction, powerful stories that develop themes of the intransigence of prejudice in both the white and black communities. It is significant, however, that Chesnutt gives his African-American characters moral agency, the power to choose a course of action, placing them in situations requiring the most profound ethical decisions. The three novels that followed, *The House Behind the Cedars* (1900), *The Marrow of Tradition* (1901), and *The Colonel's Dream* (1905), were less enthusiastically received, and Chesnutt abandoned literature to devote himself to legal stenography, the struggle for racial justice in America, and to his family. In 1928 the NAACP awarded him the Spingarn Medal. Chesnutt died in Cleveland in 1932.

Kate Chopin

Kate O'Flaherty was born on February 8, 1851, in St. Louis, Missouri, where she graduated from the St. Louis Academy of the Sacred Heart in 1868. In 1870 she married Oscar Chopin, a Creole gentleman from Louisiana, and for the next decade they lived in New Orleans, later the setting for her most important novel. Upon the failure of her husband's cotton business, the family, which included six children, moved to Clouterville, in northern Louisiana, where Oscar died of fever in 1883. The following year, Kate moved the family back to St. Louis, where she devoted herself to her writing. Her stories of passion, love, racial bigotry, and confining social conventions began appearing in the 1880s, but they did not attract widespread attention until they were collected in *Bayou Folk* (1894) and *A Night in Acadie* (1897). An early novel, *At Fault* (1890), was less successful, but her second novel, *The Awakening* (1899), proved to be a masterpiece, generally regarded as the most important work of fiction on the emerging New Woman theme. Its frank treatment of a woman's passion outside of marriage proved controversial, though, and her work briefly fell into disfavor. By 1911, however, Fred Lewis Pattee had proclaimed her the genius of the American short story, and she is now one of the most widely read writers of the period, celebrated for her frank treatment of sexuality and marriage, responsibility and freedom, and the relationship of the individual to society. She died in St. Louis, the city of her birth, on August 22, 1904.

Rose Terry Cooke

Rose Terry Cooke was writing fiction with local-color tendencies a full decade before the publication of Bret Harte's most popular stories after the Civil War, which are often taken to mark the inception of the movement. Born in Connecticut in 1827, she attended Hartford Female Seminary and served as a tutor before a small inheritance offered her time to devote to literature. In 1873 she married Rollin H. Cooke, a widower with two young daughters, and the financial support of the family fell largely to her, to what she could earn with her pen. Originally a poet, she turned to fiction to capture the language and character of her native Yankee region, and her work features the poverty, narrowness, and restricted circumstances of the women of her rural area, often in stories set in the past. She also used her fiction to address the women's issues of the day, particularly the relentless duties of the family household and the rigid social structure of New England that limited opportunities for unmarried women. The best of her work is contained in four volumes of stories, *Somebody's Neighbors* (1881), *Root-Bound* (1885), *The Sphinx's Children and Other People's* (1886), and *Huckleberries Gathered from New England Hills* (1891). Although her work was never a major success, it is notable for the accurate depiction of a region, its use of folk dialect, and its challenge to traditional values. She died at home in 1892.

Stephen Crane

Stephen Crane was born in Newark, New Jersey, in 1871, the fourteenth child of a father who was a Methodist minister and a mother who was the daughter of a Methodist bishop. The Reverend Crane died when Stephen was only eight, after which his mother supported him through her journalism, writing for religious magazines. After preparatory school at Claverack College, he spent one unsuccessful semester at Lafayette College and another at Syracuse University, where he began writing *Maggie: A Girl of the Streets* (1893), the first naturalistic urban novel in America. With the book publication of *The Red Badge of Courage* in 1895, Crane became one of the most famous writers in the world, widely sought after for his journalism as well as for his fiction and verse, which included *The Black Riders and Other Lines* (1895) and *War is Kind* (1899). His short stories, some of which rank among the best ever written in English, display an impressive range, from the naturalistic depiction of the Irish poor in the Bowery, to impressionistic evocations of adventure in the West, to vividly realistic portrayals of men at war, to satiric treatments of the themes of popular fiction. When he died of tuberculosis in Badenweiler, Germany, in 1900, he was only twenty-eight, and yet his brief career had made him one of the most important American writers of his era.

Theodore Dreiser

Theodore Dreiser was born in Terre Haute, Indiana, on August 27, 1871. After a poor and difficult childhood, Dreiser broke into newspaper work in Chicago in 1892. He read and was deeply influenced by the evolutionary theories of Herbert Spencer and Thomas Huxley. A successful career as a magazine writer in New York during the late 1890s was followed by his first novel, *Sister Carrie* (1900). When this work made little impact, Dreiser published no fiction until *Jennie Gerhardt* in 1911. He then wrote his trilogy of desire—*The Financier* (1912), *The Titan* (1914), and *The Stoic* (posthumously published in 1947). These novels deal with a financier named Frank Cowperwood, modeled after the real financier Charles Yerkes, and are harshly critical of American capitalism. There then followed a decade and a half of major work in a number of literary forms, which was capped in 1925 by *An American Tragedy*, a novel that brought him universal acclaim. He published three collections of short fiction: *Free, and Other Stories* (1918), *Chains* (1927), and *A Gallery of Women* (1929). Dreiser was increasingly preoccupied by philosophical and political issues during the last two decades of his life. He died in Los Angeles on December 28, 1945.

Paul Laurence Dunbar

The son of former Kentucky slaves, Paul Laurence Dunbar was born in Dayton, Ohio, in 1872. He was drawn to the literary life from an early age and recalled that he wrote his first poem at the age of six. He published his first book of verse, *Oak and Ivy*, in 1893 and his second, *Majors and Minors*, in 1895. A third volume based on the first two was issued under the title *Lyrics of Lowly Life* (1896) with an introduction by W. D. Howells. During his brief lifetime, Dunbar was primarily known as a dialect poet, though his talents were far more diverse, and not all nor even his best poetry was written in dialect. In addition to eight volumes of poetry, he wrote songs, plays, short fiction, essays, and four novels—*The Uncalled* (1898), *The Love of Landry* (1900), *The Fanatics* (1901), and *The Sport of the Gods* (1902). After graduation from high school, Dunbar worked as an elevator operator for four dollars a week. Later, he was briefly employed by Frederick Douglass and formed an admiring friendship with the man. After the endorsement of William Dean Howells, Dunbar's literary reputation increased, and he soon became one of the most popular poets of the day. In 1897, Dunbar met Alice Moore (later Alice Dunbar-Nelson). They were married in 1898, but there were temperamental differences and they were separated four years later. He became ill with pneumonia in 1899, and doctors detected tuberculosis. Dunbar's health steadily deteriorated, and he returned to Dayton in 1903, lonely, ill, and more pessimistic than he had been in more vigorous days. He died in February of 1906 at the age of thirty-four.

Alice Dunbar-Nelson

Alice Moore (Dunbar-Nelson) was born in New Orleans in 1875. The daughter of a former slave, her racial heritage was a mix of black, white, and perhaps Indian extraction. Dunbar-Nelson was light enough to pass for white and did so upon occasion. Nevertheless, she consciously identified herself with Creole culture and worked energetically for African-American political and social causes. Dunbar-Nelson was educated in Louisiana and supported herself teaching English; at various times she attended colleges and universities in the North. She began her literary career early, publishing poetry at a young age, but she soon turned to short fiction as her favored genre. Paul Laurence Dunbar noticed one of her poems in a Boston periodical and began a two-year correspondence with her. Eventually they met and became engaged. They were married in 1898, but the marriage was not a happy one and they separated in 1902; in 1916, she married Robert Nelson, a journalist. Dunbar-Nelson published only two collections of short fiction: *Violets and Other Tales* (1895) and *The Goodness of St. Rocque and Other Stories* (1899). She continued to write fiction and poetry after that, but, more and more, she devoted her time to political activism. She was a political organizer for black women and in 1922 headed the Anti-Lynching Crusade in Delaware. Alice Dunbar-Nelson died in Philadelphia in 1935.

Harold Frederic

Harold Frederic was born on a farm in upstate New York in 1856. He was editor of the *Utica Observer* and the *Albany Evening Journal* before going to England in 1884 as London correspondent for *The New York Times*. From this post Frederic wrote fiction ranging widely in subject matter from historical romances of the American Revolution and Civil War to satirical portraits of London society. A visit to Russia motivated him to write *The New Exodus* (1892), a condmenation of anti-Semitism. His best novels depict with psychological realism characters beset by contemporary political, economic, and religious pressures; these include *Seth's Brother's Wife* (1887), *The Copperhead* (1893), *The Market-Place* (1899), and his masterpiece, *The Damnation of Theron Ware* (1896). *Marsena and Other Stories* (1894) is a volume of short fiction dealing with the Civil War. Frederic died in 1898.

Mary Wilkins Freeman

Mary E. Wilkins was born in 1852 in Randolph, Massachusetts, where her father was a carpenter. Her mother, Eleanor, came from one of the founding families of the area. In 1867 the family moved to Brattleboro, Vermont, where Mary went to high school before attending Mt. Holyoke Seminary for a year. She established her literary reputation in 1887 with her first volume of adult fiction, *A Humble Romance and Other Stories*, which deals with village and family life, the lingering grip of a staunch Calvinism on New England thinking, and the aspirations of the young for a better life. Her second volume, *A New England Nun and*

Other Stories (1891), further advanced her reputation, as did her novel *Pembroke* (1894), a grim portrayal of the harsh values of the region. Her fiction customarily rests on a strong plot, deftly drawn characters who speak the regional dialect, and the exploration of struggles in the lives of rural women. In 1902 she married Dr. Charles Freeman, a union that seems to have been mutually supportive until alcoholism drove him into a mental institution and she sought a legal separation. In 1926, her reputation firmly established, Freeman was awarded the Howells Medal for fiction by the American Academy of Arts and Letters, and she joined Edith Wharton as the first women elected to the National Institute of Arts and Letters. She died in New Jersey in 1930.

Zona Gale

Zona Gale was born in Portage, Wisconsin, in August 1874. After her graduation from the University of Wisconsin in 1895, she worked as a journalist, first in Milwaukee and later in New York. She moved in literary circles in New York and was for a time engaged to the poet Ridgely Torrence. Her first novels, *Romance Island* (1906) and *The Loves of Pelleas and Etarre* (1907), were airy romances, but when she began to exploit regional materials in the Friendship Village stories she personally returned to her birthplace and remained there for the rest of her life. These tales possess something of the sentimentality of her earlier work, but they were written with the confidence of long acquaintance with the landscape and the people of Wisconsin. These local-color pieces were followed by grimmer novels, such as *Birth* (1918), *Miss Lulu Bett* (1920), and *Borgia* (1929); Gale adapted *Miss Lulu Bett* to the stage, and the play won a Pulitzer Prize in 1921. A committed feminist and ardent pacifist, Gale was a social and political progressive who campaigned for Robert M. La Follette and joined the Save Sacco and Vanzetti movement. In her later years she was deeply influenced by Eastern mysticism, and her fiction reflects that interest. In 1928, at the age of fifty-four, Gale married William L. Breese, and they adopted a three-year-old girl. Gale died of pneumonia ten years later.

Hamlin Garland

Hamlin Garland was a radical of the prairies whose major contributions to American literature came early in his career in his naturalistic stories of midwestern agrarian life. Born in Wisconsin in 1860, he experienced the grinding labors of farm life on the prairies of Iowa and South Dakota before moving to Boston to write his masterpiece, *Main-Travelled Roads*, published in 1891. Three years later he produced *Crumbling Idols*, a theoretical reflection on the aesthetic implications of democracy, the nature of impressionism in art and literature, and the need for a uniquely American literature. *Rose of Dutcher's Coolly* (1895) is a startling depiction of the emerging New Woman, one that seems "modern" even a century after its publication. After two decades of writing popular romances, such as *The Captain of the Gray-Horse Troop*, he turned in the final period of his life to nine volumes of autobiographical sketches, winning the Pulitzer Prize in 1921 for *A Daughter of the Middle Border*, based on the life of his mother. He died in Los Angeles in 1940.

Charlotte Perkins Gilman

Charlotte Anna Perkins was born in Hartford, Connecticut, on July 3, 1860. Her father deserted the family when she was an infant, and her childhood was filled with poverty and disillusionment. In 1884 she married the artist Charles Stetson, and their only child, Katherine, was born the following year, after which Charlotte fell into a prolonged depression. The "rest cure" she was prescribed served as the background for her most famous story, "The Yellow Wallpaper" (1892). After her divorce in 1888, she quickly became a leading feminist writer, publishing *Women and Economics* in 1898, widely regarded as the bible of rights for women, and *Man-Made World* in 1911, an analysis of the destructiveness of economic dependence on men. She also wrote a series of Utopian novels, the most famous of which is *Herland* (1915). In 1900 she married her cousin, George Houghton Gilman, and they enjoyed a happy union until his death in 1934. The next year, following her diagnosis of breast cancer, she committed suicide by taking chloroform. *The Living of Charlotte Perkins Gilman: An Autobiography* appeared in 1935.

Joel Chandler Harris

Joel Chandler Harris was born on December 9, 1848, near Eatonton, Georgia. His parents never married, and soon after his birth his father, an Irish laborer, deserted the family. In 1862, Harris began a four-year apprenticeship as a printer at the Turnwald plantation in Putnam County, Georgia, where the journal *The Countryman* was published. Through this position he was able to publish his first writing. In 1866 he began his career as a journalist, working for a number of newspapers around the South. In 1876 he began his work at the *Atlanta Constitution*, where he eventually became an editor. During this time he also married Esther LaRose. Harris was an avid student of black folklore and wrote several collections of stories based on his studies, known as the *Uncle Remus Tales*. The first volume, *Nights with Uncle Remus: Myths and Legends of the Old Plantation*, was published in 1883. Other works include *Daddy Jake, the Runaway, and Short Stories Told after Dark* (1889), *Little Mr. Thimblefinger and His Queer Country* (1894), and *The Chronicles of Aunt Minervy Ann* (1899). In 1900 Harris resigned from the *Constitution* so that he could concentrate on his fiction. He founded *Uncle Remus's Magazine* in 1906. Harris died in Atlanta in 1908.

Bret Harte

Francis Bret Harte was born in Albany, New York, in 1836. Confined by ill health from the time he was six until he was ten, he read widely in the library of his father, a schoolteacher, who encouraged his literary interests. During his early teens he worked in a lawyer's office and in the accounting room of a merchant. At about the age of sixteen he moved to California, worked as a printer, schoolteacher, and finally in a mint. He also began to publish stories and poems in various magazines. In 1857 he became a typesetter for the *Golden Era* in San Francisco and contributed short sketches to the publication. *The Californian* published his *Condensed Novels and Other Papers* (1867), which were parodies of current fiction. By 1868 he had achieved local fame and was made editor of a new magazine, the *Overland Monthly*. His story "The Luck of Roaring Camp" was published in its second issue and his reputation quickly spread across the continent. In 1871, at the request of eastern editors, he returned to New York. After great initial success, Harte fell into financial difficulties. As a consequence he was glad to accept a position as a U.S. consular agent in Crefeld, Germany, in 1878, leaving his wife and four children behind in America. Two years later he was transferred to Glasgow and eventually settled in London, where he continued writing stories and was welcomed into literary circles. He died in Camberley, England, in 1902.

William Dean Howells

William Dean Howells was born in Martin's Ferry, Ohio, on March 1, 1837. His father was a printer and newspaperman, and the family moved from town to town. As a boy he learned the skill of printer's devil; by the time he was in his teens he was setting type for his own verse. Between 1856 and 1861 he worked as a reporter for the *Ohio State Journal*. About this time his poems began to appear in the *Atlantic Monthly*. His campaign biography of Abraham Lincoln, compiled in 1860, prompted the administration to offer him the consulship at Venice, a post he held from 1861 to 1865. He married Elinor Gertrude Mead in 1862 in Paris. On his return to the United States in 1865, Howells worked in New York before going to Boston as assistant to James T. Fields of the *Atlantic Monthly*. In 1871 he became editor in chief of the magazine; in this position he worked with many young writers, among them Mark Twain and Henry James, both of whom became his close friends. He later joined the editorial staff of *Harper's* in New York, where he contributed his "Easy Chair" essays, many of which later appeared in his *Criticism and Fiction* (1891). His first novel, *Their Wedding Journey*, appeared in 1872. *The Rise of Silas Lapham* was serialized in *Century Magazine* before it was published in book form in 1885. *A Hazard of New Fortunes* was published five years later. Howells's position as critic, writer, and enthusiastic exponent of the new realism earned him the respected title of Dean of American letters. He died in 1920.

Henry James

Henry James was born in 1843 in Washington Place, New York, of Scottish and Irish ancestry. His father was a prominent theologian and philosopher, and his elder brother, William, became famous as a philosopher and psychologist. He attended schools in New York and later in London, Paris, and Geneva, entering the Law School at Harvard in 1862. In 1864 he began to contribute reviews and short stories to American journals. In 1875, after two prior visits to Europe, he settled for a year in Paris, where he met Flaubert, Turgenev, and other literary figures. The next year he moved to London, where he became so popular in society that in the winter of 1878–79 he confessed to accepting 107 invitations. In 1898 he left London and went to live at Lamb House,

Rye, Sussex. Henry James became a naturalized English citizen in 1915. In addition to many short stories, plays, and books of criticism, autobiography, and travel, he wrote some twenty novels, the first published being *Roderick Hudson* (1875). They include *Washington Square* (1881), *The Portrait of a Lady* (1881), *The Princess Casamassima* (1886), *The Tragic Muse* (1890), *The Spoils of Poynton* (1897), *The Wings of the Dove* (1902), *The Ambassadors* (1903), and *The Golden Bowl* (1904). James died in England in 1916.

Sarah Orne Jewett

Sarah Orne Jewett was born in South Berwick, Maine, in 1849, the daughter of a country doctor and a descendent of a sea-faring family. In 1865 she graduated from Berwick Academy and, inspired by Harriet Beecher Stowe's *The Pearl of Orr's Island*, began to write stories capturing the character and landscape of rural Maine. Her first sketches, many of which had appeared in the *Atlantic Monthly*, were gathered in *Deephaven* (1877) and *Country By-Ways* (1881) before the publication of her first novel, *A Country Doctor* (1884), which explores the difficulties of a woman combining a professional career with marriage. Jewett published two additional volumes of short fiction, *A White Heron and Other Stories* (1886) and *Strangers and Wayfarers* (1890), before the appearance of her masterpiece, *The Country of the Pointed Firs* (1896), often regarded as the most important work of local-color literature. In 1901 she was awarded an honorary Litt.D. degree by Bowdoin College, the first woman accorded this distinction. She had come to be recognized as a writer of eminence in regional fiction, without peer in capturing provincial life in Maine. After a head injury in a carriage accident in 1902, she never recovered her previous literary capacity. She died on June 24, 1909, at home in Maine as she had wanted, with "the lilacs in bloom and all the chairs in their places."

Grace Elizabeth King

Grace Elizabeth King was born on November 29, 1852, in New Orleans, where she lived her entire life save for the period of the Civil War. Her father was a lawyer and politician, and the King family lived comfortably in aristocratic Creole society even though they were themselves Protestants of Anglo-Saxon background. After the devastation of the war, however, they were reduced to modest circumstances, living in a working-class neighborhood. This change of stature provided the themes for her most important work, which deals with the social and psychological complexity of the South during Reconstruction, and the humiliation of a fallen aristocracy. Grace Elizabeth King began her writing career in outrage over the portrayal of the Creole gentry in the fiction of George Washington Cable, and she said she was determined to cast her society in a more favorable light, with greater sympathy for what they had endured. She did so in an early novel, *Monsieur Motte* (1888), and *Tales of a Time and Place* (1892) before the fruition of her finest work in *Balcony Stories* (1893), her most artistically successful fiction. Although she published two more novels, notably *The Pleasant Ways of St. Médard* (1916), the rest of her career was devoted primarily to the writing of historical studies of her region. She died in New Orleans in 1932.

Jack London

Jack London—his real name was John Griffith London—had a wild and colorful youth on the waterfront of San Francisco, his native city. Born in 1876, he left school at the age of fourteen and worked in a cannery. By the time he was sixteen he had been both an oyster pirate and a member of the Fish Patrol in San Francisco Bay. In 1893 he joined a sealing cruise, which took him as far as Japan. Returning to the United States, he traveled throughout the country. He was determined to become a writer and read voraciously. After a brief period of study at the University of California, he joined the gold rush to the Klondike in 1897. He returned to San Francisco the following year and wrote about his experiences. His short stories of the Yukon were published in *Overland Monthly* and the *Atlantic Monthly*, and in 1900 his first collection, *The Son of the Wolf*, appeared, bringing him national fame. In 1902 he went to London, where he studied the slum conditions of the East End. He wrote about his experiences in *The People of the Abyss* (1903). A prolific writer, he published an enormous number of stories and novels. Besides several collections of short stories, he wrote many novels, including *The Call of the Wild* (1903), *The Sea-Wolf* (1904), *White Fang* (1906), *Martin Eden* (1909), and *John Barleycorn* (1913). Jack London died in 1916, at his home in California.

Mary Noailles Murfree

Mary Noailles Murfree was born in Murfreesboro, Tennessee, in 1850. A childhood illness left her permanently lame, and perhaps as a result she turned her attention and energies to writing at an early age. The family spent their summers in the Cumberland Mountains and she developed an affectionate fascination with the Tennessee mountain folk and made them the subject of her many local-color stories. During the Civil War, she and her sister were tutored at home; after the war, she attended a boarding school in Philadelphia. Murfree published under the pseudonym Charles Egbert Craddock. A popular and well-known writer, particularly after the publication of *In the Tennessee Mountains* (1884), when her identity as a woman was revealed it caused something of a national stir. Murfree published more than ten volumes of local-color stories, including *Down the Ravine* (1885) and *The Mystery of Witch Face Mountain* (1895). She also wrote a number of novels, of which *The Prophet of the Great Smokey Mountains* (1885) is perhaps the most enduring. Murfree was able to coordinate a romantic strain, mostly exhibited in elegant and lyrical description, with an accurate ear for Appalachian dialect and a realist's eye for telling detail. She died in 1922.

Frank Norris

Frank Norris was born in Chicago in 1870 but moved to San Francisco with his parents in 1884. After studying art in Paris, Norris enrolled as an undergraduate at the University of California at Berkeley. There, under the influence of Zola's fiction, he began a novel of lower- and middle-class life set in San Francisco, which he later published as *McTeague* (1899). In 1895 and 1896 he was in South Africa and reported on the Boer War for *Collier's* and the *San Francisco Chronicle*. After being captured by the Boers he was ordered to leave the country, and he returned to California to join the staff of the magazine *The Wave*. In 1898 he went to Cuba, where he reported the Santiago campaign of the Spanish-American War for *McClure's Magazine*. Upon his return in 1899 he was employed by the publishing firm of Doubleday, Page and Company, which that year issued *McTeague* and *Blix*. He published *A Deal in Wheat and Other Stories of the New and Old West* in 1903. It was about this time that Norris conceived his plan of writing an "Epic of the Wheat," a projected trilogy examining social and economic forces in America. He completed *The Octopus* (1901) and *The Pit* (1903) before his sudden death following an appendix operation.

John M. Oskison

John M. Oskison, the son of a Cherokee mother and a European father, was born in 1874 in the Indian Territory, which covered parts of Oklahoma, Nebraska, and Kansas. He took a degree in literature from Stanford University in 1898 before going on to graduate work at Harvard. His early career was as a journalist writing for Cherokee newspapers and later for the *New York Evening Post* and *Collier's Weekly*. In 1899, however, he won a short-story contest sponsored by *Century Magazine*, and he turned his attention to fiction, eventually producing three novels, *Wild Harvest* (1925), *Black Jack Davy* (1926), and *Brothers Three* (1935). Among his other books are *A Texas Titan: The Story of Sam Houston* (1929) and *Tecumseh and His Times* (1938). Oskison was thoroughly assimilated into American society but retained his interest in his Cherokee background and often described things from that point of view, particularly with regard to the conflict of values between the two cultures, the subject of his best-known short story, "The Problem of Old Harjo." He died in 1947.

Harriet Beecher Stowe

Harriet Beecher Stowe was born in Litchfield, Connecticut, on June 14, 1811, the seventh child of Lyman and Roxanna Foote Beecher. Her family produced a number of religious leaders, teachers, and reformers, with abolitionism as one of their chief causes. For a time she attended school in Hartford, but in 1832 she rejoined her family in Cincinnati, where her father ran the Lane Theological Seminary. Her proximity to Kentucky, a slave state, made her increasingly aware of the horrors of slavery, a concern she later expressed in *Uncle Tom's Cabin*, the first important abolitionist novel in America. In 1836, Harriet married Calvin Ellis Stowe, a minister who also taught at Bowdoin College. With the publication of *Uncle Tom's Cabin*, Stowe became the best-selling author in the country, and the popular magazines competed for her work, which focused on local-color fiction and was gathered in such volumes as *The Pearl of Orr's Island, Oldtown Folks,* and *Oldtown Fireside Stories.* A popular figure to the end of her life, Stowe wrote and lectured widely until she became ill in 1878. She died on July 1, 1896, and was buried in Andover, Massachusetts.

Sui Sin Far

Edith Maud Eaton was born in England in 1865, the daughter of a British merchant father and a Chinese mother, and she was brought to the United States at the age of six. With the beginning of her writing career in the 1880s, she adopted the name Sui Sin Far ("water fragrant flower"), which she used thereafter in both her personal and professional life. Never married, she earned a living as a stenographer, journalist, and writer of short stories, many of them for children. Her stature in American literature derives from the fact that she is the first Chinese-American author, one who wrote in English, in America, about immigrants from China who had settled in the United States. Despite the virulent Sinophobia that had led to the Chinese Exclusion Act of 1882, her work appeared in the leading newspapers and magazines of her day. Her short stories present a normative perspective from within the Asian community, viewing white America as an exotic, inscrutable culture with "foreign" values new arrivals must struggle to comprehend. Although she began publishing fiction in the 1880s, she did not produce a volume until *Mrs. Spring Fragrance,* her only book, appeared in 1912. Long ignored, this volume has become the focus of renewed attention for the charm of its language, the humor and insight of its characterizations, its vivid portrayal of life within the Asian-American community, and its sensitive and perceptive exploration of biracialism in a multicultural society. She died in 1914 in Montreal, where a headstone describes her as "the righteous one who does not forget China."

Mark Twain

Samuel Langhorne Clemens was born on November 30, 1835, in Florida, Missouri, about forty miles southwest of Hannibal, the Mississippi River town Clemens was to celebrate as Mark Twain. In 1853 he left

home, earning a living as an itinerant typesetter, and four years later
became an apprentice pilot on the Mississippi River, a career cut short
by the outbreak of the Civil War. For five years, as a prospector and a
journalist, Clemens lived in Nevada and California. In February 1863
he first used the pseudonym Mark Twain as the signature to a humorous
travel letter; and a trip to Europe and the Holy Land in 1867 became
the basis of his first major book, *The Innocents Abroad* (1869). *Roughing It* (1872), his account of experiences in the West, was followed by
a satirical novel, *The Gilded Age* (1873), *Sketches: New and Old*
(1875), *Tom Sawyer* (1876), *A Tramp Abroad* (1880), *The Prince and
the Pauper* (1882), *Life on the Mississippi* (1883), and his masterpiece,
Huckleberry Finn (1885). Following the publication of *A Connecticut
Yankee* (1889) and *Pudd'nhead Wilson* (1894), Twain was compelled
by debts to move his family abroad. By 1900 he had completed a round-
the-world lecture tour, and, his fortunes mended, he returned to America. He was as well known for his white suit and his mane of white hair
as he was for his uncompromising stands against injustice and imperi-
alism and for his invariably quoted comments on any subject under the
sun. Samuel Clemens died on April 21, 1910.

Edith Wharton

Edith Newbold Jones was born into the aristocratic society of New York
in 1862, where she was educated privately prior to her marriage to
Edward Wharton in 1885. Although her work would eventually contain
verse, travel accounts, and autobiographical reflections, her highest
achievement was in the novel. She began writing fiction in the 1890s,
exploring the novel of manners with great psychological insight and a
mastery of fiction unequaled in her time by anyone other than Henry
James. She was widely regarded as among the foremost American writers of the early twentieth century. Her masterpieces in novel form include *The House of Mirth* (1905), *Ethan Frome* (1911), *Summer* (1917),
and *The Age of Innocence* (1920), for which she was awarded the Pulitzer Prize. Her short stories revolve around a "significant situation"
that often casts an individual in conflict with social conventions, and
they have won praise for their artistic control, penetrating social comment, and subtle humor. She died in France, where she had lived for
three decades, in 1937.

Constance Fenimore Woolson

Constance Fenimore Woolson was a regional writer of remarkable skill in rendering the landscape and characters of the Great Lakes region, Ohio, and the South. Born in New Hampshire in 1840, she was educated at the Cleveland Female Seminary and Madame Chegaray's fashionable New York school. Reaching maturity at the outbreak of the Civil War, the most dramatic national event in her life, she volunteered to serve in a center for convalescing soldiers. In the 1870s she spent winters in the South with her mother, visiting the Carolinas, Georgia, and Florida, and some of her best work depicts that region. Her first novel, *Anne* (1882), a drama set on Mackinac Island, was immensely popular, selling sixty thousand copies. But she is now remembered largely for her short stories, the best of which are collected in *Castle Nowhere: Lake-Country Sketches* (1875) and *Rodman the Keeper: Southern Sketches* (1880), both containing stories that had appeared in the leading magazines of the day. Her fiction, which captures local dialects and regional folkways, stressing the psychological depth of regional identity while developing themes of unfulfilled love, personal sacrifice, and alienation, brought new depth to the local-color tradition. After the death of her mother in 1879, she chose to live in Europe, where she became friends with Henry James. She died in Venice in 1894 after a suspicious fall from her bedroom window.

Madelene Yale Wynne

Relatively little is known about Madelene Yale Wynne. She was born in Newport, New York, in 1847 and died in Chicago, Illinois, in 1918. She was the daughter of Linus Yale (the inventor of the Yale lock). Wynne was obviously a multitalented woman and, evidently from an early age, devoted herself to the arts. Madelene Yale studied under George Fuller at the Boston Art Museum and later enrolled in the Art Student's League in New York City. She was principally known as a metal sculptor and lived most of her adult life in Chicago. Wynne was elected president of the Deerfield Arts and Crafts Society and was a member of the Copley Society. She was the author of two collections of short stories, *The Little Room and Other Stories* (1895) and the posthumously published *An Ancestral Invasion and Other Stories* (1920). She wrote the argument and the dialogue for the *The Magic*

Hour (A Cantata of the Seasons) (1897), and the year before her death
she published a volume of poems, *Si Briggs Talks* (1917).

Zitkala-Sä

Zitkala-Sä was born on the Pine Ridge Reservation in South Dakota in
February of 1876. Her mother was a full-blooded Sioux; her father, a
white man, deserted the family before she was born. The young Gertrude was given the last name of her mother's second husband, John
Haÿsting Simmons, but later in her life she would reclaim her tribal
name, which means red bird. Zitkala-Sä was educated in Indiana and
studied violin in Boston. Caught between cultural tribal traditions
and the dominant white culture, she explored her sense of alienation
and dislocation in a series of autobiographical essays published in the
Atlantic Monthly. She later published *Old Indian Legends* (1901), traditional Sioux tales and legends that she attempted to adapt and render
in English. She collected previously published short fiction, including
"The Trial Path," along with some new essays in *American Indian Stories* (1921). Most of her life was spent not in writing fiction, however,
but working for Indian civil rights. With her husband, Raymond T.
Bonnin, Zitkala-Sä worked in Utah for the Society of American Indians
and later in Washington, D.C., where she edited the *American Indian
Magazine*. She founded the National Council of American Indians in
1926 and served as its president until her death in January 1938.

NOTES ON THE TEXTS

The stories in this volume were drawn from the sources indicated below. Unless otherwise indicated, the texts were chosen from either the original magazine publication of a story or its first appearance in a published volume.

Austin, Mary. "The Walking Woman." *Lost Borders*. New York: Harper and Brothers, 1909, pp. 195–209.

Bierce, Ambrose. "An Occurrence at Owl Creek Bridge." *Tales of Soldiers and Civilians*. San Francisco: E. L. G. Steele, 1891, pp. 21–39.

Cable, George Washington. "Belles Demoiselles Plantation." *Old Creole Days*. New York: Scribner's, 1879, pp. 60–87.

Cahan, Abraham. "A Providential Match." *The Imported Bridegroom and Other Stories of the New York Ghetto*. Boston: Houghton, Mifflin, 1898, pp. 122–65.

Cather, Willa. "The Wagner Matinée." *Youth and the Bright Medusa*. New York: Knopf, 1920, pp. 248–72.

Chesnutt, Charles W. "The Sheriff's Children." *The Wife of His Youth and Other Stories of the Color Line*. Boston: Houghton, Mifflin, 1899, pp. 60–93.

———. "The Wife of His Youth." *The Wife of His Youth and Other Stories of the Color Line*. Boston: Houghton, Mifflin, 1899, pp. 1–24.

Chopin, Kate. "Athénaïse." *Atlantic Monthly* 78 (August 1896): 232–41; 78 (September 1896): 404–13.

———. "Désirée's Baby." *Bayou Folk*. Boston: Houghton, Mifflin, 1894, pp. 147–58.

Cooke, Rose Terry. "How Celia Changed Her Mind." *Huckleberries Gathered from New England Hills*. Boston: Houghton, Mifflin, 1891, pp. 284–315.

Crane, Stephen. "The Blue Hotel." *The Monster and Other Stories*. New York: Harper and Brothers, 1899, pp. 109–61.

———. "The Bride Comes to Yellow Sky." *McClure's Magazine* 10 (February 1898): 377–84.

———. "An Experiment in Misery." *The Open Boat and Other Stories*. London: Heinemann, 1898, pp. 211–26.

———. "The Men in the Storm." *Arena* 10 (October 1894): 662–67.

———. "The Open Boat." *Scribner's Magazine* 21 (June 1897): 728–40.

Dreiser, Theodore. "Curious Shifts of the Poor." *Demorest's* 36 (November 1899): 22–26.

———. "The Second Choice." *Free and Other Stories*. New York: Boni and Liveright, 1918, pp. 135–62.

Dunbar, Paul Laurence. "The Lynching of Jube Benson." *The Heart of Happy Hollow*. New York: Dodd, Mead, 1904, pp. 223–40.

Dunbar-Nelson, Alice. "The Goodness of Saint Rocque." *The Goodness of St. Rocque and Other Stories*. New York: Dodd, Mead, 1899, pp. 3–16.

———. "Sister Josepha." *The Goodness of St. Rocque and Other Stories*. New York: Dodd, Mead, 1899, pp. 155–72.

Far, Sui Sin. "Mrs. Spring Fragrance." *Hampton's Magazine* 24 (January 1910): 137–41.

Frederic, Harold. "My Aunt Susan." *The Copperhead and Other Stories of the North During the American War*. New York: Heinemann, 1894, pp. 247–68.

Freeman, Mary Wilkins. "A Church Mouse." *A New England Nun and Other Stories*. New York: Harpers, 1891, pp. 407–26.

———. "The Revolt of 'Mother.'" *A New England Nun and Other Stories*. New York: Harper and Brothers, 1891, pp. 448–68.

Gale, Zona. "Nobody Sick, Nobody Poor." *Friendship Village*. New York: Grosset and Dunlap, 1908, pp. 28–41.

Garland, Hamlin. "The Return of a Private." *Main-Travelled Roads*. New York: Macmillan, 1899, pp. 169–94.

———. "Under the Lion's Paw." *Main-Travelled Roads*. New York: Macmillan, 1899, pp. 197–217.

Gilman, Charlotte Perkins. "The Yellow Wallpaper." *New England Magazine* 5 (January 1892): 647–56.

Harris, Joel Chandler. "Free Joe and the Rest of the World." *Free Joe and Other Georgian Sketches*. New York: Collier, 1887, pp. 3–29.

Harte, Bret. "The Luck of Roaring Camp." *The Luck of Roaring Camp and Other Sketches*. Boston: Osgood, 1871, pp. 1–18.

Howells, William Dean. "Editha." *Harper's Monthly* 110 (January 1905): 214–24.

James, Henry. "The Beast in the Jungle." *The Better Sort*. New York: Scribner's, 1903.

———. "The Real Thing." *The Real Thing and Other Tales*. New York: Macmillan, 1893, pp. 1–41.

Jewett, Sarah Orne. "Miss Tempy's Watchers." *Tales of New England*. Boston: Houghton, Mifflin, 1890, pp. 7–27.

———. "A White Heron." *A White Heron and Other Stories*. Boston: Houghton, Mifflin, 1886, pp. 1–22.

King, Grace Elizabeth. "La Grande Demoiselle." *Balcony Stories*. New York: Century, 1893, pp. 23–35.

London, Jack. "The Law of Life." *McClure's* 16 (March 1901): 435–38.

———. "To Build a Fire." *Century* 76 (August 1908): 525–34.

Norris, Frank. "A Deal in Wheat." *A Deal in Wheat and Other Stories of the New and Old West*. New York: Doubleday, Page, 1903, pp. 3–26.

Oskison, John M. "The Problem of Old Harjo." *The Southern Workman* 36 (April 1907): 235–41.

Stowe, Harriet Beecher. "The Minister's Housekeeper." *Sam Lawson's Oldtown Fireside Stories*. Boston: Houghton, Mifflin, 1881, pp. 53–78.

Twain, Mark. "Jim Smiley and His Jumping Frog." *Early Tales & Sketches*, Vol. 2 of *The Works of Mark Twain*, Edgar Marquess Branch and Robert Hirst, eds. Berkeley: University of California Press, 1981, pp. 13–19.

———. "The Story of the Old Ram." *Roughing It*, Franklin Rogers and Paul Baender, eds. Berkeley: University of California Press, 1972, pp. 68–72.

Wharton, Edith. "The Other Two." *The Descent of Man and Other Stories*. New York: Scribners, 1904, pp. 71–91.

Woolson, Constance Fenimore. "Rodman the Keeper." *Rodman the Keeper: Southern Sketches*. New York: Appleton, 1880, pp. 9–41.

Wynne, Madelene Yale. "The Little Room." *Harper's New Monthly Magazine* 91 (August 1895): 467–73.

Zitkala-Sä. "The Trial Path." *Harper's Monthly* 103 (October 1901): 741–44.

FOR THE BEST IN PAPERBACKS, LOOK FOR THE

In every corner of the world, on every subject under the sun, Penguin represents quality and variety—the very best in publishing today.

For complete information about books available from Penguin—including Puffins, Penguin Classics, and Arkana—and how to order them, write to us at the appropriate address below. Please note that for copyright reasons the selection of books varies from country to country.

In the United Kingdom: Please write to *Dept. JC, Penguin Books Ltd, FREEPOST, West Drayton, Middlesex UB7 0BR.*

If you have any difficulty in obtaining a title, please send your order with the correct money, plus ten percent for postage and packaging, to *P.O. Box No. 11, West Drayton, Middlesex UB7 0BR*

In the United States: Please write to *Consumer Sales, Penguin USA, P.O. Box 999, Dept. 17109, Bergenfield, New Jersey 07621-0120.* VISA and MasterCard holders call 1-800-253-6476 to order all Penguin titles

In Canada: Please write to *Penguin Books Canada Ltd, 10 Alcorn Avenue, Suite 300, Toronto, Ontario M4V 3B2*

In Australia: Please write to *Penguin Books Australia Ltd, P.O. Box 257, Ringwood, Victoria 3134*

In New Zealand: Please write to *Penguin Books (NZ) Ltd, Private Bag 102902, North Shore Mail Centre, Auckland 10*

In India: Please write to *Penguin Books India Pvt Ltd, 706 Eros Apartments, 56 Nehru Place, New Delhi 110 019*

In the Netherlands: Please write to *Penguin Books Netherlands bv, Postbus 3507, NL-1001 AH Amsterdam*

In Germany: Please write to *Penguin Books Deutschland GmbH, Metzlerstrasse 26, 60594 Frankfurt am Main*

In Spain: Please write to *Penguin Books S. A., Bravo Murillo 19, 1° B, 28015 Madrid*

In Italy: Please write to *Penguin Italia s.r.l., Via Felice Casati 20, I-20124 Milano*

In France: Please write to *Penguin France S. A., 17 rue Lejeune, F–31000 Toulouse*

In Japan: Please write to *Penguin Books Japan, Ishikiribashi Building, 2–5–4, Suido, Bunkyo-ku, Tokyo 112*

In Greece: Please write to *Penguin Hellas Ltd, Dimocritou 3, GR–106 71 Athens*

In South Africa: Please write to *Longman Penguin Southern Africa (Pty) Ltd, Private Bag X08, Bertsham 2013*